U0108290

金庸小說國際學術研討會論文集

Proceedings of the International Conference on Jin Yong's Novels

Proceedings of the International Conference on Jin Yong's Novels

Copyright © 1999 by Yuan-Liou Publishing Co., Ltd.

7F-5, No. 184, Sec. 3, Ding-Chou Rd., Taipei, Taiwan

Tel: 886-2-23651212　Fax: 886-2-23657979

All rights reserved

金庸小說國際學術研討會論文集

主編——王秋桂

特約編輯——李素娟

責任編輯——李佳穎・鄭祥琳

美術設計——唐壽南

發 行 人——王榮文

出版發行——遠流出版事業股份有限公司

　　　　　　台北市汀州路三段 184 號 7 樓之 5

　　　　　　郵撥／0189456-1

　　　　　　電話／2365-1212　　傳眞／2365-7979

香港發行——遠流（香港）出版公司

　　　　　　香港北角英皇道 310 號雲華大廈 4 樓 505 室

　　　　　　電話／2508-9048　傳眞／2503-3258

　　　　　　香港售價／港幣 333 元

著作權顧問——蕭雄淋律師

法律顧問——王秀哲律師・董安丹律師

1999 年 12 月 1 日　初版一刷

行政院新聞局局版臺業字第 1295 號

售價新台幣 1000 元　　（缺頁或破損的書，請寄回更換）

版權所有・翻印必究（Printed in Taiwan）

ISBN 957-32-3813-6

金庸荼館網站

http://jinyong.ylib.com.tw　E-mail:jinyong@yuanliou.ylib.com.tw

YLib **遠流博識網**

http://www.ylib.com.tw　E-mail:ylib@yuanliou.ylib.com.tw

金庸小說
國際學術研討會論文集

Proceedings of
the International Conference on Jin Yong's Novels

主辦單位
漢學研究中心
中國時報人間副刊
遠流出版公司

贊助單位
行政院文化建設委員會
行政院大陸委員會

會議時間
一九九八年十一月四日至六日

會議地點
臺北市國家圖書館國際會議廳

序

王德威

　　一九五五年香港報人查良鏞先生以金庸爲筆名，在《新晚報》開始連載武俠創作《書劍恩仇錄》。陳家洛與香香公主的愛恨情仇，乾隆大帝的身世謎題，還有紅花會黨的呼群保義等，諸般情節人物高潮迭起，緊扣讀者心弦。隔年《書劍恩仇錄》刊畢，金庸之名已不脛而走，成爲武俠小說界的新寵。

　　《書劍恩仇錄》只是金庸初試身手之作。以後十六年間，他再接再厲，屢創高峰。《射鵰英雄傳》、《神鵰俠侶》、《天龍八部》、《笑傲江湖》等作，部部膾炙人口。金戈鐵馬、俠骨情心，傳說中的江湖世界是如此奇特瑰麗，不由我們不心嚮往之。尤其對映五、六〇年代海峽兩岸嚴峻的政治氛圍，金庸立足香港，創造了另一片書劍江山，更顯得難能可貴。這片江山一方面投射一代文壇的烏托邦欲望，一方面又緊扣臺海大陸的歷史情境；以世俗對抗正統，以說部否想教條，亦今亦古，形成了最不可思議的文學地誌。多少年後的專家學者順應西學，紛紛在主流現代中國文化、歷史裡找尋「國族寓言」，殊不知海外的金庸現象，早已獨樹一幟了。

　　一九七二年金庸的《鹿鼎記》完稿，次年即金盆洗手，退出江湖，至此金庸一共創作了十五部作品。萬千猶在興頭的讀者，固然因此爲之扼腕歎息，對金庸本人而言，卻未嘗不是明智之舉：急流勇退，原來就是武林的一大絕招。更何況金庸其實以退爲進，立意閉關以修訂他的作品。十年批閱增刪之後，十五部三十六冊的《金庸作品集》問世，精益求精，自然引起轟動。

　　而這才是金庸熱潮的眞正開始。金庸當年崛起香港，風靡海外，甚至引來學者如陳世驤、楊聯陞等都心儀不已。六〇到七〇年代，因爲種種原因，他的作品在臺灣成爲禁書。即便如此，各種改頭換面的版本，早已流行不輟。八〇年代的臺灣局勢丕變，金庸終於名正言順的光臨寶島，大受歡迎。但比較起來，金庸在大陸所造成的轟動，才眞正讓我們見識到庶民文學的力量之

一斑。「毛文學」雷厲風行了五十年，那裡敵得過幾招倚天劍、屠龍刀，還有降龍十八掌？到了九〇年代，金庸已躋身學院，成爲與魯迅、老舍、巴金平起平坐的現代作家了。與此同時，源出於金庸作品的影劇、漫畫、翻譯、電玩、有聲書、網站等種種媒體應運而生，而且無遠弗屆。郭靖與黃蓉、楊過與小龍女、東方不敗、韋小寶等衆多人物事蹟，儼然已成爲世紀末華人群體文化想像及實踐的一部分。

金庸「傳奇」於是演變爲金庸「神話」：全球化的金庸、國粹化的金庸、經典化的金庸、市場化的金庸、奇觀化的金庸、生活化的金庸……。這些有關金庸的「説法」其實不無矛盾，但在神話的光環之下，居然合縱連橫，形成綿密的網絡。作爲金庸神話的供養人及消費者，我們對其居之不疑，信以爲眞。而研究金庸神話的學問，我們謂之「金學」。近現代文學研究中有「紅學」（《紅樓夢》）、「魯學」（魯迅）、「張學」（張愛玲）。「金學」發展迅速，儼然已有後來居上之勢。

但神話何曾須臾離開歷史？金庸現象畢竟值得我們深思。白話俠義小説起自宋元，八百年來，綿延不絕。即至現代，民國前期的平江不肖生、還珠樓主，金庸同輩的臥龍生、古龍、梁羽生，都曾各領風騷。而過去二十年間，金庸全集一出，所向披靡、盡得天下風流。這其間的消長，不僅見證金氏傲人的才華器識，也更説明他麾下一種文化事業——甚或文化工業——的機制運作，空前成功。不論是自動自發還是借力使力，金庸現象都提供我們一絕佳立足點，審視廿世紀下半段中國文學（後）現代化的得與失。如前所述，金學當然打破了正統文學文化的藩籬，但它是否已形成一種新的封閉體系？金庸的成就既已稱「空前」，是否也必須要成爲曠世絕響？忝爲金迷之一，我無意唐突大師。但金庸小説既以史識史觀見長，我們頌讚之餘，又怎能不自省本身閱讀的位置？

收錄在本論文集的二十六篇文章，恰可視爲金學研究又一次的成果驗收。而上述金庸神話的威力與侷限，似乎也可在此一見端倪。這部選集分爲五輯，縱論金庸世界的宗教與科學，愛情與人物，翻譯與版本，評論與結構，還有其影響文學與社會的意義。提供論文的學者從國學耆宿到科學專家，從當代小説名人到兩性理論先鋒，眞可謂各大門派，齊顯身手。他（她）們立

意鋪陳的金學知識體系，既有天文地理，也有醫卜宗教，其他如武術技擊、歷史敍事、愛情欲望，乃至種種世路人情，無一不包羅。有些題目也許點到爲止，但金學百科全書式的架構，已隱然浮現。自魯迅以降，我們還看不到那一位作家可以號召如此規模的研究。魯迅學背後有國家機器撐腰，金學則來自民間出版業、媒體及廣大讀者群的推波助瀾。兩相比較，一個世紀的中國文學文化與生產間的脈絡，竟已有跡可循。

話說回頭，金庸的學識文筆若非深有可觀，也不會贏得如此多本行與他行學者的青睞。在「宗教與科學」一輯中，金庸作品能召喚出許多觸類旁通的研究，即是一例。學界前輩柳存仁教授據《射鵰英雄傳》爲本，指出金庸私淑《蒙古秘史》等史料，敷衍全書恢宏的歷史架構；他又追溯全眞教在宋元之際與政治間的互動關係，龐徵博引，功力非凡。與柳文相互呼應的是劉南強教授論《倚天屠龍記》與明代摩尼教的關連。金庸雅好由民間會黨、教派入手，探尋市井草莽的政治及精神寄託，由此再次可以確認。此外，洪萬生以金元數學家李冶爲焦點，討論全眞教與中世紀算學的發展；林富士分析江湖武術及醫事的互相關照；Meir Shahar 追溯氣功、武學及金庸武術的發展；還有曾志朗、莊瓊如從表意符號系統描述金庸世界的認知能量及情緒反應，都令我們一開眼界。

金庸在揮灑刀光劍影之餘，尤善寫情。楊過與小龍女的情深無悔、令狐冲與任盈盈的好事多磨，不過只是最明白的例子，已足令人驚心動魄。傳統武俠小說一向渲染英雄色彩，少有如金庸這般，對兒女之事細作文章。金庸不只寫純情癡情，也寫畸情無情。貪癡嗔怨，均由情字而起，一部《天龍八部》，恰可作如是觀。比起古典言情説部冠軍《紅樓夢》，金庸作品遠乏那種超脫智慧，但癡男怨女、生死以許的連台好戲，仍頗有與晚明「情敎」種種，互通有無之處。本書輯二中張小虹、黃宗慧二文均採西方精神分析學觀看金庸人物的情慾癥結。自戀相戀，戀物戀人，寫來頭頭是道，如能對中國傳統情欲學的幽微論證，再加琢磨，成績當更豐富。同理，陳益源專治金庸人物的不倫之戀，一樣也有續可發揮的餘地。輯二中另有陳芳英、呂宗力、及危令敦三家，就美學、語言學及倫理學的角度，分論金庸人物造型。他們由俠與情的辯證擴及其他審美及社會教化、言説的層面，取法乎上，論辯亦自可觀。

　　本書第三輯介紹金庸作品的翻譯現況及版本問題。金庸在華人讀者群中的盛名，早已見知於他國漢學界；英、日等主要語言譯本，近年陸續問世。但翻譯金庸豈是易事！武俠世界的種種玄通，只能意會，不能言傳，又何況是以他國語言迻譯。除此，金庸對中國歷史、文化的浸潤，在在考驗譯者功夫。劉紹銘、賴慈芸、John Minford 都是譯界能手，由他們現身說法談論翻譯金庸作品的得失，可謂此其時也。劉與 Minford 以《鹿鼎記》爲例，對該書所可能產生的中西文化認同及讀者反應的差距，均表示了保留的態度，語重心長。另一方面，金庸的作品歷經連載、單行本、盜版、修改重版等過程，已多次脫胎換骨。論金庸小說的版本，不僅在於追本溯源，也更在於見識其人其作自我提昇的痕跡。林保淳是臺灣武俠小說版本學權威之一，Chirstopher Hamm 是美籍金學研究的新秀，他們的議論及對話，足可見證金庸版本遞嬗間的美學及歷史動機。馬幼垣重新發掘金庸、梁羽生、百劍堂主三人當年報上以文會友的掌故，則堪稱彌足珍貴。

　　金庸作品也觸發了評者對其文筆丰采的興趣。識者早已指出金庸文辭典麗，成爲新白話文的範本。本書輯四的文章續對其敘事特徵，再加定義。大陸學者陳墨比較《唐吉訶德》與《鹿鼎記》異同，對兩作顛覆中西俠情說部的實驗，多所著墨。馮其庸細談《笑傲江湖》，看出太多有關政治、人性的微言大義，一邀讀者會心微笑。另外，張大春與廖朝陽爲金庸小說的結構是否離奇鬆散，各作建言。張是專業作家，憑一己心得及對傳統敘事學的研究，提出內行人語。廖則根據佛經要義及西方文論，力證金庸的形式特徵，直指他內容、義理上的公案。廖以《天龍八部》爲例，出入作品各個層次，爲其大開大闔的「傳奇」架構重新定位，是本論文集最具思辨深度的佳作之一。

　　論文集最後探討金庸作品與社會的互動關係。嚴家炎談論金庸的遊走雅俗之間，爲文學及文化史的述寫投下新的變數。胡小偉則就金庸筆下「顯性」及「隱性」的社會，思考正／邪、朝／野、俠／盜、文／武等傳統社會架構的生剋；行有餘力，他亦對現世社會價值的移動，多所抒發。Robert Chard 上溯草莽綠林譜系，以金庸爲集其大成者。黃錦樹則爲金學的社會影響作出「否想」。他認爲清末、五四以降新文化運動的啓蒙及平民化主張，可能並未由菁英作家及學者實現，反由像金庸這輩俗文學作家代行其是。百年來中華文化花果飄零，引來多少鄉愁浩歎；在新儒家文化復興建設事倍功半之際，金派

武俠作品卻悄悄「靈根自植」，意外結出奇花異果。

　　這本論文集的出版，無疑爲金庸作品經典化發展，再下一城。換個角度，菁英學者願意爲誼屬大衆的武俠傑作鼓掌背書，也代表了現代文學研究視野的又一擴張。一個世紀的中國紛紛擾擾，文化與政治上俗雅正邪的替換，快如電光石火。歷史敍述不及之處，小說取而代之。我們是從說部的千言萬語中，淬鍊家國想像，安頓人我關係。從世紀初魯迅的「吶喊」、「徬徨」到世紀末金庸的「笑傲江湖」，從感時憂國到快意恩仇，多少人事興廢，盡付滄海一聲笑。論中國現代性的曲折發展，可以如是！是爲序。

目　次

第一輯 宗教與科學

《脫卜赤顏》‧全眞敎和《射鵰英雄傳》

柳 存 仁

澳大利亞國立大學

摘 要

　　金庸的《射鵰英雄傳》是他的一部較早的作品，也是當時一開始就受到讀者注意的力作。它的熱鬧的情節，曲折變換的場面，後來又曾經攝成電影和電視劇，所以不止有廣大的讀者群，還有廣大的觀眾。

　　做爲是小說故事，《射鵰英雄傳》涉及的眞正史實，也包括了蒙古人未滅女眞人在華北統治的金國和偏安在東南的南宋之前，他們在荒漠草莽高原的各種活動，他們的不出世的領袖成吉思汗怎樣征服和統一蒙古各部族而被舉做大汗，蒙古大軍的遠征西域花剌子模，蒙古和金國之間的聯絡和最後無可挽回的衝突，這些情節都可從一部音譯蒙文旁注漢解的《脫卜赤顏》（舊鈔本叫做《元朝秘史》，現代譯本叫做《蒙古秘史》）裡找到重要的、新鮮的線索。本文用了很嚴謹的態度解說《脫卜赤顏》的書誌學方面的背景，和小說如何巧妙地去利用那些資料。

　　小說裡寫出江湖上的俠義人物有多少複雜的派別和恩怨，還有超出在各派之外的全眞敎，也跟那些江湖上的活動有許多藕斷絲連的關係。全眞敎自係歷史上道敎的一大支派，後來蒙古人在中原立國之後，它的信徒在道敎的許多支派中更成了一枝獨秀之勢。但是全眞敎的敎旨和活動的目的究竟是什麼？敎主王重陽死後，他的門徒們爲什麼接受金主的宣召？丘處機爲什麼認爲只有勸導成吉思汗才能夠拯救中國在苦難中的老百姓？這些繁複迷離的問題，本文也都從史料裡尋出了一個客觀的回答。

一

《脫卜赤顏》（*Tobča'an*）是蒙古文獻中紀錄早期蒙古民族在大漠裡遊牧生活的情形，從他們的遠祖神話和傳說時代的故事講起，直到征服和統一蒙古各部族成爲大汗的成吉思汗（Chingis Khan）和繼任大汗的窩闊台（Ögödei）[1] 後來的事蹟，包括成吉思汗的西征和窩闊台的滅金。這部書最初書寫的時候，大約是用蒙古化了的畏兀兒文（Uighur script）寫的，那個本子早已不存了。後來見到的，有兩個系統的本子。一個是十卷本加兩卷續書，所以叫做十二卷本，另一個是十五卷本。兩個本子所敍的事蹟，大致相同，但是十二卷本的安排，比較複雜。它的正文是蒙古文字的漢語譯音，旁邊用細字注出漢文的意思。由於時代的關係，那樣的漢文我們現代人仍是不很容易讀的。但是它的每一節文字後面，又用細字注上總譯（有的時候總譯只能說是撮譯，它會比蒙語原文或漢文旁注漏去一些瑣細的描敍）。這樣的全書共有二百八十二節，最後的一節撰書的人還說明了寫作的時、地，態度是很認眞的。另一個十五卷本，沒有正文的漢語譯音和細字注釋，僅有總譯，這是這兩個系統的本子在體製上不同的地方。兩種本子的書名都是漢文《元朝秘史》，近代做研究的文字或新的譯本多數已稱它做《蒙古秘史》，是因爲它所敍述的事迹其實發生在蒙古人征服了金朝和佔領了不少南宋的領土後建立的元朝之前許多年的緣故。這個《元朝秘史》的名稱，可能是明初的人鈔錄這書時加的名字。清乾隆間的錢大昕撰《補元史藝文志》（1791），卷二有《元秘史》十卷，又《續秘史》二卷，他說這書：

> 不著撰人。記太祖初起，及太宗滅金事，皆國語旁譯，疑即《脫必赤顏》也。[2]

這個「國語旁譯」之本，不論是刻本、影寫本或鈔本，看來指的多數是十二卷本。錢大昕疑心這書可能就是《脫必赤顏》（*Tobǐca'an*）。同卷另外一

1　這是《元史》裡尊稱的太宗。《元史‧太宗本紀》的譯名是諤格德，此從《新元史》及一般通史用的名稱。《脫卜赤顏》裡稱斡哥歹可汗。

2　《潛研堂全書》本，或《二十五史補編》第六冊本（上海：開明書店），頁8406。

條《聖武開天記》，錢大昕釋云「中書平章政事察罕譯《脫必赤顏》成書」。
又一條《太宗平金始末》，又釋云「同上」。《元史》裡叫做察罕（Chagan）
的一共有三個人，這裡指的是《元史》卷一三七說的察罕本傳，說他在皇慶
間（1312-1313）曾奉命「譯《脫必赤顏》，名曰《聖武開天記》，及《紀年纂
要》、《太宗平金始末》等書，俱付史館。」這個《聖武開天記》和後來的《皇
元聖武親征錄》可能是一部書，[3] 內容和《脫必赤顏》當然有關係。但是兩者
恐怕還不是一部書。王國維（靜安）先生《觀堂集林》卷十六〈蒙文《元朝秘
史》跋〉云：

> 此本卷首書題下，有「忙豁侖紐察脫察安」二行（仁按：王先生說的是十二卷系
> 統的本子，特別相合的是王先生故後，1935 年收入《四部叢刊‧三編》的那個影
> 元鈔本，因爲那裡面有王先生提到的顧廣圻的跋文的影印眞迹。但是王先生大概
> 不曾見這個後來歸涵芬樓並且收入《四部叢刊》的鈔本，不過顧氏的這個跋，也
> 收入他的《思適齋文集》卷十四。此外，清末葉德輝刊印的另一個十二卷鈔本，
> 也有此跋，卻略去最後的署名和時、地。），曩顧千里跋此卷，以爲撰人姓名。余
> 謂此即《元朝秘史》之蒙古語也。「忙豁侖」即蒙古，「脫察安」即《元史》之《脫
> 必赤顏》若《脫卜赤顏》。

按，此原著卷一書題下雙行注「脫豁侖紐察脫察安」（「脫」「察」二音間
又注更細字「中」字）。近賢治蒙古史的人俱已同意它是書名，拉丁化譯音爲
Mongqol-un Ni'uca Tobča'an，我們就不用多贅了。王靜安先生續引《元史‧
虞集傳》，說「有旨修《經世大典》，集請以國書《脫卜赤顏》增修太祖以來
事迹。承旨塔失海牙曰：『《脫卜赤顏》非可令外人傳者』，遂已。」這件事
不僅見〈虞集傳〉，也見《元史》卷三十五〈文宗本紀四〉，至順二年（1331）
四月，諫止的人是翰林學士承旨押不花。王先生舉〈虞集傳〉做證據說：

> 案，既稱國書《脫卜赤顏》，則當文宗時，此書尚無漢譯之本。乃〈察罕傳〉言仁
> 宗命譯《脫必赤顏》，名曰《聖武開天記》，及《紀年纂要》、《太宗平金始末》等

3　這是洪煨蓮（業）先生的推斷，參看 William Hung, "The Transmission of the Book
　　Known as *The Secret History of the Mongols*," *Harvard Journal of Asiatic Studies*, 14
　　(1951), p.470。

書,俱付史館云云。考明《文淵閣書目》卷五有《元朝秘史》、《續秘史》各二部;卷六有《聖武開天記》一部。則察罕所譯與虞集所請,自非一書。緣《聖武開天記》既宣付史館,且至明初尚存,則與虞集國書之目,塔失海牙不傳外人之言,不能相符。疑元時自有兩種《脫卜赤顏》,其譯爲《聖武開天記》者,殆即今之《元聖武親征錄》,而虞道園所請以修《經世大典》者,則今之《元朝秘史》也。[4]

　　《脫卜赤顏》的流傳問題,是很複雜的。[5] 我現在僅引用靜安先生這篇短文,說明錢大昕的舊說還不能做爲定論。好在金庸先生在他的大著《射鵰英雄傳》卷末附的〈後記〉裡,既說小說裡歐陽鋒不懂《九陰眞經》中的怪文「哈虎文缽英,呼吐克爾」等等的設想是得了「忙豁侖紐察脫必赤顏」這些怪文的啓示,[6] 我們對他這部著名作品裡參用過的不少記述蒙古人開國時期的這部重要史料,在有關的範圍內也不能不稍加說明。

　　我們上文說這個漢文舊譯本《元朝秘史》的本子有兩個系統,現在不妨把它們的情況再具體地說一說:

　　除了專門的學者,譬如藏書家、考證家、版本和書誌研究的專家之外,一般的讀書界的人知道有十五卷本的《元朝秘史》問世,都是由於清末李文田的《元朝秘史注》的流通,原書 1896 年刻入袁昶輯《漸西村舍彙刊》裡,用的是張穆校本的十五卷《元朝秘史》,張校收在楊尚文刻的《連筠簃叢書》(1847) 裡。這個十五卷本是只有總譯,沒有蒙古音的漢字,也沒有漢文旁注的。其實連筠簃本,也並不是十五卷最早的本子。最早的十五卷本,曾鈔入明永樂初編的《永樂大典》元字韻,從卷五一七九到卷五一九三,卻正是十五卷。清乾隆間錢大昕藏的十五卷本,就是他設法從《大典》中鈔錄出來的。顧廣圻爲十二卷本的元鈔本《秘史》撰的跋說:

　　《元朝秘史》載《永樂大典》中。錢竹汀少詹家所有,即從之出,凡首尾十五卷。

---

4 《觀堂集林・附別集》第三冊,《集林》卷十六（北京:中華書局,1959）,頁 765-766。
5 看本文註 3 引洪煨蓮先生的書,可知其較詳細的情況。洪先生這篇長文的下半,很細密地舉了不少假設的意見,這些洪先生也說都還是有待於證明的。洪先生此文雖然是四十多年前的著作,據我的研究蒙古史的同事羅依果教授 (Dr. Igor de Rachewiltz) 說,仍是研究《元朝秘史》的流傳最好的一篇文章。
6 金庸,《射鵰英雄傳》第四冊,《金庸作品集・8》（香港:明河社,1976）,頁 1621。

後少詹聞桐鄉金主事德輿有殘元槧本，分卷不同，屬彼記出，據以著錄於其《元
史藝文志》者是也。

　　這裡說的金德輿藏的殘元槧本，分卷不同的，一定就是一個十二卷本；
所以我們上文引的《補元史藝文志》，錢大昕也說《元秘史》十卷，《續秘史》
二卷，正合十二之數，不過那只是他之所知、所見，卻不是他所藏。他的《廿
二史考異》卷一百曾用到《秘史》的材料，這書是乾隆四十七年（1782）編
定的，卷一百是最後的一卷。他在乾隆三十八年擢詹事府少詹事，在這之前
他已補翰林院侍讀，入直上書房，自然有不少看到《永樂大典》的機會。錢
大昕以後，阮元的《四庫未收書目提要》卷二紀錄他採錄呈進之本，也有《元
朝秘史》十五卷，說「此依舊鈔影寫，國語旁譯」，這下面一句不知道他的眞
正意思。因爲據我們所知，十五卷本是沒有「國語旁譯」的。[7] 在阮元之後，
楊尚文輯的《連筠簃叢書》裡也刻有張穆校的十五卷本《元朝秘史》，清末李
文田注的《秘史》，主要的根據也是張石洲的這一個校本。

　　清代道光、咸豐間，注重中國北方和西北邊事的張穆和何秋濤都是有心
人。張穆的《蒙古遊牧記》和何秋濤的《朔方備乘》最著名，他們也可以說
是清末研究西北史地的先導者。但是清末北方的俄羅斯對中國覬覦之心更
亟，學者們關心邊防和史地的人的研究就不止是學問上的興趣了。他們的追
尋史料、旁搜遠紹，又添上了一種實用性的價值。和這些活動有關係的人，
像李文田、洪鈞、沈曾植、盛昱、文廷式，都曾研究過蒙古和元代的史料。

　　李文田注的《元朝秘史》十五卷，是到他死後（1895）大約一年左右，
才刻入袁昶的《漸西村舍叢刊》裡的，袁昶就是後來在庚子之亂時因爲在廷
議中力陳義和團的危害被西太后下令斬首的一個人。李文田注《秘史》，基本
上用的是張穆校本，是個殘缺的元槧本，但是他是有機會見過盛昱所藏的顧
廣圻校過的十二卷本的，所以也有機會參照十二卷本的漢文文字。如我們所
知，這個顧校十二卷本正文是蒙古原文的漢字譯音，李若農的蒙古語的知識
不夠，所以後來能讀蒙古文的學者們對他的疏失，不免有較切的批評。但是

7　這書近年的刊本，題傅以禮重編的，《秘史》書題下細注「連筠簃叢書本」一行就是傅
　以禮加上去的，未免亂人耳目。書前更有他光緒八年（1882）的識語。上海：商務印
　書館，1955 年本，〈目次〉，頁 1-3。

他在當時治蒙古史和《元史》，作的注文所涉及的其實是很淵博的，他在各方面的貢獻，也可從他的其他著述像《元聖武親征錄校注》，[8] 和江標輯《靈鶼閣叢書》裡收的《朔方備乘札記》一卷、《西遊錄注》一卷、《和林金石錄》一卷這些書見到一斑。[9]

　　十二卷本《秘史》，我們在上文引王靜安先生的文章已經知道明初楊士奇編《文淵閣書目》裡紀錄過《元朝秘史》和《續秘史》，但不曾說卷數。可是它說一部五冊，又續集一冊；如果每冊兩卷，這就正合十二卷之數。明末清初奉仕兩朝的孫承澤，他的《元朝典故編年考》卷九記的只是從《元朝秘史》鈔出來的元代的一些瑣細的典故，〈小序〉說「元有《秘史》十卷，《續秘史》二卷。前卷載沙漠始起之事，續卷載下燕京、滅金之事，蓋其國人所編記。書藏禁中不傳，偶從故家見之，錄續卷末，以補史所不載。」[10] 《四庫總目》的編者曾用《永樂大典》元字韻所鈔檢覈他所引的各條，文字都同，也疑心這是「元時秘冊，明初修書者或嘗錄副以出，流傳在外，故承澤得而見之耳」，說明這個十二卷本是早有的。再遲下來，清初黃虞稷的《千頃堂書目》卷四也有十二卷本的《元朝秘史》，雖然《四庫》裡並沒有收錄這部難得的、可以說得上是第一手的史料。更遲的還有乾隆間萬光泰的《元祕史略》，這書今天我們看得到的本了收在清道光十三年（1833）楊復吉輯的《昭代叢書》戊集續編裡。萬光泰這部書本身就是節略本，雖然沒有什麼可以引起考證的價值，他撰的序文卻說他根據的是一個鮑廷博藏的鈔本，也是正集十卷，續集二卷的。萬光泰的時代比顧廣圻要早四十多年。

　　今天十五卷本《秘史》的流傳，李文田的注固然收在《漸西村舍彙刊》裡，還有《皇朝藩屬輿地叢書》第五集本，和從它翻石印的上海文瑞樓本，並不難致；近代又有商務印書館的《叢書集成・初編》本。但是十二卷本，

8　收光緒中順德龍鳳鑣刻的《知服齋叢書》第三集裡，僅一卷。（在叢書用的書名題《元親征錄》）這個注的底子是何秋濤校本，李文田和沈曾植的注全載，三家的校注刻書時分別提行，很是清晰，卷末有李文田自記。《漸西村舍彙刊》裡也收《校正元親征錄》一卷（1894），就是此書，但是衹題何校，沈、李的注用小字夾注，僅有寥寥數條，也未標明何人之說。

9　《朔方備乘札記》收第二集，餘書收第四集。這三書也收入繆荃孫的《煙畫東堂小品》（1920），稱「順德師著述」。

10　《四庫全書總目》，卷八十一〈元朝典故編年考〉條引。

在《四部叢刊・三編》出現以前，卻是靠了葉德輝在光緒三十四年（1908）
刻印的觀古堂「據影鈔元足刻本」的問世。這個有蒙古文漢語注音的《蒙文
元朝秘史》的問世，在當時是震動全世界研究蒙古史的人們的一件大事。有
了它的出現，把漢語注音的文字還原變成眞正蒙古文的《蒙文元朝秘史》，多
少部研究專著和新的譯本就跟著出來了！從外文著述的角度說，法國的伯希
和（Paul Pelliot）、德國的海尼士（Erich Haenisch）、日本的那珂通世
（Naka Michiyo），以及時代稍後的白鳥庫吉（Shiratori Kurakichi），都可
說是早期領導群倫的先輩。他們能夠善用這部罕見的新書，就把西方人多年
從歐洲和中亞細亞裒集的知識和這部十三世紀中葉的蒙文原始資料有機性地
結合起來了！但是我們也不該忘記洪鈞的《元史譯文證補》。[11] 他在光緒十
三到十六年間（1887-1890）任出使俄、德、奧、荷四國大臣的時期，在歐洲
一有機會就去搜求和蒙古元代有關的歷史資料，編譯多年，死後（1893）這
部《譯證》才由他的友人陸潤庠、沈曾植替他整理印行（1897）。這裡面就包
含到今天我們也不能不注意的拉施特・哀丁（Rashīd ud-Dīn）、志費尼
（Juvainī）和多桑（C. d'Ohsson）這些人的著述。[12]

11　這書原刻之外，有《廣雅書局叢書》本（1900）。

12　拉施特・哀丁和志費尼都是波斯人。志費尼的時代稍早（1226-1283），他的祖父曾任
　　花剌子模大官，父親就替蒙古征服花剌子模後的西亞服務了。早年他曾隨父親到過
　　蒙古，後來在 1252-53 年（蒙哥，憲宗 Möngke 時）他又在和林（Karakorum，當時
　　蒙古的都城，約在今烏蘭巴托西南二百里）大汗的朝廷做事，才開始有撰寫蒙古史的
　　心願。等他回到西亞，他就跟著旭烈兀（Hülcgü，蒙哥的六弟）打仗，攻陷報達
　　（Baghdad）之後在波斯建立的蒙古人的政府做官（後來這就是伊兒汗國 Il-khans）。
　　1260 年（元中統元年，南宋景定元年）他被任做管轄從前哈里發（caliph）所有領土
　　的長官，到 1282 年（元至元十九年）才被旭烈兀的兒子阿八哈（Abaqa）免職。阿八
　　哈死後他的地位恢復，但是同一年他就死了。志費尼著名的紀載早期蒙古歷史的書
　　Ta'rīkh-i-Jahān-Gushā，在五十年代已有很好的英譯本：J. A. Boyle, *The History of
　　The World Conqueror*, 2 vols., Manchester Univ. Press, 1957. 拉施特・哀丁（1247-
　　1318）這位波斯的史家和政治家，是猶太族，改信了伊斯蘭教的。他是阿八哈汗（1265-
　　1282 在位，即元至元二年、南宋咸淳元年到至元十九年）的醫官和大臣。1298 年（元
　　大德二年）他坐了阿八哈的孫子合贊汗（Ghazan-khan）朝廷的相位，是合贊的親信，
　　對政治上頗有改革。合贊死，傳位給其弟合兒班答，稱鄂爾采圖（鄂爾采是吉祥的意
　　思），所以外文紀載多稱合兒班答爲 Ulja'ita。這時候拉施特・哀丁仍繼續做首相，但
　　是到了合兒班答的兒子不賽因（西籍多稱 Abū Sa'īd，因爲他在 1317 延祐四年即位後

　　葉德輝刻的《蒙文元朝秘史》，是從文廷式那裡鈔錄的，文廷式的本子又是從盛昱家藏的那部有顧廣圻原跋的《秘史》鈔出來的。這部從清嘉慶乙丑（十年，1805）顧廣圻教張敦仁（跋文中的「古餘先生」）向盧州知府張祥雲[13]（跋文中的「晉江張太守」）借來覆影的影鈔本，直到清光緒間（這部有顧跋眞迹的本子）歸盛昱收藏的時候，中間已經過了收藏的人多手，包括盛昱的伯祖。這些藏書家多數把他們的印章加蓋在這個本子好幾卷的首頁，傅沅叔（增湘）先生的《藏園群書經眼錄》卷四有縷細的記錄。[14] 他的《經眼錄》記錄裡還記書中有盛昱「聖清宗室盛昱伯羲之印」等兩個印章，藏書的木匣還有黃士陵用篆書題的「伯羲祭酒藏書匳」等二十六個字，說明這書是影鈔足本《秘史》十卷，續二卷。此外更有光緒癸未（九年，1883）八月周鑾詒[15]住在盛家的意園時，曾用這個鈔本和連筠簃的刻本對讀的題記。這樣說來，後來歸涵芬樓藏、印入《四部叢刊·三編》的這個影鈔本是盛伯羲家的故物，

又稱阿卜賽特·蘇爾灘的緣故，蘇爾灘即 sultan）在位時，不幸的事情就發生了。這時他遭人讒害，誣他毒死故君合兒班答，最後竟以七十多歲的高齡慘遭腰斬，「梟首通衢，分其手足，傳示各部」(《新元史》卷一〇九，〈不賽因傳〉)。這是這一位大史家慘痛的經歷。拉施特·哀丁的《集史》(*Djami el-Tévarikh*) 歷來各國史家節譯或引用它的很多，我們管它叫做《集史》，因爲它不止有敍述成吉思汗和在波斯輝煌一時的合贊汗的事迹，還有印度、歐洲和東羅馬公教教廷的描寫。《新元史》卷一〇九〈拖雷中·合贊傳〉說合贊「熟於蒙古掌故、世系、族派、姓氏，命拉施特·哀丁作史，凡述蒙古事，皆面奉教令，然後載筆。」所以他著的書有很高的史料價值；參看邵循正先生〈刺失德丁《集史》忽必烈汗紀譯述〉，北平《清華學報》，第十四卷，1947；余大鈞、周健奇譯，《史集》(北京：商務印書館，1983)。我這裡用的拉施特·哀丁和志費尼兩家的漢譯名，全是《新元史》卷一〇八和一〇九裡的名稱。《新元史》稱志費尼或云「阿塔·瑪里克·志費尼」，或云「阿累屋丁·志費尼」，因爲志費尼的全名的拉丁拼音是'Ala ud-Dīn'ata-Malik Juvainī，柯鳳蓀（紹忞）先生敍述時用古文筆法，不免撮取以順文意。其實，拉施特·哀丁也有全名 Rashīd ud-Dīn Ṭabīb，但是那一卷史傳裡叫做哀丁的人很多，所以柯先生就不嫌重複，屢用拉施特·哀丁之稱了。

13　張祥雲，字鞠園，福建晉江人，乾隆五十二年（1787）進士。

14　「《元朝秘史》十卷，續集二卷（六冊）」條，第二冊（北京：中華書局，1980），頁301-302。文中沅叔先生鈔錄顧跋，文字和《四部叢刊·三編》影印的原迹，微有少數異同。盛昱是光緒二十六年庚子（1900）逝世的，沅叔在民國元年壬子曾睹盛伯羲遺書。他另有跋文，刊《藏園群書題記》第三冊（天津，1933）。

15　湖南永明人。他和盛昱都是光緒三年（1877）的二甲進士。他的題記也見《經眼錄》這裡引的一條。

是毫無可疑的了！可是，據洪煨蓮先生的研究，《四部叢刊‧三編》本的這部
《秘史》的印章，別的都有著落，卻是尋不到一個姓盛的印章。這是很奇怪的
事。煨蓮先生說這許多印章裡有一個影印得很模糊的，也許就是盛昱的
罷？[16] 他說的模糊的印，也許指的是蓋在卷一正面書題下方的、朦朧地看到
幾個不清楚的字，前面有個「室」字，最後一字爲「藏」字，似乎就是傅沅
叔記錄的「宗室文愨公家世藏」一章，文愨公是他的伯祖敬徵的諡。因爲未
見原書，這個也祇可存疑。但是，就算這是對的，還有「盛淸宗室盛昱伯羲
之印」另一個章呢？也許這一點我們暫時也只好存疑了。涵芬樓影印的本子，
據《續集》卷二（即第十二卷）最後附的張菊生（元濟）先生的跋，其中有
四十一葉，分屬第三、四、七、八諸卷的，是用了當時北平圖書館藏的、[17]
和它行款相同的明初刊本的殘葉更換了過來，以補影鈔本和葉煥彬刻鈔本的
缺漏的。那麼，盛伯羲的另外一章，會不會因爲換葉的關係失落了呢？也許
這是不會的，因爲印章通常多僅蓋在卷首或卷末。現在涵芬樓的舊人，老輩
已經幾乎全凋落了，我們只好等待有幸運再看見原書的機會。[18] 至於文道希
（廷式），他幾乎可以說是淸末士林中的傳奇人物。他是才子、文士，也是學
問家，文史和哲學的知識很淵博，渴求新知的願念又很濃厚，所以未經整理
的著作也有時候不免失之瑣碎。他是江西萍鄉人，光緒十六年（1890）庚寅
恩科的榜眼，曾做翰林院編修、侍講，一時的聲名很盛。戊戌政變後他因爲
是新黨，又得罪過西太后，曾逃到日本去避難。但是不久，他就回到中國南
方來了。冒鶴亭（廣生）先生說：「庚子、辛丑之間，道希寓黃歇浦。其時
帶甲天地，京朝士夫多南還，若沈子培、子封兄弟，丁叔衡‧費屺懷、張季
直、暨外舅黃叔頌先生，與余輩朝夕咸集，極一時文酒山河之感。」[19] 後來文

16　本文前引洪先生文（註3），頁 445，原注 27。

17　今北京圖書館。

18　張菊生先生說他得悉北平圖書館藏有明初刊本殘葉，是從趙斐雲（萬里）先生那裡聽
　　到的。這些殘葉，原屬民國二十二年（1933）北平故宮博物院裡的舊內閣大庫裡的故
　　紙堆裡沒有整理過的殘餘物。據說其間還有板本格式和《秘史》殘葉相同的《華夷譯
　　語》，那是明洪武二十二年（1389）刊行的。

19　《小三吾亭詞話》卷一，收唐圭璋《詞話叢編》第十二冊（臺北：廣文書局版，1967），
　　頁 7-8。這裡說的子培、子封是沈曾植、曾桐兄弟；叔衡是丁立鈞；屺懷是費念慈；
　　季直是張謇；叔頌是黃紹第，也是冒鶴亭先生的丈人。

道希得病，仍回到他的故鄉江西萍鄉，鬱鬱不得志，光緒三十年（1904）他就侘傺以歿了。日本學者最初研究蒙文本的《元朝秘史》，也是拜文廷式之賜。光緒二十八年（1902）大概文廷式還住在上海的時候，他曾把他鈔本另一個副本送給在大阪的朋友內藤虎次郎（Naitō Torajirō），內藤又很快地製了一本轉送給研究蒙古史的那珂通世。1907 年那珂通世的日譯本已經用了《成吉思汗實錄》的書名在東京出版了。[20] 文廷式自己在他的《純常子枝語》裡，也有不少地方提到《元秘史》，雖然他不曾說《秘史》本子的來源。[21] 他又曾從《永樂大典》裡輯出過好幾種原本收在元天曆、至順（1329-31）間編的《經世大典》裡的著作，《經世大典》在明代中葉已經佚亡了，文廷式的幾種輯本，後來為王靜安先生收在民國初年他為上海猶太富商哈同（Silas Aaron Hardoon）出資編印的《廣倉學宭叢書》裡。[22]

　　沈子培（曾植）也是和《元朝秘史》攸關的人，雖然他注的十五卷本《元秘史補注》在他死後（1922）二十三年（1945）才由張孟劬（爾田）先生等在北平替他刊印出來，[23] 他其實和洪鈞、李文田、盛昱、文廷式、袁昶都是

20　1907 年還在葉德輝刻本之前，其實兩者用的鈔本都是文廷式供給的。參看內藤虎太郎《研幾小錄》（京都，1928），頁 160，洪煨蓮先生文，前引，頁 445 引。那珂先生仍有《成吉思汗實錄・續編》收《那珂通世遺書》（東京，1915）。

21　文廷式這書四十卷，現在流行的有揚州江蘇廣陵古籍刻印社 1990 年影印 1943 年刻本。新印本有 1979 年錢仲聯先生的序，說「此巨帙芸閣殆未經最後鑒定，故次第較亂，刊行時胥存其本眞」，說的是不錯的。但是錢序又說新印本「並撰索引，爲分類探究之便」，今本卻未見。卷首有〈簡目〉，或係原刻，其實也多有疏漏。

22　《廣倉學宭叢書・甲類》，一名《學術叢編》，名義上是姬佛陀（覺彌）編的。上海倉聖明智大學民國五年（1916）排印本，第二集收有《元高麗紀事》、《元代畫塑記》、《大元倉庫記》、《大元氈罽工物記》、《大元官制雜記》各一卷，都是文廷式輯的遺稿。靜安先生自己早年的研究文字《兩周金石文韻讀》、《唐韻別考》、《韻學餘說》，和他那些用甲骨文字考證商殷古史的像《殷卜辭中所見先公先王考》、《殷周制度論》，以及《古本竹書紀年輯校》、《今本竹書紀年疏證》、《太史公繫年考略》，還有《宋史忠義傳王稟補傳》、《清眞先生遺事》、《永觀堂海內外雜文》，也都收在這部叢書的第二集。

23　北平，圓城古學院刊本，共二冊。參看姚從吾先生〈漫談《元朝秘史》〉一文，原刊《大陸雜誌》（臺北）第 17 卷第 12 期，亦收入《大陸雜誌史學叢書》第 1 輯，第六冊，《元明史研究論集》，1966 再版，頁 295-306。姚先生此文並收在札奇斯欽先生《蒙古秘史新譯並註釋》（臺北：聯經出版公司，1979，1992）書內，作爲〈代序〉。

一輩的熟人。他自己說光緒元、二年（1875—76）間他已開始注意蒙古地理之學。[24] 光緒六年庚辰這一科他中了進士。這一科會試的第五道經策，問的是關於北方邊事，沈子培的卷子從西漢時代起源源本本地縷述下來，也破天荒用到了《秘史》裡的資料。同科的李慈銘在當時久負盛名，據說他這次考畢出闈場時曾「自詡其第五策爲通場冠」，[25] 結果這一年李悉伯中了二甲進士第八十五名，沈子培也得三甲第九十七名。後來李慈銘在他著名的《日記》裡說：「沈子培來久談，且送其行卷來。[26] 此君讀書極細心，又有識見，近日所罕覯也。其經文刻四首，皆博而有要。第五策言西北徼外諸國，鈎貫經史，參證輿圖，辨音定方，具有心得，視余作爲精審矣。」[27] 這眞是由衷的欽佩。那珂通世透過了文廷式的介紹，也跟沈子培通訊。可惜沈子培早年寫的《聖武親征錄校注》鈔本在庚子（1900）他南下時留在北京已經成爲火燼無存了。民國六年（1917）他又根據了一個明弘治殘本《說郛》裡收的《聖武親征錄》來和何秋濤校本對勘，收在《知服齋叢書》裡（參看註 8）。自然，在這之後我們還有王靜安先生的《聖武親征錄校注》。[28]

　　我們現代的人要讀《脫卜赤顏》，比前人幸運多了。前人的業績貢獻之外，現代的白話譯本或其他語文並加注釋的譯本，已經不少，十二卷本的涵芬樓影元鈔本各處圖書館也很易得，更可以增加我們對勘的興趣。金庸先生寫《射鵰英雄傳》時參考用的《脫卜赤顏》，是中國大陸出版謝再善先生漢譯的外蒙古策‧達木丁蘇隆（Damdingsurung）編輯的《蒙古秘史》，是用現代的蒙古語把原典當做文學作品看待加以改寫的。在臺灣，札奇斯欽先生的《蒙古秘

24　《海日樓文集》卷上，〈《聖武親征錄》校本敍〉云「在光緒乙亥、丙子之間」，最初讀的是張穆的《蒙古遊牧記》、沈垚的《落颿樓文稿》。

25　據王瑗仲先生（蘧常）《沈寐叟年譜》，《中國史學叢書》（長沙：商務印書館，1938），頁 15 夾注。

26　唐代舉子有投卷、溫卷的習慣或制度，這裡李慈銘指的是考試發榜後坊間刻印後可以送人的本子，李慈銘不過借用了一個典故。

27　《越縵堂日記》裡的〈荀學齋日記〉，光緒六年十月十四日己酉。

28　《海寧王忠慤公遺書》，第三集，1927，海寧王氏刊本；《海寧王靜安先生遺書》（長沙：商務印書館，1940）。這書的序文又收在《觀堂集林》卷十六，前引，頁 796-799。序中靜安先生說他以前疑《聖武親征錄》與《聖武開天記》或係一書，這裡《校注》又主張《親征錄》之成「確在〔元〕世祖之世」，舉原書癸亥年王孤部下原注「今愛不花駙馬丞相白達達」語爲證，並可參研。序作於民國十五年丙寅（1926）。

史新譯並註釋》(見註 23)大約可以說是學術價值和譯筆流暢這兩方面都能夠顧及到的，我尤其注意他的註釋裡面還引用了不少更早的時候他和姚從吾先生共同研究這部《秘史》時的一些姚先生的劄記或意見。日文方面，四十年代到五十年代小林高四郎先生 (Kobayashi Takashirō) 譯注的《蒙古秘史》和他的專著《元朝秘史の研究》，[29] 在許多方面都可以說是有了新的貢獻。但是我以爲我們更當讀一下札奇先生寫的〈介紹小林《元朝秘史之研究》並論重譯《蒙古秘史》〉這一篇涉及到關於這部《秘史》許多重要問題的文章。[30] 至於英譯的《秘史》，姚從吾先生當年所盼望過的柯立夫先生 (Francis Woodman Cleaves) 譯的 *The Secret History of the Mongols*，1982 年已由哈佛大學印行了。在這之前，在澳大利亞研究蒙古史和元史的學者羅伊果先生 (Igor de Rachewiltz)，札奇斯欽的《蒙古秘史》的譯註本序文裡已經提到他有「羅馬字復原本的問世」，他的《秘史》的英譯本，從 1971 年起也陸續在坎培拉的《遠東歷史集刊》上發表了。[31] 這兩種英譯的工作態度，都是非常矜愼嚴謹的。要是我們愛讀小說的人，想看文學情趣濃些的《蒙古秘史》，就不妨試讀一下 Paul Kahn 先生 1984 年的譯品。[32] 他的譯本是柯立夫先生的譯本的改寫，全用的詩歌體裁。札奇先生的《譯註》，有好多處已經採用了詩句體裁，但是他自己也指出如果詩的部分完全譯成詩的格式，「又容易破壞了語氣和記事的連貫性」，所以有的地方，「原文雖然是詩，但仍是以散文的格式譯寫出來」(〈自序〉，頁 23)。中國小說的傳統，如金庸先生的許多作品那樣，是時常穿插了見景生情的詩、詞、歌讚的。愛好文學的人們，以爲譯《脫卜赤顏》這樣的名著應該何去何從呢？

29　前者東京：生活社，1941 出版；後者東京：日本學術振興會，1954 出版。

30　原刊《大陸雜誌》第 12 卷第 5 期，收入《元明史研究論集》第 1 輯，第六冊，同註 23，頁 58-66。

31　"The Secret History of the Mongols," *Papers on Far Eastern History*, Canberra: Australian National University, No.4, 1971, pp.115-163; No.5, 1972, pp.149-175; No.10, 1974, pp.55-82; No. 13, 1976, pp.41-75.

32　*The Secret History of the Mongols, The Origin of Chinghis Khan*, an Adaptation of the *Yuan Ch'ao Pi Shih*, Based Primarily on the English Translation by Francis Woodman Cleaves, San Francisco: North Point Press, 1984.

二

　　《脫卜赤顏》一書，主要是記敍成吉思汗（元太祖）和窩闊台（太宗）兩個時期的事情，這些記敍的概況，姚從吾先生在他的〈漫談《元朝秘史》〉（見註 23），和前引的洪煨蓮先生的大文（見註 3）裡，都有分段的說明，[33]我們這裡不用贅述了。金庸先生的《射鵰英雄傳》是創作小說，也曾利用了《秘史》的一些資料，成爲貫穿他一部幾十萬字的作品的主要情節，卻是我們不能夠不留意的。《射鵰英雄傳》裡面，和蒙古史及一部分的元史有些藕斷絲連的地方，我們試把它略做分析如下：

1/3/116- 1/4/151；[34] 1/5/180- 185；188- 89；195- 203；1/6/223- 225；228- 229；237- 260。2/16/636- 41；3/25/1008- 1014；3/26/1047；1054-60；4/36/1407- 20；1422- 28；4/37/1444- 47；1455- 67；4/38/1471- 72；1488-1500；4/40/1553-55，1563-70。

這裡面包括的情節，是複雜的，它敍述郭靖母子怎麼會在蒙古居住；郭靖這個漢族的窮小子怎樣會認識成吉思汗的子女，特別是郭靖怎麼會被大汗看重，許爲駙馬，產生郭靖、黃蓉跟華箏公主三人之間的情愛糾纏。在爭戰方面，也有成吉思汗（帖木眞 Temüjin）在沒有做到蒙古各部族的大汗之前，跟王罕（To'oril ong-qan）、札木合（Jamuqa）等的衝突及札木合之死，而在更大的方面，又有蒙古和金國的經常聯絡和逐漸的發生衝突；蒙古的勢力日漸擴大之後，它最初的聯宋剋金的策略，它的大軍的遠征西域花剌子模（Khorezm），大軍的統帥之一漢人郭靖的勝利，到最後成吉思汗爲什麼會懷疑郭靖的可能對他不忠實，和郭靖的寡母怎樣在危急的時候自己悲痛地結束了自己的生命。這些重要的部分當然不完全是《脫卜赤顏》或《元史》的材料，有一些自然讀者們都知道它們是虛構的，但是它們無論如何是有機體生動而容易令人置信地嵌在一個龐大的故事結構之內。跟這些事件平行的，如

---

33 姚先生文見札奇斯欽先生譯《秘史》〈代序〉，頁 4-6；洪先生文見前引，頁 467-468。
34 我用的版本見註 6。這裡每條的三個號碼，例如 1/3/116，第一個是指冊數，第二個是回數，第三個是頁碼；下同。

果不是更重要的，還有作者很拿手的描寫俠義、武林的故事，那些故事的活動也絕不脫離整個大布局的要求。作者個人特別創造出來、前無繼承的武俠人物的四大幫派，東邪、西毒、南帝、北丐的驚人活躍，並不是限於這一部大書的範圍就算終止的，這些人物和線索還貫穿於作者的其他的說部，在某一部實際獨立的故事裡也往往照應到其他的著作的因果、輪廓，增加它們的可信性而能夠並行不悖。除了這幾大派之外，還有其他的各有勢力範圍的組織，像長江上游的鐵掌幫，像江南六怪他們都是，而在宗教史上特別著名的全真教，它的最早創教的人王重陽，也因武功的關係而成為最早的華山論劍時最成功的大人物。我們現在僅就那些和《秘史》或《元史》的利用有趣味的地方，作一點學術性的補述：

1/9/347 金國的趙王完顏洪烈說「大金太宗天會三年，那就是趙官兒徽宗的宣和七年了……」，自然這是小說裡方便了解的話，這時候離開徽宗時已經很多年，徽宗稱廟號，當然沒有問題。「官兒」這個名稱，《秘史・續》卷一，第二五一節稱它做「趙官」。王靜安先生《觀堂集林》卷十六有〈趙官〉一條，說「金人輒直呼宋帝之名」，所以他推測這個趙官，或指趙擴，就是南宋寧宗的名字。這當然是可能的，而「蒙古人亦以金人所呼者呼之耳」。如果王靜安的推測是對的，金庸先生這裡已把它活用了。

成吉思汗點兵出征花剌子模，據《秘史・續》卷一，第二五四節說是有成吉思汗遣派的兀忽納 (Uquna) 等一百名使臣，被回回人扣留殺害；[35] 《新元史》卷二五四〈西域・上〉說「眾四百餘，皆畏兀人」。《射鵰英雄傳》4/36/1415 卻有博爾忽 (Boroqul) 說花剌子模的狗王 (指摩訶末 Mohammed)聽了金狗王子完顏洪烈的唆使，「把大汗的忠勇使者殺了，將使者的衛兵殺了一半，另一半燒了鬍子趕回來。」照《新元史》卷一二一〈博爾忽傳〉，他在太祖十二年征禿馬惕部時，中伏遇害，是不可能在兩年後參加別的戰役的。但是完顏洪烈，這個虛構的角色，卻是《射鵰英雄傳》裡的關鍵人物。因為他是書中另一位要角楊康的名義上的父親，又是郭靖的殺父仇人。小說中郭靖那麼熱心地去參加西征，要旨也是為了想報父仇。這個完顏洪烈便注定了要做反面的角色了。完顏洪烈這個名字的創造，我想是作者很費心機的。完

35　見札奇斯欽譯的《秘史》，頁 385。

顏是女眞部族的姓，《金史》裡記載姓完顏的人很多，但是用烈字做名字的，像卷一二三的完顏斜烈（並見《元史》卷一四九），卷一一一的完顏思烈，都是有成就的人。用洪字爲名的，也有完顏洪裕、洪靖、洪熙、洪衍、洪輝，他們都是金章宗的皇子，一望而知是個貴族的好名字，可是他們都只是一兩歲就夭折了。金庸先生挑了洪烈做他的小說裡趙王的名字，看去若不經意，其實正是代表了這個角色和皇室的關係。

撒麻爾罕（Samarkand）就是漢代的康居，隋、唐時候叫做康國，但是同時已經有了颯秣建、薩末建這些音譯的名字。遼、元時代的記載或叫做尋思干，是西遼的河中府，[36]《秘史‧續》卷一，第二五七、二五九節俱作薛米思加卜；《元史‧太祖本紀一》「十六年辛巳春，帝攻卜哈兒（Bokhara）、薛迷思干等城」，和《秘史》相同。《射鵰英雄傳》4/37/1444 寫攻打花剌子模的名城撒麻爾罕時，十餘萬人連攻數日，始終不下，云：

> 又過一日，察合台（Chaghatai）的長子莫圖根（Mutugen）急於立功，奮勇進城，卻被城上一箭射下，貫腦而死。……親兵將王孫的屍體抬來，成吉思汗眼淚撲簌簌而下，抱在懷中，將他頭上的長箭用力拔出，只見那箭狼牙鵰翎，箭桿包金，刻著「大金趙王」四字。左右識得金國文字的人說了，成吉思汗怒叫：「啊，原來是完顏洪烈這奸賊！」

照《秘史‧續》卷一，第二五七節，「越過阿剌亦（Arai）[37] 去征討回回的時候」是兔兒年，即元太祖十四年己卯（1219）。《元史‧太祖本紀一》說十六年辛巳春攻薛迷思干，下之；「秋，皇子尤赤（Juchi）[38]、察合台、窩闊台分攻玉龍傑赤（Urgench）[39] 等城，下之。」這是說明攻下薛迷思干（撒

---

36 耶律楚材《西遊錄》卷上，「訛打剌（Otrar）之西千里餘有大城曰尋思干」條，向達校注（與《異域志》合刊）（北京：中華書局，1981），頁 3。李志常《長春眞人西遊記》，《道藏》本，卷上，23b；卷下，5b，6b 皆作耶米思干。

37 札奇斯欽譯注，頁 278 引姚從吾先生舊注，從德國 Erich Haenisch（海尼士）譯本 *Die gcheime Geschichte der Mongolen*，當作 Arai-pass，是在今俄國境內阿爾泰山脈中的一個山口。

38 《秘史》中他的名字叫拙赤，是成吉思汗的長子。

39 按，這個花剌子模都城的譯音，頗不統一。《新元史》卷三〈太祖本紀下〉十六年作烏爾鞬赤；札奇斯欽先生譯注本，第二五七節、注4，作兀龍格赤，《四部叢刊‧三編》

麻爾罕）和攻下玉龍傑赤（即《秘史・續》卷一之兀籠格赤，花剌子模的都
城）都在十六年，不過一個在春天，一個在秋季罷了。但是莫圖根並不是死
於這兩個戰役的。金庸先生用的莫圖根之名，大概是根據《新元史》卷一零
七〈察合台傳〉的。《新元史》用的人、地名，前後有時候不統一，在〈太祖
本紀下〉裡，他又叫做謨阿圖堪了。但是比起《元史》來，《新元史》還是較
詳細和正確的。下面三段我們可以分別地看到前述的兩個戰役，及另一段莫
圖根之死的細節。

㈠《新元史・太祖本紀下》記攻下撒馬爾干，在太祖十五年，不在十六
年。〈本紀〉云：

> 十五年庚辰，夏五月，進至撒馬爾干城。尤赤等三路之師，亦傅城下。貨勒自彌
> 蘇爾灘（按，即花剌子模之 sultan，名 Ala-ud-Din Mohammed）先居撒馬爾干，
> 聞大兵至，遁走，使其將阿爾潑汗嬰城固守。帝遣者別（Jebe）、速不台（Subotei）
> 各率輕騎追蘇爾灘，又使脫忽察兒（Toqucar）爲二將後援，帝自率諸皇子圍撒馬
> 爾干。阿兒潑汗以波斯兵出戰，中伏，大敗，康里（Kanklis）兵開門出降，阿兒
> 潑汗引親兵突圍走。帝恐康里兵反覆，仍盡誅之。……帝以蘇爾灘母土而堪哈敦
> （Turkan Khatun）（哈敦，《秘史》卷五「田迭塔塔侖……」條作合敦 khatun，指
> 貴婦人）在烏爾韃赤（即 Urgench），遣丹尼世們往論之。土而堪不答，奔馬三德
> 蘭，與蘇爾灘妻俱爲者別、速不台所獲。秋，命尤赤、察合台、窩闊台攻烏爾韃
> 赤。

㈡但是十五年這一年，烏爾韃赤並未攻下。十六年〈本紀〉繼續說：

> 十六年辛巳春，……尤赤等攻烏爾韃赤屢失利，帝駐蹕塔里堪（Talikan），尤赤等
> 以軍事來告，帝廉知尤赤、察合台素不合，改命窩闊台總諸軍，并力急攻，克之。

所以撒麻爾罕是十五年打下來的，但是花剌子模的都城之陷落，卻要到下一
年大約在二、三月之間，因爲這裡下面的文字就是說三月攻陷幾個別的城鎮

本同，説的都是一個地方。Urgench 在今俄國烏茲別克共和國境（Uzbek），阿母河
（Amu Dar'ya）流域的 Shavat 運河上，那古代舊城的遺址，在現在的城市西北約八十
哩，叫做 Kunya-Urgench 的地方。Urgench 一名，學者又或拼音作 Gurganj。

的事了。尤赤和察合台兄弟失和的事，也見《秘史·續》卷一，第二五四、二五五及跟這裡說的直接有關的第二五八節。[40] 《射鵰英雄傳》4/36/1423—26 也描寫過他們兄弟相爭相鬥，以致要兵戎相見。用蛇蟠陣來阻隔兩軍，用虎翼陣圍擒不服的人，把一場大禍消弭於無形的，正是尤赤大罵「南蠻不是好人」的郭靖；暗地裡幫忙他的真正的軍師，就是全書的女主角黃蓉。這當然是小說家移花接木的伎倆，史書裡是找不著的。以上是說明攻克花剌子模的都城是在十六年。

　　(三)莫圖根喪生的事，是在十六年九月。〈本紀〉又說：

> 八月，踰印度固斯大山（Hindu Kush），至八米俺（Bamian）。命忽都虎（Qutuqu）扼喀不爾山（Kabul）之隘。忽都虎與札剌勒丁（Jalal-un-din Munkabirni）戰於巴魯安（Baru'an），失利。九月，帝親攻八米俺城，皇孫謨何圖堪中流矢卒。帝怒，城下之後，遇生物悉屠之。改城名曰夘庫兒干。

　　這才是歷史上的莫圖根死事的真正事蹟。他不是死於攻撒麻爾罕之役的。小說的敘述把他喪生的地點改了，是要求它合乎作書的人的要求。南宋理宗時（有端平乙未，即二年，公元 1235，恰是金亡之後的一年）灌圃耐得翁著《都城紀勝》，他寫的〈瓦舍眾伎〉條，說「最畏小說人，蓋小說者能以一朝一代故事，頃刻間提破。」[41] 有更遲的署「甲戌歲中秋日錢塘吳自牧書」的序文的《夢粱錄》，這個甲戌年，可能是南宋度宗咸淳十年（1274），正是《射鵰英雄傳》描寫的兵荒馬亂、外寇來臨的時代。它的最後一節〈小說講經史〉，也說「最畏小說人，蓋小說者，能講一朝一代故事，頃刻間捏合。」[42]這是中國傳統小說給我們留下來的寶貴遺產，金庸先生運用題材，舉重若輕，可以說是得到其中三昧。

　　《元史》裡沒有給莫圖根，甚至也沒有給察合台立傳。《新元史》卷一〇七〈察合台傳〉敘述莫圖根死事，還添了下面一段很有情思的真實故事。它說：

40　札奇斯欽譯注本，頁 385-394；400-401；《四部叢刊·三編》本，《續一》，頁 21a-34b；41a-42b。

41　《東京夢華錄·外四種》（上海：古典文學出版社，1957），頁 98。

42　同上條註，卷二十，頁 313。

察合台不知莫圖根之死。一日，諸子侍食。太祖佯發怒，察合台惶懼伏地，謂如不從父命則死。太祖問：「汝此言誠否？」察合台力矢不敢妄言。太祖乃告以莫圖根之死，令勿悲哀。察合台聞言，忍淚侍食如故。既而出，痛哭野外而返。

這段描寫親情生死之感的文字，注意歷史的金庸先生不會不留心的。他果然把它收在小說第四冊附錄的〈成吉思汗的家族〉一文裡（頁1590），沒有把它融合入正文。為什麼呢？我想，察合台在歷史上是開創汗國的大人物，可是在金庸的小說裡，只是個不很重要的配角；比起拖雷（Tolui），他這個角色重要性差得遠了，雖然拖雷在書裡佔的篇幅也有限。作好的小說和寫好的散文，甚至於和寫學術研究的論文一樣，要緊的是知道取和捨。搜集材料一定要充分，但是搜集來的東西不一定要全留著，就是十分辛苦得來的材料，在這裡用得不適合的，還不如去掉它更加完美。附錄的〈成吉思汗的家世〉，它本身可以說是一部現代人改寫的《脫卜赤顏》，還加上些《元史》、《新元史》的資料，仍是不能把每一件珍寶都掛在另外一棵生氣蓬勃的大樹上面的。

《新元史·太祖紀》所說與札剌勒丁對抗的忽都虎，有傳見卷一二六，開首說「忽都虎·失吉·塔塔兒氏」，就是同書卷二五四〈西域·上〉的失吉·忽都虎（sigi-Qutuqu），也就是《秘史·續》卷一、第二五七節說的「做頭哨，與札剌勒丁對陣敗了」的失吉·忽禿忽。這個札剌勒丁，是前文提過的從撒馬爾干遁走的老蘇爾灘的兒子，他的父親畏懼蒙古兵，逃到裡海的一個荒僻的小島上死了，他就繼了位。這個札剌勒丁才是個勇悍不屈，又能指揮騎兵應戰的角色。和忽都虎這一戰而勝，大約是蒙古這趟西征唯一的一次被人打敗的戰役。《新元史·忽都虎傳》記兩軍交綏的地方在斡里俺城，說忽都虎「命軍中縛氈象偶人列士卒後，以為疑兵」，敵人望見了那些偶人，果然疑心他有後援，可是：

札拉（剌）勒丁呼曰：「我衆彼寡，不足畏也！」張兩翼而進。圍既合，札拉勒丁使其衆下馬以待，戰酣，乃悉令上馬衝突。我軍大敗，兵士死傷者衆。

這裡最後寫的幾句話，〈西域·下〉的文字和它文義全同，可是〈西域·下〉說的交戰的地點是巴魯安，《秘史》這一節也說後來成吉思汗的追兵在「巴

魯安客額兒（Baru'an-ke'er）地面下了營。」[43] 好在所描述的戰況是一樣的，我們這裡就暫不深究了。〈西域·上〉描寫成吉思汗聽說：

> 失吉·忽都虎既敗，太祖捲甲南行，軍中不及炊，皆啖生米。至嘎自尼（Ghazni）
> （這是札剌勒丁的根據地），則札剌勒丁已去。仍疾追之，及於印度河（Indus）……
> 聞其欲渡河，即夕列陣圍之。曉而戰，先敗其右翼，……未幾，左翼亦敗，中軍
> 僅七百人，猶死戰。太祖欲生擒札剌勒丁，命諸將環攻，勿發矢。札剌勒丁勒其
> 馬，至數丈高崖投入印度河，泅水而逸。獲札剌勒丁妻子，盡殺之。時十六年冬
> 也。

　　多桑（C. d'Ohsson）的《蒙古史》（*Histoire des Mongols dépuis Tchinguiz-khan jusqu'à Timour Bey ou Tamerlan*）[44] 記敘札剌勒丁投水一節說「札蘭丁見重圍不開，乃易健馬，復為最後一次之突擊。蒙古軍後卻，札蘭忽回馬首，脫甲負盾執纛，從二十尺高崖之上躍馬下投，截流而泳。成吉思汗進至河畔見之，指示諸子，言此人可供諸子效法，止將卒之欲泳水往追者。蒙古兵發矢射從渡之花剌子模兵，死者甚夥。盡殲岸上殘兵，虜札蘭丁眷屬，殺其諸子。」[45] 這頗令我想起《射鵰英雄傳》4/37/1456 歐陽鋒被困在撒麻爾罕的禿木峰頂上，「無法從這筆立千丈的高峰上溜下來，熬了幾日凍餓，情急智生，忽然想到一法。他除了褲子，將兩隻褲腳都牢牢打了個結，又怕褲子不牢，將衣衫都除了來縛在褲上，雙手執定褲腰，咬緊牙關縱身一躍，從山峰上跳將下來。」作者還用說書人的口吻說「這法子原本極為冒險，只是死中求生，除此更無他策。」這兩句代言體的話，如果拿來轉贈給札剌勒丁，恐怕也不需要移動一字。成吉思汗不許他的兵士用箭射札剌勒丁，意思就是要生擒，不要傷他的性命。小說中的郭靖卻不惜用箭去射在半空中的歐陽鋒，但是「想到相饒三次之約，箭頭對準他大腿非致命之處」，目的也是不想射死他。可是小說中的歐陽鋒，是西毒一派的領袖，郭靖以為他「身在

43　此據〈總譯〉文字。札奇斯欽先生譯注本作「到巴魯安曠野駐下」，頁 396。

44　4 vols., Les Frères van Cleef, La Haye et Amsterdam, 1834-35; ph. rep. Tientsin, 1940.

45　馮承鈞譯本上冊（上海：商務印書館，1936 年），頁 128-129；札奇斯欽《秘史》譯注本，第二五七節，注 12，頁 399。

半空，無可騰挪閃避」，誰想他「卻是眼觀四方，見箭射到，當即彎腰弓身，雙足連揮，把郭靖射上來的箭枝一一踢開」，這是寫他的武功的超絕處。可是小說裡的成吉思汗卻不知這層關節，就下令放箭，「登時萬弩同張，箭似飛蝗」，歐陽鋒「就是有千手萬腿，也難以逐一撥落」，這時「歐陽鋒見情勢危急，突然鬆手，登時頭下腳上的倒墮下來。數十萬人齊聲呼喊，當真驚天動地。只見他在半空，腰間一挺，撲向城頭的一面大旗。此時西北風正屬，將那大旗自西至東張得筆挺。歐陽鋒左手前探，已抓住了旗角，就這麼稍一借力，那大旗已中裂為二。歐陽鋒一個觔斗，雙腳勾住旗桿，直滑下來，消失在城牆之後。」

　　札剌勒丁「脫甲負盾執纛」，文字間並沒有抒寫他這些行動起了什麼作用。如果金庸先生真地借用了這些動人的史實，那他的描敍可比前人要聰明多了。他不但敍述了歐陽鋒的武功，更把大旗用得恰到好處，真能令看書的讀者和當時目擊歐陽鋒的絕活的人們同樣地「忘了廝殺」，眼張目瞪。然而這裡作者所要送給我們的訊息實不止此：他先教黃蓉看了歐陽鋒「一條褲子中鼓滿了氣」，心轉一念「已明其理」；後面更明顯地教她告訴郭靖要送撒麻爾罕城給他做一份大禮了。我們經過第二次世界大戰的人，都早已知道「郭靖傳下密令，命部屬割破篷帳，製成一頂頂圓傘，下繫堅牢革索，限一個半時辰縫成一萬頂」（4/37/1457）是要幹什麼的了。這明明是現代的事情，怎好把它移植在古代十三世紀初葉？可是作者早已安排下線索了。「撒麻爾罕城倚峯而建，西面的城牆借用了一邊山峯，營造之費既省，而且堅牢無比，可見當日建城的將作大匠極具才智。這山峰陡削異常，全是堅石，草木不生，縱是猿猴也絕不能攀援而上。」（4/37/1447）這個底子打好了在那裡，下文的發展就教讀者在心理上會同意這是唯一的打開戰局的生機了。如果我們可以挑剔一些的話，將作大匠的名稱用在這兒似乎不很確當。第一，這名詞是中國歷史上的名詞，未必是突厥種和伊朗種的花剌子模人用的官名。其次，在中國歷史上，漢代到唐、宋這個很長的階段，將作大匠或和它名稱相近、性質相同的職官很多是朝代都設置的。元代也有將作院，「掌造金玉珠翠犀象寶貝、冠佩、器皿、刺繡、緞匹紗羅異樣百色造作」，[46] 卻不關城市建築之事。

---

46 《新元史》卷五十九，〈百官志五〉，「將作院」條。

「凡營造之程式，材物之給授，銓注」這些紙面上的工作歸工部管，實際上的運作又有各式各樣的規運提點所、總管府、營繕司許多架牀疊屋的機關。不過這些興作都在統治中國全國之後，在成吉思汗的蒙古時候，還是談不到的。撒麻爾罕在中亞也是一個古城，在十三世紀的花剌子模以前，它已換過不少主人。十一世紀的時候，這個城已經有六座城門和五哩長的城牆了。那是它歸伊朗的散路祝克王朝（Seljuks）統治的時代，我們知道散路祝克的馬力克‧沙王（Malik Shah）對當時的都城伊思弗罕（Isfahan）是留過建築方面的光輝遺跡的。我們這裡能不能把建城的將作大匠試改做建城的君王呢？

　　現在還有兩個有趣味的小問題，也許可以提出來一談，就是：小說的男主角之一的郭靖做過成吉思汗的駙馬，這件事情是有可能的麼？另外一個問題是：爲什麼要姓郭？蒙古人的軍隊裡可以有漢人做它的領兵大將麼？這兩個問題，都是和《脫卜赤顏》或《秘史》及兩《元史》的記載不無關係的。

　　對於前一個問題，我想在蒙古史或《元史》裡，漢人做蒙古皇室的駙馬大約是沒有可能的。但是金庸先生的《射鵰英雄傳》寫下來的環境條件，慢慢地把各種情形滲進我們的腦子裡，幾回寫了下來之後，條件成熟了，就會教我們覺得這件事情的發生並不怎樣陌生，我們與其信其無，就不如信其有了。郭靖母子自他小時候就被帶到荒涼的大漠裡去，他跟成吉思汗的第四個兒子拖雷、女兒華箏兩人都是自小認識的，當然他又會說蒙古話，後來又立了功勞，人品又耿直、忠實，這樣的青年正是大汗要選擇好女壻的適當對象，何況他跟華箏又是自幼就有了濃烈的兄妹之情的呢？華箏這個名字當然和郭靖一樣，都是創造，不是眞實的歷史人物。不過，作家要創造人物，也得先有成熟的條件。華這個字在字源上就是花朵的花，用它做女子的名字大約不論蒙、漢都是還適合的。《秘史》卷十，第二三九節說「因爲斡亦剌惕族（Oyirad）的忽都合‧別乞（Quduqa-beki）率先來歸，並且領導他的斡亦剌惕族人前來，〔大汗〕恩賜將女兒扯扯亦堅（Ceceyigen）給了他的兒子亦納勒赤（Inalci）。」[47] 這段話也可以說明成吉思汗招女壻目的不過是要他爲我

47　這裡用的漢文名字，從札奇斯欽先生譯注本，頁357，有一二字因行文關係略有修飾。
　　十二卷本（《四部叢刊》三編）人名和札奇先生所譯微有異同，今從札奇先生。拉丁
　　文拼音從羅依果先生 Igor de Rachwiltz, *Index to the Secret History of the Mongols*,
　　Bloomington: Indiana University Publications, Uralic & Altaic Series, Vol. 121,

所用。小說 4/38/1494 成吉思汗一聽郭靖會有變，那還得了？立刻就要把他抓來斬首，說「我待你不薄，自小將你養大，又將愛女許你爲妻。小賊！你膽敢叛我？」波斯的史家志費尼稱成吉思汗是世界的征服者，世界的征服者的心裡，只有英雄成功的一面，那裡顧得別人的心理、情緒？不過，扯扯亦堅的名字，原義也是花。

　　我們若是細說女壻，女壻的地位和價值在成吉思汗的時代原是很高的，我們但看《秘史》裡面，聖旨常常把皇子和公主、駙馬放在一塊兒相提並論，就可以知道。一旦國家有什麼大事，他們也都在一起開會。[48] 這些駙馬們的數目可能是不少的。《秘史》卷八、第二〇二節，虎兒年（丙寅，1206）把各處來的百姓都安頓好了，他們都住在有氈子保護的篷帳內，就在斡難河（Onan）源頭那裡聚會，豎起了九腳白虎纛，大家共上成吉思汗可汗的尊號。這個時候成吉思汗就派定了一共九十五個人做那顏（noyat），這是官員的尊稱，又敎他們做以千爲管理單位的千戶。這九十五個名字裡，有八個名字下面稱古列堅（güregen），就是女壻，也就是駙馬。小說裡的郭靖，在帖木眞打敗了王罕和札木合、在斡難河源大會之後，因爲「立功極偉」，也是被封做千夫長，並且把華箏給他，「從明天起，你是我的金刀駙馬」的（1/6/257）。可是他還不是那顏。那顏是到了 4/36/1419 蒙古兵西征出發的時候，成吉思汗命他統率一個萬人隊，才給他的。小說還說「『那顏』是蒙古最高的官銜，非親貴大將，不能當此稱號。」但是，金刀駙馬之稱卻是不典的，可是它在我們的《楊家將》一型的傳統小說裡，也偶然會發現。

　　成吉思汗派落的八個那顏駙馬裡，有一位叫做赤古古列堅（Cigü-güregen），恐怕和《秘史・續》卷一、第二五一節的駙馬出古（Cügü-güregen），《新元史》卷三〈太祖紀〉八年的駙馬赤古，都是一個人。[49] 這

1972, p.137.

48　例如成吉思汗一死，《秘史・續》卷二鼠兒年一條，就是召集各人到客魯列河（Keluren）闊迭兀・阿剌地方（Kode'ü-aral）去開會，以便奉斡歌歹（窩闊台）爲汗，就可以知道。看札奇斯欽譯注本，頁 424。

49　《元史》卷一〈太祖紀〉八年「駙馬齊奇」大概也是同一個人；此從寒齋用的乾隆四年本《元史》。札奇斯欽先生注譯本（頁 304）引姚從吾先生的舊注，云赤古應即《元史・太祖紀》八年之駙馬赤駒，疑所引或係百衲本，仍當一查。

一節的文字我們試參考幾家的譯本，略作簡括的敍述如下：

> 後來差去招降趙官勸他歸附的主卜罕（Jubqan）等許多使臣，又被在漢人地方[50]
> 的金國皇帝阿忽台（Aqutai）所阻擋，成吉思汗就在狗兒年（甲戌，1214）再向漢
> 地出征，責問爲什麼既然歸附了，又阻止差去趙官那裡的使臣？出發時成吉思汗
> 指向潼關進兵，敎者別攻打居庸關。金國皇帝知道成吉思汗攻向潼關這個口子，
> 就派亦列（Ile）、合荅（Qada）、豁字格禿兒（Höbögetür）三個人統率軍隊去堵塞，
> 「用我們最好的弓箭手部隊人員[51] 當頭陣，不顧一切休敎他們越過嶺來！」達三
> 將疾快地就出發了。我們的兵到來時，但見到處都是漢地的兵。成吉思汗和亦列、
> 合荅、豁字格禿兒三人對陣，逼亦列、合荅兩將往後退卻，拖雷、出古駙馬兩人
> 橫衝直撞，擊退了金兵的弓箭手部隊和亦列、合荅，像拉枯摧朽似地戰勝了金兵，
> 他們留下的屍體堆積多得像堆爛木塊那樣。金國皇帝知道了打敗仗，就從中部（北
> 京）逃避到南京（汴梁）去，剩餘的殘兵餓困死的很多，苦到吃人肉。成吉思汗
> 見拖雷和出古駙馬兩人打得那麼好，就詩獎他們，賞給他們很多恩賜。

姚從吾先生以前曾經研究過《秘史》這一段原文，說狗兒年的記載和《元史·
太祖紀》及《金史·宣宗紀》所敍的年份不合，所以考定蒙古攻打潼關的事，
當在丙子年（1216），就是太祖十一年，金宣宗貞祐四年。[52] 這話是不錯的。
《元史》稱這一段「獲金西安軍節度使尼瑪哈富勒呼」，《新元史》卷三〈太祖
紀下〉稱「獲其將尼蘭古蒲魯虎」，實即一人，《金史》卷十四就說「泥龐古
蒲魯虎戰沒」了。但是這一年發生的事，不會有拖雷和駙馬出古在內，《秘史》
是把兩件事混合了記在一塊兒了。拖雷他們兩人的戰功，是在太祖八年癸酉
（1213），比攻潼關的事早了兩年多。兩《元史》所記是一樣的，不過《新元
史》卷三說「秋七月，帝自將大軍圍德興府，皇子拖雷、駙馬赤古先登克之」，

50　原文乞塔惕（Kitat）即契丹，遼時的中國北方，現在爲金人所據，故云。

51　這裡的原文是「忽剌安·迭格列」（hula'an-degelen），姚從吾先生以爲當指金時楊安
　　兒、劉二祖等的紅襖軍，引《金史》卷一〇一〈僕散安貞……等傳〉及周密《齊東野
　　語》九〈李全〉條，姚先生曾撰〈《元朝秘史》所記『忽剌安·迭格列』人（紅襖軍）
　　助金守潼關並抗蒙古人入侵事考〉，刊《中央研究院歷史語言研究所外編：董彥堂六
　　十五歲紀念論文集》（臺北，1960）；參看札奇斯欽譯注本，頁 381-382，注 4。這裡
　　的譯法見 Paul Kahn（前引，見註 32），頁 164。

52　參看註 51，札奇斯欽譯注本，頁 382，注 7。

《元史》卷一寫做「皇子圖類、駙馬齊奇」罷了（看註 49）。兩《元史》這一年也都記有者別（《新元史》）或哲伯（《元史》）攻取了居庸關的事，這一點也跟上面引的《秘史》狗兒年條說「教者別攻打居庸關」相同，倒可以互做印證。這些記載都可以說明拖雷和這一位叫做出古的駙馬是在一起打仗的，可能兩人間的感情也很好。《射鵰英雄傳》的駙馬郭靖和拖雷之間的關係，寫得比《秘史》熱鬧得多，但是它的根源，也許會是從《秘史》這一點因子發展出來的。

小說裡郭嘯天和楊鐵心兩個人的夫人都有了喜，丘處機替她們腹中的孩子起了「靖」和「康」兩個單名，要孩子們不忘記靖康之恥，這是 1/1/29 早已說明了的。只是寫書的人，為什麼要安排這兩個好朋友中有一個姓郭，將來他的兒子才會叫做郭靖呢？我想，這恐怕是作者受到了兩《元史》裡〈郭侃傳〉的影響。郭侃和他的上兩代都見〈郭寶玉傳〉（《元史》卷一四九、《新元史》卷一四六）。郭侃的祖父郭寶玉本是金國的猛安（相當於千夫長，見《金史·兵志》），蒙古兵到，他就帶軍隊歸降了。成吉思汗十四年（1219）征西域，他跟隨出征，參加過打撒麻爾罕的戰役，這也算是郭靖出征撒麻爾罕的一點助因。十六年（1221）追札剌勒丁，他也跟著追到印度。他有兩個兒子，德山和德海，德海就是郭侃的父親。德山官到萬戶，從大軍破金的陝州，死在攻潼關的時候，可能就是十一年十月撒木合（薩木哈 Samuqa）攻潼關一役。德海在金國是謀克（百夫長），父親投降後他也在太行山歸從蒙古，曾跟者別西征，後來又跟闊闊出（Kököcü）打進關中，直到凌風寨，才退出的。在窩闊台（太宗）六年，他因打仗受傷病死。

郭侃的時代較晚。太宗初年他由百戶積戰功到千戶，又因他曾押送兵仗到當時的都城和林，得了個抄馬那顏之銜。憲宗（蒙哥 Möngke）三年，他跟隨拖雷的第六個兒子旭烈兀（Hülegü）西征，攻打木剌夷（Mura'i）[53] 的

《新元史》卷二五六有〈木剌夷傳〉。木剌夷是阿剌伯語的譯音，義謂舍正路者，指的其實是伊斯蘭教十葉派（Shi'ah, Shi'ite）裡的伊斯瑪儀支派（Isma'iliya, Isma'ilism）內一個叫做阿薩辛派（Assassin）的小支派。阿薩辛就是暗殺，因為他們常用激烈的暗殺手段去對付敵人。創始的人是哈桑·本·薩巴（Hasan ibn al-Sabbah），他在十一世紀末（1090-91 間，北宋元祐五、六年，蘇軾、程頤這些人的那個時代）率他的信徒打下了在今伊朗山區的阿拉穆特堡（Alamüt），做他們的大本營。他們的這一個

時候，已頗立戰功。[54] 憲宗八年（1258）旭烈兀率領大軍進攻報達，這個回教哈里發所駐的大城（caliphate），郭侃很出力，《新元史·郭侃傳》說他「破其兵七萬，屠西城，又破其東城。東城殿宇皆構以沉檀木，舉火焚之，香聞百里。」這恐怕是蒙古兵殺戮的習俗，郭侃雖是漢人，也難免染了這種不文明的習氣，和《射鵰英雄傳》4/37/1462 看了蒙古兵的來去屠戮，忍不住向大汗求他「饒了這數十萬百姓的性命」的郭靖，就不可同日而語了。報達陷落時，哈里發（caliph）要逃走。東西兩城之間「有大河（就是體格力斯河 Tigris），侃預造浮梁，以防其遁。城破，合（哈）里發登舟，覩河有浮梁扼之，乃自縛，詣軍門降。」〈憲宗本紀〉說「旭烈兀平報達。獲哈里發木司塔辛，殺之。」這個倒霉的報達最後一位哈里發正是 Al-Musta'sim。[55] 〈憲宗紀〉的話可參看卷二五六〈報達傳〉。

　　〈郭侃傳〉裡所記的，他還有其他的功績。他曾經打到天房（默伽 Mekka, Mecca）、密昔兒（Misr，埃及 Egypte 本名），又曾奉旭烈兀命西渡海，收富浪國。這個富浪（Farang），是波斯語，可能指地中海東岸的歐洲人。《元史》卷一四九〈郭侃傳〉所記，大致和《新元史》全同；它們的共同資料可能是劉郁的《西使記》。[56]

活動中心到蒙古憲宗六年（1256）才被旭烈兀的軍隊攻落；參看《新元史》卷六〈憲宗本紀〉。〈憲宗紀〉說木剌夷「酋兀克乃丁請降，帝以木剌夷人凶悍，命旭烈兀悉誅之。兀克乃丁入朝，亦殺之於中途。」這個兀克乃丁，就是他們最後的一位大宗師 Rukn al-Din Khurshah。《射鵰英雄傳》裡附錄的〈成吉思汗家族〉的註 19（頁 1605）提到木剌夷這一派有所謂山中老人（哈桑·本·薩巴就是第一個山中老人）引誘青年，用迷藥把他們一批一批的分別抬上山頂的樂園，教他們享盡各種的樂事，相信這是天堂，然後又把他們迷昏過去，重新回到人間，再吩咐他們盡力聽命教主。行刺的奮不顧身，即使死去，就是重回天堂的時候。這個傳說從馬可波羅時已很流行，只是伊斯瑪儀支派的人仍舊不承認它的真實性。

54 照《新元史·憲宗本紀》攻克木剌夷，在六年冬天。這裡說三年，〈本紀〉三年云「六月，命……皇弟旭烈兀征報達」，是三年開始出征，不是這一年就跟木剌夷作戰。

55 《新元史》卷二五六〈報達傳〉，說木斯（司）塔辛「請沐浴就死，同死者其長子及宦者五人，皆裹以氈，置衢路，驅戰馬蹴踏而斃」。同傳也說及蒙古軍防他逃走，「軍於體格力斯河上下游，列礮船上游以防其逸」，可是並不曾提到郭侃。

56 這書的背景是憲宗三年癸丑（1253）曾命諸王錫里庫等帥師征西域法勒哈、巴哈台等國，九年（1259）常德西使錫里庫軍中沿途往返的見聞，劉郁把常德說的記敘下來，僅一卷。版本很多，如《古今說海》、《說郛》（宛委山堂本）弓五十六、《學津討原》

如果我們說《射鵰英雄傳》記郭靖西征可能有一點郭侃的影子，那麼，《新元史·郭侃傳》後面著者柯鳳蓀先生的「史臣曰」說「元之兵制，漢人無將蒙古兵者，旭烈兀平木剌夷及報達，郭侃之功在怯的不花諸將之右，其事或虛而不實。」，我想，這恐怕是過慮，至少郭侃所帶的兵，不能全是《元朝秘史》所說漢地契丹人罷？但是如果郭靖這個「虛而不實」的漢將，真地是從蒙古西征得到一點「煙士披里純」的，那麼，〈郭侃傳〉裡說的他向元世祖忽必烈（Kublai Khan）獻平宋策，「當先取襄陽，既克襄陽，彼揚、盧諸城彈丸地耳，置之勿顧而直趨臨安，疾雷不及掩耳，江淮、巴蜀不攻自平」（《新元史》卷一四六，《元史》卷一四九全同），若讓郭靖得知，恐怕比他在桃花島看見幾位師父被殺，腦中猶似天旋地轉（4/34/1317）還要傷心呢！

三

關於全真教，我以前曾寫過兩篇較長的文字，一篇〈全真教和小說《西遊記》〉，一篇〈讀蜂屋邦夫《金代道教の研究》〉，[57] 已經說過不少話，所以這裡只就和《射鵰英雄傳》有關的兩個問題，略做考究。這兩個問題是：㈠《射鵰英雄傳》雖然不止是通常所說的武俠小說（它包括的題材和識見實在很

第六集、《四庫全書·傳記類》、《叢書集成·初編》……都收入。《四庫全書總目》卷五十八《西使記》條指出《元史·憲宗紀》憲宗二年命錫喇征西域，錫喇即死在這年，下一年又派錫里庫，說《西使記》對這一點有混淆處，其實兩個名字說的都只是一回事。（殿本《元史》錫喇又刻做實喇）《四庫總目》本條又說「考〔《元史》〕〈世系表〉睿宗（按，即拖雷）十一子，次六曰錫里庫。」檢殿本《元史》卷一〇七，睿宗第六子即旭烈兀。《元史》旭烈兀無傳，《新元史》卷一〇八〈拖雷傳〉附〈旭烈兀傳〉云「憲宗二年以木剌夷凶悍無道，命旭烈兀率諸將討之。」但是卷六〈憲宗紀〉明言三年六月，「命……皇弟旭烈兀征報達」，八年，「旭烈兀平報達」，都與《元史·憲宗紀》三年六月「命諸王錫里庫……等率師征西域法勒哈」；八年「諸王錫里庫討回回法勒哈，平之」相符合。可見錫里庫當然是旭烈兀（Hülegü），而西域的法勒哈，恐怕實係報達之哈里發（Caliph）也。

57 前者原刊香港《明報月刊》第 233-237 期，1985，收入拙著《和風堂文集》下冊（上海：上海古籍出版社，1991），頁 1319-1391；後者原刊香港中文大學《中國文化研究所學報》，1994，收入拙著《和風堂新文集》下冊（臺北：新文豐出版公司，1997），頁 509-569。

深廣），但是武俠仍是它的重要成分之一，這是沒有人會否認的，我要問的是：歷史上的全真教人物，有武俠的經歷和活動麼？第(二)個問題是：《射鵰英雄傳》裡全真教各人對當時宋、金和蒙古三個政權的態度，在小說所描寫的環境和局面之下是十分清楚的：基本地說南宋是大宋，女真金是佔領中國北方大部分領土的敵國，蒙古在它不曾攻擊宋境以前是和平相處的鄰人，蒙古軍隊一攻小說裡的襄陽，就是敵人了。個人間的恩怨還有很多，但是小說布置下的局面是如此。從歷史方面來看，全真教的立場和經歷又是怎樣呢？這仍是我們可以稍做說明的。

　　我們先說武俠的問題。

　　一般記述或研究全真教的創立者王嚞的著作，從清代光緒間著《全真道教源流》的陳教友（銘珪）開始，[58] 到近歲如姚從吾先生等人的著述，[59] 多半用的《道藏》611-613《甘水仙源錄》裡面所收的金源璹[60] 的〈終南山神仙重陽真人全真教祖碑〉、劉祖謙的〈終南山重陽祖師仙跡記〉，和麻九疇的〈鄧州重陽觀記〉等幾篇文章。[61] 這幾篇文字中看到王重陽能武事是沒有問題的，如金源璹說他：

58　《長春道教源流》有光緒己卯（五年，1879）著者自序，署「羅浮酥醪洞主陳教友」。這書共八卷，其中關於創教的人王重陽（嚞）才一卷，述邱（丘）長春（處機）事蹟及弟子、法嗣的佔六卷之多。汪孝博（宗衍）先生撰《陳東塾先生年譜》記東塾（陳澧）咸豐十年庚申（1860）「閏三月初八日與陳銘珪（友珊）、葉靜軒、黎遂之同遊羅浮」，酥醪觀即在羅浮；香港：商務印書館，1964，頁82；澳門：于今書屋，1970 增訂本，頁82。《長春道教源流》近亦收入《藏外道書》，第三十一冊（成都：巴蜀書社，1994 影印本）。

59　例如姚著〈金元全真教的民族思想與救世思想〉，收入姚著《東北史論叢》，下冊（臺北：正中書局，1959），頁175-204。

60　即完顏璹，《金史》卷八十五有傳。他雅愛文事，和趙秉文、元好問等人交善，著《如菴小藁》，收他自己刪存的詩及樂府不少。他有志盡心國事，卻不得志。汴都危急議和時，他自請做副使去辦交涉，哀宗（完顏守緒）說：「南渡後（指從燕京渡過黃河到汴京）國家比承平時有何奉養？然叔父亦未嘗沾溉。無事則置之冷地，無所顧藉，緩急則置于不測。叔父盡忠固可，天下其謂朕何！」君臣相顧淚下。

61　金源璹文見卷1/2b-10a；劉文見卷1/10a-14a；麻文見卷9/16a-18a。劉祖謙的〈仙跡記〉，末署「天興元年（1232）九月重陽日謹記」，已是哀宗時，不過兩年金朝就亡了。

> 弱冠修進士舉業，籍京兆府學。又善武略，聖朝天眷間（1138-1140）收復陝西，
> 英豪獲用。眞人於是捐文場，應武舉，易名德威，字世雄，其志足可以知。還被
> 道炁充餘，善根積著，天遣文武之道兩無成焉，於是慨然入道，改今之名字矣。
> 會廢齊攝事，秦民未附，又饑饉，……（1/3a-b）

劉祖謙記他，說：

> 形質魁偉，任氣而好俠。少讀書，係學籍，又隸名武選。當天眷之初，以財雄鄉
> 里。歲且飢，人多殍亡。（1/11a）

　　以上兩段，下面節去的文字都記王重陽家曾被盜劫，後來獲得了盜首，
重陽竟置不問，里人因此敬仰他，「遠近以爲長者」。但是這和他是否應金時
的武選沒有關係，我們就不鈔錄了。陳教友力主王重陽是「有宋之忠義也」
（《長春道教源流》卷 1/25a），以爲重陽是不會應金時的武舉的，所以他更信
任麻九疇的〈鄧州重陽觀記〉說的「〔重陽〕有文武藝，當廢齊阜昌間，脫落
功名，日酣於酒」（9/17a）的話，並且說「劉豫廢後踰年，金熙宗改元天眷。
麻〈記〉稱阜昌時已『脫落功名』矣，寧於天眷而反應舉邪？」所以又下結
論說「此蓋李志源輩乞文於璹，以璹爲金源王子，爲是飾說耳！」（1/26b）
教友的話有對有不對。阜昌是劉豫稱齊帝的年號，查《宋史》卷四七五〈叛
臣五〉，劉豫在南宋建炎四年（金太宗天會八年，1130）立於大名府，次年稱
阜昌元年（南宋紹興元年，1131），二年四月始遷都汴，到八年（1137）十一
月就被廢了！廢劉豫的下一年就是金天眷元年，這一點教友是不錯的。但是
他說金源璹所以會這樣寫，是因爲請他寫這篇〈教祖碑〉的李志源等人因爲
他是金朝的貴胄，恐怕說話開罪他，所以才如此「飾說」，這話可能不確。我
們讀〈教祖碑〉原文，金源璹已經交待清楚了說王重陽歿後五十六年，「嗣法
孫汴京嘉祥觀提點眞常子李志源，中太一宮提點洞眞子于善慶二大士眞實道
行，弘揚祖道者也，懇懇求記於玉陽子友人樗軒居士」；接著這位樗軒居士就
「援筆爲之銘」了。樗軒居士是金源璹的雅號，他又是玉陽子的友人，玉陽子
就是王玉陽處一，王重陽的七個大弟子之一，樗軒跟他認識，他所聽到的王
重陽事蹟該是接近第一手的，李志源似乎不用向他進言什麼了。〈教祖碑〉的
銘文又說重陽：

　　幼之發秀，長而不群。工乎談笑，妙於斯文。又善騎射，健勇絕倫。以文非時，復意于武。戡定禍亂，志欲斯舉。文武二進，天不我與。蓋公宿緣，道氣為主。慨然入道，真仙自遇。(1/9b)

　　措辭其實跟前引的散文體的碑文是差不多的。事實上碑文所說的「收復陝西，英豪獲用」，這收復二字是金朝的人說話用的誇大詞，而所謂英豪，也是指的金方的英豪，簡言之，就是華北淪陷區可以出來賣氣力當兵的漢人罷了。如果重陽真地這樣去做，這時候他的腦子裡的動機，也不會是太單純的。客觀的紀錄告訴我們，金熙宗天眷這三年間宋、金之間的活動可真不是簡單的。先是金國表示要歸還宋朝河南、陝西的故地，最初宋方也真地接收了一些地方，不少原係陷區的金方派的漢人節制使、節度使、經略使也分別向臨安「上表待罪」，獲得宋朝的新委任，可是不久金方就叛盟了，這就是碑文說的「收復陝西」的原委。事實上，這時候在金國的區域內像後世的遊擊隊似的「太行忠義」、「兩河豪傑」的活動，還是很活躍的；但是宋方的正式軍隊像吳璘、劉錡、岳飛所統率的，雖然在各處個別地打過幾個勝仗，也不能抗命不接受堅持和議的朝廷的命令撤兵。王重陽最後的「脫落名利」、「慨然入道」恐怕跟這樣的情勢很有關係。陳教友在另段更引了清初顧嗣立編的《元詩選》[62] 收的元朝商挺的一首〈題甘河遇仙宮〉詩做證，說「據此，則重陽不惟忠憤，且實曾糾眾與金兵抗矣！」(1/26b-27a) 商挺這首五言古詩前半是這樣寫的：

　　　　子房志亡秦，曾進橋下履。佐漢開鴻基，屹然大一柱。要伴赤松遊，功成拂衣去。異人與異書，造物不輕付。重陽起全真，高視仍闊步。矯矯英雄姿，乘時或割據。妄跡復知非，收心活死墓。……

　　下文描寫的就是重陽遇二仙的故事了。這詩以王重陽和秦、漢間的張良相比況，暗示重陽的心情也和張子房相似，要推翻統治的王朝；「乘時或割據」句是說他也許曾經有過什麼行動。我想，如果重陽真地曾經領兵要造反，

62　收癸集之乙，清嘉慶戊午 (1798) 刻本，頁 1b-2a。這書共一百十一卷，也收入《四庫全書‧總集類五》。其實這首詩也見《甘水仙源錄》，10/27a。

甚至於想割據，那麼不管那是什麼朝代，去應武舉好圖謀一個上進的機會更是不足怪的了。教友先生把這幾個字的含義看得鑿實了，認爲他「實曾糾眾與金兵抗矣」，金庸先生《射鵰英雄傳》附的〈關於全眞教〉（4/1612）因爲這個看法和小說的構想很接近，也曾引了他的話。[63]

　　上面說的，僅講的王重陽一人。他「善騎射，健勇絕倫」，是所謂馬上功夫罷了，別的武功怎樣呢？我們所知還不多，只可以舉一兩個例子。《甘水仙源錄》卷二收有秦志安撰〈長生眞人劉宗師道行碑〉，述重陽吸引劉長生（處玄）信道，有這件的趣事：

> 大定己丑（按，九年，1169）之春，忽〔有人〕於鄰居壁間人所不能及處，揮灑二頌，而墨跡尚新，不留姓名。其末句云：「武官養性眞仙地，須有長生不死人。」先生（劉處玄）嘆賞其筆力遒勁，疑神物之所化成，而未能決其信情。是歲九月霜寒露清，重陽祖師杖履西行，攜丘〔處機〕、譚〔處端〕、馬〔鈺〕三仙之英度

---

63 關於王重陽早期的歷史，和〈教祖碑〉很接近的，如《道藏》75 林間羽客樗櫟道人編《金蓮正宗記》卷二〈重陽王眞人〉條云：「膂力倍人，才名拔俗。蚤通經史，晚習弓刀。當廢齊阜昌間，獻賦春官，迕意而黜，復試武舉，遂中甲科。」（2/1a）但是這裡說的時間竟在阜昌間。樗櫟道人是秦志安的號，《甘水仙源錄》7/24a-26b 元好問撰〈通眞子秦公道行碑銘〉稱秦志安所居曰樗櫟堂（7/25b）可證。這篇文字也見於元好問《遺山集》卷三十一，題〈通眞子墓碣〉，文字略有不同。志安是宋德方披雲的弟子，所以是丘處機的再傳弟子。他在山西平陽玄都觀居住幾乎十年，盡力校補金《道藏》的文字，並且增入了若干全眞教的著作，加以刊刻，對道經的流布貢獻很大。姚從吾教授也是贊成陳教友的意見，並且引《金史》卷四〈熙宗本紀〉說只有天眷元年五月有過一次「詔以經義、詞賦兩科取士」，並云《金史》卷五十一〈選舉志〉同。又引〈選舉志〉說「武選當設於皇統時，其制則見於泰和」；前引，頁 179。引的話都是正確的，但是《金史》的這些記載可能是很粗略的。例如武舉，皇統共有八年（1141—1148），皇統元年就是天眷三年的下一年。這裡指的到底是皇統的那一年呢？從熙宗的皇統元年起到章宗的泰和元年（1201），其間經歷了皇統、天德、貞元、正隆、大定、明昌、承安七個年號，共有六十個年頭，會不會這裡面失去了正確的記錄呢？又如試進士，《金史·選舉志一》說進士考試「其設也始於太宗天會元年（1123）十一月，時以急欲得漢士，以撫輯新附，初無定數，亦無定期，故二年一月、八月，凡再行焉。五年，以河北、河東初降，職員多闕，以遼、宋之制不同，詔南北各因其素所習之業取士，號爲南北選。熙宗天眷元年五月詔南北選各以經義詞賦兩科取士。海陵庶人天德二年（1150），始增殿試之制，而更定試期三年，併南北選爲一，罷經義策試兩科，專以詞賦取士。」這樣說來，前文所涉及的天眷時代，試期竟是不確定的。

海島，歷山城。先生聞之竭蹶而趨，香火而迎。祖師顧而笑曰：「壁間墨痕汝知之乎？」三子者亦相視而冰哂，方悟其頌乃神通變現之所以相驚也。(2/1b-2a)

假如我們不相信「神通變現」，我們卻相信武功高的人是能夠跑上「壁間人所不能及處」用毛筆寫字的。[64] 另一個可能和武功發生關係的事情，見《甘水仙源錄》卷一收的金源璹撰〈長真子譚真人仙跡碑銘〉。長真子就是譚處端：

> 至大定丁亥（七年，1167）仲秋，聞重陽真人度馬宜甫（鈺）爲門生，公徑赴真人所，祈請棄俗服羽，執弟子禮。真人付之以頌，便宿於庵中。時嚴冬飛雪，丹竈灰冷，藉海藻而寐，寒可墮指。真人遂展足令抱之，少頃，汗流被體，如置炊甑中。(1/29a)

《道藏》76《金蓮正宗記》卷四〈長真譚真人〉條沒有記得這麼詳細，卻說重陽「召之同衾而寢，談話親密，過於故交。比曉下床，舊疾頓愈，四體輕健，奔走如飛。」(4/1a-b) 處端本是因爲醉臥風雪中，患了風眩癱瘓的病來的，《金蓮正宗記》這麼一描寫，就像是用氣功治病似的，不見那有武功的人的妙處了。[65] 《金蓮正宗仙源像傳》的敍描略同金源璹撰的〈碑銘〉。其實在《金蓮正宗記》卷五〈廣寧郝真人〉條敍述郝大通在河北沃州（就是趙州）[66] 橋上練靜坐，一坐數年，也是一種武功兼氣功的表現。《正宗記》云：

> 重陽南歸汴梁，先生往來河北。乙未歲（大定十五年，1175，這時重陽已死了五年）乞食於沃州，方悟重陽密語，渙然開發。[67] 遂往橋上默然靜坐：饑渴不求，寒暑不變，人饋則食，不饋則否。雖有人侮狎戲笑者，不怒也。志在忘形，如此

64　參看《道藏》75《金蓮正宗記》4/4a；《道藏》76《金蓮正宗仙源像傳》29b-30a。《道藏》76 李道謙編《七真年譜》8b 僅云「祖師領丹陽、長真、長春西至萊州，化長生真人出家，訓名處玄，字通妙，號長生子。」重陽詩句中所說的「武官」，是山東東萊的武官莊。

65　《七真年譜》但云「是冬，長真真人就環內出家，祖師訓名處端，字通正，號長真子。」(7b)

66　金海陵王天德三年（1151）以後才改稱沃州。

67　這指的郝大通棄家，入崑崳山拜師時，重陽解衲衣，去了袖子才給他，說「無患無袖，汝當自成。」見《甘水仙源錄》2/20a 收徐琰撰〈廣寧通玄太古真人郝宗師道行碑〉；參看《金蓮正宗記》5/7a；《射鵰英雄傳》3/25/1018。

三年，人呼爲「不語先生」。一夕，天色昏冥，偶醉者過，以是蹴先生於橋下，默而不出者七日。人不知者以爲先生何往？忽値客官乘馬將過而馬驚躍，捶之不進。客遂墮馬，問左右曰：「橋下必有怪事！不然，何吾馬之驚也。」命左右往視之，則一道者奄然正坐，問之，則不語，以手畫地曰：「不食七日矣！」州民聞之爭往饋食，焚香請出，但搖手不應，只於橋下復坐三年。水火顚倒，陰陽和合，九轉之功成矣。乃忻然而起，杖履北遊，盤桓於眞定（今河北正定）間。(5/7a-b) 68

比起郝大通的道行來，王處一的表現像更接近武俠的所謂外功，其實，如通常講求鍛鍊身體的人們所了解的，內功和外功恐怕就是一種相關的功能。《甘水仙源錄》所收姚燧撰〈玉陽體玄廣度眞人王宗師道行碑銘〉云：

後居雲光洞，志行確苦。嘗俯大壑，一足跂立，觀者目瞚毛豎，舌撟然而不能下，稱爲鐵脚仙。洞居九年，制練形魂。其長春爲詩頌曰：「九夏迎陽立，三冬抱雪眠。」(2/14a)

雲光洞據《金蓮正宗記》5/1b 在山東文登縣鐵查山，鐵查山大概就是諸家筆下所說的查山了！丘長春送王玉陽的這首詩，在現存的《道藏》裡收的《磻溪集》裡找不著，如果它不是收在今已失傳的丘處機的《鳴道集》裡，就是根本不曾收錄過了。可是關於王處一住的雲光洞所在的查山，在全眞教的歷史上卻有一樁著名的傳說，被道教中人誇做王重陽的奇蹟的。我看這段故實，恐怕也有一部分用的是武功的招數，其餘的大部分，恐怕就是他們神道設教的靈跡了！我們現在講全眞教諸君的武功，也不妨把它分析一下看看。《甘水仙源錄》卷一收的金源璹撰〈全眞教祖碑〉，有一段云：

又於寧海塗中，眞人（按，重陽）擲油傘於空。傘乘風而起，至查山王處一菴處，其傘始墜；至擲處已二百餘里也。其傘柄內有傘陽子號。(1/7b)

這段話雖然記得或略或詳，幾乎全眞教的各種史乘中是無不具備的。《甘水仙源錄》這段的傘字印得很模糊，看去幾乎和普通的傘字差不多，別的書就淸楚多了。《金蓮正宗記》說「至四月間（按，照上文意謂大定春四月，沒有說

68 參看〈廣寧通玄太古眞人郝宗師道行碑〉，前引，2/20b—21a；《金蓮正宗仙源像傳》，40a-b；《七眞年譜》，10b。

年分），祖師將遊龍泉，借范明叔傘以蔽日。丘、劉、譚、馬先行，祖師在後可半里許。忽擲傘於空中，飄飄然起，西北而飛，不知所往。丘、劉輩驚，反走，而問其所由。曰：『搏扶搖而上，不知所以然也！』自辰至脯，傘乃墮於雲光洞前，擊破其柄，中有道號，曰『㦻陽子，名處一。』㦻音竹，篇韻中本無此字，蓋祖師之所撰也。字作七人，表金蓮七朵之數，大約擲傘處、雲光洞相去二百餘里。」（5/2a）《金蓮正宗仙源像傳》37a 又補充說「於傘柄中得詩一首，并㦻陽子三字。」傘柄中有詩，是《金蓮正宗記》不曾提過的。《七真年譜》繫這事於大定九年己丑（1169）四月，又說重陽出門的原因，是「引丹陽、長真、長春、廣寧遷居寧海州金蓮堂，途中至龍泉。」（8a）借來的傘，傘柄內會盛著㦻陽子的新道號，這非事前先有準備不可。單只一兩個人如此做佐證還不行，要更多的人深信，必須要大家通力合作。參加同行的丘處機，《磻溪集》卷三有一首七古〈度世吟〉，「擲蓋投冠予計較」等數句有夾行長注（3/3a-b），它也證實了《七真年譜》說的飛傘這件事情在大定九年己丑發生的可靠性。

仙傳（hagiography）和史傳不同，它的寫法其實比史傳寬鬆了許多，因為它並不一定要求有和許多方面徵驗的歷史真實性。但是它仍舊是有些縛手縛腳的，沒有小說創作的自由，因為它至少還要頂著一頂史傳的帽子，輕易不願意把它捨棄。從武俠的觀點看起來，這些史料，不能放開筆來說話，就不會像小說那樣有更豐富的素材可以寫得親切生動。它們所具有的一些勉強的神話性，又不會像真正的神話那樣漫天開價，彌綸六極。

四

我們現在剩下來的還有一個問題，就是從道教史的看法來說，全真教初起時它的領導者和信受奉行的人，對他們所處的變化中的境遇的反應或態度。我並不是說從南宋初到元末這兩百年來全真的活動是一貫的，譬如以十六世紀中葉盛行的章回小說所代表的時代來說，不論《水滸》、《西遊》，這些大部頭的小說中「全真」兩個字幾乎可以代表一切道士們的活動了。當時別的支派的道士們的活動在這樣的聲勢之下隱而不顯，一般性的「全真」只是抽象地涵蓋了古典性的辭藻所說的羽士或類似的稱呼罷了；這種抽象的對象

就很不易說明有沒有具體的態度。我們寧可說魯智深是有魯智深的態度的，《水滸傳》第六回的「生鐵佛」崔道成和「飛天夜叉」丘道人也應該有他們個別的態度，可是我們實在無從知道。

　　因爲史料實在不很足夠，更豐富的知識還實在有待於我們或將來的人的發掘，我們對於全眞教的創立者王嘉（重陽）在他創教的時候到底有多少程度是爲國爲民的，還有很大的部分只能說是未知數。但是我們對他的行動也還有若干部分可以肯定的地方，這些肯定多數可以從他的詩詞集裡獲得一些實證。他的生活，早期在陝西終南縣劉蔣村的事蹟我們知道的很模糊，卻仍可以用金世宗大定七年（1167）四月他自焚劉蔣村的茅庵，那年夏天他東去山東寧海州開始教化做他的生涯的下半段的標幟。這時候他已是舊曆算法的五十六歲，再過不到三年，他就死了。以後全眞教在山東及其他各地的活動，他的七個弟子（尤其是馬、丘、譚、劉）實在都曾盡出過比他本人更多更久的貢獻。但是在那麼短促的歲月，他也曾經率領各人，奔波各處，造成了所謂「三州五會」開創的局面，也確實很不容易。[69]

　　在他離開陝西之前，所謂在甘河鎮遇見了仙人（《道藏》796《重陽分梨十化集》卷下頁 6 下面詞題，是他唯一的一関詞自稱「自甘河得遇純陽眞人」的）以後，大約曾經過一個一般宗教史上說的由常人變到非常人的轉化時期，以後他就像是入了迷似地（或者說是徹悟洞明了似地）以道自任了。《道藏》794《重陽全眞集》9/11b-12a 的〈悟眞歌〉很零碎地揭露了一些重陽貧苦的出身和家世，雖然文字很短，仍可能比後人爲他寫的〈教祖碑〉一類的文字更能夠教我們稍知道一些他的教養和環境。他到了山東寧海州在街上求乞，作七絕體的詩寫在紙旗上引人注意（2/18a）。《道藏》786《漸悟集》卷上 10a 馬鈺就有詩說〈師父引馬鈺上街求乞〉，他自己也曾〈在南京乞化〉（卷下19a）。《重陽全眞集》1/6a 有七律〈化造鐵罐錢〉；6/8b 有〈漁家傲〉詞是「詠鐵甀，先生出外常攜之」；這就是討飯時用的罐子，9/9a-b 還有十首〈鐵罐

69　這三州，據丘處機《磻溪集》3/3a〈度世吟〉的注，是寧海州、登州和萊州。計開寧海州金蓮，登州玉華，萊州平等，文登七寶，福山三光；文登屬寧海州，福山屬登州，所以算起來還是三州。會社的名字有時用會，有時用社，《重陽全眞集》裡有時候還看到《玉華金蓮社》（10/18a）一類的名稱。此外，蓬萊也有玉華會，是在登州；掖縣也有平等會，是在萊州。就是文登，也有玉華社。

歌〉。丘處機的《磻溪集》裡 5/18b-19a 是一首〈芰荷香‧乞食〉，譚處端《水雲集》卷中 14a-b〈西江月〉第四首上片云：「欲入全真門戶，行住坐臥寂寞，存心乞化度中朝，塵事般般屏了。」說來這全真教學的簡直就是《射鵰英雄傳》裡丐幫的淨衣魯有腳一派。

　　從他留傳下來的文字的全部來觀察，重陽只能說是一個十分平民化（甚至貧民化）的教主，所以他的傳教的對象雖然細大不捐，可是他的教化最能影響的正是窮困的農村裡樸實的農民、小商人、家庭婦女和其他社會地位較低的階層。財主和做官宦的信眾只佔少數。他自己的詩裡所提供的信仰的道統就是十分入俗的，像「漢正陽兮為的祖，唐純陽兮為師父，燕國海蟾兮是叔主」（《重陽全真集》9/1a〈了了歌〉），這鍾離權、呂洞賓、劉海蟾三個信仰的對象正是這時候還不曾認真地進入道教的廟廊的神仙，卻是在民間信仰裡已經被逐漸滲入的偶像。王重陽那著名的四字標語酒、色、財、氣（1/18a-19a〈一字至七字詩：酒、色、財、氣〉），這四個大字直到近世，雖然許多人早已忘記它們的根源了，還時常出現在許多勞苦大眾非知識分子揮汗用的紙扇上面，只這麼四個毛筆墨字做裝飾。[70] 不管從前他是不是係學籍隸武選，重陽雖然認識一些做官的長吏或他們的部屬，在他傳教的過程裡，卻從來沒有很多的政治上的沾溉。[71]

　　王重陽死後（1170）不過十餘年間，孫不二和馬鈺夫婦就相繼死了（1182-1183），再過兩年（1185）譚處端也死去了。餘下的四人，丘處機在重陽死後曾經「入磻溪（在陝西寶雞東南）穴居，日乞一食，行則一簑，……晝夜不寐者六年。既而隱隴州龍門山七年，如在磻溪時。」（陳時可〈長春真人本行碑〉，收《甘水仙源錄》2/5b-6a）後來他仍回到龍門山終南祖庵長住。劉處玄曾經先在洛城（洛陽）東北的雲溪洞住，後來回過故鄉武官，在那裡建

70　全真弟子們的文集裡，以此為警語的很多。例如《道藏》798 譚處端的《水雲集》卷上 14a〈勸眾修持〉第二首首句，又卷上〈頌‧其二〉第一首，16a；第六首，16b。

71　關於王重陽的學問的來歷，參看拙著〈讀蜂屋邦夫《金代道教の研究》〉，收入《和風堂新文集》，下冊，前引，頁 529—556。《四庫全書總目》卷一四七〈甘水仙源錄〉條說重陽「以《孝經》、《心經》、《老子》教人諷誦」，我看在傳教的效力方面，全真教提倡讀的一些言簡意賅的短經，如《道藏》342《太上老君內日用妙經》、《太上老君外日用妙經》……說不定更實用些。

庵居住，開始爲《道德》、《黃庭》等經作注。[72] 王處一主要的活動地區仍在
山東各處，他有時候居住道觀，或是金蓮堂，常爲地方上建醮，也已有一群
弟子或住家的信眾。四個人裡郝大通是個殊異的角色。他離開趙州之後，據
說在河北灤城忽然精明《易》理，到處歡迎他演講，現存《道藏》798 他的四
卷《太古集》，除了第四卷是三十首的〈金丹詩〉之外，前面三卷盡是他的〈周
易參同契簡要釋義〉，有很細密繪製的圖象，可能是專門研究的人所愛讀的。
他暮年仍回到寧海州居住，成吉思汗七年壬申（1212）他就死在寧海州的先
天觀。[73] 他和王、丘、劉三位師兄還有一點不同的地方，就是只有他一個人
沒有受到金朝皇帝的宣召和恩寵。

　　受皇帝宣召，是全眞教的教祖王重陽和已故世的馬鈺夫婦、譚處端都不
曾有過的經歷。無論如何，王處一、丘處機、劉處玄他們三個人這時候不能
夠一點都不表示個人的態度了。劉處玄的立場似乎只是純宗敎性的。金章宗
承安二年（1197）他應詔入燕京，到了著名的天長觀，作〈感皇恩〉詞兩首，
其第二首下片云「外貧保命，隱眞居陋，亙初無相貌，勝豐厚。桑田海變，
這箇無形堅久」，最後補了一句「暗祝吾皇德齊天壽」罷了。（《道藏》785《仙
樂集》4/17a）但是王處一、丘處機他們對於被宣，卻認爲這是件巍煌的大事，
對於個人的地位和全眞一派的鞏固和中興，都有很大的意義。丘處機在「出
山」以前，曾在山中住了十五年，對於國計民生以及宗敎的前途，衡以他後
來的應蒙古皇帝的宣召，不能說沒有徹底地思考過。全眞教號稱是道敎的一
個大派，這話是我們幾百年後的人們說的，在當時王重陽提倡的三敎並尊，
「懼國法」、「孝父母」、「行平等」（俱見《道藏》342 他們所諷誦的《太上老君
外日用妙經》1a）……這些民間宗敎式的實踐從傳統的道敎觀點看起來仍然
很有點「四不相」，甚至遲到章宗明昌元年（1190）十一月還有「以惑眾亂民，
禁罷全眞及五行、毗盧」的詔書（《金史·章宗本紀一》），這也難怪王處一在
世宗大定丁未（二十七年，1187）十一月十三日初奉宣詔時作詩那樣地驚喜

72　現存《道藏》57 是他的《黃帝陰符經注》，728 是他的語錄，題爲《無爲清靜長生眞
　　人至眞語錄》，785 是他著的《仙樂集》。後者最能夠看出當年全眞教在山東傳教時集
　　體歌唱的神韻。

73　這裡用了成吉思汗的紀年，是根據《七眞年譜》17a 的記載。這一年就是金廢帝崇慶
　　元年，南宋寧宗嘉定五年。

欲狂了。《道藏》792《雲光集》2/1a 開卷這一首云：「上騰和氣徹三台，下布祥雲徧九垓。化出空中清雨降，道橫四海一聲雷！」同樣地丘處機《磻溪集》3/6a-7a〈世宗挽詞〉一首的長引，敍述他「大定戊申（二十八年，1188）春二月自終南召赴闕下」，受到種種優遇的情況，表現的是同樣的心情。處機更說世宗並且「聖旨塑純陽、重陽、丹陽三師像于宮菴，彩繪供具靡不精備。」（3/6b）這一點更是重要，因爲全眞教的王重陽和馬丹陽兩位領袖，這麼一來可以上躋於神仙呂純陽相等的位置，他們已經快要成神了。以後章宗承安二年又召見王處一和劉處玄，《雲光集》裡也有詩詞敍述（1/1b；4/12a）。

我們若是要問，在王處一、丘處機這些召見，或是和政府高官來往時，他們的談話有沒有涉及一些政事呢？我們的回答是有的，在少數的資料裡大約還可以見到一些蛛絲馬跡。王處一《雲光集》1/1a 他爲承安丁巳受第三宣時作的詩的小引說七月初三日宣見：

> 次問北征事，師答云：「戊午年即止。」後果應。

這是章宗教王處一推測一下，北征的兵事前途怎樣了。處一也好像術士似地推斷說「明年戊午（1198）就要結束了。」這是全眞教的人事後有先見之明的神化了的故事。只是，這裡說的戰爭是怎麼一回事呢？這件事情在〈章宗本紀二〉這一年裡僅有「四月……尚書省奏比歲北邊調度頗多，請降僧道空名度牒、紫褐、師德號，以助軍儲，從之」這一條紀錄，或者有些關係。其實，這裡指的是在金境北邊嘯聚叛亂的契丹人編制的糺軍，詳情見《金史》卷九十四夾谷淸臣、內族襄（即完顏襄），特別是瑤里孛迭等的傳記：「承安二年，糺軍千餘出沒剽掠錦、懿間。」（錦州和懿州，地點都在今遼寧。）軍需的費用支出很大，政府就要出賣度牒、法號，還需要上天的庇佑，七月朔章宗就要「幸天長觀，建普天大醮」了！

《甘水仙源錄》卷 2/6b〈長春眞人本行碑〉記丘處機在章宗泰和間（1201-1208）住在山東棲霞：

> 師旣居海上，達官貴人敬奉者日益多。定海軍節度使劉公師魯、鄒公應中二老當代名臣，皆相與友。貞祐甲戌（宣宗二年，1214）之秋，山東亂。駙馬都尉僕散公將兵討之。時登及寧海未服，公請師撫諭，所至皆投戈拜命，二州遂定。

這裡說的山東亂事，指的是貞祐二年楊安兒在益都造反的事。安兒本是販馬鞍的無賴，在泰和間趁金、宋攻戰時在他的本鄉益都聚眾剽掠，後來向官方投降，做到刺史、防禦史的高官。衛紹王大安三年（1211）他統率的兵該去戍邊，在半途他設計逃回山東，就又聚黨攻劫州縣。這時候僕散安貞（就是〈長春本行碑〉說的駙馬）正做山東路統軍安撫等使，曾把楊安兒從益都追趕到萊陽，可是萊州和登州都向他納降了，安兒就置官屬，稱帝號，改元天順。寧海州也曾失陷，叛眾又曾攻濰州，佔密州，整個的叛亂到貞祐三年初才算平定。這次亂事，丘處機對金朝的地方當局有過多少幫助，或者他對地方有多大的影響力量，我們還不能確知。不過，《磻溪集》1/9a-b倒是有一首題為〈承安丁巳冬至後苦雪，時有事北邊〉，提到的正是上文說及金章宗詢問王處一的北征的戰役。丘處機這首律詩最後的兩句說「月費國資三十萬，如何性命不凋殘」，我們也可以知道他對於北邊，或任何戰亂的態度了。

《射鵰英雄傳》4/37/1465-66 寫丘處機在晉見成吉思汗時乘機向他進言，用了四首丘處機的原作。這四首詩其實不是他們見面時唸的，不過應用得卻是恰到好處。頁 1466 用的「天蒼蒼兮臨下土」等二首，原題是〈憫物〉，見《磻溪集》3/10a。《磻溪集》據《道藏》本有四篇序，最遲的亦撰於泰和戊辰（八年，1208），所以兩詩所憤慨的恐怕還是山東等地的情況。頁 1465 用的「十年兵災萬民愁」一首倒是和丘處機的西行有關的，是成吉思汗十五年（庚辰，1220）冬天，處機及他的徒眾暫住在德興府（舊察哈爾、今河北涿鹿附近）龍陽觀過冬時，寫寄給燕京道友的，原詩見《道藏》1056 李志常撰《長春真人西遊記》卷上 8b-9a。還有很有趣味的一首，是成吉思汗十七年（壬午，1222）八月，丘處機從撒麻爾罕去成吉思汗駐的行在，半途在鐵門（在碣石 Kosh 南）遇見「三太子（窩闊台）之醫官鄭公」，因為是中秋，作這詩贈他，所以首句說「自古中秋月最明」，原詩見《長春真人西遊記》卷下 4a。這詩金庸先生很巧妙地拿去利用了，上半用在 1/2/75，就是丘處機上一年作的中秋詩揣在懷裡沒有寫成，卻被江南七怪之一的「妙手書生」朱聰偷了去，現在卻又在他和成吉思汗諸人相見時把全詩補足吟了出來了。他寫的並不勉強，「我之帝所臨河上，欲罷干戈致太平」，在時間地點上可說用的天衣無縫。這裡「帝所」二字，本來在古人的詩詞裡原也可以借來比喻神話中的天帝，但是又那裡比

得上丘處機這時候用的更眞切呢！

一九九八年九月，寫於坎培拉之和風堂。

Fact or Fiction:
Ming-chiao (Manichaeism) in Jin Yong's
I-t'ien t'u-lung chi 倚天屠龍記*

Samuel N. C. Lieu (劉南強)
Department of Ancient History
Macquarie University

Abstract

The paper aims to (1) chronicle the way in which Manichaeism (*Mo-ni chiao* 摩尼教) — a dualist missionary religion from the Near East — came to China in the T'ang period via the Silk Road and how it adapted itself to the Chinese cultural milieu to the extent that it became a popular but secret religion — the Light Sect (*Ming-chiao* 明教) from Sung to early Ming period, especially in the Fukien province — made famous to millions of Chinese readers by the first major work of Jin Yong. The paper will (2) focus on the survival of the sect in S. China in a close study of the only remaining Manichaean temple in Ch'üan-chou 泉州 and assess the impact the religion had on folk beliefs in the Fukien region as portrayed in the famous novel of Jin Yong and to discuss the work's historical value for our knowledge of *Ming-chiao*. The lecture will be illustrated by slides of *Ming-chiao* sites on the Silk Road and in Fukien.

---

* The author would like to acknowledge his gratitude to the Chiang Ching-kuo Foundation for International Scholarly Exchange for financial support in his research on Manichaeism in China.

I. Introduction

When I first embarked on the study of Manichaeism in both the Roman Empire and Medieval China more than twenty years ago, the most common reaction to such an esoteric endeavour from my Oxford research colleagues, especially those in Late Roman History, was, "What? Manichaeism in China? You mean the heresy to which St. Augustine was attached as a young man went all the way to China?" The second most common remark was, "You must have read the martial arts novels by Jin Yong to choose such a research topic." The latter came almost exclusively from Chinese friends, who the moment they heard that Manichaeism was known as *Ming-chiao* 明教 immediately made the connection with one of the most famous novels of Jin Yong which they had undoubtedly read in their adolescence. It was with great pleasure that in 1997 I was invited to give the Louis Cha (i.e. Jin Yong) Lecture in Hong Kong University for which I chose as my topic 'From Manichaeism to *Ming-chiao* — the East Asian transformation of Manichaeism'. It was most unfortunate that the lecture was given on a rainy evening and Mr. Jin Yong himself was not able to attend for health reasons. Nevertheless I was extremely touched to have been asked by the Chinese Department of Hong Kong University to give a lecture in honour of Jin Yong who has done more than any other modern writer to popularize the presence of Manichaeism in China.

II. Manichaeism

Manichaeism was often confused by Chinese scholars with Nestorianism — the version of Eastern Christianity which flourished in the Persian Empire under the Sassanians and which came to China after the collapse of that dynasty to the forces of Islam in the eighth century. *Ching-chiao* 景教 (the Luminous Religion) and *Ming-chiao* 明教 (the Religion of Light) sound all too similar in Chinese. Manichaeism was more indigenous to Iran than Nestorianism which was imported to the Sassanian Empire from the religious controversies which raged in the fifth century between Antioch and Alexandria in the Roman Empire. Mani (c. 216–c. 276) on the other hand grew up in a Syriac-speaking Jewish Christian sect in southern Mesopotamia — an area which was held by both the Arsacid (i. e. Parthian) and the Sassanian dynasties.[1]   He preached a universal religion which contained Christian and Zoroastrian elements and his followers practised a form of asceticism which was akin to that of Buddhism. He obtained permission from Shapur I (c. 240) to disseminate his new doctrine in an Iranian Empire which at that time stretched from the Euphrates to the Hindu Kush. By the time he suffered martyrdom under Bahram II, his religion was well established in the regions of the Roman Empire and of the Kushan Empire which bordered onto that of the Sassanians. A great artist as well as a prolific writer and indefatigable teacher, Mani left a canon of seven scriptures to his disciples as well as lecture notes and a book of drawings. His disciples took his religion into Syria, Egypt, North Africa, Italy as well as Central Asia. Though few in numbers everywhere, the Manichaean communities maintained a cellular structure which enabled them to be highly mobile and also to remain in contact with each other.

III. Manichaeism in China

Manichaeism came to China in the T'ang period from Iran via the Silk Road on which commerical activities had long been dominated by Sogdian (*hu* 胡) merchants. Our knowledge of the religion in China comes from two main types of sources. Firstly Manichaean texts in Chinese[2] found in Tun-huang of

---

1   On the origins of Manichaeism see S. N. C. Lieu, *Manichaeism in the Later Roman Empire and Medieval China*, Second Edition (Tübingen, 1992), pp. 1–120 and idem, *Manichaeism in Mesopotamia and the Roman East Religions in the Graeco-Roman World*, 118 (Leiden, 1994), pp. 1–131.

2   For an account of the discovery of the texts listed see S. N. C. Lieu, *Manichaeism in Central Asia and China* (Leiden, 1998), pp. 10–11 and 48–53.

which there are three and all are in excellent condition of preservation:

a. Texts in Britain (British Library, London)

S3969 Mo-ni *kuang-fu chiao-fa i-lueh* 摩尼光佛教法議略 (Compendium of the teaching of Mani the Buddha of Light), text reproduced in Lin Wu-shu 林梧殊, *Mo-ni chiao chi ch'i tung-chien* 摩尼教及其東漸 (2nd edn., Taipei, 1997), pp. 283-86. {Commonly referred to as *Compendium*}

S7053 *Mo-ni chiao hsia-pu tsan* 摩尼教下部讚 (Hymns for the Lower Section (e.e. Hearers?) of the Manichaean religion). Cf. Lin Wu-shu, op. cit., 287-316. {Commonly referred to as *Hymnscroll*}

b. Text in China (Beijing)

北8470 (formerly 宇56) *Mo-ni chiao ts'an-ching* 摩尼教殘經 (The Fragmentary sutra of a Persian Religion — the very first line of the text (a discourse on the Light-Mind) is not preserved and the standard title is given by modern scholars) Cf. Lin Wu-shu, op. cit., pp. 268-82. {Commonly referred to as *Traité* after the famous initial edition of this work by E. Chavannes and Paul Pelliot, "Un traité manichéen retrouvé en Chine," *Journal Asiatique*, 10e sér., 18 (1911) 499-617}

c. Text-fragment in France (Paris)

P3884 "Fragment Pelliot" = concluding part of S3969 (i.e. the Compendium) in the British Library in London (see above). Cf. Lin Wu-shu, *loc. cit.*

To these should be added a number of fragments found in Turfan and kept in Berlin collections:

a. Text-fragments (from codices) in the Turfan-sammlung

Ch 174 (T II 1917) untitled fragment. Cf. Th. Thilo, "Einige Bemerkungen zu zwei chinesisch-manichäischen Textfragmenten der Berliner Turfan-Sammlung," in H. Klengel and W. Sundermann (eds.), *Ägypten-Vorderasien-Turfan; Probleme der Edition und Bearbeitung altorientalischer Handschriften*, Schriften zur Geschichte und Kultur des Alten Orients XXIII, (Berlin, 1991), pp. 171-174 and pls. XX-XXI, figs. 22-23. For Parthian parallels see W. Sundermann, "Anmerkungen zu: Th. Thilo, Einige Bemerkungen zu zwei chinesisch-manichäischen Textfragmenten der Berliner

Turfan-Sammlung," pp. 171–172.

Ch. 258 (T II T 1319) untitled fragment. Cf. Thilo, op. cit., pls. XXII-XXIII, figs. 24–25

b. Text-fragments in the Staatsbibliothek

Ch 3138 (T III T 132) (fragment resembles but not identical to *Traité*). Cf. Y. Yoshida, "On the recently discovered Manichaean Chinese fragments," *Studies on the Inner Asian Languages*, 12 (1997): 36.

Ch 3218 (fragment resembles but not identical to *Traité*). Cf. Yoshida, op. cit., p. 36

The majority of these texts are translated from texts in Middle Iranian dialects, especially Parthian but the *Compendium* contains a number of Chinese elements and citations from Chinese texts which were clearly of Chinese origin.

Secondly a large number of important references to the religion can be gleaned from a variety of Chinese sources, especially the Dynastic Histories of the T'ang period and Buddhist historical works like the *Fo-tsu t'ung-chi* 佛祖統紀 by Chih-p'an 志磐, collections of memorials of officials like *P'an-chou wen-chi* 盤州 文集 by Hung Hao 洪皓, of Sung edicts like *Sung-hui-yao chi-kao* 宋會要輯稿 and the all important local history and gazeteer of Fu-chien viz. the *Min-shu* 閩書 of Ho Ch'iao-yüan 何喬遠.[3]　A number of inscriptions, some of which will be discussed later in the study, also add considerably to our knowledge of the subject.

The Chinese government came to know of it as a foreign religion whose priests accompanied foreign envoys from Central Asian kingdoms like

---

3　The best collection remains E. Chavannes and P. Pelliot, 'Un traité manichéen retrouvé en Chine, deuxième partie, Fragment Pelliot et textes historiques', *Journal Asiatique*, 11ᵉ ser., 1 (1913): 99–199 and 261–392 to which should be added P. Pelliot, 'Les traditions manichéennes au Fou-kien', *T'oung Pao*, 22 (1923): 193–208. The number of studies in Chinese and Japanese on the history of Manichaeism in China has grown dramatically in the last few decades. See works listed in G. Mikkelsen (ed.) *Bibliographica Manichaica*, Corpus Fontium Manichaeorum, Series Subsidia 1 (Turnhout, 1997), pp. 281–301.

Tocharistan on their missions to the T'ang court. The latter soon became concerned that this new sect was zealous for mission inside the Middle Kingdom and that it diffused under the guise of Buddhism. In 731 a Manichaean priest was ordered in to provide the court with a summary in Chinese of the doctrines and practices of the sect. A copy of his work has survived as the *Compendium* (see above). The next year saw the passing of the first imperial edict on the subject of Manichaeism, limiting its practice to foreigners in China:

> The doctrine of Mo-ni 末尼 (= Mani, i.e. Manichaeism) is basically a perverse belief (*hsieh-chien* 邪見) and fraudulently assumes to be [a school of] Buddhism and will therefore mislead the masses. It deserves to be strictly prohibited. However since it is the indigenous religion of the Western Barbarians (*hsi-hu shih-fa* 西胡師法) and other [foreigners], its followers will not be punished if they practise it among themselves.[4]

Despite the ban, the religion found followers among the Chinese. The situation changed dramatically, however, in the period after the An Lu-shan Rebellion when Mo-yu Khaghan who at the head of an army of Uighur Turks liberated Lo-yang at the behest of the T'ang government in 762 was converted to Manichaeism by Sogdian priests active at the eastern capital. An account of his conversion is given in the famous trilingual (Chinese, Sogdian and Turkish) inscription found in his capital of Karabalghasun south of Lake Baikal in 1890. Unfortunately all three versions are very Manichaeanary and the Chinese version which is the best preserved gives only a broken account of the famous conversion. Line 7 gives in a summary form the events leading to the intervention of the Uigur Khaghan in the internal politics of China, how he went to the aid of the T'ang Emperor Hsüan-tsung with his entire army and recaptured the capital of Lo-yang and how the two states made an alliance with each other. It was at Lo-yang that he came to realize (with the help of Manichaean priests) that the practices of his people were depraved and needed to be corrected by the

---

4   *T'ung-tien* 通典, 40.229c.

adoption of a new and more rigorous religion:

{Line 8} ... he (the Khaghan) took four priests with him back to his kingdom including one by the name of Jui-hsi 睿息. They propagated the Two Sacrifices (i.e. Principles) and thoroughly penetrated the Three Moments. Moreover, the *Fa-shi* 法師 (Masters of the Law, i.e. the Electi) had marvellously reached the Gate of Enlightenment and had carefully studied the Seven Volumes (i.e. the Manichaean Canon). Their skills are deeper than the seas and higher than the mountains. Their eloquence is like a cascade (lit. a suspended river). Therefore they were able to bring the Uighur (Kingdom) to the true faith [...] {fragment joined to end of Line 8?} the [Ma] histag [默] 奚悉德 (= *magister* in Latin — the third highest priestly rank in Manichaeism), then all the military governors and civilian officials [... (The Khaghan publicly declared that) he] {Line 9} now confessed his wrongful past and his wish to return to the true religion. An imperial edict publicly proclaims: "This religion is indeed marvellous but is hard to receive and support (i.e. it makes considerable demands on the believer). On numerable occasions I have confessed that in the past I was ignorant and (mistakenly) called the demons Buddhas. Now that I am cognizant of the truth, I can no longer continually repeat (the misdeeds of) the past. It is my particular wish that [...] {fragment joined to end of Line 9?} all the engravings and pictures of the demons are now ordered to be burnt. A [...] for praying to spirits and paying respects to demons [...] {Line 10} accept the Religion of Light (i.e. Manichaeism). (A land which practises) the abnormal custom of blood sacrifices will be turned into a region of vegetarians, a state which indulged in excessive killing (will be converted) to a nation which exhorts righteousness."[5]

The inscription gives the first occurrence of "*Ming-chiao* 明教" as the title or the sect rather than the more common and by now probably derogatory "*Mo-ni-chiao* 摩尼教". The Khaghan quickly requested that Manichaean temples should be set up in at least four major commanderies in China. Clearly these

---

5   *Inscription of Karabalgasun* lines 8-10. Cf. Chavannes-Pelliot, op. cit., p. 194 [reprint edn. p. 218]. The accompanying translation by Chavannes and Pelliot contains a number of errors. See the corrections by P. Pelliot in his article "Neuf notes sur des questions d'Asie Centrale," paragraphe VII. Un exemple méconnu du titre manichéen de 'maɣistag,' *T'oung Pao*, 26 (1929): 201-265.

were established for missionary purposes. That the religion found followers in China during the period of Uighur dominance is well illustrated by the following story of Buddhist origin:

> Wu K'o-chiu (吳可久), a man of Yüeh, resided in Ch'ang-an in the fifteenth year of Yüan-ho of the T'ang [820]. He began to practise Manichaeism and his wife Wang also followed his example. She died suddenly after more than a year. Three years later she appeared to her husband in a dream, saying: 'For my perverse belief I have been condemned to become a snake and I am below the *stupa* at Huang-tzu p'o (皇子陂). I shall die tomorrow at dawn and I wish you would ask monks to go there and recite for me the *Diamond Sutra* so that I could avoid other forms of suffering'. Wu disbelieved her in his dream and scolded her. She became angry and spat at him. He woke up in fright and his face was unbearably painful. His wife also appeared to his elder brother in a dream, saying, 'Pick some Dragon-tongue herb from the garden which will heal [your brother's] pain immediately when crushed and applied.' His elder brother woke up and ran to get [the herb] to give to him and he was subsequently healed. The next morning both brothers went out together and invited monks to read the *Diamond Sutra*. Soon a large snake emerged from the *stupa*, It raised its head and gazed around. It died when the reading of the *sutra* was ended. K'o-chiu returned [to the fold of] Buddhism and constantly carried with him this [i.e. the *Diamond*] *Sutra*.[6]

Manichaeism was expelled from China along with minor foreign religions like Zoroastrianism and Nestorianism in 843. However, a Manichaean priest, as we learn from Ho Chiao-yüan's account of how a Manichaean temple came to situated near Ch'üan-chou 泉州:

> In the period Hui-ch'ang 會昌 (841-846) when (Buddhist) monks were suppressed in great numbers, the religion of the light was included in the suppression. However, a *Hu-lu fa-shih* 呼祿法師 came to Fu-t'ang 福唐 (south of Fu-chou), and taught his disciples at San-shan 三山 (i.e. Fu-chien). He came to the prefecture of Ch'üan in his travels and died (there) and was buried at the foot of a mountain to the north of the

---

6   *T'ai-p'ing kuang-chi* 太平廣記, 107.727.

prefecture. In the period Chih-tao (995–997) a scholar of Huai-an 懷安, Li T'ing-yü 李廷裕, found an image of the Buddha (Mani) in a soothsayer's shop at the capital; it was sold to him for 50,000 cash-pieces, and this his auspicious image was circulated in Fu-chien. In the reign of Chen-tsung (998–1022) a Fu-chien scholar, Lin Shih-ch'ang, presented his (i.e. Manichaean) scriptures for sake-keeping to the Official College of Fu-chou 福州.[7]

The sect, as evidenced by the following story, also became well known for the ability of its priests to exorcise particularly pernicious evil spirits:

A certain man of Ch'ing-yüan 清源 by the name of Yang was Deputy Commander of the Defence Garrison of his commandery. He possessed a large house in the western suburbs [of the commandery]. Early one morning he went to the prefecture. While he was away, his family was about to eat when a goose carrying paper money came in from the gate and went straight to a chamber off the western gallery. [Someone in] Yang's family said, "This goose must have come from a temple!" They ordered their servant to chase it away. The servant, on entering the room, saw only an old man with hair tied into two tufts and a white beard. All the members of the family ran away in fear. When Yang returned and heard about this he became exceedingly angry and tried to beat it with a stick. The spirit appeared from, and disappeared into, all four corners in rapid transformations and Yang kept missing it with the stick. Yang became even more angry and said: "After I have eaten, I shall return to beat it to death." The spirit bowed, came forward and mouthed an agreement. Yang had two daughters; the elder daughter went to the kitchen to carve meat in preparation for a meal. The meat fell off the chopping board and disappeared. The daughter lashed out with the cleaver in the air in all four directions. Suddenly a large black hairy hand appeared from underneath the chopping board and said: "Please chop (me)." The daughter ran away, gasping for breath, and subsequently became ill. The younger daughter was fetching salt from a large jar when a monkey suddenly leapt out of the jar and landed on her back. She ran to the front of the hall and there lost it. She too became ill. Thereupon they sent for a shaman to erect an altar to exorcise the spirit. The spirit also erected its own altar and performed its rites

---

7 *Min-shu* 閩書, 7.32b.

so much more zealously than the shaman that the latter was unable to subdue it and left in fear. Shortly afterwards, Yang's two daughters and his wife all died. Later someone who excelled in magic, viz. [a devotee] of the Religion of Light (*Ming-chiao*), was invited to stay overnight with his scriptures. The spirit then spat at Yang, scolded him and left. Thereupon it disappeared and Yang also died in that year.[8]

In the Northern Sung period, Manichaeism emerged in South China as a secret religion and came to be derided under the blanket term of "Vegetarian Demon Worshippers" (*ch'ih-ts'ai shih-mo* 喫菜事魔). The secretive nature of the sect and its cellular structure lent itself to accusations of sedition and disloyalty:

The sect of the "demon worshipping vegetarians (sic)" is strictly prohibited by the laws. Even the family members of the offenders who are not privy to their crime are exiled to distant lands and half of the offender's property would be awarded to the informer and the rest confiscated. Nevertheless the number of followers has increased in recent times. The sect originated in Fu-chien and spread to the Province of Wen and the two Che Provinces (i.e. eastern and southern Chekiang). When Fang La rose in rebellion, the followers of the sect incited each other to rebel everywhere.

It is said that their rules prohibit the eating of meat and the drinking of wine. They do not worship spirits or Buddhas or ancestors. Nor do they entertain guests. When [a member of the sect] dies he is buried naked. However the corpse was first laid out fully-clothed and capped. Two fellow members of the sect then sit beside the corpse and one of them will ask, "Did he come with a cap?" The other will say, "No, [he did not]." They then proceed to take off his cap and in similar fashion they remove one by one his other items of clothing, until nothing is left. One of them will then ask: "What did he wear when he first came?" The other will answer: "A placenta [i.e. the clothes of the womb]." They then put the corpse into a cloth sack.

One hears it said that those who join the sect later become rich. These common folk are indeed ignorant for they do not realise that abstaining from wine and meat and lavish feasts and sacrifices and elaborate funerals will enable one to accumulate wealth. There are some who were quite poor when they first joined the sect but other members will

---

8　*Chi-shen lu* 稽神錄, ap. *T'ai-p'ing kuang-chi*, 355.2812.

help them with contributions. By accumulating these contributions, no matter how small, they can earn a comfortable living. When a member of the sect goes to or passes through another place, fellow members will provide him with board and lodging even if they do not know him. Everything is used by any member with no need for prior permission. They speak of themselves as members of one family and hence they use the term "an all-covering blanket (?)" to entice their followers.

Their leader is called the Demon King (*mo-wang* 魔王) and his assistants are called Demon Fathers (*mo-weng* 魔翁) and Demon Mothers (*mo-mu* 魔母). They all engage in luring people [to join the sect]. On the first and fifteenth of each month, each follower pays forty-nine cash pieces as incense money at the place of the Demon Father. The Demon Mother will then collect all the strings of cash and hands them over to the King Demon from time to time. The amount of money collected each year in this way is not inconsiderable.

The followers of the sect also chant the *Diamond Sutra* and take from it the verse: "They who see me (i.e. the Buddha) by visible form are following a perverse way (*hsieh-tao* 邪道)." Hence they worship neither spirits nor buddhas but revere the sun and the moon and regard them as real buddhas. When they interpret the verse: "The Dharma is even and has no gradations" they would join the word "no" [through deliberate mispunctuation] to the first part of the verse (i.e. to make it read: 'The Dharma is not even and has gradations'). Such is the way they normally interpret the *sutras*.

The word *mo* (demon) is mispronounced by the common people as *ma* 麻 [hemp] and hence their chiefs are called *ma-huang* 麻黃 (yellow hemp) or some other such term with which they substitute the appellation of *mo-wang* (Demon King). The followers are required to swear solemn oaths at the initiation. Since they regard Chang Chüch 張角 (*fl.* second century A. D.) as their original founder of the sect, they would not utter the word *chüeh* (horn) even if they are tortured to the point of death. It is said that when Ho Chih-chung 何執中 was an assistant magistrate second class of the Prefecture of T'ai, the local authorities had arrested some Demon Worshippers but they were unable to make them confess [their crime] even after detailed examination. Someone reminded them that Ho was a native of Lung-ch'üan 龍泉 commandery in the province of Ch'u where there were many followers of the [demon worshipping] sect and he would be able to determine whether the charge could be substantiated. They therefore asked Ho to investigate the case. Ho placed before them a number of miscellaneous items and asked them if they could name them. He placed a horn in the midst of these items. [The accused] named all of them but they passed over the horn in silence. This was how the case was decided.

Their refusal to pay respects to their ancestors and their practice of naked burial are detrimental to public morals. They also assert that human existence is full of misery. Hence, to terminate it by killing is to relieve misery. This is what they call "deliverance" and he who "delivers" many will become a Buddha. Therefore, once their numbers increase, they will take advantage of political chaos and rise in revolt. Their greatest crime is the pleasure they take in killing. They hate Buddhism in particular because its prohibition of killing is an offence to them.

However, the laws against them are too strict. Every time someone is prosecuted, many others are implicated. When the property of an offender is confiscated and his whole family exiled, the punishment differs little from death. As a result they are united in their effort to resist the authorities. Local officials fear them and dare not press home the charges against them. Thus the proscriptions have the opposite effect of causing their numbers to increase.

My own humble opinion is that the penalties for their crimes should be reduced in severity and the law of confiscation of their property be abolished. However, their leaders should be dealt with severely and in this way they may be subdued.[9]

The fact that the Fang La (方臘) Rebellion which engulfed much of south and central China was seen by officials as being caused by the Vegetarian Demon Worshippers led to widespread persecution of the sect. At the height of the rebellion in 1120 there was a severe crackdown in Wen-chou and the memorial detailing the confiscation of texts of the Religion of Light gives a list of titles which were undoubtedly Manichaean:

[Memorial submitted] on the fourth day of the eleventh month of the second year of the Hsüan-ho reign period [26 November 1120]

---

9   Ch'ing-ch'i k'ou-kuei 青溪寇軌 (*Traces of the bandits of Ch'ing-ch'i*), 12a2–4, ed. by Fang Shao 方勺 (1614 edn.) in *Chin-hua ts'ung-shu*, tse 12. Cf. Kao Yu-kung, "Source Material on the Fang La Rebellion," *Harvard Journal of Asiatic Studies*, 26 (1966): 223–225.

The officials say: "At the prefecture of Wen 溫 and other places are recalcitrant persons who proclaim themselves to be the 'disciples' (*hsing-che* 行者 = Sanskrit: acarin) of the Religion of the Light (*Ming-chiao* 明教)."

At present these followers of the Religion of Light set up buildings in the districts and villages of their abode which they called "vegetarian halls" (*chai-t'ang* 齋堂). In the prefecture of Wen 溫 for instance there are some forty such establishments and they are privately built and unlicensed Buddhist temples.

Each year, in the first (lunar) month, and on the day of *mi* 密 (= Pth. *myhr*) in their calendar, they assemble together the Attendants [of the Law] (*ch'ih-(fa)-che* 持(法)者, the Hearers (*t'ing-che* 聽者), the Paternal Aunts (*ku-p'o* 姑婆), the Vegetarian Sisters (*chai-chieh* 齋姊) and others who erect the Platforms of the Tao (*tao-ch'ang* 道場 = Bema?) and incite the common folk, both male and female. They assemble at night and disperse at dawn.

The scriptures and the pictures and images of the followers of the Religion of Light have titles such as these:

1. *The Sutra of exhortation to meditation* (*Ch'i-ssu ching* 訖思經)
2. *The Sutra of Verification* (*Cheng-ming ching* 證明經)
3. *The Sutra of the Descent and Birth of the Crown Prince* (*T'ai-tzu hsia-sheng ching* 太子下生經)
4. *The Sutra of the Father and the Mother* (*Fu-mu ching* 父母經)
5. *The Sutra (or Book) of Illustrations* (*T'u-ching* 圖經 = Ardhang)
6. *The Sutra of the Essay on Causes (?)* (*Wen-yüan ching* 文緣經)
7. *The Gatha of Seven Moments (or Prayers)* (*Ch'i-shih chieh* 七時偈)
8. *The Gatha of the Sun* (*Jih-kuang chieh* 日光偈)
9. *The Gatha of the Moon* (*Yueh-kuang chieh* 月光偈)
10. *The Essay on the (King of) (?) Justice* (*p'ing-wen* 平文)
11. *The Hymn for Exhorting (virtuous) (?) Men* (*Ts'e-han tsan* 策漢贊)
12. *The Hymn for Exhorting the Verification* (*Ts'e cheng-ming tsan* 策證明贊)
13. *The Grand Confessional* (*Kuang ta ch'an* 廣大懺)
14. *The Portrait of the Buddha the Wonderful Water* (*Miao-shui fo cheng* 妙水佛幀)
15. *The Portrait of the Buddha the First Thought* (*Hsien-i fo cheng* 先意佛幀)
16. *The Portrait of the Buddha Jesus* (*I-shu fo cheng* 夷數佛幀)
17. *The Portrait of Good and Evil* (*Shan-o cheng* 善惡幀)

18. *The Portrait of the Prince Royal* (*T'ai-tzu cheng* 太子幀)

19. *The Portrait of the Four Kings of Heaven* (*Ssu t'ien-wang cheng* 四天王幀)

These works and the names of the divinities are not mentioned in the Taoist or Buddhist Canons. They are full of false and fantastic sayings and they often cite from texts beginning with (the words): "Thereupon the Lord of Light..." which are different from Taoist and Buddhist scriptures.

As for the words [of the scriptures] they are hard to recognise and also difficult to pronounce. In short they demonstrate that these are demented and arrogant people who falsely concoct words and terms to deceive and mislead the uninformed masses and usurp the titles of the "King of Heaven" (*T'ien-wang* 天王) and of the "Prince Royal" (*T'ai-tzu* 太子).'

Despite the crack-down, the sect survived in South China and, as I have pointed out elsewhere, and was even accorded a degree of toleration as a form of Nestorian Christianity by Kublai Khan at the intercession of Marco Polo and his uncle Maffeo.[10]

IV. The *Ming-ch'ao* of history and the *Ming-chiao* of Jin Yong

In 1368, Chu Yüan-chang 朱元璋 entered Beijing and replaced the Yüan dynasty of the Mongols with that of his own, the Dynasty of Light (*Ming-ch'ao*). The war of liberation against the Mongols began on the lower Yangtze and the Canton region. It was not a co-ordinated movement but a series of minor rebellions led by local half-patriots and half-bandits. Many of these rebel-groups had grown out of religious societies and their rallying calls were commonly religious as well as patriotic slogans. Although the White Lotus Society played a prominent role in this confused war of liberation, the eventual victor was a leader of a group which had its origins in the Maitreya Society and had the red scarf for its insignia. Chu therefore knew better than any emperor the potential powers of such religious societies. Once his rule was firmly established, he

---

10   Cf. Lieu, *Manichaeism in Central Asia* etc., pp. 177-195.

renewed the proscriptions of the sects in an edict of 1370 which names in particular the White Lotus, the White Cloud and the Religion of Light:

Prohibition of Sorcery and Black Arts: Sorcerers who pretend to call down false divinities, write charms, cast spells over water, "support the phoenix" [i.e. perform planchette-writing], invoke the Sages, calling themselves the "Upright Master", "Grand Guardian" or "Mistress", or claim to be members of the Maitreya sect, or the White Lotus sect or the sect of the Venerable [Lord] of Light or the White Cloud sect, etc. which indulge in heterodox practices (*tso-tao*) and in distorting the truth, together with those who conceal prints and images of their deities and congregate to burn incense to them and those who meet at night and disperse by dawn and mislead and beguile the masses under false pretences of charity [shall suffer punishment]. Their leaders shall be strangulated and their followers shall receive a hundred strokes of the heavy baton and be exiled to a distance of 3,000 *li*.

Soldiers and civilians who impersonate deities, beat gongs and drums and hold religious processions shall receive a hundred blows of the heavy baton but this should only be meted out to their leaders. Village heads who know of such activities but do not inform the authorities shall receive forty blows of the bamboo cane. However, this proscription does not apply to the spring and autumn sacrifices among the people.[11]

The White Cloud Society had been nominally proscribed since 1306 and the White Lotus Society since 1309.[12] The repetition of the ban against these two sects by Chu was therefore only a renewal of the legal position of these two groups under the Mongols. Since the Manichaeans were under the protection of the laws of the Christians under the Mongols, some additional reason had to be given for their proscription and Chu found it in the name of the sect which he

---

11 *Ming lü chi-chieh fu li*, 11.9b–10a.

12 Cf. Kenneth Ch'en, *Buddhism in China* (Princeton, New Jersey, 1964), p. 430. The best critical study of the role of the Buddhist secret societies in the overthrow of the Yüan dynasty is B. J. Ter Haar, *The White Lotus Teachings in Chinese Religious History* (Leiden, 1990), pp. 16–172. See also the earlier work of D. L. Overmyer, *Folk Buddhist Religions: Dissenting Sects in Late Traditional China* (Cambridge, Mass. 1976).

said impinged on the title of his reign as they are both named after light (*ming*). In Imperial China it was gross impropriety to use any word which sounded or appeared similar to those used in the names of the ruling emperor or the dynastic title. Thus, the prefecture of Ming in Chekiang was renamed Ning-po to avoid clashing with the dynastic title. To provide the common people with safer alternatives, officials would issue at the beginning of the reign lists of synonyms with different sounds.[13]

Our knowledge of the Ming persecutions of Manichaeism, besides the edict of 1370, is largely dependent on the account of Ho Ch'iao-yüan on the Manichaean shrine on Hua-piao Hill. The relevant section reads:

> When T'ai-tsu of the Ming Dynasty (i.e. Chu Yüan-chang) established his rule, he wanted the common folk to be guided by the Three Religions (i.e. Confucianism, Taoism and Buddhism). He was further displeased by the fact that [the Manichaeans] in the title of their religion (i.e. *Ming-chiao*) usurped his dynastic title (i.e. *Ming-ch'ao*). He expelled their followers and destroyed their shrines. The president of the Board of Finance, Yu Hsin, and the president of the Board of Rites, Yang Lung, memorialised the throne to stop [this proscription], and because of this the matter was set aside and dropped. At present (i.e. *c.* 1600) those among the people who follow it practise incantation according to the "Magic of the Master [of sorcery] (*Shih-shih fa* 師氏法)" but they are not much in evidence.[14]

That the persecution of the sect was carried out under the specious excuse of that the name of the sect usurped the dynastic title is confirmed by a long funerary inscription to a Ming official, Hsung Ting 熊鼎 (1322–76), composed by Sung Lien 宋濂 (1310–1381):

> In the Prefecture of Wen there were perverse teachers who were of the Grand Religion of Light (大明教 *Ta Ming-chiao*). They built and furnished their shrines and meeting

---

13   *Min-shu* 7.32b, trans. Pelliot, 'Les traditions', p. 206.

14   *Min-shu* loc. cit.

halls in a rather extravagant manner. Idle folks [lit. those who were unemployed] flocked to join it. However, because it was blinding and misleading the masses, and its title offended (the sanctity) of the dynastic title, Hsiung memorialised [the throne for permission] to suppress it, to confiscate its property and to compel its followers to return to the land.[15]

The persecution was later lifted, as we learn from Ho Ch'iao-yüan, at the intercession of two important ministers. The shrine on Hua-piao Hill managed to escape destruction and even as late as 1445, its priests or worshippers erected an inscription exhorting the faithful to remember "Purity, Light, Power and Wisdom (i.e. the four attributes of the Father of Greatness) and Mani and the Buddha of Light."[16]   The last known reliable mention of Ming-chiao in a written source dates to the beginning of this century in Fu-chien and is found among the records of the Boxer Rebellion. In it a village-head was said to be a Manichaean was accused by Christian authorities of vandalising a Catholic church along with the Boxers.[17]   It also says that the sect had only a handful of followers.

The events of the fall of the Yüan and the rise of the Ming provided the back-drop for Jin Yong's novel *I-t'ien t'u-lung chi* 倚天屠龍記. Fully aware of the fact that his audience may not be aware of the Iranian connection, Jin Yong gives an abridged history of the diffusion of the sect in China (iii, 25.1016-17)[18] which shows clearly that the author is aware of the source material on the subject assembled by Chavannes and Pelliot and Ch'en Yüan and goes as far as quoting some of the memorials and related writings against Vegetarian Demon Worshipper translated above. He even provided the sect with a historical work of

---

15   *Chih-yüan hsü-chi*, in *Sung Wen-hsien kung ch'üan-chi*, 31.5a.

16   Cf. Wu Wen-liang 吳文良, *Ch'üan-chou tsung-chiao shih-ko* 泉州宗教石刻 (Beijing, 1957), p. 44.

17   Wang Chien-chu'an 王見川, *Ts'ung Mo-ni chiao tao Ming-chiao* 從摩尼教到明教, M.A. diss., National Tsinghua University (Hsinchu, 1991), pp. 277-8.

18   All references to the text of *I-t'ien t'u-lung chi* are to the four volume edition of 1996.

its entry and diffusion in China with a title which sounds surprisingly like the famous academic study on the subject by Ch'en Yüan 陳垣 — *Ming-chiao liu-ch'uan chung-t'u chi* 明教流傳中土記.[19]　This is not ahistorical as the Manichaeans in South China — judging from Ho Ch'iao-yüan's highly accurate account of the sect — had a good knowledge of their links with Sassanian Persia and the history of their sect under the T'ang. They must have possessed a continuous historical tradition. Jin Yong is also fully aware of the alleged link between the sect and the Fang La Rebellion — a link which was little challenged by scholars in the 1970's (iii, 25.1017). The most important scholarly influence on Jin Yong by scholars of Manichaeism is clearly a seminal article on the relationship between Ming-chiao and the founding of the Ming Dynasty published in 1940 by Wu Han 吳晗 which made an enormous impact on both serious scholarship on Ming history as well as in popular perception.[20]　In this article and in his short and popular biography of Chu Yüan-chang Wu Han made the important observation that the title of the Ming dynasty appears to be unrelated to any place — or family-name which might have been connected with Chu Yüan-chang's rise to power. The relation, Wu Han believes, is to be found in the name of the religious society which helped to propel Chu to power. It is in the light of the popular success of Wu Han's theory and his reconstruction of the early history of the Ming Dynasty that we have to understand the involvement of the sect in Jin Yong's novel and the author's reconstruction of the main historical events of the period. In order to give credibility to the sect as a driving force in the revolt against the Mongols, Jin Yong made it a movement of national proportion — at least of south and central

---

19　Ch'en Yüan's work is entitled "Mo-ni-ch'iao ju Chung-kuo kao 摩尼教入中國考" (The diffusion of Manichaeism in China) published in *Kuo-hsueh chi-kan* 國學季刊, 1/2 (Peking, 1923): 203-40.

20　Wu Han, "Ming-chiao yü ta Ming ti-kuo 明教與大明帝國," *Ch'ing-hua hsüeh-pao* 清華學報 13 (1941): 49-85 [reprinted in the author's *Tu shih cha-chi* 讀史箚記 (Peking, 1956), pp. 235-70.] and idem, *Chu Yüan-chang chuan* 朱元璋傳 (Peking, 1944).

China (iii, 25.1025; iv, 34.1389 etc.). That the "Vegetarian Demon Worshippers" as a movement certainly had followers outside Fu-chien is hinted by a famous memorial of Lu Yu 陸游, which was presented to the throne *c.* 1166 but he also emphasised that the Religion of Light was particular to Fu-chien:

> Since ancient time, the rise or cessation of banditry has been the result of famine caused by floods or drought. Pressed by cold and hunger, men would assemble by a whistle to attack and pillage, but if appropriate steps are taken, they could easily be calmed and pacified and will certainly not become a source of worry to the court. However, perverse people practising demonic sorcery deceive and beguile decent people during times of peace. They form into associations and remain settled, awaiting the right moment to rise. The harm which they cause is harder to fathom.
>
> Your servant humbly thinks that this type of people can be found everywhere. In Huai-nan 淮南 they are called "People of Two Knots (?)" (*Erh-kuei-tzu* 二檜子).[21] In the two Che 浙 they are called the [followers of] the doctrine of Mou-ni 牟尼. In Chiang-tung 江東, they are called the "Four Fruits", (*Ssu-kuo* 四果) and in Chiang-hsi 江西 they are called the "Diamond Dhyana" (*Chin-kang ch'an* 金剛禪). In Fu-chien they are called followers of the "Religion of Light" (*Ming-chiao* 明教) or ["those who observe] the Gati Fast (?)" (*Chieh-ti chai* 揭諦齋) and by various other titles. The Religion of Light is particularly prominent to the extent that it is practised and disseminated by scholars, magistrates and soldiers. Its deity is called the "Messenger of Light" and it also has names (of deities) like the "Buddha of Flesh", the "Buddha of Bones" and the "Buddha of Blood". Its followers wear white garments and black caps. They form into associations wherever they are. They possess false scriptures and demonic images and they even go to the extent of engraving print-blocks for the dissemination of their scriptures. They falsely borrowed (the names) of the officials in charge of Taoism (*Tao-kuan* 道官) like Ch'eng Jo-ch'ing 程若清 and others of the Cheng-ho 政和 period (1111–8) as revisers of their texts and (they also named) the Prefect of Fu-chou, Huang Shang 黃裳 as supervisor of the engraving (of the print blocks). They regard the sacrifices to deceased grandfathers and fathers as an invocation to the (evil) spirits. They abstain completely from food which contains blood. They

---

21　The meaning and significance of this term are both uncertain.

consider urine as holy water and use it for their ablutions. Their other demonic excesses cannot be easily enumerated. Since they burn frankincense, frankincense has risen in price. Since they eat ground-mushrooms (*chün* 蕈) and tree-fungi (*chün* 菌), these too have risen in price. Furthermore, because they practise these things together they are like glue and lacquer. If perchance they should stealthily rise (up in revolt) they would make one's heart go cold (with fright). Chang Chüeh 張角 of the Han period, Sun En 孫恩 of the Tsin 晉 dynasty (265–419) and Fang La 方臘 of more recent times are all men of this sort...[22]

The chief of the sect was given the title of "chiao-chu 教主" by Jin Yong (iv, 34. 1391), a term which is hitherto unattested in Manichaean text or in reliable sources on the sect. Jin Yong followed the Confucian writers in making the enemies of the Manichaeans refer to their leaders as "mo-tou 魔頭" which shows that Jin Yong is certainly familiar with the polemical writings against the sect (iv, 36.1462). However the term "mo-po 魔婆" for the female equivalent (iv, 34. 1406) is unattested. "Mo-mu 魔母" appears to have been the better attested term. The sect, according to Jin Yong, wore scarlet (iv, 34.1406, 1410 etc.) whereas Manichaeans were noted in the Sung and Yüan period to be "pai-yi 白衣" (wearer of white).[23]　The fact that the followers of *Ming-chiao*, according to Ho Ch'iao-yüan, had preserved special spells clearly lent credibility to the sect as repository of special martial skills. The same was believed of other secret religious societies as satirized in a poem against the "vegetarian demon-worshippers" composed during the Fang La Rebellion:

22　*Wei-nan wen-chi* 渭南文集, 5.7b–8b. Cf. French translation of this passage in *Traité* 1913, pp. 344–50.

23　Same observation also made by Lin Wu-shu 林梧殊, "Chin Yung pi-hsia ti Ming-chiao yü li-shih chen-shih 金庸筆下的明教與歷史真實," *Historical Monthly* 歷史月刊, 1996.3: 66–67. I am grateful to Mr. Wang Ch'ien-chu'an who in his critique of the original version of this article at the Conference drew my attention to this important work which is published in a popular historical journal.

金鍼引透白蓮池　此語欺人亦自欺

何似田桑家五畝　雞豚狗彘勿違時

The Golden Needle pierces through the White Lotus Pond.

Sayings like this deceive both the speaker and the listener.

How can one compare them with sayings like: "Mulberry trees should be planted in homesteads of five acres and the breeding times of chicken, pigs, dogs and swine be not neglected?"[24]

"Golden Needle" is of course a term which is often encountered in Jin Yong's novels. Ancient Persia (*po-ssu* 波斯) was the reputed home of origin of the special martial powers of the followers of *Ming-chiao* (iv, 38.1568). However, the Chinese Manichaeans always attributed the land of origin as Su-lin (蘇鄰 i.e. Assuristan) the province of the Sassanian Empire which comprises most of modern Iraq and not Po-ssu. The "Persian" link is used by Jin Yong as the land of origin of near-supernatural martial skills for the hero of the novel with the "Old Man of the Mountain" as the ultimate source (iii, 30.1200, iv, 38.1565-66 etc.). However the "Old Man of the Mountain" viz. Hasan e Sabbah, the Grand Master of the sect of the Assassins and whose exploits are made famous by Marco Polo, flourished in the time of the Crusades (11th Century) and had nothing to do with the Manichaeans. A mystical figure like him was a convenient source of arcane skills. A similar error in making Manichaeism an Iranic religion is the claim that Manichaeans were fire-worshippers like Zoroastrians (iii, 29.1175-79). This, of course, is entirely unhistorical as the mains symbols of worship by Manichaeans were the Sun and the Moon and not fire. Continuing links with the sect in Iran had been severed after the T'ang dynasty and the possibility of a special embassy of three "Persian" Manichaeans to China in the Yüan period to heal an age old schism (iii, 29.1180ff.) is nil.[25] Excavations on Hua-piao Hill by Chinese archaeologists during the 1980s in the area in front of the rustic

---

24 *Chia-t'ing Ch'ih-ch'eng-chih* 嘉定赤城志, 37.21a2-3.

25 Point also made by Lin Wu-shu, op. cit. 66.

Manichaean shrine, on which a large Buddhist temple now stands, unearthed a complete glazed bowl and a considerable number of fragments of a distinctive black earthenware pottery. Inside the complete bowl is inscribed in large letters: *Ming-chiao hui* 明教會, i.e. "The assembly of the Teaching of Light (or Light-Sect)". Some fragments examined by the author in 1993 carry the inscription *Ming-chiao pao* 明教寶, i.e. "the possession (lit. treasure) of the Teaching of Light (or Light-Sect)". These were clearly once utensils for the communal eating of vegetarian meals by the sect. No Manichaean ossuary has yet been found but it is entirely probable, as suggested by Jin Yong and the polemical texts we have examined, that Manichaeans in China exposed their dead naked[26] — a practice which would have certainly given offence to up-holders of Confucian principles. What is less certain historically is whether the Manichaeans burnt the corpses of their dead (iii, 30.1235 etc.). In one area in which fiction comes very close to fact is the tetrarchic designation of the leaders of the sect as *Ssu ta fa-wang* 四大法王 (The Four Great Kings of the Dharma) (iv, 37.509) when the term *Ssu t'ien-wang* 四天王 (the Four Kings of Heaven) was used by Chinese Manichaeans to denote the "Father of Four Faces" (i.e. the Father of Greatness) in the Manichaean cosmogony. In the Sung edict cited above the Manichaeans in Wen-chou possessed a work entitled the *Ssu t'ien-wang cheng* 四天王幀 (Portrait of the Four Kings of Heaven). The sect's vegetarianism was well known and there is little historical possibility of its leader agreeing to have meat used as filling for moon-cakes because of the prevalence of famine (iii, 25.1026). On the other hand, the Manichaeans as depicted in a miniature from Turfan, celebrated the Feast of the Bema in commemoration of their martyred founder with cakes with sun and moon symbols.[27]   Therefore a link between Manichaeans in China and the popular festive institution of the moon-cake is not altogether fanciful.

---

26   Cf. *Ibid*.

27   Cf. A. von Le Coq, *Die buddhistische Spätantike*, ii, *Die manichäischen Miniaturen* (Berlin, 1923), pl. 8b(a).

An important factor in identifying the followers of *Ming-chiao* as the predominant group of anti-Mongol rebels lies in the fact that Chu Yüan-chang joined a rebel group led by Han Shan-t'ung — a figure which appears frequently in Jin Yong's novel — whose grandfather was a member of the White Lotus Society. Han Shan-t'ung 韓山童 himself prophesied that in the midst of the present turmoil an enlightened ruler would appear to prepare for the return of the Maitreya from Tushita Heaven. He proclaimed himself the Major Enlightened Ruler (*Ta ming wang* 大明王) but was later killed in battle. His son Han Lin-erh 韓林兒 assumed the title of the Minor Enlightened Ruler (*Hsiao ming wang* 小明王). He in turn was killed by Chu who took over command of the group and eventually gained the throne. Wu Han pointed out in his influential article that the Manichaeans of the Sung, according to the Buddhist historian Tsung-chien 宗鑑, possessed a scripture entitled *Sutra on the Coming to the World of the Major and Minor Enlightened Rulers* (*Ta hsiao ming wang ch'u-shih k'ai-yüan ching* 大小明王出世開元經). This led Wu Han to suggest that Han Lin-erh had borrowed his title from the Manichaeans. Chu Yüan-chang used the symbol of light as title of his dynasty because he too had come under Manichaean influence since the Maitreya Society and the Manichaeans were closely associated.[28] Critical study of the texts by the Japanese scholar Chikusa Masaaki[29] has shown that the title of the *sutra* which mentions the Major and Minor Enlightened Rulers occurs in a list of works which were labelled Manichaean by Tsung-chien, but none of the titles correspond with any other known lists of Manichaean works. The list was most probably taken from an

---

28 Cf. Wu Han, "Ming-chiao", pp. 49-81 [259-70] and *idem*, *Chu Yüan-chang* (Beijing, 1944), pp. 105-108.

29 Chikusa Masaaki, "Kitsusaijima ('Ch'ih-ts'ai shih-mo') ni tsuite," in *Aoyama hakushi koki kinen So-daishi ronso* (Tokyo 1974), pp. 239-62 [Germ. trans. by Dr. Renate Herold in H.-J. Klimkeit and H. Schmidt-Glintzer (eds.), *Japanische Studien zum östlichen Manichäismus, Studies in Oriental Religions* 17 (Wiesbaden, 1991)] and *idem*, 'Hō Rō (Fang La) no ran to *Kitsusaijima* (Ch'ih-ts'ai shih-mo)', *Tōyōshi kenkyū* 32/4 (1973-74): 455-477.

essay by a Confucian scholar called Wang Chih 王質 on the "vegetarian demon worshippers" in Chekiang, with special reference to the Diamond Dhyana. The only tenuous link between the Maitreya Society of Chu and the Religion of Light rests on the title of one scripture from Tsung-chien's list of so-called Manichaean works and once the Manichaean origin of these works is rejected on critical grounds, Wu Han's thesis simply disintegrates.

By making a little known and highly secretive society with acknowledged exotic foreign roots as a driving force in the national revolt against the Mongols and as a key-player in the founding of the Ming Dynasty, Jin Yong has successfully combined romance with contemporary historical scholarship. In reminding his audience that the two hundred and seventy-seven year reign of the Ming Dynasty originated in a struggle for power in which the Manichaeans played a substanial part (iv, 40.1629), Jin Yong had succeeded to give flesh to the historical hypothesis of Wu Han. However, while research on Manichaeism is a continuous process of discovery, especially of new texts, and of revaluation, Jin Yong, in fictionalising the sect on a scale which its followers in China in Yüan and early Ming would never have dreamt of, had placed *Ming-chiao* in a far richer and far more lasting literary tableaux than any research historian could achieve.

全眞敎與金元數學
——以李冶（1192-1279）爲例

洪　萬　生

國立臺灣師範大學數學系

摘　要

　　本文以李冶（1192-1279）爲個案，探討全眞敎與金元算學的關連。關於研究方法，則採取數學社會史（social history of mathematics）的進路，始終視數學爲社會文化脈絡下的一種知識活動（mathematics in context）。準此，全眞敎在金元的學術環境中如何影響數學知識活動，自然是我們的主要關懷所在。無論李冶與全眞道士的交往密切程度如何，他的「天元術」研究及其支撐的社會條件，離不開全眞敎所參與、經營的學術環境，應該是毫無疑問的歷史事實。

> 　遠寺孤舟墮渺茫，雨聲一夜滿瀟湘
> 　黃陵渡口風波暗，多少征人說故鄉
> 　　　　　　　　——李冶〈瀟湘夜雨〉

一、楔　子

　　元朝朱世傑《四元玉鑑》（1303）誠然是一部偉大的數學經典，但也總結了十三世紀中國數學的輝煌。中國數學史家錢寶琮曾論及元代數學始盛終衰之外爍原因有二：蒙古人一統中原之後，「科舉制之復行與理學之普及是已。」至於元初數學所以遠勝於前，則是學者多致力於此，「雖在干戈擾攘之

際，未廢研治之功。且師承有自，學友相從，利祿之途難進，名理之樂可求。
金亡後數十年中，數學之進步遠盛前代。李冶、劉秉忠、朱世傑三家學術，
其尤爲顯著者也。」（引錢，1983b）

　　不過，由於李冶及其好友元好問與全眞教高道交往密切，所以，金元鼎
革之際，全眞教所提供的學術環境，可能間接地促成了中國北方數學的發展。
京都學派領導人藪內淸或許是最早指出這個史實的科學史家，它大大地有助
於我們了解宗敎（如道敎）與中國科學、數學的關係，值得我們再深入探討。
（參考藪，1967）

　　本文將略述金元數學家李冶（1192-1279）的數學生涯，及其歷史環境中
最重要的「制度性」因素之一──全眞道觀。本文論述，也因而假定任何一
種數學知識活動，不能從它的社會文化脈絡抽離（mathematics in con-
text）。這是本文的限定，必須首先聲明。

　　由於全眞教是道教的一個支派，因此，本文第二節將對數學與宗教的關
係做一個簡單的說明，進而轉述李約瑟（Joseph Needham）與席文（Nathan
Sivin）的爭論。接著，在第三節中，我將從制度史的觀點，鋪陳全眞教所經
營的學術環境。最後，在這樣的脈絡下，我們將試著探索李冶的學術生涯，
以及全眞教如何爲他的數學研究提供正當性。

二、數學與宗敎：數學社會史的一個側面

　　從認識論觀點來看，宗教影響科學或數學，在西方科學史上確有先例可
尋。譬如說吧，中世紀學者在基督教的學術世界中，對亞里斯多德兩部經典
《論天體》（*On the Heaven*）與《物理學》（*Physics*）的熱烈討論，就可以證
明很多科學研究的問題意識，在「言必稱上帝」的宗教文化環境中，不僅「合
法」，而且合情合理。（參考 Lindberg，1992；洪，1996）伽利略的《兩種新
科學對話錄》（*Two New Sciences*，1638），不僅模仿了歐幾里得（Euclid）
的《幾何原本》（*The Elements*）體例，師法阿基米德（Archimedes）的數
學物理進路，而且也回應了「化身」爲超級數學家的上帝對他的召喚：

　　哲學（自然）是寫在那本永遠在我們眼前的偉大書本裡的──我指的是宇宙──

但是，我們如果不先學會書裡所用的語言，掌握書裡的符號，就不能了解它。這書是用數學語言寫出的，符號是三角形、圓形和別的幾何圖形，沒有它們的幫助，是連一個字也不會認識的；沒有它們，吾人就在一個黑暗的迷宮裡勞而無功地遊蕩著。（轉引自 Kline，1972，pp. 328-329）

正因為如此，所以，探索大自然背後的數學定律，既是科學哲學的一種（認識論）主張，也是榮耀上帝的另一途徑。

回到中國數學史這一邊，我們應該可以試著釐清類似問題是否具有「歷史正當性」。誠然，中國道教的教義，是否曾經發展出類似的意識形態而影響自然哲學的進路，目前可能不是下結論的時候。更優先的問題或許是：究竟數學知識的形成與其他學問譬如《周易》的研究有沒有關係？[1] 由於《周易》是儒者與高道之士擅長的學問之一，因而激盪出金元的「天元術」也未可知。（參考藪，1984，頁 46-48）無論如何，要是沒有全真教所提供的學術環境，那麼，金元時代中國北方的數學知識活動，可能就不會那麼多彩多姿了。

不過，道教是否促成了中國科學的發展，既然曾經是李約瑟及其合作者努力想證明、而席文又極力想反駁的一個論點，本文照理不應迴避。好在 Alexei Volkov 剛剛為臺灣出版的英文期刊 *Taiwanese Journal for Philosophy and History of Science*（遠流出版公司贊助出版）客座主編「趙友欽專輯」（Volume 5, No. 1, 1998），為這個學術公案提供了一個簡要但十分有用的說明。

針對這個科學與道教議題，Volkov 選擇以元朝趙友欽（1271-1335?）作為個案來研究，是很有史識的，因為趙友欽精通經學、天文曆算及經緯數術，在科學與數學尤其表現特出，而且是一位如假包換的全真道士。根據他的徒弟陳致虛的追記，趙友欽（號緣督子）師承張模（號紫瓊子），再往上追溯李玨（號太虛子）及宋德方（1183-1247）。而後者就是全真七子馬鈺與丘處機

1　根據南宋數學家秦九韶，「聖有大衍，微寓於《易》。奇餘取策，群數皆捐。衍而究之，探隱知原。」（〈數書九章序〉）可見他的「大衍求一術」得自《周易》的啟發是很有可能的。參考李繼閔（1987）或劉鈍（1993）。事實上，在中國的歷史文化脈絡中，數學與易學的關聯，可以在焦循的著作中看得更為清楚。請參閱洪萬生主編《談天三友》（1993）。

的徒弟。(參考 Volkov，1998) 於是，在中國歷史文化中，道士、算家與談天者這幾種角色至少曾在趙友欽身上同時適用，所以，道教思想是否在認識論上啟發了十三世紀金元學者的數學與自然哲學研究？道觀對這些學者是否提供了制度化的誘因，讓他們可以「正當地」研究數學或自然哲學？這些問題意識看來頗為合情合理，剩下來的研究工作，當然就是深入探索趙友欽與全真教了。

　　無論如何，Volkov 綜合趙友欽相關的歷史研究成果，已足以在科學社會史的取向上，深化李約瑟的觀點，亦即道教在一個「共享的認知空間」(shared cognitive space) 中，成功地創造了有利於傳播中國傳統科學知識的「另類網絡」(alternative networks)。基於同一論述，Volkov 在另一方面反駁了席文的觀點，這是因為席文認為道教門徒關心宗教甚於自然哲學，所以，他們的教義與修行當然無涉「大自然的理性探索」。對席文而言，按宗教的定義來說，它本來就無關科學。(參考 Volkov，1998)

三、全真教與金元學術環境

　　金世宗大定七至九年 (1167-1169)，王重陽 (1113-1170) 以寧海全真堂為基地，創立全真教，訓誨會眾「悟理莫忘三教語，全真修取四時春」，勸人誦讀《般若波羅密多心經》、《道德清靜經》和《孝經》。事實上，它的教義是在《道德經》的基礎上，融會三教「理性命之學」。王重陽強調「儒門釋戶道相通，三教從來一祖風」，可見他始終表明「三教平等」。根據劉精誠的研究，「三教合一是唐宋以來社會思潮發展的總趨勢，北宋以來，蘇轍、張紫陽等都主張三教之說兼容並蓄，全真道的三教合一，正是順應這股社會思潮的產物。」(引劉，1993，頁 245) 所以，全真教在十二、三世紀華北地區贏得士人的注意，就知識層面來看，是很容易理解的。

　　不過，全真教的理論繼承了陳摶 (?-989) 的思想，也是讓它在金元之際，對中國北方學術文化發揮影響力的另一個重要因素。這是因為陳摶的《無極圖》對於後來道教內丹派影響很大。無論是王重陽的北宗道教或南宋白玉蟾的南宗道教，在先修命或先修性容或有所不同，但理論上都從陳摶一脈相承而來。同時，陳摶對易理象數的深入研究，為周敦頤的宇宙起源說——《太

極圖》開啓了先河，兩宋其他理學家如程頤、程顥、朱熹也都對他十分仰慕與推崇。（參考劉，1993，頁 226-227）因此，在動盪不安的亂世之中，全真道觀提供給流浪學者除了棲身之所之外，顯然也支撐「共享的認知空間」，讓他們分享了豐富的知識世界。關於這一點，後文還會略作說明。

此外，王重陽將「仙」與「全真」聯繫起來，改革道教對神仙「白日升天、長生不死」的理解。同時，他也認爲全真之意是「全其本真」，以「澄心定意，抱元守一，存神固氣」爲「真功」，要保全作爲人性命的根本要素即精、氣、神。換句話說，「全真、全氣、全神」就是最高神仙境界。正是基於這種新的詮釋，信徒的內丹修持變得比較可行，也因此獲得了廣大道徒的信賴。（參考劉，1993，頁 245）

王重陽去逝前不久，先後渡得「全真七子」丘處機（1148-1227）、譚處端（1123-1185）、馬鈺（1123-1183）、王處一（1142-1217）、郝大通（1135-1212）、孫不二（1119-1182）與劉處玄（1147-1203），並開始擴散到登州、萊州兩地成立會堂，吸收會眾。由於王重陽「家業豐厚」，自幼酷嗜讀書、才思敏捷；此外，他也習弓馬，臂力過人，1138 年曾應金初科舉武選，中甲科。（參考劉，1993，頁 243）因此，金庸小說《射鵰英雄傳》描述他們師徒都是武林高手，是極有可能的。

七子宣教時期，馬鈺、王處一、劉處玄、丘處機爲官民齋醮的次數，較重陽立教時期頻繁，會堂分布範圍也更大，全真教在金末時已蔚爲華北第一大道派，教眾占河朔人口的五分之一。（據元好問估計，參見鄭，1987，頁 114）元初，全真領袖丘處機善察天下形勢，不赴金、宋之詔，唯以七十二歲高齡率徒十八人，行程萬餘里，歷時四年，西觀成吉思汗，獲禮遇敬重，遂得以免除「大小差發稅賦」，從而成爲天下道流之宗主。平心而論，元初蒙古人在中原的政權尚未穩固，必須利用勢力龐大的全真教來招攬民心。至於全真教則順勢而爲，持牒招求，廣攬教眾，在亂世中全活人民性命財產甚多，充分表現宗教濟世精神，同時，教團勢力也因而更加壯大。（參考鄭，1987，頁 27、67）

除了在金元鼎革、社會動盪不安之際，全真教發揮了政治庇護與宗教慰藉的功能之外，它後來甚至還執掌了大蒙古國的國家祭典與國子學。根據正統道藏所載，在 1232-1254 年間，全真教曾多次爲蒙古汗廷齋醮祀香。（參考

鄭，1987，頁 85）早在丘處機進駐燕京玉虛觀時，往來即多金朝遺老與蒙古官員。處機死後，十八弟子之一的李志常（1193-1256）任都道錄，負責教門與汗廷的聯繫，頗受蒙古人器重。志常也因此得以推薦同門師弟馮志亨(1180-1254）擔任國子學總教官，他本人與楊惟中也一併奉旨擔任。楊惟中雖非道士，但與全真教接觸頻繁。由此可見，全真教已經控制了國子學。不過，這主要歸功於馮志亨擁有主持校務的學養，他早年是金朝太學生，能文善詩，與儒士交往密切，備受贊譽。（參考蕭，1996a）

　　事實上，李志常也是「以儒家者流，決意學道」。正因爲如此，他對動盪世局中流離失所的士大夫，總是隨時提供庇護：

> 時河南新附，士大夫之流寓燕者，往往竄名道籍。公（即李志常）委曲招宴，飯於齋堂，日數十人。或者厭其煩，公不恤也。其待士之誠類如此。（《甘水仙源錄》卷3，頁 0154 下，轉引自鄭，1987，頁 144）

金太宗七年，宋使徐霆訪問燕京，也看到很多士人的棲身道觀：

> 長春宮多有亡金朝士，既免跣焦（薙髮），免賦役，又得衣食，最令人慘傷也。（《黑韃事略》，頁 16 上，轉引自鄭，1987，頁 144）

入元以後，由於全真教教團內部的腐敗、對貴族官僚的影響力減弱、汗廷的猜忌、儒士的振興(以重掌國子學的控制權爲例)，以及佛道的衝突等等因素，使得全真教的勢力逐漸衰退。（參考鄭，1987，頁 141-149）儘管如此，元初名公鉅卿與全真教士長相往來者仍舊不在少數，例如楊奐、姚樞、王磐、商挺與主領陝西教事的天樂道人李道謙，又如趙著、王鶚、姚樞、王磐、竇默、王善及本文主角李冶就與道錄樊志應頗有來往。（參考鄭，1987，頁 161）

　　此外，全真教與元代漢軍世家的結合，也對流離失所的漢人學者發揮了很大的撫慰作用。譬如，全真教與（山東）東平嚴實曾修上清萬壽宮，迎請范圓曦（號玄通子，郝大通弟子）爲住持，時論以「治軍」與「掌教」並稱二人，當有以圓曦爲幕府而安撫民心之考慮。與嚴實及其幕府交往密切的全真道士還有張至偉、商挺與趙天錫等等。此外，曾爲全真教撰碑的官員頗多，其中不少是嚴實的幕府或學士，除了前述的商挺之外，還有宋子貞、王磐、徐琰、孟祺與李謙等人。（參考鄭，1987，頁 107）據孫克寬研究，嚴實在東

平興學、招置幕府，不僅只是爲了保存文化，亡金名士薈集山東，可能有政治的圖謀。除了嚴實之外，漢家世侯眞定史氏及保定張氏也競相羅致亡金遺士，於是，東平、眞定及保定遂成爲人才薈萃之地，才俊之多，絕不下於和林與燕京。「他們利用這些人才在所轄地區推行漢地傳統式的改革，恢復秩序、發展經濟、保存文化。因此，各士侯轄地，在政治、軍事、經濟、文化上都具有一定程度的自主性。」（引蕭，1994，頁 276-277）不過，召賢納士充任幕府者，還是以嚴實最多，根據王名蓀的統計，依附東平幕府的士人可考者二十一人，多數任秘書、參謀之類的幕僚官，其中就包括了元好問。（參考王，1992，頁 61-64）由此可見，李冶訪問東平搜求算書（詳見本文下節），是很有地緣因素考慮的。

四、李冶生平事跡

　　李冶，字仁卿，號敬齋，祖籍眞定欒城縣（今河北省欒城縣）。他在金明昌三年出生於金大興城（今北京市大興縣），父親李遹，母親王氏，有同父異母兄弟李澈與李滋，及兩位同胞姊妹。他原名李治，後改今名。[2]

　　李冶被史家視爲十三世紀最偉大的代數學家。（參考 Ho，1970）他的主要成就在於將宋金元時代的「天元術」集大成，爲朱世傑的「四元術」鋪路。所謂「天元術者，中國之代數術也。立一元或多元以爲未知量，使加減乘除有所憑藉，依問題所示推演條段以造方程式，解方程以得所求數也。立一元以『演段』者，世謂之天元術，立多元以『演段』者，世謂之四元術。天元、四元之於中國數學史上之貢獻，猶阿拉伯人代數之於西洋數學史也。」（引錢，1983b）

　　李冶的曾祖父及祖父都以醫爲業，因此，他的父親李遹年少時亦習醫，只是後來不願「以人命試吾術」，遂改讀律令。可是，隨後卻又認爲法家寡恩，便盡棄前學，全心全意讀六經、攻辭賦，終於成爲能詩善畫、博學多才的學

2　目前中國數學史家大都採取「李冶」之名，唯劉德權點校《敬齋古今黈》時仍取「李治」爲名。請參考他的「點校說明」，收入李治，1995，頁 1-4。又此書由畏友劉鈍代購，特在此申謝。

者。

李遹於李冶出生前一年考中金朝詞賦科進士，先後擔任縣丞與縣令，後來升任大興府推官，李冶便是在此地出生。不幸，李遹上司胡沙虎被「時人視之猶蛇虎鬼魅，疾走遠避之不暇」，爲了防避不測，爲官耿直、敢言犯上的李遹便將家小送回故鄉灤城。正值童年的李冶沒有隨行，獨自一人到灤城的鄰縣元氏（今河北元氏縣）求學。

李冶「幼讀書，手不釋卷，性穎悟，有成人之風」（《元朝名臣傳略》），李屛山曾贊譽他「仁卿不是人間物，太白精神義山骨」。金大安三年（1211），李冶二十一歲，父親在東平府（今山東東平縣）任治中，因見胡沙虎更加得勢及朝政不可爲，又惟恐胡沙虎迫害，遂辭職隱居於陽翟（今河南禹縣），以詩畫自娛，並將家眷接來同住，李冶也從河北來到河南。

大概從這時開始，李冶與元好問交往密切結爲好友。後來，兩人前往南都（即汴京，今河南開封市）拜趙秉文、楊文獻爲師，不久，雙雙文名大盛。李冶的多才多藝，較諸他的父親不遑多讓，請徵之於李冶的自述：

> 李子年二十以來，知作爲文章之可樂，以爲外是無樂也。三十以來，知搴取聲華之可樂，以爲外是無樂也。四十歲以來，知究竟名理之可樂，以爲外是無樂也。
>
> 今五十矣，覆取二十以前所讀論孟六經等書讀之，乃知曩昔所樂，曾夏蟲之不若焉。尚未卜自今以往又有樂於此以否。（《泛說》）

事實上，李冶雖年幼時即愛好算數，然而傾力研究，卻可能是在五十歲之後。他在1248年寫成《測圓海鏡》，終於成爲一代算學大師。不過，這個學術興趣也可能與他四十歲以後的顚沛流離，乃至寄寓全眞道觀有關。

金正大七年（1230），李冶赴洛陽應試，被錄取爲詞賦科進士，隨即奉派高陵（陝西高陵縣）主簿，但因窩闊台大軍攻入陝西，所以未能赴任。接著，他又調往陽翟附近的鈞洲城（今河南禹縣）當知事。金開興元年（1232），蒙古軍攻破鈞洲，李冶棄城北渡黃河，從此走上漫長而艱苦的流亡之旅。

李冶北渡後，便流落於山西忻縣、崞縣之間，過著「飢寒不能自存」的生活。根據藪內清的研究，「李冶在山西流浪之時，受到當地出現的數學之影響。金元之際，習算之人主要集中在山西南部汾河流域地區。其中平水是金朝時代出版最盛行的地方，平陽是元代道藏刊行的地方。天元術產生之處，

可以說在汾河流域。」（引藪內，1967）此外，山西在當時也是全眞道觀數目僅次於陝西、河北與河南的地方，因此，李冶在流浪時寄寓道觀是極有可能的。

北渡兩年後，李冶終於在忻縣境內的桐川定居下來，開始專心讀書，「凡天文象數，名物之學，無不研精。」（《元史新編》，轉引自孔，1988，頁 10）大概就在此時，他獲得洞淵有關勾股容圓的一部算書，「日夕玩繹」，終於對早年「無以當吾心」的「考圓之術」豁然貫通。至於編成《測圓海鏡》一書，則是他「山中多暇，客有從余求其說者，於是乎又爲衍之，遂累一百七十問。」（〈測圓海鏡序〉）此外，他也曾從東平府尋得一部算經，對於他集大成「天元術」很有啓發：

> 予至東平，得一算經，大概多明如積之術。以十九字志其上下層數，曰：仙、明、霄、漢、壘、層、高、上、天、人、地、下、低、減、落、逝、泉、暗、鬼。此蓋以人爲太極，而以天地各自爲元而陟降之。其說雖若膚淺，而其理頗爲易曉。予遍觀諸家如積圖式，皆以天元在上，乘則升之，除則降之，獨太原彭澤彥材法，立天元在下。凡今之印本復軌等書，具下置天元者，悉踵習彥材法耳。彥材在數學中，亦入域之賢也，而立法與古相反者。其意以爲天本在上，動則不可復上，而必置於下，動則徐上。亦猶易卦，乾在在下，坤在在上，二氣相交而爲太也。故以乘則降之，除則升之。求地元則反是。（引李冶，1995，頁 32）

由此可見，李冶在桐川所參與的數學知識活動，包括了算書的搜集、學者之間的討論以及師徒的傳授。誠然，《測圓海鏡》就是在這樣活潑的學術環境中所創造出來的。

在《測圓海鏡》完成後不久，李冶到太原住了一段時期，接著又流落到平定。平定侯聶珪接待他到帥府居住，十分禮遇。然而，他卻一心想回到少年求學的元氏縣定居。1251 年，他結束流浪生活，如願回到元氏縣外封龍山下隱居教學。講學之餘，他與元好問、張德輝過從甚密，常一起遊封龍山，時人因稱之爲「龍山三老」。由於張德輝曾在眞定史氏家族手下爲官，得忽必烈的信任，派任眞定學校，遂受託舉荐漢人學者，這是（1252 年）元好問、（1257 年）李冶先後應召與忽必烈王廷問對的主要原因。

會見忽必烈之後，李冶回到元氏，繼續他「愛山嗜書，餘無所好」（引王

磬語）的日子。1261 年，忽必烈聘他作翰林學士知制誥同修國史，但李冶以老病婉拒。至元二年（1265 年），忽必烈再召他出任同一官職，他勉強就職，但一年後他又以老病辭，理由是「翰林非病叟所處，寵祿非庸夫所食。官謗可畏，幸而得請投跡故山。」（《元朝名臣事略》）其實，真正的原因是他後來透露的：

> 翰林視草，惟天子命之；史館秉筆，以宰相監之。特書佐之流，有司之事耳，非作者所敢自專而非非是是也。今者猶以翰林史館爲高選，是工諛譽而善緣勢者爲高選也，我恐議者羞之。（《泛說》遺文，轉引自《元朝名臣事略》）

這種隱而不仕的態度，與他的學術事業應該是極有關係的。大概在晚年時，李冶研究數學頗爲自信，儘管在完成《測圓海鏡》之後，他面對理學家對「九九賤技」的鄙視，不無自我解嘲的心情：

> 覽吾之編，察吾苦心，其憫我者當百數，其笑我者當千數，乃若吾之所得，則自得焉耳，寧復爲人憫笑計哉？（李冶〈測圓海鏡序〉）

在 1259 年，李冶又完成了另一本數學作品《益古演段》。它是根據《益古集》（作者未被提及）「再爲移補條段，細幡圖式」而成，目的在普及「天元術」，「使粗知十百者便得入室啗其文。」（〈益古演段自序〉）這是因爲他考慮到：

> 今之爲算者未必有劉（徽）、李（淳風）之工，而偏心蹢見不肯曉然世人，惟務隱互錯糅，故爲溟悸黯黮，惟恐學者窺其彷彿也。不然則又以淺近觕俗無足觀者，致使軒轅隸首之術，三五錯綜之妙，盡墮於市井沾沾之兒及夫荒郊下里蚩蚩之民，殊可憫悼。（〈益古演段自序〉）

無論本書是不是他的課徒講義（參考孔，1988，頁 92-94），他治算的從容自得溢於言表，則無庸置疑。

從翰林院辭官回封龍山，李冶即專心著述教學，直到 1279 年病逝，享年八十八歲。他一生著述頗豐，除了前述兩部數學作品之外，據《元史・李冶傳》的記載，他還著有《敬齋文集》、《壁書叢削》、《泛說》及《敬齋古今黈》。其中前三種已亡失，僅有極小部分依附其他文獻而流傳下來。《敬齋古今黈》是一部筆記類著作，內容遍及經學、哲學、歷史、文學、天文、數學及醫學，

可以充分反映他的淵博學養。(參考孔，1988，頁 30-33)

　　《敬齋古今黈》對於我們瞭解李冶的學術生涯至爲重要，它的內容解析還有待進一步的研究。不過，從它的一些相關內容，目前我們至少可以證明：李冶相當熟悉全眞教等道教內丹派集氣功、胎息、服餌、房中、養生爲一體的修煉。譬如在本書中，李冶就萬松和尙以爲達摩無胎息法而提出反駁：

> 予謂萬松之説非也。佛乘雖深密，要不出性命二字。故知胎息法，只是以性命爲
> 一致。若謂胎息等皆妄，則凡鐙史所載機緣語句，獨非繫驢橛耶？胎息雖不足以
> 盡至理，亦至理之所依也。今一切去之，則所謂性外求命，命外求性耳。性外求
> 命，命外求性，便是不識性命。(引李冶，1995，頁 27)

此外，他也清楚說明精氣神之舍的三丹田之位置（參考同上書，頁 81）。由此可以再度說明，李冶與全眞道士交往應該十分密切才是。

五、「推自然之理，以明自然之數」

　　在《敬齋古今黈》中，李冶留下一則文字，頗能暗喻他自己中年顛沛流離之際的困頓與辛酸：

> 納紙投名媿已深，更教門外久沈吟。事窮計急燒牛尾，不是田單素有心。此詩竟
> 不知何人所作。投謁固可恥，然士當窮困，搖尾乞憐於人，亦可憫也。前輩又有
> 云，門前久立處，席上欲言時，此眞所謂不經此境，不能道此語也。(引李冶，1995，
> 頁 18-19)

這麼說來，李冶後來獲忽必烈重用而出仕，何以並不熱衷？[3] 或許他對於蒙古人的不斷征伐（包括攻宋與內戰）十分不滿（參考孔，1988，頁 27-28），不過，更重要的原因，恐怕是他自己已經在數學研究中找到安身立命之道，聞

3　根據王明蓀的研究，元人的不仕而隱可歸類爲七種：㈠以爲出仕的條件或能力不足
　　者；㈡以朝廷之政風及需要不合意者；㈢以欽羨古隱逸之士者；㈣以道不行、時不用
　　而隱者；㈤屬於類似人生觀的不仕者；㈥忠於故國之意而隱退者；㈦爲義而隱者。
　　(參見王，1992，頁 279-282) 李冶應該歸屬於第四類，不過，由於他常引述陶淵明的
　　詩歌，因此，自況古隱逸之士，當然也是一種自處之道。

達與否似乎不是他的主要考慮了。請徵之於王德淵的〈敬齋先生測圓海鏡後序〉：

> 敬齋先生病且革，語其子克脩曰：吾平生著述，死後可盡燔去，獨《測圓海鏡》
> 一書，雖九九小數，吾常精思致力焉，後世必有知者，庶可布廣垂永乎！先生於
> 六藝百家靡不串貫，文集近數百卷，常謙謙不自伐，惟於此書不忘稱異於易簀之
> 間，想有元妙內得於心者。

　　儘管如此，對李冶這樣的學者而言，起碼的社會地位與生活條件顯然十分重要。也正是如此，金元之際的全真教所經營的學術文化環境，就變得非常相干了。然則，我們究竟應該如何著手呢？或許西方數學社會史學可以給我們一點啓發。自從八十年代以來，社會史取徑的西方數學史家在相關的研究上，多半十分重視算學的認識論上的正當性（epistemological legitimacy），與算學知識活動參與者（mathematical practitioner）的社會正當性（social legitimacy）（參考 Biagioli，1989）。準此，李冶的算學研究是否受惠於金元之際的全真教？或許關鍵就在於這個歷史脈絡是否提供了有利的環境，讓李冶可以「正當地」研究算學，而不必擔心學術地位受到質疑或挑戰。

　　可是，算學何以帶給李冶這麼大的精神滿足呢？顯然，這是因爲他的所謂「自然之數」在「推求自然之理」上取得了主導作用：

> 彼其冥冥之中，固有昭昭者存。夫昭昭者，其自然之數也；非自然之數，其自然
> 之理也。數一出於自然，吾欲以力強窮之，使隸首復生，亦末如之何也已。

所以，

> 苟能推自然之理，以明自然之數，則雖遠而乾端坤倪，幽而神情鬼狀，未有不合
> 者矣。（〈測圓海鏡序〉）

另一方面，即使數學不過是一種「九九賤技」，然而，「由技進乎道」仍然是聖人所稱許的：

> 由技兼於事者言之，夷之禮、夔之樂，亦不免爲一技。由技進乎道者言之，石之

斥、扁之輪，非聖人之所與乎？（〈測圓海鏡序〉）

此外，他在解釋「內經言：腎者作強之官，技巧出焉。」時，也特別指出：

> 技雖不至於道，亦游於藝者之所貴。巧雖未至於神，亦妙萬物而爲言。不作強則
> 何以得之。（引李冶，1995，頁 96）

由此可知，無論數學是「自然之數」也好，「九九賤技」也好，李冶的「自得」
之情始終如一，無怨無悔。

李冶關於「自然之數」與「自然之理」的概念，無疑是陳摶以及其他宋
儒易數理氣論述的歷史產物。如果說他也分享了全眞教徒關於周易的研究，
應該也不爲過。此外，由上引他到東平訪得算經之說明，我們也可以發現，
如仙明霄漢等道教術語以及易卦二氣升降等周易論證，在認識論層面上如何
影響「天元術」的「如積圖式」（亦即列方程式的方法）！

總之，李冶治算的認識論上的正當性，以及作爲算家的社會正當性，都
可以在全眞教所經營的學術環境中得到合理的解釋。這兩種「正當性」當然
支撐了 Volkov 所謂的「共享的認知空間」，因此，當我們討論道教與金元數
學的關連時，一個比趙友欽更早的恰當個案，恐怕非李冶莫屬了。

六、結　論

現在，讓我們回來呼應本文一開始所引錢寶琮論斷元代數學始盛終衰的
兩個原因，也就是：科舉制度的重新實施，以及理學北上然後普及於華北地
區。誠然！不過，全眞教的式微，恐怕也是一個不可分割的因素。我們相信
儒士的重掌學術文化的主導權，對於李冶「由技進於道」的主張，一定採取
相當保留的態度；[4] 同時，科舉重開的利祿之途，又吸引了學者的全副注意
力，因此，算學又再度受到貶抑，是極有可能的。不過，從李冶逝世（1279

4　在中國歷史文化上有幾個時期，數學參與者對於數學的學術地位感到自在，也因此做
　　出更大的貢獻。這些時期分別是魏晉、宋金元以及十九世紀清代。在這些時期中，對
　　於儒士而言，算術既可以兼明，又可以專業，所以，「由技進乎道」的說法似乎也有了
　　正當性。請參考洪萬生（1982，1989，1990，1991a，1991b，1993）及劉鈍（1993）。

年）到趙友欽逝世（1335 年？）大約五、六十年之間，全眞教的餘緒究竟如
何影響元朝算學，無疑是數學社會史的絕佳題材，值得深入探索。

參考文獻

甲）中文

王明蓀

　　1992　《元代的士人與政治》（臺北：臺灣學生書局）。

孔國平

　　1988　《李冶傳》（石家庄：河北教育出版社）。

　　1996　《測圓海鏡導讀》（漢口：湖北出版社）。

朱越利

　　1991　《道經總論》（瀋陽：遼寧教育出版社）。

李　治

　　1995　《敬齋古今黈》，劉德權點校，（北京：中華書局）。

李繼閔

　　1987　〈蓍卦發微〉，收入吳文俊主編，《秦九韶與《數書九章》》（北京：北京
　　　　　師範人學出版社），頁 124-137。

李豐楙

　　1990　〈道教〉，收入王壽南主編，《中國文明的精神》（臺北：廣電基金），頁
　　　　　452-489。

李　儼

　　1955　〈唐宋元明數學教育制度〉，收入李儼，《中算史論叢》第四集（北京：
　　　　　科學出版社），頁 238-280。

周瀚光

　　1994　《李冶評傳》，收入周瀚光、孔國平著，《劉徽評傳》（南京大學出版社），
　　　　　頁 91-163。

金永植

　　1985　〈中國傳統文化中的自然知識──中國科學史研究中的一些問題〉，
　　　　　《史學評論》第 9 期，頁 59-92。

洪萬生

　　1982　〈重視證明的時代──魏晉南北朝的科技〉，收入洪萬生主編，《格物與

成器》（臺北：聯經出版公司），頁 105-164。

1989　〈十三世紀的中國數學〉，收入吳嘉麗、葉鴻灑編，《新編中國科技史演
　　　　講文稿選輯（上）》（臺北：銀禾文化事業公司），頁 142-162。

1990　〈獨特傳統 自主發展〉，收入王壽南主編，《中國文明的精神》(臺北：廣
　　　　電基金)，頁 1019-1046。

1991a　〈孔子與數學〉，收入洪萬生，《孔子與數學》（臺北：明文書局），頁 1-
　　　　12。

1991b　〈同文館算學教習李善蘭〉，收入楊翠華、黃一農主編，《近代中國科技
　　　　史論集》（臺北：中研院近史所、新竹：清大歷史所），頁 215-260。

1993　《談天三友》（臺北：明文書局）。

1996　〈科學與宗教：一個人文的思考〉，《科技報導》，1996 年 9 月 15 日。

袁　冀

1974　《元史研究論集》（臺北：臺灣商務印書館）。

1986　《元史論叢》（臺北：聯經出版事業公司）。

梅榮照

1985　〈李冶及其數學著作〉，收入錢寶琮等著，《宋元數學史論文集》（北京：
　　　　科學出版社），頁 104-148。

樊克政

1995　《中國書院史》（臺北：文津出版社）。

鄭素春

1987　《全真教與大蒙古國帝室》（臺北：臺灣學生書局）。

藪內清

1967　〈宋元時代科學技術的展開〉（許進發中譯未刊稿），收入藪內清編，《宋
　　　　元時代科學技術史》（京都大學人文科學研究所刊），頁 1-32。

1979　《中國科學文明》，李淳譯（高雄：文皇社）。

1984　《中國數學史》，鄭瑞明譯（臺北：南宏圖書公司）。

錢寶琮

1981　《中國數學史》（北京：科學出版社）

1983a　〈宋元時期數學與道學的關係〉，收入錢寶琮等著，《宋元數學史論文
　　　　集》（北京：科學出版社），頁 225-240。

1983b　〈金元之際數學之傳授〉，收入中國科學院自然科學研究所編，《錢寶
　　　　琮科學史論文選集》（北京：科學出版社），頁 317-326。

劉　鈍

　　1993　《大哉言數》（瀋陽：遼寧教育出版社）。

劉精誠

　　1993　《中國道教史》（臺北：文津出版社）。

蕭啓慶

　　1996a　〈大蒙古國的國子學〉，收入氏著，《蒙古史新研》（臺北：允晨文化實
　　　　　　業公司），頁 63 94。

　　1996b　〈元代幾個漢軍世家的仕宦與婚姻〉，收入氏著，《蒙古史新研》，頁
　　　　　　265-348。

乙）英文

Biagioli, Mario

　　1989　"The Social Status of Italian Mathematicians, 1450-1600," *History of Science* 27: 41-95.

Chemla, Karine

　　1995　"What is the Content of This Book? A Plea for Developing History of Science and History of Text Conjunctly," *Philosophy and the History of Science: A Taiwanese Journal* 4(2): 1-46.

Ho, Peng-Yoke

　　1970　"Li Chih," in C. C. Gillispie ed., *Dictionary of Scientific Biography*. New York: Charles Scribner's Sons, 18 volumes, 1970-1990.

Kim, Yung Sik

　　1985　"Some Reflections on Science and Religion in Traditional China," *Han'guk Kwahak-Sa Hakhoe-Ji* (Journal of the Korean History of Science Society) 7(1): 40-49.

Kline, Morris

　　1972　*Mathematical Thought from Ancient to Modern Times*. New York: Oxford University Press.

Lam Lay Yong and Ang Tian-Se

　　1984　"Li Ye and His Yi Gu Yan Duan," *Archive for the History of Exact Sciences* 29: 237-266.

Lindberg, David C.

　　1992　*The Beginnings of Western Science*. Chicago: The University of

Chicago Press.

Martzloff, Jean-Claude

　1997　*A History of Chinese Mathematics*. Berlin/Heidelburg/New York: Springer-Verlag

Shinji, Arai

　1998　"Astronomical Studies by Zhao Youqin," *Taiwanese Journal for Philosophy and History of Science* 5(1): 59-102.

Volkov, Alexei

　1998　"Science and Daoism: An Introduction," *Taiwanese Journal for Philosophy and History of Science* 5(1): 1-58.

一九九九年一月一日修訂稿後記：

本文提交「金庸小說國際學術研討會」（臺北：國家圖書館，1998 年 11 月 4-6日）宣讀時，原題名爲「全真教與金元數學」，承龔鵬程、李豐楙教授指正，謹此致謝。不過，作者理當對本文負全部責任。

武俠世界中的醫者*

林　富　士

中央研究院歷史語言研究所

摘　要

　　幾乎每個人都會生病或受傷，都必須仰賴醫者的救治，而武林中人由於習武練功，較少罹患一般性的疾病，但是身處刀光劍影、爭鬥激烈的環境中，受傷的機會卻又比平常人多，因此，醫者在武俠世界中是不可或缺的人物。

　　以金庸的十二部長篇武俠小說來說，幾乎每一部都有醫者出現，《飛狐外傳》更是以女性醫者程靈素爲主要的角色之一。不過，武俠世界中的醫者，畢竟和現實世界中的醫者有一些不同的面目。基本上，金庸筆下的醫者至少可以分成四類。

　　第一類是不懂武功的職業醫者。江湖人物只有在極爲緊急或特殊的情況下，才會求助於他們。即使是所謂的「名醫」、御醫、太醫，在江湖人物眼中，幾乎都具有負面的形象，不是昏庸無能，就是奸佞邪惡。

　　第二類可以稱之爲「自救自療」型的醫者。他們通常武功平平，大多隸屬某些門派而行走江湖。他們的醫療技術也不高，只能處理一些簡單的金創、外傷，或靠師門的傷藥、解毒藥，治療一些比較不嚴重的內傷和中毒。

　　第三類是以醫藥爲專業的武林人士。他們的武功高低不一，但卻精通醫術、藥物，以專業醫者的身分在江湖立足，成爲大家受傷、中毒之後求救的對象，或因擅長使用毒物而被人畏懼。另外，有些門派甚至是以醫藥爲其開宗立派的骨幹。這一類型的醫者，在江湖上有著不低的地位，沒有人敢輕易

────────────

＊本文初稿於「金庸小說國際學術研討會」宣讀後，蒙評論人李永熾教授暨蒲歆嵐小姐惠賜寶貴意見，特此致謝。

得罪他們。但是他們畢竟不以武功見長,因此,除了程靈素之外,很少成為武俠世界中的主要角色。

第四類是兼擅武功與醫藥的高手。他們往往修練了高深的內功,並因此嫻習用藥、用毒和療傷、治病的方法。

總而言之,在武俠世界中,真正的主角還是那些身具一流武功的高手。通常,他們也是一流的醫者,因為上乘的武功大多兼具治病、療傷和解毒的法門與功效。這一類高手通常又兼習其他醫術,熟悉經脈、穴道、針灸、診脈、藥物之學,因此,可以處理各種複雜的傷、病。換句話說,在虛構的(古代的)武俠世界中,只有頂尖的武功高手,才能算是一流的醫者。武功就是醫藥,醫藥也是武功,都兼具救人和殺人的功能。

一、引　言

在現實的世界中,幾乎每個人都會因為生病或受傷而有賴醫者的救治。因此,從古至今,醫者一直是社會上不可或缺的人物。至於在虛構的「武俠世界」中,由於「人物是有武功的」,而且有「激烈的鬥爭」,[1] 因此,武林人士雖然不容易罹患一般性的疾病,但是受傷的機會卻不少。所以,純粹從理論上來說,在刀光劍影的武俠世界中,醫者應該也能佔有一席之地。

但是,武俠世界畢竟是武俠世界,武林人士所需要的醫者、醫藥和醫療方式,和真實世界的芸芸眾生畢竟有一些差異。因此,本文擬藉著金庸的十二部武俠小說,[2] 揭示武俠世界中各種不同類型的醫者、醫藥和醫療方式,並探討這一種虛擬的社會情境所蘊藏的文化意涵,以及對於現代人的啟示。

---

1 根據金庸的定義,「武俠小說與別的小說一樣,也是寫人,只不過環境是古代的,人物是有武功的,情節偏重於激烈的鬥爭。」詳見金庸,〈「金庸作品集」臺灣版序〉,收入《金庸作品集》1(臺北:遠流出版公司,1987),頁1。

2 基本上,本文只限於金庸的十二部長篇武俠小說,所使用的版本則是遠流出版公司於1987年編訂、結集的《金庸作品集》,其書名和序號如下:一、《書劍恩仇錄》(1-2);二、《碧血劍》(3-4);三、《射鵰英雄傳》(5-8);四、《神鵰俠侶》(9-12);五、《雪山飛狐》(13);六、《飛狐外傳》(14-15);七、《倚天屠龍記》(16-19);八、《連城訣》(20);九、《天龍八部》(21-25);十、《俠客行》(26-27);十一、《笑傲江湖》(28-31);十二、《鹿鼎記》(32-36)。

二、武林之外的職業醫者

在真實世界裡，一般人在生病、受傷之時，雖然也會求助於巫者、道士、僧尼之流的人物，企圖以宗教的手段解除肉體上的病痛，但是，在傳統的中國社會中，大約從西元前三世紀開始，尋求職業醫者的療治，已被多數人視為正當、正確的醫療方式。[3]

然而，在武俠世界裡，這一種不會武功的職業醫者，卻是可有可無的人物。武林人士只有在極為特殊的情況之下才會求助於他們。

第一種情況是婦女分娩的時候。舉例來說，在《雪山飛狐》裡，「雪山飛狐」胡斐誕生之時，他的母親有難產的現象。其父胡一刀雖然武功蓋世，卻也一籌莫展，只好企圖找尋「穩婆」（產婆）幫忙接生，而在找不到穩婆的情形下，便以威脅利誘的方式，請來一位跌打醫生閻基（也就是後來出家為僧的寶樹和尚），才解決難題，讓胡斐呱呱墜地。[4]

第二種情況是發瘋的時候。舉例來說，在《俠客行》裡，雪山派掌門人「威德先生」白自在，由於「自大成狂」，得了瘋病。他的門人束手無策，只好去請凌霄城裡最高明的兩位大夫（南大夫和戴大夫），不過，這兩位大夫還沒來得及把脈診治，便被白自在一掌擊斃。[5]

第三種情況是不明病因、病情的時候。例如，在《倚天屠龍記》裡，崑崙派掌門人「鐵琴先生」何太沖的第五個小妾，由於全身浮腫，病重不起，卻又查不出原因，因此，何太沖便將四川、雲南、甘肅一帶最有名的七位名醫「半請半拿」的捉去替她治病。這七位「名醫」診脈之後，或說是「水腫」，或說是「中邪」，也開了一些藥方讓她試服，卻都無效。何太沖便斥之為「庸醫」，並用鐵鍊將他們鎖上。後來，張無忌到來，才查出病因在於中了「金銀血蛇」的蛇毒，並替她解毒。[6]

3　詳見林富士，《漢代的巫者》（臺北：稻鄉出版社，1988）；林富士，〈東漢晚期的疾疫與宗教〉，《中央研究院歷史語言研究所集刊》，66:3 (1995)，頁 695-745。

4　《金庸作品集》13，頁 83-85。

5　《金庸作品集》27，頁 544-546。

6　《金庸作品集》17，頁 541-544。

　　另外，在《天龍八部》裡，段譽由於初練逍遙派的「北冥神功」，能吸取他人內力，但又不知如何導引、運用，因此，當他在萬劫谷吸了五位武功高手的內力之後，便覺體內真氣鼓盪，不可抑制，只得手舞足蹈、亂走亂闖、大聲號叫，因而被認為是「中邪」，並交由大理國醫道最精的兩名太醫診治，而兩名太醫對於脈象的解讀和療法都不一樣。一個認為「脈搏洪盛，血氣太旺」，因此便用水蛭替他放血，但因段譽曾經吞入萬毒之王「莽牯朱蛤」，血中蘊含劇毒（但也百毒不侵），水蛭一吸血便即僵死。兩名太醫因此改口說段譽是中了劇毒，但一個說是「熱毒」，另一個卻說是「毒性微寒」。即使是武功高強、又通醫理的保定帝親自替他把脈，也無法診斷出真正的病因。後來，段譽還是到「天龍寺」練了「六脈神劍」，才將到處流竄的內力收入臟腑。[7]

　　第四種情況是傷（病）太重，無法自己療治的時候。這樣的例子還不少，僅舉其中幾個略做說明。第一，在《書劍恩仇錄》裡，武當派大俠陸菲青，為了避難而藏身於陝西扶風延綏鎮的總兵衙門之內，擔任教席。後來，行藏被人識破，並被「關東六魔」的第三魔焦文期以鐵琵琶手和鐵牌所傷。當他負傷逃回住處時，雖然勉力取出刀傷藥替自己療傷，但因內傷太重，以致吐血、昏厥，其徒弟李沅芷只好替他聘請名醫，購買良藥，花了兩個多月，才治好內傷。[8]

　　其次，在《書劍恩仇錄》裡，紅花會的十當家徐天宏，因被「火手判官」張召重以三枚「芙蓉金針」射中，深入附骨，痛楚難忍，以至昏迷。鐵膽莊的大小姐周綺，雖然用刀將他左肩的肉剜開，拔出金針，用草灰按住創口，拿布條縛好，但是傷口終致化膿，徐天宏因發高燒而再度喪失神智。因此，周綺只好到鎮上抓了一位曹司朋大夫前去診治。這位曹大夫雖然人品惡劣（既供給春藥，又給毒藥，讓其客戶謀色害命），但醫道頗為高明，開的藥方極為有效，徐天宏在服用湯藥之後，便慢慢好轉。[9]

　　第三，在《書劍恩仇錄》裡，紅花會的四當家「奔雷手」文泰來和他的夫人駱冰，為了逃避清廷大內高手的追殺，到鐵膽莊周仲英家中避難時，文

---

7 《金庸作品集》21，頁 220-221；393-407。

8 《金庸作品集》1，頁 7-19。

9 同上，頁 215-238。

泰來因受重傷而神智昏迷，周家便派人到鎮上請醫生。[10] 後來，文泰來還是被捕，紅花會的十四當家余魚同於是前往解救，不過，不但沒有成功，自己反受清廷侍衛的圍攻而被刀、劍、棍所傷，渾身是血，暈了過去。文泰來只好投降，要求侍衛替余魚同止血救傷，並請了醫生開藥，才保住一條小命。[11] 總之，紅花會的幾位當家，在重傷之餘，往往都由他人延醫治療。[12]

第四，在《雪山飛狐》裡，有多名武林人物圍攻胡一刀，其中七個反被砍成重傷，他們的同伴只好請來滄州鄉下小鎮的跌打醫生閻基，替他們上金創藥、止血、包紮，並給他們服用寧神減疼的湯藥。[13]

第五，在《倚天屠龍記》裡，張無忌用「雲手」絞斷了阿三的四肢，用掌力震斷了禿頂阿二的雙臂、胸前肋骨和肩頭鎖骨，用木劍削斷了「八臂神劍」方東白的一臂，他們三人雖然有「金剛門」的「黑玉斷續膏」，但療治之時，還是要請醫生替他們敷藥，並用金針治痛。[14]

第六，在《天龍八部》裡，蕭峯（喬峯）雖然武功極為高強，卻常常求助於醫生。首先是在阿朱被少林方丈玄慈以大金剛掌擊中之後，命在垂危，蕭峯雖然用了譚公的傷藥「寒玉冰蟾膏」替她敷治，但阿朱仍舊昏厥不醒。因此，蕭峯只好到鎮上請醫生診治，那位醫生在把脈之後，便宣告阿朱沒藥醫，只開了一張藥性溫和的方子。蕭峯只好將內力輸入她體內，暫時以自己的真氣替她續命，然後尋求「閻王敵」薛神醫的救治。[15] 後來，蕭峯誤殺了阿朱，又誤傷了阿朱的妹妹阿紫，一掌將她打得雙目緊閉、臉如金紙、口流鮮血。於是，蕭峯又用自己的真氣內力替阿紫續命，然後帶著她求醫，首先找上了一個在大市鎮開業的「世傳儒醫」王通治。這位王人夫在替阿紫把脈之後，卻說蕭峯有病，神智不清，心神顛倒錯亂，因為他認為阿紫已是個死人，脈息已停。幸好，蕭峯聽人說「老山人參」可以「吊一吊性命」，才用人

10　同上，頁 76-77。

11　同上，頁 190-192。

12　同上，頁 404-405。

13　《金庸作品集》13，頁 79-80。

14　《金庸作品集》18，頁 984-995、1005-1006。

15　《金庸作品集》22，頁 781-786。

參保住了阿紫的一條小命。[16]

第七，在《笑傲江湖》裡，令狐沖因被成不憂一掌擊中胸口，以致口中鮮血狂噴，又被桃谷六仙等人胡亂醫治一番，以致體內經脈大亂，形同廢人。而當江湖傳出令狐沖是任盈盈的意中人之後，群雄為了討好任盈盈，便在五霸崗群聚了千餘人，要醫治令狐沖。其中，有人提供藥物，有人則是將魯東六府中最有本事的七個名醫都綁到現場，令他們替令狐沖診脈、治病。結果並沒有任何作用，即連當世第一大名醫平一指抵達之後，雖然診出病因，但卻想不出醫治之法，甚至因思慮過度，且自愧無能救人，因而當場自殺。[17]

最後，在《鹿鼎記》裡，韋小寶略通醫藥，而且還藏有各式各樣的藥物（春藥、毒藥、傷藥、補藥都有），但當他被建寧公主打得頭破血流、身中數刀、燒掉髮辮之後，雖然還能替自己敷上金創藥，終究仍是命手下太監去請御醫替他敷藥治傷。[18] 另外，天地會青木堂的「八臂猿猴」徐天川，以在北京天橋賣膏藥維生，青木堂甚至還經營了一家回春堂藥店，因此，徐天川應該是懂醫藥之人，不過當他被雲南沐王府的「白氏雙木」（白寒松、白寒楓）掌力擊中，受了嚴重內傷之後，卻也無力醫治自己，而必須求治於跌打名醫姚春。[19]

至於求助於職業醫者的第五種情況則是，沒有藥物或不懂醫術，以致無法自己療治的時候。這一類事例也不少，僅舉其中五個略做說明。首先，在《書劍恩仇錄》裡，李沅芷偷偷地將巴豆汁放入茶水中，讓關東三魔喝了之後肚瀉不止，客店的老闆只好請醫生替他們診脈。不過，醫生卻以為是受了風寒，便開了一張驅寒暖腹的方子。而當店小二煎藥時，李沅芷又偷偷加入了巴豆和幾十種不同的藥材，關東三魔服藥之後更是慘不忍睹。[20]

其次，在《碧血劍》裡，華山派的歸辛樹夫婦雖然武功高強，但其獨子歸鍾出生之後便身染重病，歸氏夫婦不知如何醫治，只好帶著他到處訪尋名醫。而那些名醫雖然診斷出病因在於「胎傷」，可是因為欠缺千年茯苓和成形

---

16 《金庸作品集》23，頁 1087-1093。
17 《金庸作品集》29，頁 677-686。
18 《金庸作品集》34，頁 850-863。
19 《金庸作品集》32，頁 332-342。
20 《金庸作品集》2，頁 625-626。

何首烏，因此也無法加以救治。[21]

第三，在《雪山飛狐》裡，天龍門掌門田歸農的妻子（也就是「金面佛」苗人鳳的前妻）受了涼，傷風咳嗽，田歸農卻無法加以醫治，只能請醫生診治、開藥方。不過，這位夫人卻拒絕服藥，以致病亡。[22]

第四，在《天龍八部》裡，「帶頭大哥」（少林寺方丈玄慈）和丐幫幫主汪劍通，在雁門關外伏擊契丹武士蕭遠山（蕭峯之父），卻反被蕭遠山踢中穴道，動彈不得。其同伴智光大師曾嘗試替他們解穴，但任他抓拿打拍、按捏敲摩、推血過宮、鬆筋揉肌，卻一點反應也沒有，後來，只好將他們帶回雁門關內，找尋跌打傷科的醫生療治解穴，卻也解救不得，直到滿十二個時辰，才自行解開。[23]

第五，在《俠客行》裡，石破天為了掩飾他本來的面目，冒充石中玉，因而塗了藥膏，以致頸中紅腫、狀似癰疽，而其父母石清和閔柔一見之下，大為驚慌，便請了一位老醫生前來診治，結果斷為大癰，開了一些消腫、化膿、消毒的藥物，雖然對症，卻是誤診。後來，石氏夫婦又帶他去看了幾位醫生，也都診不出半點端倪。[24]

總之，從以上這些事例來看，不會武功的職業醫者，在武俠世界中，幾乎沒什麼地位。武林人士只有在無法親自動手醫護，或不知如何醫治的情況下，才會求助於他們。但是，大部分的例子都只突顯出他們的平庸、無能。他們通常不是誤診，就是束手無策，能發揮作用的只是幫忙接生、止血、治痛和治療一些外傷。其中，醫術比較高明的，似乎只有《書劍恩仇錄》裡的曹司朋和《雪山飛狐》裡的閻基，而這二人卻都是品行不端、會用藥物害人的惡醫。在金庸筆下，幾乎所有的「名醫」都變成「庸醫」或是「惡醫」，都只有負面的形象。[25]

至於他們的治療方式，大多透過把脈診斷病因、病情，然後開藥方，以

21　《金庸作品集》3，頁 330。
22　《金庸作品集》13，頁 174-175。
23　《金庸作品集》22，頁 663-666。
24　《金庸作品集》27，頁 490-494。
25　事實上，金庸曾藉喬峯之手，殺了一個沒有醫德的「名醫」。詳見《金庸作品集》22，頁 790-794。

湯藥救治。若是外傷，則主要用金創藥止血，然後包紮，有時還會利用金針止痛。比較特殊的療法是大理國的太醫以水蛭放血的方法治療段譽。無論如何，對於武林人士來說，這種類型的醫者是可有可無的，很少會成爲他們求助的對象。因爲武林人士本身大多也能掌握這些醫療的方法和藥物，有一些人的醫術甚至還超越職業的醫者，因而聞名於江湖，成爲同道求助的對象。至少，他們大多能自力救濟，或替他人進行急救。

三、自救自療的武林醫者

由於習練武功，武林人士大多比一般人強健，不易生病。但由於經常行走江湖，再加上恩怨、是非太多，因此，遭受到各種外力傷害的機會便相當多。

武林人士所受到的傷害，主要是來自同道。至於受傷的類型，基本上可分爲三種。第一種是外傷，主要是被刀、劍之類的兵器或細小的暗器所傷，以致肢體、器官受創，流血不止，疼痛不堪。或是被棍、棒之類的武器或拳、掌所擊，以致骨頭斷裂。

第二種是內傷，主要是被拳掌或內力所傷，或是因練功時不慎走火，以致臟腑、經脈受損，通常還會吐血，並陷入昏迷。

第三種是中毒，主要是中了各式各樣的毒物，並呈現各種不同的中毒反應，這也是金庸小說相當複雜而迷人的一部分。以毒物的種類來說，又可進一步細分爲四種。

第一，植物性的毒物。包括：《書劍恩仇錄》裡的巴豆；《神鵰俠侶》裡的情花和斷腸草；《飛狐外傳》裡的斷腸草、藍花、醍醐香、血矮栗和七心海棠等；《倚天屠龍記》裡的靑陀羅花、靈脂蘭；《連城訣》裡的金波旬花。

第二，動物性的毒物。包括：《碧血劍》裡的「五毒」（靑蛇、蜈蚣、蝎子、蜘蛛、蟾蜍）、鶴頂蛇和金蛇；《射鵰英雄傳》裡「西毒」歐陽鋒的杖頭雙蛇；《飛狐外傳》裡的孔雀膽和鶴頂紅；《倚天屠龍記》裡的漆裡星（黑色毒蛇）、金銀血蛇、蜈蚣、心一跳（西域毒蟲）；《連城訣》裡的花斑毒蝎；《天龍八部》裡的閃電貂、莽牯朱蛤、蝎子、冰蠶；《鹿鼎記》的毒蛇。

　　第三，人工合成或煉製的毒物。包括：《碧血劍》裡的醉仙蜜（迷藥）；《神鵰俠侶》裡的蟾蜍毒砂；《飛狐外傳》裡的碧蠶毒蠱、迷藥、三蜈五蟆煙、赤蠍粉；《倚天屠龍記》裡的毒鹽、啞藥、蒙汗藥（迷藥）、金蠶毒蠱、三蟲三草劇毒、鳩砒丸、醉仙靈芙加上青鯪香木、七蟲七花膏、十香軟筋散（迷藥）、麻藥、五毒失心散、腐蝕藥水；《天龍八部》裡的斷筋腐骨丸、斷腸散、陰陽和合散（春樂）、薰香（迷藥）、悲酥清風（迷藥）、十香迷魂散（迷藥）、三笑逍遙散、麻藥；《俠客行》裡的蒙汗藥（迷藥）、悶香（迷藥）、烈火丹、九九丸；《笑傲江湖》裡的三尸腦神丹、五更雞鳴還魂香（迷藥）、百花消魂散（迷藥）、啞藥；《鹿鼎記》裡的蒙汗藥（迷藥）、悶香（迷藥）、化屍粉、升天丸、七蟲軟筋散、千里消魂散、化血腐骨粉、百涎丸、豹胎易筋丸、百花腹蛇膏、迷春酒（春藥）。

　　第四，將毒物焠煉在暗器、兵器上或掌力之中，或是帶有陰毒的內功。包括：《射鵰英雄傳》裡的毒沙掌、子午透骨釘、附骨針、七絕針；《神鵰俠侶》裡的冰魄銀針、五毒神掌；《雪山飛狐》裡的追命毒龍錐；《飛狐外傳》裡的絕門毒針、毒砂掌；《倚天屠龍記》裡的蚊鬚針、七星釘、餵毒梅花鏢、玄冥神掌、蝎尾鉤、截心掌、餵毒喪門釘、千蛛萬毒手；《連城訣》裡的藍砂掌、蝎尾鏢；《天龍八部》裡的生死符、修羅刀、餵毒短箭、碧磷針、鍊心彈、三陰蜈蚣爪、抽髓掌、餵毒牛毛針；《俠客行》裡的黑煞掌；《笑傲江湖》裡的黑血神針、藍砂手、毒針；《鹿鼎記》裡的化骨綿掌、含沙射影（鋼針）。

　　總之，江湖人物大多免不了會有受傷、中毒的機會，因此，即使不懂醫理，也要具備簡單的醫療技術，以便在危急時自救或救人。尤其是對於外傷的救治，不外乎止血、接骨和包紮，一般狀況下，武林人士大多能自理，也因此他們大多隨身帶有金創藥。當然，比較嚴重的時候，尤其是失血過多、昏迷、疼痛、發燒這類的問題，則需要求助於職業的醫者，另以針灸、湯藥醫治。

　　此外，有一些門派或高手甚至煉製了特殊的金創藥。其中，比較有名的有：《射鵰英雄傳》裡，桃花島「東邪」黃藥師的田七鯊膽散；《飛狐外傳》裡，程靈素的止血生肌丸；《倚天屠龍記》裡，武當派的金創藥和三黃寶臘丸（續骨）、崆峒派的回陽五龍膏（續骨）、華山派的玉真散（續骨）、少林派

的玉靈散、西域金剛門的黑玉斷續膏；《天龍八部》裡，靈鷲宮的九轉熊蛇丸、譚公的寒玉冰蟾膏；《笑傲江湖》裡，恆山派的天香斷續膠；《鹿鼎記》裡，少林寺的金創藥。

至於內傷，若是高手，可以利用內功自行療傷，或替他人醫療。但是，大多數的武林人物還是有賴藥物的救治。許多門派或高手，通常也都煉製了獨特的療傷藥物，讓門徒或自己隨身備用。其中，比較有名的有：《書劍恩仇錄》裡，「天池怪俠」袁士霄的雪參丸；《射鵰英雄傳》裡，「東邪」黃藥師的九花玉露丸和無常丹；《神鵰俠侶》裡，黃藥師的九花玉露丸、全真教的九轉靈寶丸；《飛狐外傳》裡，湯沛的人參養榮丸；《倚天屠龍記》裡，「崑崙三聖」何足道的少陽丹、武當派的白虎奪命丹和天王護心丹；《天龍八部》裡，少林派的六陽正氣丹；《俠客行》裡，丁不三的玄冰碧火酒；《笑傲江湖》裡，恆山派的白雲熊膽丸、「殺人名醫」平一指的鎮心理氣丸；《鹿鼎記》裡，神龍教主洪安通的大補雪參丸和天王保命丹。除了這種人工調製、便於攜帶的藥物之外，有一些動物或植物也具有特殊的療效。例如，《碧血劍》裡的朱睛冰蟾；《神鵰俠侶》裡的九尾靈狐和千年雪參；《倚天屠龍記》裡的人血、火蟾；《天龍八部》裡的人參、熊膽、虎骨、虎筋等，都對嚴重或奇特的內傷有效。

中毒的情形則比較複雜。有些藥物只是會激發性衝動的「春藥」，有些則是會令人昏迷或喪失功力的「迷藥」，大多不會令人喪命。但是，某些特製的春藥和迷藥，也需要專門的解藥才能治癒。

真正可怕的還是那些含有劇毒的藥物、兵器和武功。有一些根本沒有解藥，中則斃命；有一些則必須服用特殊的解藥，而通常只有下毒者才有解藥或知道解毒的方法。因此，有一些精通藥物的武林高手，便利用其獨創的下毒方法（通常是用毒藥），控制其部屬或其他江湖人物，使其俯首聽命，不敢反抗。其中，比較著名的有：《天龍八部》裡，靈鷲宮的天山童姥利用生死符（事實上結合了內功、暗器和毒性）控制各幫各派的重要人物；《笑傲江湖》裡，魔教（日月神教）教主任我行利用三尸腦神丹控制其部屬；《鹿鼎記》裡，神龍教教主洪安通利用豹胎易筋丸控制其門徒。而無論是生死符、三尸腦神丹，還是豹胎易筋丸，若不定時服用解藥，則會痛不欲生、受盡折磨而死。

　　雖然大多數的毒藥、毒物都需要專門的解藥，不過，有些門派和個人還是會煉製一些解毒藥，以防萬一。其中，比較有名的有：《射鵰英雄傳》裡，「西毒」歐陽鋒的通犀地龍丸；《飛狐外傳》裡，「毒手藥王」的生生造化丹；《倚天屠龍記》裡，武當派的天心解毒丹、「蝶谷醫仙」胡青牛的牛黃血歇丹和玉龍蘇合散、崆峒派的玉洞黑石丹；《笑傲江湖》裡，五毒教（五仙教）的五寶花蜜酒。另外，特殊狀況下，也可以採食天然的藥物，像《碧血劍》裡的朱睛冰蟾、《神鵰俠侶》裡的普斯曲蛇的蛇膽、《倚天屠龍記》裡的佛座小紅蓮、《天龍八部》裡的通天草，便都具有解毒的功能。

　　總之，基於現實上的需要，療傷、治病、解毒，幾乎是每一個江湖人物必修的功課，武學著作大多也有相關的篇章，例如，在《天龍八部》裡，王語嫣便說：

> 我看過的武學書籍之中，講到治毒法門的著實不少。[26]

另外，在《射鵰英雄傳》裡，最重要的武學書籍《九陰真經》也有「療傷篇」，講的是「如何以氣功調理真元，治療內傷」。[27] 事實上，金庸在書中也指出：

> 武術中有言道：「未學打人，先學挨打。」初練粗淺功夫，即須由師父傳授怎生挨打而不受重傷，到了武功精深之時，就得研習護身保命、解穴救傷、接骨療毒諸般法門。[28]

然而，一般武林人士大多武功粗淺，醫療技術也不高明，只能處理簡易的外傷。至於內傷或中毒，則有賴其師門配製的成藥。總之，這一類型的醫者，只能療治輕傷，碰到嚴重的內、外傷或中了劇毒，只能求救於武林中的專業醫者，或有賴武功、醫術俱臻上乘的高手。

26　《金庸作品集》22，頁 595。

27　《金庸作品集》7，頁 950-951。

28　同上，頁 950。

四、武林中的專業醫者

　　武林人物自然是以各種武功見長，不過，也有一些人是以精通醫道、醫藥聞名江湖，成爲大家求治的對象。有些門派甚至就是以醫藥爲其開宗立派的骨幹，其領導人或弟子也都精於此道，以醫藥行走江湖。

　　以門派來說，比較著名的有下列幾個。

　　一、《碧血劍》裡的五毒教。其教主何鐵手（何惕守）和教中人物何紅藥等人，都是用毒、解毒的高手。

　　二、《飛狐外傳》裡的「毒手藥王」一門。包括「毒手藥王」無嗔大師，其師弟「毒手神梟」石萬嗔，其徒弟慕容景岳、姜鐵山、薛鵲和程靈素等人，都是用毒、解毒、治病、療傷的能手。

　　三、《天龍八部》裡的神農幫。該幫是以採藥、販藥在江湖上立足，擅長用毒、醫病。

　　四、《天龍八部》裡的星宿派。「星宿老怪」丁春秋和他的門人都擅於用毒，令人畏惡。

　　五、《笑傲江湖》裡的百藥門和五仙教（五毒教），號稱江湖上的兩大毒門，擅長下毒和解毒之道。

　　以個人來說，以醫術、毒術揚名立萬的則有十個左右。

　　一、《射鵰英雄傳》和《神鵰俠侶》裡，「南帝」一燈大師的師弟天竺神僧，號稱「治傷療毒，天下第一」。

　　二、《飛狐外傳》裡的「毒手藥王」無嗔大師，雖以擅於用毒聞名，但也精於醫治之道，著有《藥王神篇》。

　　三、《飛狐外傳》裡的程靈素，也就是「毒手藥王」的小弟子，不僅承繼了其師的毒術、醫術，而且還青出於藍，培育出「七心海棠」。事實上，她也是這部書的靈魂人物。

　　四、《倚天屠龍記》裡的「蝶谷醫仙」胡青牛，外號「見死不救」，主要以醫術見長，並在醫學上大有發明創見，著有《帶脈論》和《子午針灸經》。

　　五、《倚天屠龍記》裡的「毒仙」王難姑，也就是胡青牛的妻子，擅長用

毒，著有《毒經》，對於醫道、毒術和武功之間的關係，有獨到的論述。[29]

六、《天龍八部》裡的「閻王敵」薛神醫（薛慕華），被認爲是「當世醫中第一聖手」，喜歡結交江湖人物，以替人治病換取武功。

七、《俠客行》裡的「著守回春」貝大夫（貝海石），因久病而成良醫，爲長樂幫的要角。

八、《笑傲江湖》裡的「殺人名醫」平一指，他的醫寓中掛著一幅大中堂，寫明：「醫一人，殺一人。殺一人，醫一人。醫人殺人一樣多，蝕本生意決不做。」據說，沒有他治不好的人，而他「殺人醫人，俱只一指」。[30]

九、《鹿鼎記》裡神龍敎的陸高軒大夫，不僅能療傷、治病、解毒，藥箱裡還有打胎藥。

這些人物之中，像貝海石、平一指等人，都有不錯的武功，其他則武功平平。但是，他們令江湖中人印象深刻的，都是用毒、用藥、療傷、治病的本領，這也是大家不敢輕易招惹、得罪他們的原因。因爲，醫藥和武功一樣，既能救人也能殺人。不過，他們的醫療方法，基本上和一般的職業醫者並無不同，大多是利用診脈斷定病因、病情，並利用針灸和藥物救治，只是他們的手段比較高明，因此能聞名於世。然而，在武俠世界中，眞正一流的醫者，其實還是那些武功和醫術都是頂尖的高手。

五、兼擅武功與醫藥的高手

對於武林人士來說，一般的金創、外傷只是小事，眞正不易處理的是嚴重的內傷和中毒，因此，比較深奧的武功（內功），大多兼具防病、治病、療傷、驅毒的心法。例如，在《碧血劍》裡，袁承志修練了華山派的混元功之後，雖然時日尚淺，尚未有成，但「身子已出落得壯健異常，百病不侵」。[31]

其次，在《射鵰英雄傳》裡，郭靖腰間挨了楊康一刀，前胸又被歐陽鋒

29　王難姑認爲：「一人所以學武，乃是爲了殺人，毒術也用於殺人，武術和毒術相輔相
　　成。只要精通毒術，武功便強了一倍也還不止。但醫術卻用來治病救人，和武術背道
　　而馳。」詳見《金庸作品集》17，頁490。

30　《金庸作品集》29，頁577-578。

31　《金庸作品集》3，頁86。

的蛤蟆功擊中，命在垂危之際，便是靠《九陰眞經》「療傷篇」所載的法門，在密室之中，七日七夜，由黃蓉助他運氣療傷，才告痊癒。[32]　而黃蓉被鐵掌幫幫主裘千仞的鐵掌擊中雙肩之後，身受重傷，性命垂危，則是郭靖背著她求救於段皇爺（一燈大師），在一燈大師用一陽指替她點遍全身穴道之後，才保住性命。[33]

第三，在《神鵰俠侶》裡，小龍女在修習《玉女心經》的內功時，因爲受到干擾，驚怒交集，以致氣息逆轉，口中鮮血狂噴，身受嚴重內傷，但後來的療傷工作，主要還是依賴這門功法。[34]

第四，在《倚天屠龍記》裡，張無忌身中玄冥神掌之後，已無藥可醫，連張三丰、「蝶谷醫仙」都無能爲力。最後，還是靠修練《九陽眞經》中的九陽神功，才用自身眞氣驅盡體內的寒毒，解除痛苦。後來，他還利用九陽神功替明教的楊逍、韋一笑及五散人逼出體內玄陰指的寒毒，治好他們的內傷。[35]

第五，在《天龍八部》裡，大理段家的六脈神劍不僅是威力強大的劍法（劍氣），更是上乘的內功，具有解毒、療傷的功效，段譽原本苦於體內眞氣亂竄，也因修練了六脈神劍才解除痛苦。[36]

第六，在《天龍八部》裡，少林寺《易筋經》的神功也具有解毒、療傷的強大功能。游坦之飽受阿紫的各種折磨，又身中冰蠶的劇毒之後，還能活命，並且成爲武林高手，便是修練了這門神功的緣故。[37]

第七，在《天龍八部》裡，逍遙派的逍遙神功也具有絕佳的療傷、治病功能。當逍遙派掌門無崖子將其七十餘年修爲的逍遙神功（北冥眞氣）灌輸到虛竹身上之後，「聰辯先生」蘇星河（無崖子的大徒弟）便告訴虛竹，以此神功「治傷療病，可說無往不利」，而虛竹也以此治好少林大師和風波惡等人

32　《金庸作品集》7，頁 940-951。

33　同上，頁 1191-1195。

34　《金庸作品集》9，頁 222-224、271。

35　《金庸作品集》16，頁 397；《金庸作品集》17，頁 626；《金庸作品集》18，頁 901。

36　《金庸作品集》21，頁 398-407。

37　《金庸作品集》23，頁 1189-1204。

的內傷和寒毒。[38]

第八，在《笑傲江湖》裡，令狐冲身受重傷之後，無法醫治，不過，華山派的紫霞神功、魔教任我行的吸星大法，和少林寺《易筋經》的內功，都被認爲可以治癒他的傷勢。後來，令狐冲先後練了吸星大法和《易筋經》的內功，才完全恢復正常，並且功力大進。[39]

第九，在《鹿鼎記》裡，韋小寶中了老太監海大富的毒藥，原本是無藥可救的。但是天地會總舵主陳近南（陳永華）卻以其「內功」，將他體內的毒逼了出來，才保住韋小寶的小命。[40]

總之，修練混元功、九陰眞經、九陽神功、一陽指、玉女心經、六脈神劍、易筋經、逍遙神功、紫霞神功、吸星大法這一類的武學，不但可以使人成爲一流的武功高手，其內功心法更可以療傷、治病、解毒，不僅可以殺人，也可以救人。因此，在武林之中，一個武功上乘的高手，往往僅憑精湛內功，便夠資格做一個傑出的醫者。事實上，在金庸筆下，這一類的高手，通常不僅能以內功替人治病、療傷，還精通醫藥。例如，在《碧血劍》裡，金蛇郎君不僅武功蓋世，還學會了五毒敎用毒、解毒的本領，成爲江湖中人聞風喪膽的人物。

其次，在《射鵰英雄傳》和《神鵰俠侶》裡，桃花島的「東邪」黃藥師和大理國的「南帝」一燈大師，不僅是排名前五名的頂尖高手，而且精通醫道、醫術，常能替人療傷、治病。黃藥師更親自調製了一些療傷治病的藥物（如九花玉露丸、田七鯊膽散），而且還煉製有毒的暗器（如附骨針）。此外，也是五大高手之一的「西毒」歐陽鋒，則擅長解毒、用毒，其杖頭雙蛇，毒性奇烈無比，殺人無數，連「北丐」洪七公都差點因而喪命。至於全眞敎的丘處機，武功也不弱，而且還精通醫道。

第三，在《神鵰俠侶》裡，古墓派的「赤練仙子」李莫愁，非但武功不凡，而且還擅長用毒、解毒，擁有一部《五毒秘傳》，練成了毒性強烈的冰魄銀針和五毒神掌，傷人無數。絕情谷谷主公孫止，也是個武學高手，同時也

---

38 《金庸作品集》24，頁 1361-1365。

39 《金庸作品集》29，頁 467-472、738；《金庸作品集》30，頁 902；《金庸作品集》31，頁 1677。

40 《金庸作品集》32，頁 326-327。

是用藥的能手，谷中便設有煉藥的丹房和藏藥的芝房，擁有可以解除情花之毒的絕情丹和其他藥材。此外，「金輪法王」更是精通武功、醫藥和毒術。

第四，在《倚天屠龍記》裡，武當派祖師爺張三丰的武功是數一數二的，然而，他在醫藥方面也有不凡的成就，不僅能以內功替人療治內傷、外傷，還煉製了不少解毒、療傷的丹藥（如天心解毒丹、白虎奪命丹、三黃寶臘丸、天王護心丹）。不過，在武功和醫藥方面的造詣都到達頂極的，應該是張無忌。他不僅得到「蝶谷醫仙」胡青牛的親傳，還苦讀古典醫經和各種醫方書籍，並且承繼了「毒仙」王難姑的《毒經》，精通用毒、解毒之道。因此，在學成絕世武功之前，便已四處行醫救人。後來，更學會了《九陽真經》上的武功和明教的武功心法「乾坤大挪移」，不僅使自己天下無敵，也強化了他替人療傷、治病的功力。此外，蒙古公主趙敏也不差，不僅能打善鬥，而且擅於使毒，身上常帶有各種毒藥（如十香軟筋散、七蟲七花膏）和傷藥（去腐消肌膏、黑玉斷續膏），更能用藥物控制各大門派的高手，逼他們傳授本門的武功。

第五，在《天龍八部》裡，萬劫谷谷主鍾萬仇，武功也不弱，家中也設有藥房，儲藏各種藥物，其中甚至有春藥「陰陽和合散」，而且還豢養了一隻具有毒性的閃電貂。不過，真正兼具高深武功和醫藥知識的，應該是逍遙派一脈。蘇星河曾對剛入門的虛竹說：

> 師弟，本門向來並非只以武學見長，醫卜星相，琴棋書畫，各家之學，包羅萬有。你有一個師姪薛慕華，醫術只懂得一點皮毛，江湖上居然人稱「薛神醫」，得了個外號叫做「閻王敵」。[41]

事實上，在這部書裡，幾個武功和醫術俱一流的高手都是逍遙派的。第一代有掌門人無崖子，其師姐靈鷲宮的天山童姥和師妹李秋水，武功都出神入化，也都精通醫術，天山童姥更擅於用藥物控制江湖群雄。第二代則有無崖子的大弟子「聰辯先生」（「聾啞老人」）蘇星河、二弟子「星宿老怪」丁春秋和三弟子虛竹，其中虛竹更兼習天山童姥的武功和醫術，成為最傑出的一位。第三代則有蘇星河的徒弟薛慕華，人稱「薛神醫」，不過，此人武功還不在高手之列，只因精通醫藥而揚名立萬。

---

41 《金庸作品集》24，頁 1361。

　　第六，在《俠客行》裡，俠客島的龍島主和木島主，不僅武功頂尖，而且還能將「斷腸蝕骨腐心草」和其他藥物熬煮成「臘八粥」，對於練武之人大有補益，而其門人也能調製毒藥、藥酒，可見他們對於醫藥之道也有不錯的造詣。

　　第七，在《笑傲江湖》裡，魔教教主任我行也是兼擅武功和用藥的高手，而其女任盈盈似乎也不差，不僅武功有一定的程度，還能替令狐冲把脈看病，甚至能以琴曲（清心普善咒）緩解令狐冲的痛苦。

　　第八，在《鹿鼎記》裡，宮中太監海大富也有資格稱得上是武功和醫藥俱佳之人，其藥箱中更有千奇百怪的藥物。其次，天地會的陳近南不僅武功極高，以「凝血神抓」稱雄武林，而且還精通以內力驅毒療傷之法，並擁有解毒靈丹。不過，醫藥知識的水平和其武功成就不相上下的，應該是神龍教教主洪安通。他不僅武功高強、出手狠毒，還能運用各種毒藥（如豹胎易筋丸、百涎丸）和補藥（如大補雪參丸、天王保命丹）掌控其徒眾，使其俯首聽命。至於韋小寶，雖然嘻皮笑臉，不曾認真學習過武術或醫術，但東摸西碰的，再加上因緣巧合，武功其實也已不含糊，而他下藥的本領雖然不能算是高手，但是對於石灰、化屍粉、毒藥、迷藥、春藥、瀉藥，卻也運用自如，勉強可以進入高手的行列。

　　總之，在武俠世界裡，只有這一類的醫者才接近完美無瑕，才能預防或醫治各種的疾病和傷害，或利用其武功和醫藥打敗敵人。他們是最可愛的醫者，也是最可怕的殺手。

六、結　語

　　總結來說，武林人物通常比較不容易生病，主要的危害是來自武林同道的武功和毒物。在是是非非、恩恩怨怨、打打殺殺、奸奸詭詭的江湖中，任何高手都免不了會受傷或中毒。因此，江湖人物往往必須兼習醫藥，一方面可以自救救人，另一方面則能以藥（毒藥）制敵、殺人。

　　在武俠世界中，雖然也有一些不懂武功的職業醫者，但是，他們的角色大都不很重要，江湖人物只有在極為緊急或特殊的情況下，才會求助於他們。即使是所謂的「名醫」、御醫、太醫，在江湖人物眼中，幾乎都具有負面的形

象，不是昏庸無能，就是奸佞邪惡。換句話說，尋常的醫術和藥物只能治療一般的疾病，無法滿足江湖人物的需求。

江湖人士最需要的，是能療治內、外傷的靈丹妙藥和上乘內功，以及可以辟毒、解毒的藥物和功法。不過，限於資質和機緣，每個人所能擁有的醫療知識和能力也有所不同。

最差的一種，武功平平、醫療技術也不高，只能處理一些簡單的金創、外傷，或靠師門的傷藥、解毒藥，治療一些比較不嚴重的內傷和中毒。這一種自救自療型的人物，應佔武林醫者中的多數。

更高一層的是，武功高低不一，但卻精通醫術、藥物，以專業醫者的身分在江湖立足，成為大家受傷、中毒之後求救的對象，而有些門派甚至是以醫藥為其開宗立派的骨幹。這一類型的醫者，在江湖上有不錯的地位，沒有人敢輕易得罪他們。但是，他們畢竟不以武功見長，因此，除了程靈素之外，很少成為武俠世界中的主要角色。

武俠世界中，真正的主角還是那些身具一流武功的高手。通常，他們也是一流的醫者，因為上乘的武功大多兼具治病、療傷和解毒的法門與功效。而這一類高手往往又兼習其他醫術，熟悉經脈、穴道、針灸、診脈、藥物之學，因此，可以處理各種複雜的傷、病。

總而言之，在虛構的（古代的）武俠世界中，只有頂尖的武功高手，才能算是一流的醫者。武功就是醫藥，醫藥也是武功，都兼具救人和殺人的功能。至於在真實的（現代的）世界裡，武林高手似乎不再是一流的醫者。但是，醫藥仍是一種強有力的武功，能救人也能殺人，更能控制人的身心。因此，在我們的世界裡，只有一流的醫者才是真正的武林高手。

這種差異，也許是真實世界與虛構世界之間原有的分別，[42] 但是，似乎也是時移境遷的結果。中國到了西元前第三世紀的時候，已發展出一套有關人體生理的臟腑、經脈理論，以及以氣為主的身體觀。以診脈判斷病因、病情，以針灸、藥方、導引治病，也從西元前第三世紀之後逐漸成為正統的醫療方式。另外，舊有的神仙術和養生術（類似現代所謂的「預防醫學」或「保

42　武俠世界和真實世界之間的差異，依李永熾教授之見，頗類似人類學家 Eliade 所說的「神聖」（sacred）與「世俗」（profane）世界的分別。

健學」），也因道教在西元第二、三世紀之後大力倡導、發展而有新的突破，氣功、內丹、丹藥也成爲中國傳統醫學的一部分。因此，在傳統中國社會中，要成爲一個一流的醫者，基本上，必須熟知人體的經脈、穴道、嫻習針灸、導引、氣功之術，並能調製、運用各種藥物。而一些修練內功（內丹）的人士（以道士爲最多），便大多具有這些知識和技能，他們不一定以替人療傷治病爲業，卻往往是一流的醫者。[43] 金庸的武俠小說既以宋到清的傳統中國社會爲背景（詳見附表一），其武俠世界中，當然只有武功高手，才是一流的醫者。至於在現代的社會裡，大致來說，中國傳統的醫療體系已喪失原有的典範和主流地位，因此，在醫療事務上，即使是武功高手也很少有用武之地。他們的黃金時代已經消逝，目前只能活躍在金庸虛構的武俠世界裡。

---

43 關於中國的傳統醫學，詳見 K. Chimin Wong（王吉民） and Wu Lien-teh（伍連德），*History of Chinese Medicine*, second edition (Shanghai: National Quarantine Service, 1936)；Paul U. Unschuld, *Medicine in China: A History of Ideas* (Berkeley: University of California Press, 1985)；陳邦賢，《中國醫學史》（上海：商務印書館，1937）；馬伯英，《中國醫學文化史》（上海：上海人民出版社，1994）；鄭曼青、林品石編著，《中華醫藥學史》（臺北：臺灣商務印書館，1982）；傅維康，《中國醫學史》（上海：上海中醫學院出版社，1990）；史蘭華等編，《中國傳統醫學史》（北京：科學出版社，1992）；范行準，《中國醫學史略》（北京：中醫古籍出版社，1986）；趙璞珊，《中國古代醫學》（北京：中華書局，1983）；李經緯、李志東，《中國古代醫學史略》（石家莊：河北科學技術出版社，1990）；俞慎初，《中國醫學簡史》（福州：福建科學技術出版社，1983）；姒元翼，《中國醫學史》（北京：人民衛生出版社，1984）；賈得道，《中國醫學史略》（太原：山西人民出版社，1979）；郭成圩主編，《醫學史教程》（成都：四川科學技術出版社，1987）；陝西中醫學院主編，《中國醫學史》（貴陽：貴州人民出版社，1988）；北京中醫學院主編，《中國醫學史》（上海：上海科學技術出版社，1978）；甄志亞主編，《中國醫學史》（上海：上海科學技術出版社，1984）；王樹岐、李經緯、鄭金生，《古老的中國醫學》（臺北：緯揚文化，1990）；陳勝崑，《中國傳統醫學史》（臺北：橘井文化事業股份有限公司，1992）。

附表一：《金庸作品集》基本資料表

序號	書名	時代背景	主要人物	寫作年代	備註
1(1-2)	《書劍恩仇錄》	清高宗乾隆年間 (1736-95)	乾隆皇帝、陳家洛、霍青桐、紅花會眾當家	1955	
2(3-4)	《碧血劍》	明毅宗崇禎年間 (1628-44)	袁承志、溫青青、金蛇郎君、何紅藥、玉眞子	1956	
3(5-8)	《射鵰英雄傳》	南宋寧宗時期 (1195-1224)	郭靖、黃蓉、楊康、穆念慈、東邪、西毒、北丐、南帝、中神通、全眞七子、江南七俠	1957-59	
4(9-12)	《神鵰俠侶》	南宋理宗時期 (1225-64)	楊過、小龍女、郭靖、黃蓉、東邪、西毒、北丐、南帝、周伯通	1959-61	
5(13)	《雪山飛狐》	清高宗乾隆45年(1780)前後	胡一刀、苗人鳳、胡斐、苗若蘭	1959	
6(14-15)	《飛狐外傳》	清高宗乾隆年間 (1736-95)	胡斐、程靈素	1960-61	
7(16-19)	《倚天屠龍記》	元順帝至元2年(1337)前後	張三丰、張無忌、趙敏、武當七俠、明教中人	1961	
8(20)	《連城訣》	無特定年代。似乎是清代(1644-1911)	狄雲、戚芳、水笙	1963	
9(21-25)	《天龍八部》	北宋哲宗時期 (1086-1100)	喬峯、段譽、虛竹、慕容復、游坦之、王語嫣、阿朱、阿紫	1963-66	
10(26-27)	《俠客行》	明代？	石破天、石中玉	1965	
11(28-31)	《笑傲江湖》	無特定年代。似乎是明代晚期(1600-1644)	令狐冲、任盈盈、任我行、東方不敗、岳不羣、岳靈珊、林平之	1967	
12(32-36)	《鹿鼎記》	清聖祖康熙年間 (1662-1722)	康熙皇帝、韋小寶、神龍教教主、陳近南	1969-72	

Martial-Arts Fiction and Martial-Arts Practice:
The Concept of *Qi* in Jin Yong's Novels*

Meir Shahar

Department of East Asian Studies

Tel Aviv University

Abstract

The twentieth-century witnessed the flowering of the Chinese genre of martial-arts fiction (*wuxia xiaoshuo* 武俠小說). To what extent did the evolution of this genre mirror the development of the martial-arts themselves? Can we detect similarities between the twentieth-century fiction of the martial-arts and their contemporaneous practice? This paper will examine this question from the perspective of a prominent representative of this genre, Jin Yong 金庸 (1924-), who is considered by many as one of the greatest Chinese novelists of the twentieth-century.

Even though most fighting techniques in Jin Yong's novels are the product of his own creative imagination, his martial-arts fiction is related to twentieth-century martial practice. Jin Yong's novels include textual borrowings from martial-arts manuals; his protagonists engage in fighting techniques that are sometimes widely practiced, and some of these protagonists have been borrowed themselves from the, largely legendary, genealogical trees of contemporary martial-arts schools. Perhaps most significantly, the martial-arts as presented in

* I am grateful to Noga Zhang-hui Shahar for her help, and to the Israel Science Foundation for its financial support.

his novels are largely premised upon the internal circulation of *qi* 氣. In this respect, his fiction mirrors the profound transformation that the Chinese martial-arts underwent beginning in the Qing period, namely the incorporation of *daoyin* 導引 techniques of *qi*-circulation into martial-training.

The intimate relation between Jin Yong's martial-arts fiction and the realm of martial-arts practice, doesn't shed light on his genius as an artist. However, it might help us unravel an important cultural development which we witness in contemporary China — the flowering of a martial-arts culture, the foundations of which can be traced back to the early Qing. This martial-arts culture is largely premised upon the internal circulation of *qi*, and it has both a dimension of practice, and a dimension of fictional representation.

I. Introduction

In one of the climactic moments of Jin Yong's 金庸 (1924-) *Extraordinary Beings* (*Tianlong babu* 天龍八部), Duanyu 段譽, who is the novel's principal protagonist, discovers inside a mysterious cave a jade statue of a divine maiden. Like Baoyu 寶玉, after which he has been fashioned, and with which his name resonates,[1] Duanyu is consumed by admiration to women, which he considers as superior to men. Perhaps for this reason, the discovery of the lifelike images touches the depths of his soul. Overcome with emotion, he kneels in front of it.

Inadvertently, Duanyu's romantic impulse transforms him into a martial-artist. This is because from his kneeling posture Duanyu chances upon a tiny inscription on the maiden's feet. It reads: "After kowtowing to me a thousand times, even if you experience a hundred deaths you will have no regrets." All too happy to comply with this instruction and worship the lovely

---

1   The influence of the *Dream of the Red Chamber* (*Honglou meng* 紅樓夢) is apparent in the novels of Jin Yong, who points to the former as one of his sources of inspiration; see his interview with Lin Yiliang 林以亮, dated August 22 1969, and reprinted in *Zhuzi baijia kan Jin Yong*, sanji 諸子百家看金庸三輯 (*The Various Thinkers and Hundrel Schools Examine Jin Yong's Fiction*, Third Collection), ed. Shen Dengen 沈登恩 (Taipei: Yuanjing, 1985), 47.

creature, Duanyu prostrates himself on a small mat, which he finds spread in front of the statue. By the time he completes his prostrations, the mat is torn to shreds, revealing underneath it an ancient book, which endows Duanyu with invincible powers. This sacred book contains the secret fighting methods of the "Free and Easy Sect" (Xiaoyao pai 逍遙派).[2]

In many ways this episode is characteristic of Jin Yong's writing. Its plot is full of surprising turns, connecting as it does the veneration of beauty with hidden martial techniques. We find in it mysterious caves and sacred books, love and invincible fighting methods. Perhaps most significantly, the protagonist of this episode is, from the perspective of martial-arts fiction, an anti-hero: Duanyu is, at least initially, much more interested in romance than in warfare.

All of these elements are vintage Jin Yong. All but one. There is one item in this episode that isn't the product of Jin Yong's imagination. This is the book discovered by Duanyu, or, more precisely, the name of the sect which martial techniques it purports to disclose: the "Free and Easy" (Xiaoyao). Gymnastic techniques titled the "Free and Easy" are common in twentieth-century Chinese martial-arts.[3] These techniques derive from a Ming-period manual of physical education, attributed to one "Free and Easy" (Xiaoyaozi), and titled *The Free and Easy's Gymnastics Formula* (*Xiaoyaozi daoyin jue* 逍遙子導引訣). This manual, which enjoyed considerable popularity during the Ming — it is preserved in several editions — teaches a combination of external limb movement with internal circulation of *qi* 氣.[4] Ultimately, of course, the title of this manual,

---

2 *Tianlong babu* (1963-7; revised edition, Hong Kong: Minghe, 1978), 2.68-70.

3 Including such techniques as "The Free and Easy Walking Technique" (Xiaoyao buxing gong 逍遙步行功), and "The Free and Easy's Method of Moving the Eyes" (Xiaoyaozi yun jing fa 逍遙子運睛法); see respectively: *Zhongguo qigong daquan* 中國氣功大全 (*Comprehensive Compendium of Qigong*), ed. Zhang Youjun 張有寯 et al. (Tianjin: Tianjin renmin, 1993), 339-41, and *Zhongguo qigong gongfa daquan* 中國氣功功法大全 (*Comprehensive Compendium of Qigong Techniques*), ed. Lou Yugang 樓羽剛 et al. (Beijing: Zhongyi guji, 1993), 241.

4 See *Xiaoyaozi daoyin jue* in Zhou Lüjing 周履靖, ed., *Yimen Guangdu* 夷門廣牘 (The Recluse's Extensive Records) (Wanli edition; photographic reprint, Shanghai: Hanfenlou, 1937). The

like its presumed author's sobriquet, derive from the "Free and Easy Wandering" (*Xiaoyao you* 遊) chapter of the *Zhuangzi* 莊子.

Thus, into a fictional narrative which is the product of his own creative imagination, Jin Yong has inserted a term borrowed from the realm of martial-arts practice. This phenomenon is not atypical of Jin Yong's writings, which attest a close connection between fictional representation and practice in the Chinese martial arts. Jin Yong's fictional protagonists engage in fighting techniques which are widely taught, and these protagonists themselves have sometimes been borrowed from the literature produced by martial-arts practitioners. Furthermore, the discussion of the martial-arts in Jin Yong's novels is sometimes elucidated by quotations from martial-arts manuals. In this respect, then, Jin Yong's fiction is the product of Chinese martial-arts history, and his novels mirror the shape that the martial-arts have taken by the mid-twentieth century.

Jin Yong himself acknowledges his indebtedness to the literature produced by martial-arts practitioners. When asked about his familiarity with the martial-arts, he usually responds that even though he isn't a practitioner, he does read martial-arts manuals, which occasionally serve as a source for his writings. Consider his following comment, from an interview, dated 1969, with Lin Yiliang 林以亮:

> As for martial-arts (*wushu* 武術) manuals, I am somewhat familiar with some. They include illustrations as well as written explanations. If, for example, I write something that concerns a hand-combat technique (*quanshu* 拳術), I may consult some manuals of

---

Xiaoyaozi daoyin jue exists also in several other Ming anthologies, sometimes under a different title; see *Zhonghua Daojiao da cidian* 中華道教大辭典 (*The Comprehensive Dictionary of Chinese Taoism*), ed. Hu Fuchen 胡孚琛 et al. (Beijing: Shehui kexue, 1995), 1060; see also *Zhongguo gudai tiyu shi* 中國古代體育史 (*A History of Chinese Physical Education: The Classical Period*), ed. Guojia tiwei tiyu wenshi gongzuo weiyuanhui 國家體委體育文史公作委員會 (Beijing: Beijing tiyu xueyuan 北京：北京體育學院, 1990), 414 note 2.

hand-combat. I read about these forms of hand-combat, and elaborate upon them a little.[5]

Highlighting the correspondence between Jin Yong's fiction of the martial-arts and their contemporary practice is not to deny that most of the fighting-techniques in his novels, like their fanciful names, are the product of his own literary imagination.[6]   Nonetheless, the measure of similarity between his fiction and contemporary fighting methods offers us an interesting vantage point from which to examine the former. It suggests that the evolution of the Chinese martial-arts might have influenced the development of the literary genre to which Jin Yong's works belong. It would appear that martial-arts fiction, (as I would render this genre's Chinese name: *wuxia xiaoshuo* 武俠小說), hasn't grown independently of martial-arts practice.[7]   At least in Jin Yong's case, the fiction of the martial-arts is related to their contemporaneous performance. Let us consider a few examples:

In his *The Eagle-Shooting Heroes* (*Shediao yingxiong zhuan* 射鵰英雄傳), Jin Yong introduces a fighting method called Iron-Cloth Shirt (Tiebu shan 鐵布衫). As described in the novel, this method is meant to harden the body so that it becomes as impenetrable as "cast bronze and forged iron." Thus the practitioner's

---

5   Reprinted in *Zhuzi baijia kan Jin Yong*, sanji, 41.

6   As he himself emphasizes; see *Ibid*.

7   This rendition of the genre's name depends upon the component *wu* ("martial"); other English renditions, such as "chivalric fiction" or "gallant fiction," allude to the element *xia*, (sometimes translated as "knight errant"). On nineteenth and twentieth century martial-arts fiction see, among others, Chen Pingyuan 陳平原, *Qiangu wenren xiake meng* 千古文人俠客夢 (*The Literatus' Ancient Knight-errant Dream*) (Beijing: Renmin, 1992), pp. 42-204; Wang Hailin 王海林., *Zhongguo wuxia xiaoshuo shilue* 中國武俠小說史略 (*A Brief History of Chinese Martial-Arts Fiction*) (Taiyuan: Beiyue wenyi, 1988), pp. 99-120, 134-261; Ning Zongyi 寧宗一, *Zhongguo wuxia xiaoshuo jianchang cidian* 中國武俠小說鑑賞辭典 (*A Connoisseur's Dictionary of Chinese Martial Arts Fiction*) (Beijing: Guoji wenhua, 1992); and James J. Y. Liu, *The Chinese Knight-Errant* (London: Routledge and Kegan Paul, 1967), pp. 116-121, 124-137.

own skin would be transformed into an armor, making him largely invulnerable.[8]   As it happens, both the name of this body-hardening technique and the semi-fantastic claims for its efficacy predate Jin Yong's fiction. An invulnerability technique variously referred to by the names Iron-Cloth Shirt and Armor of the Golden Bell (Jinzhong zhao 金鐘罩) has been practiced in the North-China plains since the mid-eighteenth century at the latest. This technique — or, more accurately, *these* techniques, for there have been variations in its practice — has been relied upon by such rebel armies as the Eight Trigrams (in 1813), the Big Sword Society, (precursor to the Boxers United in Righteousness) (in the mid-1890s), and the Red-Spear Militias (During the Republican Period). Some of these armies even sought in it protection from firearms.[9]

The Iron-Cloth Shirt continues to be a popular martial technique to this day, and it figures prominently in contemporary martial-arts manuals.[10]   The latter usually explain it in terms of the internal circulation, within the body, of the psycho-physical force of *qi*, for which reason they tend to classify the Iron-Cloth Shirt as a form of "hard *qi*-technique" (*ying qigong* 硬氣功). The practitioner, it is argued, is capable of directing his *qi* to a given bodily location,

---

8   See *Shediao yingxiong zhuan* (1957-9; revised edition, Hong Kong: Minghe, 1976), 2.87, 4.161.

9   The term "Iron-Cloth Shirt" probably predates the actual *practice* of the martial-techniques to which it now refers. To the best of my knowledge this term first appeared in Shen Defu's 沈德符 (1578-1642), *Wanli yehuo bian* 萬曆野獲編 (*Private Gleanings of the Wanli Reign*) (Beijing: Zhonghua, 1959), 28.722. On the practice of Iron-Cloth Shirt/Golden-Bell Armor type invulnerability exercises in nineteenth and twentieth century peasant armies see: Joseph W. Esherick, *The Origins of the Boxer Uprising* (Berkeley: University of California Press, 1987), 55, 96-8, 104-9, 227; Susan Naquin, *Millenarian Rebellion in China: The Eight Trigrams Uprising of 1813* (New Haven: Yale University Press, 1976), 30-31, 320 note 125; and Elizabeth J. Perry, *Rebels and Revolutionaries in North China 1845-1945* (Stanford: Stanford University Press, 1980), 186-97.

10   See, for example, Yang Liancun 楊連村, *Jinzhong zhao, tiebu shan* 金鐘罩鐵布衫 (*The Golden-Bell Armor; The Iron-Cloth Shirt*) (Beijing: Beijing tiyu xueyuan, 1990); see also *Zhongguo qigong daquan*, 533, 540-44, and *Zhongguo qigong gongfa daquan*, 748-9, 731-6.

which is thereby hardened and becomes impenetrable. This explanation for the efficacy of Iron-Cloth type techniques dates back to the mid-eighteenth century, when Zheng Xie 鄭燮 (1693–1765) wrote of one, Wei Zizhao 魏子兆, who would direct his *qi* to a specific spot in his body, "whereupon even swords and axes were unable to penetrate it."[11]

If the Iron-Cloth Shirt is premised upon the internal circulation of *qi*, then this is also the case with another fighting technique which Jin Yong borrowed from the realm of martial-arts practice: the Primordial-Chaos Palm (Hunyuan Zhang 混元掌). In his *The Sword Stained with Royal Blood* (*Bixue jian* 碧血劍), Jin Yong describes the latter as combining the internal refinement of *qi* with the external development of hand-combat skills. "Having practiced both externally and internally," he explains, "one's every move and every maneuver would naturally be accompanied by internal power. Thus, without even thinking about it, one would triumph and overcome his adversary."[12] This interpretation of the Primordial-Chaos Palm closely corresponds to its presentation in twentieth-century practitioners' manuals. This is, for example, how the *Comprehensive Compendium of Qigong Techniques* (*Zhongguo qigong gongfa daquan* 中國氣功功法大全) describes the Primordial-Chaos Palm, (to which it refers by the slightly different appellation of Primordial-Chaos Cinnabar Technique (Hunyuan dan gong 混元丹功)):

> The Primordial-Chaos Cinnabar Technique belongs in the *qigong* methods that include [external] movement (*donggong* 動功). Inside it cultivates the essence (*jing* 精), the vital energy (*qi* 氣), and the spirit (*shen* 神). Outside it cultivates the muscles, bones, and skin. Having mastered it, doesn't only protect one's health and strengthen his body, it also has the effect of endowing him with inexhaustible power, of the type obtained through hard *qigong* (*ying qigong*).[13]

---

11   Quoted in Lin Boyuan 林伯原, *Zhongguo tiyu shi* 中國體育史 (*A History of Chinese Physical Education*) (Beijing: Beijing tiyu xueyuan, 1987), 1:380.

12   *Bixue jian* (1956; revised edition, Hong Kong: Minghe, 1975), 3.86.

13   *Zhongguo qigong gongfa daquan*, 128.

The similarity between the martial-techniques as described in practitioners' manuals and as portrayed in Jin Yong's fiction suggests that, in some cases, he has relied on the former. Instances of textual borrowing further evince the close connection between this author's fiction and martial-arts textbooks. Thus, for example, the discussion of Taijiquan in Jin Yong's novel *The Heaven Sword and the Dragon Sabre* (*Yitian tulong ji* 倚天屠龍記) (hereafter: *Heaven Sword*) betrays the textual influence of Yang Chengfu's 楊澄甫 (1883–1936) *The ten important points for* [*Taiji*] *quan technique* (*Quan shu shiyao* 拳術十要). The novel includes a Taijiquan formula, which is made of the section-headings of Yang's manual. It reads:

> The energy at the top of the head should be light and sensitive,
> (*xu ling ding jin* 虛靈頂勁)
> Sink the chest and raise the back.
> Relax the waist and let fall the buttocks,
> Sink the shoulders and drop the elbows.[14]

This isn't the only example of textual borrowing in the *Heaven Sword*, several chapters of which are dedicated to the history, and theory, of Taijiquan. The novel contains a list of the various Taijiquan postures, such as "Grasp Sparrow's Tail" (Lanquewei 攬雀尾), "Single Whip" (Danbian 單鞭), "White Crane Cools Wings" (Baihe liangchi 白鶴亮翅), "Play Guitar" (Shouhui pipa 手

---

14   Compare: *Yitian tulong ji* (1963; revised edition, Hong Kong: Minghe, 1976), 24.964, with *Quan shu shi yao* in *Taiji quan lun* 太極拳論 (*Treatise on Taiji quan*) (n.d.; photographic reprint, Beijing: Zhongguo shudian, 1992), 7b–9a. The *Quan shu shi yao* includes oral instructions by Yang Chengfu, which were recorded by his disciple Chen Weiming 陳微明. My translation follows that of Douglas Wile in his *T'ai-chi Touchstones: Yang Family Secret Transmissions* (Brooklyn, New York: Sweet Ch'i Press, 1983), 11–2. Jin Yong added two characters to the third phrase, apparently in order to maintain a balance of four characters per phrase.

揮琵琶), "Embrace Tiger, Return to Mountain" (Baohu guishan 抱虎歸山), and so on.[15] These fanciful names haven't been invented by Jin Yong. As the common designations for Taijiquan postures, they appear in numerous manuals of this school.[16]

Jin Yong's discussion of Taijiquan leads us to another type of borrowing in his writings — that of figures revered within the martial-arts community. At least some of Jin Yong's narratives revolve around figures that he borrowed from the genealogical trees of martial-arts schools. This is the case, for example, with the novel *Heaven Sword*, which features the legendary founders of Taijiquan, the Song-period Zhang Sanfeng 張三丰 and his seven disciples. Thus, both the fighting methods and the protagonists of the *Heaven Sword* were borrowed from the literature produced by martial-arts practitioners. The fighting methods are described in Taijiquan manuals, and, at least some of the protagonists, derive from what might be described as the hagiographic literature of Taijiquan transmission.[17]

The legend according to which Taijiquan was invented by the Song-period Taoist, Zhang Sanfeng, has been discredited by scholars as early as the 1930s. It is generally accepted today that the origins of Taijiquan can't be traced earlier than the seventeenth-century — some five-centuries after Zhang Sanfeng, whose

---

15   *Yitian tulong ji*, 24.963, 24.981-2.

16   My rendition of the postures' names follows that of Douglas Wile in his *Cheng Man-Ch'ing's Advanced T'ai-Chi Form Instructions, With Selected Writings on Meditation, the I-Ching, Medicine, and the Arts* (New York: Sweet Ch'i Press, 1985), 55-100.

17   The legend according to which Taijiquan was created by Zhang Sanfeng dates from the late nineteenth-century at the earliest. Some late-Qing and Republican-period Taijiquan manuals are even attributed to Zhang Sanfeng, and have him expound the principles of the art in the first person; see, among others, *Zhongguo gudai tiyu shi*, 417; Tang Hao 唐豪 and Gu Liuxin 顧留馨, *Taijiquan yanjiu* 太極拳研究, (*Researches into Taijiquan*) (1964; reprint, Beijing: Renmin tiyu, 1992), 10 note 3; and Douglas Wile, *Lost T'ai-chi Classics from the Late Ch'ing Dynasty* (Albany: State University of New York Press, 1996), 108-11; see also the texts translated by Wile, *Ibid*, 86-9.

historicity itself is uncertain.[18]　However, for our purpose here the question of Taijiquan transmission isn't as significant as Jin Yong's preoccupation with it. For the latter evinces his acquaintance with the literature produced by Taijiquan practitioners. Indeed, in a comment appended to the narrative, the *Heaven Sword*'s implied author acknowledges his reliance upon the genealogical writings of Taijiquan. The comment is interesting, for in it the implied author shares with his readers artistic considerations, which informed the very narrative they are reading:

> According to ancient records, Zhang Sanfeng's seven disciples were Song Yuanqiao 宋遠橋 (Song Remote-Bridge), Yu Lianzhou 俞蓮舟 (Yu Lotus-Boat), Yu Daiyan 俞岱巖 (Yu Tai-Mountain Cliff), Zhang Songxi 張松溪 (Zhang Pine-Stream), Zhang Cuishan 張翠山 (Zhang Green-Mountain), Yin Liheng 殷利亨, and Mo Shenggu 莫聲谷 (Mo Resonant-Valley). Yin Liheng's name must derive its meaning from the *Classic of Changes'* (*Yijing* 易經) expression: *Yuan heng li zhen* 元亨利貞 ("He shall have fundamental prevalence and find it fitting to practice constancy").[19]　However, it doesn't resemble the names of the other six disciples. For this reason I have replaced it here by another name, which characters are nonetheless similar to Liheng in shape: Liting 梨亭 ([Yin] Pear-Pavilion)."[20]

No doubt many more cases of correspondence between Jin Yong's fiction and martial-arts manuals can be examined. Nonetheless, even the limited number of examples thus far surveyed probably suffice to demonstrate Jin Yong's

---

18　See among others, Tang Hao and Gu Liuxin, esp. 1-5, 10 note 3; *Zhongguo gudai tiyu shi*, 417-8; Lin Boyuan, 1:369-71; and Xi Yuntai 習雲太, *Zhongguo wushu shi* 中國武術史 (*A History of Chinese Martial-Arts*) (Beijing: Renmin tiyu, 1985), 220-22.

19　See *Yijing*, hexagram 49; *A Concordance to the Yi Jing*, Harvard-Yenching Institute Sinological Index Series, Supplement no. 10 (1966; reprint, Taipei: Ch'eng-wen, 1973), 30. English translation by Richard John Lynn, *The Classic of Changes: A New Translation of the I Ching as Interpreted by Wang Bi* (New York: Columbia University Press, 1994), 444.

20　*Yitian tulong ji*, 3.124.

indebtedness to the literature produced by martial-arts practitioners. These examples suggest that the martial-arts in Jin Yong's fiction weren't created *ex nihilo*. Rather, his protagonists engage in martial techniques that have been widely practiced during the twentieth century. In this sense Jin Yong's novels illustrate the intimate relation between practice and fiction in the contemporary martial-arts. Furthermore, we can probably advance one step beyond this preliminary conclusion, for all of the instances thus far examined share one common trait: They are all premised upon the psycho-physical force of *qi*. The techniques of the Free and Easy, the Iron-Cloth Shirt, the Primordial-Chaos Palm, and Taijiquan, all stress the internal circulation of *qi*. In order to appreciate the significance of this common motif, we need briefly survey one of the dominant trends in the evolution of the late-imperial and modern martial-arts.

II. *Qi* in Martial-Arts Practice

Historians of Chinese physical education usually agree that the Qing period signifies a turning point in the history of the martial-arts. This is because the Qing-period witnessed the merging together of two, up until then, by and large distinct traditions of physical education: The tradition of hand combat with its various forms of boxing and wrestling, and the tradition of classical gymnastics, usually referred to in the scholarly literature by the generic terms *yangsheng* 養生 ("nourishing the vital principle") and *daoyin* 導引 (literally: "guiding and directing").[21]   The latter mirrors one of the defining characteristics of Chinese classical gymnastics: Its emphasis upon the "guiding and directing" (*daoyin*) of *qi*. The practitioner concentrates his mental faculties and regulates his breath thereby circulating his *qi* within the body. In this respect Chinese classical

---

21   On the Qing-period combination of the martial-arts with classical gymnastics see: Lin Boyuan, 1: 371, 1:373, 1:378-9; and *Zhongguo gudai tiyu shi*, 377, 417-9; regarding the case of Taijiquan see also Tang Hao and Gu Liuxin, 1-2, 5-6.

gymnastics is a form of meditative practice, premised upon a psycho-physical force — *qi*. (It should be noted, however, that, in addition to the internal circulation of *qi*, some *daoyin* exercises include external-limb movements).[22]

The roots of *daoyin* gymnastics can be traced back to the first centuries b.c. e., (the term itself appears already in one of the *Zhuangzi*'s outer chapters).[23] From its very beginnings this gymnastic tradition was considered to be of therapeutic value, both in preventing and in curing disease, for which reason *daoyin* exercises figure prominently in the classics of Chinese medicine, such as the *Huangdi neijing* 黃帝內經 (*The Yellow Emperor's Classic of Medicine*), (compiled during the Han, but including earlier materials as well).[24]　During the first centuries of the common era, *daoyin* gymnastics were further developed within the emerging Taoist religion, which sanctioned them as an integral element of its self-cultivation regimen. Taoist mystics such as Sima Chengzhen 司馬承禎 (647-735) considered the training of *qi* a prerequisite for the mystical union with the Tao.[25]

Even as they were widely employed for therapeutic and religious purposes, *daoyin* gymnastics remained largely divorced of pugilistic ends prior to the Qing period. The available information doesn't permit us to trace the integration of

---

22　Already during the first centuries c.e. the term *daoyin* carried two slightly different meanings: a) It was used as a generic term for all forms of gymnastics premised upon the circulation of *qi*, (whether or not these gymnastics technique include — in addition to *qi*-circulation — also external limb movement; and b) Some texts use it only in reference to those forms of gymnastics that *in addition* to the internal circulation of *qi* include external limb movement; see *daoyin* in *Zhonghua Daojiao da cidian*, 1031; see also Catherine Despeux, "Gymnastics: The Ancient Tradition," in *Taoist Meditation and Longevity Techniques*, ed. Livia Kohn (Ann Arbor: Center for Chinese Studies, The University of Michigan, 1989), 225-61.

23　*Zhuangzi*, chapter 15; see A. C. Graham, *Chuang-tzu: The Inner Chapters* (London: Unwin Paperbacks, 1986), 265.

24　See Despeux, 241, and Lin Boyuan, 1:89.

25　See Ute Engelhardt, "Qi for Life: Longevity in the Tang," in *Taoist Meditation and Longevity Techniques*, 263-96.

qi-circulation techniques with methods of boxing and wrestling earlier than the seventeenth-century, for which reason scholars have concluded that the traditions of *daoyin* gymnastics and hand-combat remained largely distinct all through the late-Ming. Admittedly Tang-period tales do describe Taoist mystics whose fighting skills are related to methods of self-cultivation. However, in their case the "nourishing of the vital principle" (*yangsheng*) is related to swordsmanship rather than boxing or wrestling. In addition, the tales in question — unlike Qing-period fighting manuals — do not detail specific methods of *qi*-circulation, and, furthermore, their methods of self-cultivation are largely dependent upon magic potions of various kinds, enabling their protagonists, among other feats, to fly or become invisible at will.[26]

The Qing-period integration of the ancient *daoyin* gymnastics with techniques of hand-combat has had a profound impact on the contents, as well as the very purpose, of the martial-arts. *Daoyin* gymnastics enriched the martial-arts with medical significance, and contributed to them a meditative aspect. *Qi*-circulation techniques transformed the martial-arts from a regimen of physical exercise into a method of psycho-physical training, which was no longer intended for warfare alone. Lin Boyuan, one of the leading historians of Chinese gymnastics, summarizes this process as follows:

> During the Ming-period, the various fighting schools stressed each one technique only,

---

26 See, for example, the Tang tales "Lanling laoren" 蘭陵老人 ("The Old Man of Lanling") and "Nie Yin'niang" 聶隱娘 ("Nie Yin'niang") in Li Fang 李昉 (925-996), ed., *Taiping guangji* 太平 廣記 (*Extensive Records Compiled During the Taiping Period*) (Beijing: Renmin wenxue chubanshe, 1959), 195.1464-5, and 194.1456-9 respectively. The former tale is probably by Duan Chengshi 段成式 (ca. 800-863), in whose *Youyang zazu* 酉陽雜俎 (*Miscellaneous Fare from Youyang*) it was anthologized; the latter probably by Pei Xing 裴鉶 (825-880). Both stories have been translated by James J. Y. Liu in his *The Chinese Knight-Errant*, pp. 93-4, and 89-90 respectively. On Taoist motifs in tales of knight-errantry see Cui Fengyuan 崔奉源, *Zhongguo gudian duanpian xiayi xiaoshuo yanjiu* 中國古典短篇俠義小說研究 (*Research into Traditional Chinese Tales of Knight-Errantry*) (Taipei: Lianjing, 1986), pp. 237-56.

and they all specialized in actual fighting. By contrast, the Qing-period schools of fighting usually combined various techniques. In particular, Qing-period fighting methods were closely integrated with the teachings of *daoyin* ("guiding and directing") and *yangsheng* ("nourishing the vital principle"). This integration was motivated by a double-purpose: Firstly, it added efficacy to these methods in terms of fighting; secondly, it strengthened the body, and it assisted in the prevention, as well as the healing, of disease.

Many Qing-period martial-arts manuals contain chapters dedicated to the discussion of *qi* and the training of *qi* (*lianqi* 練氣). Most fighting-schools stressed the significance of the training of *qi*, and many martial-artists combined their fighting practice with training in *daoyin* and *yangsheng* techniques...

The widespread integration of *daoyin* practice and martial-arts practice during the Qing demonstrates that the recognition of *daoyin*'s efficacy became more common. *Daoyin* practice transformed the martial arts in terms of their contents, forms of practice, and usages alike. The martial-arts were no longer an activity meaningful only as a fighting technique. Rather, the martial-arts were transformed into a physical activity that has many forms of training, that enhances both skill and strength, and that is efficacious both in preventing, and in healing, disease. Evidently, by Qing times the martial-arts evolved into an entirely unique system of physical training.[27]

One of the Qing-period schools of fighting that demonstrates the integration of the martial-arts with *daoyin* gymnastics is Taijiquan, which, as we have seen above, figures in Jin Yong's *Heaven Sword*. Eminent historians such as Tang Hao, Gu Liuxin, and Lin Boyuan point out that this school integrated techniques of hand-combat with the psycho-physical methods of *qi*-circulation.[28] The editors of the influential *History of Chinese Physical Education* summarize this dual ancestry of Taijiquan as follows:

From the perspective of its form, the Qing-period popular Taijiquan belongs to the martial-arts' methods of hand-combat (*quanshu*), and it does bear the characteristics of a

---

27   Lin Boyuan, 1:378-9.

28   See Tang Hao and Gu Liuxin, 1-2, 5-6, and Lin Boyuan, 1:371.

fighting method. However, in terms of its substance it belongs in the physical education tradition of "nourishing the vital principle" (*yangsheng*). It is the product of our country's ancient *daoyin* techniques' evolution.[29]

Taijiquan theoretical compositions stress the significance of *qi*-circulation. Some of these compositions describe the circulation of *qi* in general terms only, but some, such as Li Yiyu's 李亦畬 (1832–92) "Song of the Circulation of Qi" ("Shenqi yunxing ge" 神氣運行歌) describe the precise course of the *qi* within the practitioner's body. Here are the opening lines of Li's poem, in Douglas Wile's translation:

> The *qi* is like the waters of the Yangtze,
> As it flows eastward wave upon wave;
> Arising from the "bubbling well" point in the ball of the foot,
> It travels up the spine in the back.
> Arriving at the *niwan* 泥丸 in the center of the brain,
> It returns to the *yintang* 印堂 between the brows.
> The mind leads the *qi*,
> And never leaves it for an instant.
> For example, if you want to raise your right hand,
> The mind-*qi* first reaches the armpit.
> Then following the kinetic energy,
> You will feel the mind-*qi* in the pit of the elbow.
> Turning over your hand,
> The *qi* will arrive at the *neiguan* 內關 point on the inside of the arm above the wrist...[30]

During the late-Qing, Taijiquan writings such as Li's poem, circulated among practitioners in the form of hand-written manuscripts, and it was only several decades later, during the Republican period, that the literature of this

---

29   *Zhongguo gudai tiyu shi*, 417.

30   Wile, *Lost T'ai-chi Classics*, 55; the original is reproduced in *Ibid.*, 132–3.

school was first published.[31]　The latter period witnessed the publication of numerous manuals belonging to other schools as well, and many of these evince a similar emphasis on the training of *qi*. Thus, for example, the *Secret Formulas of the Shaolin Fighting Technique* (*Shaolin quanshu mijue* 少林拳術秘訣) (1915) opens with a chapter titled: "Unraveling the Subtleties of the Qi-Techniques" ("Qigong chan wei" 氣功闡微),[32]　and its contemporary, the *Secret Formulas of the Shaolin Internal Art* (*Shaolin neigong mijue* 少林內功秘訣), by Jiang Shihun 姜使魂, elaborates at great length on the superiority of the "internal arts" (*neigong*) of *qi*-circulation over the "external arts" (*waigong*) of limb-movement. Jiang Shihun explains that the former are harder to master exactly because they depend upon the training of the mind:

> In practicing the internal art, the beginning is extremely difficult. It isn't like the external art, which involves only the exercising of the body, and in which, if only you are diligent and not remiss, you are certain to achieve results. This is because the internal art lays emphasis upon the circulation of *qi* (*yunqi* 運氣): When I want the *qi* to reach my back, then it fills my back. When I want the *qi* to reach my arms, then it fills my arms. It goes where directed by one's mind (*yi* 意), and there is nowhere it can't reach. Only then can one reap the internal art's benefits...
> What is known as "using the spirit to control the *qi*" (*yi shen yi qi* 以神役氣) means

---

31　The earliest printed edition of Taijiquan writings dates from 1912, but some manuscripts (including Li Yiyu's song) were published as late as the 1980s and 1990s; see Wile, *Lost T'ai-chi Classics*, esp. 33-8.

32　The *Shaolin quanshu mijue* (Shanghai: Zhonghua shuju, 1915) is available in a photographic reprint (Tianjin: Tianjinshi guji shudian yingyin, 1988), and in a punctuated reprint (in Wu Gu 無谷 and Liu Zhixue 劉志學, eds., *Shaolin si ziliao ji* 少林寺資料集 (*Compilation of Materials on the Shaolin Monastery*) (Beijing: Shumu wenxian, 1982)). The opening eight chapters of the *Shaolin quanshu mijue* (including the chapter "Qigong chan wei") derive from a work titled *Shaolin zong fa* 少林宗法 (*The Classical Method of Shaolin Fighting*), which was first published in 1911; see Tang Hao 唐豪, "*Shaolin quanshu mijue* kaozheng" ("Research into the *Secret Formulas of the Shaolin Fighting Technique*"), reprinted in Wu Gu and Liu Zhixue, *Shaolin si ziliao ji*, 270-1.

that practice should begin by thinking (*xiangnian* 想念). If I want the *qi* to flow into my back I should have my thought reach it, before my *qi* does. Even though the *qi* hasn't reached it, the spirit already has. If one practice thinking in this way for a long time, the *qi* is certain to gradually follow the spirit, so that they reach the desired spot together."[33]

The growing significance of *qi*-training in the Republican-period martial-arts is evinced by their reliance upon a term, the origins of which can be traced back to the Tang dynasty: *qigong* (*qi*-techniques).[34] In the course of the twentieth century this term has enjoyed increasingly wide currency, and, in recent decades, it has figured in the titles of scores of publications, which usually treat it as a general designation for all forms of fighting and healing based upon the manipulation of *qi*.[35] Most *qigong* manuals are divided into disparate

---

33   Jiang Shihun, *Shaolin neigong mijue* (n.d.; photographic reprint, Hualian: n. d.), 13. Its patriotic fervor, and open hostility to the Qing dynasty, indicate that the *Shaolin neigong mijue* was published during the Republican era, (see especially the chapter: "Those Who Practice the Martial Arts Must Uphold the Laws and Love the Nation" ("Lian Wugong zhe xu shoujie aiguo" 練武功者須守戒愛國)).

34   On the Sui and Tang period provenance of the term, see *qigong* in *Zhonghua Daojiao da cidian*, 967.

35   Kunio Miura concluded that "it was not until the fifties and sixties that Qigong became known and available to larger segments of the [Chinese] population;" see his "The Revival of *Qi*: Qigong in Contemporary China," in *Taoist Meditation and Longevity Techniques*, 335. Among recent Qigong publications see *Zhongguo qigong daquan*; *Zhongguo qigong gongfa daquan*; *Zhongguo chuantong qigong xue cidian* 中國傳統氣功學詞典 (*A Dictionary of Traditional Chinese Qigong Studies*), ed. Zhang Wenjiang 張文江 and Chang Jin 常近 (Taiyuan: Shanxi renmin); *Qigong jingxuan* 氣功精選 (*A Selection of Qigong Writings*), ed. Jin Guan 金冠 et. al. (Beijing: Renmin tiyu, 1981); *Qigong jingxuan xupian* 氣功精選續篇 (*Sequel to A Selection of Qigong Writings*), ed. Tao Xiong 陶熊 et. al. (Beijing: Renmin tiyu, 1985); *Ying Qigong dianxue shu* 硬氣功點血術 (*The Techniques of Hard Qigong and Nodal Points*), by An Zaifeng 安在峰 (Beijing: Beijing tiyu daxue, 1990); and *Baojian qigong* 保健氣功 (*Therapeutic Qigong*), by Tang Shilin 唐世林 (Beijing: Gaodeng jiaoyu, 1993).

sections dedicated to fighting and healing of various sorts — healing of self, and of others, preventive, as well as remedial. One underlying principle common to many of these healing, and fighting, techniques is the practitioner's ability to concentrate his *qi* into a specific location in his body, where it is employed either for a therapeutic, or a combative, purpose. The *qi* gathered into the practitioner's fingers, for example, can be transmitted into a patient's body for healing ends, or employed to harden the fingers so that they injure an adversary.

Whether it is intended for therapeutic or martial ends, modern Qigong derives from traditional Chinese medicine in that it conceives of specific bodily points that are responsive to treatment (and conversely susceptible to injury). These nodal points, known in the classical medical terminology as *xue* 穴 (literally: hole), provide the sites for acupuncture treatment, and it is to them that the Qigong master directs his therapeutic, as well as his combat, skills. The following description, from a manual dated 1993, illustrates the reliance of *qigong* techniques upon the concept of nodal points. It concerns a *qigong* method called the Shaolin Technique of the Golden-Needle Finger (Shaolin Jin zhen zhi 少林金針指), which can be employed either for fighting or for healing:

The "Shaolin Golden-Needle Finger" is one of the Shaolin hard Qigong (*ying qigong* 硬氣功) techniques. Its special features are the use of the mind (*yi* 意) to guide the *qi*, the combination of *qi* and [external] force (*li* 力), and the use of *qi* to strengthen force (*yi qi zhuang li* 以氣壯力). As a fighting technique it can be used to drill holes in stones, and target an adversary's nodal points. As a therapeutic method it can be used to emit *qi* into a patient's nodal points thereby curing disease. Thus one reaches the state in which: "One breath of *qi* cultivated inside,
is matched by the cultivation of muscles, bones, and skin outside"
(*nei lian yi kou qi* 內練一口氣,
wai lian jin gu pi 外練筋骨皮)

Those who practice this technique shouldn't fear hardships. They should be persistent and diligent, and need strictly adhere to the warriors' morality (*wude* 武德). Every morning and every evening they should choose a quiet place, where the air is fresh.

They should exhale the body's dirty *qi*, and then "circulate the *qi*" (*yunqi*).[36]

Qigong isn't the only term, the twentieth-century vogue of which reflects the centrality of *qi*-training in the contemporary martial-artist; another is *neijia* 內家 ("internal school"), which first appeared in Huang Zongxi's 黃宗羲 (1610–95) "Wang Zhengnan muzhi ming" 王征南墓志銘 ("Epitaph for Wang Zhengnan") (1669).[37] In the course of its complex history, *neijia* has meant different things to different authors. However, at least some nineteenth-and-twentieth-century sources use this term to designate those systems of fighting that like Taijiquan rely upon the internal power of *qi* and the susceptibility of an adversary's nodal points. Other martial-artist manuals treat *neijia* as an adjective, which is applicable to any martial-artist — regardless of his affiliation which a specific fighting school — who excels in *qi*-circulation. It is in this vein that the founder of Sun-style Taijiquan, Sun Lutang 孫祿堂 (1861–1933), explains: "In breathing there is a difference between the internal and external schools. In fighting-techniques there are no such schools. He who excels in cultivating his *qi* (*yangqi* 養氣) belongs to the internal school. He who doesn't should be classified in the external school."[38]

Thus, the twentieth-century ubiquity of such terms as *qigong* and *neijia* is the product of a lengthy process in which the martial-arts gradually absorbed the ancient *daoyin* techniques of *qi*-circulation. Historians of Chinese physical education have pointed out that this process has had a profound impact on the Chinese martial-arts, which have been transformed into a unique system combining martial, and therapeutic, goals. What I will suggest here is that this evolution of martial-arts *practice* is mirrored in Jin Yong's martial-arts *fiction*. In the novels of this twentieth-century author *qi* is presented as one of the primary

---

36   *Zhongguo qigong gongfa daquan*, 688.

37   In *juan* 8 of Huang Zongxi's *Nanlei wending* 南雷文定 (*Huang Zongxi's Authorized Writings*), Congshu jicheng chubian edition (Shanghai: Shangwu, 1935-7).

38   Quoted in *Zhongguo gudai tiyu shi*, 377.

vehicles of the martial-arts. Many of the fighting techniques described in Jin Yong's novels are premised upon, or, at the very least, are accompanied by, the circulation of *qi*. Indeed, in his fiction, this is all too often mastery of *qi* that distinguishes between the fully accomplished, and the less accomplished, warriors.

However, before I survey briefly the role of *qi* in Jin Yong's fiction, a caveat regarding this term's occurrence in China's military classics is necessary. To argue that the Qing-period witnessed the integration of hand-combat techniques with methods of *qi*-circulation isn't to deny that the term *qi* appears already in pre-Qing military writings. *Qi* in the sense of morale, or fighting spirit, is considered one of the primary factors of warfare in the "Seven Military Classics" (Wujing qishu 武經奇書), which reflect the strategic thought of ancient China.[39] It appears as early as the maxim "a whole army may be robbed of its spirit" (*sanjun ke duo qi* 三軍可奪氣) in Sunzi's *Art of War* (*Sunzi bingfa* 孫子兵法) (fifth century b.c.e.?),[40] and it is discussed extensively in the Yuan-or-Ming-period novel of strategy *Three Kingdoms* (*Sanguo yanyi* 三國演義).[41] What is new in late-Qing martial-arts manuals isn't the very appearance of the term *qi*, the manipulation of which as "fighting spirit" has been pondered in a thousands-years old military tradition, but rather the discussion of *qi* as a psyhco-physical entity, which through prescribed techniques of internal circulation may enhance an individual warrior's pugilistic ability.

39　See Ralph D. Sawyer, *The Seven Military Classics of Ancient China* (Boulder: Westview Press, 1993), esp. 121–3.

40　*Sunzi bingfa*, chap. 7; English translation by Lionel Giles, *Sun Tzu on the Art of War* (1910; reprint, Taipei: Dunhuang, 1985), 65.

41　See Robert P. Gray, "An Analysis of the Role of *Qi* in Military Strategy as Outlined in *Three Kingdoms* (*Sanguo yanyi*)," *B.C. Asian Review* 9 (Winter 1995/6): 77–119.

III. *Qi* in Jin Yong's Fiction

Perhaps the best illustration of the ubiquity of *qi* in Jin Yong's novels is this concept's role in explaining invulnerability. All too often when he seeks to account for a protagonist withstanding a blow, the narrator resorts to the notion of internal *qi* power. It is therefore not uncommon to find in Jin Yong's fiction such sentences as: "luckily so-and-so practiced the internal-art (*neigong*), and therefore he wasn't injured by that blow," or: "so-and-so cultivated the internal-strength (*neijing* 內勁), for which reason his nodal point (*xue*), though targeted, wasn't affected." Thus, if he only wishes to keep a favorite character alive, the author may turn to the hidden power of *qi*, which concept becomes an expedient tool for rationalizing the result of any martial confrontation.

The notion of *qi* provides the ultimate explanation for the outcome of battles regardless of specific fighting techniques. That is, the narrator may account for the result of a given match by the concept of "internal power," even as he fails to name the fighting technique by which it is manipulated. In addition, however, we find in Jin Yong's fiction specified methods that are premised upon the concept of *qi*. These include, among many others, the techniques, discussed above, of the Free and Easy, the Iron-Cloth Shirt, the Primordial-Chaos Palm, and Taijiquan. Let us briefly review two additional examples:

Jin Yong's novel, *The Eagle-Shooting Heroes* (*Shediao yingxiong zhuan* 射鵰英雄傳), features an anti-hero, who shares certain characteristics — such as an ineptitude for the martial-arts — with the above-mentioned *Extraordinary Beings'* protagonist, Duanyu. This is Guo Jing 郭靖, who becomes a martial-artist by learning to *sleep*. A mysterious Taoist teaches him a technique of bedtime *qi*-circulation, which endows him with extraordinary powers. The Taoist explicates his sleeping art as follows:

> When thought is fixed desire expires, when the body is emptied, the *qi* circulates, when the mind dies, the spirit (*shen*) becomes alive, when *yang* flourishes, *yin* is eliminated...

Before going to sleep, one's mind should be emptied and illuminated. It shouldn't contain as much as a thread of thought. One should sleep on the side, in a curled-up position. Breathing needs be continuous. Inside, the soul shouldn't be agitated, and, outside, the spirit shouldn't wander off.[42]

Even though Jin Yong's protagonist, Guo Jing, is unaware of it, sleeping methods are not uncommon in contemporary *qigong*. Usually referred to by the generic terms "lying-down techniques" (*wogong* 臥功) or "sleeping techniques" (*shuigong* 睡功), these methods have an ancient pedigree in the Chinese gymnastic and religious tradition: their antecedents may be traced back to the *Pillow-book Methods* (*Zhenzhong fang* 枕中方) of the seventh-century Taoist Sun Simiao 孫思邈;[43]   they are associated with the tenth-century Taoist Chen Tuan 陳摶; and they are recorded in detail in a sixteenth-century manual of gymnastics, Zhou Lüjing's 周履靖, *The Red-Phoenix Marrow* (*Chifeng sui* 赤鳳 髓).[44]   Following the twentieth-century revival of *qi*-related techniques, these sleeping methods became fashionable anew, as is attested, for example, by the "Lying-Down Chan [Meditation] Method" (*Wo chan fa* 臥禪法), which, despite its name, evinces no Buddhist influence. The *Comprehensive Compendium of Qigong* (1993) describes it as follows:

The ancients held that a person's inborn *qi*,[45]   is often lost during sleep. If one doesn't sleep carefully then his essence (*jing* 精), his *qi*, and his spirit (*shen* 神) would have nothing to rely upon. By practicing often this method one would be able to secure his

---

42   *Shediao yingxiong zhuan* (1957-9; Reprint: Hong Kong: Mingbao, 1976), 5.207.

43   See Kunio Miura, 346.

44   The *Chifeng sui*, (which techniques are attributed in part to Chen Tuan), was compiled by Zhou Lüjing, and is included in his *Yimen Guangdu* (see above, note 4). It has been translated into French by Catherine Despeux, *La moelle du phénix rouge: santé et longue vie dans la Chine du XVIe siècle* (Paris: Guy Trédaniel, Éditions de la Maisnie, 1988).

45   I am amending *zhenwu* 眞無 to *zhenyuan* 眞元; in this context, the latter's meaning of *yuanqi* 元 氣 (inborn/original *qi*) appears more appropriate.

essence (*gu jing* 固精), guard his *qi* (*shou qi* 守氣), nourish his spirit (*yang shen* 養神), and keep intact his self (*quan zhen* 全眞). This "Lying-Down Chan [Meditation] Method" is none other than the method of the "Five Dragons' Winding Bodies." It has been transmitted ever since the Northern-Song [master] Chen Tuan, and to this day many of those who nourish the vital principle use it.

Method of practice: The formula says: You should lie down on your side — either the left or the right are all right — with your head facing eastward. You should bend one arm, and support your face with the palm of your hand, keeping the passage into the ear unobstructed. Keep your waist and back straight, and massage your abdomen with one hand. One leg needs to be straight, the other, bent up — like a winding dragon, like a curled-up dog, unperturbed and self-possessed.

Prior to your mind (*xin* 心) falling asleep, your eyes should. Achieving the ultimate, and guarding the essence, naturally your *qi* would return to its roots, and naturally your breathing would be cultivated. Breathing would be in tune without being regulated. The *qi* would yield without being controlled.[46]

As for Guo Jing he is astonished by the effectiveness of the sleeping art. His previously mediocre martial exercises, executed clumsily despite his laborious efforts, are suddenly transformed. As if by miracle, each and every movement of his is now accompanied by internal vigor, and performed with precision and grace. Thus, Jin Yong's protagonist comes to realize that the bedrock of *qi*-circulation is much more significant than any specific combat technique. Having mastered the fundamental art of *qi*, he describes it in terms very similar to those found in twentieth-century martial-arts manuals, namely in terms of the practitioner's ability to control the flow of *qi* within his body: "[The Taoist] taught me to sit down and breath slowly," says Guo Jing. "He also told me not to think of anything except this puff of air that goes up and down inside my belly. At first I couldn't do it, but recently it really seems as if there is a warm mouse

---

46   *Zhongguo qigong daquan*, 244; Compare also the "Sleeping-Immortal Technique" (*Shuixian gong* 睡仙功) in *Zhongguo qigong gongfa daquan*, 60-61.

squirming his way to and fro inside my body. It's really fun!"[47]

Guo Jing's realization of the power of *qi*, is shared by an entire fighting school, presented by Jin Yong as premised upon this internal force. Appropriately named the Qi Sect (*Qizong* 氣宗), this school figures in the opening chapters of *The Laughing, Proud Wanderer* (*Xiao'ao jianghu* 笑傲江湖), in which it is described as locked in a deadly struggle with its arch-rival, the Sword Sect (*Jianzong* 劍宗). The protracted war between these two schools, which mirror different conceptions of the martial-arts, lasts for generations, until the two meet in a decisive battle from which the Qi Sect emerges as victorious. Indeed the superiority of the *qi* is visually demonstrated by the Qi-sect marters, who effortlessly smash steel swords with their bare hands.

Many years after the decisive battle from which they emerged victorious, one of the Qi-Sect leaders, Lady Yue 岳, explained to her disciples how, drawing on the power of *qi*, their school was able to overcome its Sword-Sect adversaries. Her explanation is interesting for it weaves the classic rhetoric of "substance" (*ti* 體) and "expediency" (*yong* 用) into a discussion of the power of *qi*:

> That year atop the Jade-Maiden Peak our school encountered in a decisive battle the great masters of the Sword-Sect: Their swordsmanship was of a myriad deceptions, and their swordplay of countless transformations. And yet your patriarch, who relied on his training in the Purple-Clouds *Qi*-Method, was able to overcome cunning with simplicity, and subdue movement with quiescence.[48]   He completely defeated more than ten great masters of the Sword Sect, and secured our school's correct martial-teachings' foundations, which won't be uprooted for a thousand years! You should all ponder deeply and realize through practice the exhortations that you have heard today from your master. This school of martial-arts considers the *qi* as substance (*ti* 體) and the sword as expediency (*yong* 用). It regards the *qi* is primary (*zhu* 主), and

---

47   *Shediao yingxiong zhuan*, 5.213.

48   *Yi jing zhi dong* 以靜制動; this formula appears already in the earliest extant account of the *neijia* school, Huang Zongxi's (1610-1695), "Wang Zhengnan muzhi ming;" see above note 37.

the sword is secondary (*cong* 從). It holds *qi* as its principle (*gang* 綱), and the sword as a detail (*mu* 目). If one hasn't succeeded in his *qi* training, then, even if his sword technique is good, eventually it will be of no use to him.[49]

The examples discussed so far probably suffice to demonstrate the significance of *qi* in Jin Yong's martial-arts fiction. Was he the first author in this genre to rely upon *qi*-circulation as a tool of warfare? A survey of *qi*-fighting throughout the evolution of martial-arts fiction is beyond the scope of this paper. Nonetheless, it should be noted that *qi*-premised techniques are mentioned in at least some martial-arts novels that were written during the 1920s, the very same period that witnessed the publication of numerous *qi*-related martial-arts manuals. Passages such as the following one, from Zhao Huanting's 趙煥亭 (1877-1951) novel *The Complete Tale of the Fabulous Knights' Utmost Loyalty* (*Qixia jingzhong quanzhuan* 奇俠精忠全傳) (1923-27), suggest that the ubiquity of *qi* in Jin Yong's fiction is the result of a process which began as early as the so-called "Old-Style" (Jiupai 舊派) martial-arts fiction of the Republican period. Future research will determine to what extent they are typical:

> In this world only quiescence can subdue movement.[50] This is all the more so with the techniques of the martial-arts, which must begin with this principle. This means that the art of sitting cross-legged in quiet meditation should be the starting point for regulating, and training, the strong-*qi* (*gangqi* 罡氣). If one has begun with this principle, and has become proficient in this technique, then he would be able to circulate, and use, his strong-*qi*. In between exhaling and inhaling, and throughout his entire body — three-hundred-and-sixty degrees — wherever the mind (*yi* 意) goes the *qi* would follow. Using the *qi* to protect his body, one would be able to compete in agility with monkeys, and his skills of attack would equal those of birds of prey... Indeed, the stories of old

---

49   *Xiao'ao jianghu* (1963; reprint, Beijing: Sanlian, 1994), 9.342-3.

50   *Tianxia shi wei jing neng zhi dong* 天下事惟靜能制動; we find here a variation on Huang Zong-xi's expression *Yi jing zhi dong*, which Jin Yong quotes as well; see above note 48.

concerning skilled knights, aren't just people's empty-talk![51]

IV. *Qi* and Fantasy

Why is it that the efficacy of *qi* is highlighted as much in Jin Yong's fiction? Is it only that the prevalence of *qi*-training in the practice of the martial-arts is mirrored in his fiction of the latter? Or can we single out specific functions of *qi* in furthering this author's writings as fiction? Firstly, the concept of *qi* probably contributes to the shaping of character in Jin Yong's novels. This is because the notion of internal power dispenses with the external manifestations of physical strength, such as a large physique and built-up muscles, thereby enabling a character-type that is very much favored by Jin Yong: the young scholar (*shusheng* 書生) whose martial skills are hidden behind the facade of the refined literatus. The protagonists of this twentieth-century author need not be provided with the colossal body of a Lu Zhishen 魯智深, from the early-Ming novel *Water Margin* (*Shuihu zhuan* 水滸傳), in order for them to excel in fighting. Indeed, their features are sometimes so refined, that their adversaries underestimate their military skills. The *Heaven Sword*'s protagonist Du Dajin 都大錦, for instance, is astonished by the appearance of the renowned Zhang Cuishan: "In the warriors' world of recent years," he ponders, "Zhang Cuishan's great name has been praised by numerous people, all of whom said that his martial skills are outstanding. Who would have thought that he is actually this type of a cultured, refined, unable-to-withstand-the-wind weakly youth! (*wenzhi binbin, ruo bu jin*

---

51   Zhao Huanting, *Qixia jingzhong quanzhuan* (1923–7; reprint, Chengdu: Bashu shushe, 1990), 21. 169. At least one scholar argues that this was Zhao Huanting who introduced the notion of *qi* as an invincible pugilistic weapon into the genre of matial-arts fiction; see Ye Hongsheng 葉洪生, *Ye Hongsheng lun jian: wuxia xiaoshuo tan yilu* 葉洪生論劍：武俠小說談藝錄 (*Ye Hongsheng Discusses the Sword: Talks on the Art of Martial-Arts Fiction*) (Taipei: Lianjing 1994), 36.

feng de shaonian 文質彬彬弱不禁風的少年).[52]

Numerous critics have pointed out that one of Jin Yong's greatest achievements has been the integration of culture (*wen* 文) and warfare (*wu* 武) in the genre of martial-arts fiction. His novels are regarded by many as embodying traditional Chinese culture, in that his protagonists engage in the literatus' pursuits: poetry, calligraphy, *qin* 琴 (zither) music, and encirclement chess (*weiqi* 圍棋, or go).[53]   What I will suggest here is that the combination of culture and warfare in the persona of the martial-artist is related to the latter's reliance upon the power of *qi*, which enables the fulfillment of an ancient dream — that of a scholar whose refined appearance conceals invincible powers. Interestingly, here too we find a correspondence between martial-arts entertainment fiction and martial-arts practitioners' textbooks. Beginning in the Qing-period, and increasingly so during the twentieth-century, practitioners' literature sought to demonstrate the internal powers of *qi*, by portraying outstanding warriors who are outwardly frail-looking. The semi-miraculous feats of these martial-artists — recorded in practitioners' manuals, collections of lore, and general encyclopedias — amount to what may be described as the hagiographic literature of the martial-arts. Here is an early example from the *Gujin tushu jicheng* 古今圖書集成 (*The Comprehensive Collection of Ancient and Modern Charts and Writings*) (1725):

> Zhang Songxi was as gentle as a Confucian scholar. He was respectful to others, and his body seemed so delicate that it appeared hardly capable of carrying his cloths... Once he instructed several young men to bring from the garden several large stones — each weighing several hundred pounds — and pile then up. He said: 'I am a useless old man of seventy. Nonetheless, I will try to amuse you, gentlemen.' Thereupon he lifted his left hand and struck with its side. All three stones were split in two. His skills were this

---

52   *Yitian tulong ji*, 3.111.

53   See, for example, Chen Mo 陳墨, *Jin Yong xiaoshuo yu zhongguo wenhua* 金庸小説與中國文化 (*Jin Yong's Fiction and Chinese Culture*) (Nanchang: Baihuazhou wenyi, 1995).

extraordinary![54]

The notion of the genteel martial-artist, whose frail-looking body hides invincible *qi*-power, leads us to another function of *qi* in Jin Yong's novels. This mysterious internal force adds a touch of magic to protagonists and plots alike, thereby serving to enwrap the narratives with an aura of the extraordinary. I will suggest that, in this respect, *qi*-related fighting contributes to the dimension of fantasy in the writings of Jin Yong.

The magic aura which surrounds the concept of *qi* in Jin Yong's fiction underscores an interesting conundrum pertaining to our very understanding of this term: how is it possible for *qi* to add an extraordinary dimension to novels, if it is perceived itself as ordinary, that is inherent in each and every one of us? To be sure the term *qi* hasn't had one meaning only throughout the lengthy — two millenniums and more — period in which it has been in use. This key concept in the Chinese philosophical and medical traditions has meant different things to different authors, as is attested, if by nothing else, by its diverse English renditions: breath, pneuma, vital force, vital spirit, and vital energy, to name just a few. However, one attribute of *qi* has probably remained constant throughout its history — it has been regarded as an integral aspect of the natural phenomena it animates. In this respect, terms such as "supernatural," or "extraordinary" are inapplicable to it.

A comparative note might be in order here. The Western monotheistic tradition conceives of a god who created nature, and is himself external to it. This "supernatural" god is thus capable of "supernaturally" interfering in nature. By contrast, the Chinese world-view hasn't recognized an external creator, and by this yardstick it has no place for the "supernatural." "It should be remembered," notes Needham, "that for the characteristic and instinctive Chinese world-view

---

54   *Gujin tushu jicheng* 古今圖書集成, ed. Jiang Tingxi 蔣廷錫 et al. (1934; photographic reprint, Taipei: Dingwen shuju, 1977), yishudian 藝術典, chapter 810, the *quan bo* 拳搏 section, p. 59665b.

in all ages there could be nothing supernatural *sensu stricto*. Invisible principles, spirits, gods and demons, queer manifestations, were all just as much part of Nature as man himself, though rarely met with and hard to investigate."[55] It is for this reason that some scholars prefer the term "supernormal" over "supernatural" in the Chinese context.[56]

Returning to the concept of *qi*, if — as the narrator in Jin Yong's novels would probably acknowledge — it is ordinary, (in that it is inherent in us all), in what sense does it contribute a magic aura to works of fiction? I would suggest that the notion of *qi* carries supernormal connotations in Jin Yong's fiction in two ways: Firstly, even as the *qi* is inherent in us all, it is presented as accessible only to the very few. Outstanding martial-artists alone are capable of exhausting the limitless potential of their internal *qi*, which is thus extraordinary in that it is extraordinarily difficult to tap. Secondly, those few who possess the secret methods for harvesting the power of *qi*, are thereby capable of performing feats hailed by the narrator and protagonists alike as exceptional. I will try to illustrate these supernormal aspects of *qi* by two examples drawn from the novel *Extraordinary Beings*:

The first example concerns methods of fighting with invisible rays of *qi*, which the practitioner emits from his fingertips. Described by the narrator as fencing with the "formless *qi*-sword" (*wuxing qijian* 無形氣劍) these methods enable the adept to overcome a distant adversary, without ever coming into physical contact with him. Their names tinged with religious aura, the formidable techniques in question are for the most part attributed in the novel to Buddhist monasteries. Three methods, for instance, are ascribed to the Shaolin Monastery: The Peerless Kalpa Finger (Wuxiang jie zhi 無相劫指); the

---

55 Joseph Needham, *Science and Civilization in China* (Cambridge: Cambridge University Press, 1956), 2:377.

56 See John Kieschnick, *The Eminent Monk: Buddhist Ideals in Medieval Chinese Hagiography*. Kuroda Institute Studies in East Asian Buddhism, no. 10 (Honolulu: University of Hawaii Press, 1997), 96-7.

Palmyra-Leaf Finger (Duoluo ye zhi 多羅葉指; *duoluo* is the Chinese transliteration of the Sanskrit *tāla*, or palmyra, which leaves have been used in India for the writing of scriptures); and the Flower-Holding Finger (*Nianhua zhi* 拈花指).[57] The latter name alludes, as the narrator explains, to a famous legend concerning the origins of the Chan school: Once when the Buddha Śākyamuni was preaching the doctrine, he held in his fingers a golden lotus blossom for all to see. Only Kāśyapa understood his meaning and smiled, whereupon the Buddha announced: "I possess the True Dharma Eye, the Marvelous Mind of Nirvāṇa, the True Form of the Formless, the Subtle Dharma Gate that does not rest on words or letters but is a special transmission outside of the scriptures. This I entrust to Mahākāśyapa."[58]

The supernormal dimension of *qi*-fencing is attested by the protagonists themselves, who refer to this form of fighting by such expressions as "unbelievable" (*bukesiyi* 不可思議). Equally important as an indication of its extraordinary nature, *qi*-fencing has been mastered by no more than a handful of warriors worldwide. Indeed, the secret methods for emitting *qi*-rays are encoded in ancient manuscripts, themselves hidden in secluded monasteries, the residents of which regard them as their most sacred possessions. Thus, for example, the Heavenly-Dragon Monastery (*Tianlong si* 天龍寺) in the outskirts of Dali, Yunan, treasures the only existing manual of the Six-Channels Spiritual Sword (*Liumai shenjian* 六脈神劍), which enables the practitioner to emit simultaneously six deadly rays of *qi*, generated via six different *qi*-circulation tracks within his body.[59]

---

57 *Tianlong babu*, 10.413-5.

58 This famous formula, which Jin Yong inserted into his narrative, appeared for the first time in the *Zongmen liandeng huiyao* 宗門聯燈會要 (*A Collection of Essential Materials from the Chan Sect's Successive Records of the Lamp*) (1183); this is Heinrich Dumoulin's translation in his *Zen Buddhism: A History*, translated into English by James W. Heisig and Paul Knitter (New York: Macmillan, 1988), 1:9.

59 *Tianlong babu*, 10.424-5.

The following passage illustrates the supernormal overtones that accompany the description of *qi*-swordplay in Jin Yong's *Extraordinary Beings*. It concerns the Dharma-King of the Tibetan Tubo 吐蕃 kingdom, who is competing against the Heavenly-Dragon Monastery's monks. The competition's religious aura is enhanced by the Tibetan king's pseudo-Sanskrit name, Jiumo zhi 鳩摩智, which has been fashioned, probably, after that of the Buddhist translator Jiumoluohsi (Kumārajiva 鳩摩羅什) (fl. 385-409):

With his left hand Jiumozhi picked a Tibetan incense-stick, and with his right one he grabbed several of the wooden chips that were spread on the floor. He squeezed them gently into a small pile, into which he inserted the incense-stick. In this manner he inserted one after the other six Tibetan incense-sticks, which together formed a line. The distance between one incense stick and the next was about one foot. Jiumozhi himself proceeded to sit down, crossed-legged, at a distance of approximately five feet behind them. Suddenly he rubbed his hands a few times, and spread his palms forward. The heads of the six incense-sticks instantly shone — they were all simultaneously kindled! Everybody present was greatly astonished. They realized that the power of this person's internal strength (*neili* 內力) has already reached an unbilievable sphere (*bukesiyi di jingjie* 不可思議的境界).

The smoke that rose from the Tibetan incense-sticks was of emerald-green hue, and it gradually floated upwards in six perfectly straight lines. Jiumozhi's palms appeared to be holding an invisible ball. As they started emanating internal power, the six rays of emerald smoke gradually began curving towards the outside. They separated so that each line of smoke was directed at one of Jiumozhi's six Heavenly-Dragon Monastery adversaries: Kurong 枯榮, Benguan 本觀, Benxiang 本相, Benyin 本因, Bencan 本參, and the Baoding 保定 Emperor. Jiumozhi was using a form of palm-power, known as the "Flames' Blade" (Huoyan dao 火焰刀). Even though it is an empty and intangible force, which can't be grasped, still it can invisibly kill a person. Indeed, no power is more formidable...

The six columns of emerald smoke continued to float towards Benyin and the others, and when they reached a distance of three feet from them, they suddenly stopped and moved no more. Benyin and the rest were flabbergasted. They considered that to rely upon internal strength to send emerald smoke isn't so difficult. However, to have floating and unstable vapor congeal in mid-air is ten times more difficult.

Bencan pointed with his little finger, and a stream of *qi* gushed out of his Shaochong 少衝 nodal-point directly towards the emerald smoke. Having met the pressure of this internal strength, the smoke column shot back at an incomparable speed towards Jiumozhi. It approached as near as two feet from him, when the internal strength in the latter's "Flames' Blade" increased so that the smoke could advance no further. Jiumozhi nodded, and exclaimed: "Your fame hasn't spread in vain..."[60]

If the narrator and his protagonists alike consider *qi*-fencing techniques as extraordinary, then they certainly accord a similar status to another method, which draws not on one's own *qi*, but rather on his adversary's. This is a method of inhaling an opponent's *qi*. Those rare individuals who master it, are presented in the novel *Extraordinary Beings* as practically invincible: Whomever they encounter, they can rob of his vital energy, which they can proceed to use for their own ends. Indeed, their hapless victims are glued to them, until drained of their last drop of *qi*.[61]

Like the methods of *qi*-fencing, the technique of *qi*-stealing is shrouded in mystery. It has been preserved in a single manuscript, itself hidden in a mysterious cave, underneath a divine maiden's statue, (where the above-mentioned Duanyu, acting on his romantic impulse discovered it). Like the description of *qi*-fencing methods, that of the *qi*-inhalation technique is impregnated with religious significance, even though in this case the terminology used is Taoist, rather than Buddhist. The name of the *qi*-inhalation method, "North-Ocean" (Beiming 北冥), like the imagery used for its depiction, derive from the "Free and Easy Wandering" chapter of the *Zhuangzi*:[62]

As to consuming water and grains and storing them in the belly, every new-born is

---

60　*Tianlong babu*, 10.418-9.

61　See, for example, *Tianlong babu*, 5.213-4, 9.387-8.

62　*Zhuangzi*, chapter 1; Graham, 43.

capable of that, and needs no training. However, as to using the Shaoshang 少商 nodal point to inhale another person's internal strength, and then going on to store this acquired vigor in one's ocean of *qi*, this can only be accomplished by the North-Ocean Divine Method of the Free and Easy Wandering, Righteous Sect. It takes one day only for whatever water and grain a person has consumed to be dispersed to the outside. By contrast, when we inhale another's person internal vigor, one percent inhaled is one percent saved. Nothing leaks to the outside. The internal ocean of *qi* keeps growing infinitely, until it becomes as immense as the North Ocean and the Lake of Heaven (Tianchi 天池). So much so, that it is large enough for the thousand-miles Kun 鯤 fish to float in.[63]

Techniques of *qi*-stealing and *qi*-fencing demonstrate that the notion of *qi* contributes to the dimension of fantasy in Jin Yong's fiction. Even though this internal force is inherent in us all, its description in his novels carries supernormal overtones. The *qi* is presented both as extraordinarily difficult to tap, and, once released, extraordinarily powerful. This literary fancy of the *qi*, brings us back to the question of latter's role in practice: Could it be that supernormal overtones accompany the concept of *qi* not only in martial-arts fiction, but also in martial-arts practice? That is, could it be that some martial-arts practitioners attribute to their inherent *qi* extraordinary qualities? And, if so, can we perceive in their practice of the martial-arts a dimension of ritual performance intended to induce this supernormal force, which is located within their own bodies?

I will not try to address here the question of the supernormal aspect of *qi* in martial-arts practice. This issue, which pertains to the religious dimension of the martial-arts, goes far beyond the scope of this paper. Still I would mention that some of the most fantastic forms of *qi*-warfare in Jin Yong's novels do have their correlates in martial-arts practice. For instance, we have seen that, in the novel *Extraordinary Beings*, techniques of *qi*-fencing are premised upon the concentra-

---

63   *Tianlong babu*, 5.202; the image of the Kun Fish, like that of the Lake of Heaven derives from
the *Zhuangzi*, chapter 1; see Graham, 43.

tion of *qi* in one's fingertips, and, at least three of these — the Peerless Kalpa Finger, the Palmyra-Leaf Finger, and the Flower-Holding Finger — are attributed to the Shaolin Monastery. Interestingly, it is not uncommon to find twentieth-century martial-arts methods that are ascribed to the same temple, and are intended for the concentration of *qi* in the fingertips. As early as 1915, the *Secret Formulas of the Shaolin Fighting Technique* hailed the formidable powers of the Shaolin Single-finger Technique (*Yi zhi gongfu* 一指功夫),[64] and manuals published during the 1990s praised similar techniques, referred to by such names as the "Shaolin Finger Chan ［Meditation］ Technique" (*Shaolin zhi chan gong* 少林指禪功), and the "Shaolin Technique of the Golden-Needle Finger" (the latter has been mentioned above).[65]   Whether or not these techniques of finger-premised *qi*-fighting have carried in practice the same supernormal overtones that they do in fiction will have to be determined by future research.

V. Conclusion

A study of the fighting techniques in Jin Yong's novels suggests that the evolution of Chinese martial-arts fiction isn't unrelated to the history of Chinese martial-arts practice. Evidence of the latter's influence on Jin Yong's fiction is abundant: His novels include textual borrowings from martial-arts manuals, his protagonists engage in fighting techniques that are widely practiced, and some of these protagonists have been borrowed themselves from the genealogical writings of martial-arts schools. Perhaps most significantly, the martial-arts as presented in his novels are largely premised upon the internal circulation of *qi*. In this respect, his fiction mirrors the profound transformation that the Chinese martial-arts

---

64   *Shaolin quanshu mijue* (1915; reprint, Tianjin: Tianjinshi guji shudian yingyin, 1988), 97–8. (On the *Shaolin quanshu mijue* see above, note 32).

65   See *Zhongguo qigong gongfa daquan*, 662, 688, and *Zhongguo wushu dacidian* 中國武術大辭典 (*Comprehensive Dictionary of Chinese Martial Arts*) ed. Zhongguo wushu dacidian bianji weiyuanhui 中國武術大辭典編輯委員會 (Beijing: Renmin tiyu, 1990), 338.

underwent during the Qing period, namely the incorporation of *daoyin* techniques of *qi*-circulation into martial-training.

The intimate relation between Jin Yong's martial-arts fiction and the realm of martial-arts practice, doesn't shed light on his genius as an artist. However, it might help us unravel an important cultural development, which we witness in contemporary China — the flowering of a martial-arts culture, the foundations of which can be traced back to the early Qing. This martial-arts culture is largely premised upon the internal circulation of *qi*, and it has both a dimension of practice, and a dimension of fictional representation.

認知能量，情緒指標與一心兩用

——金學中的認知心理面面觀

曾志朗　　莊瓊如

國立陽明大學通識教育中心

摘　要

　　本文是以科學的方法，針對三個認知的方向（認知能量、情緒指標與一心兩用）來討論《書劍恩仇錄》（約 43 萬字）、《射鵰英雄傳》（約 75 萬字）、《神鵰俠侶》（約 80 萬字）、《天龍八部》（約 100 萬字）、《鹿鼎記》（約 99 萬字）五部金庸小說。

　　首先討論的是：金庸的寫作模式是否受到人類認知系統的規範。在金庸眾多小說作品集中，以上述五部小說爲例，每部小說字數雖長短不一，但每部小說所出現的字頻（Types）卻都在四千三百字左右。可見金庸的寫作模式與古今中外的大文豪一樣，仍然無法打破人類認知系統的先天限制。

　　再者，人們讀小說，思路除了跟著作者安排的故事情節走外，在情緒感受上，也會隨著劇情而起伏。本研究根據正負向情緒字彙出現頻率，提出情緒指標的公式，根據此公式的分析，五部金庸小說在情緒指標上的確有其差異性。一般而言，多數讀者認爲《鹿鼎記》故事輕鬆詼諧，屬於正向情緒的小說，而《書劍恩仇錄》比起《鹿鼎記》，在情緒指標上確實平穩了許多。

　　最後，金庸的創意隨處可見，其中雙手互博拳術的提出不得不令人爲之驚嘆。在心理學「注意力」的研究中，有選擇性注意的問題，也有一心兩用的問題，而這兩者都有如何由訓練變成精練的效益問題。金庸極富創意的提出心思太巧的人無法學會雙手互博拳術的看法，這個理念與近年來認知心理學的尖端研究領域是不謀而合的。

因此，由這三個（認知能量、情緒指標與一心兩用）不同的認知心理學層面來看，金庸小說中確實蘊含了許多寶藏，等待讀者們來挖掘！

一、引　言

看金庸的小說，對多數人而言，是充滿了情、意、智、美、知的感受。而對研究人類認知系統的心理學家而言，卻有另外一層的享受。他們往往可以在金庸那充滿創意的想像力中，找到人類智慧的精華。他對人物的定性、對事物的洞見，以及對歷史的重解，無一不表現出他個人認知系統的融合與運作的彈性。底下我們由三個面向來檢視他的認知系統之內涵。

二、金庸小說中所顯示的認知系統的規範

語言是人類智慧的表徵，而文字的寫作是表達智慧的最高能耐。從八千年前到現在，文字的演變由圖形到一套表音或表意的符號系統，使人類的智慧突破了時空的限制，可以把記憶由腦海中移到身體之外而得以永生（科技的進步使永生的意義更爲明顯，例如光碟）。這個演化的「奇蹟」帶動了人類六千年的文明進展，使人類可以把寰宇的森羅萬象納入掌控。但這個顯然是擁有無限潛能的智慧可以改造周邊的事物，卻仍然沒能改變自己的本體。醫事科技使我們可以換心、換牙、換肝、換腎、換……，就是還沒有辦法換那智慧的中樞——腦，帶來的後果就是認知運作總是跟不上資訊革命的腳步！

我們的認知系統對資訊的處理會形成一個先天的瓶頸，是被心理學實驗上一再證實的，曾志朗在「三」與「七」的聯想的那篇文章中，曾經這麼說過：「無論就人類演化的歷史而言，或就個人成長的歷程而言，『數』觀念的發展反映著心智活動的成熟，也代表著人對外在世界的掌握。由一到三，由三到七，人類經歷了兩次資訊傳遞的瓶頸，而兩次也都能以組集的方式解困。但文明的進展並不止於如此而已。」（見曾志朗著，《用心動腦話科學》，頁235）我們可以從金庸小說所用的字數的頻率去切入，來理解「文明的進展不止於此，而認知系統卻不是無所規範」的事實。

我們的一位朋友鄭錦全教授，在美國伊利諾大學敎書做研究，他一直對

古今小說中的認知規範有興趣，於是就設計了一套電腦程式，可以把整本小說中的字頻計算出來。他的計算結果確實證實了古今中外的小說作品，所用的字數是有規範的，單看全部小說的總字數是不準的。例如《理性與感性》的總字數是 120,735，但其中不同的字只有 4,199；《傲慢與偏見》的總字數是 123,270，但不同的字是 4,146；最有趣的是傑克倫敦的《白牙》總字數是 32,361，但不同的字是 3,431，所以人類所能使用的不同的字似乎有一定的限制，證實了每一位作家的認知能量是有所規範的！鄭教授的想法給了我們一個啟示：我們應該可以用他的程式與方法來檢視金庸小說，看看他是否也受到類似的先天規範。於是就和鄭教授聯絡，鄭教授慨然地把他設計的程式寄來提供我們使用。

　　我們選了金庸的五部小說，有的長（如《天龍八部》），有的短（如《書劍恩仇錄》），利用鄭教授的程式，算出了這五部小說各自的全部字數，也算出每一部所使用「不同字數」之總數。結果是：金庸在每一部所使用的不同的字大約在四千三百多字上下。這可看出聰明多學如金庸，也不能打破認知系統的先天規範。古今中外的大文豪大多受制於同樣的限制（見表一）。金庸和《紅樓夢》的曹雪芹比起來，不相上下，都屬於這個規範的上限人物。

　　此外，我們也可以把這五部小說最常出現的二十個字列印出來（見表二）。其中有十四個字共同出現在五部小說中，表示金庸使用語文的一致性還是相當高的。從這些結果，我們看到了語文資訊傳遞的瓶頸還是存在的。它的深義必須再進一步的分析，才能釐清。總之，有了這程式，要做的以及可做的事還很多哩！想想看現代的文書處理已經在改變人們寫作的習慣，同一個螢幕下可以開啟多個視窗，人們就不再受制於線形的寫作方式。也許下一世紀的作家將會突破這個字數的規範，到時候人們的想像力會有所不同嗎？不同的工具不同的表現方式，會使我們由先天的認知能量的限制中走出來嗎？下一個世紀應該會有答案！我們在這裡就提出了一套解謎的方法。

三、以情緒指標來評比金庸小說的正、負向情緒

　　讀金庸的小說，總讓人手不釋卷，讀者的情緒當然也跟著小說中的情節而起伏。小說看完了，讀者對故事內容有所領會，有時更迫不及待地要講給

別人聽。但除了故事的情節所敍明的內容之外，讀者也會對那本小說興起整體的情緒感知。例如，多數人看完《鹿鼎記》的總體印象是歡喜、鬧笑，全是正面的情緒；但讀完《書劍恩仇錄》，卻隱隱約約地總是感到哀愁、淒涼的負向情緒。認知心理學者總是希望以一客觀的方法去表達每一本小說的情緒指向。因為唯有建立客觀的指標，才能深入分析各部小說的情意結構。

上一節所談到並使用的電腦程式，給我們一個可能建立觀察指標的方法。既然這個程式可以幫我們列出全書中各個字使用的頻率，那我們就可以把書中出現的正向情緒字（如喜、樂、笑、悅、愉、愛、歡）及負向情緒字（怒、哀、悲、憤（忿）、怨、哭、苦、恨、厭、愁）都找出來，並且把它們出現的次數也一併記下來。有了字的出現次數就可以得到其百分比。再把所有正向情緒字的百分比加起來，得到正向情緒的總體百分比；同樣，我們也可以用相同的方法計算負向字的總體百分比。最後，以負向情緒的總體百分比去除正向情緒的總體百分比，得到的就是一客觀的情緒指標（Emotional Index）。這個指標的數字越大，表示小說的喜劇成分越高（見表三）。

我們以這個方法去評比上面所提到的五部小說，把結果列在表三。正如我們所預計的，《鹿鼎記》的情緒指標最高，表示它的字裡行間充滿了喜氣；而《書劍恩仇錄》果然有最低的情緒指標，表示小說的內容較為沈重。事實上也是如此，《鹿鼎記》讓讀者想起韋小寶的嘻皮笑臉及調皮搗蛋；而回想起《書劍恩仇錄》，則香香公主的哀亡、霍青桐的怨意，以及陳家洛的無奈都突現在心頭。此外，為了建立上述指標的生態效度（Ecological Validity），我們也以七點量表的方式，請五十位大學生（都是金庸迷）就這五部小說的總體印象來評比它們的正、負向情緒，所得到的排列由《鹿鼎記》到《書劍恩仇錄》，和前面所說的用情緒字數所算出的排列次序完全吻合。證實了我們以客觀的方式建立的情緒指標，是符合讀者的總體印象的。

有人說情緒的感覺反映的是讀者個人的主觀意識，應該是很難以客觀的方法去測量的。但是我們以很簡單的字頻為根據，所推算出來的情緒指標，卻能被為數眾多的金庸小說所肯定。這當然表示人類的情緒絕對不是那麼不可捉摸！其穩定性是可以通過統計上的檢測的。對寫小說的作者而言，這應該是個好消息。只要好好的掌控用字遣詞的技巧，則讀者的情緒是可以與之共鳴的，作家們不可不察！當然，建立客觀的指標只是個起步。我們可以根

據這個原則，去把每一部小說的情節作進一步的情意分析，看起來「感性」與「理性」確是可以融合的！

四、雙手互搏拳術的創意與認知的彈性

金庸小說裡，各路的拳法都蘊涵相當的傳統武術概念，令讀者不但對中國武術的多元多樣感到驚佩，更重要的是由金庸所描繪的各門各派之「拳術」與「拳意」的區辨中，感受到「功能與形式」（Function and Form）之間的互動關係。這實在是點出了近年來認知科學家對創意的基本了解。我的實驗室中的一些有關兒童智慧表徵的發現，也證實了創意其實是根植在個人對所要做的事有解析其形式與功能的能力上。《笑傲江湖》中華山思過崖山洞中的繪圖，點出各家各派的拳法、劍法、槍法的精華，其實就是在說明，別的行家只要能掌握那特定拳法中的「形式與功能」的互動關係，那麼再神奇的拳法也是即時可破的！

這樣的瞭解不得不讓我們感到金庸眞是「看透了」人的認知系統，並對其運作的彈性有很精闢的理解。他本人的創意也隨處可見，其中對「雙手互搏拳術」的提出眞是令人歎為觀止。現代的認知心理學研究者只要讀到金庸對雙手互搏拳術的描述，馬上就會認為金庸簡直就是最先進的人類資訊傳遞（Human Information Processing）理論的代言人。因為在近三十年，認知心理學有個相當重要的研究課題，就是「注意力」（Attention）的類別與特性。其中除了對「選擇性注意力」（Selective Attention）的廣泛研究外，也對「分散注意力」（Divided Attention）做了相當深入的探討。

「分散注意力」俗稱「分心」，討論的是一個人能否有效地做到「一心兩用」的問題。其實這問題牽涉到整個腦神經如何分工的一些細節。對於個人是否可能做到「只有一個腦，卻有兩個心智系統」（One Brain, Two Minds）的想法，一直是哲學思辨上的大議題。馬戲班的各種特技表演，充滿了一心兩用或多用的事實，但一般人要做到「一手畫方，一手畫圓」卻是非常困難的。即使是因為非常嚴重的癲癇而必須把連接兩腦皮質之間的胼胝體切開的裂腦病人（Split-Brain Patient）也要在非常高壓力的情況下才會產生裂腦徵狀。所以，那些耍特技的人如何做到那麼有效的「一心多用」，總是令認知

神經心理學家百思不解。因此，對於能成功的做到 Divided Attention 的心理特質，就要一一去釐清。

在對雙手互搏拳術的敘述裡，金庸提出了一個非常具有想像力的心理特質，例如他認爲「心思」太巧的人（如黃蓉），不管是再聰明，也是不可能學會一心兩用的。只有那些沒有「心機」的人（如老頑童周伯通、小龍女及郭靖）才能一下子就掌握了一心兩用的原則。這個觀點直指心理學研究裡最中心的議題——即「個別差異」的問題。生物界的行爲特質就是各有千秋，人類智慧能力的多元也是近年來所有研究者的共識。有些人長於語文，有些人長於空間組合的能力，也有些人長於音樂節奏的創作與欣賞，更有些人長於數理邏輯及人際關係等（見遠流出版的《經營多元智慧》一書）的社會現實；在金庸小說人物中都歷歷如繪，道盡人間百態！

但金庸所提出的「個別差異」的另類思考，在「雙手互搏拳術」裡是有更深一層的意義的。他已經把我們帶到了認知歷程的核心，提出了策略與運作（Strategy and Operation）之間的分野。心理學家在思考這個問題時，已經漸漸能掌握「執行者」與「監控者」的兩層建構。在執行者的層次（Executive Level），一心兩用是較容易完成的，只要在輸入或輸出的兩組運作是基於兩個不同的管道，則干擾就會降低；在監控者的層次上（Monitoring Level），一心兩用就非常難。在這個所謂後設（Meta）認知的層次，一心兩用牽涉到自動化運作以及由意識狀態變成無意識狀態的精神領域裡。最近的一些實驗發現，上層策略的介入，會使本來是自動化的運作又轉換成意識控制下的序列處理（Serial Processing）。換句話說，像黃蓉這樣心思巧、心眼多，而心機又深的人，是絕對學不會要求一心兩用的雙手互搏拳術的！神算子瑛姑就更不用談了！反而是那心思空空蕩蕩的郭靖，就能把運作的系統整個放到「執行者」的層次。沒有心思，就沒有干擾。

雙手互搏拳術的構思，真是金庸創意的表現。他對一心兩用的詮釋，與現代認知心理學在注意力的個別差異的研究發現上是不謀而合的！

五、結　語

認知心理學關心人類智慧系統的運作，而寫作就是人類智慧運作的一項

最特殊的表現。在這篇討論金庸小說的論文裡，我們針對三個認知面向，以科學的方法來觀察金庸的認知系統之表徵。首先我們要問的是，金庸的寫作是否受到認知能量的規範。以《書劍恩仇錄》、《射鵰英雄傳》、《神鵰俠侶》、《天龍八部》、《鹿鼎記》五部小說為例，我們看到，小說字數的數量相差很大，但是所使用的字頻卻總是保持在四千三百字上下。所以，無論小說的長短與內容的豐富與否，金庸的認知系統是有所規範的，和曹雪芹比較起來，是差不多的！再者，上述五部小說常使用的字數幾乎完全雷同。第二，我們再看這五部小說的情緒指標確實是有差異的，如大家所料到的，《鹿鼎記》是比較會讓讀者產生正向情緒的小說，而《書劍恩仇錄》就顯得有比較平穩的情緒表現了。這也反應了我們以字頻的統計為根據的情緒公式是有心理上的意義的。最後，我們要為金庸小說中的創意之合理性感到敬佩。雙手互搏拳術的提出就是個最佳的創意，而這個理念與近年來認知心理學的尖端研究領域是不謀而合的。在注意力的研究中，有選擇性注意的問題，也有一心兩用的問題，而這兩者都有如何由訓練變成精練的效益問題。金庸更異想天開的提出心思太巧的人沒有辦法學會雙手互搏拳術的看法，這是心理學的個別差異問題，而目前確有實驗證據指出金庸的想法可能是正確的。綜合這些認知心理學不同層面的說明，我們必須承認，金庸的小說是心理學家的寶藏！

表一

Title	Tokens	Types
書劍恩仇錄	435,313	3,685
射鵰英雄傳	757,561	4,210
神鵰俠侶	802,426	4,092
天龍八部	1,022,633	4,439
鹿鼎記	994,522	4,163
紅樓夢前 80 回	496,855	4,293
紅樓夢後 40 回	234,980	3,217
紅樓夢 120 回	731,835	4,501
史記	533,505	5,122
風俗通	34,431	2,716
桃花扇	80,121	3,315
日知錄	459,357	5,225
漢書	742,298	5,833
三國志	377,807	4,388
後漢書	894,020	6,161

表二

書劍恩仇錄			射鵰英雄傳			神鵰俠侶			天龍八部			鹿鼎記			中研院新聞語料字頻統計		
9372	2.153	一	14183	1.872	一	15475	1.929	一	20108	1.966	不	18737	1.884	不	340512	2.355	的
6859	1.576	不	13206	1.743	不	14635	1.824	不	18746	1.833	一	18175	1.828	道	160234	3.464	一
6566	1.508	道	11772	1.554	的	12285	1.531	是	18445	1.804	的	17888	1.799	了	117216	4.274	不
6448	1.481	了	11737	1.549	道	11838	1.475	的	16485	1.612	是	17580	1.768	一	114733	5.068	在
5626	1.292	的	11540	1.523	是	11771	1.467	道	15501	1.516	道	17115	1.721	的	109366	5.824	人
5394	1.239	是	11448	1.511	了	10917	1.360	了	15380	1.504	了	16114	1.620	是	106582	6.562	有
5384	1.237	人	7971	1.052	他	9021	1.124	過	12589	1.231	人	14331	1.441	小	98293	7.241	中
5139	1.181	來	7784	1.028	人	8084	1.007	他	10981	1.074	我	10785	1.084	人	92102	7.879	會
4244	0.975	他	6846	0.904	這	7903	0.985	人	10087	0.986	你	10648	1.071	章	90378	8.504	是
3591	0.825	上	6708	0.885	來	7105	0.885	這	9945	0.972	這	10337	1.039	寶	87186	9.107	國
3521	0.809	這	6487	0.856	我	6904	0.860	我	9790	0.957	他	10173	1.023	這	86699	9.706	為
3454	0.793	在	6070	0.801	在	6641	0.828	你	9080	0.888	大	10130	1.019	大	83354	10.283	大
3300	0.758	大	5777	0.763	你	6404	0.798	來	8842	0.865	來	10077	1.013	你	76679	10.813	十
3110	0.714	我	5686	0.751	上	6310	0.786	楊	8006	0.783	之	9991	1.005	我	75722	11.337	以
3058	0.702	你	5376	0.710	靖	6122	0.763	大	7120	0.696	說	9719	0.977	他	68644	11.812	年
3013	0.692	家	5355	0.707	郭	5785	0.721	在	7046	0.689	中	9331	0.938	來	66262	12.270	出
2805	0.644	去	5326	0.703	大	5575	0.695	之	6632	0.649	在	8006	0.805	說	65677	12.724	公
2746	0.631	見	5179	0.684	下	5506	0.686	中	6611	0.646	得	7659	0.770	子	63985	13.167	日
2626	0.603	手	5105	0.674	黃	5314	0.662	得	6471	0.633	下	7549	0.759	上	60532	13.586	行
2620	0.602	下	5000	0.660	得	5235	0.652	上	6445	0.630	子	7171	0.721	得	60164	14.002	時

表三

書　名	Cognitive Capacity		Emotion Index		
	Tokens	Types	P.E.	N.E.	P.E./N.E.
書劍恩仇錄	435,313	3,685	0.394	0.207	1.125
射鵰英雄傳	757,561	4,210	0.461	0.216	2.134
神鵰俠侶	802,426	4,092	0.423	0.376	1.903
天龍八部	1,022,633	4,439	0.384	0.234	1.641
鹿鼎記	994,522	4,163	0.479	0.184	2.603

備註：
P.E.(Positive Emotion)＝喜、樂、笑、悅、愉、愛、歡
N.E.(Negative Emotion)＝怒、哀、悲、憤（忿）、怨、哭、苦、恨、厭、愁

第二輯 愛情與人物論

問金庸情是何物
——禮物、信物、證物

張 小 虹

國立臺灣大學外國語文學系

摘 要

　　「問世間，情是何物，直叫生死相許」一直是金庸武俠世界中的愛情主題曲，而本篇論文不直接談情說愛，而欲改變提問之方式，以「情是何物」談論愛情與物件間的關聯性。在文本取樣上集中於《射鵰》與《神鵰》，在理論援引上兵分二路，一以文化人類學 Marcel Mauss 對 the gift 之探討，延續至後現代物質消費的相關理論；另一條路數則以精神分析為主，涵括 Freud 對 fetishism 與 Lacan 對 the gift of love 之理論。

　　在此分析架構之下，將以二個基本問題展開對金庸文本之閱讀：㈠object 既指人也指物，那「慾望客體」（人）到「慾望物件」（物）的轉換在心理與文化社會層面的機制為何？㈡愛情之「空無」（nothingness）是否即「空無一物」（no-thingness），而記憶的物質性基礎又如何與物件互為托寓？此二問題意識將在具體之文本分析中鋪展，援引之例包括瑛姑—老頑童—段皇爺之間的錦帕與玉鐲、楊康與穆念慈的定情繡鞋、李莫愁贈陸展元的錦帕等。此「情事」即「物事」不僅在小說情節發展與情愛關係上舉足輕重，也具精神分析的「小物件」（objet a）與文化人類學上「禮物」（the gift）之特質而富饒深究之趣味。

一、引　言

嗜讀金庸者皆知，其令人入神入癡、廢寢忘食之魔力，不僅在於武俠世界的奇幻詭秘，更在於箇中癡兒女的情思入扣，看金庸是看俠義更看纏綿。而金庸的言情功夫，便是在刀光劍影中嫵媚演練郎情妾意，讓武俠與愛情成為相互提喻的虛構傳奇，一般危機四伏、一樣驚心動魄。[1]

於是「問世間，情是何物，直教生死相許？」幾乎就成了金庸武俠情愛世界的主題曲，其殷切探問、不得其解之慨然，雖屬文法上的「修辭問句」（rhetorical question），但卻也勾起許多批評家的錯愛與投射，旁徵博引從民族文化、倫理道德到性心理、婚姻、個性等諸多面向之決定因素，正經八百地論證貪嗔癡的社會文化心理演繹。而本篇論文則是要重新回到「情是何物」的問題之上，以一種調皮搗蛋的方式歪讀「情」與「物」的關係，亦即由愛情癡、妄、惑、迷的「形而上」討論，移轉到愛情禮物、信物、證物「形而下」的物質性基礎，鋪陳愛情物質論與武俠戀物學的發展可能。

因而本篇的理論亦即「禮」論，既是文化人類學從莫斯（Marcel Mauss）以降對「禮物」（the gift）之討論，也是精神分析學派自拉岡（Jacques Lacan）以降對「愛的禮物」（the gift of love）之延展。在此「禮」論架構下，將以金庸的《射鵰英雄傳》與《神鵰俠侶》為主要分析文本，以「情是何物」為起點，引發一連串的理論質疑：「慾望客體」（object of desire）與「慾望物件」（object of desire）的差異性為何？如果 object 既可指涉情人又可指涉情物，那由情人到情物在文化與心理上的轉換機制又為何？而在主體與客體若即若離、不即不離的愛情關係中，什麼是「非主非客」（abject）與「小客體（物件）」（*objet a*）的差異，你儂我儂的地獄與天堂之別？而愛情的「空無」（nothingness）是否亦即一種「空無一物」（no-thingness），那記憶的物質性基礎又如何與物件互動托寓？

而這一連串「情事」與「物事」的探問，將隨著《射鵰》與《神鵰》中六個主要物件陸續推展：靖康短劍、楊家鐵槍、鴛鴦錦帕、紅花錦帕、翡翠

1　有關武俠小說中言情傳統之源流，可參見陳墨《情愛金庸》引言，頁 3。

小鞋、樹皮兒衫。「情是何物」不再是只可意會不可言傳、拈花微笑的不說之說，「情是何物」的物質性可貫穿生與死、愛與恨、歷史與傳奇，由兵器到繡鞋、槍法到衣衫，既是禮物、交易與社會結盟的憑證，更是愛情、戀物與武俠敘事的源由，國仇家恨、兒女情長盡在其中。

二、靖康短劍：邊界戀物與武俠敘事

　　《射鵰》與《神鵰》以兩柄短劍所引發的世代恩仇貫穿全局，短劍既由武俠敘事所產生，也啓動著武俠敘事之發展，爲典型「物事」與「敘事」相生相滅之例證。誠如史都爾（Susan Stewart）所言，敘事乃「一種慾望的結構，一種既創生又區隔其客體—物件的結構，因而一再銘刻意符與意旨間的裂縫，也以此爲象徵體系之生發所在。」（ix）此裂縫存在於意符與意旨間，亦如同存在於敘事與客體—物件間，「所謂伊人，在水一方」，所謂短劍，流離輾轉，語言符號對意旨的無能捕捉，一如敘事對客體—物件的無法合一，裂縫所帶來的匱缺（lack）與失落（loss），正是以懷舊歸鄉（nostalgia）啓動語言敘事不斷塡補的動力慾念。

　　那麼此兩柄啓動敘事的短劍由何而來，自當回返敘事之中去尋。話說宋朝臨安府牛家村住著一對義結金蘭、八拜之交的兄弟郭嘯天與楊鐵心，他們因緣巧合與全眞教長春子丘處機在雪夜裡不打不相識而結緣，因郭妻李萍與楊妻包惜弱皆有孕在身，二人遂請丘道長爲未出世的孩兒命名：

> 丘處機微一沉吟，說道：「郭大哥的孩子就叫郭靖，楊二哥的孩子叫作楊康，不論男女，都可用這兩個名字。」郭嘯天道：「好，道長的意思是叫他們不忘靖康之恥，要記得二帝被虜之辱。」
>
> 丘處機道：「正是！」伸手入懷，摸出兩柄短劍來，放在桌上。這對劍長短形狀完全相同，都是綠皮鞘、金呑口、烏木的劍柄。他拿起楊鐵心的那柄匕首，在一把短劍的劍柄上刻了「郭靖」兩字，在另一把短劍上刻了「楊康」兩字。（《射鵰》29）

而丘處機走後，郭嘯天與楊鐵心又將刻了名字的短劍相互掉換，約定若都生男則結爲兄弟，若都生女則結爲姊妹，若一男一女則短劍便成指腹爲婚的文

定之禮。

因此，丘處機的兩柄「攣生」短劍在此經歷了兩個層次的交換（exchange）過程。在第一個層次上，以禮物形式由丘處機之手轉移到郭、楊二人之手，既是給未出世孩子的見面禮，也是以殺敵防身的短劍訂下日後傳其功夫的師徒名份；在第二個層次上，兩柄短劍又在這對「但願同年同月同日死」的結拜兄弟之間交換，爲未出世的孩子訂下兄弟、姊妹或夫妻的名份。

這種透過交換短劍以確立關係名份的方式，不禁令人想起文化人類學家莫斯在其經典之作《禮物》（*The Gift*）一書中對交換模式的探討。莫斯指出，許多前資本主義社會乃是以「禮物」與「回禮」（countergift）的儀式性交換，建立贈者與受者間的盟約與連繫，所謂有送有還、禮尚往來，氏族部落中人與人之間的關係於此存焉。但這種「禮物交換」（gift exchange）模式的重要性，不僅在於標示出有別於「商品交換」（commodity exchange）模式的另一種經濟與文化活動，[2] 更在於其凸顯出人與物的相互銘刻與不可分離性。如莫斯所言，被交換之物件有「名姓、個性與過往」（55），乃擬人化的存有，見證著契約與盟誓之建立，絕非資本主義社會所標榜的人與物之截然對立與二分。[3]

2　有不少批評家指出莫斯的「禮物交換論」有浪漫化初民社會之傾向，尤其是低估禮物交換在經濟交易層面的角色。而「禮物」與「商品」也往往被簡化爲「個人化」與「客體化」的二元對立，前者以社會關係爲中介，強調互惠與結盟；後者以金錢爲中介，專注利潤與成本；而晚近的討論重點則由「禮物交換」與「商品交換」的對立性移轉到其可能的相似性，見 Appadurai 11-12。

3　這種人與物的分離對立，不僅可被置於西方資本主義的社會脈絡之下審視，更可由此牽扯出與早期資本主義同期發軔的西方殖民擴張主義。批評家史達利布拉斯（Peter Stallybrass）就曾以「戀物」（fetish）一詞源於 *fetisso*（十六、十七世紀葡萄牙與荷蘭人在西非黃金海岸與非洲土著進行交易時的貿易用語，指土著以身上所穿戴之衣物配飾，見證商業交換的契約）爲出發，探討由啓蒙時期以降「歐洲主體」（the European subject）之建構，乃對立於非洲式人—物—巫的糾纏不清：「戀物的概念惡魔化了一種可能性，一種視歷史、記憶與慾望必須物質化爲物件的可能性，那些被觸摸、被愛憐、被穿戴的物件。」（186）歐洲主體必須是一個超越主體，不滯於物乃致可以黃金交換船隻、交換槍炮、交換煙草、交換蔗糖以獲取利潤。換言之，殖民擴張與資本主義之可怕處，不在其物質主義，而在其「去物質主義」（dematerialization），以超物質與超感官的抽象型式進行價值交換。史達利布拉斯此種「視歷史、記憶與慾望，必須物質化爲物件」的戀物閱讀方式，正是本文所欲有樣學樣的，然而有關中國資本主義與帝國擴張和戀物理論的關連，則是本文有待補強之處。

因此，「禮物交換」強調的是「互惠性」（reciprocity）與「結盟性」（solidarity），以物串起人與人的關連，物的流通亦即社會關係的流通。以兄弟結義爲例，鐵木眞與札木合的三次「結安答」便皆是以禮物交換進行之：

> 鐵木眞和札木合是總角之交，兩人結義爲兄弟時，鐵木眞還只十一歲。蒙古結義爲兄弟，稱爲「結安答」，「安答」即是義兄、義弟。蒙古人習俗，結安答時要互送禮物。那時札木合送給鐵木眞一個麀子髀石，鐵木眞送給札木合一個銅灌髀石。髀石是蒙古人射打兔子之物，兒童常用以拋擲玩耍。兩人結義後，就在結了冰的斡難河上拋擲髀石遊戲。第二年春天，兩人用小木弓射箭，札木合送給鐵木眞一個響箭頭，那是他用兩隻小牛角鑽了孔製成的，鐵木眞回贈一個柏木頂的箭頭，又結拜了一次。兩人長大之後，都住在王罕部中，始終相親相愛，天天比賽早起，誰起得早，就用義父王罕的青玉杯飲酸奶。後來鐵木眞的妻子被擄，王罕與札木合出兵幫他奪回，鐵木眞與札木合互贈金帶馬匹，第三次結義。（《射鵰》128）

而鐵木眞之子拖雷也與郭靖在河邊結安答，郭靖贈予拖雷母親李萍親手縫製的紅色繡紋汗巾，拖雷則贈予郭靖他平日素在頸中所帶的黃金項圈，汗巾與頸圈雖爲身外之物，但皆有親情與身體的銘刻，在交換中更見證了相親相愛、互相扶助的兄弟盟誓。

也莫怪乎鐵木眞與札木合日後翻臉成仇之際，必須先行送還禮物以斷總角之交的名份與恩義：

> 鐵木眞心想：「你旣已知道此事，我跟你更是永無和好之日。」從懷內摸出一個小包，擲在札木合身前，說道：「這是咱們三次結義之時你送給我的禮物，現今你收回去罷。待會你拿鋼刀斬在這裡。」說著伸手在自己脖子裡作勢一砍，說道：「殺的只是敵人，不是義兄。」嘆道：「我是英雄，你也是英雄，蒙古草原雖大，卻容不下兩個英雄。」札木合拾起小包，也從懷裡掏出一個革製小囊，默默無言的放在鐵木眞腳邊，轉身下山。
>
> 鐵木眞望著他的背影，良久不語，當下慢慢打開皮囊，倒出了幼時所玩的箭頭髀石，從前兩個孩子在冰上同玩的情景，一幕幕的在心頭湧現。他嘆了一口氣，用佩刀在地下挖了一個坑，把結義的幾件禮物埋在坑裡。
>
> 郭靖在一旁瞧著，心頭也很沉重，明白鐵木眞所埋葬的實是一份心中最寶貴的友

情。(《射鵰》243-244)

箭頭髀石所召喚的，自是成長記憶中同杯而飲、同被而睡的身體親密，更勝骨肉兄弟。退還禮物亦即「割袍斷義」，由義兄義弟情份轉為誓不兩立的仇敵，有趣的是埋葬結義禮物的行為，既是象徵意義上的埋葬記憶過往，更是一種「禮物戀物論」(fetishism of the gift) 的除魅儀式，斬斷人—物—巫的牽繫。

　　正如這對有著相同綠皮鞘、金吞口、烏木劍柄的短劍一般，禮物交換既可成就結拜兄弟，亦可牽成結髮夫妻。短劍作為文定之禮的可能，並未因郭、楊兩家皆生男孩而消失，反倒是在楊鐵心死後，刻有郭靖名字的短劍以遺物之形式落入楊鐵心義女穆念慈之手，此短劍不僅使穆見匕首如見義父，更不斷提醒著她義父遺命將其婚配郭靖之安排。也莫怪乎黃蓉要處心積慮地「比武奪劍」：劍之為物所代表的名份與承諾，其重要性並不亞於郭靖的人與心。所幸穆念慈執意義父已在「比武招親」時將其許配給楊康，而慨然將刻有郭靖之短劍贈與黃蓉（另一個以劍為文定之禮贈與的退讓方式，自是小龍女以淑女劍贈郭芙，以配對楊過的君子劍）。當然，黃蓉在「解決」郭靖短劍之後，日後還需處理郭靖做為成吉思汗「金刀」駙馬一事。

　　禮物交換，也可在同一關係中由兄弟結義轉為夫妻定情的盟誓。像黃蓉與郭靖在張家口初識，黃蓉打扮成衣衫襤褸、身材瘦削的少年，兩人雖萍水相逢卻言談投契，郭靖便贈黃蓉黑色貂裘與汗血寶馬，自是「車馬輕裘與朋友共」的最佳寫照。但這張家口訂交的禮物，也由黃蓉的回復女兒身而變成定情之物，尤其是汗血寶馬，不僅陪伴著黃蓉、郭靖日後的患難生死與共，更成為夫妻恩愛情深的表徵，就連黃蓉親自為次女郭襄縫製的褓褓之上，亦是「湖綠色的緞子，繡著一隻殷紅的小馬」(《神鵰》1085)。

　　但更重要的是，這對短劍除了做為《射鵰》、《神鵰》二書在敘事啟動與禮物原型上的功能外，更是二書「邊界戀物」(border fetish) 的代表。此處的「邊界戀物」乃援引史拜爾 (Patricia Spyer) 的說法：「既非此地亦非他方，既非過去亦非未來，既非隱無亦非無庸置疑地現存，邊界戀物之概念意在凸顯無法解決之擺盪、永不歇息的前後來回和標明戀物形構的文化、商業與政治之越界。」(1)史拜爾所談之文化歷史脈絡，自是西方與非洲交易互動的人—物關連，而今挪用此概念於不同文化歷史脈絡之中，無非是想強調「邊

界戀物」所能引發有關承認與否認、隱無與存有的心理機制，以及模糊邊界劃分與鬆動主客對立的僵局。

　　故由此角度切入，靖康短劍做為「邊界戀物」而言，不僅界於大宋與金兵的邊界，也界於歷史與傳奇的邊界、尋常社會與武藝社會（舒國治語）的邊界，更界於言志與言情的邊界。一對短劍帶出了曾親赴西域見成吉思汗的長春子丘處機，以及其他六位於史有名有姓的全真道士；但一對短劍也帶出了江南七怪，純粹武俠小說虛構時空的俠客，雙方相約各授其徒以競賽。換言之，一對短劍貫穿了歷史與傳奇，一邊是碑文、書籍中記載流傳的全真七子，一邊是武林一派的江南七俠，虛實之間既是歷史的傳奇化，也是傳奇的歷史化。而「靖康」的命名，更是把國仇家恨銘刻於人際關係之上，民族情感與私人情感的相互擺盪、公領域與私領域的不斷越界。

　　由全真七子到江南七怪，由靖康之恥到郭靖、楊康，歷史不再只是武俠小說的背景，武俠小說也不再只是亂世浮生的逃避，《射鵰》與《神鵰》二書中歷史與傳奇的越界擺盪，乃物質化為一對短劍，既以禮物交換方式串連結義或結髮關係，更以邊界戀物方式啟動敘事慾望。

三、楊家鐵槍：家族系譜與相思戀物

　　如果丘處機所贈之靖康短劍有貫穿身世、世代、恩怨情仇的戀物功能，那在《射鵰》開場與短劍先後出現的另一兵器鐵槍，則展開戀物以遺物型式運作之面向，另一引爆父系系譜與相思戀物的輻輳點。話說郭嘯天與楊鐵心之為「忠義之後」，皆可由其所使兵器與槍法瞧出端倪。郭嘯天乃梁山泊好漢地佑星賽仁貴郭盛的後代，使的是家傳戟法，只不過變長為短、化單為雙；而楊鐵心的先曾祖楊再興乃岳飛麾下名將，在小商橋力戰金兵、壯烈殉國。丘處機原以為郭、楊二人乃喬扮村夫的官府鷹犬，也是靠楊鐵心使出七十二路楊家槍法，才得以驗明「忠義之後」的正身。

　　故而鐵槍做為父系系譜驗明正身的憑證，不在於鐵槍本身的形貌與價值，真正的「傳家寶」乃是以槍法之型式建立傳承：傳子不傳女的楊家槍法自是驗證了楊鐵心乃楊家嫡傳的身份。武俠小說的特色之一，乃是將武功本身建立系譜，既可是家族系譜，也可是派別系譜。而武功所建構之家族系譜

與派別系譜自有其異同之處。以家族系譜而言,冠父姓乃入族譜之先決條件,而所冠之父姓又在整個承嗣傳統上具「提喻」(synecdoche)、以部分代替全體之功能。如楊鐵心之姓楊,並不足以完全說明其為名將楊再興之後,因而楊家槍法的武功本身具有父姓般同等的提喻功能與系譜位置。而家傳武功與父姓除了在系譜提喻功能上的相同性外,卻是以極為不同的方式呈現血緣關連;父姓乃血緣關連的「隱喻」(metaphor),而武功則是血緣關連先化為抽象的武功路數,再肉身化為身體髮膚的規訓與鍛鍊,此肉身物質性基礎乃凸顯了武功上身的毗鄰性,而成為血緣關連的「轉喻」(metonymy)。

　　而就派別系譜而言,則是以非血緣關連所建立之純武功承嗣傳統,師徒名份乃以武功路數傳承,同門師兄姊弟妹的「擬」血緣關連也以學習相同武功為認親方式。譬如說「古墓派」之歸類類同於姓氏的隱喻性(傳女不傳男的古墓派戒律該是父系系譜的另一反面),而小龍女、楊過在實際演練「玉女心經」的招數時,則又是另一種肉身證道(武)、道(武)成肉身式的轉喻。

　　雖然鐵槍和短劍一般具「邊界戀物」之功能,也牽帶出有關家族系譜與派別系譜的討論,但鐵槍在《射鵰》中的驚鴻一瞥,卻是開展物件做為記憶與慾望物質性基礎的新面向。話說「風雪驚變」之後,楊鐵心之妻包惜弱輾轉成為金國六王子完顏洪烈的妻子,這由村婦到王妃的社會身份轉變,也伴隨著牛家村到皇宮的地理位置轉變。「驚變」不僅是夫妻離散、流落異鄉,更是所有分類系統、人際關係的大混亂,而包惜弱「處變不驚」的心理機制,乃是透過「地點複置、時間固置」的戀物方式,承認且否認分離、斷裂與變易。她令大金國趙王府親兵千里迢迢趕赴臨安府牛家村,專程取來舊居中一切家私物品,從破櫈爛椅到鐵槍犁頭,一件不缺。「風雪驚變」後的時空斷裂,乃由「收集」(collection)即「回憶」(recollection)的物質形式重新對焦,再建故鄉的歷史空間性。此種感官知覺的重建既是以舊居置換皇宮,也是舊居與皇宮的疊影,同時承認與否認的戀物雙重意識。

　　故楊鐵心與包惜弱分離十八年後的重聚場景,便充滿了時空易位的「詭秘」(the uncanny)氛圍,不是恍若隔世,而是好似一切凝止未曾變動、未曾發生:

　　　楊鐵心在室中四下打量,見到桌櫈櫥床,竟然無一物不是舊識,心中一陣難過,

眼眶一紅，忍不住要掉下眼淚來，伸袖子在眼上抹了抹，走到牆旁，取下壁上掛
著的一根生滿了銹的鐵槍，拿近看時，只見近槍尖六寸處赫然刻著「鐵心楊氏」
四字。他輕輕撫摩槍桿，嘆道：「鐵槍生銹了。這槍好久沒用啦。」王妃溫言道：
「請您別動這槍。」楊鐵心道：「爲甚麼？」王妃道：「這是我最寶貴的東西。」
楊鐵心瀟然道：「是嗎？」頓了一頓，又道：「鐵槍本有一對，現下只賸下一根
了。」王妃道：「甚麼？」楊鐵心不答，把鐵槍掛回牆頭，向槍旁的一張破犁注
視片刻，説道：「犁頭損啦，明兒叫東村張木兒加一斤半鐵，打一打。」

王妃聽了這話，全身顫動，半晌説不出話來，凝目瞧著楊鐵心，道：「你……你
説甚麼？」楊鐵心緩緩的道：「我説犁頭損啦，明兒叫東村的張木兒加一斤半鐵，
打一打。」

王妃雙腳酸軟無力，跌在椅上，顫聲道：「你……你是誰？你怎麼……怎麼知道
我丈夫去世那一夜……那一夜所説的話？」（《射鵰》369-370）

物是舊物、人是舊識，一切時間記憶凝止在生離死別前一夜的家常對話，犁
損依舊未打，但刻著「鐵心楊氏」的鐵槍卻已生銹，時間終究侵入這凝止的
時空，一如楊鐵心一身的風霜侵磨。包惜弱捨王府畫棟雕樑的樓閣，卻戀物
許多破爛老舊的桌檯櫥床，而舊物竟也真召回魂縈夢牽的舊人，垂淚話當年。

但鐵槍之爲相思戀物—遺物的感官物質性，卻在《射鵰》中有更進一步
的發揮。此次乃是透過丘處機之眼所呈現包惜弱與鐵槍間的互動關係。

貧道晚上夜探王府，要瞧瞧趙王萬里迢迢的搬運這些破爛物事，到底是何用意。
一探之後，不禁又是氣憤，又是難受，原來楊兄弟的妻子包氏已貴爲王妃。貧道
大怒之下，本待將她一劍殺卻，卻見她居於磚房小屋之中，撫摸楊兄弟鐵槍，終
夜哀哭；心想她倒也不忘故夫，並非全無情義，這才饒了她性命。（《射鵰》441）

包惜弱之所以逃過死劫，乃由其深情所致，不愛才識博洽、吐屬俊雅的金國
王子完顏洪烈卻朝思暮想粗豪「先」夫楊鐵心，「撫摸楊兄弟鐵槍，終夜哀
哭」。這「撫摸」舊人舊物的動作，卻在包惜弱殉夫自盡後，也同樣出現在完
顏洪烈身上。而這一次則是透過黃蓉之眼所呈現完顏洪烈在包惜弱故居思憶
故人的場景：

黃蓉見光亮從小孔中透進來，湊眼去看，只見一隻飛蛾繞燭飛舞，猛地向火撲去，

> 翅兒當即燒焦，跌在桌上。完顏洪烈拿起飛蛾，不禁黯然，心想：「若是我那包
> 氏夫人在此，定會好好的給你醫治。」從懷裡取出一把小銀刀、一個小藥瓶，拿
> 在手裡撫摸把玩。（《射鵰》954-955）

銀刀與藥瓶乃包惜弱之物事，更是十九年前二人初識結緣、包惜弱救治完顏
洪烈所用之物。包惜弱「撫摸」鐵槍，完顏洪烈「撫摸」銀刀藥瓶，這人與
物的親密肌膚碰觸，對比於丘處機與黃蓉的遠觀視覺位置，既標示出遠／近、
視覺／觸覺之差異，更凸顯相思戀物─遺物在意像與「再現」（rcprcscnta-
tion）之外的物質性基礎，觸手可及、撫摸把玩的感官知覺形式。

　　正如馬克思視戀物爲「感官慾望的宗教」（the religion of sensuous
desire），人類情感乃爲感官與物件間的物質性辯證：官能感應力讓人受苦受
難，亦即受制於他者他物。而物質性與眞實、記憶、慾望的相互穿透，也正
是柏格森（Henri Bergson）在《物質與記憶》（*Matter and Memory*）中所
欲探究之核心，記憶若是「心靈與物質的交點」(13)，那所謂「物質」便更是
界於物與再現間的意像積累。或用巴特勒（Judith Butler）的話說，英文
"matter" 既指「物質」也指「表意」，既可是眞實的幻象式建構，也可是幻
象的物質性基礎。

　　一把鐵槍的物質性與表意性，從提喻式、隱喻式、到轉喻式的家族武功
系譜，從相思戀物─遺物的睹物思人、撫摸把玩，最後盡皆集結於楊康不住
撫摸生父楊鐵心遺物的時刻，這一次依舊是透過黃蓉之眼所呈現之場景：

> 只見他手中拿著一條黑黝黝之物，不住撫摸，來回走動，眼望屋頂，似是滿腹心
> 事，等他走近燭火時，黃蓉看得清楚，他手中握著的卻是一截鐵槍的槍頭，槍尖
> 已起鐵銹，槍頭下連著尺來長的折斷槍桿。（《射鵰》504）

黃蓉看見錦袍金冠的小王爺完顏康手握楊鐵心的斷槍頭，只道是與穆念慈有
關，將此睹物思親誤讀爲「撫摸槍頭相思」。而眞正困擾小王爺心中的卻是「完
顏康」與「楊康」的身份擺盪，一是認賊作父卻有享不盡的榮華富貴，一是
認祖歸宗當立報父母及家國之血海深仇。鐵槍的槍法未能成爲其武功的派別
系譜，但鐵槍上刻的「楊氏」卻強制其歸屬家族系譜，更何況鐵槍上還沾著
其生父生母的鮮血。而終究未能認祖歸宗的楊康，日後也因用鐵槍頭殺死歐

陽克而賈禍，更慘死於鐵槍廟，這一切冥冥中似有命定。

四、鴛鴦錦帕：愛情信物與復仇證物

　　前二節對短劍與鐵槍的討論，已由禮物訂盟擴展到遺物詔命的面向，雖能凸顯武俠小說中兵器的戀物化，但對「情之爲物」的愛情戀物學卻有未逮之處。故以下的討論，將由殺伐爭鬥的兵器，轉到小閣梳妝的愛情信物—手帕、繡鞋之流的私密與親暱，探一探由情人到情物的輾轉流離，摧心相思的未老先白首。

　　貫穿《射鵰》與《神鵰》愛情私密信物的頭籌，自非鴛鴦錦帕莫屬。話說當年全眞教掌門王重陽赴大理國與段皇爺切磋武學，師弟周伯通卻與劉貴妃在後宮研習點穴功夫，因肌膚相親、日久生情而闖下大禍。東窗事發後，王眞人將周伯通綑縛段皇爺跟前請罪，但段皇爺卻以學武之人義氣爲重、女色爲輕，而願將劉貴妃「割愛相贈」，然周伯通卻絕計不從。此段往事在日後皈依佛門的一燈大師段皇爺心中，依然歷歷在目：

> 一燈大師卻並不在意，繼續講述：「周師兄聽了這話，只是搖頭。我心中更怒，說道：『你若愛她，何以堅執不要？倘若並不愛她，又何以做出這等事來？我大理國雖是小邦，難道容得你如此上門欺辱？』周師兄呆了半晌不語，突然雙膝跪地，向著我磕了幾個響頭，說道：『段皇爺，是我的不是，你要殺我，也是該的，我不敢還手。』我萬料不到他竟會如此，一時無言可對，只道：『我怎會殺你？』他道：『那麼我走啦！』從懷中抽出一塊錦帕，遞給劉貴妃道：『還你。』劉貴妃慘然一笑，卻不接過。周師兄鬆了手，那錦帕就落在我的足邊。周師兄更不打話，揚長出宮，一別十餘年，此後就沒再聽到他的音訊。（《射鵰》1219-1220）

在這個兄弟之義大於男女之情的場景中，我們看到的不僅是周伯通退還錦帕的「絕情」，更是男性同盟 (male homosocial bond) 下「兄弟如手足，妻子如衣服」的「絕情」。劉貴妃不僅要傷心其一片痴心托寄的錦帕被情郎遺棄在地，更要痛心自己如禮物一般在皇夫與情郎間推送拒受、割愛相贈，若《水滸》必須「殺女人」以成兄弟之邦，那《射鵰》此情此景莫不是要以「贈女人」以全兄弟之義。

　　而更反諷的是，周伯通桃／逃之夭夭後，[4] 劉貴妃一時失魂落魄、呆立一旁，落在段皇爺足邊的錦帕便自然被段皇爺拾起，瞧見帕上織就的鴛鴦戲水圖與「四張機，鴛鴦織就欲雙飛。可憐未老頭先白。春波碧草，曉寒深處，相對浴紅衣」的題詞。劉貴妃與周伯通的定情之物，此時透過第三者的眼與手呈現，而這第三者也正是這椿三角愛戀關係中的另一方，這種集妒嫉、悔恨、繾綣深情於一物的當下此刻，正是情何以堪的戲劇化高潮所在。

　　這件情物的圖文並茂，皆是以鴛鴦喻愛侶，姑且不論「春波碧草，曉寒深處，相對浴紅衣」可能引起被翻紅浪的私密性意涵，也暫時不管「可憐未老頭先白」在日後劉貴妃身上的一語成讖，題詞中最富饒深趣的，莫過於「鴛鴦織就欲雙飛」一句。此句之所以具體而微所有愛情信物之精要，不在於鴛鴦的傳統譬喻或雙宿雙飛的祈願嚮往，而在於此句動詞形態上的幽微婉轉，在前一個動作「織就」與下一個動作「欲雙飛」之間的凝止，過去式與未來式之間的「化剎那為永恆」。愛情的戀物亦如戀屍，情物的木乃伊化，乃是將天雷地火的剎那凝止，託寓在詩畫之中變為永恆。所謂「生死相許」未必要刎頸為紅顏或殉情赴黃泉，而是愛情戀物的本身亦即一種死亡形式，凝止（stasis）即天長地久。故而「欲雙飛」的唯美，不在於飛不成或天涯單飛，也不在於欲／慾之不得故輾轉反側，而是被繡「死」在錦帕上的一對鴛鴦，自是可以天長地久、天荒地老地「欲」雙飛。

　　鴛鴦錦帕圖文上的戀物凝止，不正也帶出了錦帕做為「愛的禮物」的交換與流通方式。依拉岡的精神分析而言，愛即一種禮物，以「理想化」與「昇華」的方式增累所愛之人的價值，所愛之人遂由一般血肉之軀幻化為理想原型，成為「慾望中不可能的非客體」（the impossible nonobject of desire），能成功抹去主體所有對存在空無、匱缺與失落的恐懼認知，彷彿回返母體剝

4　周伯通的拒女色於千里之外，常被論者評為「性心理殘疾」（陳墨 25-26），或以「武癡」一言以蔽之。但若就「情癡」與「武癡」的巧妙對應而言，我們是否也可異想天開地論證，武俠世界所強調的「童子功」乃是一種自戀模式，功力如慾力（libido）一般，不可固置在他人他物之上耗損，而盡皆在於強化自我（enrichment of the ego）。如果更調皮一點，那周伯通每次聽瑛姑要尋來時的屎遁，是否也是一種肛門期的固置，一如決口不談情愛的洪七公在口腹之慾上的口腔期固置呢？

離、主體砍頭之前想像期的豐美圓滿。[5]

　　故鴛鴦錦帕之爲「愛的禮物」可有兩個層次的思考。就第一個層次而言，錦帕是劉貴妃身與心的轉喻，皆送給了被理想化的愛人周伯通。就第二個層次而言，劉貴妃的慾望「客體」周伯通與慾望「物件」錦帕間有更爲繁複的置換取代關係：愛情你儂我儂的想像期圓滿幻象，否認了匱缺與失落，但當慾望客體消失或分離時，慾望物件遂以戀物形式取而代之，繼續否認匱缺與失落，更否認消失與分離。劉貴妃親手縫製與題詞的鴛鴦錦帕，原是渴望愛人周伯通貼身攜帶、寸步不離（否認距離與匱缺）；而愛人消失後，錦帕物歸原主劉貴妃，成爲曾經滄海的憑證與誓言，迷離撲朔記憶中不可懷疑的物質性眞實。

　　而《射鵰》、《神鵰》中的錦帕傳奇更在愛情銘刻上加添了喪子之痛。周伯通走後，劉貴妃十月懷胎產下一子，一日卻被蒙面刺客震斷經脈。段皇爺本想出手醫治，但卻又躊躇再三，深恐在華山二次論劍之前大耗元氣，錯失獨魁群雄的良機。但在劉貴妃苦苦哀求下，遂又起惻隱之心，正如一燈緩緩追憶道：

> 她見我答應治傷，喜得暈了過去。我先給她推宮過血，救醒了她，然後解開孩子的襁褓，以便用先天功給他推拿，那知襁褓一解開，露出了孩子胸口的肚兜，登時教我呆在當地，做聲不得。但見肚兜上織著一對鴛鴦，旁邊繡著那首「四張機」的詞，原來這個肚兜，正是用當年周師兄還給她那塊錦帕做的。（《射鵰》1225）

定情之物的錦帕，現在成了定情之產物嬰兒的襁褓，自是情深纏綿的一番心意，但看在段皇爺眼中，那繡著一對頭頸偎倚著頭頸的鴛鴦錦帕，卻是私情與私生子的罪證，難以寬恕。劉貴妃便在瞬時急白了頭髮，絕望之餘舉起匕

5　依拉岡體系而言，主體因進入語言的象徵秩序而「無頭」（headless），而愛的理想化則阻止主體體認到己身之空無（Silverman 44）。但同時拉岡「愛的禮物」也以「宮廷騎士之愛」（courtly love）爲範模，強調因愛戀客體已被提昇至「小客體（物件）」的不可企及之處，故無法納入己身、眞正擁有，主體與「小客體（物件）」的距離反倒在這種極端情況中，成爲強化象徵秩序割裂而非想像豐美圓滿的運作，主體不因「小客體（物件）」而承認／否認無頭、匱缺存有，反倒是每次對無法獲取「小客體（物件）」的空手而返，造成了主體的無頭、匱缺存有。

首插在孩子心窩解其痛苦，並毒誓日後要將用同一匕首戳在段皇爺的心口。

果然十幾年後，已改稱瑛姑的劉貴妃前來尋仇，送給一燈大師的見面禮之一，便是這錦帕做成的嬰兒肚兜：「錦緞色已變黃，上面織著的那對鴛鴦卻燦然如新。兩隻鴛鴦之間穿了一個刀孔，孔旁是一灘已變成黑色的血跡。」（《射鵰》1229）變黃的錦緞象徵歲月的流逝，而燦然的鴛鴦卻是凝止不老的愛情如新。但此愛情信物也同時成為復仇證物，鴛鴦之間的刀孔與血跡，見證的是段皇爺因妒絕情、逼劉貴妃手刃親子的人倫慘劇，這愛與恨的記憶具皆化為一方錦帕肚兜、耳提面命。十幾年來劉貴妃念茲在慈的錦帕，既是愛的相思戀物，對距離與親密、分離與重聚的雙重意識迷離交錯，也是恨的偏執意念，貫徹始終。錦帕遂以其鴛鴦圖文與刀孔血跡的物質性基礎表意，頂住遺忘。

但我們不要忘記，瑛姑在錦帕肚兜之前送上山去的物事尚有一樁，雖不及錦帕如此戲劇化地交織愛恨情仇，卻一樣是件會說話、會表意、有「名姓、個性與過往」的愛情信物。一只女子戴的玉鐲，羊脂白玉的圓環，乃是當年劉貴妃入宮之時，段皇爺所贈的定情之物，瑛姑此番送上山來，自是斬斷情緣由夫妻變仇敵的告知，但接到玉環的一燈大師，卻因物思情更覺惘然。雖一燈已然是斬斷紅塵的得道高僧，但依舊下意識地「豎起左手食指，將玉環套在指上，轉了幾圈」（《射鵰》1210）。這不經意的小動作，可以只讀成「物事」與「敘事」的啟動方式，也可以有另一番潛意識閱讀的尋幽訪勝。這裡倒不是要以性意象對號入座，而是一陽指上的羊脂白玉，無法不讓人在剛柔陰陽間穿鑿「百鍊剛化為遶指柔」的深情想像，這種「撫摸把玩」的感官知覺形式是記憶的肉身，也是以物相傳的慾望。

但不論動情或入定，瑛姑─一燈─老頑童的三角愛戀關係卻在《神鵰》書末有著最溫柔的結局。不是破癡化孽，也非無憂無怖，而是經過八十年的愛情長跑，三人已是也無風雨也無晴的近百之人，遂能返老還童，三小無猜，同在萬花谷中隱居，養蜂種菜，蒔花灌田，真真個白首偕老。

五、紅花錦帕：外納式與內涵式情愛的兩極交鋒

如果說一方鴛鴦錦帕道盡了瑛姑、一燈與老頑童間的愛恨牽纏，那另一

方紅花錦帕則是另一個三角關係的情海生變。一織白首鴛鴦同棲共眠，一繡紅花綠葉相偎相依，皆是情人間從縫製、贈與到攜帶上的肌膚相親、欲語還休，但「風月無情人暗換，舊遊如夢空腸斷」，錦帕的由愛轉恨，卻也有不堪回首當年的淒厲怨毒。

　　《神鵰》中，赤練仙子李莫愁鍾情於少俠陸展元，在陸妻何沅君的婚禮上揚言日後定來尋仇，十六年後雖陸展元已病死而何沅君亦自刎殉夫，李莫愁仍執意滅門陸家莊以洩恨。是夜萬籟俱寂中，忽聞李莫愁歌聲輕柔唱道：「問世間，情是何物，直教生死相許？」但她在殺陸展元之弟陸立鼎之前，卻竟然躊躇再三，無法下手：

> 李莫愁眼見陸立鼎武功平平，但出刀踢腿、轉身劈掌的架子，宛然便是當年意中人陸展元的模樣，心中酸楚，卻盼多看得一刻是一刻，若是舉手間殺了他，在這世上便再也看不到「江南陸家刀法」了，當下隨手揮架，讓這三名敵手在身邊團團而轉，心中情意纏綿，出招也就不如何凌厲。(《神鵰》32)

武功高強、行事毒辣的女魔頭李莫愁，此時不是殺人不眨眼，而是看著「江南陸家刀法」不眨眼，心旌搖蕩地觀刀法憶故人。而真正讓李莫愁顧念舊情、刀下留人的，則是陸展元死前交與其弟、其弟死前交與甥女程英、後被武三娘撕成兩半分另半給女兒無雙的一方錦帕：「手帕是白緞的質地，四角上都繡著一朵紅花。花紅欲滴，每朵花旁都襯著一張翠綠色的葉子，白緞子已舊得發黃，花葉卻兀自嬌豔可愛，便如真花真葉一般。」(《神鵰》42) [6]

　　這塊紅花綠葉錦帕正是當年李莫愁精心繡就、贈予意中人陸展元的定情之物，李莫愁以大理國最著名的紅色曼陀羅花自喻，以「綠」「陸」同音將綠葉比陸郎，自是與劉貴妃錦帕上的鴛鴦浴水圖與〈四張機〉題詞有異曲同工的相依相偎之妙。但同一塊錦帕在召喚李莫愁昔日濃情蜜意時，也同時提醒

---

[6] 此睹物思人、顧念舊情（手下留情）的戲碼，不也在晚近美國總統柯林頓的緋聞案中一再搬演嗎？柳文思基送給柯林頓的領帶禮物，不僅出現在柯林頓宴晤江澤民的國宴之上，也出現在出庭大陪審團會議的白宮僕役長身上，而當柳文思基自己出席大陪審團會議時，柯林頓當日則在另一個社交場合聚會上打著柳贈之領帶。而更有趣的當然是柳的白宮實習禮物，一件沾了總統精液的藏青色洋裝被當成愛情信物般收藏，也在日後成為比對 DNA 的辦案證物。

刺激著她情變被棄的不堪下場。過去許多批評家在論及李莫愁因情所苦而殺人無數時，總慣以一句「情生癡、癡生妄、妄生怨、怨生毒」一言以蔽之，但若我們要深究李莫愁究竟「傷」在何處而所以日後要不斷傷人，那就不得不回到移情別戀的創傷現場：

> 心中一動，少女時種種溫馨旖旎的風光突然湧向胸頭，但隨即想起，自己本可與意中人一生廝守，那知這世上另外有個何沅君在，竟令自己丟盡臉面，一世孤單淒涼，想到此處，心中一瞬間湧現的柔情蜜意，登時盡化爲無窮怨毒。（《神鵰》44）

對李莫愁而言，情之傷人正在於「丟盡臉面」，由自戀的受創到顧影自憐的淒涼。小說中不斷描呈李莫愁爲出色美人，「美目流盼、桃腮帶暈」，「明眸皓齒、膚色白膩」。而失戀則像是「丟盡臉面」的毀容，將一切華美錦繡破壞殆盡。如果「外納」（excorporative）式的愛戀關係，是將自己如紅花錦帕般「交」出去，無怨無悔；那自戀「內涵」（incorporative）式的愛戀關係，則是與紅花錦帕間形成一種海市蜃樓般的映鏡關係，錦帕如魔鏡，沈醉愛河時便是情人眼中、魔鏡之前的曠世美女，而情斷緣絕後則鏡裂人毀、怨毒一世。

故紅花錦帕的精神分裂，正在於既讓李莫愁瞧見美麗多情的自己，也驚瞥殘毀被棄的自己，「紅花綠葉」召喚的既是理想化的愛情「小客體（物件）」（*objet a*），也是因「被棄」（cast off）而強遭排除的「非主非客」（abject）。故而紅花綠葉錦帕雖一時保住了程英與陸無雙的命，卻未必能在日後再讓李莫愁手下留情。

> 楊過又從懷中取出兩片半邊錦帕，鋪在床頭几上，道：「這帕子請你一並取了去罷！」李莫愁臉色大變，拂塵一揮，將兩塊帕子捲了過去，怔怔的拿在手中，一時間思潮起伏，心神不定。程英和陸無雙互視一眼，都是臉上暈紅，料不到對方竟將帕子給了楊過，而他卻當面取了出來。
>
> 這幾下你望我、我望你，心事脈脈，眼波盈盈，茅屋中本來一團肅殺之氣，霎時間盡化爲濃情密意。程英琴中那「桃夭」之曲更是彈得纏綿歡悅。
>
> 突然之間，李莫愁將兩片錦帕扯成四截，說道：「往事已矣，夫復何言？」雙手一陣急扯，往空拋出，錦帕碎片有如梨花亂落。（《神鵰》599）

此時兩個半塊錦帕已被重新銘刻，程英與陸無雙各自在不讓對方知曉的情況下「贈帕」給楊過，自是對其情深一片，寧可己亡也要楊郎平安無恙的心意。原李莫愁贈陸展元的定情之物，現倒成了一對表姊妹不約而同芳心託屬的信物。但如今這「小客體（物件）」與「非主非客」的精神分裂，使得心神不定的李莫愁終將錦帕扯爲碎片，往事的煙消雲散莫非眞在於愛情信物的屍骨無存？

但如果如前所述「鴛鴦織就欲雙飛」與「花紅欲滴」皆是戀物如戀屍般的愛情凝止，那麼有屍骨無存的愛情信物，是否也有屍骨無存的愛人遺骸呢？在《神鵰》開場和李莫愁一般前來陸家莊尋仇的，尚有昔日大理國將軍、一燈大師門下漁樵耕讀的農夫武三通，他在得知義女阿沅已入土爲安的消息後，竟挖墳盜屍，其目的並非毀屍洩憤，而是癡情地要再見義女一面。如此恐怖駭人的舉止，或可用其早已失心發瘋一語帶過，但「戀屍」的瘋狂行徑，卻因武三通頸上所掛之圍飾而再次展現戀物即戀屍的連帶：

> 那人滿頭亂髮，鬍鬚也是蓬蓬鬆鬆如刺蝟一般，鬚髮油光烏黑，照說年紀不大，可是滿臉皺紋深陷，卻似七八十歲老翁，身穿藍布直綴，頸中掛著個嬰兒所用的錦緞圍涎，圍涎上繡著幅花貓撲蝶圖，已然陳舊破爛。（《神鵰》8）

錦緞圍涎是義女阿沅小時的用品，而今被武三通愛屋及烏地帶在身上，在亂倫禁忌的運作下，武三通所戀之物不是亭亭玉立、嬌美可愛的何沅君之衣裳飾品，反倒回返孩童時期可摟可抱、天眞無邪的父女親情想像。錦緞圍涎之上不僅有花貓撲蝶圖，更有阿沅的口涎鼻涕，而今自是加雜著武三通的涕淚與涎液。此戀物之瘋狂大抵也不下於挖墳盜屍的瘋狂，一是執意她未死，一是執意她未長大，死的人與死的物盡皆神靈活現在武三通的身上心裡。

當然另一個能與此處同等驚怖駭人的戀屍戀物，大概要算鐵屍梅超風的人皮九陰眞經了。當郭靖幼時以短劍無意中刺中銅屍陳玄風的肚臍罩門後，眼已瞎的鐵屍梅超風原本怕師兄陰間冷淸而欲殉情，卻因摸到短劍上的「楊康」二字而欲先報此仇。然黑風雙煞原本爲桃花島黃藥師門下的同門師兄妹，卻因互通款曲，在竊得師父的「九陰眞經」下半部後亡命天涯。然陳玄風雖與梅超風有夫妻之親，卻決意不肯出示眞經原本，怕她貪多務得、走火入魔，

故皆是自己參悟習練之後，再行轉授妻子。故在陳玄風猝死之後，報仇心切的梅超風自是努力在丈夫遺體之上找尋真經：

> 我仔細的摸索，原來他胸口用針刺著細字和圖形，原來這就是「九陰真經」的秘要。「你怕寶經被人盜去，於是刺在身上，將原經燒毀了！」是啊，像師父這般大的本事，真經也會給咱們偷來，誰又保得定沒人來偷咱們的呢？你這主意是「人在經在，人亡經亡」。我用匕首把你胸口的皮肉割下來，嗯，我要把這塊皮好好硝製了，別讓它腐爛，我永遠帶在身邊，你就永遠陪著我。（《神鵰》394）

硝製的人皮既是「九陰真經」的武學秘要，也是情郎永不腐爛的身體部分，黑風雙煞雖心狠手辣、惡事做絕，平日也粗魯互喚「賊漢子、臭婆娘」，但一句平鋪直敘的「我永遠帶在身邊，你就永遠陪著我」，卻道盡所有戀物者的癡狂，毛骨聳然中好一個「人在情在，人亡情未亡」的生死相許。「九陰真經」是武功戀物學的至寶，而人皮則是水裡來、火裡去、生相隨、死相依的部分愛人遺體，《射鵰》做為一部情意纏綿的武俠小說而言，人皮「九陰真經」這種屍中之屍、寶中之寶，該是愛情戀物與武學戀物中令人拍案稱奇、嘆為觀止的結合。

六、翡翠小鞋：偷心與竊物

　　前兩節以兩方錦帕做愛情信物的細節閱讀，而本節愛情私密信物的焦點則轉到與身體更為貼密的繡鞋。錦帕為愛人而縫製，以圖與詞託寓絲羅；而繡鞋則更像錦緞圍涎，多了身體的分泌、排泄與氣味，且更較圍涎具性意涵上的想像空間。而本節討論更是要以繡鞋為出發，探究偷心與竊物在禮物層次上的巧妙轉合，丟了心的人失魂落魄，掉了物的人倉皇失措，一隻繡鞋便貫穿了比武招親的熱鬧與殺人滅口的兇殘，既是嫁女的禮物也是嫁禍的證物。

　　化名為穆易的楊鐵心，帶著義女穆念慈四處「比武招親」，只道小女及笄、未許婆家，不圖富貴，只望是個武藝超群的好漢，凡能勝得穆念慈一拳一腳者，即將其婚配。小王爺完顏康馳馬而過，與生父見面不相識，卻因一時輕浮貪玩而下場比試。先是一時大意，被穆念慈扯下半截錦袍長袖，後用掌抓

鈎穆念慈手腕、抱在懷裡輕薄：

> 那少女急了，飛腳向他太陽穴踢去，要叫他不能不放開了手。那公子右臂鬆脱，
> 舉手一擋，反腕鈎出，又已拿住了她踢過來的右腳。他這擒拿功夫竟是得心應手，
> 擒腕得腕，拿足得足。那少女更急，奮力抽足，腳上那隻繡著紅花的繡鞋竟然離
> 足而去，但總算掙脱了他的懷抱，坐在地下，含羞低頭，摸著白布的襪子。那公
> 子嘻嘻而笑，把繡鞋放在鼻邊作勢一聞。(《射鵰》286)

只見完顏康披上錦袍，將繡鞋放入懷中就要離去，既拒穆易的許婚也拒歸還
繡鞋，對他而言此「采頭」不能不留，其輕薄放肆的行徑，就連站在一旁觀
戰的郭靖也不免催其還鞋，而和完顏康纏鬥了起來。

　　不論這場比武招親是如何由喜事一樁變得血濺當場，但繡鞋定情卻是穆
念慈與楊康一段孽緣的開啟。在眾目睽睽的擂台之上，一對璧人比試拳腳，
「只見那公子滿場遊走，身上錦袍燦然生光；那少女進退趨避，紅衫絳裙，似
乎化作了一團紅雲」(《射鵰》284)，而有趣的是比武中無意奪自對方身上的
物事 (一截斷袖與一隻繡鞋)，卻成為日後相思戀物的愛情憑證。紅花繡鞋自
是比紅花錦帕、鴛鴦錦帕有更豐富的文化與性意涵。鞋同音於「諧」與「偕」，
故婚俗納采上多用鞋與銅鏡當吉祥物，取其「同偕到老」之意，而同時鞋也
一直是佛洛依德在談論「性戀物」(sexual fetishism) 上重要的轉喻式替
代。[7]

　　但這場比武招親所凸顯的性別交易，卻不是只有被楊康強行取走的「采
頭」繡鞋而已，比武招親的真正采頭當然是穆念慈的身體，贏了她才能贏得
她。如此的思考方式，自然讓我們把繡鞋做為楊康、穆念慈二人之間「定情」
禮物的閱讀，擴展為穆念慈做為穆易與完顏康之間「定親」(定下翁婿關係)
禮物的閱讀。(雖然楊鐵心與楊康本就為生身父子不需另行「定親」；也雖然
因完顏康擂台輕浮而令穆易不恥) 前面我們已由莫斯的「禮」論，談及各種
經由交換禮物而建立之人際關係與情感連帶，而莫斯之後將其「禮」論發揚
光大的第一人，自非李維史陀 (Claude Lévi-Strauss) 莫屬，他的《親族基
本結構》(*The Elementary Structures of Kinship*) 便是將莫斯原有的物品

7　有關精神分析「性戀物」的討論，可參閱《慾望新地圖》，頁 10-18。

交換加入性別的面向，點撥出不同男性氏族間關係之建立乃是以交換女人行之。

換言之，穆易比武招親爲的不是義女的終生幸福，穆易比武招親的眞正目的是爲尋訪故友郭嘯天之子，或其他能人異士助其雪恥復仇，而義女之爲采頭禮物，正在於建立兩個男人之間的關係名份。我們看見的不僅是白底紅花錦旗上繡著「比武招親」四個金字，我們也看見了「錦旗左側地下插著一桿鐵槍，右側插著兩枝鑌鐵短戟」（《射鵰》280）。只是被交換之禮物自己有了主見，不僅將義父遺物（刻著郭靖名姓的短劍）送給了黃蓉，更千里尋郎，夜夜在楊康窗外瞧著影子出神。

穆念慈的情竇初開，一片春心盡皆在相思戀物上纏綿，這番自言自語、失魂落魄，看在黃蓉眼中也不禁大大稱奇：

> 只聽得房中微微風響，她眼睜一線，卻見穆念慈在炕前迴旋來去，虛擬出招，繡帕卻已套在臂上，原來是半截撕下來的衣袖。她斗然而悟：「那日她與小王爺比武，這是從他錦袍上扯下的。」但見穆念慈嘴角邊帶著微笑，想是在回思當日的情景，時而輕輕踢出一腳，隔了片刻又打出一拳，有時又眉毛上揚、衣袖輕拂，儼然是完顏康那副又輕薄又傲慢的神氣。她這般陶醉了好一陣子，走向炕邊。（《射鵰》502-503）

繡帕變衣袖，自是回返當日擂台現場，只是此時穆念慈一人分飾二角，既是輕薄挑釁的少年，也是含羞低頭的少女。周伯通「分心二用，左右互搏」的心法，在這裡倒成了「分身二用，左右互薄（輕薄）」，套上情人的衣袖變成情人，再與自己拳腳纏綿，衣袖戀物成了相思劇場的道具，栩栩搬演。

而那廂的楊康也因穆念慈款款深情而動心，動了心的楊康竟也如穆念慈一般顛倒，而與愛人物事「戀人絮語」了起來：

> 完顏康目送她越牆而出，怔怔出神，但見風拂樹梢，數星在天，回進房來，鐵槍上淚水未乾，枕衾間溫香猶在，回想適才之事，眞似一夢。只見被上遺有幾莖秀髮，是她先前掙扎時落下來的，完顏康撿了起來，放入了荷包。（《射鵰》507）

與穆念慈的一番溫存，讓楊康心魂俱醉，鐵槍已不是認祖歸宗／背祖忘宗的遺物掙扎，而是沾有愛人淚水的物事，與留有愛人溫香的枕衾並置。而放入

荷包中的愛人秀髮，則又是一則性戀物的佳話。[8] 相思的勾魂懾魄，將愛人身上的物事迷魅化，既見物如見人，也觸物如觸人。像後來楊康被困，囑穆念慈將其腰帶刻上「完顏康有難，在太湖西畔歸雲莊」去求援，大難當前之際穆念慈卻依然「撫摸腰帶」而神馳：

> 想在不久之前，這金帶還是圍在那人腰間，只盼他平安無恙，又再將這金帶圍在
> 身上；更盼他深明大義，自己得與他締結鴛盟，親手將這帶子給他繫上。痴痴的
> 想了一會，將腰帶繫在自己衣衫之內，忍不住心中一蕩：「這條帶子，便如是他
> 手臂抱著我的腰一般。」霎時間紅暈滿臉，再也不敢多想。（《射鵰》537-538）

套上愛人的衣袖一如繫上愛人的腰帶，既是愛戀憧憬也是身體感應，愛戀幻象的物質基礎與物件之上的愛戀幻象，總是這般卿卿我我、難捨難離。

但不論是繡鞋、衣袖、秀髮或腰帶，皆無力反轉穆念慈與楊康的坎坷情路，而他們因繡鞋招親結緣而特意雕製的一對玉鞋，卻在日後一場故佈疑陣、殺人嫁禍的場景中，成為偵破懸案的關鍵線索。歐陽鋒與楊康計殺江南五怪，將其棄屍在黃藥師亡妻之墓中，佈置成五怪盜墓寶未果而遭東邪擊斃的場面，使得郭靖與黃藥師反目成仇、黃蓉左右為難。而此天衣無縫栽贓一事的破案線索，卻是妙手書生朱聰死時緊緊握在手中的一隻翡翠小鞋，正面鞋底有「比」字、反面有「招」字。好在黃蓉聰穎慧黠，總算從其中猜出此乃楊康與穆念慈私訂終身的定情之物而破案。

玉鞋的香豔典故、浪漫傳奇，楊康與穆念慈各執「比」、「招」與「武」、「親」的　隻，以成雙成對。但怎知朱聰在臨死之前施展妙手，從兇手楊康懷中取得此物。朱聰此舉當是要以此翡翠小鞋為證物線索，盼沉冤大白，但卻也牽扯出另一種偷竊與禮物之間微妙的關連。《射鵰》開場便有跛子曲三在雪地上擊殺朝廷命官，只因他往皇宮大內盜取金器玉器與卷軸，卻又正氣凜然地說道：「這些物事，是我去臨安皇宮中盜來的。皇帝害苦了百姓，拿他一些從百姓身上搜括來的金銀，算不得是賊贓。」（《射鵰》17）但如果這些金銀算不得是賊贓，那日後的敘事也告訴我們曲三亦非俠盜，郭靖與黃蓉誤闖傻姑家中密室療傷，才驚見各式價值連城的珠玉珍寶、青銅器與書畫卷軸，

---

8 有關頭髮戀物的討論，亦可參閱《慾望新地圖》，頁 13-14。

而曲三即其師兄曲靈風，其不惜爲「蒐集」珍玩而葬命，只爲師父黃藥師好此道而意求其歡心。

堆滿異寶珍品的密室，令人不禁想起另一個壙室：「壙室中壁間案頭盡是古物珍玩、名畫法書，沒一件不是價值連城的精品。黃藥師當年縱橫湖海，不論是皇宮內院、巨宦富室，還是大盜山寨之中，只要有甚麼奇珍異寶，他不是明搶硬索，就是暗偷潛盜，必當取到手中方罷。」（《射鵰》772）黃藥師這番將明珠美玉、翡翠瑪瑙盡皆供在亡妻的壙室之中，自是情深意重的表現，但這由師到徒皆一般以「蒐集」、「搜羅」名義行之的竊盜行爲，與喪身壙室之中、素以偷竊爲武功見長的妙手書生又有何差別？

這些明偷暗盜若從精神分析的角度視之自是另有端倪，「所謂的偷竊癖，常可回溯到孩童因缺乏愛的證明而覺受傷或無人重視的事實……偷竊癖爲失去的快樂找到替代的快樂，而同時是對造成此種所謂不公不義之人的報復。精神分析顯示在我們這些病人的潛意識中存在著相同的衝動，強行將未收到的『禮物』據爲己有。」（Karl Abraham qtd. in Pinch 142）這裡並非要以精神分析爲黃藥師、曲靈風、朱聰等人對症下藥，反倒是要回到先前莫斯「禮」論的架構開開玩笑。正如道格拉斯（Mary Douglas）爲莫斯《禮物》一書所添之前言〈無免費之禮物〉，那秘室與壙室之中「盜竊」而來的禮物，該是唯一有借無還，既不建立互惠與結盟關係，也不需禮尚往來的「純」禮物了（那洪七公在御膳房中的大快朵頤，難不成也是「天底下沒有白吃的午餐」之反證）。而更有趣的是，妙手書生這不請自取楊康懷中的禮物，不也正是楊穆定情的信物，不正也成了黃蓉神算破案的證物嗎？翡翠小鞋由禮物、信物到證物的身份轉換，既是愛情也是栽贓更是兇殺的痕跡，竟帶出偷心與竊物在戀物學上難以軒輊的曖昧。

七、樹皮兒衫：絕情古墓與衣衫記憶

在英文裡有個對記憶的物質性基礎最佳之語言表達："memories"，既指「記憶」也指衣衫之上手肘膝蓋處所造成的「摺痕」。在歷數過各種結拜、定情的物事之後，讓我們回到神鵰俠侶本身，看一看楊過與小龍女之間情愛記憶的衣衫摺痕。

楊過與小龍女聚散依依，身雖離、心常繫，終南山下活死人墓一別後，楊過便是帶著一身由姑姑傳授的武藝與一身由姑姑縫製的衣衫闖盪江湖。然衣久必舊，看在暗戀楊過的程英眼裡，自是心憐不捨，逐熬夜縫製一件針腳綿密的青布長袍給楊過換上。一直要到李莫愁的道袍被老鐵匠馮默風的鐵錘鐵拐燒得衣不蔽體而楊過慨然贈袍之時，衣衫做為情愛專一投注的祕密才被揭曉。

> 程英見楊過將自己所縫的袍子送給李莫愁，當時情勢緊迫，那也罷了，但他新袍底下仍是穿著那件破破爛爛的舊袍子，顯見這袍子因是小龍女所縫，他親疏有別，決不忘舊。程英心中微微一酸，裝作渾不在意。(《神鵰》631)

而後小龍女與楊過重逢絕情谷，楊過的舊袍子又被樊一翁抓出個大破洞，小龍女也就在眾目睽睽之下、殺機四伏之中，從懷中取出針線包，拿小剪刀在自己衣角上剪下一塊白布替楊過縫補，「當二人同在古墓之時，楊過衣服破了，小龍女就這樣將他拉在身邊，替他縫補，這些年來也不知有過多少次。」(《神鵰》716)

而這件破破爛爛、補了又補的袍子，居然在楊過與公孫綠萼被公孫止打下鱷魚潭時，又先後為公孫綠萼與裘千尺遮身蔽體，直到裘千尺逼婚未果，楊過與小龍女攜手離去之際，才由公孫綠萼雙手捧來歸還：

> 楊過心想留在這裡徒然多費唇舌，手指在劍刃上一彈，和著劍刃振起的嗡嗡之聲，朗聲吟道：「熒熒白兔，東走西顧。衣不如新，人不如故。」挽起一個劍花，攜著小龍女的手轉身便走。
> 綠萼聽著「衣不如新，人不如故」那兩句話，更是傷心欲絕，取過更換下來的楊過那件破衫，雙手捧著走到他面前，悄然道：「楊大哥，衣服也還是舊的好。」
> 楊過道：「謝謝你。」伸手接過。(《神鵰》804-805)

「衣不如新，人不如故」，然故人所贈之衣，就是破爛襤褸也要真心愛惜；「兄弟如手足，妻子如衣服」，楊過這件由妻子縫製的衣服，卻是千金不換、比自己手足尚珍貴的身體物質記憶。

然而這個會破損污舊的衣衫記憶，卻在另一個時空以另一種轉換的形式借屍還魂。十六年後楊過再臨絕情谷舊地，苦候多日、焦心如焚，仍未見小

龍女現身，遂心傷腸斷地縱身躍入深谷之中。那知谷底有深潭，潭邊大樹排列著數十個蜂巢，而樹皮也曾爲人所剝去，楊過一路推敲，竟尋得茅屋一間：

> 舉步入內，一瞥眼間，不由得全身一震，只見屋中陳設簡陋，但潔淨異常，堂上只一桌一几，此外便無別物，桌几放置的方位他卻熟悉之極，竟與古墓石室中的桌椅一模一樣。他也不加思量，自然而然的向右側轉去，果然是間小室，過了小室，是間較大的房間。房中床榻桌椅，全與古墓中楊過的臥室相同，只是古墓中用具大都石製，此處的卻是粗木搭成。
>
> 但見室右有榻，是他幼時練功的寒玉床；室中凌空拉著一條長繩，是他練輕功時睡臥所用；窗前小小一几，是他讀書寫字之處。室左立著一個粗糙木櫥，拉開櫥門，只見櫥中放著幾件樹皮結成的兒童衣衫，正是從前在古墓時小龍女爲自己所縫製的模樣。他自進室中，撫摸床几，早已淚珠盈眶，這時再也忍耐不住，眼淚撲簌簌的滾下衣衫。（《神鵰》1598-1599）

令楊過大吃一驚的，自是此屋內陳設乃古墓石室的翻版，寒玉床、長繩、書几與樹皮衣衫一件不差。想來小龍女能幽居深谷十六年，靠的不只是古墓派玉女功養生修煉少語少事、少喜少愁的規條，更用的是昔日包惜弱「地點複製、時間固置」的方式，以承認且否認變易的心態，活在凝止的戀物時空。

　　古墓自身本就結合「子宮」與「墳墓」的想像，而今小龍女在絕情谷底複製古墓，起居作息猶如昔日在古墓一般，自是谷底無歲月的時空靜止之法。木櫥裡用樹皮結成的兒童衣衫，更具體而微地表徵了這種戀物凝止的心理機制，莫怪乎小龍女與楊過在劫難重重、生離死別後重聚，飽歷憂患、大悲大喜的楊過早已兩鬢如霜，但看在屏絕思慮欲念而容貌未變的小龍女眼中，卻是溫柔一句：「不是老了，是我的過兒長大了。」（《神鵰》1599）而這變與不變、成年與孩童、時間的流逝與凝止，更在楊過因喜極忘形而跳上大樹連翻觔斗時更形彰顯：

> 小龍女從身邊取出手帕，本來在終南山之時，楊過翻罷觔斗，笑嬉嬉的走到她身旁，小龍女總是拿手帕給他抹去額上汗水，這時見他走近，臉不紅，氣不喘，那裡有什麼汗水？但她還是拿手帕替他在額頭抹了幾下。（《神鵰》1600）

翻觔斗是楊過幼年習以爲常的頑童作爲，而手帕拭汗則是小龍女慣常的疼愛

動作，只是昔日頑童已是今日武功精湛的神鵰大俠，翻觔斗之時早以上乘輕功，在半空中矯夭騰挪，那有汗水可拭？正如憂心悄悄、兩鬢星星的中年人，那需兒衫來試？而小龍女依舊用樹皮手帕拭汗、用樹皮經絡織衣，都是以不變應萬變的戀物凝止。

而這變與不變的奧妙，又更是《神鵰》中武功與愛情間的玄學。過去在談論武功與愛情之關連時，論者最常以「玉女心經」最後一章的雙劍合璧為例，武功必須以情愛為底，必須是情意相通、未結絲蘿的愛侶之間眉來眼去、心有靈犀，在亦喜亦憂、亦甜亦苦中冒死以相救，全力彌補對方的破綻（破綻是否即是一種匱缺，而愛情武功的消弭破綻，是否亦即一種想像期的豐美圓滿？）。而對比於這種在武功搏擊生死關頭的男歡女悅，自是楊過日後「黯然銷魂掌」的形單影隻、形銷骨立。「玉女心經」中的花前月下、撫琴按蕭、小園藝菊、松下對弈，如今皆成了「黯然銷魂掌」中的徘徊空谷、行屍走肉、廢寢忘食、孤形隻影，前者以成對圓滿否認匱缺，後者則是情愛剝離後的無盡匱缺、盡皆在目。

但在這裡想另闢蹊徑的，倒不是愛情與武功、圓滿與匱缺的對應，而是要用變與不變的辯論方式，探問武功物質性與愛情物質性的差異。就武功物質性而言，其旨在於「變」。楊過從全真教內功口訣、古墓派玉女心經、九陰真經、歐陽鋒蛤蟆功、洪七公打狗棒法到黃藥師的彈指神通、玉簫劍法，每有奇遇便內力玄功大增。而楊過身體的物質性也隨年長成人、練功、斷臂等機緣而變化，甚至在性別社會化的過程中，也由原先陰柔嫵媚的美女拳過渡到獨孤求敗既鈍且拙的玄鐵劍。但相對於武功而言，愛情的物質性基礎卻是強調歷久彌新的「不變」，鴛鴦燦然如新、紅花花紅欲滴、會壞會舊的繡鞋「木乃伊化」為翡翠不壞之身，而會爛會破的衣衫也「古墓化」為樹皮兒衫。天若有情天亦老，地若有情地亦荒，難不成戀物凝止便是在有情天地間尋天荒地老的唯一方式？

八、結　語

以上有關《射鵰》、《神鵰》二書中物事與敍事、愛情與戀物間的糾纏，由靖康短劍、楊家鐵槍談到了鴛鴦錦帕、紅花錦帕、翡翠小鞋與樹皮兒衫，

間歇牽連出箭頭髀石、汗血寶馬、銀刀藥瓶、白玉手環、錦緞圍涎、人皮眞經、錦袍斷袖、荷包秀髮、刺字金帶等諸多物事，但就二書中可能之禮物、信物、證物的各式例證，確有未盡詳數之處。像洪七公以「打狗棒法」與打狗棒傳黃蓉，楊過以三根玉蜂針贈郭襄及在其生日宴會上所贈之三件厚禮，王重陽與林朝英的書信禮物往來與化情爲功、以功喩情的心意，或是書中所載各種傳師授徒、承續衣缽的江湖因緣，雖未能一一細部論述，但大抵不脫禮物交易、武俠敍事、兄弟締盟、男女鴦配的討論模式。

　　而就文中有限揀選的幾件禮物、信物與證物而言，歷史、記憶與慾望皆物質化爲物件，事件本身的「不可重複」(unrepeatable)，卻轉化爲物件本身的「可被敍述」(reportable) 與「可被攜帶」(portable)。隨身攜帶的歷史、眼見爲憑的記憶，與化爲觸手可及之物的慾望，愛情物質論與武俠戀物學的虛實眞幻盡皆在此。而在我們手中「撫摸把玩」的《射鵰》、《神鵰》二書，是否也是後設形式上的一種禮物、信物與證物呢？書前盡皆以詩畫碑帖、陶瓷木俑等古物彰顯歷史，是否也是一種化物事爲敍事的邊界戀物書寫呢？戀物癖、偷竊癖又與歷史癖、考據癖有何別何異呢？《射鵰》、《神鵰》二書，既可以是具使用價值、交換價值與符號價值的商品，在書市、傳媒、網路與學術會議之中流通，也可以是具情感價值的戀物，承載成長記憶與慾望投射。入癡武俠奇情，縱橫文史趣言，難不成問「金庸」情是何物的初衷，竟也是戀物化「金庸」的始末。

　　問世間，「金庸」是何物？

參考書目

金　庸
　　1987　《射鵰英雄傳》（臺北：遠流出版公司）。
　　1989　《神鵰俠侶》（臺北：遠流出版公司）。
舒國治
　　1998　《讀金庸偶得》（臺北：遠流出版公司）。
陳　墨
　　1997　《情愛金庸》（臺北：雲龍出版社）。

張小虹

　　1996　《慾望新地圖》（臺北：聯合文學出版社）。

Appadurai, Arjun

　　1986　"Introduction: Commodities and the Politics of Value." *The Social Life of Things*. Ed. A. Appadurai. Cambridge: Cambridge UP, 3-63.

Bergson, Henri

　　1988　*Matter and Memory*. Trans. N. M. Paul and W. S. Palmer. New York: Zone Books.

Butler, Judith

　　1993　*Bodies that Matter: On the Discursive Limits of 'Sex'*. New York: Routledge.

Douglas, Mary

　　1990　"Foreword: No Free Gifts." *The Gift*. Marcel Mauss. Trans. W. D. Halls. New York: Routledge. vii-xviii.

Mauss, Marcel

　　1967　*The Gift: Forms and Functions of Exchange in Archaic Societies*. 1925. Trans. Ian Cunnison. New York: Norton.

Pinch, Adela

　　　　　"Stealing Happiness: Shoplifting in Early Nineteenth-Century England." Spyer 122-49.

Silverman, Kaja

　　1996　*The Threshold of the Visible World*. New York: Routledge.

Spyer, Patricia

　　1998　"Introduction." *Border Fetishisms: Material Objects in Unstable Spaces*. Ed. Patricia Spyer. New York: Routledge. 1-11.

Stallybrass, Peter

　　　　　"Marx's Coat." Spyer 183-207.

Stewart, Susan

　　1993　*On Longing: Narratives of the Miniature, the Gigantic, the Souvenir, the Collection*. Durham: Duke UP.

他不看她時她在嗎？
——以《天龍八部》中段正淳身邊的女性為例
談自戀、戀物、攻擊慾

黃　宗　慧

國立臺灣大學外國語文學系

摘　要

　　本論文由精神分析的觀點出發，解讀金庸小說《天龍八部》中段正淳身邊的女性因失去所愛而展現的種種「變態」面向——如自戀、戀物及攻擊慾等等。筆者以為，欲理解這些心理現象，斷不能從父權的思考出發，認定女性心性便有自戀及拜物的傾向，而善妒及好勾心鬥角等特質又使女性特別容易互相為難，甚至如我們在小說中看到的，自相殘殺。依據精神分析的理論來思考這些看似專屬女性的病象，將能發現其成因與個人觀看／認同的模式密切相關：局限在想像認同中的主體，不分男女，都特別容易產生自戀、戀物的情結或發展出過強的攻擊慾，而即使一般觀察顯示，女性確實較男性容易困於想像認同的階段，這其中也有社會文化因素的介入，不能僅以性別天性使然來解釋。為釐清以上的概念，本論文除闡述法國精神分析師拉岡提出的想像認同相關理論外，並以金庸筆下自戀的馬夫人、執戀山茶的王夫人、以及其他數位困陷愛恨情愁而產生侵略或報復行為的女子為例，來說明由想像出發的觀看／認同模式所造成的現象及其危險所在。藉由對金庸小說的精神分析式閱讀，期能打破傳統女性主義論述對男性中心的武俠小說的撻伐，以更細膩的分析來解釋這些負面女性形象背後的成因與問題，並進一步開發女性主體由此困境中掙脫的可能性。

一、前　言

　　在武俠小說所呈現的陽剛世界中，女性角色所被分派的「任務」一直頗為固定，也就是為男主角在忠孝節義、武林恩怨的情節之外勾勒另一條愛恨情仇的支線，而在這樣的情況下，女性角色也就難免被類型化，她們的存在意義往往是依附在男性角色身上的，而所言所行也常常是為了爭取男性的鍾情；本論文雖然也是從一個看來相當女性主義的詰問——「他不看她時她在嗎？」——出發來研究《天龍八部》中段正淳身邊的女性，但要申述的卻不是金庸小說如何牴觸了女性主義的訴求。雖然如果我們要列舉金庸小說中願意為男主角生、為男主角死的女性角色，可以舉出不少的例子，但一來金庸小說所形塑的女性角色類型變化其實頗多，以某些例子來斷定金庸對女角的刻劃出自父權中心主義並不甚公允；二來這樣的批評實在屢見不鮮，以至於似乎具有女性主義的意識便無法享受閱讀金庸小說的樂趣。本論文因此希望跳出將武俠小說看成女性主義者要誓師討伐的讀（毒）物這樣的傳統，藉由檢視小說中負面的女性角色其觀看／認同的方式，積極地釐清：金庸筆下某些負面形象的女性角色她們的認同模式到底出了什麼問題，以至於陷溺在依附男性而生的處境中難以自拔？透過精神分析的閱讀方式，有沒有另一種有別於這些女子所採取的觀看方式，可以將（女性）主體自愛慾情仇的狹隘空間中釋放出來？

　　「他不看她時她在嗎？」這樣的一個問題其實是挪用拉岡（Jacques Lacan）的精神分析思考所發出的詰問。在科學界，Bohr 提出量子力學此一學說，認為一個物理量只有在當它被測量之後才是實在的；之後，持反對觀點的 Einstein 表示，一個嚴謹的物理理論應該要區別「客觀實體」以及這個理論運作的觀點，客觀實體應獨立於理論而存在，Einstein 問道：「難道月亮只有在我看她的時候才存在嗎？」拉岡的精神分析傾向接受量子力學提出的反省，肯定了主體的觀看與否及觀看方式在在影響到他所看到的結果，如此一來，「我不看月亮的時候，她就形同不在」便不再是荒謬絕倫的說法。如果武俠小說中的世界可以看做是中國傳統社會的縮影，而女性的存在依附於男性而生又幾乎是武俠世界中的必然，從精神分析的觀點來看，我們會發現，

的確是有某種觀看／認同方式特別容易使女性被定位／將自己定位於這種「他不看我時我彷彿不存在」的處境，而《天龍八部》中段正淳的眾情人所展現的侵略、報復等行爲與這種觀看方式更有著密切的關係：這些女子觀看自身及他者的模式顯然頗有問題，以至於段正淳「不看她」（不將之視爲慾望的客體）的時候，就導致其主體存在意義的虛無，甚至種種毀滅性的舉動。透過對金庸文本的分析及對精神分析相關理論的釐清，本論文將試圖證明，只有當這些依附男性而生的女性角色體會到慾望主體的眞相其實是「我不看它時它就等於不在」，她們才能逆轉「他不看我時我就不存在」的宿命。

在《天龍八部》中，與段正淳有過一段情的女子在他離去之後幾乎仍過著被過去情感牽絆、沒有主體性可言的生活：或者如秦紅棉自名幽谷客，大有自戀自憐「絕代有佳人，幽居在空谷」（第七回，金 268）之意，在隱居的生活中則不時練著段正淳曾傳授她的五羅輕煙掌來回味過去；或者如王夫人在山莊種滿茶花，以此爲留住遠去的情人的方式；或者如段正淳的元配刀白鳳，因丈夫處處留情而出家，成了云空未必空的玉虛散人；不過這些爲情所困的女性顯然有別於傳統描繪下願意爲男主角犧牲一切的癡情女子，因爲她們幾乎都有著極強的攻擊慾與報復心：每練一次五羅輕煙掌就要發一次脾氣的秦紅棉以追殺段正淳其他情人爲終生職志；嗜種茶花的王夫人不是憐花葬花的溫柔女子，而是慣將負心漢處死做花肥的狠角；而刀白鳳則以委身「天下最醜陋、最汙穢、最卑賤」的男子來報復丈夫的薄倖；至於段正淳的情人中最令人髮指、由愛生恨地將段正淳肩頭肉都咬下的馬夫人康敏，更是一個不可忽視的角色，自負美貌的她竟因爲喬峯正眼也不瞧她一眼就設下毒計加害他。喬峯看不看她眞的有那麼要緊嗎？何以他對康敏美色的視若無睹竟然釀成後來一連串的悲劇？我們不妨就從極度自戀的康敏開始，來看看自戀的觀看模式究竟是如何進行的、又會造成什麼樣的後果。

二、一切從自戀開始

馬夫人惡狠狠的道：「你難道沒生眼珠子嗎？憑他是多出名的英雄好漢，都要從頭至腳的向我細細打量。有些德高望重的人，就算不敢向我正視，乘旁人不覺，總還是向我偷偷的瞧上幾眼。只有你，只有你……哼，百花會中一千多個男人，

就只你自始至終没瞧我……洛陽百花會中，男子漢以你居首，女子自然以我爲第
一。你竟不向我好好的瞧上幾眼，我再自負美貌，又有什麼用？那一千多人便再
爲我神魂顛倒，我心裡又怎能舒服？」（第廿四回，金 1024）

　　關於自戀，最通俗的詮釋便是個體對自我的過度愛戀。至於自戀與女人
之間的關係可以說是淵源久遠，不但現在普遍的社會價值觀仍然認爲女性比
男性來得自戀，精神分析大師佛洛依德更早已指出女人與自戀有著不解之
結。按照精神分析的理解，自戀是一種由自身，而非他人來激起性覺醒的現
象，有原初自戀（primary narcissism）和次發自戀（secondary narcissism）
之分：前者指的是嬰兒期喜歡自己的身體，以自己的身體做爲慾力（libido）
的對象，從而獲得滿足；後者則是指兒童期以後，個體將自己原應外投的慾
力收回，由愛戀別人轉而愛戀自己，從而陶醉於自我想像之中。根據佛洛依
德的看法，次發自戀基本上自然是一種女性的特質，因爲女性的陽具欽羨
（penis-envy）會使她們感覺到先天上劣於男性，而爲了補償這種匱缺感，女
性就會不由自主地在後天上尋求對抗這種失落感的方式，因而高度地關懷、
欣賞、愛戀自己的容貌。相對的，男性既然不受陽具欽羨之苦，也就較少呈
現出自戀的傾向。做出這樣的推論之後，佛洛依德還特別強調這並非出自他
個人詆毀女性的慾望（Gay 555）：女性，特別是外貌好看的女性，分外會藉
由自戀來尋求自我滿足，因爲社會對於她們可以選擇的愛戀對象實在是強加
了太多限制；她們不但因此特別有自戀的傾向，而且在感情的模式中也是需
要被愛，而不是主動去愛（Gay 554）。在此，用陽具欽羨來斷言女性會因感
到自身的匱缺而發展成過度自戀，實在有本質論的嫌疑，我們當然可以指控
這是男性精神分析師對女性的污名化，然後一舉切斷女人與自戀間由來已久
的強制聯結，但佛氏關於社會的種種箝制會把女性推向自戀一途的這項觀
察，其實是頗值得重視的。當父權社會予以女性重重制約，使其做爲主體的
慾望與行動多受打壓而不得滿足時，女性是否有可能傾向於把自己當成一個
被慾望的客體，藉由把被壓抑的愛戀與慾望投注於自己身上來得到滿足，也
因此即使當她在面對愛戀對象時，也往往是延續著自戀的模式，希望被愛、
被注視，而不懂如何主動去愛？以下精神分析式的閱讀也許可以提供我們一
些線索。

　　和段正淳有過一段情、嫁給馬大元、色誘白世鏡及全冠淸的馬夫人康敏，其所做所爲可以說是把自戀發展到極至的具體代表，陳墨評其爲「自戀成狂」──「她的一生只愛她自己。她的美貌，她的智慧，她的心願，她的花衣服，她的情郎……她的她的！一切都是她的！……她從來也沒有愛過丈夫馬大元；也從來沒有愛過其他的人（甚至包括段正淳），並且永遠也不可能愛除自己以外的任何人！」（《情愛金庸》211）──恐怕沒有任何讀者會有異議。不過康敏的自戀是否「已經是不可理喻，從而一般的人無法猜知她內心的究竟，她的言行舉止，也無法被人所預料、所理解」（《情愛金庸》211-12），倒也不見得那麼絕對，從精神分析的觀點來看，我們可以一窺這種自戀機制的運作方式。在康敏的例子裡，我們會發現一個疑點：如果自戀指涉的是像西方那希塞斯（Narcissus）愛上自己水中倒影的例子一樣，那種自信地認定自己就是最值得愛戀的對象、不假外求的狀態，那麼自戀成狂的康敏大可以不受任何外界的影響，肯定自己是最美貌的女子，至於在她口中不算什麼東西，「不過是一群臭叫化的頭兒，有甚麼神氣了？」的喬峯看不看她，又何損她對自己美貌的認定？從這個弔詭的現象，我們正可以追索出自戀的觀看模式本身如何的脆弱：不但需要仰賴他者的凝望來支撐，更是侵略與攻擊慾的本源。

　　不同於佛洛依德以本質論的陽具欽羨理論來解釋自戀，法國精神分析巨擘拉岡以鏡像階段（mirror stage）來闡釋自戀的機制如何形成及運作，顯然更具有啓發性。對拉岡而言，六到十八個月的幼兒對自己的鏡像即有特殊的迷戀：人類的出生就解剖學而言，其實屬於一種特殊的早產（premature birth），亦即在系統發育尚不完整、尚帶有母體殘留體液時便已出生。這個有所欠缺的主體卻能在鏡子中認出自己的形象並且表現出對鏡像的無窮興趣，究其因，是要藉由鏡像所提供的完形（Gestalt）來實現自己期望成熟的目的，換句話說，鏡像認同乃是一個「從不足到期待」(from insufficiency to antici-pation)的過程，主體藉此將其實並不完整的身體透過鏡像所提供的幻覺形象延伸爲全形(Lacan 1977: 3-4)。這樣的原初自戀雖然是主體最早期的認同方式，因此負有不可或缺的階段性使命，但是精神分析也同時強調不能久滯於此階段，而必須接受伊底帕斯化的過程，進入象徵體系之中。鏡像認同到底有什麼樣的問題，使得精神分析理論不斷強調走出鏡像期的重要性？拉岡對此的解釋是，當主體透過鏡像認同來認識自己的時候，他其實也同時發生了

異化（alienation）的現象（Lacan 1993: 39）：因爲他畢竟是靠著那外於自身的他者（other）才認識到自己的存在，因此「我是完整的」此鏡像幻覺成立的同時，也是「我是分裂的」這個事實被揭露的時刻；鏡像認同的弔詭便在於「我就是他者」（Lacan 1993: 39）。正因身體形象從匱缺延伸到完整的期待過程是建立在內部衝突矛盾的鏡像認同上，這種主體內在的衝突所造成的結果便是「攻擊性的競爭」（aggressive competitiveness, Lacan 1977: 19），主體和他的鏡像既同一又分離的這種情境將使他成爲「自己的敵對」（a rival to himself, Lacan 1977: 22）。說得更淺白些，就是主體要靠鏡像他者才能成立自己的這個現象，會使他憂心被他者所取代或控制，因此對他者產生攻擊的慾望。泰瑞莎・布南（Teresa Brennan）因此表示：雖然主體是透過對自己身體的執戀才建立分離主體（a separate being）的，但這種將自己視爲全能的幻想也必將帶來企圖操控（鏡像）他者的慾望（98-99）。職此之故，如果自戀的想像認同稍後不能被象徵認同所取代的話，將會使主體在對待他者時，始終與之處於在想像層次不斷角力的關係之中，既要靠他者來確立自己的存在，又唯恐他者威脅自我的生存，就此陷入嫉妒、偏執、不斷攻擊的危險中。

　　回到金庸小説的文本，我們可以說康敏的表現正吻合自戀模式所造成的種種苦果。乍看之下，康敏已經極度自滿其美貌，喬峯看不看她有什麼關係？經過精神分析對自戀的解讀，我們可以知道喬峯看不看康敏對她而言當然是大大的有關係：因爲自戀並不是我們所想像的那樣一個穩定及自給自足的結構，反而在根本上就是需要某種「外援」才能成立的——那希塞斯也需要水中的倒影才能自詡爲最值得愛戀的慾望標的物。康敏先前能自誇爲百花會中群芳之冠，是因爲無數男子眼中都流露了對她姿色的傾慕，這些英雄好漢、德高望重之人因此都如同她的鏡子，印證了她是值得被慾望的、被愛的這樣的自戀信念，但是正因爲自戀要建立在這種他者的凝望之下，所以康敏自恃美貌的信念絕對不是不可搖撼的；我們看到，當喬峯竟然對康敏視而不見時，康敏的自信就受到了嚴重的衝擊：當康敏指責喬峯「眼光在我臉上掠過，居然沒停留半刻，就當我跟庸脂俗粉沒絲毫分別。僞君子，不要臉的無恥之徒。」（第廿四回，金 1024）時，她的言語間已經充分流露出她的不確定與不安全感，她不能肯定她是不是眞的有別於庸脂俗粉之姿，而這樣的不安是她

所不能接受的，因此只有靠攻擊喬峯——認定喬峯不看她的原因是出於假正經、逞英雄、是僞君子，而不是因爲她自己眞的不夠吸引人——來解決這種不安。其實康敏心裡是否相信自己的說詞？答案應該相當明顯：自戀機制本身結構性的脆弱使康敏無論如何自負美貌，都還是不能自給自足，必須透過與他者的鏡映關係才能完成從不足到期待的過程，而這個期待一旦被喬峯破壞，她無法承受自身不足的結果，便是轉而用攻擊他者來說服自己「不是我不夠好，是他有問題」。

　　康敏在全書中的份量雖然不重，但出場時卻總是令人印象深刻，這除了是因爲她策劃以陷害喬峯及段正淳的毒計招招陰險之外，也因爲她連招供自己的罪行時都顯得那麼志得意滿。當她告訴段正淳自己爲什麼要陷害他時，她先說了一個自己小時候如何害了「花衣服的相思病」的故事，敍述自己過年時盼不到新衣服，又眼見隔壁江家姊姊有新衣可穿，便如何偷偷到隔壁江家剪壞別人的新衣服：

> 我拿起桌上針線籃裡的剪刀，將那件新衣裳剪得粉碎，又把那條褲子剪成了一條條的，永遠縫補不起來。我剪爛了這套新衣新褲之後，心中說不出的歡喜，比我自己有新衣服穿還要痛快。（第廿四回，金 998）

康敏這番話的目的當然是爲了進一步告訴段正淳，她不只對花衣服如此，對人也是如此，如果得不到，就要毀掉：

> 我要叫你明白我的脾氣，從小就是這樣，要是有一件物事我日思夜想，得不到手，偏偏旁人運氣好得到了，那麼我說甚麼也得毀了這件物事。小時候使的是笨法子，年紀慢慢大起來，人也聰明了些，就使些巧妙點的法子啦。（第廿四回，金 999）

這番自述不僅在字面上透露出，康敏得意洋洋於會使聰明法子，是一種嚴重自戀的表現，更重要的是再次展現了自戀所導致的侵略慾。

　　自戀模式中「有他就沒有我」的互斥關係是如此不穩定，以致於主體總是想著要取得主控的位置（Lacan 1993: 93），對待他者的態度也因此充滿攻擊慾，滯留在想像的層次不斷與他者進行拼個你死我活的爭鬥，這也正是精神分析中所說的「邪惡之眼」（evil eye）的運作邏輯：「嫉妒」（*invidia*）這個拉丁字乃是以「去看」（*videre*）爲字根，拉岡據此將嫉妒與觀看做一連結，

表示嫉妒是充滿了貪婪慾念的邪惡之眼與生俱來的力量。而嫉妒與「渴望」、「想要」（*avoir envie*）不能混爲一談，因爲在嫉妒中，慾望的運作並非指向主體眞正需要的東西，而是當主體覺得別人的形象看來比自己完滿時，就會自覺黯然失色，更因此覺得他者威脅了自己的生存，從而產生嫉妒的情結，不管自己到底需不需要別人所擁有的那樣東西，就按照別人的慾望複製自己的慾望，對別人的慾望物產生邪惡的貪念（Lacan 1981: 115-16; Lacan 1993: 39），我們甚至可以說，邪惡之眼在沒有看到別人有那樣自己沒有的東西之前，根本不覺得自己那麼想要那樣東西，然而一旦看到別人有自己沒有，別人比自己完整這樣的感覺就會使他認定自己是眞的極度渴望那樣東西。康敏的極度自戀自然也會使她的渴望化爲一雙邪惡之眼，完全撇開需要的問題，任由毀滅性的慾望蔓延。陳墨在評論康敏的「新衣情結」時，曾表示康敏這個情結的關鍵在於她想要的是「新」衣服，而段正淳、馬大元、喬峯等等都只是一件一件的新衣服，她想穿就穿想脫就脫，並進一步表示「想要穿新衣服，這本是人類的一種極普遍的慾望，女性尤其如此」（《人性金庸》101）。姑且不論想穿新衣是否爲女性特有的慾望，這裡特別值得注意的其實是「想穿新衣」這個情結所透露出的需要（need）與慾望（desire）的差距。穿衣，是保暖禦體的基本需要問題，穿「新」衣卻不是，沒有人非需要新衣不可，所以對新衣的「需求」其實已經是進入慾望層次的問題了，至於康敏對新衣服的慾望，更不折不扣的是出自她邪惡之眼的貪慾：如果康敏是單純的想要新衣服，她再不擇手段，也應該會選擇去偷走衣服據爲己有，而不是以剪爛別人的新衣服爲樂。事實上，康敏稍早的言談間就已經透露了她對新衣服的渴求根本是一種與需要無關的慾念作祟：當被康敏下了藥的段正淳醉醺醺地表示，如果知道當年的康敏如此渴望新衣，要他送十套二十套給她都不成問題時，康敏的回答是，「有十套、二十套那就不希罕啦。」（第廿四回，金 998）這裡當眞道破了邪惡之眼的觀看模式——重點根本不在於有多少衣服，而是當東西不是你的、你得不到的時候，它就特別顯得希罕！拉岡在闡釋邪惡之眼的時候，所舉的例子便是，已經不需要母親哺乳的哥哥如果看到弟弟在吸吮母乳，由於邪惡之眼的作祟，依然會嫉恨地看著弟弟（Lacan 1981: 116）。康敏對得不到的新衣、對擁有眾多情人的段正淳所展現的幾近變態的渴望也是一樣的心態：她自認爲爲新衣服害了相思病、認爲自己深愛著段正淳，但

又會去把衣服毀掉、想把段正淳害死，這種愛恨綜合的矛盾正是自我與他者（鄰居姊姊、段正淳其他情人）爭鋒的鏡映關係中，嫉妒的邪惡之眼必然造成的現象。

當社會價值觀傾向於把女性與自戀連結的時候，對某些女性主義流派而言，全面挑戰父權價值體系、歌頌被父權體系污名化的女性特質一直是抗爭的途徑之一，不過就自戀這個特質而言，我們發現這種反向的歌頌恐怕不是很理想的一種方式，我們透過康敏來檢視的自戀機制足可說明自戀可能造成的災害。而康敏最後竟然因爲在鏡中看到自己被阿紫毀容的醜陋模樣而氣絕，更無巧不巧地爲過度自戀、沈溺虛幻脆弱的鏡像所帶來的惡果，做了一個最好的註解。

三、從想像認同到戀物癖

比起馬夫人康敏，段正淳的其他情人雖然不至於自戀至此，卻多也困在想像認同（imaginary identification）的處境中不能自拔。前面已談過鏡像期與自戀等理論，而這裡所說的想像認同其實便是指自戀與鏡映關係所在的場域，用拉岡的圖表來說明，就是圖示 L（schema L; Lacan 1993: 14）中，連接 oo'（o 爲代表自我的 ego，o'代表對應於鏡像自我的他者）的軸線。

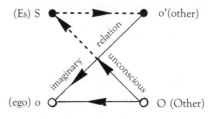

在這個關係圖中，主體所在的位置是在 S，相對於主體而言，眞正的他者則是代表象徵秩序與潛意識的大他者（Other），而主體的建立也是透過與大他者（Other）互動所完成的，[1] 但是主體最原初的建立方式就是想像的鏡像認

---

1 拉岡對此的解釋如下：「這個圖示意指潛意識主體的條件端賴所有在大他者的場域中開展（unfolded）出來的東西。所有在那裡開展的東西都被串鏈、發聲（articulated）成爲像不定向滑動的論述（潛意識就是大他者的不定向滑動論述）」（1977: 193）。

同，也就是會把從 o'（他的鏡像、相對於他的小他者）那裡所看到的，當成是主體的所在，從而建立自我（ego），這也就是圖中從 S（主體）出發的線為何先指向 o'（小他者），之後又沿著想像的軸線到達 o（自我）（Dor 161-64），而 oo'所構成的想像軸線同時也形成了一道語言牆（the wall of language），[2] 使大他者與主體被分隔在遙遙相對的兩端，主體因此也不易直接企近自己潛意識的真相，這也就是為什麼從大他者發出的線條經過語言牆的阻隔後會成為虛線；而精神分析的目的就是要讓主體理解到想像認同的虛妄，才能於象徵秩序中安身立命。所謂在象徵秩序中安身立命，是必須超越自我與小他者間剪不斷理還亂的關係，瞭解到自己所面對的他者們同樣也是一個個的主體，有其獨立的慾望運作模式，因此想用一己的自我去控制管束他們必定是徒勞無功的，唯有接受這個現實，才能在面對分離（separation）——不管是原初母子共生幻象的結束，或是認清鏡像和自己的區隔，或是接受失落所愛之物——之後，在象徵秩序中尋求種種的替代，展開自己做為主體的慾望辯證過程。

　　在《天龍八部》中，段正淳的情人們在與愛人分離之後，顯然都沒有辦法在象徵秩序中找到自己的定位，她們的生命意義建立在被段正淳視為慾望客體之上，只有當段正淳這個小他者持續給予如鏡像對自己的凝望時，她們的自我才能穩固下來，一旦失去了他者的凝望，主體就或者因為自我完形的無法確立變得惶惶不安、或者要靠攻擊他者來勉力維持住自我的完整；前者如甘寶寶與阮星竹，後者如刀白鳳、秦紅棉、王夫人。段正淳情婦之一的俏藥叉甘寶寶雖然再嫁，卻幽怨度日，初見段譽時，連聽到他的大理口音、獲知他姓段都足以使她思及故人而神思恍惚，忘記身陷險境的女兒（第二回，金 79-80），後來再與段正淳相遇時，雖然力圖謹守已婚婦人之份際，但卻不時可以看出她難忘舊情而哀怨不已（第九回，金 379-380）；而阮星竹對段正淳的癡戀更是到了即使被他用花言巧語所哄也甘心的地步：「『我叫你永遠住

2　oo'的想像軸線之所以會構成語言牆是因為語言其實分成所述（statement, the enounced）與能述（enunciation）的不同層次，所述是字面的意義，能述則是經過主體慾望仲介的發言位置，而想像認同的關係無法區辨這兩者的區隔，因此所進行的對話只是一種「空洞的言說」（empty speech），阻斷了主體與大他者之間「完整的言說」（full speech）（Lacan 1993: 14）。

在這兒，你也依我嗎？……你就是說了不算數，只嘴頭上甜甜的騙騙我，叫我心裡歡喜片刻，也是好的。你就連這個也不肯。』說到了這裡，眼眶便紅了，聲音也有些哽咽。」（第廿二回，金 928-929）至於段正淳的元配刀白鳳，她的攻擊性則表現在報復的慾望上；她不惜「找一個天下最醜陋、最污穢、最卑賤的男人來和他相好」（第四十八回，金 2014）以報復段正淳——得不到丈夫完整的愛，就寧可作賤自己，強迫自己委身於讓她乍見之下驚恐不已、要轉身逃開的叫化子。刀白鳳這麼做，看似給了段正淳一個最好的教訓——他一生風流，私生女無數，但到頭來很諷刺的是，他視如己出的唯一兒子段譽竟是妻子與別人私生的，而他還爲了保護這個兒子不惜讓慕容復把他的眾情人全部殺掉！然而刀白鳳的一生其實何嘗有其做爲一個主體的意義？她又何嘗因爲遂行這樣的報復稍微減輕了自己被丈夫背叛的痛苦？更不堪的是，她自己因丈夫的出軌而傷心欲絕，所以認爲用同樣的方式就可以達到報復丈夫的目的，但其實段正淳至死都不知道段譽的身世，又怎會被她的報復行動所傷害？刀白鳳所得到的報復快感，終究不過是來自於自己想像的投射：「你對不起我，我也要對你不起。你背著我去找別人，我也要去找別人。你們漢人男子不將我們擺夷女子當人……我一定要報復，我們擺夷女子也不將你們漢人男子當人」（第四十八回，金 2013），結果我們看到，這自暴自棄的一次出軌，並不能使刀白鳳就此脫離爲段正淳所負的陰影，只是徒然在自我與他者的角力中亦步亦趨地受制於他者的所作所爲，在攻擊他者的時候也傷害了依附他者而生的自己。

　　接著看秦紅棉。秦紅棉的生命似乎以追殺段正淳的其他情人爲目的，行徑雖不似康敏般變態，卻也是攻擊慾極強的例子，她不但把自己的生命浪擲在追殺情敵上，也灌輸女兒木婉清天下男子皆薄倖的觀念，要她立下毒誓，若有人見了她的臉，假如不殺這個人就得要他娶她，而丈夫若是負心又必須親手殺了他，一旦有違誓言、下不了手的話，就得自刎（第四回，金 161），這樣一種在女兒身上複製自己偏執的思考的行徑，表面看起來是保護女兒以免她受一樣的苦，其實也暴露出秦紅棉對自己被拋棄一事不曾忘却，更無法擺脫被拋棄之痛苦，女兒若是眞的遇上負心漢而將他殺了，倒也是可以爲她帶來替代性的滿足——自己不能（不忍）手刃段正淳，但卻希望天下負心漢能夠死盡！另一個希望天下負心漢都死盡而且更爲變態的角色自然就是王夫

人阿蘿。事實上，王夫人的侵略慾及變態行徑可說不遜於馬夫人，而她所表現出來的一項其他女子沒有的變態傾向則是戀物癖（fetishism），以下我們就來看看這種心理機制和想像認同的鉤聯。

關於戀物癖，佛洛依德所提出的解釋依然是充滿陽物理體中心（phal-logocentrism）的色彩，對他而言，戀物癖中受到崇拜愛戀的物神（fetish）基本上是陽具的替代品：

> 正常的情況下這陽具應該被放棄，而物神就是特地設計用來防範陽具消失的東西。說得更淺白些，物神是母親的陽具的替代品——小孩子一度相信母親（和他一樣）有陽具，但基於種種我們並不陌生的原因，他可能不願放棄這陽具。之後所發生的現象，就是小男孩拒絕承認他發現女性沒有陽具的這個事實。不，這不可能：因爲如果女性是因爲被去勢才沒有陽具的話，那麼他自己擁有的陽具豈不也處境危險？爲了反叛這樣的情況，他對陽具這個特別的器官本能的防護，使他的自戀情結油然而生。（SE XXI 152-153）

也就是說，佛洛依德認爲戀物癖是小男孩爲了否認（disavow）去勢恐懼所發展出來的傾向。正常的情況下，接受了去勢恐懼的小男孩會進入伊底帕斯化的過程，知道不能依附在母子共生的想像階段，也就是說戀母有可能會使他的強大對手——父親——將其去勢，所以小男孩會發展出對父親的認同，以期自己長大後能夠擁有母親以外的其他女性作爲其慾望客體；而戀物癖者則是從這樣的常軌中逃逸，他們對自己的陽具所投注的自戀使其不能處理瞥見女性生殖器所造成的去勢恐懼，因此選擇相信女性也是有陽具的，爲了要否認這個他們明明已經看見的事實，戀物癖者所採取的折衷之道——當然不是在意識層次選擇這麼做，而是根據潛意識法則的引導——便是堅持相信女性有一個不同於他原先所認定的陽具，也因此替代陽具功能的物神就出現了，透過這個物神，他把原先應投注於生殖器官的性滿足轉從物神身上得到。佛洛依德認爲男性戀物癖的對象物常常是女性的內褲，原因在於那是女性把衣物卸盡、露出沒有陽具的眞相的前一刻，在這一刻，他還是可以相信女性是有陽具的（phallic），所以他選擇了這個關鍵物爲物神（SE XXI 155）。

關於戀物癖這個問題，法國女性精神分析師克莉斯提娃（Julia Kris-teva）也做了一番值得參考的補充。根據克莉斯提娃的論點，戀物癖的確和

鏡像期的自戀情結有關。小孩對鏡像投注驅力（drives）的原初自戀期，奠定了後來他可以區分人我、自身與外物的基礎：小孩最早安置／確立（posit）的物件（object）便是鏡像中的自我，而認識到鏡像畢竟外於自身之後，他將能接受與母親分離的經驗，在象徵秩序中一一安置／確立其他物件／客體的存在，也就是展開他象徵表意（signify）的過程，利用語言的表意來昇華原初的失落感（Kristeva 1984: 46）；但是鏡像期的經驗如果不能被適當的轉化發展，那麼就有可能變爲窺視狂（scopophilia），始終需要一面鏡子或替代鏡子功能的受話者（addressee）；或者是變成戀物癖者，抗拒承認他發現母親被去勢的這件事，運用戀物癖的機制使陽物母親（phallic mother）的存在可以確立。克莉斯提娃認爲其實戀物癖也許不是在發現母親被去勢的時候才出現的，更早期對自己鏡像的依戀、不能將鏡像與實際身體分離開來的問題也將造成戀物癖的形成（1984: 63）。總之，不論是因爲不能與母親分離所以認定其爲陽物母親，或是深陷於鏡像誤識之中所造成的戀物癖，都是一種透過戀物回返自體快感（autoeroticism）的機制（Kristeva 1984: 65），是正常的表意功能停滯的一種表現，因爲表意功能是要主體學習用語言去指涉，同時瞭解使用語言就是接受失落（必然是當下缺席（absent）的東西才需要靠語言來再現（represent），的這個事實，而戀物癖者卻不使用語言，而使用物件（object）來表意（Kristeva 1984: 64）。

　　在以上的理論中，佛洛依德的看法因爲傾向生物決定論，因此令人不解的是如果從對陽具有無的在意來解釋戀物癖的產生，那麼本來就沒有陽具，也就是沒有去勢恐懼的女性是否就不會有戀物癖的出現？克莉斯提娃的補充則把戀物癖連結到鏡像期所發生的問題（disorders in the mirror stage）之上，因而可以解釋兩性都有可能出現戀物癖。其實，如果我們按照拉岡對佛洛依德去勢效應的修正來看這個問題，會更爲清楚；拉岡認爲去勢效應並不必定指小孩對失去陽具的恐懼，而是小孩與母親分離的經驗中，發現自己不是母親唯一愛著的對象（因爲還有父親），母親有著他所不瞭解的、不可知的慾望，因此深感自己一定失去了什麼東西（Lacan 1957-1958, seminar of January 15, 1958, qtd. In Dor 115）這樣的一種原初失落，換句話說，戀物癖不必然只發生在不承認母親在生理上被去勢的男孩身上，也發生在明知已然失落了愛物卻不願意接受失落或分離經驗的任何主體身上。王夫人對蔓陀

山莊的茶花所投注的特殊情感，正是一種戀物癖者與物神的關係，用以否認情郎段正淳已經不在身邊的事實。

　　用來讓自己對失落視而不見的物神具備了什麼樣的特質呢？這裡我們可以參考馬克斯在分析商品物神化的現象時所提供的看法：「在金幣作爲交易媒介的階段，貨幣本身依舊帶有使用價值的色彩。但因在頻繁的交易流通過程中金幣本身的物質性會不斷耗損，變得越來越名不符實──金幣本身所代表的價值不符現有的實質──遂導致金幣後來逐漸爲銅幣、鎳幣、甚至紙幣所取代。也就是說，整個貨幣的流變是往愈來愈名不符實的方向走 (Marx 11-14)，變得越來越鬼魅。正如齊傑克 (Slavoj Žižek) 所言，錢幣擁有一種難以言喻、崇高 (sublime) 的『非物質肉身性』(immaterial corporeality)──縱使肉身不斷消磨耗損，但它所象徵的價值依舊恆常不變(18)。」(Chiou 106) 簡單的說，物神必須超越該事物本身原本的價值、對主體產生無法名狀的特殊魅力，也就是必須產生溢乎其「物質肉身」的吸引力。那麼什麼樣的東西特別可能成爲物神？它通常必須和主體不願與之分離的對象有所關連。段譽曾經猜測到王夫人分外喜愛茶花的原因「定是當年爹爹與她定情之時，與茶花有什麼關連」(第四十七回，金 1985)，這個推測後來在王夫人死前從段正淳與她的對話中得到證實：「我對你的心意，永如當年送你一朵蔓陀花之日。」(第四十八回，金 2032) 王夫人當年與段正淳在姑蘇的蔓陀山莊定情，段正淳離去後山莊依然種滿大理的山茶花，而且就連後來她用計要擒拿段正淳時，所購置的莊子也是種滿了茶花，茶花的布置還和當初一模一樣，這些都足以證明王夫人對茶花的喜愛不只是喜歡茶花本身，其實更是在延續對段正淳的情愛，否則她也不會連品種都不懂卻還是癡戀著段譽眼中一盆盆的俗品茶花──把大理人嘲諷命名爲「落第秀才」的雜色茶花視爲至寶、把白茶「紅妝素裹」、「抓破美人臉」都當成「滿月」……等等，王夫人的「焚琴煮鶴」、「不懂山茶，偏要種山茶」(第十二回，金 493) 在段譽看來十分無稽，但其實只要瞭解茶花對王夫人的象徵意義，就可以理解何以她愛茶花卻不識茶花本身「物質肉身」的價值。王夫人或許本來就已極愛茶花，但是茶花被提升到物神的地位，卻定是段正淳的離去所造成的，藉著大理盛產的茶花，住在蔓陀山莊的她與住在滿是茶花的鎮南王府的段正淳之間，也彷彿還有著聯繫。

　　段譽曾經揣測，王夫人「一捉到大理人或是姓段之人便要將之活埋，當

然是爲了爹爹姓段，是大理人，將她遺棄，她懷恨在心遷怒於其他大理人和
姓段之人。她逼迫在外結識私情的男子殺妻另娶，是流露了她心中隱伏的願
望，盼望爹爹殺了正室，娶她爲妻」（第四十七回，金 1985），其實除此之外，
王夫人動輒把大理段氏的人、在外另有情婦又不肯殺妻另娶的人捉來活埋做
茶花花肥的這種行徑，也可以看出王夫人絕不只是單純地喜愛茶花：透過茶
花來思念、埋怨、痛恨段正淳，無非都是處心積慮地用茶花來維繫住與段正
淳的一絲關係。王夫人原本也要將闖入山莊的段譽折磨至死再做成花肥，卻
因他說起茶花頭頭是道便願意設宴款待他，在席間段譽侃侃而談茶花的正品
副品如何區分、有哪些名種，王夫人聆聽得悠然神往之際，自言自語了一句
「怎麼他從來不跟我說。」（第十二回，金 496），這裡實在是點破了茶花在王
夫人心中如此重要的關鍵所在：分離已成事實卻不能接受，戀物癖者只有憑
藉著物神，停滯在分離之前的完滿幻象中，而無法在象徵秩序中開展自己慾
望的辯證。而連王夫人想計擒段正淳時，也是利用過去段正淳所吟過的詩詞
「春溝水動茶花白，夏谷雲生荔枝紅」、「青裙玉面如相識，九月茶花滿路開」
（第四十七回，金 1979-1980）做成填字遊戲，企圖引段正淳入甕，她牢記當
年與茶花／段正淳有關的種種，始終停留在過去回憶的心態，不言自明。

　　不論是自戀或是戀物，困在想像認同的層次中等待他者的凝望來成立自
我的結果，便是主體的極度異化、有紓解不完的攻擊慾。段譽感嘆父親的舊
情人，包括自己母親，個個脾氣古怪（第四十七回，金 1996），實非無的放矢。
最後這些女人（除了康敏之外）全部同歸於盡的場景中，特別加以刻劃、也
因此分外值得玩味的，便是王夫人的死：當慕容復殺了阮星竹、秦紅棉、甘
寶寶卻仍不能使段正淳屈服時，王夫人雖然是慕容復的舅母，卻也開始心驚
有性命之虞，此時段正淳對她柔聲道：「阿蘿，你跟我相好一場，畢竟還是
不明白我的心思。天下這許多女人之中，我便只愛你一個……你外甥殺了我
三個相好，那有什麼打緊，只須他不來傷你，我便放心了。」段正淳這番話
使王夫人害怕莫名，因爲她知道段正淳恨她至極，才會故意說反話想讓慕容
復把她也殺了，但是之後的變化則更爲戲劇性：

> 王夫人素知道外甥心狠手辣……只要段正淳繼續故意顯得對自己十分愛惜，那麼
> 慕容復定然會以自己的性命相脅，不禁顫聲道：「段郎，段郎！難道你眞的恨我

入骨，想害死我嗎？」

段正淳見到她目中懼色、臉上戚容，想到昔年和她的一番恩情，登時心腸軟了，破口罵道：「你這賊虔婆，豬油蒙了心，卻去喝那陳年舊醋，害得我三個心愛的女人都死於非命，我手足若得了自由，非將你千刀萬剮不可……」他知道罵得越厲害，慕容復越是不會殺他舅母。

王夫人心中明白，段正淳先前假意對自己傾心相愛，是要引慕容復來殺了自己，爲阮星竹、秦紅棉、甘寶寶三人報仇，現下改口斥罵，已是原諒了自己。可是她十餘年來對段正淳朝思暮想，突然與情郎重會，心神早已大亂，眼見三個女子屍橫就地，一柄血淋淋的長劍對著自己胸口，突然間腦中一片茫然。但聽得段正淳破口斥罵……比之往日的山盟海誓，輕憐密愛，實是宵壤之別，忍不住珠淚滾滾而下……（第四十八回，金 2031）

最後王夫人更在段正淳斥罵不休的情況下，自己猛然撞向慕容復的劍尖結束生命，不但段正淳要吃驚何以王夫人不解他的斥罵是要救她一命，讀者可能也極驚訝於王夫人竟神智不清、顛三倒四至此，先前還知道段正淳若假意示好才是恨她的表現，瞬時間竟然又認爲段正淳如此嚴厲的話語是恨她的表現。這一段的曲折寫得極細緻，我們就此可以再次看到想像認同造成的問題。先前說過，當主體困在 oo' 的想像軸線上時，這軸線會形成一道語言牆，阻隔了真正對話的進行——每一個主體的語言行動其實都受到了慾望的穿透，必須放在代表大他者的象徵體系中才能理解，不能只從自我的位置出發，以想像投射的方式理解字面上的意思。王夫人起初意識到這一點，知道段正淳語言中的慾望是要置她於死地，但是當段正淳心軟改口罵她時，她卻因爲心神已亂，分不清楚段正淳口頭上的辱罵是否正是他的真心，因此把自己棄婦哀怨自傷的心情——「你從前對我說過甚麼話，莫非都忘記了？你怎麼半點也不將我放在心上了？」（金 2031）一股腦投射到段正淳身上；說話者的發言位置、發言慾望這些東西都被摒除在想像軸線之外了，此刻段正淳所說的話聽在王夫人的耳朵裡之所以只具有字面上的辱罵仇恨之意，實在是因爲王夫人幾近偏執的狀態，使她所聽見的成爲一種「錯覺的言說」（delusional speech），自己心裡懷疑、焦慮、認爲對方會如此看待自己的種種信息，會反向地透過錯覺中的小他者之口被主體接收 （receiving somewhere her own message in an inverted from the small other ; Lacan 1993: 52-53)。而偏執的想像認同所造成的結果，自然是使王夫人認定段正淳不但離棄她還恨她，因而決定自戕，王夫人想聽的，畢竟是段正淳「輕憐蜜愛」之語，和阮星竹一樣，即使是口頭說說騙她，她也高興——王夫人就在段正淳許下不可能實現的承諾：明天就去大理無量山中的玉洞雙宿雙飛，之後，滿臉喜色的死去。

四、女人何苦為難女人？

陳墨在評析金庸小說中失戀的女子為「憂傷的情魔」時，提到了一個他認為「怪。但這就是女性」（《情愛金庸》50）的現象，這個現象，就是失戀的女人「不去恨應該恨的人（拋棄她的男人、薄情的男人或不愛她的男人），而卻偏偏要去恨那不該恨的人（她的情敵、她的同類，那個得到或『奪了』她的情郎的女人）」（《情愛金庸》57）。陳墨舉出了不少例證，如《碧血劍》中的何紅藥不恨金蛇郎君夏雪宜、不恨自己盲目，卻恨透了夏雪宜所愛的溫儀；《神鵰俠侶》中的李莫愁「也像何紅藥、王夫人、秦紅棉、甘寶寶、阮星竹……等等所有的女性一樣並不恨男人，不真的恨那『薄情郎』，而是恨自己的同類，恨另一個女子將自己的情郎奪去。以為別的女人是『小賤人』、『狐媚子』、『騷狐狸』云」（《情愛金庸》54）。這種女人為難女人的現象在《天龍八部》中的確是甚為明顯，我們在第八回就已經看到秦紅棉與刀白鳳正面交手，雖然眼見段正淳出手相救自己的情敵時，兩人分別不滿地向段正淳進攻，但是當她們見到對方向段正淳攻擊時，又都同時要迴護郎君，即使她們之後發現段正淳是假裝受傷，思及「這傢伙最會騙人」，兩人又聯手向他進攻，但是對段正淳出手時，卻絕非像攻擊情敵時那樣，招招意圖置對方於死地。在第廿三回中秦紅棉原先意圖行刺阮星竹，在阮星竹的軟語感動下，表面上化敵為友，共同把馬夫人康敏視為使段正淳負心的罪魁禍首：「秦紅棉恨恨的道：『我和段郎本來好端端地過快活日子，都是這賤婢使狐狸精勾當……』阮星竹沈吟道：『那康……康敏這賤人，嗯，可不知在哪裡。妹子找到了她，妳幫我在她身上多刺幾刀。』」（金 986）稍後我們將發現兩女的同仇敵愾並不真摯，彼此都只是假作對對方毫無戒心之狀，事實上阮星竹對秦紅棉隱瞞了

段正淳的行蹤，而秦紅棉也知道她在使詐，兩女之間短暫的姊妹相稱畢竟是爾虞我詐而非相濡以沫。第四十七回，王夫人聽說段正淳又和別的女人同行，勃然大怒地質問：「⋯⋯他丟下了我，回大理去做他的王爺，我並不怪他，家中有妻子，我也不怪他，誰叫我識得他之時，他已是有婦之夫呢？可是他⋯⋯可是他⋯⋯你說他又和別的女人在一起，那是誰？那是誰？⋯⋯哼，這賤女人模樣兒生得怎樣？這狐媚子，不知用甚麼手段將他迷上了。」（金 1996-97）這些女人之間的恨意可說是非常分明，然而她們對共同的負心漢的心情恐怕卻一致多類似王夫人：「對他即使有怨懟，也多半是情多於仇。」（第四十八回，金 2006）

　　對於武俠小說中充斥的這種女人為難女人的例子，難道我們只能感嘆這就是非理性的女人特別會製造的怪現象嗎？或許也不盡然。《天龍八部》中段正淳眾情人們一致表現出來的對情敵的恨、對情人的寬容，與其用性別決定論推斷是因為失戀的女性必然會如此，不如說還是她們觀看／認同模式的結構性問題使然。前面已經說過，段正淳的情人們多停留在想像認同的層次，而因為想像認同中的自我完形只是從不足跨越到期待所產生的幻象，這種不穩定會使自我必須不斷與小他者進行爭鬥來保障自己無所匱缺的錯覺，從這個角度來看這些女子恨其他的女子而不恨段正淳的原因，或許就不是那麼怪異難解了：如果她們痛恨段正淳、真的把他看成厚顏無恥、到處留情、花言巧語的負心漢，那麼她們豈不也等於承認愛著段正淳的自己是盲目的、愚蠢的、和無恥之徒廝混的同一等人？而自己到現在心裡仍眷戀段正淳這個惡人，豈不是更為不堪？可是如果她們恨的是情敵，情況就不同了，把情敵貶為賤女人、狐狸精，她們不但保全了「情郎只是一時被狐媚所惑才誤入歧途」、「他不是不愛我」這樣的幻覺，也可以免於面對心底的焦慮：是不是我有甚麼不夠好所以他才又去愛別人？換句話說，想像認同「有他就沒有我」的結構性缺陷，將為主體製造出「打壓他就可以確保我」的錯覺，這恐怕才是這些女性彼此憎恨殘殺的深層原因。也就是說，問題的關鍵並不在於女性之間互相打壓貶抑是女性本質使然，而是任何過度耽溺想像認同的人都容易發生的現象。

　　不過我們還是得問，那麼女性是不是就是這種比較容易耽溺想像認同的人呢？法國女性主義者依莉佳萊（Luce Irigaray）很不滿意的，就是精神分

析的理論所導出的答案似乎是肯定的。依莉佳萊認爲，佛洛依德用伊底帕斯化的過程來解釋主體的形成，表示小男孩的戀母情結將會在父親帶來的去勢恐懼下受到阻止，因而發展出較強的超我（super-ego），知道要控制不應有的慾望，進入主體化的正常過程，但女孩因爲本來就已經被去勢，不會受到去勢恐懼的威脅，所以戀父的情況不論持續多久都無所謂，甚至女性對父親或男性長輩那種孩童式的依賴（infantile dependency）也是一直被允許的，因此女性的超我就變得較弱；這整套理論似乎表示女性的象徵認同較差是一種宿命、女性不像男性那樣具有社會及文化中較被肯定的種種正面價值（Irigaray 39-40）。佛洛依德用陽具的有無來推斷象徵認同的發展順利與否當然是大有可議之處的，但是他關於女性的戀父、依賴情結多被允許的這項觀察卻是相當重要的。事實上我們知道，不要說是武俠小說所描繪的中國古代社會了，即使到如今，社會的價值還是普遍地允許、甚至鼓勵女性的依賴情結，當女性一直被「潛移默化」爲應該被保護疼愛、被男性慾望的客體時，想要超越想像認同的幻象、進入象徵秩序成爲主動愛慾的主體也就變得格外困難。因此問題不在於歸咎女性生理條件會使其超我軟弱、道德價值觀較低、喜歡與女性同類鬥爭，而在於檢討整個社會環境所能提供的條件是否根本在很多方面是不利於女性主體發展的。

　　除了佛洛依德之外，克莉斯提娃關於主體形成的理論也指出了女性主體發展的不利情況。克莉斯提娃認爲，孩童若要瞭解到母親並不是和他共生的一部分、接受與母親分離的事實，很重要的一個步驟是完成象徵性的弒母（matricide），唯有透過這一個步驟，自主自發的主體（autonomous subject）才能成立（1989: 27）；反之，主體如果把母子共生狀態的結束看成是失去了自己的一部分，就會被這種自戀傷痕（narcissistic wound）帶入憂鬱情結之中，無法進入象徵層次的主體發展。有鑑於此，主體必須進行象徵性的弒母，至於母親已死的原初失落，則要用昇華（sublimation）的方式來處理。然而昇華的方式是什麼呢？克莉斯提娃表示，對異性戀男性或同性戀女性而言，就是將死去的母親（當然是比喻的說法）當成愛慾的客體（erotic object），透過愛戀其他女性來重新收復母親這個失落物，另外，以藝術創作的方式來達到昇華的目的更是克莉斯提娃甚爲讚許的一種方式（1989: 28）。但是根據克莉斯提娃的看法，女性想完成象徵性弒母是困難重重的，「因爲我就是她

（母親），她就是我」（1989: 18）：女兒與母親在性別上的直接認同使得她不容易透過弒母來成立她的主體。女兒的主體性，在弒母障礙的爲難之下，難以發展。

在這裡特別要說明的是，雖然許多女性主體性的發展顯得較男性遲滯，的確和無法脫離依賴母親的況狀極爲相關，但這種女兒與母親在性別上的直接認同並不只是生理上的必然性所能解釋的，它同時被社會文化的意識型態所穿透：例如家庭及社會環境對女孩成爲「賢妻良母」的要求，便是女兒被強制（但不見得在意識層次感受到這種強制性）與母親做認同的原因之一。因此，即使精神分析的理論導引我們注意到女性在象徵認同上的困難、解釋了自戀的情況多發生在女性身上的原因，我們更必須強調的是，這並不是一種本質論的劃分，女性所受到的社會限制、昇華的管道較爲局限等因素絕對與許多女性爲何難逃想像認同的牽絆有很大的關係。女人如果爲難女人，並不是像部分評家所認爲的那樣，是女人的天性，而是在內化了男性中心的價值觀之後，女性習慣靠著男性的凝視來決定自己的價值。試問是不是因爲「女爲悅己者容」這樣的價值觀深植在女性心中，所以《俠客行》中的梅芳姑才會在發現不被石清所愛之後，把原本自詡姣好的容貌毀掉？而馬夫人得不到喬峯的凝望就覺得自己再怎麼自負美貌也沒有用，是否使我們警覺到，一個無時不忘攬鏡自照的自戀女人根本不見得是真正自我肯定的女性主體？也許她根本是透過男性的眼睛來看自己、惶惶不安於是否符合美的標準、是否能成爲慾望的客體而已？當我們重新檢討自戀的結構之後，會發現不論是把自戀歸爲女性本質的父權意識型態，或是想把自戀歌頌爲女性自信自愛的主動表現的部分女性主義流派，都有其無法觀照到的盲點。

五、結　語

一開始，我們便看到，存在於肉眼與凝視的辯證中的，不是巧合，而是，相反的，誘餌。每逢，在愛戀中，我索求一個凝望，令人深深不滿的，總是佚失的，便是——你絕不能從我看你的那個位置來看我，反過來說，我所看到的絕非我想看的。

（Lacan 1981: 102-103）

　　如果陷溺想像認同的女性所犯的錯誤，在於認定「他不看我時我就等於不存在」、把生命的價值建立在被慾望（to be desired）之上，那麼什麼樣的認知可以有助於跳脫想像認同的局限呢？前言中提到了量子力學的反省，就是一個很好的起點。當齊傑克把量子力學的思考引進精神分析的框架時，所舉的例子正是引起 Einstein 與 Bohr 爭議的「光的波粒二象性」的實驗：Einstein 設計了一個電子通過雙狹縫干涉的實驗——當雙狹縫開啓時，從屏幕出現的亮點可以知道電子垂直方向的動量，分別關上其中一個狹縫，就可以知道電子的確實位置；但是 Bohr 發現，如果關上其中任何一個狹縫，實驗的狀態就完全改變了。當雙狹縫開啓時，不管是眞的有兩個電子分別通過狹縫，或者電子其實是一個個發射出來的，最後都會在屏上形成波的干涉條紋；假如輪流開啓一個狹縫，去觀察電子究竟經過那個狹縫，最後幕屏上卻不會再有干涉條紋了；「這好像是說單一的電子（必須通過兩個狹縫之一的粒子）『知道』另一個狹縫到底有沒有打開，因此有不同的因應方式：如果另一個狹縫是開著的，它就呈顯波的型態，如果關著，它就呈顯正常粒子的型態。甚至於一個電子好像也知道自己是否正被觀測著……這個實驗要暗示的是什麼？」（Žižek 221）這個本來是 Einstein 用來反駁量子力學的理想實驗，經由 Bohr 的解釋在今日已成了說明測不準關係和互補原理的標準範例；我們在此當然不是要探討這門深奧的學問，而是要隨著齊傑克一起問，這個物理學的爭議所暗示出的哲學性思考是什麼？

　　Einstein 堅信，有一個離開知覺主體而獨立存在的客觀世界，是一切自然科學的基礎，因此也一直想駁倒 Bohr 的觀點。爲 Einstein 立傳的作家 A. Pais 回憶道：「有一次和 Einstein 同行，他突然停下來，轉身問我是否眞的相信，月亮只有在我去看它的時候才存在？」[3] 如果我們回答，「月亮只有在我看它的時候才存在」似乎顯得無稽荒謬，但是在精神分析的觀點裡這個答案卻不是沒有意義的。齊傑克便用光的波粒二象性的實驗來引申精神分析的相關概念：「我們（主體）對事物的認知會影響並且改變該事物本身：我們不能認定每樣事物均包含了自身的本質，以爲不論我們怎麼看它，它『就

3　關於本論文中提到 Einstein 與 Bohr 的爭議係取材自「沒有人看月亮時她是否還在哪兒？」（www.phys.ntu.edu.tw/～cwhuang/pub/phys/EPR/eprl.htm＃secl）。

是在那裡』……一件事物之所以完全變成『它自己』,同時會受外在的環境如何『注意到它』(take note of it) 所影響。這種事物和外在的構成關係,不就像『象徵實踐』(symbolic realization)的邏輯一樣?某一件事物要算數、要變得有效,都是透過外於自身的象徵秩序將之加以定位後的結果。」(Žižek 222-23)[4] 就像在以上的實驗中,如果粒子和波的性質不曾被一套特定的象徵鑄模 (symbolic matrix) 定義為互斥的、矛盾的 (Žižek 225),那麼實驗的結果是否還是那麼令人困擾不解呢?在這裡齊傑兄所點出的其實是精神分析非常強調的觀念,也就是對象徵定位的理解:我們在象徵秩序中的定位並不是一成不變的本質,而是透過主體、他者與大他者之間的繁複互動 (如前述的 L 圖示) 才決定的。有了這樣的認知,主體才不至於被釘死在一個固定位置上,落入宿命的本質論中,而能夠展現主體的能動力,瞭解自我與他者的關係是如何被語言、慾望、文化建構等不同因素所穿透。

　　再舉一個簡單的例子來說明在想像認同中以為可以「獲得」他者的凝望來肯定自己是多麼虛妄的想法。飛蛾翅膀上的假眼原本當然是為了嚇阻捕食者,但是我們不妨想想,在不把飛蛾當成獵物的狩獵者眼中,那眼狀斑點是不是形同瞎的呢?因為其實只有在打算獵食飛蛾的他者眼中,飛蛾的眼狀斑點才變得看得見東西 (Božovič 171-72)。簡單的說,這個例子要強調的便是,他者的凝望這種東西,其實是我從他者的位置想像出來的 (imagined by me in the field of the Other, Lacan 1981: 184),就像飛蛾的假眼如何會產生瞪視的效果呢?只有當捕食者把自己的慾望讀入牠的位置時,本來只是個斑點的東西才成為假眼;任何的凝望也都像假眼發出的效果一樣,凝望並不是來自飛蛾翅膀上斑點的「本質」,也因此無從被「獲得」。只有瞭解到這一點時,主體才有機會脫離渴望他者看自己一眼的窘境,轉而肯定自己作為一個慾望主體的身分:如果我總是想成為被慾望的客體,就必須因應他者的眼光,變成他想要看的樣子——其實我永遠不可能真正知道他是怎麼看我的,因此結果我只能徒然困在「他不看我時我等於不在」的處境中,但是當我肯定「我不看它時它可能形同不在」時,我卻可以變成一個有行動力的主體。

4　齊傑克根據這個實驗所推出來的哲學性反省,其實連此處提到的論點在內共有五項,有興趣的讀者可以參考其 *The Indivisible Remainder* 一書,頁 220-31。

當然這個層次的認知不是要我們反向地變成獨我論的自大狂，認為自己的看法對他者有舉足輕重的影響，而是指去瞭解自己對外在事物的觀望方式、自己的慾望投射等等，在在影響到我所看到的結果、我所誤以為一成不變的客觀現實，如此才能一方面肯定自己的主體性，一方面理解象徵秩序的可造性。

在《賞析金庸》中陳墨評道：

> 《天龍八部》這部小說，是一部有關人心、人性、人生與人世的深刻的寓言——其「大悲大憫、破孽化癡」的意義正在這裡。……，可以說，這部《天龍八部》浸透了佛家的哲學思想與美學思想。它的內容來自人性——或對人性的認識——中的貪、嗔、癡的種種病態的深刻的揭示；它的意義來自對這種貪、嗔、癡的「人性之毒」及由此而造成的「人生之苦」與「人世之災」的揭發與破解；它的境界來自於對這種人生、人世、人心與人性的大悲憫與大超越。（《賞析金庸》269-70）

而精神分析的理論雖極其艱深繁複，但秉持的理念其實卻與此相當近似，便是對潛意識——舉凡慾望、毀滅、恐懼、空無、不可能的面向——的意識（the consciousness of its unconscious）（Kristeva 1991: 191）。例如雖然知道人與人之間的凝望無可避免地攙雜有想像的投射與慾望的穿透等成分，我們還是應該盡可能透過自我與他者在象徵秩序中的辯證關係，去勘破其中想像的虛幻，以免被一己的執念所困，陷入想像、自戀、攻擊的惡性循環中。段正淳身邊的女性自然無一可以超越這樣的困境，而其實不能超越想像認同的又何止武俠小說中的女子而已？不論性別身分如何，如果缺乏對人自身黑暗面的認知，都很容易墮入這樣的迷障中。藉由跳出性別本質論來解讀這些女子悲劇的形成原因，本論文冀望就此開啟女性主義閱讀與金庸小說之間的溝通空間，在拒絕父權意識型態對女性的樣板化之際，能同時品評閱讀金庸小說的無窮樂趣。

＊本論文的完成，要特別感謝妹妹宗潔代為蒐集相關資料以及她的辛苦校閱。

引用書目

金　庸

　　1997　《天龍八部》（臺北：遠流）。

陳　墨

　　1997　《情愛金庸》（臺北：雲龍）。

　　1997　《人性金庸》（臺北：雲龍）。

　　1997　《賞析金庸》（臺北：雲龍）。

Božovič, Miran

　　1992　"The Man Behind His Own Retina." *Everything You Always Wanted to Know About Lacan (But Were Afraid to Ask Hitchcock)*. Ed. Slavoj Žižek. London: Verso. 161-177.

Brennan, Teresa

　　1993　*History After Lacan*. London: Routledge.

Chiou, Yen-bin

　　1995　"Reading Specters: On Derrida's Desire to Be an Inheritor and His Intervening Reading." *Chung-Wai Literary Monthly* 24.2 (July): 102-115.

Dor, Joël

　　1997　*Introduction to the Reading of Lacan: The Unconscious Structured Like a Language*. Trans. Susan Fairfield. Ed. Judith Feher Gurewich. Northvale: Jason Aronson Inc.

Freud, Sigmund

　　1961　*The Future of an Illusion: Civilization and its Discontents and Other Works. Standard Edition of the Complete Works of Sigmund Freud, Vol. XXI*. Trans. and Ed. James Strachey. London: Hogarth.

Gay, Peter, ed.

　　1989　*The Freud Reader*. New York: Norton.

Irigaray, Luce

　　1985　*This Sex Which Is Not One*. Trans. Catherine Porter and Carolyn

Bruke. Ithaca: Cornell UP.

Kristeva, Julia

　1984　*Revolution in Poetic Language*. Trans. Leon S. Roudiez. New York: Columbia UP.

　1989　*Black Sun: Depression and Melancholia*. Trans. Leon S. Roudiez. New York: Columbia UP.

　1991　*Strangers to Ourselves*. Trans. Leon S. Roudiez. New York: Columbia UP.

Lacan, Jacques

　1977　*Écrits: A Selectoin*. Trans. Alan Sheridan. New York: Norton.

　1981　*The Four Fundamental Concepts of Psycho-Analysis* (1973). Ed. Jacques-Alain Miller. Trans. Alan Sheridan. New York: Norton.

　1993　*The Psychoses: The Seminar of Jacques Lacan, Book III (1955-1956)*. Ed. Jacques-Alain Miller. Trans. Russell Grigg. New York: Norton.

Žižek, Slavoj

　1996　*The Indivisible Remainder: An Essay on Schelling and Related Matters*. London: Verso.

金庸小說人物的「不倫之戀」

陳　益　源

國立中正大學中文系

摘　要

　　叔嫂之戀、父女之戀、師生之戀、兄弟之戀、同性之戀，這些「不倫」情事，頻頻出現在兼擅言情的金庸武俠小說裡，使得金庸小說的情愛世界更加五彩繽紛，也使得大家對金庸在前衛與保守之間的定位感到好奇。

　　金庸小說人物的「不倫之戀」，例如《書劍恩仇錄》中的余魚同與四嫂駱冰，《神鵰俠侶》中的武三通與養女何沅君，小龍女與徒弟楊過，《天龍八部》中的段譽與妹妹木婉清、鍾靈、王語嫣，乃至《鹿鼎記》中的韋小寶與義嫂阿珂……，一再把情不自禁的男歡女愛，推向倫理與道德的邊緣，這在小說的寫作技巧上，不能不說是作者的一記「險招」。金庸出此「險招」，頗為有效地製造了人性本能與社會規範的高度衝突。金庸彷彿慣於運用這樣的衝突，以增加他作品的戲劇張力；至於他化解這樣的衝突的手法，則似乎有點公式化。

　　本文著重鈎稽金庸小說的「不倫之戀」情事，探討它們在小說裡所發揮的美學作用，並擬藉由比較研究，透視作者對於畸戀題材的認知與局限，讓金庸小說情愛世界重要的一隅，可以得到正確的評價。

一、前　言

　　金庸小說於武俠之外，又擅言情，故而作家三毛說她與金庸的作品有著

一樣的本質；[1] 研究者也寫專書加以論述，[2] 肯定金庸小說之所以膾炙人口，成功的愛情描寫無疑是重要因素之一。

　　在金庸小說的情愛世界裡，百花齊放，而且扣人心弦，然而本文準備討論的只是其中的不倫之戀。所謂「不倫之戀」，意指違背倫常的戀情，日本語雖常用以指稱外遇，但本文並不以婚外情爲論述重點，而是想集中在數樁幾近亂倫的事件上，包括叔嫂之戀、父女之戀、師生之戀、兄妹之戀，以及特殊的同性之戀，這是要聲明在先的。

　　其次，亦該表明的是，金庸小說人物固有幾近亂倫的演出，但作者行文雅潔，即使描寫韋小寶和七個女人在揚州麗春院的那場大床春光，也只是以「胡天胡帝」一語帶過，[3] 簡直比「大旨談情」的愛情名著《紅樓夢》還要純情，所以金庸曾說：

> 韋小寶與之發生性關係的女性，並没有賈寶玉那麼多，至少，韋小寶不像賈寶玉那樣搞同性戀，既有秦鐘，又有蔣玉菡。[4]

這話前半句不對，後半句不全。因爲賈寶玉與之發生性關係的女性其實沒有韋小寶那麼多，和賈寶玉搞同性戀的則不只秦鐘和蔣玉菡二人。[5] 不過，金庸小說的性描寫的確比《紅樓夢》還要節制，這是事實。

　　在中國古典小說中，《紅樓夢》居然比《水滸傳》、《金瓶梅》更適於拿來跟金庸武俠小說相提並論其間的不倫之戀，這是很奇妙的。除了《紅樓夢》

1　三毛曾對金庸說：「你豈止是寫武俠小說呢？你寫的包含了人類最大的，古往今來最不能解決的，使人類可以上天堂也可以下地獄的一個字，也就是『情』字。」她又說：「我跟金庸先生的作品雖然不同，就這點來說，本質是一樣的，就是寫一『情』字。」見《夢裡花落知多少》（臺北：皇冠出版社，1981 年 8 月），頁 282。

2　如陳墨《金庸小說的情愛世界》（合肥：安徽文藝出版社，1993 年 5 月，臺灣版易名爲《情愛金庸》，臺北：雲龍出版社，1997 年 7 月）、陳沛然《情之探索與神鵰俠侶》、吳靄儀《金庸小說的情》（收入臺北遠流出版公司的《金庸茶館》叢書，1997 年 10 月二版、1998 年 5 月初版）等。

3　見於《鹿鼎記》第三十九回。《鹿鼎記》新版曾對舊版的時距略作修訂，但仍沒有細寫，參見倪匡《再看金庸小說》（臺北：遠流出版公司，1997 年 7 月二版），頁 49-51。

4　語見《鹿鼎記‧後記》（臺北：遠景出版公司，1981 年 9 月初版），頁 2132。

5　詳參陳益源，〈《紅樓夢》裡的同性戀〉，收入陳益源，《從嬌紅記到紅樓夢》（瀋陽：遼寧古籍出版社，1996 年 7 月），頁 320-345。

之外，本文基於討論的需要，偶而還要引用若干被視爲「等而下之」的古典豔情小說來作比較，此等作法對金迷而言看似「不倫不類」，但不如此，又難以彰顯金庸運用畸戀題材的技巧與局限，所以也要請讀者鑒諒。

以下就讓我們一起來看看，金庸如何一再把情不自禁的男歡女愛，推向倫理與道德的邊緣，製造人性本能與社會規範的高度衝突。這樣的衝突，既引發出小說人物的痛苦抉擇，對作者與讀者而言，無疑也都是一種嚴酷的考驗。

二、叔嫂之戀

金庸在三十歲那年（1955）寫作他的第一部武俠小說《書劍恩仇錄》（又名《書劍江山》）時，就穿插了一場不倫的叔嫂之戀來吸引讀者。

書中紅花會十四當家「金笛秀才」余魚同，暗戀四義兄文泰來的妻子駱冰，每次私自悔恨「心如禽獸」，就用匕首往臂上刺一刀，五、六年來已經刺得「臂上斑斑駁駁，滿是疤痕」，終於在鐵膽莊外趁駱冰昏睡之際摟抱熱吻一番。駱冰羞憤交集，但憐他癡心，既往不咎。余魚同則自傷自憐，自悔自責，「覺堂堂六尺，罪行無恥，直豬狗之不若，突然間將腦袋連連往樹上撞去，抱樹狂呼大叫」，從此身懷罪孽，自稱是「千古第一喪心病狂有情無義人」（自傷對駱冰有情，自恨對文泰來無義），直到冒死搭救文泰來，把一張俊俏的臉燒得焦黑醜陋，又拒刁蠻佳人李沅芷於千里之外，出家去當和尚，依舊覺得自己「喪心病狂，早就該死了」。

《書劍恩仇錄》（二十回）描述這場余魚同單戀四嫂駱冰的不倫之戀，從第二回不斷延續到第十五回，可見金庸經營之用心，難怪陳墨在他的幾部金庸研究中對此總是一提再提，並說這是金庸的一記奇招，也是一記險招、一記絕招：

> 技藝高超的金庸卻始終把握著分寸，沒有把余魚同變成壞人，而是一個有缺點的好人，到最後還不失爲一個「犯了錯誤的好同志」。余魚同的愛和失禮，在道德上也許是不光彩的，但在人性上是完全可以理解的。……余魚同是這部小說中刻劃得最爲成功的人物形象。因爲它不僅揭示了愛的本質，也寫出了人性的真實性及

其複雜性。[6]

嚴格說來，余魚同還只是《書劍恩仇錄》的次要人物，而他居然能被稱爲「刻劃得最爲成功的人物形象」，這大概正是金庸穿插這樁叔嫂的不倫之戀的奇絕之處吧。

提到叔嫂之戀，《水滸傳》第二十四回潘金蓮挑逗小叔武松的情節是大家耳熟能詳的，小說重要人物武松的英雄形象的建立，跟他毫無掙扎地痛叱「嫂嫂休要這般不識羞恥」自然有關；《紅樓夢》第十二回王熙鳳毒設相思局，把那平兒口中的「沒人倫的混賬東西」、企圖染指嫂子的賈瑞，捉弄個半死不活，也有助於塑造鳳姐潑辣的形象。這些單向的叔嫂之戀情節的安排，看來都跟小說人物形象的刻劃關係密切。《書劍恩仇錄》跟傳統小說的差異在於：《水滸傳》、《紅樓夢》的作者都給予有意引發不倫的一方（潘金蓮、賈瑞）嚴厲的懲罰，而余魚同「卻得到了作者最終的同情和寬恕」。[7] 潘金蓮、賈瑞也可謂癡心者（賈瑞甚且至死不渝），偏偏二人都是欲重於情，與正面人物余魚同的情重於欲大不相同，未獲《水滸傳》、《紅樓夢》作者的同情和寬恕，是因爲他們本是作者筆下的反面人物。

余魚同、駱冰的義叔嫂之戀，按理不比《水滸傳》、《紅樓夢》的親叔嫂之戀、堂叔嫂之戀來得驚世駭俗，但由於金笛秀才是一正面英雄人物，所以金庸不得不大費周章地替他解套。不像另一小說《射鵰英雄傳》中的反面人物西毒歐陽鋒，「歐陽克是他與嫂子私通而生，名是姪兒，其實卻是他的親子」，[8] 作者就用這簡單幾句話，便足以讓他的邪惡翻案無門了！有人對「關於歐陽鋒的私生活，《射鵰英雄傳》說得很少」感到奇怪，[9] 我看倒不足爲奇。

6　陳墨，《人性金庸》（臺北：雲龍出版社，1997 年 12 月），頁 7。

7　同前註，頁 37。

8　語見《大漠英雄傳》（即《射鵰英雄傳》，臺北：遠景出版公司，1980 年 5 月初版）第二十六回，頁 1049。

9　吳靄儀，《金庸小說的男子》（臺北：遠流出版公司，1997 年 2 月初版），頁 140。

三、父女之戀

被倪匡稱爲「情書」的《神鵰俠侶》,在情魔李莫愁哀唱「問世間,情是何物」的主題曲下,幾乎寫遍了各種男女之情。[10] 第一回登場的,即是武三通暗戀養女何沅君成瘋的不倫之戀。何沅君自幼孤苦無依,被武三通、武三娘夫婦收養在家,認作義女,憐愛有加;後來她不顧武三通的強力反對,堅持要跟原是李莫愁的意中人的陸展元成親。金庸解釋說:

> 原來何沅君長到十七八歲時,亭亭玉立,嬌美可愛,武三通對她似乎已不純粹是義父義女之情。以他武林豪俠的身份,自不能有何逾份的言行,本已內心鬱結,突然見她愛上了一個江南少年,竟是狂怒不能自己。[11]

「固執得緊」的武三通,既阻止不了養女對於愛情的追求,又氣她臨別前居然哭也不哭,曾經和李莫愁去大鬧婚禮,被大理天龍寺高僧鎮住,要他們保新婚夫婦十年平安。「憤激過甚」的武三通,從此心智失常,一直瘋瘋癲癲,十年之期一到,就去嘉興要找陸展元算帳,聽說陸氏夫婦已亡,還以手挖墳,說非要見上一面不可……。

這位曾是一燈大師座下四大弟子之一的武三通,最後瘋成滿頭亂髮、滿臉皺紋的德性,模樣狼狽不堪——頸中兀自掛著何沅君兒時所用的那塊錦緞圍涎。倪匡斥之爲「老混蛋」,因爲他認爲「一個男人,愛上了自己從小養大的一個有著義女名分的小女孩」,是不尋常的,駭人聽聞的。[12] 不過,仔細品味上引金庸的解釋,武三通雖然情不自禁地產生畸戀之情,但他畢竟並未「有何逾份的言行」,那股幾近亂倫之愛起初是鬱結在內心深處,並沒有演變成性侵害。從這點來看,他要比失戀後殺人成狂的李莫愁「理性」多了。

武三通對何沅君的癡戀,雖無血緣上的亂倫危機,但確實觸犯了「名分」,爲傳統倫理所不容。金庸另一部小說《白馬嘯西風》,提到喬裝成計老人的壯

10　詳參倪匡,《我看金庸小說》(臺北:遠流出版公司,1997 年 7 月二版),頁 40-44。
11　語見《神鵰俠侶》(臺北:遠景出版公司,1980 年 5 月初版),頁 24。
12　詳見倪匡,《五看金庸小說》(臺北:遠流出版公司,1997 年 8 月二版),頁 28-35。

年男子馬家駿，與小孤女李文秀相依爲命十年，「兩個人就像親爺爺、親孫女一般」，後來還爲她犧牲生命，儘管她已「深深愛上了別人（哈薩克少年蘇普）」。金庸對馬家駿這段奇特的感情不肯明講，卻又寫道：

> 這十年之中，他始終如爺爺般愛護自己，其實他是個壯年人。世界上親祖父對自己的孫女，也有這般好嗎？或許有，或許沒有，她不知道。[13]

作者欲蓋彌彰，讀者倒很容易就猜出馬家駿對李文秀「感到的是男女愛情」。[14] 同樣是長輩對孤女滋生莫名的男女之愛，同樣是孤女長大以後自己心有所屬，但馬家駿即使在臨終前對李文秀表明愛意，亦無不倫，因爲他們沒有正式「名分」之累；武三通則不然，他旣不能把對義女的愛埋藏心底，又無法不去干涉何沅君的選擇，除了逼瘋自己之外，是註定還要背負「不倫」的罪名的。

幸虧何沅君沒有《笑傲江湖》中岳靈珊對岳不羣的戀父情結，[15] 否則武三通的罪孽恐怕還要更加沉重。我看金庸似乎沒有要把武三通寫成「老混蛋」的意思，這個不該愛上養女的老男人，比他筆下那位想害自己親生女（公孫綠萼）來討好李莫愁的父親公孫止，或活埋親生女（凌霜華）並於棺木上塗毒只爲奪取寶藏祕訣的父親凌退思，[16] 顯然「可愛」得多。

四、師生之戀

師生關係雖然不在「五倫」之列，但在中國傳統倫理道德觀念裡，師生之戀絕對是傷風敗俗的不倫行徑。清朝中葉，男老師（袁枚、陳文述）招收

---

13 語見《白馬嘯西風》，收在《雪山飛狐》（臺北：遠景出版公司，1983 年 4 月初版），頁 417。

14 吳靄儀，《金庸小説的情》（臺北：遠流出版公司，1998 年 5 月初版，頁 116。

15 令狐冲曾對任盈盈說他小師妹岳靈珊：「崇仰我師父，她喜歡的男子，要像她爹爹那樣端莊嚴肅，沉默寡言。」岳靈珊後來愛的是林平之，任盈盈對令狐冲說：「正好林平之就像你師父一樣，一本正經，卻滿肚子都是機心。」見《笑傲江湖》（臺北：遠景出版公司，1980 年 10 月初版）第三十六回，頁 1494。

16 故事見於《連城訣》（原名《素心劍》，臺北：遠景出版公司，1980 年 2 月初版）第三回。

女弟子尚且被衛道人士（章學誠）嚴加抨擊，[17] 更何況是把故事背景設定在「南宋理宗年間」的那個《神鵰俠侶》的年代呢？金庸在《神鵰俠侶》這部情書中安排小龍女和楊過這對女老師、男弟子彼此愛戀，並且兩度大聲公開宣布要結爲夫妻，理所當然是要被當時的江湖社會所不齒的。

　　第一次，在陸家莊上，「於什麼禮法人情壓根兒一竅不通」的小龍女說出「我自己要做過兒的妻子」一番言語時，現場數百人「臉上都是又驚又詫、又是尷尬、又是不以爲然的神色」；輪到楊過表態時，他：

> 大聲說道：「我做了什麼事礙著你們了？我又害了誰啦？姑姑教過我武功，可是我偏要她做我妻子。你們斬我一千刀、一萬刀，我還是要她做妻子。」[18]

這番話語驚四座，直到與小龍女攜手出莊，群雄仍望著二人背影，「有的鄙夷，有的惋惜，有的憤怒，有的驚詫」。

　　第二次，在重陽宮裡，小龍女命在旦夕，仍掛念楊過孤苦伶仃，沒人陪伴；楊過要她明白自己的心意：

> 大聲說道：「什麼師徒名分，什麼名節清白，咱們通通當是放屁！通通滾他媽的蛋！死也罷，活也罷，咱倆誰也沒命苦，誰也不會孤苦伶仃。從今而後，你不是我師父，不是我姑姑，是我妻子！」[19]

重陽宮中數百名出家清修道人聽了，「無不大是狼狽，年老的頗爲尷尬，年輕的少不免起了凡心。各人面面相覷，有的不禁臉紅。」待他倆肆無忌憚地在重陽宮後殿拜堂成親，則更惹得「全眞教上下人等無不憤怒」。

　　金庸於《神鵰俠侶》一再聲明「其時君臣、父子、師徒之間的名分要緊之極」（第十一回）、「宋人最重禮法，師徒間尊卑倫常，看得與君臣、父子一般，萬萬逆亂不得」、「當時宋人拘泥禮法，那裡聽見過這般肆無忌憚的叛逆之論」（第十四回），卻又刻意使小龍女、楊過這場不倫之戀白熱化，屢屢製造愛情與倫理的激烈衝突，最後還讓失貞（第七回）的小龍女、斷臂（第三

17　詳參劉達臨，《縱橫華夏性史──古代性文明搜奇》下冊（臺北：性林文化公司，1995年11月），頁361-366。

18　同註11，頁551。

19　同前註，頁1127。

十四回）的楊過，突破「禮教大防」，成就「師生之戀」，創造出一個勇於追求愛情、敢於享受愛情的新典範。影響所及，直到現在，「楊過與小龍女」仍然是多數讀者最羨慕的一對有情人。[20]

　　有人說，楊過、小龍女結爲夫婦，金庸特別註明「小龍女年長於楊過數歲，……到二人成婚之時，已似年貌相若」，並補充「婚後別離一十六年，……久別重逢，反顯得楊過年紀比她爲大了」，未免拘泥，主張：

> 若相愛可以忘年，不必規限於世俗之見，又何必鄭重解釋外貌誰長誰幼？蕭伯納
> 喜劇《康狄達》中，少年詩人愛上中年婦人，爲她婉拒，她勸他道：「你要對自
> 己說：我三十歲時，她是四十五歲；我六十歲時，她七十五……」少年接口：「一
> 百年後，我們是同一個年歲。」這才是超脫世俗之見。[21]

這樣的說法言之成理。不過轉而設想，如果小龍女年紀大過楊過太多，甚或達到「枯楊戀」（老妻少夫）的地步，羨慕這對偶像情侶的讀者恐怕就要大爲減少了！如果再依法律觀點來看，完全不考慮年紀的話，也可能與現代法律相牴觸。文學作品超脫傳統世俗之見的同時，在許多地方還是得合於當下世俗，才能被大家所接受，金庸小說用心拿捏男女主角年貌這一細節，應該有其必要才對。

　　又有人說，楊過、小龍女的愛情之所以能戰勝禮教大防，是因爲「在現代生活中，這一條師生不能戀愛、結婚的倫理已經不存在了」，所以作者盡可以毫無思想包袱及道德負擔地放手寫去。[22] 這樣的說法也很有道理。然而換個角度想想，如果小龍女、楊過的師生角色對調，換成男老師楊過、女弟子小龍女的話，他們當初遭遇挫折與後來受到歡迎的程度，難道還會跟現在完全一樣嗎？可見作者在處理這椿師生之戀時，還是頗具匠心的。金庸自己也清楚「師生不能結婚的觀念，在現代人心目中當然根本不存在」，不過他另有

20　「金庸茶館」電腦網站 1998 年 9 月曾有「最羨慕金庸小說中的那一對有情人？」投
　　票活動，結果「楊過與小龍女」獲得第一，「令狐冲與任盈盈」次之。詳見《中國時
　　報》，民 87 年 9 月 14 日，第 9 版。
21　吳靄儀，《金庸小說的女子》（臺北：遠流出版公司，1998 年 2 月初版），頁 129-130。
　　金庸的註明補充原文，見於《神鵰俠侶》第三十九回，頁 1609-1610。
22　陳墨，《金庸小說的情愛世界》，頁 182。

幾句話值得我們深思：

> 然則我們今日認爲天經地義的許許多多規矩習俗，數百年後是不是也大有可能被
> 人認爲毫無意義呢？[23]

五、兄妹之戀

　　武俠小說裡描寫「師兄妹」恩怨情仇者，是司空見慣的，涉及婚外情的師兄妹間的不倫情節（例如：金庸《雪山飛狐》中田靑文與師兄曹雲奇私通、《倚天屠龍記》中成崑與師妹陽夫人私通），也不怎麼稀奇。至於親兄妹間，若有亂倫行爲發生，那可是天大的醜聞了，處理這類敏感題材的文學作品，也便因而格外引人注目。金庸武俠小說裡，難道有這樣的倫理悲劇嗎？

　　金庸的短篇小說《鴛鴦刀》，發明了一種「夫妻刀法」，林玉龍、任飛燕這對寶貝夫妻空知招數，卻因感情不合而使不上力，倒是由靑年戀人袁冠南、蕭中慧學以致用。孰料袁、蕭二人訂下婚約以後，才發現二人的生母同爲晉陽大俠蕭半和的夫人：

> 蕭中慧聽得袁冠南叫出一聲「媽」來，身子一搖，險險跌倒，腦海中只響著一個
> 聲音：「原來他是我哥哥，原來他是我哥哥……他是我哥哥……」[24]

「心如刀絞」的蕭中慧，眼看不能跟同父異母的袁冠南成親，又不得不在緊急情況下與哥哥合使「夫妻刀法」禦敵，眞是情何以堪！故事的結局是，後來證實他們的母親與蕭半和並無夫妻之實，二人這才破啼爲笑，不過倒委屈了蕭半和，使他在大庭廣眾下吐露出「在十六歲上便淨了身子」去當太監的祕密。

　　後來金庸寫作《天龍八部》時，類似的兄妹不倫之戀危機再度出現。《天龍八部》男主角之一的段譽，有個風流老爸段正淳，貴家公子出身、不通世務俗禮的他，也是個情癡情種，專情於王語嫣，兼及鍾靈、木婉淸等人，頗

23　同註 11，頁 1671。

24　語見《鴛鴦刀》，收在《雪山飛狐》（臺北：遠景出版公司，1983 年 4 月初版），頁 299。

似《紅樓夢》裡的賈寶玉。[25] 賈寶玉固然「素行不良」，卻向無兄妹亂倫之虞，因爲他根本沒有親妹妹；段譽則不然，緣於風流老爸四處撒情播種，使得他的心上人都一一變成了親妹妹，並引發出接連不斷的亂倫危機。

先是發誓第一個見她容顏者非殺即嫁的木婉清，好不容易與段譽訂下夫妻之約，卻由段正淳親口告訴她：「你不能和譽兒成親，也不能殺他」、「因爲段譽是妳的親哥哥」！這項打擊使她痛不欲生，獨自走向無量山山腳下的江邊，並落入四大惡人之首段延慶的手中。接著段延慶與段正淳情敵之一的鍾萬仇，使計將木婉清、段譽困於石室，讓他倆服下猛烈春藥「陰陽和合散」，企圖陷害「段正淳的親生兒子和親生女兒同處一室，淫穢亂倫」，做爲報復。幸經華赫艮等人挖通地道，拿鍾萬仇之女鍾靈和木婉清掉包，令鍾萬仇「自作自受」。誰知這位鍾靈竟然也是段正淳的私生女，亂倫罪惡始終揮之不去（以上情節見於第七至九回）。後來，王語嫣、段譽枯井定情（第四十五回），同樣還是得飽嚐亂倫罪行的煎熬，因爲他們仍舊是同父異母而不自知的親兄妹。

該如何化解這接踵而至的亂倫危機呢？金庸安排的不是別人，正是段正淳的元配、段譽的母親刀白鳳，這位擺夷女子當初惱恨丈夫用情不專，心想：

> 我要找一個天下最醜陋、最污穢、最卑賤的男人來和他相好。你是王爺，是大將軍，我偏偏去和一個臭叫化相好。[26]

她如此作賤自己，並懷孕生下了段譽，而那個臭乞丐正是段延慶。這個祕密，直到第四十八回，才由刀白鳳娓娓道出，以拯救段譽免遭親生父親段延慶的毒手，並且一舉消弭段譽與王語嫣、鍾靈、木婉清的亂倫憂慮。

原來《天龍八部》裡兄妹幾近亂倫的悲哀，正如段譽所謂：「是上代陰錯陽差結成的冤孽」。這樣的手法和《鴛鴦刀》如出一轍，都是作者先故弄玄虛，藉小說人物的痛苦掙扎牽動著讀者閱讀的情緒，然後再以另一椿孽情來化解不倫，釋放大家沉重的負擔。

25　吳靄儀曾撰文比較「段譽與賈寶玉」，並且肯定兩者的確很像，詳參《金庸小說的男子》，頁 67-74。

26　語見《天龍八部》（臺北：遠景出版公司，1979 年 11 月初版），頁 2014。

　　說穿了，金庸小說根本沒有兄妹不倫之戀存在！不像古龍的武俠小說，
貨眞價實地去書寫同胞兄妹成親的聳人情節。[27]

六、同性之戀

　　金庸小說不存在眞正的兄妹不倫之戀，倒是曾有同性之戀的描寫，見於
《笑傲江湖》東方不敗與楊蓮亭的身上。

　　東方不敗趁任我行苦研「吸星大法」時篡位成功，當上了日月神教教主，
之後練成《葵花寶典》，號稱武功天下第一。在黑木崖上，任我行、任盈盈父
女和向問天、令狐沖四人聯手也打他不過，他是不忍看到男寵楊蓮亭受傷才
分心落敗的，臨死之前說道：

> 唉，冤孽，冤孽，我練那《葵花寶典》，照著寶典上的祕方，自宮練氣，煉丹服藥，
> 漸漸的鬍子沒有了，說話聲音變了，性子也變了。我從此不愛女子，把七個小妾
> 都殺了，卻……把全副心意放在楊蓮亭這鬚眉男子身上。倘若我生爲女兒身，那
> 就好了。[28]

他的男寵楊蓮亭，先前任盈盈說他「只二十來歲年紀，武功旣低，又無辦事
才幹」，第三十回初次亮相則是「身形魁梧，滿臉虯髯，形貌極爲雄健威武」。
「自宮」後變得男不男、女不女的東方不敗面對他的粗聲粗氣，始終百依百順，
死前還不忘請任我行饒楊蓮亭一命。

　　《笑傲江湖》裡，「揮劍白宮」苦練武功祕笈的，還有一個林平之，不過
他沒有搞同性戀。[29] 金庸說他不喜歡東方不敗，所以把他女性化了，刻意將
這個男人寫得不像男人，[30] 但關於他與楊蓮亭的同性戀行爲，除了嗲聲嗲

27　古龍《名劍風流》一書，描寫殺人莊莊主姬苦情、墨玉夫人姬悲情二人，既是同胞兄
　　妹，也是結髮夫妻，他們姬家人都很驕傲，總認爲自己家人才是最優秀的，所以世代
　　均採兄妹成親，生下來的子女卻往往是白癡或瘋子。

28　同註15，第三十一回，頁1291。

29　同上註，見第三十五回。林平之練的是《辟邪劍譜》，雖然沒搞同性戀，但也導致心
　　理變態。

30　同註10，頁73。

氣、親暱服侍的幾個畫面之外，實際上並未再加著墨。這段武林男同性戀故事，有人說是「神來之筆」、「看來又絕不噁心」，[31] 有人則說「讀得人又噁心又歎息」，[32] 各家看法不一。

　　現代武俠小說中，深入描寫同性之戀的極少，這大概跟它通常被視爲不倫有關，像古龍《畫眉鳥》那樣敍述不倫的女同性戀者的作品，是很罕見的。[33]

　　中國古典小說中，清代的《紅樓夢》、《品花寶鑑》有同性戀描寫，這是眾所週知的，而早在明代末年，實已出現《龍陽逸史》、《弁而釵》、《宜春香質》三部描寫露骨的同性戀小說專書了。[34] 其中，《弁而釵》二十回分「情貞」、「情俠」、「情烈」、「情奇」四紀，那〈情俠紀〉五回歸爲古代男同性戀武俠小說，亦無不可；《宜春香質》二十回分「風」、「花」、「雪」、「月」四集，那〈風集〉第二回不僅是男同性戀故事，主角且爲師生，不倫至極。

　　這麼比較起來，在同性之戀題材的選擇和書寫的內容上，金庸小說顯然是保守多了。

七、結　語

　　以上大體按金庸小說創作先後順序，鉤稽闡述其涉及不倫之戀的人物與情節。聚合這些以幾近亂倫爲主題的故事段落，我們不難看出金庸從第一部作品《書劍恩仇錄》以降，不斷地在他的武俠小說中運用不倫之戀的情欲題材。

　　一直到 1972 年最後完成的《鹿鼎記》，他還是不忘在那荒唐的大床春光秀裡，安排叔嫂近乎不倫的鏡頭，說那韋小寶把剛結拜的葛爾丹王子的女人

31　金庸，〈小說創作的幾點思考〉（金庸在「金庸小說與二十世紀中國文學」國際研討會閉幕式上的講話），《明報月刊》33：8（1998 年 8 月），頁 49。

32　曹正文，《金庸小說人物譜》（臺北：知書房出版社，1996 年 10 月），頁 59。

33　古龍《畫眉鳥》，乃其《楚留香傳奇》的第三部，書中寫到神水宮主人水母陰姬是個同性戀者，宮南燕既是她的女弟子，也是她的性伴侶，爲了獨占她，還殺了她的舊日情人雄娘子。

34　詳參陳益源，〈明末流行風——小官當道：明代的三部同性戀小說〉，《聯合文學》13：4（民 86 年 2 月），頁 41-44。

阿琪也抱上床去，心中反覆交戰，到底還是放過了這位二嫂。[35] 結果跟《書劍恩仇錄》余魚同、駱冰叔嫂之戀一樣，都只是「虛驚一場」罷了！

　　刻意製造人性情欲與倫理道德的高度衝突，是金庸小說塑造人物形象時慣用的一種手法。余魚同（駱冰）、武三通（何沅君）、楊過（小龍女）、段譽（木婉清）……等正面人物，歷經「高度衝突」的嚴酷考驗，情感逐漸豐富起來，性格也豐滿許多，雖不能全美，卻又更加符合眞實的人性，而這也正是金庸所勇於嘗試的。[36]

　　當然，金庸設下「衝突」以後，還得預留替這些正面人物解套的空間，所以我們看到他的尺度始終徘徊在義叔嫂、養父女、假兄妹和沒有血親關係的師生之戀上，而不會出現像古龍《名劍風流》那種親兄妹亂倫的描寫，因爲他努力要塑造的並非醜惡的反面人物。反面人物的醜惡，原本比正面人物的美好，更適於利用不倫之戀來作呈現，但金庸寫起歐陽鋒、東方不敗的不倫，倒是幾筆就帶過去，頗爲出人意表，而這也是金庸與眾不同的地方吧。

　　在中國古典豔情小說裡，除了《宜春香質》等同性戀專書之外，亦不乏細膩描寫亂倫的作品，像寫私弟、私翁、私伯、私叔、私姪等「所私者十有二人」的《癡婆子傳》，寫武則天姑姪相通、穢亂皇宮的《濃情快史》，寫阮大鋮家翁媳、兄妹淫亂乃至有一游氏父子誤戲龍陽的《姑妄言》等等，[37] 其故事人物全皆猥瑣不堪。與眾不同的金庸，不走這條老路，他改以不倫之戀來刻劃正面人物的情欲與修養，道德觀念顯得格外強烈。

　　金庸說過「小說並不是道德教科書」，[38] 但他也承認小說：

35　金庸說韋小寶——忽然想到：「朋友妻，不可欺。二嫂，你是我嫂子，咱們英雄好漢，可得講義氣。」將阿琪又抱到廳上，放在椅中坐好，只見她目光中頗有嘉許之意。韋小寶見她容顏嬌好，喘氣甚急，胸脯起伏不已，忽覺後悔……當下又抱起阿琪，走向內室。走了幾步，忽想：「關雲長千里送皇嫂，可沒將劉大嫂變成關二嫂。韋小寶七步送王嫂，總不能太不講義氣，少兩美就少兩美罷，還怕將來湊不齊？」於是立即轉身，又將阿琪放在椅中。——見於《鹿鼎記》第三十九回，頁 1651。

36　金庸曾說：「一般武俠小說的男女主角總是差不多完美，所以我就試著寫男女主角雙方都有缺憾，看看是否可以。」語見陸離，〈金庸訪問記〉，收入杜南發等，《諸子百家看金庸（伍）》（臺北：遠流出版公司，1997 年 10 月二版），頁 21。

37　以上所言諸書，均收入陳慶浩、王秋桂主編，《思無邪匯寶》（臺北：臺灣大英百科公司，1994 年 9 月—1997 年 8 月）。

38　同註 4。

　　大致上它是反映作者個人對社會的價值觀念。書中主角常常要面臨許多選擇，透過這些選擇，作者把他的道德觀念傳播出來。[39]

觀察金庸小説人物不倫之戀的安排，以及書中主角的選擇，我們看到了金庸前衛的一面，也看到了保守的地方。前者主要表現在不倫題材的運用和正面人物的創造技巧上，他特別擅於包裝偶像，連小龍女、楊過師生年貌需調整的細節都注意到了；後者則見於不倫之戀的虛假和若干觀點的局限，譬如曹雪芹可以讓不倫事件真的在賈府發生，可以讓賈寶玉既愛女子也愛男人，金庸卻常常只是故意製造緊張，而且不容「韋小寶這小傢伙」[40] 亂搞同性戀。

　　話雖如此，曹雪芹是曹雪芹，金庸是金庸，我們不能要求金庸寫《紅樓夢》，我們只是在談金庸小説人物的「不倫之戀」而已。

---

39 語見王力行，〈新聞文學一戶牖〉，收入杜南發等，《諸子百家看金庸（伍）》，頁 72。
40 金庸説：「事實上，我寫《鹿鼎記》寫了五分之一，便已把『韋小寶這小傢伙』當作了好朋友，多所縱容，頗加袒護。」語見金庸，〈韋小寶這小傢伙！〉，收入倪匡，《三看金庸小説》（臺北：遠流出版公司，1997 年 8 月二版），頁 212。

絕世聰明絕世癡

——《笑傲江湖》中的藝術與人物

陳　芳　英

國立藝術學院戲劇系

摘　要

　　情之所鍾，正在我輩，所以哀樂過人，不同流俗。

　　在動盪混亂的社會中，人人欲求此心的安頓，有的人執著於現世的名位權勢，汲汲於稱霸天下，號令群雄；有的人勘透禮法的空虛頑固，渴慕精神的自由解放，寄情於光明鮮潔的藝術。然而江湖險惡，欲進者，種種機謀狡詐之事當前，欲退者，又往往無所逃於天地之間，貪嗔癡愛、恩怨情仇，繆轇萬方而不可解，終至怪誕驚狂，以身相殉。

　　孤山梅莊江南四友，沉溺於琴棋書畫酒，一旦至寶當前，身家性命一概不要，甘犯魔教教主東方不敗禁令，與令狐沖比劍。而衡山劉正風、魔教曲洋，琴簫相合，傾蓋相交，卻不見容於正邪兩道，於是攜手赴死，以眞血性噴薄出凜然生氣，從容而美麗。風淸揚以其強韌的個性，自我放逐數十年，終不忍獨孤九劍湮沒無傳，將劍法盡授令狐沖，之後再度飄然遠引。

　　余滄海、左冷禪、岳不羣，紛紛亂亂地爭奪武功秘笈及盟主之位，眞小人與僞君子纏鬥不休，人性的畏瑣卑汙在光明正大的口號中，遂行陰謀。任我行和東方不敗則爲了日月神教的教主之爭，各自練就陰狠奇詭的武功，並因而身毀人亡。在彼此爭鬥的過程中，權力機制藉象徵符號和儀式行爲施展到極致。

　　藝術的眞義若是精神的大自在、大解放，則風淸揚「無招勝有招」的劍法傳授，確如庖丁解牛，技中見道。只是，令狐沖領略了藝事的自由解放，

在生命中是否也能自由自在地笑傲江湖呢？

> 一切有爲法　如夢幻泡影
> 如露亦如電　應作如是觀

一

情之所鍾，正在我輩，所以哀樂過人，不同流俗。

宗白華論晉人藝術特質時，特別拈出「一往有深情」一語，所謂：

> 深於情者，不僅對宇宙人生體會到至深的無名哀感，擴而之，可以成爲耶穌釋迦
> 的悲天憫人；就是快樂的體驗也是深入肺腑，驚心動魄；淺俗薄情的人，不僅不
> 能深哀，且不知所謂眞樂。[1]

金庸筆下人物，每多深情不悔者，情之所至，或投注於人，或投注於事，或投注於物，貪瞋癡愛、恩怨情仇，繆轕萬方而不可解，終至怪詭驚狂、粉身碎骨，也在所不惜，眞個是「人生自是有情癡，此恨不關風與月」。

《笑傲江湖》論及藝術的篇幅，較金庸其他作品爲多，藝術在此，不只是深情所寄，也是死生以之的對象。衡山派掌門「瀟湘夜雨」莫大先生胡琴隨身，「琴中藏劍，劍發琴音」。梅莊四友黃鍾公、黑白子、禿筆翁、丹青生對琴棋書畫酒的癡迷執著，大概用得上「無與倫比」四字考語，相形之下，綠竹翁、祖千秋對酒和酒器的斤斤講求，只能算是具體而微了。小說男女主角令狐冲、任盈盈相識相知相惜，也肇因於琴，終於結下死生契闊、白首偕老的姻緣。最驚心動魄的，當然是魔教長老曲洋和衡山派劉正風，琴簫訂交，卻引來所謂「名門正派」圍殺，爲了珍重面對音樂時光風霽月的磊落胸懷，琴簫相諧無可取代的情誼旣不見容於無知濁世，兩人選擇了「雙手相握，齊聲長笑，內力運處，迸斷內息主脈，閉目而逝。」[2] 而金庸筆下最令我動容的人物，當推風清揚。他自我放逐數十年，不與人事，還是一念不忍，出洞授

1　宗白華，〈論世説新語和晉人的美〉，《美學的散步》（臺北：洪範，1981），頁 59-84。
2　《笑傲江湖》第 1 冊，頁 276。

了令狐冲獨孤九劍，淡淡一句「只是盼望獨孤前輩的絕世武功不遭滅絕而已。」[3] 令人但覺宇宙荒寒，根觸無邊。明知小說人物不過虛構，動情處卻遠勝世間眞實人物，我有古琴二張，一張即命名曰：「風清揚」，月朗風清之際，拂絃彈奏〈普庵咒〉，常不免懷想華山頂上，飄飄下崖的瘦削身影。

　　令狐冲、任盈盈雖因琴曲結緣，但在生命的重大時刻，他們在乎的是兩心如一，便是天長地久，即使當下天崩地裂也毫不介懷，更不要說價值連城的綠綺古琴或琴譜了。倒是幾位人入中年，已屆初老，或年事已高的豪傑俠士，對藝術一事割捨不下，這卻也不能僅以「執著」一詞論斷之。江湖風波險惡，在歷經了各種打殺、機心之後，早已勘透禮法規矩的空虛和頑固，他們要從自己的眞性情眞血性裡發掘人生的眞意義眞道德，藝術的純美潔淨，遂成爲「唯一」。人到中年，才能深切體會到人生的意義、責任，並反省人生的究竟，哀樂之感也才得以深沉。走過得失榮辱之後，劉正風想金盆洗手，江南四友自求隱居西湖，風清揚早已遁跡華山之巔。經過掙扎反省才擁有心的大解放大自由，更以深沉的哀樂之情，執著守候唯一放不下，卻也是讓此心能有所掛搭的某種光明晶瑩的愛戀。在這樣的精神解放自由中，「人心裡面的美與醜，高貴與殘忍，聖潔與惡魔，同樣發揮了極致。」[4] 因此，曲洋爲尋得〈廣陵散〉舊譜，連掘二十九座魏晉前古墓；江南四友爲獲得〈廣陵散〉、二十局棋譜、張旭〈牽意帖〉和范寬〈谿山行旅圖〉，甘犯東方不敗禁令，安排令狐冲與任我行比劍。當然，美之極，亦即雄強之極，對藝術的執著既無法放棄，則曲洋與劉正風的攜手赴死，宛若殉道，從容而美麗，其眞血性噴薄而出的凜然生氣，夭矯雄健、震心澈骨。

二

　　令狐冲雖得風清揚傳授獨孤九劍，但因身受重傷，內力全失，盈盈既不知去向，自己又被師父岳不羣逐出華山門牆。固然方證、方生兩位大師慈悲，願授易筋經助其療傷，但令狐冲年少氣盛，不肯改投別派，拜別兩位大師，

3　同註2，頁415。
4　同註1。

萬念俱灰地步出少林。生既無懼，死亦何懼，莫名其妙地打抱不平，結識魔教右使向問天，與黑白兩道混戰一場。之後，又懵懵懂懂地隨向問天到西湖梅莊，向問天是籌畫周全，利用令狐冲救任我行，令狐冲卻一無所知，無可無不可的與眾人比劍。《笑傲江湖》第十九回〈打賭〉、二十回〈入獄〉，比試過程極是凶險，讀來則煞是好看。金庸在此，極盡炫學之能事，對琴棋書畫稍有涉略的讀者，更是莞爾失笑，頷首擊節，讀之再三。

　　且說令狐冲與向問天來到西湖，穿過孤山老幹橫斜、枝葉茂密的梅林，莊院大門先有虞允文題「梅莊」二字，預告了莊院主人的儒雅風流。進入大廳，一幅墨意淋漓、繪著仙人背影的中堂，題款是「丹青生大醉後潑墨」，令狐冲歎賞「這字中畫中，更似乎蘊藏著一套極高明的劍術」，順利引出好畫嗜酒的丹青生。二人談酒論交，則之前令狐冲流連洛陽東城小巷竹舍，聽綠竹翁暢談酒道，得識天下美酒來歷，及黃河岸旁柳樹之下與祖千秋論杯，都成了此一關目的伏筆了。而爲了暢飲冰鎮吐魯番葡萄酒，丹青生自然不得不將練過「玄天指」的二哥黑白子請了出來。此時向問天出示北宋范寬〈谿山行旅圖〉、唐張旭〈率意帖〉、圍棋名局、晉嵇康〈廣陵散〉，逼江南四友與令狐冲比劍，琴棋書畫至寶當前，四友既沉迷日久，豈能禁得起撩撥？身家性命一概不要，十二年閒居清福也就在他們答應比試的同時，化爲煙塵了。論述這四樣藝術奇珍，以及比試之際藝術、武功合一的描寫，金庸委實發揮炫學的功力，令人歎賞。

　　炫學之作，自古有之。其一，如希臘曼尼匹安式諷刺詩文（Menippean Satire）：

> 這類文字不以情節曲折取勝，而專事以百科全書式的文采知識，盡情逆轉嘲諷時人時事中的缺憾。荒誕不經的冒險，千奇百怪的人物列傳，似是而非的「學術」論爭，皆是其引人入勝處。至於對宗師大儒、典章經籍的揶揄，則更爲精華所在。[5]

當然這類作品的作者，本人需有極高的才情學識，方足以玩弄各家人物學說於股掌之上；中國近代作家，唯錢鍾書近於此類。其二，則是在作品中大量

5　見王德威，《衆聲喧嘩》（臺北：遠流，1988），頁 145-146。

闌用各種知識，以示博學，及加強說服力，傳統詩詞歌賦引經據典，即此類也。近代捷克作家米蘭‧昆德拉亦此中高手，並往往旁出側枝，故意造成「離題」（digression）的效果。臺灣當代作家朱天文《荒人手記》、〈世紀末的華麗〉，也都達到一定效果。其三，則純屬虛構，卻因不斷堆疊各種符碼，造成似真的效果。王德威論李永平《吉陵春秋》，謂「它是原鄉傳統流傳數十年後，一項最吊詭的特技表演。」「形式本身的玩耍試驗，才是該書最大的成就。它顯示有心人可以閑熟的擺弄原鄉作品中的各種修辭符號，而不必汲汲追尋鄉土的本質或根源問題。」[6] 最傑出的「表演者」、可以說是當代的記號學大師、義大利的安伯托‧艾可，他的三部小說《玫瑰的名字》、《傅科擺》、《昨日之島》，無一不是充塞各種符號、似是而非的歷史考證。張大春討論《昨日之島》的〈不登岸便不登岸〉「探索被禁制的知識」一節中云：

> 這個在東西方不約而同出現的書寫傳統所著意者，訴諸以敘述體處理、開拓、擴充，甚至不惜杜撰、虛擬、捏造所謂的「知識」。不論「知識」被宗教或政治打壓、縮減、剝削或利用到如何荒謬貧弱的地步，這個書寫傳統都能夠保存或製造出種種超越於禁制之外的智慧。[7]

基於同樣的自覺，張大春以近作《本事》宣示它對大師艾可不遑多讓的姿態。

金庸的炫學，是屬於第二類的，而且已經到了「隨心所欲而不踰矩」的境界。每部小說的附圖、圖片說明、後記，在在都顯示他縝密的考證工夫；《射鵰英雄傳》的附錄和後記，尤其具現了史學家的意圖。他無意以假亂真，更無意杜撰、虛擬、捏造史實和知識，即使是作為小說必要的「虛構」，雖不必對號入座，卻也不免暗示「此中有人，呼之欲出」。當然，就像金庸夫子自道，[8] 寫《笑傲江湖》時，自然而然反映了文化大革命的狀況，但用意不在影射，而是想藉由書中人物，刻劃人性和政治生活中的普遍現象。至於諸書論列事物的博學多聞，正是讀者閱讀金庸小說的一大樂趣。

讀《天龍八部》，無法忽略貫穿全書對茶花的討論，彷彿看完該書，人人

6　王德威，《小說中國》（臺北：麥田，1993），頁 272。

7　張大春，〈不登岸便不登岸〉，安伯托‧艾可《昨日之島》（臺北：皇冠，1998 導讀），頁 9-23。

8　金庸，《笑傲江湖》〈後記〉。

都不由自主地成了茶花的癡愛者。《笑傲江湖》中,令狐冲和綠竹翁、祖千秋、丹青生三次談酒論杯,雖不必如金聖歎評點六才子書,大聲疾呼一論如何、再論如何、三論又如何,卻也是值得拍案驚奇的場景。飲梨花酒用翡翠杯、葡萄酒用夜光杯,本不足為奇,及至飲高粱用青銅酒爵、百草酒用古藤杯,則別開生面,使不識酒者雖未必一飲為快,卻因而覺得酒中自有無窮滋味。至於識酒者讀至四蒸四釀的吐魯番美酒陳中有新、新中有陳,恐怕忍不住要舉觥浮白了。

　　梅莊比劍一場,是炫學離題之作,金庸寫得神采飛動,堪稱絕唱。四友各有所嗜,其癡愛對象不同,性格也因之有別,比武鬥劍時,更呈現了不同的特質和局限。丹青生自稱酒第一,畫第二,劍第三。好酒而爽朗不拘小節,作畫使劍每多破綻,由畫意衍生的「潑墨披麻劍法」敗在令狐冲手下,也不過瀟灑豁達的說聲:「咱們再喝酒。」禿筆翁是四友中最「癡」的吧,善使判官筆,又將書法名家的筆意化入武功之中,正如任我行所說:

> 臨敵過招,那是生死繫於一線的大事,全力相搏,尚恐不勝,那裡還有閒情逸致,講究什麼鍾王碑帖?[9]

偏生遇著識字無多的令狐冲,什麼〈裴將軍詩〉、〈八濛山銘〉、〈懷素自敘帖〉,一概不知,既無文字障,就不受筆劃拘束,從中攪和,禿筆翁筆路窒滯,內力改道,鬱怒之餘索性不打了,大筆醮酒,在牆上寫就殷紅如血的詩句,倒也天真浪漫。黑白子是善奕之人,算計日久,性格也變得陰沉狡詐,和令狐冲、向問天的應對也好,比試也好,都因「機關算盡太聰明」而左支右絀,更何況早就心存歹念,暗中求任我行傳授吸星大法,反於日後被令狐冲吸盡功力,骨骼斷絕,只剩皮囊。黃鍾公朝夕與琴曲相伴,沉穩雅穆,「七絃無形劍」未能動搖令狐冲分毫,自是神態蕭索,得知令狐冲實因內力盡失,對琴音無所感應,大喜過望之餘,也生惜才之念,想推薦「殺人名醫平一指」或少林方證「易筋經」,並將師父遺物療傷丸藥相贈。及至任我行以「三尸腦神丹」相逼,自盡身亡,不失豪傑襟度。「人在江湖,身不由己」,想遠離是非,隱居孤山而不可得,只有以身相殉了。

9　同註2,第2冊,頁844。

正如黃鍾公臨終之語：

> 我四兄弟身入日月神教，本意是在江湖上行俠仗義，好好做一番事業。但任教主
> 性子暴躁，威福自用，我四兄弟早萌退志。東方教主接任之後，寵信奸佞，鋤除
> 教中老兄弟。我四人更是心灰意懶，討此差使，一來得以遠離黑木崖，不必與人
> 勾心鬥角，二來閒居西湖，琴書遣懷。10

　　任盈盈在任我行失蹤之後，爲求自保，也爲了遠離黑木崖東方不敗創下
的歌功頌德行徑，與綠竹翁避居洛陽東城小巷，撫琴遣懷。因緣際會，替令
狐冲證明〈笑傲江湖之曲〉實爲琴簫之譜，不是劍譜，洗去令狐冲偷盜「辟
邪劍譜」的嫌疑，並授〈清心普善咒〉（即〈普庵咒〉）助其療傷。〈普庵咒〉
和〈笑傲江湖之曲〉遂成二人日後相守之際重要的溝通媒介，書中更以〈碧
宵吟〉、〈有所思〉點出二人情懷，當令狐冲告別綠竹小舍時，盈盈彈〈有所
思〉相送，纏綿之致，不言可喻。

　　書中對「瀟湘夜雨」莫大先生著墨不多，首度出場時，是劉正風金盆洗
手大典之前，在茶館中露了一手「迴風落雁劍」，一劍削斷七隻茶杯。再次出
現，則是劉正風被大嵩陽手費彬追殺，莫大先生以「百變千幻衡山雲霧十三
式」殺死費彬。莫大先生劍招變幻，猶如鬼魅，來去亦無跡可尋，只有幽幽
胡琴聲相隨。其後告知令狐冲，盈盈囚居少林之事，並代爲護送恆山弟子。
及至嵩山比武奪帥，因容讓岳靈珊，反被岳靈珊以圓石擊斷肋骨，吐血遠避。
群豪齊聚華山思過崖後洞觀看石壁劍招，中了埋伏，莫大先生幸而全身而退。
令狐冲、盈盈成親之日，莫大先生特別往奏〈鳳求凰〉，以申賀意。胡琴之聲，
本自淒淸，莫大先生奏來更覺悲涼，劉正風曾對曲洋表示，和莫大不睦，只
是性子不投，

> 師哥奏琴往而不復，曲調又是儘量往哀傷的路上走。好詩好詞講究樂而不淫，哀
> 而不傷，好曲子何嘗不是如此？我一聽到他的胡琴，就避而遠之。11

莫大先生骨瘦如柴，雙肩拱起，像一個時時刻刻便會倒斃的癆病鬼，武功怪

10　同註2，第3冊，頁903。
11　同註2，第1冊，頁274。

詭，喜歡胡琴這種樂器，倒也相稱。

劉正風自許當今之世，按孔吹簫，不作第二人想，而撫琴奏樂，曲洋當屬第一，二人琴簫相和，傾蓋相交。雖然一在魔教，一在衡山，聯床夜話多次，彼此仰慕敬重，原以爲退出江湖，便可以遠離門派是非，豈知天不從人願，金盆傾倒，洗手之舉已不可爲。當嵩山陸柏問及魔教曲洋，劉正風當著滿堂英雄豪傑，回道：「不錯！曲洋曲大哥，我不但識得，而且是我生平唯一知己，最要好的朋友。」這是何等的胸襟氣魄！知己必能肝膽相照、同生共死，天下既無容身之處，二人將共同創製的〈笑傲江湖曲〉琴譜簫譜託付令狐冲，自絕身亡，雖說不無遺憾，卻是悍然無悔的。藝術的自由、莫逆於心的友誼，以鮮血塗染，自是悲壯，但在紛紛擾擾的人世也終究是無瑕的「完成」。

華山一派，原分氣、劍兩宗，各自爭勝，終於導致兄弟鬩牆，自相殘殺。玉女峰上的一場惡鬥，雙方折損高手二十餘位，劍宗大敗，幸而未在比鬥中身亡者，有的橫劍自盡，有的退居山林，華山自此由氣宗接掌，大堂「劍氣衝霄」的匾額，也改成了「正氣堂」。比劍之前，氣宗畏懼劍宗高手風淸揚，於是捏造消息，將他騙往江南，待得風淸揚回到華山，已是骨肉相殘，舊友零落之後了。風淸揚自此心灰意冷，飄然遠引。江湖中人雖知其名、聞其藝，卻不知他是生是死，人在何方。令狐冲被師父岳不羣罰在玉女峰思過崖山洞中面壁一年，坐在洞中大石上，見石壁左側刻有「風淸揚」三字，揣度是本門前輩，卻何以不曾聽師父提起。岳靈珊上崖探望，令狐冲陪岳靈珊演練「玉女劍十九式」，一時大意將岳靈珊的碧水劍彈墮深谷。月光之下，悔恨良久，風淸揚身著一襲青袍，初現俠蹤，將「玉女劍」演示一回，這是令狐冲初次見識華山派劍招精妙之處。其後田伯光欲擒令狐冲下崖，風淸揚終於現身，白鬚青袍，神氣抑鬱，臉如金紙。自此十餘日，風淸揚傳授劍招和劍道，使獨孤九劍不致失傳，也成就了令狐冲日後修爲。

獨孤九劍是獨孤求敗一生武學精華，自總訣式、破劍式、破刀式，乃致破槍式、破鞭式、破索式、破掌式、破箭式、破氣式，只攻不守，有進無退，當他仗劍天涯，欲求一敗，甚或求一對手逼他迴守一招而不可得，自是無敵於天下，卻也有無盡的寂寞吧。

風淸揚傳授令狐冲的，當然不只獨孤九劍，而是劍「道」，也是藝術與生

命之道。風清揚可以自我放逐數十年，當然是個性中有極其強韌的一面，他性格跳脫，年紀已大而英氣猶在，月旦天下人物，褒貶華山門下，言詞犀利而字字鞭辟入裡。他所強調的「人使劍法，不是劍法使人」，講「悟」，講「忘」，以及最精采的「無招勝有招」劍理，無非追求個性、劍術、藝術的大自由，下文當再論述。令狐冲在孤山梅莊對丹青生的「制敵機先」，對黑白子的「只攻不守」，固然已窺獨孤求敗和風清揚劍法堂奧；對禿筆翁時因識字無多，遂不受拘制，對黃鍾公因內力盡失，於琴音中蘊藏內力不生感應，都可以說是誤打誤撞，卻正是「無招勝有招」的神髓所在。風清揚云：

> 等到通曉了這九劍的劍意，則無所施而不可，便是將全部變化盡數忘記，也不相干，臨敵之際，更是忘記得越乾淨徹底，越不受原來劍法的拘束。[12]

三

如果說，在江湖凶險的刀劍生涯中，追慕光明鮮潔的藝術，是屬於出世的渴望；則現世最難割捨的貪愛愚癡，便是名位與權勢。以武論高下的世界，練就獨一無二的絕世神功，是取得名位權勢的不二法門。家傳、本門的武功要練到登峰造極，自不待言，天下難求的武功秘笈，也無不意圖盡收己手，方能稱霸武林，貴為盟主，號令群雄。既有稱霸之心、權位之念，秘笈是只有自己可得，不是用來切磋的，若有他人妄想爭勝，將之導入歧途或趕盡殺絕，都成了必要之惡。《笑傲江湖》正具現著秘笈的搶奪和權位的追逐，誼屬同源的「辟邪劍譜」和「葵花寶典」則為其間的關鍵。

青城派掌門、松風觀觀主余滄海首先發動攻勢，帶著青城弟子一舉挑了「福威鏢局」福州總局和各省分局，除林平之外，林家慘遭滅門，不外是為了「辟邪劍譜」口訣。華山派掌門君子劍岳不羣螳螂捕蟬，黃雀在後，先派弟子勞德諾、女兒岳靈珊隔岸觀火，偵察青城派行止，之後收錄林平之入門，並納為女婿，用心與余滄海同出一轍。塞北明駝木高峯想乘機獲利，不過是「插花」而已。令狐冲在石洞中觀習各派劍招，又得風清揚傳授獨孤九劍，劍法

12　同註2，第1冊，頁415。

大進，以致蒙受偷盜「辟邪劍譜」的嫌疑，當岳不羣取得劍譜後，索性將罪名坐實到令狐冲身上了。岳不羣練成辟邪劍法，刺瞎左冷禪，當上五嶽劍派盟主；東方不敗習得「葵花寶典」，位居日月神教教主；爲了擁有「正教」與「魔教」至高無上的尊貴之位，自宮習劍，二人深夜捫心自問，是否眞的悍然無悔呢？

左冷禪／岳不羣、任我行／東方不敗，是兩組權力鬥爭的主角。嵩山派掌門左冷禪在泰山、恆山、衡山實力稍弱，華山派又因內鬨元氣大傷的情況下，輕而易舉成爲五嶽劍派盟主。五派同氣連枝，聯手結盟，與少林、武當鼎足而三，本可維持武林一定程度的平衡與安定。但權勢的滋味使人的野心不斷膨漲擴張，左冷禪想進一步將五派合一，自任掌門，封禪台比武奪帥，籌之已久，勢在必行。在此一目的下，擋我者死。先以結交魔敎曲洋爲藉口，逼死衡山劉正風，之後鼓動華山劍宗封不平、叢不棄、成不憂與岳不羣爭奪掌門位置，挑撥泰山玉璣子奪下天門道人掌門鐵劍，如此處心積慮，原以爲成功在望，豈知眞小人終不及僞君子，還是由岳不羣笑吟吟贏得五嶽掌門。

任我行本是魔敎教主，習練「吸星大法」時眞氣逆行，東方不敗趁機奪取大權，將任我行囚禁西湖之下一十二年。任我行明知「葵花寶典」之病，故意送給東方不敗，造成東方不敗的性別錯亂。任我行脫困後，重登黑木崖合眾人之力擊潰東方不敗，再掌魔敎。如果東方不敗是造反派，任我行便可謂復辟成功。

所有的權勢機制當然是靠象徵符號和儀式行爲來完成的。[13]「象徵符號可以是物品、動作、關係、甚至是語句」，[14] 前文提及泰山派以鐵鑄短劍爲掌門「符號」，鐵劍一但易手，天門道人也失卻了掌門身份。左冷禪更以令旗爲個人地位代表，五色錦旗上綴滿了珍珠寶石，揮動時發出燦爛寶光，持旗者也躊躇滿志、顧盼自得。具有政治策略的人（Political Man），同時也就是運用象徵辦法的人（Symbolist Man）。

日月神教表明了欲屠恆山一派的意圖後，少林方證、武當冲虛率領兩派弟子上山馳救。因任我行武功太高，須奈他不得，武當弟子安排太師椅一張，

13　亞伯納・柯恩《權力結構與符號象徵》一書，有深刻討論。
14　同上註引書。

設計要引爆火藥，將任我行炸死：

> 但見那椅套以淡黃錦緞製成，金黃色絲線繡了九條金龍，捧著中間一個剛從大海中升起的太陽，左邊八個字是「中興聖教，澤被蒼生」，右邊八個字是「千秋萬載，一統江湖」。那九條金龍張牙舞爪，神采如生，這十六個字更是銀鉤鐵劃，令人瞧著說不出的舒服。在這十六個字的周圍，綴了不少明珠、鑽石，和諸般翡翠寶石。簡陋的小小庵堂之中，突然間滿室盡是珠光寶氣。[15]

冲虛又特別說明：

> 這機簧的好處，在於有人隨便一坐，並無事故，一定要坐到一炷香時分，藥引這才引發。那任我行為人多疑，又極精細，突見恆山見性峰上有這樣一張椅子，一定不會立即就坐，定是派手下人先坐上試試。這椅套上既有金龍捧日，又有什麼「千秋萬載，一統江湖」的字樣，魔教中的頭目自然誰也不敢久坐，而任我行一坐上去之後，又一定捨不得下來。[16]

要引第一魔頭入彀，也只有投其所好，備上象徵地位與威勢的坐椅，虛位以待了。

「正教」各派欲誅任我行而後快，原因之一，是不忍天下英雄盡皆折腰跪拜，口頌諛詞，高呼「聖教主千秋萬載，一統江湖」，殊不知凡此儀式，正是任我行、東方不敗宣示其權勢時不可或缺的象徵行為與儀式。

任我行、向問天、令狐冲和任盈盈在上官雲引領之下，登上黑木崖，一路重重高山，層層絞盤，好不容易到得崖頂，漢白玉巨大牌樓橫在眼前，在陽光下發出閃閃金光，任性飛揚慣了的令狐冲，都不免肅然起敬，其排場架勢，嵩山、少林均不能望其項背，遑論其餘。進了牌樓，經一條筆直的石板大路才到大門，先到後廳見過總管楊蓮亭，經上官雲幾番懇求，獲准入覲教主。穿過執戟武士交叉平舉亮晃晃的長刀，眾人從刀陣下弓腰低頭而行，再經八桿槍疾刺而至的威嚇，終於進入大殿。尚未見到教主，已受如此折辱，教主與教眾的權利關係已明明白白擺著，眾人也只能敢怒而不敢言。殿堂闊

15　同註2，第4冊，頁1662。
16　同註2，第4冊，頁1662-1663。

不過三十來尺，縱深卻有三百來尺，長殿彼端高設一座，顯然是教主座席，
殿內無窗，殿口點著明晃晃的蠟燭，教主座席卻只有兩盞油燈，火焰忽明忽
滅，教主面目模糊，天威自是難測。金庸因文化大革命而生感慨，寫東方不
敗時，往往有毛澤東身影；導演徐克直接將毛澤東〈沁園春〉指為東方不敗
之作，在影片中大吟大唱，刻意牽合，令人失笑。金庸此處由天安門一路寫
進中南海，以空間的廣袤深邃，營造東方不敗的威嚴神祕，不要說毛澤東，
古今帝王都沒有這個排場，金庸之筆又塑造了璀璨和陰森交錯的典型。至於
紅衛兵以「忠」字自許，胡亂喊些「主席萬壽無疆」的無知言詞，經金庸稍
作點染，作為權力法則（Power Order）的襯托符號，實有萬鈞之力。

　　魔教中人言必稱「教主文成武德，仁義英明，中興聖教，澤被蒼生，千
秋萬載，一統江湖」，本是噁心肉麻之極，但唸誦日久，已被制約，竟至自然
而然的順口說出，流暢已極。觀見教主一律跪拜，頌聲大作，任我行取代東
方不敗重登教主之位，初時還不適應，滿心煩惡，很快就居之不疑，遍體通
泰，日後更變本加厲，「教主」之上再加一「聖」字，表示出自己遠遠超過東
方不敗。令狐冲感歎道：

> 　　我當初只道這些無聊的玩意兒，只是東方不敗與楊蓮亭所想出來折磨人的手段，
> 　　但瞧這情形，任教主聽著這些諛詞，竟也欣然自得，絲毫不覺得肉麻！[17]

任我行後來在朝陽峯上，聽著屬下諛詞如湧，雖覺言語未免荒誕不經，但「聽
在耳中，著實受用」，一時之間，也覺得諸葛亮、關雲長、孔夫子都不能與自
己相提並論，

> 　　教眾見他站起，一齊拜伏在地，霎時之間，朝陽峯上一片寂靜，便無半點聲息。
> 　　陽光照射在任我行臉上、身上，這日月神教教主威風凜凜，宛若天神。[18]

任我行就在此刻「但願千秋萬載，永如今日」的自我祈願中，口吐鮮血，從
仙人掌上摔了下來，氣絕而亡。任我行的聰明才情，也算一代梟雄，他所追
尋的，也是至高無上、獨一無二的──只不過不是光明鮮潔、回歸內心的藝

17　同註2，第4冊，頁1296。
18　同註2，第4冊，頁1650。

術境界，而是現世的權勢名位，但，哪有什麼是千秋萬載的呢？也是癡絕吧。

四

《莊子‧養生主》庖丁解牛一節，[19] 曾是古今以來許多初讀《莊子》的人目眩神迷、難以忘懷的篇章，也是思考中國藝術精神的重要依據。[20] 當文惠君贊賞解牛之技時，庖丁回答：「臣之所好者道也，進乎技矣。」然而庖丁所謂的「道」，是在「技」中完成的，經過十九年的學習體悟，由技巧的解放得到自由，「臣以神遇而不以目視，官知止而神欲行」，然後「恢恢乎其於遊刃必有餘地矣」，解牛成為無所繫縛的精神遊戲。風清揚傳授令狐冲的劍道，正可由此細細體會。

授完獨孤九劍後，風清揚特別提醒令狐冲：同一劍法，同是一招，不同人使出，威力強弱大不相同。獨孤求敗仗劍天涯，欲求一敗而不可得，是因他已將這套劍法使得出神入化，令狐冲雖也學會，使劍時若不熟練，畢竟還是敵不了當世高手，若再苦練二十年，便可和天下英雄一較短長了。藝術的創作，是由技巧、技術中完成的。熟練之後，方能去掉斧鑿痕跡，也才能「悟」、才能「忘」。「悟」與「忘」是學習到創作之間，極為重要的途徑。徐復觀《中國藝術精神》曾舉《莊子‧大宗師》南伯子葵問乎女偊，及《莊子‧達生》梓慶削木為鐻兩則，[21] 說明學道工夫與藝術家創作的工夫全無二致，必須經過「外（忘）天下」、「外物」、「外生」、「忘吾有四肢形骸」的次第，學劍而

---

19 《莊子‧養生主》：庖丁為文惠君解牛，手之所觸，肩之所倚，足之所履，膝之所踦，砉然嚮然，奏刀騞然，莫不中音。合於桑林之舞，乃中經首之會。文惠君曰：「譆，善哉！技蓋至此乎？」庖丁釋刀對曰：「臣之所好者道也，進乎技矣。始臣之解牛之時，所見無非牛者。三年之後，未嘗見全牛也。方今之時，臣以神遇而不以目視，官知止而神欲行。依乎天理，批大郤，導大窾，因其固然，技經肯綮之未嘗，而況大軱乎！良庖歲更刀，割也；族庖月更刀，折也。今臣之刀十九年矣，所解數千牛矣，而刀刃若新發於硎。……雖然，每至於族，吾見其難為，怵然為戒，視為止，行為遲。動刀甚微，謋然已解，如土委地。提刀而立，為之四顧，為之躊躇滿志，善刀而藏之。」（《莊子集釋》，臺北：河洛，1974 年）
20 徐復觀《中國藝術精神》論莊子與道，即由庖丁解牛切入。
21 同上註引書，頁 54-56。

能將變化盡數忘記，才能無所施而不可，而忘得越乾淨徹底，才越不受原來劍法約束。

令狐冲被田伯光殺得十分狼狽時，風清揚隨口念了三十招華山劍式，要令狐冲試演一遍，因腳步方位全不相干，使出第一招「白虹貫日」，第二招「有鳳來儀」就出不了手。風清揚傳劍第一式就是「行雲流水，任意所之」，風清揚又進一步說明「學招時要活學，使招時要活使」，不但要各招渾成，更要出手無招。劍招再渾成，只要有跡可尋，敵人便有機可乘，如果根本並無招式，敵人又如何來破你的招式？這「根本無招，如何可破」替令狐冲開啟了生平從所未見，連做夢也想不到的新天地，這種自由解放的精神，正是最高藝術的體現。

超越了劍招的拘泥，得到心的大自在，才有可能將「無招勝有招」發揮到淋漓盡致。日本禪僧澤庵和尚，曾教誨他的武士弟子柳生但馬守，「要把心永遠保持流動狀態」。[22] 當武士站在他對手前面，他並不想到他的對手，不想到他自己，也不想到對方劍的動作；他只是站在那裡，持著他的劍，忘卻了所有技巧，讓心像一面鏡子，對方心裡的每一個動靜都在其中反映出來，而自己立刻知道如何攻擊對方。風清揚傳劍時曾說：

> 「料敵機先」這四個字，正是這劍法的精要所在，任何人一招之出，必定有若干微兆。他下一刀要砍向你的左臂，眼光定會瞧向你左臂，如果這時他的單刀正在右下方，自然會提起刀來，畫個半圓，自上而下的斜向下砍。
>
> 唯一的法子便是比他先出招，你料到他要出什麼招，却搶在他頭裡。敵人手還沒提起，你長劍已指向他的要害，他再快也沒你快。[23]

「料敵機先」加上「根本無招」，令狐冲在孤山梅莊小試身手，攻得黑白子四十餘招未能還手，連任我行也不肯相信：「豈有此理？風清揚雖是華山派劍宗出類拔萃的人才，但華山劍宗的劍法有其極限。我絕不信華山派中，有那一人能連攻黑白子四十餘招，逼得他無法還上一招。」[24] 令狐冲領會了劍道奧

22　見鈴木大拙、弗洛姆著，孟祥森譯，《禪與心理分析》（臺北：志文，1972），頁45。
23　同註2，第1冊，頁404-405。
24　同註2，第2冊，頁846。

妙，總算不辱獨孤九劍、風清揚傳人之名，在劍法上得到自由和解放，生命中，是否也能自由自在地笑傲江湖呢？

金庸《笑傲江湖・後記》云：「在中國的傳統藝術中，……追求個性解放向來是最突出的主題。時代越動亂，人民生活越痛苦，這主題越是突出。」沉浸在藝術中，確實有其精神上的自由、安頓，一旦與危慄萬變的世界相接，便又震撼動搖、剎那崩毀。江南四友、劉正風、曲洋、東方不敗、令狐冲、風清揚，於所愛戀之事，死生相殉，終究是癡。

> 一切有爲法　如夢幻泡影
> 如露亦如電　應作如是觀

引用書目

王德威
　　1988　《眾聲喧嘩》（臺北：遠流）。
　　1993　《小說中國》（臺北：麥田）。
金　庸
　　1982　《笑傲江湖》（臺北：遠景）。
宗白華
　　1981　〈論世說新語和晉人的美〉，《美學的散步》（臺北：洪範），頁 59-84。
亞伯納・柯恩著，宋光宇譯
　　1987　《權力結構與符號象徵》（臺北：金楓）。
徐復觀
　　1974　《中國藝術精神》（臺北：學生）。
張大春
　　1998　〈不登岸便不登岸〉，安伯托・艾可《昨日之島》（臺北：皇冠），頁 9-23。
郭慶藩輯
　　1974　《莊子集釋》（臺北：河洛）。
鈴木大拙、弗洛姆著，孟祥森譯
　　1972　《禪與心理分析》（臺北：志文）。

人間何處無小寶？

——試談《鹿鼎記》中的粗口與韋小寶的形象塑造*

呂　宗　力

香港科技大學人文學部

摘　要

《鹿鼎記》中的韋小寶武功三流，侃功和應變能力一流。小寶生長於揚州的妓院，自幼耳濡目染，加上絕佳的資質，所習侃功，屬市井粗口一類，雖不登大雅之堂，卻極生動傳神，對營構故事氣氛，塑造人物性格，關係甚大，不可或缺。小說中人物身分背景的定位，情節的推進，氣氛的調節，都常有賴於精心構思的粗口和插科打諢。

粗口在《鹿鼎記》中的特殊重要性，緣起於小說主人公韋小寶的形象定位：一個生於單親家庭，長於妓院，後又因緣際會，混跡於宮廷；自小見多識廣，深受民間文化熏陶，又過早嘗到人生的艱辛，機巧狡獪遠勝於尋常大人的「市井小人」。連篇粗話不僅是他粗鄙無文形象的註冊商標，更同他打架的成名招數拗手指、拉辮子、咬咽喉、抓眼珠、扯耳朵、捏陰囊一樣，都是他自幼練成的生存絕技。

韋小寶的形象雖然依稀有舊日上海小癟三小流氓的影子，但鴻運當頭之外，身具異稟，也可算是市井中的傑出人才。他的性格豐富多面，精細謹慎有心計，反應敏捷記性極佳，頭腦和手腳都異常靈活，講義氣也又講實惠。愛面子、愛占便宜，但不忘給人留下三分餘地。看似膽小怕死，但遭遇強敵

＊本文承蒙王邦雄教授講評並提供寶貴意見，修改後的題目，也受到他的啟發。謹此誌謝。

時又死豬不怕燙，有一股狠勁、潑皮勁。常以豪言壯語、粗口穢語充好漢、自我壯膽，但又會倚小賣小，表現出儇懶狡黠兼具童真的一面。雖然平時張嘴便是粗話，但如仔細觀察就會發現，說粗口於他不單純是粗野天性的流露，也常常是克敵制勝的技巧。出口占人便宜或許是他病態敏感和自卑心態不自覺的洩露，粗口中的自嘲、自賤、自我貶損則流露出「失父一族」的失落。韋小寶形象之有趣更在於小說作者令他由一籍籍無名的市井小子「上達天聽」，興風作浪，令得他的「傳記」幾乎等同一部康熙朝的政治編年史。康熙與韋小寶的交情，是令這種「荒謬」情節成為「可能」的關鍵所在。而這一對「王子與貧兒」交情之肇始及其深化，相當程度上有賴於韋小寶說粗口髒話、插科打諢的天份。作者就這樣有意識運用「中華上國多采多姿，變化無窮」的粗口髒話，令一個「活生生、鮮跳跳」的市井英雄韋小寶躍然紙上。

一、前　言

　　嬉笑怒罵是人之常情，粗口髒話是社會文化的組成部分。古今中外，概莫能外。《史記》中的劉邦，曾有「輕士善罵」的名聲；白描風俗世情的元雜劇及《金瓶梅》、《水滸傳》、《紅樓夢》、《兒女英雄傳》等明清小說，也常利用鮮活的粗口髒話營造氣氛，令人物的對話更生動活潑。[1] 金庸寫小說，有心發揚傳統說部風格。他塑造的小說人物中，能熟練運用粗口髒話的不在少數。《神鵰俠侶》中的楊過，《笑傲江湖》中的令狐冲和桃谷六仙，都有令人激賞的表現。《鹿鼎記》[2] 中的韋小寶武功不入流，侃功和應變能力一流，在這方面的造詣可說是登峰造極，傲視群雄。粗口髒話在《鹿鼎記》中的特殊重要性，緣起於小說作者對主人公韋小寶形象的定位。

二、韋小寶的形象定位與粗口髒話在《鹿鼎記》中的重要性

　　據一些社會語言學家和心理語言學家的觀察，對語言的運用反映出一個

1　陳克，《中國人說話的俗趣》（臺北：百觀出版社，1995），頁 286-290。
2　本文所引金庸《鹿鼎記》為香港明河社 1995 版，以下簡稱明河本。

人的教育背景、社會地位、職業、智力、價值觀、所屬的社會或次文化團體等。[3]　（"The type of speech chosen was extremely self-revealing!!"[4]）講粗口是學習而得的語言習慣。這種習慣可追溯到幼兒牙牙學語的時期。當幼兒意圖表達不適、沮喪等情緒時，他／她會使用從父母及其他長輩處學得的表示不快情緒的表達方式，如粗口。[5] 當兒童逐漸了解到粗口的禁忌性質時，他／她會進一步有意識或下意識地運用這些禁忌語言，用以自我強調、探測長輩的反應，或激怒長輩。[6] 而當步入青少年成長期，歸屬於某一個同輩團體（peer group），獲得他們的接納、認可就成為他／她最看重的身分認同。而獲得接納的捷徑之一是使用這個團體的語言，包括他們說話的方式、態度，常用的辭彙。如果這個團體慣常使用粗口髒話，他／她就要常說粗口髒話。[7]

　　不同於金庸小說中的大部分男主人公，韋小寶不具備赤膽丹心的大俠風範，不是忍辱負重的民族英雄，不算特立獨行我行我素，或風流或專情的奇男子，甚至也不是一個因曠世奇遇而練成絕世武功的傻瓜。他只是一個市井小人，生長於妓院，後又因緣際會，混跡於宮廷；深受民間文化熏陶，機巧狡獪遠勝於尋常大人的「市井小人」。[8] 他在長輩或同輩影響下形成的語言習慣，相當粗俗。

　　韋小寶出身於一個單親家庭，與他朝夕相處的母親是一個妓女。他和母

3　Timothy Jay, *Cursing in America: A Psycholinguistic Study of Dirty Language in the Courts, in the Movies, in the Schoolyards and on the Streets* (Philadelphia: John Benjamins Publishing Company, 1992), p. 87.

4　Marlene Carpenter, *The Link between Language and Consciousness: A Practical Philosophy* (Lanham: University Press of America, 1988), intro. vii.

5　同註3，頁20。

6　Joyce Brothers, "What 'dirty words' really mean," William Vesterman ed., *Discovering Language* (Boston: Allyn and Bacon, 1992), p. 84.

7　同註4，頁52。

8　韋小寶奉旨護送建寧公主到雲南完婚，與吳三桂女婿夏國相有過一段交道。夏國相領教了小寶的粗口功夫之後心想：「這小子胡說八道，說話便似個市井流氓，那裡有半分大官的樣子？」（明河本，頁1287）又，「康熙本想嚇他一嚇，好讓他知道些朝廷的規矩，哪知這人生來是市井小人，雖然做到了一等公、大將軍，無賴脾氣卻絲毫不改。」（明河本，頁2063）

親之間日常交談，也會互相「爛婊子，臭婊子」「小王八蛋」的亂叫亂罵。9
他的童年生活在妓院中度過，「妓院是一個十分奇異的地方。那裡人來人往，
光怪陸離，紙醉金迷，燈紅酒綠。客人們千金買笑，揮金如土；但有時又非
常嗇嗇，斤斤計較。出入風月場中的客人東西南北，五光十色，因此小寶耳
濡目染，自小便見多識廣，過早嘗到人生的艱辛。」這種特殊的環境和特殊
的人生經歷，形成小寶的特殊性格，令他「在思考問題時有一種獨特的思維
定勢。如見到皇宮及其他漂亮房屋，總想到應該是妓院。見到漂亮的女人，
喜歡將她們和麗春院的妓女作對比。打仗和比武，他看成是賭博、交易。總
之，他的思維活動離不開幼年時在妓院的生活經歷。」10 甚至他的人生終極理
想，也是要在揚州開辦大過麗春院的妓院。韋小寶熟知的南腔北調的粗口髒
話，多半是在揚州的妓院中學來的。

　　妓院是市井的一部分，但不是韋小寶人生課程的唯一課堂。他在揚州四
處走動，接觸各色人等，比妓女接觸面更廣。加上喜歡聽書，因此雖然不識
字，肚中裝的料可不少。「揚州市上茶館中頗多說書之人，講述《三國志》、
《水滸傳》、《大明英烈傳》等等英雄故事。這小孩日夜在妓院、賭場、茶館、
酒樓中鑽進鑽出」，聽書聽得多了，「書中英雄常說的語句便脫口而出」。11
韋小寶在聽書時學到的，恐怕也不只是英雄的豪言壯語。不同於經文人整理
出版的通俗小說讀本，民間藝人在市井、鄉野說書，多帶葷口（粗口髒話，
與性有關的笑話）。像當時大多數的鄉野民眾，市井小民，韋小寶未曾有機會
接受任何正規的學堂教育，但卻從民間文化和實際生活中獲取人生經驗，社
會經驗，歷史經驗，建立起自己的價值觀。正如陳墨在《金庸小說人論》中
所說：「韋小寶有不少的師父，然而他的真正的師父是他的生活，是他的整
個的生存環境和文化傳統下的人間現實。他不知環境的意義，更不知文化為
何物，但卻本能地、自然地、沒有任何思想和精神負擔地適應著這種環境，
按現實的遊戲規則去辦事、去生活。」12 在這樣的生存環境和文化傳統的熏陶
下，韋小寶所習得的表達思想、發洩情感、與人溝通的言語，自然更不可能

9　明河本，頁 1620-1623。

10　金戈，《韋小寶啟示錄》（廣州：花城出版社，1998），頁 12。

11　明河本，頁 54。

12　《金庸小說人論》（南昌：百花洲文藝出版社，1995），頁 246。

是詩云子曰，只能是粗俗話語及髒話。

　　韋小寶是揚州人。揚州方言極具地方特色。《鹿鼎記》以流暢的北方官話爲敍述語言，並未故意凸顯揚州方言，除了韋小寶的口頭禪「辣塊媽媽」。「辣塊媽媽」即揚州方言中的三字經。[13]　「辣塊媽媽」最早在第二回中出現，凡三見。第一次出自鹽梟之口，以表明這一幫會的地方色彩。[14] 另兩次出於韋小寶之口，都不是存心罵人，而是在身處險境，氣急敗壞的情形下脫口而出。[15] 據心理語言學家的研究，早年學會的粗口髒話在一個人的記憶中保留最久，使用也最頻繁。[16] 韋小寶雖然通曉南腔北調的粗口，有時甚至會模仿北方官話，究竟以揚州方言爲母語，一到緊急關頭，作爲自然反應，母語三字經便脫口而出。

　　如茅十八要作弄韋小寶，脫手放開小寶坐騎的韁繩，揮鞭往那馬後腿打去。小寶當時倒騎在馬背上，抓住馬尾，嚇得口中大叫：「乖乖我的媽啊，辣塊媽媽不得了，茅十八，你再不拉住馬頭，老子操你十八代的臭祖宗，啊喲，啊喲……」[17] 韋小寶初入上書房，偵察《四十二章經》之所在，面對成排書架上的千萬冊書，當即倒抽了口涼氣，暗叫：「辣塊媽媽不開花，開花養了小娃娃！」[18] 當海老公揭穿小寶的眞實身分時，小寶竭力抵賴，「顫聲道：『不……不是！辣塊媽媽的，當……當然不是。』心中一急，揚州話衝口而出。」[19]

　　在中俄談判時，韋小寶苦於說羅剎話辭不達意，無法發揮他強詞奪理的本領，唬住俄方代表費要多羅，便以揚州話罵道：「辣塊媽媽，我入你羅剎鬼子十七八代老祖宗。」這一句話出口，揚州的罵人粗話便流水價滔滔不絕，將費要多羅的高祖母、曾祖母，以至祖母、母親、姊姊、外婆、姨媽、姑母，

13　中文粗口中，以三字經應用最普遍。他媽的，他媽媽的，他奶奶的，皆可歸諸三字經，不必以字數限。「辣塊」一詞，是第三人稱指示代詞，意爲那裡或哪裡。「辣塊媽媽」即所謂國罵「他媽的」。

14　明河本，頁49。

15　明河本，頁76、79。

16　同註3，頁156。

17　明河本，頁76。

18　明河本，頁155。

19　明河本，頁218。

人人罵了個狗血噴頭。他說話猶似一長串爆竹一般，連中國官員和雙方譯員也是茫然不解。韋小寶這些罵人的說話，全是揚州市井間最粗俗低賤的俗語，揚州的紳士淑女未必能懂得二三成，索額圖、佟國綱等或爲旗人，或爲久居北方的武官，卻如何理會得？[20] 韋小寶大罵一通之後，心意大暢，忍不住哈哈大笑。可知粗口對韋小寶而言確實有宣洩的功用，小寶的揚州小痞子本色於此亦暴露無遺。

　　在特殊情形下，揚州粗口還有特別功用。如韋小寶等遇上那武功高得一塌糊塗卻無理可喻的歸辛樹一家，祇好冒充吳三桂姪子騙他們，這時揚州粗口就用得上了。(因吳三桂也是揚州府人)「辣塊媽媽，我的伯父平西王不久就要打到北京來。你們要是得罪了我，平西王可要對你們不客氣了！」[21] 當然，作爲具代表性的揚州三字經，「辣塊媽媽」在《鹿鼎記》中更多是用作韋小寶的口頭禪，正如「老子」之於茅十八，「他媽的」之於群雄、侍衛。[22]

　　除了三字經，小說中還可見到韋小寶常用的其他揚州粗口，如小娘皮，刮刮叫，別別跳，狗皮倒灶，鹹鴨蛋，乖乖龍的東，豬油炒大蔥。[23] 這些方言粗口大大豐富了韋小寶的語言和形象。

　　《鹿鼎記》中粗口髒話之出現頻率、粗野程度和運用之妙，在金庸小說中無可置疑，位列榜首。這些粗口出現的場合多與韋小寶有關。金庸精心設計的這些粗口髒話凸顯了韋小寶的出身環境及其文化背景，令這個市井小人的形象不僅鮮活，而且可信。

　　小說中說到韋小寶在揚州市井間身經百戰，成名絕招有扭手指、拉辮子、

20　明河本，頁 2022-2023。

21　明河本，頁 1713。

22　如鰲拜向康熙說蘇克薩哈是大大的奸臣，非處以重刑不可。韋小寶心道：「辣塊媽媽，我單聽你的聲音，就知你是個大大的奸臣。」(明河本，頁 162) 小寶助康熙誅鰲拜，蒙太后召見，命他進去磕頭。小寶肚中暗罵：「他奶奶的，又要磕頭！你辣塊媽媽的皇太后幹麼不向老子磕頭？」(明河本，頁 193)「辣塊媽媽的六品七品，就是給我做一品太監，老子也不做。」(明河本，頁 194)

23　韋小寶初次在宮中行走，驚歎皇宮的富麗堂皇，「乖乖龍的東，在這裡開座院子，嫖客們可有得樂子了。」(明河本，頁 121) 在中俄談判時，索額圖向小寶解釋當年蒙古拔都汗征服莫斯科的歷史，「韋小寶聽得眉飛色舞，擊桌大讚：『乖乖的龍的東！原來莫斯科果然是屬於中國的。』」(明河本，頁 2034，表示高興) 鄭克塽告訴小寶阿珂心中有他，「韋小寶大喜，道：『好！那就滾你媽的臭鴨蛋罷！』」(明河本，頁 1866)

　　咬咽喉、抓眼珠、撒石灰、扯耳朵、鑽褲襠、捏陰囊、背後捅刀子、躲在桌子下剁人腳板。這些都是小癟三小流氓打架的慣用伎倆。小癟三小流氓打架，不管什麼上三招還是下三濫，欲達目的，不擇手段。難怪當茅十八指責小寶為救他而撒石灰迷敵人眼睛，還躲在桌子下剁人腳板，是下三濫，不光彩，非英雄好漢所為時，小寶理直氣壯地駁斥茅十八的迂腐：

> 你奶奶的，若不是老子剁下幾只腳板，只怕你的性命早沒了，這時候卻又怪起我來。
>
> 用刀殺人是殺，用石灰殺人也是殺，又有什麼上流下流了？要不是我這小鬼用下流手段救你，你這老鬼早就做了上流鬼啦。
>
> 你說打架要憑真實武功，我一個小孩子，有什麼真實武功？這也不許，那也不許，還不是挨揍不還手？[24]

　　韋小寶的這種價值觀，來自他自己的生活體驗及他所熟悉的市井小民的集體意識。「韋小寶自小在妓院中長大，妓院是最不講道德的地方。後來他進了皇宮，皇宮又是最不講道德的地方。在教養上，他是一個文明社會中的野蠻人。為了求生存和取得勝利，對於他是沒有什麼不可做的，偷搶拐騙，吹牛拍馬，什麼都幹。做這些壞事，做來心安理得之至。喫人部落中的蠻人，決不會以為喫人肉有什麼不該。」[25] 連篇粗話不僅是韋小寶粗鄙無文形象的註冊商標，更同他打架的成名招數拗手指、拉辮子、咬咽喉、抓眼珠、扯耳朵、捏陰囊一樣，都是他自幼在妓院市井練成的生存和自我保護絕技，也是他日常生活中不可或缺的部分。[26] 要寫好韋小寶這樣的人物，怎可以少了他的粗口髒話？

24　明河本，頁 82-84。

25　金庸，〈韋小寶這小傢伙〉。轉引自施愛東，《點評金庸》（廣州：中山大學出版社，1995），頁 11。

26　對韋小寶而言，說髒話已是他一日不可或缺的娛樂。如他被海大富公公帶入宮中，「不覺已有兩個月，他每日裡有錢可賭，日子過得雖不逍遙自在，卻也快樂。只可惜不能污言穢語，肆意謾罵，又不敢在宮內偷雞摸狗，撒賴使潑，未免美中不足。」（明河本，頁 152）天地會的錢老本雖與韋小寶素昧平生，進宮送豬，一說開粗口，小寶立刻「覺得這錢老闆談吐可喜，很合自己脾胃。」（明河本，頁 375）

三、粗口髒話表現出韋小寶的狠勁、潑皮勁

　　韋小寶在《鹿鼎記》中第一次亮相，就表現出他與眾不同的性格。當一名私鹽販子打韋小寶媽媽韋春花的耳光，還罵她「他媽的臭婊子」時，「驀地裡大堂旁鑽出一個十二三歲的男孩，大聲罵道：『你敢打我媽！你這死烏龜、爛王八，你出門便給天打雷劈，你手背手掌上馬上便生爛疔瘡，爛穿你手，爛穿舌頭，膿血吞下肚去，爛斷你肚腸。』」[27] 他接著又鑽入鹽梟的胯下，抓住那人的陰囊，使勁猛捏。

　　韋小寶的這一舉動，令他的一生從此改變。如果私鹽販子打韋春花時，小寶不曾挺身而出，怒罵鹽販子，也就不會引來鹽販子要惡狠狠地打他，小寶也許就不會毫不猶豫地站在茅十八一邊，茅十八也就不會與小寶做朋友並帶他上京城，那麼以後的所有傳奇故事也就不會發生，韋小寶終其一生，不過是一個市井小混混，最好也許做到妓院老闆，或者黑社會老大。

　　值得注意的是，雖然還只是一個十二三歲、未經大世面的少年，韋小寶面對強悍的敵人，已能毫無懼色，透出一股狠勁、潑皮勁，受到他人欺侮或自覺受到欺侮，必會反擊。有些學者認為，咒罵行為的心理功能之一是希望以非武力的手段報復、懲罰侵犯者（getting even），令對方道歉或停止侵犯，也令受傷害者得到補償，恢復心理平衡。這既是被壓抑情緒、憤怒的宣洩（to let off steam），也是一種自我克制的表現。[28] 由於體力和武功的差異，《鹿鼎記》中的韋小寶幾乎不可能對大多數的侵犯者採取武力反擊，所以他宣洩憤怒、反擊敵人的手段主要是罵粗口髒話。[29] 至於對方威脅他說：「我一拳

27　明河本，頁50。此處韋小寶用的是咒罵式粗口。據人類學家及心理語言學家、社會語言學家的研究，咒罵（cursing）起源於咒語，與原始巫術有關。其目的是召喚一種超自然的力量，對施咒對象造成肉體或精神的傷害。（參閱 Jay，同註3，頁2；陳克，同註2，頁287。）咒罵語的傷害力，取決於被咒罵對象對這種超自然力量的信仰程度，以及當時的語境。即使被咒罵者不完全相信咒罵語的超自然力量，施罵者的強烈動機、語氣，所選用辭彙的侮辱性質及由此引起的旁觀者對被咒罵者的鄙視，也會加強咒罵語的傷害力，即如小說所描繪的這一幕場景。

28　同註3，頁74、106-107。

29　見明河本，頁52。又明河本，頁72：韋小寶「保護」茅十八離開妓院，擺脫私鹽販

打死你，我一腳踢死你」這等言語，他幾乎每天都會聽到一兩次，根本就沒放在心上。[30]

韋小寶這股光棍潑皮的狠勁韌勁，甚至也常用在追求「愛情」上，面對喜歡的女人，賭咒發狠，死纏爛打。小寶對阿珂一見鐘情，設計將阿珂帶入少林寺。他想摸她的手，卻又不敢，「眼見她美麗的纖手從僧袍下露出來，只想去輕輕握上一握，便是沒這股勇氣」，但又不知道如何表達自己的情感，只有忍不住罵道：「辣塊媽媽！」[31]

他後來對阿珂賭咒發誓，非要娶她：「皇天在上，后土在下，我這一生一世，便是上刀山，下油鍋，千刀萬剮，滿門抄斬，大逆不道，十惡不赦，男盜女娼，絕子絕孫，天打雷劈，滿身生上一千零一個大疔瘡，我也非要娶你做老婆不可。」[32]

韋小寶爲找機會接近阿珂，不惜殷勤服侍九難師太，追隨左右。但阿珂同鄭克塽陪九難師父喫飯，卻不許韋小寶同桌，小寶心道：「這位鄭公子陪著你，你就多喫幾碗飯，他媽的，脹死了你這小娘皮。」「你是一心一意，要嫁這他媽的臭賊鄭公子做老婆了，我韋小寶豈肯輕易罷休？你想殺我，可沒那麼容易。待老子用個計策，先殺了你心目中的老公，教你還沒嫁成，先做了寡婦，終究還是非嫁老子不可。老子不算你是寡婦改嫁，便宜了你這小娘皮！」[33]

鄭克塽被平西王府的人捉去，又爲馮錫範救回，阿珂喜出望外，與鄭克塽摟抱在一起。韋小寶見到，胸口如中重擊，心中立誓：「你奶奶的，我今生今世娶不到你臭小娘爲妻，我是你鄭克塽的十七八代灰孫子。我韋小寶是王九蛋，王八蛋再加一蛋。」

的追蹤，又助茅擊敗滿清官兵。茅十八卻嫌他使用「下三濫」手段，不再認他做朋友。小寶氣極敗壞，破口大罵。茅十八長臂伸處，便將他後頸抓住，提了起來，喝道：「小鬼，你還罵不罵？」韋小寶雙足亂踢，叫道：「你這賊王八，臭烏龜，路倒屍，給人斬上一千刀的豬玀……」他生於妓院之中，南腔北調的罵人言語，學了不計其數，這時怒火上衝，滿嘴的污言穢語。

30　明河本，頁 73。
31　明河本，頁 941。
32　明河本，頁 939。
33　明河本，頁 1065。

　　常人身歷此境，若不是萬念俱灰，心傷淚落，便決意斬斷情緣，另覓良配，韋小寶卻天生一股光棍潑皮的狠勁韌勁，臉皮既老，心腸又硬：「總而言之，老子一輩子跟你泡上了，耗上了，陰魂不散，死纏到底，就算你嫁十八嫁，第十九嫁還得嫁給老子。」[34]

　　韋小寶在「熱戀」中賭咒發誓罵粗口的表現，是很有趣的心理現象。一，如上所述，咒語的力量取決於施咒者和被咒者對所召喚的超自然力的信仰程度。韋小寶雖然是一個極現實的小混混，常有褻瀆神靈的舉動，對自己賭的咒發的誓卻頗懷警懼之心。所以這些咒語誓言應是他真實心聲的流露。二，不倫或違反倫常的性行為（deviant sexual act）在中西文化中都是咒罵語的重要內容，[35] 而「男盜女娼，絕子絕孫」、「寡婦改嫁」、「十八嫁，十九嫁」，都是中國傳統社會視為不倫的與性有關的行為，韋小寶卻表示滿不在乎，「老子不算你是寡婦改嫁，便宜了你這小娘皮！」「就算你嫁十八嫁，第十九嫁還得嫁給老子。」他對性和婚姻的這種觀念，相當值得探討。三，粗口髒話的真實意義，不能僅由語義學來判斷，還要注意語境。一般認為，與性或性行為有關的粗口髒話都是負面的、侮辱性的。但西方心理語言學家觀察到，在性行為過程中，性伙伴之間常使用粗口髒話，增進氣氛；關係愈親密，粗口用得愈多。[36] 中國民間俗語有所謂「打是疼，罵是愛」、「打情罵俏」，《聊齋誌異》也有類似的描寫。《鹿鼎記》中一些粗口髒話，如「辣塊媽媽」、「小娘皮」，在這種語境下，所表達的不是憎惡的情緒，而是喜愛、疼愛的情緒。

　　韋小寶表現出的潑皮性格，頗符合筆者所認識的舊日上海小癟三小流氓形象。這等人極在乎面子，一失面子，即無顏在同類中立足。故好勝，常表現得好勇鬥狠，撒石灰抓辮子摳眼睛下絆子，無所不用其極。即使對手過於強大，武力不敵，他們也不輕易言敗，軟硬不喫，胡攪蠻纏，甚而以小賣小，令對方無從下手。但因社會閱歷豐富，頗具小聰明，深明好漢不喫眼前虧之道理，所以與人爭鬥，多是動口不動手。韋小寶罵街撒潑發狠，其實常是以進為退，以攻擊來自衛，背後隱藏著心虛、恐懼、無奈和無力感。所謂「毫

34　明河本，頁 1158-1159。
35　同註 3，頁 78。
36　同上註，頁 177、241。

無懼色」，只是外表功夫，心中實不能無懼。眞到敵人以死相脅，他說不定就會自己退縮，保命第一。

四、韋小寶粗豪面目的背後

心理學家 Joyce Brothers 在討論青少年愛湊在一起講粗口髒話的原因時指出，講粗口髒話於他們可視爲一種自我性教育。青春期的少男少女對自己身體所發生的生理變化，也常會感到擔憂與恐懼。爲了克服這種恐懼感，他們就湊在一起講粗口髒話、黃色笑話和故事。這樣他們就可不必單獨面對這些困擾。[37] Brothers 進一步指出，各種形式的粗口髒話其實都是爲掩飾恐懼而戴上的面具（mask of fear）。一個缺乏安全感的人很容易感到受威脅，而他／她本能的自衛行爲，就是使用污言穢語。[38] 韋小寶撒潑發狠罵粗口的背後，也隱藏著心虛、恐懼、無奈和無力感，所以他經常以滿口粗話來充好漢、自我壯膽。

韋小寶初出道時，年幼力弱，卻不肯示弱，還要行走江湖，充一下好漢。這自然是對書場戲臺上「英雄俠義」行爲的模仿。當遇上江湖人物，書場上英雄常說的話自然而然脫口而出：「他媽的，殺就殺，我可不怕，咱們好朋友講義氣，非扶你不可。」[39] 但心中未嘗不在打鼓。而當心事被人說中時，自更須以粗口掩飾，顯得理直氣壯，令對方不能不信。如茅十八與韋小寶初識，懷疑他會向官府通風報信，領取賞金，小寶怒罵：「操你奶奶！出賣朋友，還講什麼江湖義氣？」心中卻在想：「倘若眞有一萬兩、十萬兩銀子的賞格，出賣朋友的事要不要做？」頗有點打不定主意。[40] 韋小寶這個人物的眞實性就在於此：他想學英雄、講義氣，但也不想喫虧，不想阻住自己的財路。

當著外人的面，小寶更是粗話不離口，裝出一付剌兒頭的樣子（尤其當

37　同註6，頁84。

38　同上，頁85-86。

39　這話是對茅十八說的。見明河本，頁54。又，明河本，頁62：茅十八問小寶喝不喝酒，「韋小寶從來不喝酒，這時要充英雄好漢，接過酒瓶就喝了一大口，只覺一股熱氣通入肚中，登時大咳起來。」

40　明河本，頁59。

他的臭事被外人見到時）。[41] 後來他雖然見多識廣，官高爵尊，但當謊話被人抓住漏洞，難以自圓其說時，以粗口掩飾，先發制人，仍不失為「不怕舊，只怕受」的好橋段。如韋小寶信口編造歌頌神龍教主的「古碑文」，被陸高軒、胖頭陀等視為討好教主的絕佳機會，將小寶騙上了神龍島。小寶連自己的名字都不認識，自然讀不出石碑上的「蝌蚪文」。他心下一橫，對陸高軒大聲說道：「老子狗屁不識，屁字都不會寫，什麼『洪教主壽與天齊』，老子是信口胡吹，騙那惡頭陀的。你要老子寫字，等我投胎轉世再說，你要殺要剮，老子皺一皺眉頭，不算好漢。」[42] 雖說心知闖下大禍，有生無死，也要先佔些口舌上的便宜，為自己壯一下膽。

作者為韋小寶性格所設計的這一面非常有趣。作為一個非武非俠的市井潑皮，憊懶無賴，雖年少而「其機巧狡獪早已遠勝於尋常大人」，[43] 居然贏得不少讀者的喜愛，其中的部分原因，可能即如蔡祥所說：「這同金庸對人物的分寸把握上有關。金庸始終把韋小寶定位在一個半大孩子上進行描寫，因此韋小寶不失童真一面。」[44] 一個十二三歲的少年張嘴就是粗話或草莽豪語，老三老四，為自己壯膽，令人忍俊不禁之餘，不由心生同情。

五、韋小寶的粗口髒話與「精神勝利法」

韋小寶受人欺侮或感到需要自我掩飾時喜用粗口，也同他的「面子」觀念有關。

「面子不是個人內在的自我評價過程，個人必須從他人對自己的評價中確知其面子，它是社會學的而非心理學的建構。」「面子在中國社會的存在非常廣泛、實際而具體。深深的涉入中國人社會的每一層面，它是一種非常精細的規範，中國人的社交往來，莫不以之為繞行的核心。」而不同副文化或

41　如小寶初次見到雲南沐公府家將時的表現。見明河本，頁 76。
42　明河本，頁 778。
43　明河本，頁 558。
44　〈在無賴與童真之間〉，《明報月刊》，33：8 (1998.8)，頁 30-31。

次文化的圈子中,也有各自著重的面子事情。[45]「韋小寶自幼在市井中廝混,自然而然的深通光棍之道……市井間流氓無賴儘管偷搶拐騙,什麼不要臉的事都幹,但與人爭競,總是留下三分餘地。」[46] 這就是市井中人理解的面子。如前所說,市井中行走的小癟三小流氓極在乎面子,一失面子,即無顏在同類中立足。身處有利地位而不肯給對方留點面子,即是逼對方無路可走,難免鋌而走險,市井光棍皆知為不智。但如果對方真不肯留面,失面這一方就要採取挽回面子的因應行為,包括攻擊、懲罰對方,令對方失面。咒罵對方,就是為挽回面子而採取的一種因應行為,[47] 如我們在「粗口髒話表現出韋小寶的狠勁、潑皮勁」一節中所討論的。

但如果強弱懸殊太大 (如對方社會地位太高,勢力太大,武功太高,體魄太強等等),弱者連出聲咒罵都不敢,就祇好作自我心理調整,以取得補償。那就是中國人很熟悉的「精神勝利法」,以麻木自慰和自我陶醉,維持自尊。最有名的例子莫如魯迅創造的阿 Q。他在打不過別人時,最常用的「精神勝利法」就是暗自嘀咕:「你是我兒子,我是你老子。兒子打老子。」[48]

以粗口髒話佔對手便宜,是阿 Q 自我安慰,「精神勝利」的絕招。漢語中的粗口,其實很多都是以佔對手便宜為訴求的。而按中國人的傳統價值觀,作別人的長輩就是最大的便宜。許多學者都指出,在這方面阿 Q 與韋小寶之間有著不可分的文化血緣關係。[49] 如韋小寶和茅十八被海老公抓住,二人口中被塞了布塊,用黑布蒙了眼睛放入轎中抬走。海老公的武功太高,小寶連口出污言都不敢,「只好自己心下安慰:『他媽的,老子好久沒坐轎了,今日孝順兒子服侍老子坐轎,真是乖兒子、乖孫子!』但想到不知會不會陪著茅十八一起殺頭,卻也不禁害怕發抖。」[50]

45　陳之昭,〈面子心理的理論分析與實際研究〉,楊國樞主編,《中國人的心理》(臺北:桂冠圖書出版公司,1988),頁 156、157、169。

46　明河本,頁 411。

47　朱瑞玲,〈「面子」壓力及其因應行為〉,楊國樞、黃光國主編,《中國人的心理與行為(一九八九)》(臺北:桂冠圖書出版公司,1991),頁 182-183。

48　所以 Marlene Carpenter 說,咒罵源起於某種無力感,某種對被遺棄被忽視的恐懼感。見註 4 引書,頁 18。

49　如施愛東,《點評金庸》,頁 7-9。

50　明河本,頁 104。

後來韋小寶冒充小桂子，託身宮中，受海老公之命，設法混入御書房，「忽有個難以抑制的衝動：『他媽的，這龍椅皇帝坐得，老子便坐不得？』」「他初坐下時心中怦怦亂跳，坐了一會，心道：『這椅子也不怎麼舒服，做皇帝也沒什麼了不起。』畢竟不敢久坐。」[51]

當韋小寶被海老公揭穿身分後，他心想：「西洋鏡已經拆穿，老烏龜既知我是冒牌貨，宮中是不能再住了。只可惜四十五萬兩銀子變成了一場空歡喜。他奶奶的，一個人哪有那樣好運氣，橫財一發便是四十五萬兩？總而言之，老子有過四十五萬兩銀子的身家，只不過老子手段闊綽，一晚之間就花了個精光。你說夠厲害了吧？」肚裡吹牛，不禁得意起來。[52] 四十五萬兩銀子的身家一朝化水，這個不久前還身無分文、以揩油喫剩飯為生的市井少年居然可以即刻揭過，當無事發生，他自我安慰的段位可算相當之高。

六、韋小寶以粗口髒話自嘲

一個弱者受欺侮時，無力作實際反抗，不得不以「精神勝利法」安慰自己，有時不失為一種自我心理治療的手段。但如不肯承認自己的弱點，長期以精神勝利法欺騙自己，那是一種自我麻痺，有害無益。韋小寶高明過阿Q許多，其中一個原因就是他並未沉溺於自我安慰而不可自拔，直至自我毀滅。他對自己的地位、處境、能力有比較清醒的判斷，對人情世故有比較深刻的了解，能夠按現實的遊戲規則去處事、去生活。他會通過自嘲認識自己的不足和弱點，承認別人的長處，從而化解心中的不平之氣。[53] 他也會有意識地以粗口在別人面前自我作賤、自我貶損，在宣洩憤懣情緒的同時，以自己獨特的方式將痛苦轉嫁給他人，從而減輕自己內心的壓力；又能有意識地通過自嘲化解或減低對手的敵意，同人套近乎、拉關係、換取信任，為自己謀求好處。

韋小寶與康熙交往不久，雖在打架時口頭上仍不服輸，心中卻已承認：

---

51 明河本，頁 158。

52 明河本，頁 222。

53 據心理學家的研究，自嘲屬於一種事先避免「沒面子」或事後挽回「面子」的「自我防衛」的因應行為。見朱瑞玲，〈「面子」壓力及其因應行為〉，頁 199。

「韋小寶，你這小王八蛋，這一下你可給小玄子比下去啦。你武功不及他，定力也不及他。」[54] 正因爲小寶心甘情願地承認康熙的長處，他在與康熙交往過程中，對兩人間的不平等關係，始終能保持平衡的心態。

韋小寶善於拍馬屁，給別人戴高帽，自己則相當清醒，雖不討厭別人諂媚之詞，卻不輕易因而暈頭轉向。小寶奉旨赴雲南，見到名妓陳圓圓。圓圓有求於韋小寶，又感激小寶爲她喊冤叫屈，稱小寶大才子。韋小寶這時頗有自知之明，忙稱自己是「狗屁才子韋小寶」。[55]

小寶心恨鄭克塽追求他的心中人阿珂，唆使天地會群雄戲弄並綁架鄭克塽。阿珂求小寶救回鄭克塽。小寶應承去救，心中卻罵道：「他奶奶的，老子遇到的美貌妞兒，總是求我去救她的心上人。老子這冤大頭可做得熟手之極，只怕『冤大頭功』也練得登峰造極了。」[56] 沉溺於三角戀愛中的冤大頭很多，能像韋小寶這樣清醒認識到自己在三角關係中所處不利地位而又不怕自嘲的恐怕不多。他不但對戀愛失敗的心理承受能力很強，而且不輕易氣餒，屢敗屢戰。這一方面是因爲韋小寶能以自嘲化解排洩心中的「冤氣」，另一方面也是因爲他洞察人情世故，看問題相當現實，以及他那在妓院中養成的對性行爲和女人的特殊價值觀：「他在妓院之中長大，見慣了眾妓女迎新送舊，也不以爲一個女子心有別戀是什麼了不起的大事，什麼從一而終，堅貞不二，他聽也沒聽見過。」[57]

說起在妓院中養成的對女人的特殊價值觀，許多學者都觀察到韋小寶的一個很特別的罵人習慣：小說中韋小寶多次叫別的女人「媽媽」或「好媽媽」。他叫人媽媽，其實就是罵人爲婊子。因他自己的母親是揚州麗春院的妓女，他則是一個如假包換的「婊子養的」，是一個地地道道的「小雜種」。有的學者認爲這是韋小寶的特殊罵人技巧，頗似阿Q罵假洋鬼子，除了自己覺得好笑，一點效果都沒有。[58] 也有學者認爲，這裡固然含有罵人的意思，但更主要的還是表現了他的認識論（價值觀），不然，他又何以會娶建寧公主這一小

54　明河本，頁184。

55　明河本，頁1308。

56　明河本，頁1113。

57　明河本，頁1159。

58　因別人聽了不懂，不能眞正起到罵人的效果。見施愛東，《點評金庸》，頁11。

婊子爲妻？他雖然以叫別人「媽媽」來罵人，也以叫「媽媽」來表示高興、依戀、熱愛、親近；在韋小寶的心目中，其實婦女就等於妓女，他並不在乎婊子不婊子的。[59]

在各類汚言穢語中，與性有關的粗口髒話最具傷害力、最具侮辱性。[60]按照社會生活中的語言規範，與性有關的辭彙，包括性器官，一般性行爲乃至不倫性行爲，都是平時說話需要忌諱的，萬一要說，也要採用委婉的、隱晦的隱語。但一旦那些隱語廣泛流行，它們也成爲禁忌的對象，人們需要發明新的隱語。[61] 陳克對性粗口現象的解釋是：性衝動是無意識的，非理性的。當人類組成社會之後，這種無意識的非理性的衝動就被納入既定的社會規範之中，時時受到約束。大多數社會中不直接談論性，而代之以諸多隱語，反映了社會規範在語言上對性衝動的一種約束。而髒話和咒罵是對語言規範的衝破，是本能的發洩。[62] Jay 認爲，性器官和性行爲被公認爲骯髒、令人厭惡的，所以將一個人貶低爲性器官或將之與不倫性行爲聯繫起來是一種嚴重的侮辱。(如英文粗口中的 prick, cock, cunt, motherfucker, pigfucker, go fuck yourself 等。)[63] Carpenter 指出，多數人內心深處對性存有自相矛盾的態度。這種態度令得人們視性以及與性相關的語言爲禁忌，而涉及性的辭彙也都被視爲髒話。[64] 這種對性和性行爲的自相矛盾心態和視性及性

59　陳墨認爲，在韋小寶的心目中，婦女等於妓女。他對一切女性，包括母親、丫鬟、公
　　主、郡主、夫人、皇后、妓女，都是「一視同仁」的。在他的「辭典」裡，「媽媽」
　　就是妓女。他想罵人，就叫別人是「媽媽」。而在他高興的時候，他也叫人「媽媽」，
　　表示他對她的依戀、熱愛與親近。誰能分得清「媽媽」與「妓女」之間的非語詞方面
　　的差異？更能說明問題的是，他也總喜歡 (暗地裡) 叫人是婊子。他叫建寧公主是小
　　婊子，皇后是老婊子，俄羅斯索菲亞公主是洋婊子或騷婊子。這裡固然含有罵人的意
　　思，但更主要的還是表現了他的認識論。不然，他又何以會娶建寧公主這一小婊子爲
　　妻？他實在是不在乎婊子不婊子，只在乎她們都是女人。見《金庸小說情愛論》(南
　　昌：百花洲文藝出版社，1996)，頁 255。

60　見註 3 引書，頁 5；見註 2 引書，頁 305。

61　鳥、馬、老二、傢伙、那玩藝兒本來是對男女性器官的委婉說法，但流行開來之後就
　　成了髒話。

62　見註 2，頁 305。

63　見註 3，頁 77-78。

64　見註 4，頁 24、25、83。

行為為禁忌，源自人們對性的一些錯誤觀念。Carpenter 說，「沒有髒話，只有髒念頭」；「髒話之所以醜惡，並非因為它們提及性，而是因為它們暗示了一種狹隘、機械式的施與受的性觀念。」[65] 陳克在分析漢語中最流行的髒話「他媽的」時也指出：這句話的原意是「我與你母親發生性關係」。按照傳統的價值觀，它有三層含義：一，中國人看待性關係從來不是平等的，而是男人對女人的「使用」，非家庭關係的「使用」便是極大的佔便宜，女人幾乎是一件家庭財產；二，母親是每個人感情最集中的長輩，侮辱對方的母親是對人感情最大的傷害；三，與對方的母親發生關係，意味著做對方的父輩，在講究孝道的傳統社會中，輩分的變動意味著對身分的極大貶低。幾乎所有其他罵人髒話都是從「他媽的」衍生出來，罵的對象可以換成對方的奶奶、姐妹等，皆為家庭中的女性成員。[66] 至於將代表不倫性行為的烏龜、王八、婊子等頭銜冠於對方家庭長輩的頭上，則是更嚴重惡毒的侮辱。

但韋小寶的性愛觀顯得相當特別，對妓院、嫖客、婊子、操來操去這一類平常人避之如蛇蠍的污穢辭彙，有特殊的親切感，[67] 哪怕牽涉到他自己的母親或先人，也顯得毫不介意。韋小寶在通喫島上和施琅等見面，說起鄭克塽，小寶罵道：「操他奶奶的！」忽然哈哈大笑，說道：「咱們平日罵人奶奶，這人的奶奶實在有些冤枉。只有操鄭克塽的奶奶，那才叫天造地設。」施琅聽著受用，也罵：「韋爵爺這話對極，咱們都操他奶奶的。」小寶說，旁人都好操，唯你施將軍操不得，因你的功名富貴，都是從這老虔婆身上得來的。施琅滿臉通紅，心中怒罵：「老子操你韋小寶的奶奶。」韋小寶心道：「瞧你臉色，心中自然在大操我的奶奶，可是我連爹爹是誰也不知道，奶奶是誰更加不知道，你想操我奶奶，非操錯了人不可。你心中多半還想做我老子，那麼我奶奶便是你媽，你操我奶奶，豈不是你跟自己老娘亂七八糟，一塌糊

65　同上，頁 82-84。

66　見註 2，頁 305-306。

67　韋小寶這種怪異的習慣，當與他自小長大的環境有關。「自盤古開天闢地以來，膽敢罵皇太后為『老婊子』的，諒必寥寥無幾，就算只在肚裡暗罵，也不會很多。韋小寶肆無忌憚，就算他自己母親，打得他狠了，也會『爛婊子，臭婊子』的亂叫亂罵。」（明河本，頁 229）小寶母親則慣常稱小寶「小王八蛋」。（見明河本，頁 1620-23）

塗？」笑吟吟的瞧著他。[68] 這樣的話題對一般人來說，可能是很具侮辱性的，韋小寶居然能心平氣和，淡然處之，甚至自得其樂。[69] 莫非他真的認爲「婊子」是一個完全中性的辭彙，全無侮辱性，也不在乎自己是「婊子養的」嗎？[70]

當假太后差柳燕押韋小寶去取《四十二章經》時，小寶對柳燕說：「是嗎？你想做我娘，我覺得你跟我娘當眞一模一樣。」在這種場合，「婊子」決不是一個中性辭彙，而是罵人的話。[71] 韋小寶惡作劇地叫了九難師太「媽媽」之後，心中先是得意：「你在我胸口戳了這一下，這時候還在痛。我已叫了你好幾聲媽媽，就算扯直了。」但得意之下，又向師太瞧了一眼，見到她高華貴重的氣象，不自禁的心生尊敬，「好生後悔叫了她幾聲『媽媽』」[72] 可見在多數情形下，韋小寶是把叫女人「媽媽」即婊子當成一種罵人的技巧，而非以叫「媽媽」來表示高興、依戀、親近。那麼他爲什麼不但不避諱「婊子」這類髒字，反而拿來當口頭禪，須臾不離口呢？

韋小寶內心深處，對自己母親是婊子，自己是婊子養的這件事，感受頗爲矛盾。一方面他自幼已習慣於與母親互罵「爛婊子」、「小王八蛋」，日常接觸的也多是婊子、老鴇、龜奴，人生理想是開大妓院，對婊子並無特殊厭惡，對當小雜種也不那麼深惡痛絕，所以才不那麼在乎以「媽媽＝婊子」來自嘲。他在宮中初遇沐王府小郡主，先叫她「好妹子」，小郡主不肯認。他又道：「那麼是好姐姐。」小郡主仍不肯認。「那麼是我好媽媽。」韋小寶說她「是我好媽媽」，一邊是在罵她「小婊子」，一邊也在想：「做婊子也沒有什麼不好，我媽媽在麗春院裡賺錢，未必便賤過他媽的木頭木腦的沐王府中的郡主。」[73]

68　明河本，頁 1921。

69　甚至當他母親接嫖客的時候，韋小寶也可輕鬆自嘲，保持一種「平常心」。「從前我偷看瘟生嫖我媽媽，今晚偷看老婊子（指皇太后）接客。」（明河本，頁 576）當他作爲欽差大臣來到揚州，他並沒有想過要設法將他母親從妓院中「解救」出來。他微服私訪麗春院，知道母親正在陪客，第一個反應是：「辣塊媽媽，不知是哪個瘟生這當兒在嫖我媽媽，做我的乾爹。」走進母親的房中，見床上被褥比以前更破舊，他的感想是：「媽媽的生意不大好，我乾爹不多。」（明河本，頁 1614）

70　這種罵法是雙刃的，「媽媽」等於婊子，既罵了別人，也等於罵自己是婊子養的、小雜種。

71　明河本，頁 569。

72　明河本，頁 1015。

73　明河本，頁 392。

這是他自小養成的價值觀念。此之所以他當上大官後，對他母親繼續操皮肉生涯並不介意，甚至對「不知是哪個瘟生這當兒在嫖我媽媽，做我的乾爹」也表現得不十分在乎。[74]

但另一方面，以他的人生經驗，韋小寶也明白做婊子和婊子養的在別人眼中是受鄙視的，是丟人現眼的。上文提過，他人生第一次交到的江湖朋友是茅十八，他自然視這段友情極其可貴。但當茅十八因不值他使用「下三濫」手段殺死清廷軍官史松，罵他：「小雜種，你奶奶的，這法子哪裡學來的？」金庸這樣描寫韋小寶的反應：「韋小寶的母親是娼妓，不知生父是誰，最恨的就是人家罵他小雜種。」立即惡毒地回罵：「你奶奶的老雜種，我操你茅家十七八代老祖宗，烏龜王八蛋，你管我從哪裡學來的？你這臭王八，死不透的老甲魚……」「你這賊王八，臭烏龜，路倒屍，給人斬上一千刀的豬玀……」[75] 熟悉韋小寶粗口語言的讀者應該了解，雖然小寶肚中南腔北調的污言穢語無數，若非傷了心或感到受了大侮辱，他通常不會用如此惡毒的粗口髒話對付朋友。韋小寶反應如此激烈，當然是恨茅十八揭痛了他內心深處的傷疤。

陶宮娥數次救他，並要認他做侄兒。「韋小寶心想：『我娘做婊子，茅十八茅大哥是知道的，終究騙不了人。要騙出人家心裡的話，總得把自己最見不得人的事先抖了出來。』」於是主動對陶宮娥說：「有一件事十分倒霉。」「我沒爹爹，我娘是在窰子裡做婊子的。」[76] 韋小寶一心要討好未來丈母娘，當陳圓圓說自己命薄，出於風塵時，小寶立即說：「我跟你志同道合，我也是出於風塵。」但他隨即醒覺，怕心上人阿珂會就此瞧不起他，趕緊補一句：「我只跟你一個兒說，對別人可決計不說，否則人家指著我罵婊子王八蛋，可喫不消。在阿珂面前，更加不能提起。」[77]

由此看來，韋小寶在以「媽媽＝婊子」自嘲自虐時所表現出來的破罐破摔、死豬不怕燙的心態，很可能是對自卑感的一種掩飾。語言表達習慣是人們內在意識的外化。用得最頻繁的辭彙常常意味著它對使用者有特殊的意

74　見註 68。

75　明河本，頁 72。

76　明河本，頁 618。

77　明河本，頁 1311。

義。習慣性使用的粗口「口頭禪」，聽似滿不在乎，很可能暴露了使用者潛意識中揮之不去、難以釋懷的焦慮心結。[78] 韋小寶平時看似天不怕地不怕，一股潑皮勁兒，心中其實深藏著自卑。如他初遇沐王府小郡主沐劍屏時，表示對她很鄙視：「你是郡主娘娘，很了不起，是不是？你奶奶的，老子才不將你放在眼裡呢！」「辣塊媽媽，臭小娘皮。」[79] 這種無來由的「鄙視」，其實是一種預防失面的自我防衛：「你是郡主娘娘，心中一定瞧不起我這小太監，我也瞧不起你，大家還不是扯直？」[80] 當他以叫人｜媽媽」即婊子自嘲自虐，有意識地以粗口在別人面前自我作賤、自我貶損，宣洩憤懣情緒的同時，他更希望的是以自己獨特的方式將這種屈辱感轉嫁給他人，從而減輕自己內心的壓力，取得心理補償。

　　劉心武將韋小寶與阿 Q 同歸為失父一族，認為不同之處只在於韋小寶所演出的，「是一齣絕大的喜劇，乃至鬧劇。他甚至也沒有強烈的尋父意識，在失父的狀態中，度過了自己貌似幸運實為顢頇的人生。」[81] 但從韋小寶對師父陳近南的莫以名狀的親近感，[82] 可知他的內心深處其實一直有著「尋父」的需求：「他從來沒有父親，內心深處，早已將師父當作了父親，以彌補這個缺陷，只是自己不知道而已；此刻師父逝世，心中傷痛便如洪水潰堤，難以抑制，原來自己終究是個沒父親的野孩子。」[83] 金庸小說中的主人公，多屬失父一族，多有失父的焦慮、尋父的需求。[84] 韋小寶雖然在這方面表現得比

78　參見註 3 引書，頁 156。心理學家 Brothers 認為，頻繁使用性粗口是心理失調的癥狀之一。見註 6 引書，頁 85。
79　明河本，頁 379。
80　明河本，頁 381。
81　〈失父一族的典型〉，《明報月刊》33：8 (1998)，頁 27。
82　以韋小寶的個性、人生抱負，與陳近南可說是南轅北轍，冰火不相容。陳近南初收韋小寶為徒，及任命他為天地會青木堂主，完全抱著一時利用的打算。後來師徒之間的投緣及真摯感情（對韋小寶來說是絕無僅有的不含任何功利考慮的感情），以及小寶於師父不幸被害時之痛不欲生，雖說是作者的著意鋪排，但也並不違反情理，其基礎即在於小寶對父愛的渴求。
83　明河本，頁 1864。
84　「金庸小說的主人公的形象雖個性不同，但他們的身世卻有一種突出的相似點，那就是他們大多數出身孤苦。陳家洛雖出生仕宦之家，但被母親送到了江湖，孤獨地尋摸著自己的人生。袁承志的父親被冤死，母親也不知在哪兒。胡斐出世後幾乎父母雙雙

較「豁達」甚至麻木，但並非沒有尋父的潛意識。或許正因為尋父不成功，韋小寶才會下意識地頻頻自嘲自虐，以舒緩內心的張力，維持心態平衡。

韋小寶「不學有術」的一大本領是善於與人拉關係。他在這方面頗有天份，一點就透。所謂「說好話又不用本錢」，[85]「拍馬屁不用本錢」，[86]「花花轎子人抬人」，[87] 都是他在現實生活中領略到的人際溝通技巧。說好話、拍馬屁之外，他的另一絕招就是用粗口表示親熱，迅速縮短人際距離。他對天地會群雄、眾御前侍衛說話，就是如此。[88] 但更妙的是，他還能有意識地通過自嘲化解或減低對手的敵意，同人套近乎、拉關係、換取信任，為自己謀求好處。

如韋小寶無意中殺死鰲拜後，以一個市井小流氓，因緣際會，被陳近南任命為有崇高江湖地位的天地會靑木堂主。他自己很清醒地認識到，他屬下的好漢們面子上對他客氣，其實頗有點瞧不起他。不久靑木堂與雲南沐王府發生衝突，他屬下的玄貞道人不想他參預其事，說：「這並不是什麼大事，韋香主不在這兒主持大局，想來也不會出什麼岔子。」韋小寶眉精眼企，沒有把玄貞的假客氣當補藥喫，笑道：「道長，自己弟兄，你也不用捧我啦。韋小寶雖然充了他媽的香主，武功見識，哪裡及得上各位武林好手？」「這幾句話說得人人心中舒暢，大家對這個小香主敬意雖是不加，親近之心卻陡然多了幾分。」[89]

這一招未必是韋小寶的獨創。市井之徒間溝通，常行此道。但小寶以一

死去。郭靖之父在他出生之前就死了……楊過父母雙亡。張無忌父母雙全，但在他幾歲時也雙雙自殺。狄雲、令狐冲都是來歷不明的孤兒。李文秀童年時父母雙亡，只身流落回疆。袁冠南、蕭中慧的父親都已死去，袁冠南與母親又失散了。石破天被養母養大，但受盡了苦楚，且童年時與養母失散，到後來也不知自己的父母是誰。蕭峯母親死亡、父失蹤。盧竹一直不知父母是誰，等他知道誰是他父母，其父母卻於同一天自殺。」（陳墨，《金庸小說人論》，頁219-220）

85　明河本，頁400。

86　明河本，頁794。

87　明河本，頁1610。

88　心理語言學家已觀察到，在特定的語境下（包括說話時的場合、語調、說話者與聽話者的關係等），粗口髒話可表示親暱，拉近人際關係，在同單團體中強化歸屬感。參見註3引書，頁13。

89　明河本，頁366。

目不識丁的市井少年，驟登高位，大富大貴，仍能不爲虛情假意所蒙蔽，不惜自我貶損以娛人，有此心計城府，可謂難得。

七、粗口髒話凸顯了韋小寶市井式的狡點機敏

　　韋小寶運用粗口髒話的天份及其爐火純青的功力，在與朋友或敵人鬥嘴時發揮到極致，充分顯現出小說作者爲他設計的狡點機敏的市井傑出人才形象。前面說過，韋小寶在《鹿鼎記》中表現出的性格，頗符合筆者所認識的舊日上海小癟三小流氓形象。這等人社會閱歷豐富，頗具小聰明，深明好漢不喫眼前虧之道理，所以與人爭鬥，多是動口不動手。不動手而欲折服對手（至少在自我感覺上折服對手），唯有充分發展鬥嘴的狡點本領，在嘴頭上佔盡對方的便宜，從而獲得「精神勝利」。亦因此，小癟三們在鬥嘴方面千錘百煉，花樣百出，極富天份。說髒話於他們不單純是粗野天性的流露，更常常是克敵制勝的技巧。韋小寶在對付敵人時，不僅出口就是粗口髒話，似足潑皮，而且能因人制宜，因地制宜，抓住對方的痛腳，發揮惡毒陰損之極致。

　　上文提過，小寶因母親被私鹽販子毆辱，曾甚惡毒地反罵。但稍後小寶想起此事，又「氣往上衝」，因躲入廂房，以茅十八爲保護傘，有恃無恐，便再次惹是生非，罵道：「賊王八，你奶奶的雄，我操你十八代祖宗的臭鹽皮……你私鹽販子家裡鹽多，奶奶、老娘、老婆死了，都用鹽醃了起來，拿到街上當母豬肉賣，一文錢三斤，可沒人買這臭鹹肉……」[90] 這段髒話令私鹽販子大怒，因他罵得「惡毒陰損」。所謂惡毒，是小寶不但使用升級三字經，[91] 而且公開向對方叫陣，[92] 令對方處於不能不反擊卻又不敢反擊的尷尬境地，

90　明河本，頁 52。

91　不但罵娘，而且罵奶奶、十八代祖宗，是爲升級。在第二十六回的殺龜大會上，小寶曾罵吳三桂：「我操他十九代祖宗的奶奶！」（明河本，頁 1009）

92　用三字經罵人，即使升級到老祖宗，如果冠於三字經前的代詞是第三人稱，則還有轉圜餘地，因朋友吵架都可能使用這類語言。但如使用的是第二人稱，如不是朋友之間鬥嘴，或上司喝斥下級，則可能被視爲公開挑釁和叫陣。所以在罵人的份量上，他媽的和你媽的，他奶奶的和你奶奶的，絕不能等量齊觀。被罵者如不及時對「你媽的」或「你奶奶的」作出反擊，是極丟臉的，將被視爲膽小鬼。在北方許多地方，這類髒話通常會以武鬥收場。金庸對此習俗似也注意到了。如第七回，天地會青木堂會眾爲

心中的惱怒可以想見。所謂陰損，是小寶機敏過人，因人制宜，就鹽罵鹽。所謂「鹽皮」，即是鹽屍。至於老母豬，專指下過豬崽的母豬。這類母豬肉有異味，即使不臭不爛，賣得極便宜，在集市上亦乏人問津。在這短短一段咒罵中，韋小寶不但「不倫」地性侵犯對方家庭的女性長輩、成員，影射對方的祖先，而且將之與對方的職業特性聯繫起來，大大觸犯了對方的禁忌。熟練運用這樣惡毒陰損的髒話，是小寶獨到的武功。這一細節活劃出他的潑皮憊懶兼狡點。

　　就算不是對付敵人，只是朋友間鬥嘴，韋小寶也半點不肯喫虧，必想方設法，機巧百出，令對方落入其彀中而初不覺。其中一種高明的罵人或鬥口技巧，是佔對手便宜。上文提過，漢語中的髒話，很多都是以佔對手便宜為訴求的。而按中國人的心理，作別人的長輩就是最大的便宜。茅十八常用的「老子」，雖說是口頭禪，其實也是在佔別人便宜。[93] 很難想像如果他有機會見到所景仰的天地會主陳近南，還敢開口閉口「老子」。有名的三字經，其實多省略了那個動詞。要那個別人的媽或奶奶或十八代老祖宗，其實就是做別人的老子，爺爺或老祖宗，仍是想佔別人便宜。你想佔別人便宜，別人自然也要佔你便宜，老子、三字經滿天飛，結果如不是以拳頭分高下，則往往是平分秋色，沒有贏家。要想不戰而屈對手，在鬥嘴中令對方無還口餘地，甚至被罵而不自覺，從而佔盡便宜，便要腦筋夠活，反應夠快，口齒夠伶俐。施愛東指出，江南民間互相開玩笑鬥嘴，常用設計巧妙的討便宜套子，叫你防不勝防。[94] 金庸也善用這種討便宜套子，凸顯主人公的機智。如《神鵰俠

推舉新香主而起爭執，崔瞎子罵賈老六：「操你奶奶的，除非是你想作弊。」賈老六怒道：「你小子罵誰？」崔瞎子怒道：「是我罵了你這小子，卻又怎麼？」賈老六指著他喝道：「我忍耐已久，你罵我奶奶，那可無論如何不能忍了。」說著就把鋼刀拔出，要同崔瞎子比劃。（明河本，頁284）私鹽販子是蘇北人，自然懂此規矩，理應對此類謾罵飽以老拳。

93　雖然「老子」在漢語粗口中已被濫用，有時只是口頭禪，並無特定含義，但有時卻是有心運用，以達致罵人或佔便宜的目的。如茅十八與鹽梟衝突之初，鹽梟中的老者客氣地請教他的姓名。茅十八答曰：「你爹姓什麼叫什麼，老子自然姓什麼叫什麼。好小子，連你爺爺的姓也忘記了。」（明河本，頁50）

94　《點評金庸》，頁222-226。施愛東講了一個民間的討便宜套子：假如有一天晚上，你獨自在路上行走，突然前面來了一個鬼，後面來了一隻狼，你往前往後都沒處逃，這時候如果給你一支箭，請問你將選擇射誰？你如果回答「我射狼」，這就中套子了，

侶》中楊過用江南頑童常用的討便宜套子，令得霍都王子叫楊過「爺爺」，罵自己是「小畜生」。《倚天屠龍記》中范遙佔滅絕師太便宜，趙敏佔波斯智慧王便宜，都用精心設計的話中帶話的圈套，常可令人處於兩難境地，無論怎麼回答，都會墮入術中。比起上述人物，韋小寶的反應更快，腦筋更活。他奉康熙之命，炮轟神龍教，令教主及教中人恨他入骨，設計抓他上島。韋小寶先是大拍洪教主及洪夫人馬屁，再是挑撥離間，顛倒黑白，並用討便宜套子和兩難問題，誘使陸高軒和瘦頭陀說錯話，激起洪教主的不滿，最後造成神龍教的內鬨。[95]

　　在《鹿鼎記》中，茅十八是講粗話佔便宜的高手。茅十八在故事開場時與私鹽販爭執。私鹽販說茅不講理，茅說：「我講不講理，跟你有甚相干？莫非你想招郎進舍，要叫我姐夫？」[96] 這是一句繞彎子的罵人話，佔雙重便宜：睡你家的女人，身分還比你尊長。[97] 而韋小寶則是高手中之高手，佔人便宜的技巧更高。嬉笑怒罵，皆成文章。[98] 粗野老江湖如茅十八，亦常被他玩弄於股掌。

　　韋小寶在粗話上的造詣，得益於自小在揚州妓院以及市井中的浸潤，「南腔北調的罵人言語，學了不計其數。」[99] 他的粗口和插科打諢往往是金庸的神來之筆。在第二回中，小寶給茅十八講故事，繞了一大圈，把茅十八繞成烏龜王八，茅開始還有警覺，繞到後來，竟不敢斷定小寶佔了他便宜，因「或許雲南江中眞有毛王八亦未可知。」[100] 其中的關鍵，在於毛和茅同音異字，無證據說此毛便是彼茅。這是非常典型的江南頑童的鬥嘴伎倆：佔了別人的

　　因爲這等於是說：「我色狼！」若你回答「我射鬼」，你也逃不出圈套，「我色鬼」同
　　樣不是句好話。

95　明河本，頁 1464-1470。

96　明河本，頁 51。

97　金庸對此非常清楚：「當時北方習俗，叫人大舅子、小舅子便是罵人。」（明河本，
　　頁 657）

98　如第八回，小寶被任爲青木堂香主，與天地會諸香主會議，大家以粗口大罵吳三桂，
　　「韋小寶大喜，一聽到這些污言穢語，登時如魚得水，忍不住插口也罵。說到罵人，
　　韋小寶和這九位香主相比，頗有精粗之別，他一句句轉彎抹角、狠毒刻薄，九位香主
　　只不過胡罵一氣，相形之下，不免見絀。」（明河本，頁 317）

99　明河本，頁 72。

100　明河本，頁 92。

口頭便宜，別人還不能醒悟，或起了疑心卻無法坐實，是為高手。

又如茅十八與韋小寶一搭一檔，在平西王府的人面前挖苦吳三桂，用的是市井中罵人常見的諧音遊戲，而小寶在事先毫無預謀的情形下，配合茅十八罵人，反應一流，好似演出一段即興的相聲段子。「茅十八大聲道：『喂，小寶，你可知道世上最不要臉的是誰？』韋小寶道：『我自然知道，那是烏龜兒子王八蛋！』他其實不知道，這句話等於沒說。茅十八在桌上重重一拍，說道：『不錯！烏龜兒子王八蛋是誰？』韋小寶道：『他媽的，這烏龜兒子王八蛋，他媽的不是好東西。』說著也在桌上重重一拍。茅十八道：『我教你個乖，這烏龜兒子王八蛋，是個認賊作父的大漢奸……這大漢奸姓吳，他媽的，一隻烏龜是吳一龜，兩隻烏龜是吳二龜，三隻烏龜呢？』韋小寶大聲道：『吳三龜！』茅十八大笑，說道：『正是吳三桂這大……』」[101]

韋小寶佔人便宜，喜歡設計圈套，令人自己墮入而不覺。如韋小寶初入天地會，對會眾祁彪清說：「我認得你媽！」祁覺得奇怪，問道：「你怎麼會認得我媽？」韋小寶道：「我跟你媽是老相好，老姘頭。」[102]

他尤其喜歡與女人鬥嘴佔便宜。「跟女人拌嘴吵架，他在麗春院中久經習練，什麼大陣大仗都經歷過來的，那裡會輸給人了？」[103] 即使面對自己朋友或喜歡的人，也改不了這種惡習。方怡隨沐王府人攻入皇宮，為韋小寶所救。她年歲稍長，閱歷豐富，對韋小寶的頑童習性深具警惕，數次揭穿、破解了小寶的討便宜套子，但最後終於墮入圈套。當方怡問韋小寶姓名時，小寶自稱姓吾叫老公。精明如方怡，叫了兩句「吾老公」才發現，這三個字原來是另外一層意思。[104] 韋小寶對「一見鍾情」的阿珂也不例外，求愛時還惦著繞彎子用話把她套住。[105]

韋小寶是個嘴上喫不得虧的人，事事都要佔別人便宜。茅十八自願收韋小寶為徒，教他上乘武功，小寶卻搖頭：「不成，我跟你是平輩朋友，要是

101　明河本，頁 78。

102　明河本，頁 287。

103　明河本，頁 442。

104　明河本，頁 442-450。

105　小寶對阿珂說的是：「我一心一意要讓你孫子叫我做爺爺，今天倘若騙了你，你兒子都不肯叫我爹爹，還說什麼孫子？」（明河本，頁 942）

拜你為師，豈不是矮了一輩？你奶奶的，你不懷好意，想討我便宜。」[106] 不學武功，是韋小寶一貫的原則。他後來成為武林絕頂高手陳近南、九難師太的弟子，除了一套逃跑功夫，仍是什麼武功也不肯練。他一來懶散慣了，下不得苦功夫；二來胸無大志，當妓院老闆，何需上乘武功？三來自恃聰明，憑一張利嘴，一肚詭計，已足以縱橫天下，何需武功？

但初出道的韋小寶在當時拒絕拜茅十八為師，卻有更微妙的心理因素。那時的小寶，出身低賤，日夜在妓院、賭場、茶館、酒樓中鑽進鑽出，靠替人跑腿買物，揩點油水，討幾個賞錢，聽聽白書，揚州市井之間，人人均當他是小騙子，平時給人辱罵毆打，無人瞧他得起，誰也不把他當個人看。[107] 然而這個市井少年在心底深處也有自己的夢想。他聽說書先生說英雄故事，聽得多了，對故事中的英雄好漢極是心醉，腦子裡浸滿了義氣兩字，時時幻想自己也是個大英雄、大豪傑。[108] 可是，義氣對於當時的小寶來說，是一種奢侈品。於是韋小寶賭錢之時，雖「十次中倒有九次要作弊騙人，但對賭友卻極為豪爽。」「若有人輸光了，他必借錢給此人，那人自然十分感激，對他另眼相看。韋小寶生平偶有機會充一次好漢，也只在借賭本給人之時。那人就算借了不還，他也並不在乎，反正這錢也絕不是他自己掏腰包的。」[109] 這次借著共同對付鹽梟為契機，好不容易真正有了表現義氣、充一充好漢、實現自尊的機會，他又豈肯輕易放棄？所以當茅十八問他：「怎地你不叫我老爺、大叔，卻叫我老兄？」韋小寶即刻有強烈的反應：「你是我朋友，自然叫你老兄。你是他媽的什麼老爺了？你如要我叫你老爺，鬼才理你？」[110] 其實韋小寶平日為了生活，沒少叫大爺裝孫子，這一次那麼敏感，怕喫虧，怕在輩分上比茅十八矮了一輩，也是因為他將有生以來第一次同江湖好漢的友情看成天下最寶貴的東西。他不稀罕什麼五虎斷門刀法，只希望和茅十八平輩論交，做好朋友。

當韋小寶平步青雲，富貴逼人，自信與閱歷與日俱增之後，他雖然仍具

106　明河本，頁 84。
107　明河本，頁 120。
108　明河本，頁 132。
109　明河本，頁 124。
110　明河本，頁 58。

童心，愛佔人口頭便宜，但對偶爾被人佔便宜，也就不那麼敏感了。當形勢需要時，韋小寶甚至故意讓人佔點口頭便宜，以便保命脫身。他逃出雲南返回京城途中，遇上武功高得一塌糊塗卻又有理講不清的神拳無敵歸辛樹一家，不惜冒充吳三桂侄子，蒙混過關：「老子曾對那蒙古大鬍子罕帖摩冒充是吳三桂的兒子，兒子都做過，再做一次侄兒又有何妨？下次冒充是吳三桂的爸爸便是，只要能翻本，就不喫虧。」[111]

韋小寶市井式的狡黠機敏不僅表現於以粗口佔人便宜或有企圖地讓人佔點便宜，也表現於在不同場合，靈活運用粗口，以達到自己的特殊目的。他初識茅十八，就要人家帶他去京城。茅十八不肯，小寶就說：「你不敢帶我去，自然因為怕我見到你打輸了的醜樣。你給人家打得爬在地下，大叫：『鰲拜老爺饒命，求求鰲拜老爺饒了小人茅十八的狗命。』給我聽到，羞也羞死了！」[112] 這是利用粗口激將。韋小寶奉旨衣錦還鄉，微服夜訪麗春院，神龍會徒化裝成龜奴妓女，要擒拿小寶。小寶看出蹊蹺，笑問：「『院子裡還有烏龜婊子沒有？通統給我叫過來。偌大一家麗春院，怎麼只你們五個人？只怕有點兒古怪。』那臉孔黃腫的妓女向陸高軒使個眼色。陸高軒轉身而去，帶了兩名龜奴進來，沙啞著嗓子道：『婊子沒有了，烏龜倒還有兩只。』韋小寶暗暗好笑，心道：『婊子、烏龜，那是別人在背後叫的，你自己做龜奴，怎能口稱『婊子、烏龜』？就算是嫖院的客人，也不會這樣不客氣。院子裡只說『姑娘、伴當』。我試你一試，立刻就露出了馬腳。』」[113] 這是利用粗口察奸。

八、粗口髒話培育了韋小寶與康熙的友誼

正如陳墨所指出，康熙與韋小寶的交情，是這部書的情節基礎，至關重要。韋小寶一生最重要的機遇，便是生於妓院而遇於宮廷。倘若不是遇於宮

111　明河本，頁 1716。

112　明河本，頁 74-75。

113　明河本，頁 1645。

廷，韋小寶只不過是一個市井流氓潑皮混帳雜種王八蛋而已。[114]

中國歷史上以聖明著稱的康熙大帝與市井小人韋小寶，這一對「王子與貧兒」的友誼關係，當然是金庸的藝術創作，於史無徵。但作者寫出的這層友誼，卻不能說是無稽之談。金庸在《鹿鼎記》後記中說：「在康熙時代的中國，有韋小寶那樣的人物並不是不可能的事。」[115] 而康熙交了或希望交一個像韋小寶這樣的朋友，也不是不可能的事。

對於《鹿鼎記》中描述的韋小寶與康熙皇帝之間的親密關係及其深刻友誼的性質及原因，學者們已有不少討論。如金戈認為，兩人在初遇時，彼此間的地理距離是零（康熙隱去皇帝的身分，自稱小玄子，小寶則毫不了解皇宮內情）。年齡差不多，都是十幾歲，在這個年齡上的孩子容易互相接近；年齡相仿也迅速拉近感情上的距離。最主要的，是兩人都有交朋友的願望。皇帝也許是世界上最孤獨的人。康熙還要受制於太后和鰲拜。他要擺脫這種屈辱的命運，需要一個可以託付生死的朋友。[116] 陳墨對這一現象的討論更為透徹。他指出，《鹿鼎記》寫出了，寫活了，寫深刻了康熙形象中的另一面——真正人性及其少年心理——而這另一面則正與韋小寶有關。康熙與小寶的友誼，固然是因為韋小寶屢立大功而又忠心耿耿，但更重要的則是，在這個世界上，康熙唯有在韋小寶一人面前才能如此輕鬆快活不需任何正經嚴肅，而可以隨口說「他媽的」及「老子」從而深刻地體驗人生之樂。少年人愛玩愛鬧，乃是人之天性，皇帝乞丐，均無分別。在康熙心裡，韋小寶實在是一個奇珍異寶，極為難得。總角之時陪他打架不但是一件大大的功勞，簡直是超過了一切。韋小寶的存在與康熙的身心健康並獲天性之樂都有極為重要的關係。對於康熙而言，韋小寶的小流氓習性或小流氓氣可以說正是對大皇帝的禁錮心態的一種衝擊和一種補充，這種放蕩不羈、不擇手段更不擇言辭的天性對康熙而言正是一種可羨慕的人生境界。更何況韋小寶的流氣本身就是市井氣就是俗氣就是生活氣息與生命氣息呢。再往深處挖掘，康熙每每把韋小寶當成是他的一個「替身」。這兩個藝術形象有著內在的相通與相似之處。可

114　《金庸小說人論》，頁 154-158；《金庸小說賞析》（南昌：百花洲文藝出版社，1991），
　　　頁 318。

115　明河本，頁 2132。

116　《韋小寶啓示錄》，頁 40。

以說韋小寶的性格在某種意義上正代表了康熙的性格的內在世界的某一深層次。[117]

　　對康熙和韋小寶之間友誼作全面探討，也許會涉及社會學、心理學、行為科學等多個層面。本文僅就粗口髒話在兩人友誼形成過程中的作用略作鉤沉。在《鹿鼎記》中，康熙對市井粗口的了解及喜愛程度是隨著與韋小寶的交往而逐漸加深的。小寶初識「小玄子」時，不知其帝王身分，與其比武，不敵而投降。他站起身後，「罵道：『他媽的，你……』小玄子臉一沉，喝道：『你說什麼？』神色間登時有股凜然之威。韋小寶一驚，尋思：『不對，這裡是皇宮，可不能說粗話……我說他媽的粗話，便露出了他媽的破綻，拆穿了西洋鏡。』」[118] 可知那時的康熙，尚未習慣於市井粗話。

　　無論身在皇宮、寺廟還是妓院，無論面對皇帝、高僧還是江湖粗漢，韋小寶本性所在，是戒不了講粗話的。與韋小寶相處日久，聽的粗口多了，而且多是表達巧妙、活龍活現的粗口，少年康熙漸漸習慣粗話，感染到粗話的魅力，品出這種下層社會語言的活力。有一次，韋小寶在康熙面前用三字經罵吳三桂，康熙哈哈大笑，說道：「你人挺乖巧，就是不讀書，說出話來粗裡粗氣，倒也合我的意思。他媽的，你爺兒倆給我乖乖的吧，哈哈，哈哈！」韋小寶聽得皇帝居然學會了一句「他媽的」，不禁心花怒放。[119] 自那以後，康熙見到韋小寶，就忍不住爆粗口，說三字經。對康熙而言，爆粗口並不是為了罵人，而是一種偷食禁果的娛樂。所以別人說粗話，多用以表達憤恨不滿的情緒，康熙說來卻高興有趣。

　　康熙派韋小寶去追蹤刺客，許久不見他回來。所以一見小寶回來，「臉有喜色，罵道：『他媽的，你死到哪裡去啦？』」[120]

　　韋小寶拍康熙馬屁，亂用成語，引得康熙哈哈大笑：「原來是堯舜禹湯，他媽的，什麼鳥生魚湯！」[121]

　　韋小寶決定和盤托出太后的秘密，老老實實將自己的來歷向康熙交代。

117　《金庸小說賞析》，頁 325-332。
118　明河本，頁 149。
119　明河本，頁 481。
120　明河本，頁 511。
121　明河本，頁 561。

康熙笑道：「他媽的，你先解開褲子給我瞧瞧。」[122]

　　韋小寶在五臺山以身護駕，被九難師太捉去。脫身回宮後，「康熙大喜，拉住了他手，笑道：『他媽的，怎麼今天才回來？』」[123]

　　康熙與韋小寶說起平定三藩之後，諸大臣一定會拍馬屁、上尊號，小寶說：「哪幾個官兒請皇上加尊號，誰就是馬屁大王。」康熙笑道：「對！那時候老子踢他媽的狗屁股。」[124]

　　韋小寶因違背聖旨，不肯反天地會，在通喫島避難多年。最後領康熙密旨還京，回到皇宮，一見康熙面就大哭，康熙心腸也軟了，笑道：「他媽的，你這小子見了老子，怎麼哭將起來？」[125]

　　茅十八誤以爲韋小寶害死陳近南，入京行刺被擒。韋小寶趕進宮求情，願以自己的爵祿功勞贖茅十八之罪。康熙又好氣，又好笑，喝道：「他媽的，你站起來！」板起了臉：「你奶奶的，老子跟你著地還錢。」[126]

　　韋小寶「知道每逢小皇帝對自己口出『他媽的』，便是龍心大悅。」[127] 如果不小心得罪了皇帝，祇要聽得「他媽的」三字一出口，便知道皇帝怒氣已消。[128] 更加著意迎其所好，髒話粗口層出不窮，甚至教會康熙罵假太后「老婊子」。「康熙勤奮好學，每日躬親政務之際，由翰林學士侍講、侍讀經書詩文，只是詩云子曰讀得多了，突然說幾句『他奶奶的』、『屁滾尿流』，倒也頗有調劑之樂。」[129] 但他雖貴爲天子，這種娛樂祇能與韋小寶分享。他逐漸變得一日不可無小寶。這固然是因爲他充分信任小寶，可以讓小寶爲他做許多不便差其他人做的事，但共享說粗話的快樂，無疑也是一個重要原因。韋小寶奉旨去五臺山，又從神龍島脫險，回到皇宮，康熙喜孜孜的道：「他媽的，小桂子，快給我滾進來，怎麼去了那麼久？」「這『他媽的』三字，他只在韋

122　明河本，頁 591。

123　明河本，頁 1162。

124　明河本，頁 1782。

125　明河本，頁 1955。

126　明河本，頁 2063。

127　明河本，頁 1771。

128　明河本，頁 2098。

129　明河本，頁 997。

小寶面前才說，已憋得甚久。」[130]

　　正是在這種特殊背景下，康熙給在通喫島上避難的韋小寶發出了兩道妙絕古今的聖旨。第一道旨，是六幅畫，描繪小寶的六件大功。第一幅正是兩個小孩當年扭打比武的情形，擒鰲拜、保順治、救康熙尙在其次。韋小寶自然明白，「和康熙玩鬧比武本來算不得是什麼功勞，但康熙心中卻是念念不忘。至於炮轟神龍教、擒獲假太后、捉拿吳應熊等功勞，相較之下便不足道了。」

　　第二道密旨，更是前無古人，後無來者。稱呼、行文，處處配合韋小寶的修養、理解力；字裡行間，康熙與韋小寶之間的特殊情誼呼之欲出。小說作者透過髒話粗口所表達的康熙對小寶那份眞摯的親暱、思念，令文辭華麗、冠冕堂皇的翰苑傑作亦難望項背：

> 小桂子，他媽的，你到哪裡去了？我想念你得緊，你這臭傢伙無情無義，可忘了老子嗎？（作者原註：「中國自三皇五帝以來，皇帝聖旨中用到『他媽的』三字，而皇帝又自稱爲『老子』，看來康熙這道密旨非但空前，抑且絕後了。」）
>
> 你不聽我話，不肯去殺你師父，又拐帶了建寧公主逃走，他媽的，你這不是叫我做你的便宜大舅子嗎？……我就要大婚啦，你不來喝喜酒，老子實在不快活……
>
> 小玄子是你的好朋友，又是你師父，鳥生魚湯，說過的話死馬難追，你給我快快滾回來吧！[131]

　　作爲衝破社會語言規範、宣洩本能的一種手段，說粗口罵髒話並非市井小人的特權。漢高祖劉邦不但罵過「豎子」，也罵過「乃母」；曹雪芹也不忌諱在《紅樓夢》中寫出「把你媽一奁」這樣的句子。[132] 康熙雖生爲天潢貴胄，自幼受師傅的嚴格教訓，熟讀經史，於其少年時代，難免產生逆反心態，渴望偷食禁果；再加邂逅滿嘴粗口的韋小寶，面對同輩次文化的壓力和魅力，頗難壓抑藉爆粗口宣洩一下的慾望。所以韋小寶與少年康熙的友誼，始於打架和爆粗口，又隨康熙對粗口熱愛程度的加深而愈益深化。在康熙的教導和

130　明河本，頁 842。

131　明河本，頁 1894-1896。

132　見註 2，頁 306。William Vesterman 指出，認爲教養不夠、辭彙貧乏的人才講粗口，其實是一種誤解。難道莎士比亞的辭彙貧乏嗎？他的作品中也不乏粗口。

庇護下，韋小寶在皇宮中和官場上如魚得水；韋小寶說粗口髒話、插科打諢的天份及市井粗俗文化的強勁生命氣息，則令深宮中長大的少年天子體驗到一種放蕩不羈的人生境界。粗鄙無文的市井小人與漢學修養深厚的聖明天子因而藉粗口發現一條相互溝通、交流、了解的管道，培育起一份看似荒謬細想卻又合乎情理的深厚情誼，並為彼此人格的完成，各盡一份力量。這份情誼令一個籍籍無名的市井小子「上達天聽」，興風作浪，參預當時種種政治、軍事、外交事件，演義出一部洋洋白萬言的另類「康熙朝編年史」。

九、結　語

雖然大量脫口而出的粗口髒話暴露了韋小寶的市井本色、粗野天性，小說作者屢屢暗示，說髒話於韋小寶有時是克敵制勝減壓拉關係的手段，他的粗口常常是有的放矢、深具心計的。韋小寶的形象定位雖然只是個市井小人，但鴻運當頭之外，身具異稟，也可算是市井中的傑出人才。他的性格複雜多面，精細謹慎有心計，反應敏捷記性極佳，頭腦和手腳都異常靈活，講義氣也又講實惠。愛面子、愛佔便宜，但不忘給人留下三分餘地。看似膽小怕死，但遭遇強敵時又死豬不怕燙，有一股狠勁、潑皮勁。常以豪言壯語、粗口穢語充好漢、自我壯膽，但又會倚小賣小，表現出慵懶狡黠兼具童真的一面。韋小寶年幼力弱又偷懶，不肯花氣力學武功，但卻時時要在強敵面前逞能，不肯喫虧，面臨大敵，通常動口不動手，亦是他揚長避短聰明之處。不分場合對象，出口佔人便宜，或許是他病態敏感和自卑心態不自覺的洩露；粗口中的自嘲、自賤、自我貶損則時時流露出「失父一族」的失落。韋小寶形象之有趣更在於小說作者令他由一籍籍無名的市井小子「上達天聽」，興風作浪，令得他的「傳記」幾乎等同一部康熙朝的政治編年史。康熙與韋小寶的交情，是令這種「荒謬」情節成為「可能」的關鍵所在。而這一對「王子與貧兒」交情之肇始及其深化，相當程度上有賴於韋小寶說粗口髒話、插科打諢的天份。所以，小說作者精心構思、有意識運用的「中華上國多采多姿，變化無窮」的粗口髒話不僅有助於鎖定韋小寶的形象定位，揭示他的出身、文化背景，而且有助於凸顯韋小寶的形象，推進小說的情節，調節故事的氣氛，令一個「活生生、鮮跳跳的」市井英雄躍然紙上。

　　《鹿鼎記》是金庸最後一部也是最具爭議性的長篇小說。韋小寶則是金庸所創作的最具爭議性的人物。這些話都是老生常談了。大部分論者同意《鹿鼎記》是一部反武俠小說，韋小寶是一個反英雄，或搗蛋鬼，或小流氓。韋小寶滿嘴的粗口髒話，也為他的搗蛋鬼小流氓形象定了位。至於作者為什麼要選一個搗蛋鬼或小流氓作為他封筆之作的主人公，也已有許多假設或討論。陳墨認為：「當我們隨著揚州麗春院妓女韋春花的兒子韋小寶這一十足流氓無賴的人物走進神秘森嚴莊重典雅的皇宮內院，我們對封建王朝的全部的神秘感及由之產生的嚴肅莊重的歷史感全都被小說作者擊得粉碎。當我們看著小寶這一不學無術的小丑弄臣處處逢凶化吉、遇難呈祥，進而大紅大紫、飛黃騰達，我們就會對歷史的價值、歷史的必然規律等等產生根本的懷疑。這正是這部小說的價值與藝術之所在。」[133]　「中國的封建社會的黑幕，尤其是封建王朝的宮廷的黑幕，也正需要這種幽默而深刻的奇異目光才能穿透。」[134]　所謂「荒誕所投影的正是歷史」，[135]　大約也是這個意思。從這個角度探討下去，很可能會揭發出小說作者對中國歷史的理解頗有憤世嫉俗的傾向。

　　如果說陳墨、吳予敏、林崗所強調的是《鹿鼎記》在顛覆傳統歷史觀方面的意義，施愛東著眼的則是《鹿鼎記》對文學作品所創造的武俠世界的顛覆：「眾人罵了一陣，聲音漸漸歇了下來，突然有個孩子大聲叫道：『我操他十九代祖宗的奶奶！』群雄本來十分憤恨，突然聽到這句罵聲，忍不住都哈哈大笑。」把嚴肅靜穆的英雄大會當作了罵街的場所，很具諷刺意味。英雄大會、除奸大會簡直是胡鬧。真正誅殺吳三桂的是康熙。《鹿鼎記》通過流氓的勝利，政治的力量顯示，反襯了武林人物的失敗。如袁承志所說：「武功強只能辦些小事，可辦不了大事。」[136]

　　以上諸家的分析，各有其立論的依據和理路。《鹿鼎記》敍述文體中的黑色幽默和嘲諷色彩也能夠支持以上的論點。我們在此無意爭辯。本文祇是建議試從另一個角度來觀察這部小說：如果說《鹿鼎記》「顛覆」了傳統的歷史

<hr />

133　《文學金庸》（臺北：雲龍出版社，1997），頁283。
134　《金庸小說賞析》，頁322。
135　《明報月刊》，33：8（1998），頁29。
136　《點評金庸》，頁55-56。

觀或武俠文學觀，它所「顚覆」的不過是歷史學家和作家精心建構的觀念體系。如果說韋小寶的粗俗言行及其成功故事代表著一連串的「荒謬」，作者有意以「幽默而深刻的奇異目光」穿透荒謬，揭示歷史的本質，我們似乎很應該想一想，我們對「正常」或「荒謬」的定義本身，是否值得商榷。

　　無可置疑，金庸在創作這部小說和韋小寶這個人物時，較多運用幽默誇張的語言，包括髒話粗口；形象的設計也有漫畫化的傾向。但正如上文的討論所顯示，小說中大量粗口的選擇和運用相當具眞實感、生活感。小說雖然以第三人稱敍述，但其故事情節，除了第一回用以交代歷史背景，其餘各回，自始至終圍繞韋小寶，單線發展。換句話說，整部小說實際上是以韋小寶這個市井小人的視角和價值判斷標準來觀察詮釋康熙朝的歷史的。而大量「粗鄙無文」的俗語粗口也正可看作是作者有意選用的一套不同於上流社會精緻文化的話語系統。[137]　這就使《鹿鼎記》的創作宗旨與作者所創作的其他既武且俠兼義之小說大相逕庭。正如沈雙所觀察到的，「《鹿鼎記》無論在人物刻劃還是在作者對讀者的了解、期待方面，都是圍繞著『市井』這個想像的空間而考慮的。而作者又是巧妙地一步一步引誘我們接受『市井小人』的價值觀念，試圖從他們的角度來看問題。」[138]　從這個角度去看，我們也許可以說，《鹿鼎記》其實是　部長篇民間傳奇，所反映的是市井小人對歷史所作的詮釋和價值判斷。在他們眼裡，無所謂「顚覆」，無所謂「荒謬」，歷史、政治、英雄，眞實的人生，本來就是那麼回事，韋小寶之流，才是他們熟悉的類型，心目中的英雄。正如王邦雄先生在這次研討會上所說：「英雄回到人間，人間處處有韋小寶」。[139]

137　這套民間話語系統並非小說作者的杜撰，而是眞實的存在。本文作者曾生活於鄉間及工場，親身領略過那種粗俗「下流」然而極具活力的話語。在特定語境下，粗口髒話常常不再是宣洩憤怒、沮喪情緒的惡毒咒罵，而成爲生動鮮活的語言創作或遊戲，具有特殊的美學價值。

138　〈評閔福德的《鹿鼎記》英譯本〉，《明報月刊》，33：8（1998），頁73。

139　身居偏遠鄉村，三餐不繼的中國農民常理所當然地假設：「皇上的日子好舒坦，頓頓喫餃子。」東北鄉間的天眞兒童會這樣憧憬：「毛主席天天能喫到粉條燉肉。」我們能簡單地批評他們這種對宮廷生活的詮釋和判斷是「荒謬」的嗎？

楊過和他的問題

危　令　敦

香港科技大學人文學部

摘　要

　　本文主要從德、體兩個角度討論孤兒楊過在成長過程中所犯的「錯誤」以及「改正」的辦法，探討小說中個人與群體的關係，兼及小說所表露的父權意識。楊過之「過」有二：首先，他認賊作父，以爲生父楊康是頂天立地的英雄，因而一心一意要爲父報他的。在未探明生父死因的前提下，指（代）父爲賊，差點害死郭靖。雖然楊康是他的生父，從文化象徵的角度來看，郭靖才是眞正的「父親」，因爲他具有眞正的「父之名」。楊過成長的重要關鍵，就是要認識「父親」，接受他的價值觀，才能成長爲眾人所接納的「英雄」。其次，楊過背叛全眞教，轉投古墓派，迎娶師父，亦冒犯了「父之名」。楊過巧遇神鵰，是解決此一「錯誤」的關鍵。經神鵰指導，他擺脫古墓派之陰柔影響，重新確立男性身分，並練成絕世武功，凌駕在小龍女之上，成爲一代宗師，逆轉兩人的師徒關係。他還行俠仗義，抵禦外侮，爲國立功，終於平衡、抵消他的過失，重新爲社會所接納。

一

　　楊過的問題，從他的名字可見端倪。所謂「過」者，既指涉其父楊康之過對他的影響；亦提示了他少年時期狂傲獨行，冒犯世俗禮法之「過」。他的問題，正如「神通廣大」的黃蓉所言，是由兩個難解的死結引起的：「一是

他父親的死因，一是跟他師父的私情。」[1]　（838頁）楊過既是《神鵰俠侶》的主角，又是問題人物，小說就得設法處理他所引發的矛盾，解開死結。小說的故事時間（story time）長達二十多年，讓楊過由少年步入壯年，從邊緣人物變成一代宗師；看來，楊過的問題，需要他經歷磨練、逐步成長才能「糾正」過來。換句話說，楊過的問題，以及矛盾的化解，都可以從個人成長的角度來考察，進而申述小說裡個人與群體、男性與女性的關係，最後理出小說的構思和意識形態。

談到個人的成長，不免令人想到成長小說。[2] 成長小說的觀念源自德國，自有其歷史、文化的特性，本文無意強行比附，只想借助此一觀念，作為分析楊過的問題的出發點。[3] 所謂成長小說，背後有一個信念，就是小說裡的人物，有自我完善的可能。這種自我完善的過程是漸進、不斷累積、而且是完全的。理想的個人成長，包括德（moral）、智（intellectual）、體（physical）、情（emotional）、靈（spiritual）各方面。在經歷此一過程後，個人終於有所成就，亦成功融入社會。[4] 對於楊過而言，道德（德）與武功（體）是他「改過」、成長的兩大關鍵。[5] 以下的討論，就循這兩條線索展開。

1　本文的討論根據的是香港明河社出版的《神鵰俠侶》（1996年第22版）、《射鵰英雄傳》（1997年第21版）及《笑傲江湖》（1997年第18版）。

2　黃錦樹的文章〈否想金庸：文化代現的雅俗、時間與地理〉亦有提到從成長小說看金庸作品的角度。

3　關於成長小說觀念在德國的起源以及運用的諸種問題，可以參考：Fritz Martini, "Bildungsroman — Term and Theory;" Jeffrey L. Sammons, "The Bildungsroman for Nonspecialists: An Attempt at a Clarification;" in *Reflection and Action: Essays on the Bildungsroman*, ed. James Hardin (Columbia: U of South Carolina P, 1991), pp. 1-25; pp. 26-45。

4　"Introduction," *The Voyage in: Fictions of Female Development*, ed. Elizabeth Abel, Marianne Hirsch, and Elizabeth Langland (Hanover and London: UP of New England, 1983), pp. 5-6。

5　武俠小說中的體，即強身健體的武術。情雖是小說情節的主線，本文的論述重點卻不在兩人偏離文化規範的情，而是小說如何處理兩人重返社會、為群體所接納的過程。兩人的愛情與文化規範有衝突，可以說是「地下情」。正如馬國明所說：「《神鵰俠侶》引人入勝的情節都在地下發生的。終南山下的墓穴是其一，絕情谷是其二，而且絕情谷下另有洞天。楊過和小龍女相隔十六年重逢的地點又是懸崖下的洞穴。《神鵰俠侶》以寫情而聞名，但如果其中的愛情情節不是在地下發生，會否同樣吸引？」〈金庸與金

二

　　要討論德，得從楊過的出身談起。第二回他出場的時候，小說就點明了他是孤兒一名；到了第四回，更進一步說他是遺腹子。[6] 孤兒的處境，是一種欠缺。從敍述學的角度來看，欠缺會引發論述；[7] 楊過的故事，必須從此展開。楊過所缺，或者楊過所需，是什麼呢？第二回亦為我們提供了暗示。此回最匪夷所思的事件，是神智昏亂的歐陽鋒一定要把初相識的楊過收為兒子。看來，楊過雖然父母雙亡，父親的缺席才是故事的重點；西毒強人所難，逼楊過認他為父，表明了填補父親空缺的迫切性。即使楊過沒有主動尋父，義父亦不請自來。換句話說，小說認為，楊過生命所缺，就是父親。[8] 他需要一個怎麼樣的父親呢？

　　從楊過的角度來看，歐陽鋒武功非凡，又善待自己，當然勝任有餘。可是，從小說的邏輯來看，要為人父，並非只靠武功與愛心這麼簡單。且不說歐陽鋒的武術邪門，僅從他倒練九陰真經，使得經脈逆行、穴道位移、神智不清一事，已足以令他失去為人義父的資格。在小說的前十一回，歐陽鋒反覆提問：「我是誰？」一個連自我認知都有障礙的人，是否可以扮演父親的角色，成為少年楊過的模仿對象？小說顯然不樂觀，要不然，為什麼歐陽鋒不許楊過與他同行？其實，歐陽鋒一出場就倒立行走，未嘗不可視為其身不正、價值觀顛倒的暗喻。

　　歐陽鋒的義父角色，嚴格來說，只是一種過渡；他只出現幾次，扮演臨時的保護者，就亡命華山上了。小說想藉他帶出的，其實是楊過認識父親的

融〉，《路邊政治經濟學》（香港：曙光圖書公司，1998），頁 41-80。情為何物，坊間有不少討論，可以參看：陳沛然，《情之探索與神鵰俠侶》（臺北：遠景，1985）；吳靄儀，《金庸小說的情》（香港：明窗，1997）。

6　關於孤兒的討論，可參看周英雄，〈男女與親子的心理關係——獨占花魁的深層意義〉，《小說・歷史・心理・人物》（臺北：東大，1989），頁 99-120。

7　Robert Con Davis, "Critical Introduction: The Discourse of the Father," in *The Fictional Father: Lacanian Readings of the Text*, ed. Robert Con Davis (Amherst: The U of Massachusetts P, 1981), pp.1-26。以下引用戴維思文章，即此文。

8　楊過生母穆念慈在他十一歲時方染病身亡，但小說從未提及楊過感念母恩或家教的事。

主題。學者戴維思（Robert Con Davis）的說法，可以幫助我們分析楊過的處境。戴氏論及西方文學裡敍述與缺席父親的關係時，以荷馬史詩《奧德修紀》（*The Odyssey*）為例。令他特別感興趣的，是詩中一段著名的對話。奧德修還在海上漂流的時候，女神雅典娜曾問他的兒子帖雷馬科：「你真是奧德修的兒子嗎？」帖雷馬科的回答一語雙關，頗為精警：「家母確實這麼說，我卻不曉得。認識父親的，準是個聰明的兒子。」[9] 戴氏認為，父親一詞，在《奧德修紀》裡可以有兩個層次的含義。第一個層面所指，是生埋上的父親，帖雷馬科與奧德修相認的一幕是一例。第二個層面所指，是父親所象徵的文化規範。[10] 認識這一層意義的「父親」，意味著接受群體認可的價值觀念；能做到這一點，才算「聰明的兒子」。

　　奧德修身為父、王，擁有權力地位，處事主動，可以說是象徵意義上的「父親」。但他犯過錯誤，在攻打特洛伊城時求勝心切，盜走護城神像，闖下破壞文明的大禍而遭天譴，要在海外流浪十年。[11] 戴氏認為，奧德修的苦難，既是一種懲罰，亦是一個重新學習的過程；只有在飽經苦難、重新了解文明的意義之後，他才可以回家，恢復原來的地位。從象徵意義來說，破壞文化習俗的奧德修，只是一名「兒子」。「兒子」的處境意味著被動狀態（passivity），而「被動」一詞，在拉丁文裡的詞根（passivus）是「能吃苦」（being capable of suffering）的意思。處處被動的角色，只有重新認識、認同「父親」，方能進而成為「父親」。戴氏指出，文化的規範，如果借心理分析的術語來說，就是「父之名」（name of the father）。[12]

9　"My mother certainly says I am Odysseus' son; but for myself I cannot tell. It's a wise child that knows its own father." Homer, *The Odyssey*, trans. E. V. Rieu (Baltimore: Penguin Books, 1946), p. 30。書名及人名從楊憲益的譯法，見楊譯，《奧德修紀》（北京：中國工人出版社，1995）。

10　戴文側重父權的分析，曾經受到女性主義學者的批評。本文從他的論述出發，因為他的看法，頗能説明《神鵰俠侶》此種意識形態。對戴文的批評，見 Beth Kowaleski-Wallace and Patricia Yaeger, "Introduction," *Refiguring the Father*, ed. Patricia Yaeger and Beth Kowaleski-Wallace (Carbondale and Edwardsville: Southern Illinois UP, 1989), pp. ix-xxiii。

11　見戴氏文章第 6 頁所引用的希臘傳統説法。

12　「父之名」，亦就是「父親的法規」，兒童必須就範的法規。關於「父之名」，可以參看杜聲鋒，《拉康結構主義精神分析學》（香港：三聯，1988），頁 127-146。

如果歐陽鋒不能扮演父親的角色，那麼，楊過需要怎樣的一個父親呢？

三

楊過的名字是郭靖起的，取「人孰無過，過而能改，善莫大焉」之義。
（頁 550）這番解釋在英雄大會上道來，冠冕堂皇，直指楊過欲娶小龍女的「過
錯」。但楊過的命名，遠在他「犯錯」之前；實際所指，應爲楊康的過失。亦
就是說，楊過一出生，就已經烙上了恥辱的印記，自己卻懵然不知。郭靖的
命名，大有父過子承的意味──楊過，表字改之，聽起來的潛台辭，好像是
楊康的過失，要楊過來改正一樣。不僅如此，父親有錯，連兒子的人格也可
疑起來。黃蓉不是說過，楊過的「本性不好」麼？（頁 445）後來她甚至坦言：
「我心中先入爲主，想到他作惡多端的父親，總以爲有其父必有其子，從來就
信不過他。」（頁 1159-1160）

郭、黃兩人的想法，有血統論的意味，箇中隱含的消息是：父親的榮辱，
亦就是兒子的榮辱，難以迴避。[13]《奧德修紀》何嘗不然？奧德修遠行未歸，
登徒子乘機登堂入室，騷擾其妻潘奈洛佩；帖雷馬科忍無可忍，乃出門尋父，
後來更與父親聯手，屠殺這些追求者。帖雷馬科要捍衛的，是父親的名聲，
亦是他自己的名聲。社會的倫理，或曰「父之名」，不容動搖。

然而，楊過從未見過生父，也不了解他的爲人。在他的想像裡，一直以
爲父親是個正面的角色，可堪追隨的楷模。知道父親被人殺死，他的反應是
要爲父報仇，以雪恥辱。（頁 379）楊過復仇的意願，是推動小說敍記層

---

13 孟子所列的五倫──亦就是社會結構中的主要角色關係──以父子之倫爲首。而在傳
　　統的單（父）系親族組織中，個人之間的關係，不論長幼，有如網絡，互相牽連；個
　　人之榮辱毀譽，關係全族，父子關係，更無例外。見李亦園，〈社會結構價值系統與
　　人格構成〉，《文化與行爲》（臺北：臺灣商務，1995），頁 84-93。父子的密切關係，
　　亦可參看杜維明的討論：Tu Wei-ming, "Selfhood and Otherness in Confucian
　　Thought," *Culture and Self: Asian and Western Perspectives*, ed. Anthony J. Marsella,
　　George Devos and Francis L. K. Hsu (New York and London: Tavistock, 1985), pp.
　　231-251。

(diegetic level) 內事件發展的自發動機 (auto-motive) 之一。[14] 在尚未探明生父的爲人以及死因的前提下，楊過從傻姑口中得知生父大概喪生在黃蓉和郭靖的手裡，就三番四次的想伺機復仇，幾乎鑄成大錯。楊過不了解生父楊康，而想爲他報仇，和他不了解義父歐陽鋒，依然稱他爲父一樣，都犯了「認賊作父」的錯誤。楊康與歐陽鋒，都是《射鵰英雄傳》裡作惡多端、武林不容的歹角。甚至連神智不清的歐陽鋒，在臨死之前，也有自知之明的時候。在《神鵰俠侶》第十一回，歐陽鋒在華山火拚洪七公時，突然靈光乍現，指著對方說：「他是歐陽鋒，歐陽鋒是壞人」（頁 422）。歐陽鋒的妙語，似乎預示了身負「父仇」的楊過，在爲父報仇的過程中，最終將無法逃避眞相，必須面對生父的眞面目，指出「他是楊康，楊康是壞人。」

　　楊康雖然間接的死在黃蓉手裡，黃蓉卻非楊過的殺父仇人，郭靖與楊康之死更是毫無關聯。楊康之死，是一種天理報應──即外來動機 (hetero-motive) 使然，並非其他角色的行爲所能決定的。在《射鵰英雄傳》第三十六回，楊康使九陰白骨爪偷襲黃蓉，手指全插在黃蓉身披的軟蝟甲的刺上。刺上原來染有南希仁的毒血，楊康因此中毒身亡。而南希仁等江南五怪，正是給楊康設計的毒計害死的。黃蓉說的「天網恢恢」，正是此意。（《射鵰》頁1399）既然郭靖夫婦與楊康之死無關，爲什麼小說一再拖延眞相，讓楊過不斷的尋找機會，殺害郭靖──而不是黃蓉？

　　郭靖的地位非常重要，因爲他與楊康、歐陽鋒三人都是父親角色的候選人。郭靖亦在第二回出現，要當楊過的代父。他的資格比歐陽鋒強，因爲郭

14　「報」是傳統中國社會人際關係的基礎，參看：Lien-sheng Yang, "The Concept of Pao as a Basis for Social Relations in China," *Chinese Thought and Institutions*, ed. John K. Fairbank (Chicago and London: The U of Chicago P, 1957), pp. 291-397。「報」的觀念在傳統小說敍事上的功能亦相當重要，見高辛勇的研究：Karl S. Y. Kao, "*Bao and Baoying*: Narrative Causality and External Motivations in Chinese Fiction," *Chinese Literature: Essays, Articles, Reviews* 11 (1989): 115-138。本文運用的「自發動機」及「外來動機」(hetero-motive) 的概念，源出此文。前者指人物性格、動機對小說事件情節的影響，比如說報仇或報恩；後者指人物無法掌握的情節動力，比方說，天理報應。兩種不同的動機雖然都由作者掌握，但也有一定的區別。「自發動機」涉及人物欲望及抉擇，本身有一定的邏輯可循，不可完全脫離客觀現實；而「外來動機」則多出自作者構思及意識形態的考慮 (compositional and ideological motivations)，主觀性比較強。

楊兩家世交，楊康生前與郭靖又是結拜兄弟，關係非同一般。況且，郭靖的武功與歐陽鋒不相伯仲。所以小說安排郭靖在楊康死後，替楊過命名。後來兩人再次相遇，郭靖知道楊母身故，就把他帶回桃花島撫養。[15] 在英雄大會上，郭靖更當眾表明自己的代父身分。楊過欲娶小龍女，郭靖勃然大怒，罵道：「我當你是我親生兒子一樣，決不許你做了錯事，卻不悔改。」後來楊過堅拒認錯，郭靖幾乎一掌把他擊斃。(頁551-552)

　　郭靖扮演代父，自然有情節編排上的考慮。小說一再押後楊康的死亡眞相，無非經營懸念和戲劇衝突。讀者急著要知道的是：楊過會不會犯錯？——他究竟會不會誤殺郭靖？更重要的是，在對命案眞相起疑之後，楊過究竟還能不能下手？同爲孤兒，楊過的處境，顯然沒有傳統文學裡的趙氏孤兒那麼好辦。他不僅要念及郭靖的「撫養敎誨之恩」，(頁1635) 還要提心吊膽，恐怕自己誤殺忠良。(頁828、845-46) 趙氏孤兒爲父報仇，端的是義無反顧。他可以置養父二十年的撫育之恩於不顧，毫無心理負擔的把他逮捕、行刑。趙氏孤兒之所以能夠這麼乾脆俐落，恐怕在於屠岸賈是個罪大惡極的歹角，而孤兒的生父與祖父都是無辜的受害人吧！[16]

　　但是，從本文的角度來考慮，小說安排郭靖扮演代父，自有解說文化觀念的功能。楊過爲人處世無規範可循，因爲伺機刺殺郭靖，所以有機會仔細觀察郭靖的品行。郭靖是眾人公認的英雄，而所謂英雄，指的往往是道德英雄 (moral hero)。道德英雄與綠林好漢不同之處，即在膽色、武藝、領導才華之外，還擁有忠誠、無私兩大品質。[17] 在楊過成長的過程裡，郭靖提供的

15　在命名與偶遇之間，郭靖居然沒有過問穆念慈與楊過兩母子的生活，以致於後來穆念慈病死，楊過要流落嘉慶，偷雞摸狗的混日子。至於將楊過送到終南山以後，郭靖更是不聞不問。楊過鬧出背叛全眞的大事，也要等到後來的英雄大會，見到楊過與全眞道士勢成水火，才大吃一驚。以郭靖對楊康父子的深厚感情以及道德義務來看，並不合理。這些恐怕都是小說情節粗疏之處。

16　趙氏孤兒的果斷決絕，使現代的讀者不安，必須爲他的行爲作一番解釋。見 Joseph S. M. Lau, "Duty, Reputation, and Selfhood in Traditional Chinese Narratives," in *Expressions of Self in Chinese Literature*, ed. Robert E. Hegel and Richard C. Hessney (New York: Columbia UP, 1985), pp. 363-383。

17　詳見 Paul Zweig, *The Adventurer: The Fate of Adventurer in the Western World* (Princeton: Princeton UP, 1974), pp. 34-47。

正是「德」的啓示。郭靖爲人正直，從不諱言楊康當殺；（頁 872）即使楊康的死因未明，楊過也不得不懷疑生父的爲人。小說這麼寫楊過的內心活動：

> 他和我爹爹義結金蘭，交情自不尋常，但終於下手害他，難道我爹爹眞是個十惡不赦的壞人麼？」他自小想像父親仁俠慷慨，英俊勇武，乃是天下一等一的好男兒，突然要他承認父親是個壞人，實是萬萬不能。可是在他內心深處，早已隱約覺得父親遠遠不及郭伯伯，只是以前每當甫動此念，立即強自壓抑，此刻却不由得他不想到此節了。（頁 846）

從引文可見，楊過愈了解郭靖，他就愈懷疑生父，難以下手。

顯然，郭靖才是眞正的「父親」，因爲他代表了書中眾人認可的價值觀。他一再強調的「爲國爲民，俠之大者」，正是忠誠無私的「德」，也是維護大多數（漢）人利益的處世之道。[18] 不僅如此，在私交的層面上，郭靖亦有大

---

18 小說裡這種爲大多數人謀福利的觀點，和楊中芳對中國人的「自我」的分析，相當接近。依照他的說法，中國傳統理念以至社會教化，都很側重個人與群體的密切關係。他說：「社會的秩序與和諧是建築在每個人將『自己』由『個己』（按：即以自身實體爲界限的狹窄『自身』的稱呼）不斷地轉化爲包容整個社會的『自己』（按：泛指廣義的『自身』，既包括『個己』，亦包容特定的『別人』）。」他還進一步指出：「在中國傳統哲學的理念中……『社會』固然也是『個人』的組合，但是內裡各個『個人』却不是完全獨立的。『社會』本身藉人倫關係把『個人』組合成一個緊密、有層次的結構。每一個『個人』都有一個無形的關係網，使他與『社會』中部分其他人有不同緊密程度的關聯。個人的行爲必須依在這個網絡中，自己對他人所背負的責任和義務來行事。因爲，在中國這種『社會』與『個人』關係的架構中，如果『社會』中每一個『個人』都能履行他的社會責任及義務，整個『社會』即可運作自如，向前發展。在這個構想之中，『社會』中的『個人』必須有一個劃一的信念，那就是：『社會』幸福是『個人』幸福的先決條件。整個『社會』的進步可以帶動內中『個人』向前進步。社會規範及法律是用以限制及懲罰那些不能堅持這個信念，以致不能履行他對社會的責任及義務的人。如何確保每一個『個人』都能堅持這個信念，在於道德教育及內化，在於對『個人』的『自己』進行超越及轉化。最終使『個人』與『社會』在前進的方向上，變爲一致。」見〈試論中國人的「自己」：理論與研究方向〉，收在楊中芳、高尚仁編，《中國人・中國心——人格與社會篇》（臺北：遠流，1997），頁 93-145。亦可參看註 13 杜維明的文章。金庸本人的看法是：「在武俠世界中，男子的責任和感情是『仁義爲先』。仁是對大眾的疾苦怨屈充分關懷，義是竭盡全力做份所當爲之事。引伸出去便是『爲國爲民，俠之大者』。」見金庸，〈小序：男主角的兩種類型〉，吳靄儀，《金庸小說的男子》（香港：明窗，1997）。

俠風範，肯捨己爲人。比如說，在第二十一回，楊過有心在蒙古軍中害死郭靖，郭靖卻拚死來相救被蒙古高手糾纏不放的楊過，令他深爲感動而「不念舊惡」。(頁 875) 楊過的心理變化，雖然欠缺說服力，但小說想道出的，不外乎郭靖的行爲端正，無論在公在私，都叫楊過心服口服。所以，楊過成長的第一個重要關鍵，就是要認清社會認可的價值觀──亦就是解決「德」的問題。只有在此前題下，楊過雖然未知生父的死亡眞相，也能暫時放下所謂「父仇」，避免了第一個「錯誤」。

　　楊過練成曠世武功以後，行俠仗義，抵禦外侮，郭靖的影響不小。楊過行俠仗義的事蹟，除了屢救郭靖妻女及武氏兄弟以外，大都在第三十三回的「風陵夜話」裡，由旁人一一道來。至於抵禦外侮，在第三十六回有殲敵兩千，火燒敵糧，力保襄陽的壯舉；在第三十九回更立大功，在千軍萬馬之中克法王，救郭襄，斃大汗，一氣呵成。蒙古大軍一退，郭靖攜楊過之手進城。俠之大者，德之完成，在百姓爲楊過呈上的一杯美酒裡得到見證。

　　然而，天下沒有不是的父母。即使生父大奸大惡，楊過也不能遺棄他，只有寄望自己立品揚名，稍減其過。在兩次立功的空檔之間，楊過重遊葬父之地，終於有機會聽到生父的劣行及慘死的經過。生父心術不正，叛 (宋) 國害 (漢) 民，幾乎就是郭靖的反面；即使是生父，也難以認同他的價值觀念。楊過羞憤難言，不在話下。不過，柯鎮惡安慰他的話，有他的道理：「楊公子，你在襄陽立此大功，你父親便有千般不是，也都掩蓋過了。他在九泉之下，自也歡喜你爲父補過。」(頁 1549) 正因楊過沒殺郭靖，又爲國立功，他才有資格在這個時候替父親改立墓碑。將原來丘處機刻的「不肖弟子楊康之墓」，改爲「先父楊府君康之墓」；「不肖」之處由自己承擔，在墓碑上刻下「不肖子楊過謹立」。此時的楊過，名震天下；楊康之過，終於由楊過改正過來。(頁 1551)[19]

19　這顯然是「子爲父隱」的變奏 (《論語・子路》)。關於「天下無不是的父母」的討論，可以參考錢穆，《晚學盲言》上冊 (臺北：東大，1996)，頁 316-321 。註 13 提到的杜維明的文章，也有討論這個問題。

四

楊過在襄陽城頭接受百姓歡呼的時候，多少往事，都湧上心頭；最有感觸的，還是少年時代與「父親」的瓜葛。他心想：

> 二十餘年之前，郭伯伯也這般攜著我的手，送我上終南山重陽宮去投師學藝。可是我狂妄胡鬧，叛師叛教，闖下了多大禍事！倘若我終於誤入歧途，哪有今天和他攜手入城的一日？（頁 1636）

這裡說的「叛師叛教」，是楊過的第二個「錯誤」。當年，趙志敬尚未露出本來面目，楊過的反抗、叛教、轉投古墓派，均被視為欺師滅祖、罪大惡極的行為。楊過初涉江湖，不懂規矩，背叛師門──或者說冒犯「父之名」──自然成為他少年時期的母題。在桃花島上，他已有唐突祖師爺爺的前科。當時柯鎮惡要他交代歐陽鋒的下落，他寧死不依，還大罵柯鎮惡為「老瞎子」，結果吃了郭靖一記耳光，還要離開桃花島。這是楊過第一次被逐出師門。（頁 97-99）

　　令楊過罪加一等的事，是後來與小龍女相戀，而且不知天高地厚，在公開場合表態。一個非君不嫁，一個非卿不娶的宣言，在他人眼中，無疑是挑戰社會、破壞人倫的勾當，故此有「逆倫」或「亂倫」之說。（頁 546）[20] 楊

---

20 事實上，兩人的「逆倫」或「亂倫」的關係，除了表面上的師徒名分以外，還有另一種潛在的「母子」關係。（頁 282）比較明顯的一幕，是兩人在絕情谷下相見的描寫。楊過進到小龍女獨居的茅屋內，見一木櫥，拉開櫥門，「只見櫥中放著幾件樹皮結成的兒童衣衫，正是從前在古墓時小龍女為自己所縫製的模樣。」雖然楊過初識小龍女時只有十三四歲，但兩人在絕情谷上分別時，早已結為夫妻，楊過恐怕也有十八歲了。小龍女深谷幽居十六年，思念的居然不是懂得男歡女愛的楊過，而是「兒童」期的楊過，頗不尋常。後來兩人相見，小龍女說的話，更像母親。楊過說：「龍兒，你容貌一點也沒變，我却老了。」小龍女答道：「不是老了，是我的過兒長大了。」（頁 1609）由於兩人並無血緣關係，這種潛在的「亂倫」關係，恐怕只是對男孩依賴母親／女性的一種焦慮。男孩能否擺脫母親／女性的影響、成長為男人，是人類學及心理分析研究經常觸及的問題。見下文關於體的討論。

過魯莽倒也罷了，連身爲人師的小龍女也不懂世俗禮法，後果相當嚴重。[21]
小說寫得很清楚：

> 若是他師徒倆一句話也不説，在什麼世外桃源、或是窮鄉荒島之中結爲夫婦，始
> 終不爲人知，確是與人無損。只是這般公然無忌的胡作非爲，却有乖世道人心，
> 成了武林中的敗類。(頁 551-552)

早在武林大會之前，李莫愁已嘲笑兩人「亂倫犯上」、「做了禽獸般的苟且之
事」，(頁 389) 大會上趙志敬更乘機把他們罵爲「禽獸」，(頁 548) 會後武氏
兄弟在背後把他們叫做「師不師、徒不徒」的「狗男女」。(頁 570) 兩人的愛
情之所以犯眾怒，從戴維思的理論來看，亦因爲他們冒犯了「父之名」。儘管
小龍女身爲人師，在違反世俗禮法一事，與楊過並無分別，同樣淪爲「兒子」，
必須遭受懲罰。事實上，小龍女與楊過相親相愛，觸犯了本門的規條。在第
二十八回的洞房花燭夜，楊過自認是全眞派的忤逆弟子，亦不忘指出小龍女
是古墓派的叛徒。古墓派原來不許招收男弟子，更不准掌門嫁人；兩大規條，
小龍女都沒遵從，所以感嘆：「咱二人災劫重重，原是罪有應得」。(頁
1132)[22]

　　爲什麼楊過的第二個「過失」那麼嚴重，而他卻義無反顧、視死如歸？
這個問題與習武有關。上文談德，已經涉及體的問題。楊過身爲孤兒，經常
「遭人白眼、受人欺辱」；(頁 62) 不懂功夫，終究是一種嚴重的欠缺。他在
童年時憧憬的父親形象，是個慈祥的保護者。小說寫道：

> 他從兩三歲起就盼望有個愛憐他、保護他的父親。有時睡夢之中，突然有了個慈

21　楊過並非不知世俗禮法的厲害，只是「不服氣」，小龍女則是「一無所知」。(頁 551)
　　所以小說寫兩人「一個不理，一個不懂」。(頁 502) 小龍女不懂世事，同深居簡出固
　　然有關，但我們亦不能忽略她亦是孤兒的事實。(141 頁) 小龍女身邊只有避世的女性
　　(師祖、師父與丫鬟)，沒有入世的角色。小龍女所缺，恐怕和楊過一樣，也是父親的
　　角色。

22　小龍女的説法並不全對，因爲她不是完全不守門規。第七回寫道：「古墓派師祖……
　　傷心之餘，立下門規，凡是得她衣缽眞傳之人，必須發誓一世居於古墓，終身不下終
　　南山，但若有一個男子心甘情願的爲她而死，這誓言就算破了。不過此事絕不能事先
　　讓那男子得知。」既然楊過願意爲小龍女而死，誓言就算破了。(頁 254) 小龍女唯一
　　的「錯誤」就是收了楊過爲徒。

愛的英雄父親，但一覺醒來，這父親又不知去向，常常因此而大哭一場。(頁 62)

父親的愛心固然不可少，自衛的本事更重要。楊過對武功的需求，從他與歐陽鋒的交往裡可以看出來。歐陽鋒的行為怪異，楊過起初並不願意認他作父。但後來歐陽鋒替他驅毒，憐愛有加，才覺得親切起來。但歸根到底，楊過甘當歐陽鋒的兒子，是因為歐陽鋒的武功高強。歐陽鋒小試身手，咭咭的叫三聲，就信手推倒半堵土牆，叫他瞧得目瞪口呆。更為難得的是，歐陽鋒願意把自己「生平最得意的武功」傳授給他。(頁 63) 飽受欺凌的楊過，豈能不感動？所以在歐陽鋒要離開的時候，楊過願意相隨。雖然歐陽鋒不能帶上他，楊過也請他早日回來。甚至在歐陽鋒走後，楊過知道郭靖等人忌憚歐陽鋒的功夫，亦暗自歡喜。

在楊過成長的過程裡，凡是不肯指點武藝的師長，他都充滿疑心與敵意，郭靖、黃蓉和趙志敬屬此類。凡是真心傳授武功的師父，則感恩圖報，完全死心塌地，歐陽鋒和小龍女屬此類。在小說的最後一章，眾人附和郭靖的提議，到華山為洪七公掃墓。來到山上，眾人弔祭洪七公，只有楊過念舊情，在拜過洪七公後，和小龍女到歐陽鋒墳前跪拜。歐陽鋒所教僅為皮毛，楊過尚且感恩不盡；小龍女將古墓派武功，悉數傳給楊過，楊過內心的感激，可思過半。楊過生命所缺，小龍女毫無保留的供給，恩同再造。儘管後來兩人相愛，楊過願意生死相隨，不能說沒有報恩的成分。這種感激之情，亦是推動敘記層內事件發展的另一個自發動機——楊過甘冒天下之大不韙，緣由在此。23

楊過對武功，求之若渴；但饑不擇食，亦會出問題。歐陽鋒的功夫，本

---

23 且舉兩個例子。第五回裡有這麼一段：「楊過大為欽服，說道：『姑姑，明兒你把這本事教給我好不好？』小龍女道：『這本事算得什麼？你好好的學，我有好多厲害本事教你呢。』楊過聽得小龍女肯真心教他，登時將初時的怨氣盡數拋到了九霄雲外，感激之下，不禁流下淚來，哽咽道：『姑姑，你待我這麼好，我先前還恨你呢。』小龍女道：『我趕你出去，你自然恨我，那也沒什麼希奇。』楊過道：『倒不為這個，我只道你也跟我從前的師父一樣，儘教我些不管用的功夫。』」(頁 195) 後來又有一段：「小龍女道：『你跟全真教的師父打架，不肯討一句饒，怎麼現下這般不長進？』楊過笑道：『誰待我不好，他就是打我，我也不肯輸一句口。誰待我好呢，我為他死了也是心甘情願，何況討一句饒？』」(頁 198) 高辛勇在文內也有提到(頁 120、124)，傳統小說的男女之愛，往往產生於感恩圖報之意。

來就邪門；再加上歐陽鋒未能發揮父親的功能，指點楊過為人處世之道，楊過兩次藉此自衛，未見其利，反見其害。第一件事發生在桃花島上，楊過被武修儒兄弟欺凌，危急之中使出蛤蟆功自保，結果誤傷武修文，亦暴露了他與歐陽鋒的關係，使他幾乎命喪柯鎮惡杖下。由於柯鎮惡與歐陽鋒是死敵，事發之後，郭靖不便留楊過在島上，只好將他送去全真教學藝，因而引發種種江湖恩怨。

　　楊過與全真教結怨，與蛤蟆功也有關係。楊過瞧不起武功不及郭靖的全真弟子，鄙夷之情形諸於色，招來師父趙志敬的毆打責罵。楊過不甘受辱，憤而咬斷師父食指。能有此勁道，實拜歐陽鋒傳授的內功秘訣所賜。楊過桀驁不馴，也因此種下禍根，趙志敬不但不傳授武功，而且還要他的好看。趙志敬特地安排他參加全真眾徒的比武大會，讓他出醜，還遭到師兄鹿清篤毒打。為了自保，楊過再次使出蛤蟆功，結果又把師兄打至奄奄一息。事至如此，楊過只好溜之大吉，鬧出了背叛師門、轉投小龍女門下的一場風波。

　　儘管如此，蛤蟆功的道德取向問題還小，古墓派武功的性別取向才是楊過的真正問題。小龍女願意收他為徒，他自然感激不盡，發奮修習；對於武功的性別取向，卻不甚了了。楊過的熱心，小說並不認同。古墓派的功夫由林朝英所創，三代傳人都是女子；玉女心經更是專門剋制男性（全真派）的一門武功。[24] 小說的描寫，也刻意凸顯古墓派功夫女性化的一面，由楊過來使，不免有點彆扭。事實上，楊過使玉女劍法的時候，小說已有偷鳳轉龍之嫌：

> 小龍女教導楊過的架式，都帶著三分孃娜風姿。楊過融會貫通之後，自然而然的已除去了女子神態，轉為飄逸靈動。（頁 517）

武功裡的性別取向，到了楊過耍起美女拳法，招架達爾巴的金杵時，就更為突出。僅靠美女拳法，未必能制服得了強悍的敵手；在黃蓉點撥之下，楊過使出九陰真經的移魂大法，迷惑對方，令對方隨著美女拳法起舞。這麼一來，兩個男人的比武，因為都使起女子拳法，變成了鬧劇。一老一少的效顰之作，使在場的各路人馬尷尬不已。有文為證：

24　這也是馬國明的觀察。

> 楊過這麼一笑，達爾巴已受感染，跟著也是一笑。只是楊過眉清目秀，添上笑容，更添風致，那達爾巴顴骨高聳，面頰深陷，跟著楊過作態一笑，旁觀衆人無不毛骨悚然。……這時楊過將美女拳法施展出來，或步步生蓮，或依依如柳，達爾巴依樣模倣，只將衆人看得又是驚駭，又是好笑。（頁 528-529）

小說彷彿藉此指出：楊過年少，尙未定「性」，扮起女兒態來，形同遊戲，猶可接受；要是他年紀再大些，還使美女拳法，效果會不會像達爾巴一樣，令人駭然失笑？甚至，如果他浸淫日久，會不會變成像東方不敗那種「不男不女的妖異模樣，令人越看越是心中發毛」？（《笑傲江湖》頁 1286）性別曖昧所引起的尷尬，甚至恐懼，在此表露無遺。楊過在江湖上初次亮相，技驚四座，亦同時暴露了他的男性主體的潛在危機。[25]

　　楊過從小龍女習武，進而墜入情網，在小說裡引起相當的不安。這道難題，怎生解決是好？

五

　　詹明信（Fredric Jameson）在一篇討論大眾文化的文章裡指出：大眾文藝並非完全物化的商品，對於社會上的焦慮與不安，自有其處理方式。大眾文藝裡備受忽略的，是烏托邦的成分。引起不安的社會問題，往往會在文藝作品中透過幻想圓滿解決。最後，原有的社會秩序得到恢復、肯定，製造出天下太平的幻象。[26]

　　楊過在小說裡鬧出的「逆倫」之事，解決的方式也頗具烏托邦色彩。上文提及楊過行俠仗義、爲國爲民的事跡，這些都是他的德行。雖然行俠不一

25　「不男不女」的性別曖昧可以說是一種禁忌，因爲性別未曾定位的人，是尚未社會化的人。更何況，男人學了玉女拳法，有機會淪爲「第二性」？可以參考游靜關於電影《東方不敗》中性別政治的討論，〈歡迎大家收看〉，《今天》28 (1995)：153-160。梁秉鈞也有談到這個問題，見也斯，《香港文化》（香港：青文書屋，1995），頁 43-45。馬國明亦指出：「值得注意的是在金庸的世界裡，只可能有男性或女性，不可能有雙性，連不男不女也不可能。」

26　Fredric Jameson, "Reification and Utopia in Mass Culture," *Social Text 1* (1979): 130-148。

定需要武力，但在武俠小說裡，沒有武功，或者功夫不好，事情都不太好辦，遑論伸張正義。[27] 楊過後來修練得來的內力和武藝，正是小說化解矛盾的關鍵。

楊過的絕世武功，來自神鵰。在第二十三回，楊過初遇神鵰，見鵰有難，出手相助，成爲好友。後來楊過被郭芙斷臂，於迷亂中投奔大鵰；神鵰報之以李，救他一命，更授以上乘武功。神鵰幫助楊過，是自發動機的運作；但神鵰的出現，亦可視爲外來動機的介入。從敘述學的角度來看，神鵰的功能是「資助者」（donor），目的是爲主角提供扭轉乾坤的「神物」（magical agent）。[28] 小說裡的兩種「神物」，都同體有關：一是強身健體的蛇膽，二是劍魔獨孤求敗幾乎失傳的武功。拜師學藝曾是楊過煩惱的根源，但神鵰的出現，使小說避開了這個問題。劍魔人已不在，楊過要學他的功夫，只有靠神鵰的誘導，在搏擊中間接的修習。神鵰並非人類，從它練武，不算背叛師門。何況神鵰具靈性，有超自然的意味？[29] 從武術的道德體系來看，劍魔的武術中立，無關正邪，學來無妨。我們甚至可以說，他的武術超乎功利，幾乎是「爲武功而武功」的。[30]

楊過練就劍魔的本事，至少有三個作用；而這三個作用，都爲他立身揚名鋪路，可以看出意識形態的運作。第一個作用是讓楊過以武行俠、抵禦外辱，既鞏固了眾人認可的價值觀，亦爲他贏得道德威望以及伴隨而來的無形權力。第二個作用是建立楊過的男性主體，進而達到第三個相關的作用：逆轉他和小龍女的輩分／尊卑關係，從而抗衡、甚至消解「亂倫」、「逆倫」之說，使兩人的關係規範化。

如果劍魔的武功，在道德取向與歐陽鋒的蛤蟆功有分別的話，在性別取向上，則同小龍女的古墓派武功南轅北轍。劍魔的武功同古墓派武功的差異，

---

27 參看陳平原，《千古文人俠客夢》（北京：人民文學，1992），頁 23-41。

28 V. Propp, *Morphology of the Folktale*, trans. Laurence Scott (Austin: U of Texas P, 1988), p. 39。中譯出自高辛勇，略有改動，見《形名學與敘事理論》（臺北：聯經，1987），頁 32-33。

29 金庸在小說的〈後記〉裡寫道：「神鵰這種怪鳥，現實世界是沒有的。」（頁 1672）

30 劍魔亦是武癡，雖有報仇行俠的行逕，但顯然並非其形象描寫的重點。有自白爲證：「縱橫江湖三十餘載，殺盡仇寇，敗盡英雄，天下更無抗手，無可奈何，唯隱居深谷，以鵰爲友。嗚呼，平生求一敵手而不可得，誠寂寥難堪也。」（頁 930）

在意識形態上最大的作用，是改變楊過武功的路向，確立他的男兒身分。沒有鵰「兄」（頁 929、1065）的啓蒙，[31] 楊過恐怕無法擺脫女性（武功）的掌握，邁出成長爲男人的第一步。小說雖然沒有道出劍魔的性別，但他的武功的男性形象呼之欲出。楊過隨神鵰練功，學到的盡是硬朗功夫，同古墓派功夫形成強烈對比。如果古墓派的武功「柔靈有餘，沉厚不足」、（頁 215）「輕柔有餘，威猛不足」，（頁 517）那麼劍魔的武學，則沉潛剛猛，可以補楊過之「陰虛」。大鵰與楊過練功，沒要他抓麻雀，一開始就要他掄七八十斤的玄鐵重劍，還逼他在山洪裡練勁力。這種強調氣力、重兵器的硬功夫，和古墓派講究靈巧迅速的功架，確有天淵之別。經過數月的苦練，到楊過出山的時候，已非同小可。

在題爲「鬥智鬥力」的二十七回，楊過要鬥的，是力。當時圍攻小龍女的都是男人，楊過不再以女性的功夫與他們周旋，更不施展輕功迴避。這一回的描寫，簡潔粗獷，楊過那種與陰柔靈巧完全對立的陽剛狠拙，幾乎就是他的男性主體宣言。值得留意的是，幾個使重兵器的對手，輸得最慘。尼摩星使用十來斤的鐵杖，被楊過一擊而高飛二十餘丈；連尼摩星賴以支撐的單拐，也因楊過以劍壓住他的肩膀，不斷陷入地裡，無法拔起。金輪法王的五個金屬飛輪，通通被楊過劈去。更狼狽的是，後來金輪法王委頓在地，楊過揮劍就砍，法王的兩名徒弟分別以金杵和鋼扇抵擋，卻支撐不住。楊過的力氣簡直天下無敵，難怪身爲師祖的丘處機，亦要承認楊過的厲害，說道：「楊過，你的武功練到了這等地步，我輩遠遠不及。」（頁 1122）

楊過的功夫大進，除了確定他的男兒身外，還有另一個更重要的作用。楊過要在江湖上得人敬重，他的功夫必須超越小龍女；即使兩人在名義上不能逆轉原來的師徒關係，至少楊過要在武學上有所成，方能符合男尊女卑的社會習俗。事實上，小龍女的師父身分，從一開始就沒人願意相信。大家都認爲，小龍女漂亮（「容貌俏麗」、「嫵媚嬌怯」）、年輕（「年紀尙較楊過幼小」、「比楊過年紀更輕」），根本不可能是楊過的師父。這一點在第十三、十四回的英雄大會上特別明顯。（頁 510、531）何況在二十六回之前，小龍女的功夫尙淺，臨陣經驗不足，儘管初生之犢不怕虎，也未能鎭懾群豪。若與大師過招，

---

31 鵰「公公」、鵰「爺爺」是後來的叫法，見 1336 頁。

處境尤其凶險。第五回與丘處機只過一招，已知不敵。第十三回與金輪法王惡鬥，更是險象環生，後來還要楊過、郭靖分別出手相救，才倖免於難。

　　小龍女的功夫傳自林朝英。如果小龍女未能勝任，祖師奶奶的功夫又怎樣？儘管書中角色一再稱頌她聰明過人，自創的古墓派武功非凡，小說似乎無意讓古墓派的功夫獨步天下。她的玉女素心劍法，並非純粹的一派功夫，而是玉女劍法與全真劍法的合璧。在二十六回以前，小龍女與楊過遭遇強敵，往往要聯手合力，使出兩門劍法，方能自保。與金輪法王（第十四回）和絕情谷主（第二十回）的交手，莫不如此。雙劍合璧固然威力大增，但兩人已經不再是單憑古墓派的劍法退敵，還用上了老對頭的劍法。在第二十六回，小龍女以一敵眾，場面慘烈，靠的還不是一人使兩股劍法？小龍女懂得一心二用，還得多謝全真派的老頑童周伯通。沒有他傳授的絕技，小龍女恐怕也撐不下去。

　　楊過跟神鵰學的武功就不同了。劍魔名為獨孤求敗，自然走遍天下無敵手。這種氣概與林朝英足不出戶、潛心練武、只求破一派功夫的心眼，截然不同。小說隱含的價值判斷，不言而喻。難怪劍魔的武功，楊過只不過學了幾天，就已經發現遠勝古墓派的劍法：「越是平平無奇的劍招，對方越難抗禦。比如挺劍直刺，只要勁力強猛，威力遠比玉女劍法等變幻奇妙的劍招更大。」（頁1073）

　　到他第一次出山，已經可以獨力退敵，把圍攻小龍女的武林高手打個落花流水。多年以前，在終南山上，小龍女從全真教的手裡救走楊過。當年的楊過不懂武術，卻已有「男子漢保護弱女子的氣概」；他想保護的，居然是「武功不知要比他高出多少」的小龍女。（頁202）這是小說裡反覆出現的另一個楊過的母題。小說並沒有忘記讓楊過實現他的夢想——他在小龍女激戰九大高手的時候及時趕到，使小龍女分心，身受重傷，好讓他大顯身手。楊過的「氣概」，終於得以盡情表達。

　　這是楊過與小龍女關係的重要轉捩點。楊過終於可以採取主動，掌握兩人關係。惡戰過後，他意識到小龍女可能命不久矣，於是在眾人面前宣告：

　　什麼師徒名分，什麼名節清白，咱們通通當是放屁！通通滾他媽的蛋！死也罷，活也罷，咱倆誰也沒命苦，誰也不會孤苦伶仃。從今而後，你不是我師父，不是

我姑姑，是我妻子！（頁 1127）

這一番話妙在「是」字。從言語行動理論來看，楊過此語貌似「斷言式話語」
（constative utterance），卻有「履行式話語」（performative utterance）的
神髓。一段看似描述的話，卻有要求眾人承認兩人夫妻之實。不僅如此，楊
過言出必行，立即在重陽宮裡拜堂成親。儘管婚禮並不得體，也未得眾人的
認同，有效性存疑；[32] 但對拜堂的新人來說，卻是米已成炊，名分已變。小
龍女從此由師父變爲妻子，也樂於如此——至少小說是這麼寫的。且看兩人
逃出重陽宮的一段：

> 楊過低聲道：「你指揮蜜蜂相助，咱們闖將出去。」小龍女做了楊過妻子，聽到
> 他說話中含有囑咐之意，心中甜甜的甚是舒服，心想：「好啊，他終於不再當我
> 是師父，真的當我是妻子了。」當即應道：「是！」聲音極是溫柔順從……（頁
> 1135）

在此之前，楊過未有能力掌握兩人關係，說話的方式並不一樣。在第七回，
小龍女被歐陽鋒點穴，於黑暗中失身給尹志平，還以爲是楊過。事後小龍女
問楊過，是否以她爲妻。楊過身爲弟子，又不知就裡，豈敢胡言？只好結結
巴巴的叫師父、喊姑姑，小龍女一氣之下，遠走他方。在第十四回的英雄大
會上，郭靖自作主張，要把郭芙許給楊過，楊過只有婉卻。兩人的戀情是由
小龍女來宣布的：「我自己要做過兒的妻子，他不會娶你女兒的。」（頁 547）
語氣斬釘截鐵，但畢竟未成事實，僅爲意願而已。楊過爲兩人的戀情抗辯，
說的話也同樣用了「要」字——比「是」字軟弱多了：「我做了什麼事礙著
你們了？我又害了誰了？姑姑教過我武功，可是我偏偏要她做我妻子。你們
斬我一千刀、一萬刀，我還是要她做妻子。」（頁 551）

---

32 小說中的言語行動與現實中的言語行動並沒有太大的差異，見 Gerard Genette, *Fiction and Diction*, trans. Catherine Porter (Ithaca and London: Cornell UP, 1993)，
p. 33。關於「斷言式話語」、「履行式話語」以及後者是否得體的討論，見 Sandy
Petrey, *Speech Acts and Literary Theory* (New York and London: Routledge, 1990),
pp. 3–21; J. L. Austin, "Performative-Constative," *The Philosophy of Language*, ed. J.
R. Searle (Oxford: Oxford UP, 1971), pp. 13–22。「斷言式話語」及「履行式話語」
是周英雄的譯法，見〈從語用談小說的意義〉，《小說・歷史・心理・人物》，頁 7–8。

　　二十七回的楊過已非吳下阿蒙，但功夫未勝小龍女，亦未爲國立功。他在德、體兩方面的成長仍未完成，二人的姻緣還要受阻。小說再次棒打鴛鴦，這一趟可是望穿秋水的十六年。這是兩人三次分離最漫長的一次。同情兩人遭遇的讀者不免要問：絕情谷上，小龍女是否眞的無計可施，一定要出此下策，要楊過枯等十六年，才可以救他一命？小龍女自己身中劇毒，當眞無可救藥？這漫長的十六年，莫非有其他作用？

　　楊過形單影隻，又一次回到鵰兄身邊，心無旁騖，潛修武學。這次漫長的離別，是他成長的第二階段。他不僅練成劍魔武功的最高境界，（頁 1331-1336）還逆武學通理而行，自創黯然銷魂掌。（頁 1423）到他第二次出山，功夫更上層樓，一燈大師、（頁 1409）周伯通、（頁 1426）黃藥師（頁 1540）幾位老前輩都要佩服。不僅此也，楊過還行俠仗義，保衛襄陽。無論道德武功，他已臻至善。從戴維思的理論來看，楊過已經擺脫「兒子」的被動狀態，變成掌握主動權的「父親」。也只有在這種情況下，小說方才讓兩人於絕情谷底相會。兩人的重逢，是人物的自發動機使然——若非小龍女爲楊過自盡，她也不會吃到潭中白魚，治好劇毒。要不是楊過鶼鰈情深，他亦不會躍下深淵；如果沉潭不深，見不到冰窖，也見不著小龍女。兩人的重逢，依小說所言，亦是外來動機使然——若非「蒼天眷顧」，（頁 1612）兩人何以重逢？楊過的感喟「好心者必有好報」，（頁 1612）小龍女說的「冥冥之中，自有天意」，（頁 1161）正是此意。外來動機的介入，是否完全是天意的運作？內裡是否另有乾坤？

　　換個角度來討論，或許可以窺見箇中玄機。十六年的分離導致楊過功夫大進，但小龍女的武功卻一點也沒有長進。[33]　（頁 1614）在第二次保衛襄陽

33　馬國明的說法倒也直截了當，他認爲：「從學武功的角度而言，金庸顯然是性別歧視。他的小說極之細緻地描述男性人物如何練成絕世武功，對女性人物學武的過程則鮮有提及。即使提及也是因爲練的是邪門的武功，如《倚天屠龍記》的珠兒（殷離）和《天龍八部》的阿紫。金庸的主觀意圖當然無法知道，亦不用深究。學武情節上重男輕女的客觀結果是讀者完全投入男性人物的角色裡。」後來又加上一段：「吳靄儀說金庸不理解女性。其實不是不理解，而是害怕，尤其害怕女性學了武功。」金庸小說是否「害怕」女性學武，尚可商榷。《神鵰俠侶》主要講述楊過成長的故事（儘管題目包括小龍女在內），而成長故事的作法，依據的往往是男性的模式，並不一定適合女性。關於這個問題，可以參考註 4 的文章。男性的成長模式，自然受到社會結構的左右。

的戰役中，她只扮演小小的配角，馳騁沙場的是楊過。值得留意的是楊過與
金輪法王的一戰。楊過因爲夫妻重逢，心情愉快，生平絕學無法使出，幾乎
血濺當場。只有在生死關頭，念及夫妻永訣的哀慟時，他的黯然銷魂掌方才
自發而出，五招之內，奪法王性命。此段描寫，惹人遐思。如果小龍女的武
功追求「合」的最高境界，楊過的曠世武學及威力卻由「離」而生。前者溫
馨纏綿，但不能剋敵；（頁 564-565）後者孤獨淒苦，卻可以獨步武林。楊
過（男孩）成長的秘密，恐怕在此：楊過（男性）若不離開小龍女（母親／
女性），難成大器。[34]

　　到華山論英雄時，小龍女和楊過的武學高下正式定案。此時的楊過，不
再是任人魚肉的孤兒；他不僅與郭靖（父輩），甚至還同黃藥師、老頑童、一
燈大師（祖輩）平起平坐，攀上江湖五絕的寶座，成爲一代宗師。一旦楊過
名列五絕，意味著大家承認他的武學成就超越小龍女，即使兩人的師徒名分
不除，兩人的地位已經完全倒置。

武俠小説裡的傳統社會，與中國傳統社會有相似之處。據李亦園的看法，後者是「父
系 (patrilineal)、隨父居 (patrilocal) 與父權 (patriarchal)」的社會。見註 13 李文。
吳靄儀對金庸作品的評價，比較接近成長小説的討論。她認爲：「金庸小説的女子雖
然多姿多采，但是在他的著作中的主要作用只是點綴及引入愛情成分，愛情與美貌就
是金庸女子的唯一事業，在大男人的世界裡，男子愛女子的因素，也不過是她長得美
麗及對他溫柔，但男子的角色則完全不同，他要有事業、有道德生命、追尋人生目標，
他要面對如何在現實世界裡安身立命，在這個過程中，他做出一些行動，對社會造成
若干後果，而這些後果，又使他的發展受到某些影響。在真實世界，是個人與社會之
間互相影響，在小説世界，就是人物帶動情節。」見吳靄儀，《金庸小説的男子》1。

34 如果從兩人潛在的「母子」關係來考慮，楊過離開小龍女，象徵著男孩離開母親。人
類學及心理分析研究都有提到，原始部落的男性啓蒙儀式，實際作用是從母親——女
性手中奪走男孩，讓他們遠離女性，並且通過一系列象徵脫胎換骨的成長儀式，過渡
爲男人。此種象徵儀式相當繁複，周期也多，過程漫長，可以從八至十二歲左右開始，
綿延十多年。參看：Fritz John Porter Poole, "The Ritual Forging of Identity:
Aspects of Person and Self in Bimin-Kuskusmin Male Initiation," *Rituals of Man-
hood: Male Initiation in Papua New Guinea*, ed. Gilbert H. Herdt with an Introduction
by Roger M. Keesing (Berkeley, Los Angeles and London: U of California P, 1982),
pp. 99-154; Theodore Lidz and Ruth Wilmanns Lidz, *Oedipus in the Stone Age: A
Psychoanalytic Study of Masculinization in Papua New Guinea* (Madison, Connecticut:
International Universities P., Inc., 1989)。既然楊龍二人沒有血緣關係，楊過成長（成
了大俠）以後，兩人就可以重聚。

　　黃藥師推薦小龍女爲五絕之中的話，不能當眞，因爲他是故意和老頑童
鬧著玩的。且聽黃藥師怎麼說：

> 楊夫人小龍女是古墓派唯一傳人。想當年林朝英女俠武功卓絕，玉女素心劍法出
> 神入化，縱然是重陽眞人，見了她也忌憚三分。當時林女俠若來參與華山絕頂論
> 劍之會，別説五絕之名定當改上一改，便是重陽眞人那「武功天下第一」的尊號，
> 也未必便能到手。楊過的武藝出自他夫人傳授，弟子尚且名列五絕，師父更加不
> 用説了。是以楊夫人可當中央之位。（頁 1645）

話很動聽，但小龍女一婉拒，黃藥師立刻轉而提名黃蓉。鬧了半天，還是五
個男人把五絕分了。不管怎樣，黃藥師對「楊夫人」還是非常客氣的。此一
稱謂出自前輩之口，效果同絕情谷上程英、陸無雙等小輩叫「楊大嫂」自然
大不相同。楊過既已立德，又擁有絕世武功，與小龍女的關係亦合乎文化規
範，自然得到眾老的首肯。有趣的是，小說還意猶未足，讓小龍女越活越年
輕，楊過越長越蒼老。（頁 1609-1610）　楊過的問題，無論大小，都「糾正」
過來了。

　　兩人重新爲群體所接納，楊過的奇遇作用最大。然而，小龍女也有功勞。
比如說，在第二十五回，小龍女行俠仗義，打救了全眞教的老前輩周伯通。
此舉不但化解了全眞派險些叛國的危機，亦拆穿了趙志敬的本來面目。一個
品行不正的人，本來就沒有資格爲人師父，楊過「欺師滅祖」的罪名，亦隨
之煙消雲散。小龍女既然成了全眞教的恩人，楊過轉投她門下的陳年舊事，
識相的也就不會再提了。

六

　　本文討論了楊過的成長，主要側重他「改正」的一面。從性格的塑造、
角色的自發動機著眼，楊過是個重私情的人；但是如果從情節的發展、外來
動機的介入來看，小說容不得他這名主角只顧個人、輕忽群體。他的成長過
程，實際上也就是他的不羈野性被文化駕御的過程；少年楊過的問題，也在
這磨練過程中一一化解。收服楊過的文化，其實也就是父權的文化。從楊過
的男性定位，與小龍女關係的微妙轉變，到篇末統領武林的人選來看，莫不

如此。郭靖是《神鵰俠侶》中父權的代表，形象還很正面；楊過爲父權文化鉗制，雖然委曲，依然接受。不過，楊過和小龍女的戀情，帶來的衝擊不小。小說爲了處理這道難題，已經大費周章。據馬國明的研究，《天龍八部》和《笑傲江湖》以後，父權文化分崩離析，人文景觀大不相同。不過，這是後話了。

第三輯 翻譯與版本

《鹿鼎記》英譯漫談

劉　紹　銘

香港嶺南大學翻譯系

摘　要

就譯者的名氣和出版社的地位而言，1997 年香港牛津大學出版社出版的 *The Deer & the Cauldron* 都可說是「譯林盛事」。

原著是金庸的《鹿鼎記》，譯者是閔福德（John Minford）教授。

閔福德譯作甚豐，以與霍克思（David Hawkes）合譯《石頭記》（*The Story of the Stone*）最廣為人知。

金庸武俠小說，風靡華文讀者。但譯成英文，西方讀者是否可以接受呢？《鹿鼎記》作者本人並不樂觀。閔福德則認為「事在人為」。他相信英語世界的讀者會從閱讀《鹿鼎記》得到樂趣，一如中國讀者通過翻譯，看司各特（Walter Scott）、大仲馬（Alexandre Dumas）和司蒂文森（Robert Louis Stevenson）等人的作品，可以看得津津有味一樣。

本文將從民族和文化「情意結」的角度，去探討西方讀者對《鹿鼎記》的反應問題。

一

閔福德英譯《鹿鼎記》，從開始構想到牛津版 *The Deer & the Cauldron* 第一冊在1997年面世，[1] 已近十年。我個人對此翻譯盛事，一直關心得要緊。

---

1 Louis Cha, *The Deer & the Cauldron: The First Book*, trans. John Minford, Hong Kong: Oxford University Press, 1997.

原因有細說的必要。

首先，這跟我的職業有關。在我 1994 年回到香港嶺南大學（前香港嶺南學院）服務前的二十年，都在美國教書。所開的中國文學課程，除研究院的科目外，其他教材均爲英譯。每學期爲學生開書單，都傷透腦筋。一來選用的「名著」，不一定有英譯。二來即使有譯本，文字不一定清通可靠。

但更頭痛的是，即使所有我們認爲是名著的作品都有英譯，外國學生也不見得受用。譯作等身的英國學者詹納（W. J. F. Jenner）就慨嘆過，魯迅的地位和作品，對中國學生說來是一回事，拿給不知有漢的外國學生看，又是另一回事。[2]

語文的隔膜，是個原因。不說別的，〈孔乙己〉中的孔乙己，名字就有千絲萬縷的歷史文化關係，非翻譯所能解決的。

要外國讀者看得下去的中國文學作品，除了文字因素外，還要講內容。層次高一點來說，閱讀這些充滿「異國情調」的作品，會不會增加他們對人生的了解？

俗一點說，這些作品，讀來過不過癮？

說這些話，實在洩氣，也失學術尊嚴。但擺在眼前的事實，卻現實不過。今天的學子，無不以「顧客」身份自居。中國文學是中文系學生的必修科，老師要教什麼，就念什麼。

外系學生無此限制。他們來上課，原因不外兩種。一是爲了滿足求知慾。這類學子，至情至聖，因此鳳毛麟角。如果學校以「盈虧」的生意眼光作準則，一門課最少要有十個學生選修才能開班的話，那做老師的，絕不能把這類學生看作「基本顧客」，因爲他們可遇不可求。

比較可靠的，是那些爲了湊學分而來的外系學生。一般大學爲了符合「通識教育」的宗旨，規定所有學生必修若干人文科的課。中國文學正好是人文學科的一門。

在中文課程以選修學生多寡來決定學科價值輕重的今天，仍能苦撐下

2　W. J. F. Jenner, "Insuperable Barriers? Some Thoughts on the Reception of Chinese Writing in English Translation," in *Worlds Apart: Recent Chinese Writing and Its Audiences*, ed. Howard Goldblatt, Armonk, N. Y.: M. E. Sharpe, 1990, pp.177-197.

去，靠的就是要爲湊學分而來的「散兵游勇」。

本科生讀中國文學，不管念得下去或念不下去還是要念下去。

「散兵游勇」呢，總不會這麼輕易受擺佈，因爲除了中國文學，還有別的人文學科可選擇。作品讀來不過癮，是否還會繼續上課，實在很難說得準。

究竟這些「游離分子」要看那些東西才能看得下去，也是無法揣測的。根據詹納的經驗，作品要引起他們注意，得要在內容與形式上給他們一種「與別不同」的感覺。也就是他所說的 different。

怎樣才算 different？

他說如果要在 1949 年前成名的作家中挑選，他會選譯沈從文，特別是寫湘西風土人情那系列。這類作品不但外國人看來 different，連一向以爲自己熟悉本土風貌的中國人，讀來也會覺得耳目一新。

另外一個詹納想到要推薦的作家是老舍。沈從文最難忘情的是山水；老舍筆下的人物，都在都市紅塵中打滾。

這二家的小說，相映成趣。

除此以外，上榜的還有蕭紅（《呼蘭河傳》和《生死場》）及路翎（《財主底兒女們》）。

以上的論點，是詹納教授的「一家之言」。問題也出在這裡：他認爲是 different 的作品，外國學生和讀者不見得就念得下去。說來說去，讀者對作品的承受能力，關乎個人的教育程度、藝術品味和生活經驗。

在感情認同方面，作品本身的文化成分與讀者的「種族」（ethnic）背景，有時會互相干擾，影響到美學上的獨立判斷。

關於這一點，討論到英譯《鹿鼎記》的讀者反應時，將再補充。

二

英譯《鹿鼎記》的試行版（兩回），1993 年在澳洲國立大學學報《東亞史》發表。[3] 閔福德私下相告，譯者掛的雖然是他一個人的名字，但實際的翻譯工

3　John Minford, trans., *The Deer and the Cauldron: The Adventures of a Chinese Trick-ster. Two Chapters from a Novel by Louis Cha*, reprinted from *East Asian History* 5

作，霍克思教授一直參與其事。第一回〈縱橫鈎黨清流禍　峭蒨風期月旦評〉就是出自他的譯筆。

原來這位世界知名的《楚辭》和《石頭記》譯者，在閔福德翻譯計畫中扮演的竟是「幕後英雄」角色。

我收到閔福德寄來的試行本，如獲至寶。記得我當時第一個反應是：要看 different 的中國文學作品的讀者有福了。

武俠小說英譯，不自閔福德始。而且翻譯的對象，也不限於金庸。我對《鹿鼎記》英譯如此重視，簡單的說，是因爲這一本 different 類型的中國文學作品，英譯深慶得人：閔福德曾與霍克思合譯《石頭記》（後四十回），他是位 different 的翻譯學者。

閔福德這位 different 的譯者特別適合翻譯在武俠小說類型中「離經叛道」的《鹿鼎記》，他的英文造詣「異樣」的風流，措詞遣句，處處得心應手，當然是先決條件。另外一個原因，是他的文學趣味：他對離經叛道的作品和人物偏愛有加。

這可在他爲試行本所寫的長序看出端倪：

> 韋小寶是中國小說中難忘的角色。一如孫悟空、賈寶玉、阿 Q 這類人物那樣給人留下深刻印象。[4]

齊天大聖，反動祖宗。怡紅公子，「于國于家無望」。癩子阿 Q，左道旁門。他們所代表的一切，都與儒家「先天下之憂而憂」的承擔精神背道而馳。

事實上，外國學者中像閔福德對中國文化「離經叛道」的一面如此另眼相看的，相當普遍。儒道二家，在西方世界較受重視的，多是老莊。唐詩的詩聖詩仙，總是李白領風騷。

在文學作品裡追求 different 的經驗，反映西方人不愛隨波逐流、崇尚「個人主義」精神。

閔福德當然不是韋小寶。但作爲這位「反英雄」轉生到英語世界的引渡

(June 1993), Canberra: Institute of Advanced Studies, Australian National University, 1994.

4　John Minford, Translator's Introduction, in *The Deer and the Cauldron: The Adventures of a Chinese Trickster. Two Chapters from a Novel by Louis Cha*, p.10.

人，閔福德可以拒絕認同這小子的各種荒唐行徑，但卻萬萬不能討厭他。

譯者過的，是一種「借來的生命」，靠的是緣份。自己有話要說，從事創作好了，但如果覺得自己的話了無新意，或者話說得不像人家那麼漂亮、那麼恰到好處，最好找代言人。

所謂「借來的生命」，就是這個意思。

有關譯者與作者「緣份」之說，閔福德在近作 "Kungfu in Translation, Translation as Kungfu" 一文，[5] 舉例具體而微。

其中一例，是霍克思譯《石頭記》因緣。霍氏為了全心全力投入這項「十年辛苦不尋常」的譯作，不惜辭去牛津大學講座教授的職位。

閔德福認為嚴復的「信、雅、達」三律，扼要切實，永不會過時。若要補充，或可從錢鍾書說，再加一律：「化」。

「化」的英譯，閔福德提供了兩個：transformation 或 transmutation。

要達「化」境，需要在重鑄、重塑、重組（recasting）諸方面下工夫。

他拿了曹雪芹自認「風塵碌碌、一事無成」而感懷身世的序言，與霍克思的譯文對照，赫然發覺空空道人竟坐在威爾斯鄉下一間牧人的房子內，「蓬牖茅椽，繩床瓦灶」，喝 hot Whisky Toddy。

霍克思退休後，有一段時間隱居威爾斯。曹雪芹坐著喝熱酒的羊倌屋，應該是他的鄉居。

閔福德這一招，是「拱雲托月」。他要說的，無非是譯者投入原著的感情世界越深，譯文越能進入「化」境。

我們細讀霍氏譯文，的確正如閔福德所說，絲毫不露翻譯痕跡。如果曹雪芹的母語是英文，*The Story of the Stone* 的英文，配得上說是他的手筆。

三

但在翻譯史上，像曹雪芹與霍克思這種配搭，的確講緣份。

5　John Minford, "Kungfu in Translation, Translation as Kungfu," in *The Question of Reception: Martial Arts Fiction in English Translation*, ed. Liu Ching-chih, Hong Kong: Centre for Literature and Translation, Lingnan College, 1997, pp.1-40.

「緣」是天作之合。閔福德譯《鹿鼎記》，也有緣份：他忍不住喜歡韋小寶這角色。

他看《鹿鼎記》，看得過癮，因此決定帶小寶「西遊」，希望英語世界的讀者也能分享譯者的樂趣。

據他在試行本的序言說，他譯《鹿鼎記》的志趣，如此而已。

閔福德使盡多年修煉得來的翻譯「功夫」，務使英語讀者能像他一樣地投入韋小寶的世界，這個宏願，可以達到麼？

要知真相，得做讀者反應調查，或者看書的銷量數字。這些資料既付闕如，我們只能循別的途徑，推測英譯《鹿鼎記》對西方讀者的閱讀經驗可能產生的效果。

首先，以翻譯論翻譯，閔福德譯文得到沈雙這樣的評語：

> 僅從譯者對細節、名詞、敍事者的語氣和節奏的重視上，就不難看出閔福德的確試圖重現金庸整體的小說世界。譯者曾經戲稱金庸的敍事風格是「具有欺騙性的流暢」。其實他的譯文也具有同樣的風格，因為譯文的流暢是在譯者嚴謹的解釋、周密的考慮，以及將近六年的翻譯和校對的基礎上達到的。雖然譯文讀起來很像讀金庸的白話文言文的感覺，既典雅又通俗，任何有一定翻譯經驗的讀者都可以不時在文中發現譯者獨具匠心的痕迹。6

雖然沈雙也指出了譯文若干不逮之處，如沒有襯托出「韋小寶舉止言行有著深刻的反諷和寓言的意義」（頁 75），但大體來說，他給予譯文相當高的評價，這可從以上引文看出來。

有關《鹿鼎記》英譯之得失，在沈雙的文章出現以前，有 Liu Ching-chih（劉靖之）編的特輯：*The Question of Reception: Martial Arts Fiction in English Translation*（英譯武俠小說──讀者反應與迴響）。裡面有五篇專論談到翻譯的技術問題。

要討論譯文的細節，即使僅是抽樣，也見繁瑣。不說別的，單是「江湖」一詞的英譯，已公案連連，難望有什麼結論。閔福德在中文典籍上窮碧落下黃泉，深究其義，自己是融匯貫通了，可在英文偏找不出一個所謂 dynamic

---

6　沈雙，〈評閔福德的《鹿鼎記》英譯〉，《明報月刊》，33:8（1998.8），頁 71。

equivalent 來。由此我們可以看出在兩種語文之間，有許多東西是難劃對等號的。

「少年子弟江湖老」，說的是滄桑。江湖究竟何所指，在作者而言，一說成俗。但譯者卻不能裝糊塗，好歹也得自己拍板定案。在《鹿鼎記》的範圍內，他用了 the Brotherhood of River and Lake，可說只是因時因地制宜的選擇。

不過，要知《鹿鼎記》的翻譯能否達成他與讀者分享的願望，先得要弄清楚他要爭取的，是那一類讀者。這一點，他在 "Kungfu in Translation, Translation as Kungfu" 一文有交代。

他心儀的，是韋理（Arthur Waley）那類翻譯家：那類講究譯者作者緣份和讀者反應的翻譯家。韋理終身從事中日文學翻譯。據閔福德所說，他最受不了的，是「漢學家」──那種專愛在「江湖」英譯上鑽牛角尖的人。這類「好事者」上門找他，說不定他會一語不發就消失在自己的玫瑰園中。

閔福德是《石頭記》後四十回的譯者，英文造詣，有大家風範。他因迷上了韋小寶而翻譯《鹿鼎記》，說明了譯者作者間很夠緣份。條件既這麼配合，那麼韋小寶西遊，會不會像當年韋理帶孫悟空以 Monkey 名義西征那麼熱鬧呢？

《鹿鼎記》英譯分爲三冊，尚有兩冊未出版，因此現時尚無答案。不過，如果拿 Barbara Koh 在《新聞周刊》[7] 的書評作推測的話，韋小寶西行，會有風險。

Barbara Koh 一語道破：單是那長達十七頁的人名、地名、術語和年代紀事表已令人「目爲之眩」。

當然，對中國歷史、文物和政制全無興趣的讀者，可以把這些資料擱在一邊。《鹿鼎記》既是 martial arts fiction，最少在武鬥場面有瞄頭的。

可惜的是，正如 Barbara Koh 所說，像「南海禮佛」、「水中捉月」，或「仙鶴梳翎」這些功夫招數，譯成英文，在文化背景截然不同的讀者看來，實難明其「草蛇灰線」。

---

7 Barbara Koh, "A Trinket for the West: will Louis Cha Win over Readers in English?" *Newsweek*, 11 May, 1998, p.61.

金庸自己承認全不懂功夫。這些招數，也許全屬子虛烏有。如果看的是原文，明知是假，因其術語頗見「詩意」，想也不會見怪。

看翻譯過來的術語，卻不是這回事。Monkey Picking Fruit（猴子採桃），原文語意相關，既雅且俗。要用注釋一一解說，那與韋理譯《西遊記》和霍克思譯《石頭記》所代表的傳統則背道而馳。

不解釋，那麼猴子採桃，尋常事耳，沒什麼看頭？

功夫之於武俠小說，猶如男歡女愛之於言情作品，一樣是不可或缺的元素。《鹿鼎記》雖屬「反武俠小說」的類型，但一樣離不開武打，而且還好戲連場。

如果 Barbara Koh 的看法反映了一般英語讀者的觀點，那小寶西遊，場面恐怕會冷落。正如這位書評人所說，書中的連番廝殺，看多了，也敎人煩厭。

四

英譯《鹿鼎記》難討好外國讀者，除了上述各種技術困難外，還有一個障礙：因爲這是一本徹頭徹尾的中國成年人童話。書中的大漢情懷，濃得不可開交。

《紅樓夢》也是一本「很中國」的書，但曹雪芹的出世思想，雖不能說放諸四海而皆準，卻有相當普遍性。寶玉的前世今生，是色是空、好是了、了是好的認知最戲劇化的演繹。「白茫茫一片眞乾淨」的境界，對渴求解脫的西方讀者，一樣有莫大的吸引力。

《鹿鼎記》的情節，以「反淸復明」爲架構。正如天地會的誓言所載：「會齊洪家兵百萬　反離韃子伴眞龍」。可是，由於讀者在本書所認識的康熙，是透過韋小寶對「小玄子」的情感而擠濾出來的，因此讀者即使是漢人，也會在不知不覺間受到小寶感染，跟這位「韃子」皇帝認同起來。

漢人跟「異族」的種種恩怨，正好給予從來沒有什麼「民族大義」襟懷的韋小寶縱橫捭闔、呼風喚雨的空間和機會，也製造了人情上的矛盾和衝突。書中許多驚險百出、扣人心絃的段落，就是這種矛盾和衝突所產生的。

能夠掌握到這些微妙關節，會增加對全書宏觀的了解。但對外國讀者而

言，漢族和滿族過去那段歷史過節，既陌生、又遙遠，跟自己實難拉上什麼風馬牛的關係。因此興趣泛泛。

《鹿鼎記》令西方讀者覺得「異化」，這又是一個例。

法國學者 Jacques Pimpaneau 有此一說：

> 中國的武俠小說常見外國人穿插其間。瀰漫於這種作品的，是一段段漫長的抗「夷」滅「狄」仇外史。在金庸的小說中，各路英雄好漢開始合力抗清。後來康熙得了民心，被推爲賢主，只好找俄國人上台充數，當壞蛋。[8]

Pimpaneau 的話，說得不錯。但要知道這部小說的「仇外」部分怎麼「異化」西方讀者，危令敦在〈小寶西遊？試論《鹿鼎記》英譯〉[9] 一文所舉的幾個例子，說得更爲具體：

> 英語讀者難以接受的，恐怕還是《鹿鼎記》後半部所渲染的滿清帝國鼎盛時期的國力。……在第四十六回，口沒遮攔的小寶對施琅道：「男子漢大丈夫，總要打外國鬼子了不起。中國人殺中國人，殺得再多，也不算好漢。」（頁 90-91）

《鹿鼎記》神化韋小寶，的確無所不用其極。話說他「征服」了羅刹公主蘇菲亞後，離開時還送上自己裸體石雕像，讓公主在宮中觀摩賞玩。「據說後來石像毀於宮廷政變，其下體殘片流入民間，成爲羅刹婦女撫拜求子的聖物，十分靈驗云云。中華的男性及民族沙文心態，表露無遺。」（頁 91）

小寶與羅刹公主那段香火緣，是「征服異族」的具體表現。因此所謂「仇外」實在男女有別。正如危令敦所說：

> 《鹿鼎記》雖然允許小寶胡天胡帝，但拒絕讓中華女性成爲洋人的欲望對象。小寶親娘身陷風塵經年，迎送的嫖客之多，漢滿蒙回藏都有，儼然中華「民族團結」的大使。在接客的「大是大非」問題前，韋母充滿「民族大義」，訓斥起小寶來，

8　Jacques Pimpaneau, "Chinese Wu-hsio hsia-shuo and Their Western Counterparts"（談中西武俠小說），收入劉紹銘、陳永明編，《武俠小說論》上卷（香港：明河社，1998），頁 363。

9　危令敦，〈小寶西遊？試論《鹿鼎記》英譯〉，劉靖之編，《英譯武俠小說——讀者反應與迴響》（香港：嶺南學院文學與翻譯研究中心，1997），頁 83-94。

絕不含糊：「你當你娘是爛婊子嗎？連外國鬼子也接？辣塊媽媽、羅刹鬼、紅毛鬼到麗春院來，老娘用大掃帚拍了出去。」（頁 92）

難怪危令敦擲筆嘆道：「閱讀至此，英語讀者能不駭然？」（頁 92）

《鹿鼎記》流露的大漢沙文主義，身為譯者的閔福德，當然比一般的「英語讀者」先知先覺。他在《鹿鼎記》英譯本的序言就告訴讀者，金庸對自己的中國血統，非常驕傲，而這種「引以為榮」的心態，在他所有的作品中表露無遺。

且抄他一段自白：

> 宋偉傑博士專門研究我的小說，……他說我不知不覺地把漢文化看得高於其他少數民族文化。我的確是如此，過去是這樣看，現在還這樣看。……少數民族學習漢文化時，放棄一點自己的文化，並不吃虧，反而提高了。少數民族的文化也影響漢文化。[10]

滿洲人「放棄」了自己文化，因此不再是「韃子」，而是漢人的同胞，漢滿互相通婚，再無誰「征服」誰的問題。

羅刹人如「歸順」中國，衣冠文物也向「天朝」看齊，自然也可以做咱們的「同胞」。

但他們「怙惡不悛」，拒受文明洗禮，「婦道人家」只好在《鹿鼎記》中受小寶「征服」！

由此我們認識到，西方讀者看《鹿鼎記》，要看得像中國人那麼「過癮」，在心態上先要「歸化」中國，最少在精神上做個「炎黃子孫」。

閔福德教授嫻熟中國史，深知《鹿鼎記》所流露的「大漢沙文主義」，是「隔代遺傳」的記憶，因此見怪不怪。

其他英語讀者呢？套用英國人一句口頭禪 'they wouldn't be amused' 一點也不覺得好玩。

韋小寶的確是個 different 的角色，但看來不會在西方受歡迎。

10　金庸，〈小說創作的幾點思考〉，《明報月刊》，1998 年 8 月號，頁 49-50。

Louis Cha through the Translator's Eyes

John Minford
Department of Chinese and Bilingual Studies
Hong Kong Polytechnic University

Abstract

Having embarked on the translation of Louis Cha's Martial Arts novel *The Deer and the Cauldron* (*Ludingji* 鹿鼎記) in 1991, and having now completed the first two of the three volumes of the translation, for Oxford University Press (HK), I thought this seemed a good moment to pause and reflect on the whole project. What are the things that seem to have gone well, to have worked in the translation, and what are the lessons that can be learned from this? What have been some of the responses so far, and to what extent are they helpful? Where should the project go from here?

I look at a dozen or so passages from the *Second Book* (due for release towards the end of November) where I feel reasonably pleased with the result. (This is not an exercise in self-congratulation. One could also deduce from it that I feel reasonably displeased with all the rest — all hundreds of pages of it!) Just as it has not always been the "best" Tang poets who come over "best" in translation (Du Fu, for example, translates poorly, whereas Bo Juyi has fared excellently, and "Cold Mountain" best of all), so it is not necessarily those things that Chinese readers like the most about this book, or indeed those things that the Chinese author himself thinks most highly of in his own work, that come over best in English.

If there are any conclusions, they seem to be that the translator of Chinese popular fiction is in general far too timid, and that if we are to succeed in captivating the avid readers of *Wild Swans* with translations of actual Chinese material, and not abandon them to yet more in-house editorial rewrites of semi-autobiographies that never existed in Chinese in the first place, then we probably have to be far more radical in our approach, braver in what we allow ourselves to do to our original texts.

I. Preamble: Author, Text, Translator and Reader

The translator is an unusual kind of reader. He is obliged to read very closely. In order to do his job properly, he needs to find out what everything means (as far as possible), to wrestle with every detail.[1]　By contrast, the ordinary reader and the casual critic can, if he so wishes, skate cavalierly over difficulties, scarcely bothering to glance over his shoulder, carried along by the sheer momentum of the plot or the intensity of the emotion.

The reader of (say) a novel is a free agent, able to do as he pleases, to pick and choose, to surf through repetition and seek pleasure, slowing down to savour those moments that most nearly match his own predilections. This is one of the things that makes the experience of reading so intensely enjoyable: to be able to pick up a book at random, when one is in the mood, and sit there with a glass by one's side, lazing on one's favourite terrace (or in one's favourite wilderness), from which from time to time one may look up and catch a glimpse of the sun setting at the far end of the valley. If the book captures one's imagination, one may stay up late into the night, rising only to replenish one's glass (as silently as possible, in order not to disturb sleeping members of the family, whose irritability might spoil one's reading pleasure). If on the other hand the book fails to please, one can place it back on the shelf without fear of incurring reproach. After all,

---

1　I refuse to be constrained by considerations of gender in my use of the personal pronoun. Of course "he" includes "she".

one has paid for the thing (or something of the sort).[2]

The translator-as-reader can do none of these things with a clear conscience. He is locked in.

The translator is also an unusual kind of writer. Not for him the freedom to roam wherever the pen and his whim take him. He is from the very outset deeply and consciously involved in a joint enterprise and bound by ethical and contractual obligations, not only to the original author, but also to new readers as well as to not-so-new readers, who may have acquired high expectations from preceding readers of the original text.[3]   He is married, with two different sets of children, one on the way, the other inherited.

Where the chemistry between author and reader is haphazard, casual, spontaneous, personal, the interaction between translator and reader is very different. Here prior expectations are dominant, much of the talk is of duties and failings, and the invisibility required of the translator prohibits any other relationship. And yet, in an undeniable sense, it is the translator's voice that speaks in the translation.

Finally, the chemistry between author and translator is itself unpredictable. Here too the strains of expectation and fidelity can take their toll. This sort of relationship, and the unrelenting intimacy it implies (would any author want a

---

2   Alberto Manguel's A *History Of Reading* (Penguin, 1996) is a superb study of the many pleasures of the act of reading, and itself a joy to read. Manguel himself is a fine translator.

3   This is precisely the danger with the initial readers of Louis Cha in English. They may have acquired expectations from readers of the Chinese version (e.g. they may be non-Chinese-reading expatriate children of Chinese-reading parents — I deliberately avoid using the term Overseas Chinese, which implies that Chinese can never truly experience exile); or they may themselves be fully Chinese-Literate and have already read the Chinese version. Such readers are almost bound to be disappointed. Since the Hong Kong edition of *Deer* (*First Book*) has until very recently been legally unobtainable outside Hong Kong, it is too early to judge the reaction of the true English-reading public. However, despite its unavailability of it has already been selected (in December 1998) by both the Times Literary Supplement and the Observer as one of their "Books of the Year".

reader to live in such close contact with his book?), make heavy demands both on the translator's stamina and invention, and simultaneously on the text being translated and the tolerance and broad-mindedness of its author. It must be galling for an author to have liberties taken with his text, even if he himself acknowledges that they should be taken. It must be hard to let go. After all, it is his baby.

In the case of popular fiction, it is a more than usually peculiar symbiosis, between author and translator. The pleasure of reading a popular novel is often inseparable from the enjoyment of the peculiar style of the original storyteller. The reader gets used to hearing that voice, it wins him away from competing leisure activities (watching TV, going to a football match, going out for a walk or drink with a friend, etc). Picking up such a novel can be as compulsive as switching on a favourite talk-show — which one does for the sake of hearing the voice and seeing the face of one's favourite talk-show host. Both are extremely habit-forming. There is comfort in knowing that, come what may, whatever may have happened during the day, however unpleasant one's boss may have been, however bad the pollution, etc. etc., there is still a good Agatha Christie novel waiting at home to be finished. And when storytelling is as closely linked to history and national culture as is the case with Chinese Martial Arts fiction, it can be a habit very peculiar to its own original environment. All of this constitutes a huge challenge for the translator. He is purveying a national drug for an international market.

Louis Cha's novels have been a runaway success in the Chinese-reading world, creating a powerful mystique and generating countless by-products.[4] The

---

4   Some of these by-products themselves have produced startlingly interesting material for students of translation. In the English subtitles to the Hong Kong *Deer*-movies staring Zhou Xingchi, Wei Xiaobao is introduced as "Bond-Wilson Bond", and Oboi becomes "O'Brien"! That the anti-hero's sub-title should so effortlessly contain a reference to one of the great popular heroes of our time, and that the Manchu villain of *Deer* should have become Irish (is there even perhaps an unwittingly Nabokovian half-reference to the Inquisitor in Orwell's *1984*?) — to such wild transmutations, to such feats of crazed genius, I can never hope to aspire!

world should prepare itself for the advent of the Cha Theme Park.[5]   This phenomenally successful marketing in itself is no guarantee of the quality of the books themselves. (After all, look at Indian films. Their huge success in the Indian sub-continent, and their sheer quantity, does not mean that they are ever going to be more widely watched and appreciated beyond that sphere.) There is a growing chorus of voices claiming "serious", "high-brow" literary status for Cha's oeuvre. I find some of their claims far-fetched and opportunistic. They seem to be climbing onto a band-waggon. I am sticking for the time being (until someone convinces me otherwise) to the more modest view I have held all along (to which Cha himself has publicly subscribed in print), that Cha is a brilliantly successful story-teller, with a knack for using the traditional language of Chinese storytelling combined with a flair for imaginatively visualised situations and cleverly devised plots. He also taps instinctively into a range of Chinese archetypes which enable his books to produce a feeling of intense cultural euphoria in his Chinese consumers. The figure nearest to him in European literature is Alexandre Dumas, père. I don't go to a Cha novel for lyricism, philosophy, religious vision, or deep insights into human nature and society. This is not to diminish his achievement. What he does he does superbly well.

I ventured into this Cha Arena several years ago, perhaps rashly. I did so partly at the suggestion of a number of friends who were themselves Cha-addicts (in the original Chinese context), partly out of my own curiosity. I had some sense of the huge challenge confronting any translator undertaking what many thought was an impossible task. I thought then that I had the embryo of an idea of how do it. In the end time and the actual reactions of real English-speaking readers will tell. It is too soon to be able to predict those reactions.

---

5   Surely it would far better to build a Cha Theme Park on a large site in Kowloon, than to turn over the still almost (apart from the airport) unspoilt island of Lantau to Disney.

II. Work and Progress

The first years (beginning in 1991, when I was still living in France) I spent familiarising myself with the detail of the text I had chosen to translate (*Ludingji* 鹿鼎記), writing a lengthy synopsis and compiling lists of characters, background historical information, etc. I also began to read as widely as possible in the literature of English historical romance. Then I devised some basic ways of proceeding, and began making some headway with the actual translation, greatly assisted in this by my friend David Hawkes. This continued during a 15-month stay at the Australian National University in 1993-4. Subsequently I had an opportunity in Hong Kong beginning in 1995, to create a little research group, consisting of a number of young Chinese readers, graduates of the translation programme at my own university, with whom I could explore certain ideas, not specifically about *Deer*, but about the whole business of translating Martial Arts fiction in general.[6] We tried out bits of translation, circulating them and discussing them at regular meetings. It was a sort of translators' focus group. These young readers taught me a huge amount about Cha, as he is perceived in his home-town. They helped me to identify some of the qualities that appeal so strongly to his native audience. They also helped me to understand to what a large extent the Cha phenomenon is non-literary (or rather, extra-literary). Readers do not react to his novels like normal readers of fiction (even popular fiction). They seem to be stunned, mesmerised.

6　This workshop was funded by the Hong Kong U.G.C. It is my conviction that Cha' work depends for its lasting appeal on the fact that it is read by young people, who then return to it again and again during their adult life, recollecting the glow that surrounded the reading of their youth. In this respect it is similar to the work of writers such as Stevenson, Rider Haggard, Buchan and Conan Doyle. It exists (along with many other wonderful stories) on "the borderline between children's and adult literature": John Rowe Townsend, *Written for Children* (Penguin revised edition, 1983), 67.

Instead of Deer, we actually used the opening chapters of the earlier Cha novel *Shediao yingxiong zhuan* (we called it *Eagles*) as the raw material, trying out different approaches and seeing if they worked.[7]   Some interesting ideas were thrown up in the course of our discussions, some of which stuck. One example is the use of the word "Abbé" for the sort of roving Taoist master, suggested by Sharon Lai.

As we went along we also explored the language of chivalry, romance, adventure and combat as it exists within the English-language tradition, on the basis that translation is rooted in the empirical art of comparative rhetoric (finding the comparable written means to achieve a comparable writer's goal). We steeped ourselves not only in the language and lore of *wuxia xaiaoshuo* 武俠 小說, but also in the annals of European chivalry:

> My beloved squire, and George my dwarf, I charge you that henceforth you never call me by any other name but the Right Courteous and Valiant Knight of the Burning Pestle; and that you never call any female by the name of woman or wench but fair lady, if she have her desires; if not, distressed damsel; that you call all forests and heaths deserts, and all horses palfries.[8]

We reminded ourselves that there exists in the English (and French) language not just a storytelling vocabulary of romance and adventure, but also a jargon of swordcraft almost as colourful and esoteric as that of the Chinese Martial Arts:

---

7   A sample of this can be found as an appendix to the Special Issue of the Hong Kong *Translation Quarterly*, 1997. That issue also contains many of the papers delivered at the Lingnan Symposium of March 1996.

8   Beaumont & Fletcher, *The Knight of the Burning Pestle*, quoted by A. R. Hope Moncrieff, *The Romance and Legend of Chivalry* (reprint London, Studio Editions, 1993), 77–78. As Moncrieff points out, the farce was itself prompted by Cervantes.

Le bottc de Nevers, lc coup de Jarnac, the imbrocata at the head, the rinverso tondo; the flanquonade... There was a belief in the undoubted efficacy of those "secret thrusts", of that "universal parry", of those ineluctable passes, which every master professed to teach. These precious secrets remained long, among a certain class of shady swordsmen, and objects of untiring study, carried on with much the same faith and zest as the quest of the alchemist for his power of projection, or of the Merchant Adventurer for El Dorado... There was an almost superstitious belief in "secret foynes", in the *botte secrète* of certain practised duellists.[9]

We collected and rehearsed some of the traditional repertoire of the novelist of action and adventure, creating generous wordlists to refresh our memories for possible use in translation:

Scouting; recoiled; part company; pell-mell; retreating slowly down the passage; sauntered over; capered; pacing briskly up and down the room; swaggered...

To go post-haste to Kettley; strode lithely; down the great stairway they stole; drew her aside into an alcove; into which B had inadvertently stumbled; stormed into the room; he took a step towards her; briskly; he fell into step beside the fellow; he lengthened his stride for home; he pursued his way; meandered; at that P stalked out of the room, leaving his father a prey to indecent mirth; he bustled away; presently she relented and tripped downstairs to the drawing room; he gave chase; I skirted the old city; hurtled full length to the floor; went sprawling down as I did so; I lay low; I broke cover...

Using long and short blades to the utmost of their lethal capacity; one of the cardinal actions of regulated swordplay, the lunge; they were hewn down like sheep; Men, and beasts likewise, when stricken with a mortal wound, will run, and run on, blindly, aimless, impelled by the mere instinct of escape from intolerable agony; began laying about him with his sword; being held at bay; had not given ground; polished off his enemy; the sudden onslaught; an ill-favoured shaft; she was spread-eagled against the cart; retreating, parrying and riposting for all he was worth; pounding brawny fists on the table; utterance and breath were abruptly choked by the iron fingers that locked

---

9   Encyclopedia Britannica, Eleventh Edition (1910), Egerton Castle, article on "Fencing", 249.

themselves about his throat.[10]

Even seemingly obscure and exotic touches such as Old Hai's decomposing power (so useful, in many a tight spot during the plot of *Deer*, along with Trinket's magic dagger and adamantine waistcoat) turned out to have their corresponding references.[11]

During the course of this invaluable workshop, in early 1996, we all of us participated in a lively symposium at Lingnan College, where several scholars from around Hong Kong and from elsewhere in the world gathered to brood on the "reception" of Martial Arts fiction in English. Some fascinating insights were shared from a variety of perspectives.

Simultaneously with all of this, I had the pleasure of following the extensive reading and innovative thoughts of a young doctoral student from Taiwan, Sharon Lai, whose work finally bore fruit in an excellent dissertation on "Translating Martial Arts Fiction". During our many discussions over a period of three years, we debated many historical and practical questions relating to the translation of Chinese popular fiction. Among the many illuminating discoveries we made during this time was the eighteenth-century Percy/Wilkinson version of *Haoqiuzhuan*, *The Pleasing History*, which (so it turned out) foreshadowed many of our own conclusions. Those gentlemen did by instinct (the well-cultivated instinct of the mid-eighteenth century man-of-letters) what very few translators of Chinese fiction have managed to do since: they produced a

---

10 This is a sampling from voluminous wordlists gathered from such books as Macdonald Fraser's Flashman novels, and his wonderful romp *Pyrates*; Jeffrey Farnol's *The Broad Highway*, and *Black Bartlemey's Treasure*; Rafael Sabatini's *Scaramouche*, and his story "The Scapulary", Stanly Weyman's *Under the Red Robe*, Georgette Heyer's *Patch and Powder*, Baroness Orczy's *The Scarlet Pimpernel*; Anthony Hope's *The Prisoner of Zenda and Rupert of Hentzau*; P.C. Wren's *Beau Geste*; D.K. Broster's *Flight of the Heron*; Conan Doyle's *The White Company*; R.L. Stevenson's *The Black Arrow*, Alexandre Dumas' *The Three Musketeers* (in English translation); Kingsley's *Hereward the Wake*; Patrick O'Brien's *Master & Commander*.

11 See Arthur Machen's classic *The Novel of the White Powder*.

version of a Chinese novel that succeeded in captivating the imagination of the European reading public (including Goethe). Their work was promptly translated into French, Dutch and German. I can see no better model. And yet with the increasing specialisation of Sinology, their achievement has been neglected and belittled as amateurish.

None of these activities would have born any fruit without a publisher. Once Oxford University Press in Hong Kong had bravely decided to take on the series (1996),[12] the process of editing the typescript of the *First Book* of *The Deer and the Cauldron* began. I was very fortunate to have assigned to me as an editor by O.U.P. someone who had already accumulated considerable editorial experience with translations from Chinese, and had recently written her own popular romance based on the story of the classic drama *The Western Chamber*.[13] I learned a great deal from her scrupulous and imaginative editorial work, and the book profited enormously by it. Finally, with the much-publicised launch in October 1997 of the *First Book* of *Deer*, came a huge amount of Hong Kong media attention and discussion of the translation.[14] From this exposure I learned at first hand to what extent I was enmeshed in a public event.

---

12   For the record, some sixty international publishers declined to publish the work, before Oxford agreed.

13   Rachel May, *Love in a Chinese Garden* (Harlequin, Toronto, 1997).

14   Articles appeared in *Ming Pao Daily*, *Ming Pao Weekly*, *Ming Pao Montly*, *Oriental Daily*, *Reader's Digest* (Chinese edition), and *South China Morning Post*. I should perhaps say that Barbara Koh, in her *Newsweek* article of May 11, 1998, "A Trinket for the West", with its statement that I "rubbed out hundreds of characters and much of the historical background", does get things a little bit wrong. In the *First Book*, there is not in fact a single character or cameo left out. The translation is integral. Even in the *Second Book*, which is considerably abridged, her statement is exaggerated. Unfortunately her comments were then repeated word for word in the pages of the *Guangzhou Ribao*, and I was castigated for having "betrayed" the text. One of her reservations about the translation concerned the glossaries, lists of characters, maps that were placed at the front of the book (I had pleaded with Oxford to put them at the back). She found this material daunting. I agree, it is. But without it, would readers have been able to follow the story at all?

All in all, this has been a period of quite intensive scrutiny and self-reflection. The fruits of that reflection are fed back into the ongoing process of translation. What I intend to do here is simply to pick out a number of passages from the *Second Book* (shortly to be published) where I feel reasonably happy with the result, and see if there is any rhyme or reason in the resultant selection, if there are any general lessons to be learned.[15]

1. Trinket in Action

As an anonymous reader remarks on one of the countless Cha websites,[16] Trinket, Wei Xiaobao韋小寶, is the kind of friend who would have had not the slightest qualm about helping himself to your money and then your wife (in that order, obviously). Translating *Deer* is to a very large extent about how to represent this obnoxious brat in English. The author himself was from the outset aware that this last novel had been hijacked by Trinket, and nowadays tends to be somewhat apologetic about having spawned such a monster. I partially

---

15   Since the *Second Book* is still unpublished (it is due out towards the end of November), I will allow myself to quote at some length. Another (and perhaps more provocative) article could be devoted to the problems posed by inconsistencies in the Chinese text itself. For example, during a substantial section of the text now translated as the *Second Book*, two of Trinket's companions, Doublet (Shuang-er) and Wurtle (Yu Ba), keep popping up unexpectedly, and then melting away without any explanation. This sort of thing happens all the time in *Deer*. "Ordinary" readers are probably not too bothered by it; the translator however has a hard time. This would be a perfect subject for an article along the lines of John Sutherland's wonderful "Puzzles in 19*th*-century and Classic Fiction", in the Oxford World's Classics — "Where does Fanny Hill keep her contraceptives?", etc. I remember finding Sutherland's earlier study of Thackeray, *Thackeray at Work*, one of the best books ever written on the craft of the novelist. I wish there were books like that written about Chinese fiction.

16   Someone should make a study of these sites, as a socio-literary phenomenon (perhaps they already have). Just as Cha's work in serialisation and book form (let alone film, TV, strip-cartoon, animated film and computer game) has defied existing categories of conventional literature, it now seems to be the first Chinese oeuvre to be disseminating itself on the Internet (interesting Freudian slip — I typed Inertnet).

sympathise. He is absolutely obnoxious. But for all his less likeable characteristics, Trinket lives triumphantly, and much of the novel's life stems from his anarchic antics.

I have been taken to task recently, in the august columns of the *Ming Pao Monthly* 明報月刊, for not having recognized the true significance of the novel, and in particular for having produced a simplistic version of its protagonist, Trinket. I must confess that I was not surprised at this. There is a tradition of Chinese resentment towards translators of Chinese literature (Waley's *Monkey* is another case; more recently the neo-Orientalist camp has taken David Hawkes to task for his *Stone*).[17] It is somewhat like the feeling of outrage at seeing a daughter marry a barbarian (i.e. a non-Chinese). Cultural possessiveness is still a strong Chinese trait. Let me say that my unequivocal priority with *Deer* has been to create a picaresque Chinese novel that is fun to read in English; the ironic, satirical import of the work (of which I am more than aware) should come across with little difficulty if and when the reader's attention has been engaged. As for Trinket, so far from having a simplistic view of this young man, I continue to marvel at my own willingness to allow this monster to set foot in my study, given the grave reservations I have always had about his character! For me the enduring fascination of Trinket is precisely that such a worthless individual should be so attractive. His recurring sadism and opportunism (to select only two from the endless catalogue of his faults) are enough to alienate the most forgiving reader. And yet we read on. Why?

Re-reading the following short extract, from the opening scene of the *Second Book*, I am relatively happy with the profile and voice of Trinket. What a

---

17 See Lydia Liu's position in *Translingual Practice: Literature, National Culture, and Translated Modernity — China, 1900-1937* (Stanford University Press, 1995), and my own (by now ancient) piece entitled "Translation as Treason", *Bulletin of the Hong Kong Psychological Society*, 1986. My more recent "Death in Macau: In Defence of Orientalism" is to be published later this year by Wilhelm Fink, Munich, in a volume entitled *Translation — Interpretation* (Proceedings of the Academie du Midi Conference, Covilha, Portugal, 1998).

horror! And yet...

Trinket discovers Fang Yi (English chapter 10, Chinese chapter 11)

As she said this she gave Trinket a gentle push, and he vaulted through the window. He found himself in front of a female form in black, lying huddled up on the ground just below.

'Come on. Up you get. Or the guards'll mince you into little pieces and use you to stuff dumplings...'

'I don't mind! One day someone will avenge me.'

'Stubborn little tart, aren't you!' said Trinket, 'Anyway, they won't kill you straight away. First they'll strip all your clothes off and...rape you.' 'Then finish me off now!' spat the voice furiously.

Trinket smiled.

'I've got a much better idea. Why don't I strip your clothes off, and rape you myself.'

As he said this, he bent down and made as if to put his arms around the girl. She tried to slap him angrily on the face, but was too badly wounded to manage more than feeble sort of tap. Trinket laughed. He lifted her up in his arms and helped her through the window and into the room. The Little Countess limped forward, and staggered with her to the bed. Trinket was about to climb back into the room himself, when suddenly he heard another barely audible voice coming from near his feet.

'Lau...Laurel Goong-goong, that girl...that girl...you...you mustn't...'

It was the guard who had been sent flying by the Empress Dowager. He was still alive, though badly wounded and incapable of movement.

'I suppose he's right really,' thought Trinket to himself. 'I ought to hand the girl in. But then what about the Little Countess? They might find out about *her*!'

The decision was quickly taken. He pulled out his dagger, and stabbed the guard in the chest.

'Sorry about that,' said Trinket, to the unfortunate corpse. 'Forgive me. If only you'd kept your mouth shut, I wouldn't have had to kill you.'

He searched every inch of the nearby garden for any further survivors, but only found five more corpses, three of them Palace Guards, two intruders. He heaved the body of one of the intruders up onto the window-sill, its head protruding into the room, its feet hanging outside into the garden. Then he stabbed it a few times in the back with his dagger for good measure.

'He... he's one of our people,' said the Little Countess in a frightened voice. 'He was dead already. What did you need to do that for?'

Trinket humphed.

'I had to. If you want me to save that smelly tart of a sister of yours.'

'*You're* the smelly one, not me!' protested the girl, from where she lay on the bed.

'How would you know?' asked Trinket.

'Your whole room stinks!'

'It smelled nice enough, till you arrived.'

The Little Countess interrupted them.

'Would the two of you please stop? You don't even know each other! Sister, what are you doing here? Did you come...to rescue me?'

'No, we didn't even know you were here. When we found out that you'd disappeared, we searched everywhere, but it was hopeless...'

She was already out of breath.

'Why don't you just shut up!' said Trinket.

'And if I don't shut up? What are you going to do to me then?'

'Nothing,' replied Trinket. 'You'll wear yourself out sooner or later. Oh dear! The Little Countess is such a nice, gentle girl; but you're — '

'No, no, you don't understand,' the Little Countess hurriedly interposed. 'She's really very nice.'

She went on:

'Sister, are you badly hurt?'

'Of course she is,' said Trinket. 'I told you, she's a third-rate little kungfu slut, and she obviously can't fight for peanuts. I shouldn't think she'll live more than three hours. She'll probably die before dawn.'

'No! She mustn't! My...my *darling*... You must save her, *please*!'

'I would rather die!' growled the girl. 'I don't need any favours from him! Little Countess, why do you keep calling him...calling him *that*?'

'Calling me what?' asked Trinket.

The girl didn't fall for it.

'Little *ape*! That's what *I'll* call you!'

'Well, in that case, we can be Mr and Mrs Ape!'

Trinket was an old hand at this kind of whore-house repartee. He had heard no end of it at Vernal Delights as a small boy. The girl tried to ignore him, and lay there panting in pain.

Trinket took a candlestick from the table, and proposed that he should examine her wounds.

'Don't you *dare* look at me! *Don't!*' she cried.

'Stop screaming like that! Do you want the guards to come running in here and rape you?'

Trinket approached her with the candlestick in his hand. Through the blood smeared all over her face he could make out that she was a young woman of extraordinary beauty, about seventeen or eighteen years old.

'So, the smelly little tart turns out to be quite a babe!'

'Don't be so rude about my sister!' protested the Little Countess. 'She...she *is* beautiful.'

'All the more reason for me to marry her!' said Trinket.

The girl protested vehemently, and struggled to sit up and hit him. But the pain was so great that she could only gasp, and collapse onto the bed again.

As far as matters sexual and matrimonial were concerned, theoretically Trinket knew it all. As a child he had heard such things endlessly discussed in the whore-house — by other people. But he had never taken them seriously himself. Even now he didn't actually *mean* to marry the girl, or have sex with her, not in any real sense; he was just having a bit of fun at her expense, baiting her, enjoying her reaction.

In that last paragraph, the narrator's voice, i.e. Louis Cha's voice, returns, to reimpose a certain style and seriousness of tone on the proceedings, as befits the Chinese storyteller (repository of an important part of the tradition); Trinket, on the other hand, has got to be nasty, foul-mouthed, and yet somehow still charismatic, throughout.[18]

---

18   Margaret Ng, herself a well-established Cha critic, and Hong Kong's most polished bilingual
     journalist (as well as being a prominent lawyer and independent member of the Legislative
     Council), made what was for me a fascinating revelation in one of her articles for *Ming Pao Daily*

2. Trinket the Impostor

The reader derives great pleasure from the various identities under which Trinket is obliged to masquerade during the novel. This is potentially the most inventive dimension of *Deer* as a work of fiction. Often the identities are in contradiction with one another, and this leads to suspense, irony, and farce. Sometime this *commedia dell'arte* (cf. "The Servant of Two Masters") cries out for playful intervention by the translator, as in this scene where Trinket is posing as the new Abbot of Pure Coolness Monastery on Wutai:

Lamas at the Gate (English chapter 16)

> 'Father Abbot,' said Brother Cordial, speaking for the others, 'those lamas who have gathered down below obviously intend no good to our monastery. The Brothers want to know what you are planning to do about it.'
>
> 'I thought about it a lot, but I couldn't come up with any plan,' said Trinket, 'so I decided to have a bit of a nap. "The calamity from which there is no escape has come upon us. We must except reversity with meekness and remit our throats to the knife."' (He was trying, not altogether successfully, to remember some words from a sutra.)
>
> Even Brother Simple was not convinced that this was the best answer to their predicament.
>
> Trinket eyed Brother Cordial and asked him if he had a better idea.
>
> 'We could try to break out with Brother Wayward and the other two when it's dark and smuggle them through their lines somehow under cover of darkness,' said

---

that appeared after the translation of the *First Book*. She put her finger on a place where Cha had in fact revised an early edition to modify Trinket's behaviour and make it more acceptable (instead of his cutting out Oboi's tongue, in order to silence him, he merely stabs him in the throat). She had noticed this change as a result of yet another change introduced in the translation. I (at the suggestion of my editor) had altered Cha' amended version (the stabbing of Oboi in throat) and instead had Trinket "ramming the handle of the dagger down Oboi's throat", on the grounds that this was a far more plausible method to have been used by Trinket to *silence* the great Manchu warrior (rather than *kill* him). If I had known about the earlier tongue-cutting version, I would certainly have reverted to it.

Brother Cordial. 'I don't think they intend any harm to the other monks.'

'All right,' said Trinket. 'Let's see if we can sell this to the Venerable.'

The five of them made their way to the little temple.

A young novice who attended to the needs of the three senior monks ran inside to announce them.

The Venerable Yulin had been told only that the new Abbot was a young monk from the Shaolin Monastery but had no idea of his identity. Seeing now, for the first time, that it was Trinket, he and the other two at once guessed that his presence in the monastery must be part of some plan of the Young Emperor's to protect his father. After exchanging greetings, Yulin made Trinket sit on the central prayer-mat while he and Brother Wayward stood respectfully on either side of him. Reflecting that he was being waited on by an ex-Emperor and that even Kang Xi could not be seated in the presence of his own father, Trinket had some difficulty in suppressing a smirk of satisfaction as he invited them both to sit down.

'Father Abbot,' said Yulin when they had done so, 'I should have called on you after your installation. It seems wrong that *you* should now feel obliged to call on *me*.'

'That's all right,' said Trinket cheerfully, 'I know you don't like being disturbed. I wouldn't have come *now* if there hadn't been an emergency.'

Yulin didn't ask him what the emergency was.

'Brother Cordial,' said Trinket, 'will you explain the situation to these reverend Brothers?'

Brother Cordial proceeded to explain, in grave and respectful terms, that they were being besieged by a couple of thousand lamas, whose object, he believed, and the Father Abbot had seemed at first to agree with him, was the kidnapping of Brother Wayward.

Yulin closed his eyes and appeared to be meditating. After a minute or two he opened them again and spoke.

'And what are you proposing to do about this, Father Abbot?'

'Our Lord Buddha said: "If *I* don't go to hell, who *will*?"' Trinket replied, ransacking his memory for a few more scraps of sutra. 'We should prepare to offer our necks to the sword. In other words, if we don't have our heads cut off, who *will*? If there was no life there'd be no death, and if there was no dust there'd be no spick and span. And vicey versy. The sword is a void. And the void is a sword. Let us offer our necks to *their* swords in that spirit. Therein lies wisdom. In the beginning was the Void. I mean, the Word. I mean, the Sword. Here endeth the first lesson.'

The Venerable Yulin said nothing. Brother Simple was impressed. The other three Shaolin monks, though decidedly unimpressed, were beginning to suspect that Trinket was up to something.[19]

Anyone comparing this with the original will see at once how far the translation has strayed from the original text. I am totally unrepentant. Probably if I were starting all over again I would do this a lot more often. In places such as this the translator should surely be happy to be Homo Ludens, and should allow himself more opportunities to invent Trinketian fun and games.[20]

3. Trinket the Friend

It is often pointed out that the one endearing quality Trinket possesses is his capacity for friendship, although his only true friend seems to be the Emperor Kang Xi 康熙. The scene in which Trinket reveals to Kang Xi that he has been posing as a eunuch all along is both funny and touching:

Trinket Comes Clean (chapter 12)

Trinket looked at him. To think that one day his friend the Emperor might himself be in grave danger! The Old Whore was a ruthless enemy, and there was definitely a diabolical plot of some kind afoot in the Palace. She had kept a man hidden in her room, disguised as a woman! One day she might try to kill the Emperor himself. And concerning all of this, the Emperor — his friend the Emperor — was utterly in the dark. Suppose he himself, Trinket, were to die at the Old Whore's hands? Then there would be no one left to warn the Emperor. He had a duty to tell him everything he

---

19 I should add (to further complicate matters) that this section of the translation is mostly the work of my collaborator, David Hawkes. The penultimate paragraph only is mine — and was endorsed by my editor.

20 In that sense I would invoke the noble tradition of the seventeenth-century English version of Rabclais done by Sir Thomas Urquhart (he died laughing, it is said, of joy at the accession of Charles II).

knew! He had visions of Kang Xi's body lying dead on the ground, his bones all broken. He suddenly burst into tears.

'What's the matter?'

There was a concerned smile on the Emperor's face. He patted Trinket on the shoulder.

'You want to stay with me, don't you? Don't worry, that can be arranged. In a few days' time, when she's better, I'll have a word with her. To tell the truth, I really miss you too!'

Trinket put the cakes on the table and took hold of both of Kang Xi's hands. His voice trembled:

'Misty — can I call you that again?'

Kang Xi laughed.

'Of course you can! I always said that when there was no one else around we should drop the formalities. I know what it is: you want to fight, don't you? Come! On guard!'

As he said this, he turned his hands around, and adopted an upside-down grip.

'It's not that,' said Trinket. 'Fighting can wait. It's something else, something very important. Something I need to tell my dear friend Misty. Something I could never talk about to His Majesty... His Majesty would certainly chop my head off.'

Kang Xi found all this highly intriguing. He put his hands on Trinket's shoulders and guided him to the edge of the bed, where they sat down together side by side.

'Come on then, speak up!'

'Promise you'll be Misty, not Majesty?'

'Promise. At this moment I'm your good friend Misty, I'm no one's Majesty! I can tell you, being a Majesty all day long, without a single real friend in the world, can be very tiresome.'

'All right then,' said Trinket, 'I'll tell you. And even if you want to chop my head off, you won't be able to.'

Kang Xi smiled.

'Why ever should I want to chop your head off? Why should one friend want to kill another?'

Trinket heaved a long sigh, and began:

'Well, here goes. First of all, I'm not really Laurel. I'm not really a eunuch at all.

The real Laurel is dead. I killed him.'

'*What?*'

Kang Xi looked utterly flabbergasted.

Trinket proceeded to give him a brief account of his life to date: where he had been born, how he had been captured and brought into the Palace, how he had blinded Old Hai Dafu, how he had impersonated, and then killed, Laurel, and how Old Hai had taught him kungfu.

Kang Xi's first reaction was hysterical laughter.

'Tamardy! Come on then! Undo your trousers and let's have a look!'

He needed more than his friend's word. Trinket did as he was told. He untied his trousers and let them fall to the ground.

Kang Xi was now able to see with his own eyes that Trinket was decidedly overqualified for the role of eunuch... He roared with laughter, and made light of the whole thing.

'This *is* a rum state of affairs! Well well well! I think we can let bygones be bygones — after all, killing a junior eunuch isn't *that* serious an offence! But what about the future? We obviously can't have *you*, in your current state, running around the Palace like a eunuch any more, that's for sure! I shall have to see about making you an Intendant of the Palace Guards or something. Dolong's been pretty incompetent anyway.'

Trinket did his trousers up again.

The voices of Hugh Laurie (cf. "Bugger on in!") and Rowan Atkinson were never very far from my mind here. Especially Laurie as the Prince Regent. With *Black Adder* Ben Elton probably did more to popularise English history than anything since *1066 and All That*.

4. Trinket the Romantic

Occasionally we are given glimpses of Trinket the sentimental (almost nauseatingly so) love-sick teenager:

A Journey to the Sea (English chapter 14)

As they travelled, he and Fang Yi chatted on every subject under the sun. In the Palace, they'd been closeted together in the same room, but the Little Countess had always been with then, which had cramped their style, and made Fang Yi rather reserved. Now, as they rode slowly along side by side (with the rest of the party tactfully lagging a long way behind them), she behaved quite differently, talking happily and smiling gaily. In the Palace, Trinket had made a big thing of calling Fang Yi his wife, but that had been mainly to tease her. Perhaps he had been a tiny bit flirtatious. But he was only very slightly in love, if at all. Today it was different. Meeting her again, seeing once more the tantalizing expression on her face when she got angry, the delightful way she had of talking and smiling, he couldn't help falling head over heads in love with her. After half a day's ride, she was flushed with exertion, and tiny beads of sweat stood out on her face. Trinket found her beauty utterly bewitching. He kept staring at her, transfixed.

'What's the matter with you?' asked Fang Yi lightly.

'Dearest sister! You...you just look so beautiful. I think...I think...'

'Think what?'

'Don't get angry when I say it,' said Trinket.

'If you're serious, I won't get angry; but if you're being silly again — '

'I think...if you *really were* to become my wife, I'd be the happiest person alive!'

Fang Yi glowered coldly at him, and turned away.

'Dear sister, what's wrong?' he asked anxiously. 'Are you cross with me?'

'Of course I am! Very cross indeed!'

'But I'm being very, *very* serious,' said Trinket. 'I *really* mean it.'

'And what about me? Listen to you! *Really* this...*really* that...anyone would think you were the only person in the world who mattered! What about me? Don't I *really* exist? Didn't I *really* mean what I said? In the Palace, I promised to serve you for the rest of your life! Don't you think *that* was real?'

At that moment Trinket was blissfully happy. If he'd been riding on the same horse as Fang Yi, he would have squeezed her tight, and kissed her on her lovely check. As it was, he just took her left hand in his right.

'I'll be faithful to you for a thousand years, no, ten thousand years!'

'How could you possibly? Silly boy!'

Fang Yi gave a peal of laughter, and turned away. But she left her hand in his, and

Trinket felt as if he would burst with joy.

Time flew as they rode along and chattered together on their journey. That evening, they stopped at a largish country town and took lodgings for the night in a inn. The next morning, Trinket asked Wurtle (who had been keeping discreetly in the background) to hire a large cart, and now he and Fang Yi were able to sit side by side during their journey. When he talked of love, and put his arm round her waist and kissed her on the cheek, she did not resist. But she refused to allow him any further intimacy. Trinket had no firsthand experience of such things, and was more than satisfied with what she granted him. His only desire in life was that their journey would never come to an end, and that the cart would rumble on and on to the end of the world with him sitting inside it, his arm round his fair love.

The joys of sweet love had chased all thought of duty from Trinket's mind: his Imperial commission, the *Sutra in Forty-Two Sections,* even the Old Emperor on the Wutai Mountains — all these things were quite forgotten. In his dazed state of infatuation, Trinket was oblivious of the passage of time, and of how far they had been traveling.

One evening, their cart finally arrived at the sea. Fang Yi took him by the hand and walked with him to the shore, talking to him softly.

'Why don't you and I sail across the sea? Would you like to do that? Shall we explore the world together? We could live a magical life, like a pair of immortals? What do you say?'

As she spoke, Fang Yi held his hand and rested her head softly on his shoulder, leaning on him gently.

Trinket put his arm round her waist, for fear that she might fall. Her silken hair brushed against his face, he felt her slender body tremble slightly. He was somewhat taken aback by this sudden proposal. The whole idea of setting sail and crossing the ocean struck him as decidedly dangerous. But in the circumstances, in the glowing halo of romance that enveloped them, how could he possibly say no?

This is an effective scene that helps us become better acquainted with our susceptible anti-hero. Here is a young man whose affections are as fickle as his kungfu. Needless to say, it is all a trap — and all the more effective for that.

5. Making Fun of the Barbarians

During the whole course of the *Second Book* (chapters 11–30 of the Chinese text), there is a great deal of fun had at the expense of a number of non-Han figures, mostly Tibetans, but also Mongols, and other ethnic minorities. I don't think one need become too uptight about this. This is after all a widespread type of humour. There are Irish/Polish/Maori/Jewish/Chinese jokes to be found the world over. Why not Tibetan and Mongol? (Perhaps that is why it seems to work quite well in English?)[21] It is only when such humour serves a racist or chauvinist end that it becomes objectionable.

A typical example can be found in chapter 16:

A Mongol Prince and a Grand Lama from Tibet (English chapter 16)

A few days after this exchange, Trinket and Brother Simple were in the latter's cell discussing some fine points concerning the swordsmanship practised by the two girls when one of the Prajna Hall monks came in to say that they were wanted by the Abbot in the monastery's main hall.

When they arrived, they found thirty or forty visitors there, three of them sitting with the Abbot, the rest standing. Of the three sitting with the Abbot, the first was a young man in his early twenties who, to judge from his dress, appeared to be a Mongol nobleman; the second was a tall, thin, red-robed lama of middle years; and the third was a fortyish military man wearing the uniform of a high-ranking officer. Of the thirty or forty men standing behind them, some were army officers, some were lamas, while a dozen or so of them were dressed in civilian clothes but looked as if they might have had some sort of military training and knew how to fight.

'Ah, Father,' said Father Wisdom as Trinket entered, 'our monastery has some distinguished guests today. This gentleman is His Highness the Mongol Price Galdan: this is the Grand Lama sDe-srid Sangs-rgyas-rgya-mtsho from Tibet — in China he is known as Father Sangge; and this is Brigadier Ma Bao, who is on the staff of his Highness the

---

21   I also think the outlandishly funny Tibetan transcriptions (introduced in the translation) are a wonderful stroke of luck for the translator.

Satrap of Yunnan.'

'And this,' he said, turning to the three men he had just introduced and pointing to Trinket, 'is my Brother in the Truth, Father Treasure.'

All those present were more than a little surprised at hearing this disreputable-looking juvenile introduced as an equal-ranking colleague of the Abbot. The Mongol Galdan laughed out loud.

'Such a little Father! Very amusing.'

Trinket pressed his palms together and bowed.

'Such a big Prince! Very funny.'

'What is funny about me, please? I should like to know,' Prince Galdan said angrily.

'What's amusing about *me*, then?' said Trinket. And he sat down unconcernedly in the chair next to the Abbot.

It was clear from the look of the others present that they didn't know what to make of him.

'Well, gentlemen,' said Father Wisdom, 'to what do we owe the honour of this visit?'

'The three of us all happened to be passing through this area,' said the Grand Lama Sangge. 'We have heard of the famous Shaolin Monastery and we all come from obscure and backward places, so we decided to call on you in the hope that we might have the benefit of your instruction.'

Unlike the lesser lama Brother Bayen, whom Trinket had run into on an earlier occasion on Wutai, this one spoke like an educated Chinese and with a passable Peking accent.

'You are too polite,' said Father Wisdom. 'Mongolia, Tibet, and Yunnan all have distinguished traditions of Buddhist teaching. I cannot believe that we in this monastery can have anything to teach you.'

Sangge had, of course, been referring to the Martial Arts for which the Shaolin Monastery was famous. Whether the Abbot had misunderstood him or was only pretending to do so would be hard to say.

'All the world has heard of the seventy-two incomparable fighting skills of the Shaolin Monastery,' said Prince Galdan. 'Could you not get your monks together to give us a little demonstration?'

'You mustn't believe all the things that people say about us,' said Father Wisdom. 'All our monks here, without exception, devote their lives to the pursuit of Zen as a means of obtaining enlightenment. Although it is true that a number of them devote some of their time to training in kungfu, they do so only as a means of keeping their bodies fit and their minds alert. We attach no special importance to such exercises.'

'Are you not being a little devious, Abbot?' said Prince Galdan. 'We would like only to see a demonstration of the seventy-two skills. We do not intend to steal them from you. Why be so grudging?'

'If you gentlemen wish to discuss the Buddhist *Dharma* with us, I will gladly summon the Brothers,' said Father Wisdom, 'but not for a demonstration of martial skills. That is something expressly forbidden by the rules of our Order.'

Prince Galdan's eyebrows went up.

'It seems that the reputation of this monastery is a hollow sham. It is — how do you Chinese say? — not worth fart.'

'We are indeed taught that this world we live in is a hollow sham,' said Father Wisdom smiling gently. 'Not worth a fart, as you put it. What you say about the reputation of this monastery is of course correct.'

Prince Galdan had not expected so mild a response. He pointed, laughing, at Trinket.

'So. And this little monk, too, he is not worth fart?'

Trinket smiled cheerfully back at him.

'I'm certainly not worth as much as *you*, Your Highness,' he said. 'So, if I'm not worth a fart, it's safe to say that Your Highness *is* worth a fart. A big fart.'

Prince Galdan leapt up in a rage and was on the point of striking him. But then he reflected that the only reason this little monk had such high standing in the monastery must be that he was exceptionally skilled in Martial Arts. With some difficulty he restrained himself and sat down again.

'There are much worse things than not being worth a fart,' said Trinket, 'Owing hundreds and thousands of taels and not being able to pay them back, for instance — that's much worse.'

'How true!' said Father Wisdom, 'My brother has stated a profound truth. It is the law of karma that evil actions incur a debt of evil and good ones a good reward. Not to be worth a fart, that is to have incurred neither good nor evil karma. How much better to be owing neither good nor evil than to have incurred an infinite debt of evil karma! The parable is an excellent one.'

Brother Simple was glad to hear the Abbot praising his saintly young companion.

'I have learned much from Father Treasure since I have been working with him,' he said. 'Although he is so young, he has advanced far along the path towards enlightenment.'

The two older men's praise of this impertinent little monk struck Galdan as a deliberate provocation. He leap up once more, determined this time to do him an injury. Before he could hurt him, however, Father Wisdom's long sleeve shot out and he stepped back and sat down heavily in his seat. How it had happened he did not understand. It felt as if he had been blown back by a small but powerful wind.

All this time Trinket had not even moved. This was partly from fright and partly because he was not expecting the attack and had not had time to respond. To Father Wisdom and Brother Simple, however, he appeared to have shown remarkable restraint. Father Wisdom now launched into a short homily, interlarded with quotations from the Buddhist scriptures, on the virtues of impassivity, ending with further commendation, in which Brother Simple joined, of Trinket's spiritual advancement. This so enraged Galdan that he suddenly interrupted with a barked-out order that none of the Chinese present could understand.

'Hanisbal nimahong kanubidigar!'

A number of the Mongol henchmen behind him raised their arms and there was a rapid succession of little flashes as nine metal darts sped one after the other through the air, three towards the Abbot, three towards Brother Simple, and three towards Trinket. Despite the lack of warning, neither Father Wisdom nor Brother Simple was hurt. Father Wisdom disposed of the three aimed at him by flicking his long sleeve; Brother Simple caught the three aimed at him by slapping his hands on them as if he was catching flies; but Trinket, once again taken unawares, sat motionless as the darts hit his chest and fell — *tink tink tink* — on the floor. Once more the wonderful waistcoat had saved him, though one of the darts had landed near the newly-healed stab-wound on his chest and hurt so intensely that it cost him a great effort not to cry out.

This blend of "barbarian fun" and Trinketian mischief, larded with the sort of Zennery that Western readers (thanks to the work of two generations of translators and popularisers, and especially the writings of Daisetz Suzuki and Alan Watts) can actually understand (while at the same time enjoying the sensation of sampling the exotic), makes for a successful scene in translation.[22]

6. Making Fun of the Barbarians Again

Another example occurs in chapter 18, this time involving an aboriginal hill tribe, who play a crucial role in another of Trinket's pranks:

Manzi, goowah tooloo! (English chapter 18)

'Sst!' said Shaker. 'Put out the lights!'

Instantly all the candles in the hall, except for a little one on the altar which they somehow missed, were extinguished. Trinket seized the Green Girl's hand.

'Come on, wife, quick! We must hide.'

The Green Girl tried to disengage her hand.

'Don't call me that!' she hissed. 'That wasn't a real wedding. It doesn't count.'

'Of course it counts,' said Trinket. 'Once you've done all that kowtowing, there's no undoing it.'

A chorus of inhuman yells and cries outside caused her to draw closer to him. No longer resisting, she ran hand in hand with him to the shrine at the back of the hall and crouched down with him behind the altar. Suddenly the hall was lit up again with the light of blazing torches as a throng of some thirty of forty yelling warriors burst inside. They were the strangest-looking creatures imaginable, naked except for the animal skins round their waists and their feathered head-dresses, their faces and bodies patterned all over with warpaint. Wild Manzi! What were these savage tribesmen from the forests of Yunnan and the Burmese border doing in North China? The Green Girl cowered against Trinket's body, so close that he could feel her trembling.

The crowd of savages halted, and a big man who appeared to be their leader looked round imperiously.

'Chinee man — bad!' he said. 'All kill!' *Goowah tooloo abaslee!*'

'*Goowah tooloo abaslee!*' the other savages shouted menacingly.

---

22 Again, this section (and the subsequent six!) are the work of my collaborator. Some might justifiably suggest that there's a lesson to be learned from that too...

Shaker Wu had lived all his life in Yunnan and had picked up a few words of the Yee language spoken by many of the aboriginal tribesmen in that area, but had no idea what language these painted savages were speaking.

'We Chinee man good man,' he ventured in his pidgin Yee. 'Not kill!'

The Manzi chief shook his head uncomprehendingly.

'Chinee man — bad. All kill!' he insisted. 'All kill! *Goowah tooloo abaslee!*'

'*Goowaho tooloo abaslee!*' shouted the other Manzi, and instantly set upon the members of the wedding party, including the unfortunate Sir Zheng, who to them was a 'Chinee man' like the rest.

7. And Again

Another effective scene (occurring earlier in the text) involves making fun of Tibetans and humiliating Trinket's rival in love, the dashing Young Zheng:

Sa-sa-satisfaction! (English chapter 17)

'On knees!' shouted one of the lamas. 'Surrender, or cut off heads!'

But the men had courage enough to continue. Some of them put up their fists and some of them picked up benches to defend themselves with. The four lamas went back to where Sangge was sitting and flung down their knives so that they stuck quivering in the table. Then they moved in a slow and deliberate manner towards the men. Presently there were shrieks and cries and Trinket realized with horror that the lamas were systematically breaking the men's legs. Soon all of them lay groaning and helpless on the floor amidst the overturned tables and the broken crockery. To begin with Trinket had felt rather pleased to see Zheng and his companions being humbled, but now he was really frightened and wondered whose turn it would be next. The lamas went back to their own table, however, pulled out and resheathed their knives, and sat down as if nothing had happened.

'Waiter!' Sangge shouted towards the kitchen. 'Let's have some wine! What's happened to our dinner?' (Unlike the lesser lamas accompanying him, Sangge spoke fluent Chinese.)

He called several times, but there was no response.

'Holy yak butter!' shouted one of the lamas. 'Not bring dinner, we burn house down!'

This threat brought the proprietor to the kitchen door.

'Yes, yes, Your Reverence, immediately,' he said, and turned to address the trembling waiter inside. 'Quickly, boy, quickly! Take the wine and the dishes to Their Reverences!'

Trinket looked to see how the White Nun was reacting to this sudden change of fortune. She was slowly sipping tea from her cup and appeared to be totally unaware of what was going on around her. The Green Girl, on the other hand, was ashen-faced and there was terror in her eyes. Young Sir Zheng's hue was changing from blue to white by turns. He was standing with his hand on his sword, but the hand was trembling. Though honour told him that he should fight, it seemed uncertain whether honour or fear would prevail. The sinister Sangge observed this with a mocking laugh and, getting up from his table, went over to confront him. Young Zheng jumped back a pace and held up his sword in front of him.

'Wha-wha-wha-what do you want?'

His voice was husky with fear.

'What I want has to do with this nun here and nobody else,' said Sangge. 'Who are you? Are you her disciple?'

'No,' said Zheng.

'In that case, if you know what's good for you, you'll keep your nose out of this,', said Sangge.

'I mu-must ask you for your name,' Zheng stammered. 'I shall be requiring sa-sa-sa-, sa-sa-sa — '

'What will you be requiring? Satisfaction?'

'Ye-yes.'

Sangge threw his head back and roared with laughter. When he had finished laughing, he flicked the sleeve of his robe in young Zheng's face. Zheng made a feeble pass at him with his sword, whereupon Sangge, with the greatest of ease, knocked the sword flying from his hand, seized him by the collar, and forced him down on to a bench. Then he pressed a point on the back of his neck so that he could no longer move.

'Now sit there like a good boy!' he said, and returned, laughing, to his own table to rejoin the other lamas.

I have to confess (unrepentantly) to a shade of Tintin here. Observant readers will have noticed this here and there in the *First Book*. I don't think Cha should be afraid of being compared with Hergé. Nor should we forget that it is not only young readers who enjoy Tintin (and its excellent English translation).[23]

8. Sutras and Dragon Lines: Plot Mechanics

Like it or not, there is an enormous amount of sheer plot mechanics in *Deer*. Cha has a penchant for complex plots. He loves to tease his reader, to play games. I recall on one occasion talking to him over lunch about Anthony Hope's novel *The Prisoner of Zenda*, a historical romance set in Ruritania, enormously popular when I was a boy (made into a film at least three times, with Douglas Fairbanks Jr. [1937], Stewart Granger [1952] and Peter Sellers [1979]). Cha remarked that he found the plot of the novel too simple. The same could, I suppose, be said of some of Dumas' plots (by comparison with Cha's). But one sometimes cannot help wondering if *Deer* might not have benefited from *less* complexity of plot, and *more* complexity (or depth) of characterisation and setting. The Western reader certainly would benefit from more leisurely scene-setting descriptions of Yangzhou and Peking. It seems to be one of the consequences of the serialised form (*roman feuilleton*) in which the novel first appeared that the author often seems to be improvising as he goes along; and another consequence, that he is constantly having to remind his reader of details of the plot from several numbers back.[24] This sometimes makes for laborious

---

23　It is interesting (in the context of the ethics of translation and adaptation) to note that in the animated film version of *The Blue Lotus*, the Japanese villain virtually disappears. The animated series was made with the Japanese market in mind.

24　It is interesting to compare the time scale of Cha's feuilleton output with that of Dumas père. During the heyday of the French feuilleton (1842-1848), Dumas produced *Les Trois Mousquetaires* and its two sequels, *Vingt ans après* and *Le Vicomte de Bragelonne: La Reine Margot, Joseph Balsamo; Le Comte de Monte-Cristo; Le Chevalier de Maison-Rouge; La Dame de Monsoreau;* and *Les Quarante-Cinq*. According to legend, Dumas wrote with four separate pens at once, and a waiter stood by his side ladling soup into his open mouth, to save time. See F. W. J. Hemmings,

reading in the book version, although Chinese readers seem inclined to be tolerant.[25]

Be that as it may, the translator is obliged to deal with plot mechanics. It is part of the contract. Sometimes it seems uncontrived and unproblematic, as in this scene between Auntie Tao and Trinket:

The Eight Sutras, the Dragon Line, and the Mystic Dragons (English chapter 12)

As she said this, Auntie Tao cracked the whip loudly in the air.

'And the reason my Shifu entered the Palace was to lay hands on the Eight Sutras.'

'Eight?'

'That's right. One for each of the Banners. The Chief of each Banner — Plain White, Yellow, Red, and Blue; Bordered White, Yellow, Red, and Blue — has his own copy.'

'That makes sense,' said Trinket. 'The two I saw at Oboi's were different colours. One was yellow with a red border, one was plain white.'

'Yes. The Sutras match the colours of the Banners.'

Trinket was thinking to himself:

'I've got five of them. That means there are still three more knocking around somewhere. But I still don't know what's so special about these Sutras. I'm sure Auntie Tao knows. I must try and get it out of her somehow.'

He acted stupid again.

'So I suppose your Shifu's Shifu   your Grand-Shifu — must have been a very

---

The King of Romance (London, 1979), 117.

25 I have found that Chinese readers of Cha's work in general seem liable to go into a sort of trance, and suspend most of their critical faculties. It is almost as if Cha could write anything about anything, and they would still be happy. My friend the modernist poet Gu Cheng, normally a highly critical reader, was a Cha-addict. His wife used to beg me not to lend him any more Cha novels, as he always stayed up through the night reading them. It is as if the books are invested with an aura that renders them immune to normal critical judgement. Much of the recent so-called "critical" literature produced about Cha's work (*Jinxue*) is little more than repetitious eulogy.

devout Buddhist. These Sutras must be very valuable. The writing's probably done in gold or something.'

'No, that's not it,' said Auntie Tao. 'Dear boy, what I'm going to tell you today must never go any further than you. I want you to swear.'

Swearing was something that came easily to Trinket. He could swear his head off about something in the morning, and have forgotten all about it by afternoon. And besides, why should he want to go telling anyone else about the Sutras, when his aim was to collect the remaining three for himself?

'If I, Trinket Wei,' he began, 'should ever betray the secret of the Eight Sutras to another living soul, may I be struck dead, and die a horrible death, just like that foul turtle the Old Whore kept in her bedroom dressed up as a maid...'

'Come what may, one thing's for sure,' he thought to himself. 'I'll never be like *that* creature! No one'll catch me dressing up as a woman and getting into bed with the Old Whore!'

Somehow, to Trinket's way of thinking, that thought let him off the hook...

'That's a strange kind of oath to swear,' said Auntie Tao with an amused smile, 'Well, listen while I explain this thing to you. When the Manchus came in through the Great Pass, they never thought they would end up ruling China. There were so few of them. They thought they would do a bit of marauding and then head back to the North-East. So they just grabbed whatever treasure they could lay their hands on. There was a huge amount of it. The person in command of all the Manchu forces at the time was the Regent Dorgon uncle of the Emperor Shun Zhi. But the Banners were powerful, and each Manchu Banner had its own Head. The Banners held a Coucil, and at the Council they drew a map of the place where they would bury their Manchu treasure. Each of the Eight Banner Heads was to keep a map — '

Trinket leapt to his feet excitedly and cried out.

'I've got it!'

The cart wobbled and he sat down again promptly.

'Each of the Eight Sutras has a map hidden in it!'

'Almost, but not quite. Who knows?' said Auntie Tao. 'Only the Eight Banner Heads who were present at the Council meeting know the exact secret. Even Princes and Great Ministers don't know. My Shifu told me that the hill where the treasure is buried lies on one of the Dragon Lines that controls the destiny of the Manchu people.

This Dragon Line has enabled them to set one of their own kind on the throne and rule China.'

'What's a Dragon Line?' asked Trinket.

'It's a line of power in the earth,' replied Tao. 'The Manchu ancestors were buried in this hill. Their sons and grandsons have prospered, and have conquered China. My Shifu told me, if only we can find that hill, and break the Dragon Line, not only can we throw the Tartars off the throne of China, but we can send them back for ever to their homeland, to die there. My Shifu, and my Grand-Shifu before her, gave their lives in the quest for this knowledge. That's how important it is. And somehow or other the secret lies hidden in those Eight sutras.'

'How did your Grand-Shifu come to know all this about the Manchus?' asked Trinket.

'It's a long story. She was the daughter of a Chinese father living in the North-East. She was taken into captivity by the Head of the Bordered Blue Manchu Banner. She said that when the Manchus took Peking, there was a lot of argument among the Banner Heads. Some of them wanted to conquer the whole of China. Others thought that such a conquest would be too great an undertaking, and that it would be safer to take whatever they could carry and go back to the North-East. In the end it was Prince Dorgon who decided: they would stay and establish their dynasty, but at the same time they would carry off a huge treasure and bury it somewhere beyond the Pass. Then if the day ever came when they were forced to retreat, they would have something to fall back on.'

'So you mean they were *afraid* of us Chinese?

'Of course they were! They still are. It's just that we won't stand up against them together. Dear boy, you are the Emperor's favourite. If with your help we can find out where the Sutras are hidden, and get our hands on that treasure, we will be able to strike a double blow! We will have broken the Manchu Dragon Line, and with the treasure we will be able to pay for the soldiers and the weapons we need. Then we'll soon have them on the run!'

None of this patriotic fervour found much of an echo in Trinket's opportunist heart. But the thought of all that treasure lying somewhere ready for the taking...That was a different matter.

'Auntie,' he asked breathlessly, 'are you saying that the Sutras tell where the treasure is hidden?'

The exposition of this important (if ultimately disappointing — it leads nowhere) strand in the plot (the eight Sutras and the secret hidden in them) is rather effective, coming as it does in the encounter between the family-less Trinket and his newly acquired foster auntie. But in many other instances my overall impression is that the translator needs to do a great deal more by way of re-organising the plot material for his less "tolerant" (because as yet less addicted?) English-language readers. I recall a conversation with Cha some years ago in which we discussed this issue of abridgment. He had been approached by the French sinologist Jacques Pimpaneau (a mutual friend), who wanted Cha to abridge one of his novels himself, for the purposes of eventual translation. Cha told me he considered the idea, but concluded that he would not be able (or willing?) to do it. Quite apart from abridgment, it might also be helpful to provide Plot Briefings ("What's happened to the Sutras Now?" and "How Many Identities Does Trinket Have Now?"), and Plot Synopses (in a fun format). My collaborator David Hawkes has made a beginning in this direction in his work on the *Second Book*, in some cases drastically curtailing chapters, dovetailing episodes, and even amalgating characters. He even provided me with a very helpful Sutra Summary. I must confess that I am a lot more hesitant and incompetent at doing this kind of thing (abridgment). But I believe it has to be done.

9. Plot Mechanics Again

Another instance of effective plot exposition is in the dramatic confrontation between the White Nun (the one-armed Princess Royal) and the Old Whore (the fake Empress Dowager). A number of crucial facts are communicated in their dialogue, without the reader's tolerance being stretched too far.

White Nun meets Old Whore (English chapter 17)

The Empress Dowager was trembling violently. A vision of the Donggo sisters writhing in agony on their beds was swimming before her eyes.

'I am not a Tartar,' she said, 'I'm a Chinese.'

'Don't be absurd!' said the White Nun, and began to move away.

'But I am!' said the Empress Dowager. 'I really am a Chinese. I hate the Tartars.'

The White Nun halted.

'Oh?' she said. 'Why?'

'It's...it's a secret. I'm not allowed to tell anyone.'

'In that case you'd better keep it to yourself.'

The Empress Dowager's terror of a cruel death now drove out all her other fears.

'I'm an impostor,' she said. 'I'm not the Empress Dowager.'

The White Nun went back to her chair and sat down again. Trinket was beginning to think that the Empress Dowager was an even better liar than himself; but presently, as her story unfolded, it appeared that she was telling the truth.

She was the daughter of Mao Wenlong, a Ming general who had fought against the Manchus on the frontier for several years. Her real name was Mao Dongzhu. When both her parents were killed, she was taken into the Palace and entered the service of the Empress, the Princess of the Borjigit clan who had become the Emperor Shun Zhi's wife. There, after years of service, she had learned to imitate the voice and gestures of her mistress so well that in the end she was able to impersonate her.

'My face is false, too,' she said, and sitting down at her dressing-table, she soaked a tissue in some sort of liquid preparation she got from a gilded jar and rubbed it vigorously on her cheeks. After waiting a few moments, she peeled off two skin-covered pads, one from each side of her face. Even the White Nun gasped. The round, fat face of the Empress Dowager had turned into that of a gaunt, hollow-eyed woman.

'It certainly is a remarkable transformation,' said the White Nun. 'But when you supplanted the Empress, couldn't her other attendants spot the difference? And what about the Emperor?'

'The Emperor was infatuated with Lady Donggo, he never went near the Empress,' said this woman who called herself Mao Dongzhu. 'As for her women and her eunuchs: when I first gained control over her, before I began impersonating her, I made her dismiss them and replace them with others, so that when I took over, the ones around me were all new. I avoided going out of my apartments as much as possible; but even when I had to, Court etiquette forbids Palace staff to look members of the Imperial family in the face when they are addressing them, so that if they ever did get to look at me, it would have been from a distance, too far away for them to tell the difference.'

So far the White Nun had seemed convinced; but now, suddenly, she thought of something.

'Just a minute. You said the Emperor didn't go near you; yet you have a daughter.'

'She isn't the Emperor's,' said Mao Dongzhu. 'Her father was a Chinese. He used to stay with me sometimes in the Palace disguised as one of my women. He...he... not long ago he fell ill and died.'

Trinket and Aunt Tao gave each other a nudge. This at least they knew to be untrue.

The White Nun shook her head.

'I don't think you're telling me *all* the truth.'

'When I've just told you a shameful secret like that, Your Reverence?' said Mao Dangzhu. 'How can you doubt me?'

'What about the real Empress Dowager?' said the White Nun. 'You say you have never killed anyone. Surely you have *her* blood on your hands?'

'She is alive and well,' said Mao Dongzhu.

This was a great surprise.

'But in that case, aren't you afraid of being found out?' said the White Nun.

By way of an answer, Mao Dongzhu went up to a carpet that covered part of the wall and pulled on a tasselled cord that hung beside it. The carpet rolled up revealing the doors of a large closet, to which she applied a little golden key. She opened the doors and there, lying down inside under a bed-cover of silk brocade, was the body of a woman. The White Nun gave a little gasp.

'Is this the Empress Dowager?'

'Have a look!' said Mao Dongzhu, bringing a candle over so that the White Nun could get a better view.

The woman's face looked ill and completely bloodless. Apart from that, though, it bore a striking resemblance to what the false empress Dowager had looked like before she removed the skin-pads from her checks. The woman opened her eyes slightly, then quickly closed them again.

'I shall never tell you,' she said faintly. 'Why don't you kill me?'

'I've never killed anyone,' lied Mao Dongzhu. 'You know I wouldn't kill you.'

She closed and locked the closet and let down the carpet.

'I take it you've been keeping her shut up in here for several years,' said the White Nun.

'Yes.'

'So what is the information you want to get out of her? It can only be for the sake of what she knows that you have kept her alive so long. As soon as you have it, presumably, you will kill her.'

'I am a Buddhist,' said Mao Dongzhu. 'The Lord Buddha forbids us to take life.'

'Do you take me for a three-year-old?' said the White Nun contemptuously. 'It is extremely dangerous for you to keep her here. She has only to cry out and you would be lost.'

'I tell her that if she does so I shall kill the Emperor. She is very loyal to him.'

'Why don't you use that threat to obtain the information you want?'

'She says if I do so she will stop eating and starve herself to death.'

'Come now,' said the White Nun, 'you still haven't told me what this information is that you want to get from her.'

The answer was still some time coming, and when it did it was only partly true. It did, however, to some extent, tally with what the White Nun had already learned from Aunt Tao. The Aisingioro clan, to which the Manchu Imperial family belonged, had started out in the Long White Mountains of Liaodong. Geomancers claimed to have demonstrated that their rise to power and eventual occupation of the whole of China was thanks to the favourable *fengshui* of their old home. Anyone who dug up the Dragon Line in this area would be able to overthrow the Manchu power. The exact position of this Dragon Line was a secret that the Old Emperor had confided to his Empress — the woman locked in the closet — as he lay dying. This was the information that Mao had all these years been trying to extract from her.

'Geomancy is a superstition,' said the White Nun. 'It was misgovernment that brought down the Ming Empire. Oppression drove the people to rebel. This much I have learned during my travels. It had nothing to do with Dragon Lines.'

'I'm sure you are much cleverer than I am,' said Mao. 'Perhaps there is nothing in this Dragon Line business. On the other hand, suppose there is? Isn't it worth a try?'

'You are right,' said the White Nun. 'Even if there is nothing in it, the Tartars themselves seem to believe it. If we could get hold of the secret, it would certainly weaken their morale. So this is what you have been trying to find out from the Empress Dowager?'

'Yes,' said Mao, 'but no matter what I say or do, I can't get the wretched woman to tell me.'

10. Action

There is a general category of successful scenes in *Deer*, which I have labelled *Action*. It seems to me that a large number of episodes owe their success (in both Chinese and English) to their initial conceptions as "action scenes", lending themselves to visualisation and involvement on the part of the reader/ spectator, somewhat like good action scenes in a film (we must always remember Cha's formative years in the cinema trade). Perhaps one can even generalise and say that scenes conceived in the *storytelling* mode tend to suffer from longueur and to become boring in English; while scenes *cinematically* conceived fare much better.

For example, most of (English) chapter 14, on Snake Island, works quite well in English, it seems to me. Even the sections about calligraphy and the bogus inscription are never tedious, because they are ingenious, humorous, and well integrated into the action. The secondary figures (Doctor Lu, Fat Dhuta, the Leader and Madame Hong) have just enough individuality to keep the scene going. The only weakness is during the protracted mutiny scene, where it seems to me that Cha has given in to his tendency to say in twenty pages what could have been done in two. In Chinese he carries this off by the sheer charm of his language — the storyteller's Midas Touch.

Another typical action scene is in (English) chapter 17, when Trinket comes up with yet another of his "cunning plans" (involving a more than usually subtle and nasty use of that old favourite, the Decomposing Powder):

In the Sorghum Field (English chapter 17)

Trinket knelt down with his back to the others, laid the Sutra on the ground in front of him, and got out the severed hand, glancing over his shoulder from time to time to see how far the lamas had got in their preparations. When he had unwrapped the hand, he took out his dagger and cut some strips of flesh from it which he laid carefully on the Sutra. By this time the lamas had lit the sorghum and it was beginning to blaze. Smoke drifted towards the cave, making their eyes water and causing them to cough.

'Hey!' he called out over his shoulder. 'I've got the sutra here. If you don't put that out, I'll throw it in the fire.'

'That will keep them busy for a while,' he thought, taking out the little phial of Decomposing Powder. He didn't know if the powder would take effect on living bodies, but he thought it was worth a try. He remembered that there had to be blood for it to start working, which is why he now shook some of it on the flesh he had sliced from the hand. He glanced out at the lamas, who were thowing flat stones and earth on the burning sorghum and stamping out the flames, then back at his handiwork. The flesh strips were sizzling slightly and oozing yellow droplets. So far so good, but he needed a little time. He got to his feet and stood with the other two to face the lamas.

'Throw out that Sutra *now!*' shouted Sangge, when the fire was thoroughly extinguished.

'My Shifu will let you have it if you'll promise to use it properly,' Trinket called back. 'It's very precious. It comes from the Palace. There's a secret locked up inside it, and anyone who can unlock it will have the power to convert the whole world to the Buddhist faith.'

He glance down behind him at the Sutra. The strips of flesh were fast dissolving in a pool of yellow liquid.

Sangge knew that the secret contained in the Sutra had nothing to do with the propagation of the faith; but he also knew that the copy he had already sacrificed so much to obtain had in fact been taken from the Palace, and he was sure this was the one. He was trembling with excitement to think that it was now almost within his grasp.

'Tell your Shifu, the conversion of the world is very dear to my heart,' he said.

'My Shifu read through this copy of the Sutra, but she couldn't discover the secret,' said Trinket. 'She says that if *you* are able to discover it, you must promise to share it with monks and nuns everywhere, not just be selfish and keep it to yourselves.'

'Of course,' said Sangge. 'Tell her she can set her mind at rest. I am perfectly willing to give that undertaking.'

'If *you* can't work out what the secret is,' said Trinket, 'she says you are to hand it over to the Shaolin Monastery. And if the monks of the Shaolin Monastery can't make it out, they are to hand it over to the Pure Coolness Monsatery on Wutai. And if the monks on Wutai can't make it out, they are to hand it over the Zen Wisdom Monastery in Yangzhou.'

'Certainly,' said Sangge. 'I promise to abide by all of these conditions.'

It seemed obvious to him from all this that the White Nun had no inkling of the Sutra's real value. They could make what conditions they liked! Once he had the Sutra, he would dispose of the lot of them.

Trinket glanced down once more and was delighted to see that the flesh had entirely dissolved and the yellow liquid had been absorbed into the cover of the book. He doubled up the cloth in which the hand had been wrapped to protect his own hands with while he picked it up.

'Here it comes, then — your precious Sutra!'

He lobbed it for Sangge to catch, then hurriedly threw away the cloth. But Sangge suspected a trap and allowed it to fall to the ground. It was the other two lamas who picked it up, pouncing on it, and fighting each other to hold it and have a look.

'Hey, you guys!' Trinket shouted. 'Look at you! You've got centipedes on your faces!'

The lamas instinctively brushed at their faces with their hands but could feel nothing there. Stupid brat, they thought. They took the book over to Sangge.

'Look, Father,' (they were speaking Tibetan now), 'is it the book we have been looking for?'

'Let's take it over there,' said Sangge. 'We need to have a good look to make sure they haven't given us a fake.'

They sat down with it at some distance from the cave.

'It's wet,' said Sangge. 'We'll have to be extra careful we don't tear the pages.'

He began turning them over carefully, using only the tips of his fingers. While they were all looking at the book, one of the lamas unconsciously scratched his neck and suddenly became aware that his fingers were itching. Sangge and the other lama, too, felt their fingers itching, but at first paid no attention. The itching grew more insistent, however, and when they looked, they noticed that the tips of their fingers were wet with some yellow liquid.

'Strange!' they said. 'Where's this coming from? Surely it's not from the book?'

At that point the cheeks of Sangge's two companions started itching unbearably and they began furiously scratching themselves. When Sangge looked up from the book, he saw that there were bloody scratch-marks on both men's cheeks. The itching of his own fingers was now intolerable. Then he realized what the cause was and dropped the book in horror.

'Aiyo!' he cried. 'The book is poisoned!'

The yellow liquid was dripping like blood or sweat from his fingers. He wiped them frantically on the ground. The scratch-marks on the faces of the other two were now deep red furrows. Their cheeks not only itched now but hurt as well. When they saw blood on their finger-ends and drops of greasy yellow liquid dripping from their chins, they began to howl and scream and presently threw themselves to the ground, clutching their heads and writhing in agony.

In Sangge's case it was only his fingers that were affected, but finding that the tips were no better for all his dabbing and wiping and that they continued to ooze yellow liquid, he tore off his robe, wrapped the poisoned book in it, and rushed off with it under his arm to look for water.

Trinket was relieved to see Sangge run off into the distance, but the sufferings of the other two were more than he had bargained for. A quick thrust through the ribs with his dagger would, he thought, be doing them a kindness; but just as he was about to act on this merciful impulse, the men jumped up, mad with pain, and began running round in circles. Then, as if acting on the same impulse, they rushed to the cliff and began banging their heads against it. They banged and banged until both of them were unconscious.

It was then that Trinket ran over to finish them off. But the sight that met his eyes was so terrible that for a while he stood gazing down in horror, trembling too violently to carry out his purpose. The men's faces had been completely eaten away: eyes, lips, cheeks, nose were gone, leaving only traces of red scum and a few sinews on the white bones.

I think we have to confess that here (as rather often in *Deer*) part of the fascination is the sheer nastiness of it. The book is not for readers who find the frequent inflicting of pain distasteful.

11. Action Again

Another characteristically successful scene is in English chapter 18, where Kang Xi and Trinket find the Fake Empress Dowager with her gender-ambiguous lover.

The Emperor Receives a Revelation (English chapter 18)

'There are no rats in here,' said the false Empress Dowager; but Trinket had already rushed over and rolled up the carpet by tugging on the tasselled cord.

'Rat or no rat,' said Kang Xi, 'I'm sure I heard something in there. Better open it, Laurie, and have a look.'

Trinket tried the fastening, but it was locked.

'What sort of game are you two playing at?' said the false Empress Dowager testily. 'You can see I'm not well. I'm not in the mood for all this horseplay in my bedroom.'

'Game? That's it!' said Kang Xi gaily. 'It's Princess Ning again. We were playing hide-and-seek and I couldn't find her. I bet she's hiding in that closet. Can you tell us where we can find the key?'

'I've told you, I'm not in the mood for this foolery,' said the false Empress Dowager. 'Now please just get out of here and leave me in peace.'

'It could be an assassin,' said Kang Xi excitedly. 'Better force the lock, Laurie.'

Trinket's metal-slicing dagger made quick work of the lock, but when he looked inside the closet he found only the bedding that the captive Empress Dowager had been lying in.

'She must have killed her,' he thought.

Rummaging among the bedclothes for some sign of their former occupant, he thought he saw the corner of a book. Sure enough, when he lifted the bedclothes up, there underneath was a copy of the now familiar *Sutra in Forty-Two Sections*. He covered it up again hastily and glanced round to see if Kang Xi had noticed. But Kang Xi was staring fixedly at a hump in the coverlet of the false Empress Dowager's bed — an extremely large hump that could not possibly be part of her anatomy.

Kang Xi at once assumed that the hump must be the real Empress Dowager. He had better act quickly, he thought, before the false one decided to kill her — if she had not done so already.

'Why!' he cried, striving as best he could to give an impression of boyish glee, 'you've had the Princess there with you all the time, hidden inside your bed! Laurie, come here and pull her out!'

Trinket rushed over and plunged a hand beneath the covers. But what it made contact with, to his considerable astonishment, was not the real Empress Dowager but a man's hairy leg which presently shot out from under the covers and kicked him hard in the chest. As he reeled backwards with a cry of pain, an extraordinary, comical figure bounced out of the bed. It was a naked man, but his body was so extremely fat and his legs so extremely sort that he looked more like a huge ball of flesh than a human being. He gathered up the false Empress Dowager, bedclothes and all, in his stumpy arms and shot out of the bedchamber, running, in spite of his burden and his dwarfish legs, at what seemed like superhuman speed. Three of the eight guards outside the building were knocked flying by him as he passed; the other five pursued, but he was over the garden wall in a trice and out of sight. Kang Xi, who had followed, called to them to come back and wait outside as before.

Trinket meantime, having recovered from the first shock of the blow, had had time to go back to the closet, retrieve the Sutra from underneath the bedding, and hide it inside his gown.

Kang Xi re-entered the bedchamber.

'So what do you make of that?'

'It looked like a monster,' said Trinket. 'A spook of some sort.'

'No, no, it was a man,' said Kang Xi. 'Didn't you see? Very short and fat, but it was a man all right. It must have been her lover.'

Trinket grinned, but Kang Xi looked serious.

'Where's the real Empress, then?'

'There's a secret compartment in the bed,' said Trinket.

He threw off the bedclothes and removed the lid of the receptacle in which the false Empress Dowager had kept her treasures, but this time the only thing in it was the gold-inlaid Emei stiletto which had been Hai Dafu's undoing. He thought for a bit.

'We could try taking the bottom of the bed out.'

Kang Xi helped him lift out the boards which made up the base of the bed. It was, as it turned out, an inspired guess, for there underneath, lying on a narrow mattress with only a thin coverlet over her, was the body of a woman. There could only have been a few inches between the bed-boards and her face.

'Light a candle,' said Kang Xi. (It was too dark inside the bed to make out who she was.)

What they saw when Trinket brought a lighted candle to shine on her were the rounded features that the false Empress Dowager in her disguise had tried to imitate. They helped her up into a sitting position. The woman opened her eyes but then quickly closed them again, dazzled by the light.

'Who...' she said faintly, 'who...?'

'This is His Majesty the Emperor,' said Trinket. 'He has come to rescue Your Majesty.'

'The Emperor?' said the woman, then gave a great sobbing cry and threw her arms round Kang Xi's neck.

12. Action with a Twist

The transvestite human meat-ball brings us to a quality in Cha's action scenes that can be guaranteed to sustain reader interest across language and cultural barriers — the element of oblique sexual play, or confusion. Here Cha is in his picaresque element. A good example is to be found in chapter 15, during Trinket's brothel-escapade from the Shaolin Monastery.

Green Girl and Blue Girl again, in Strange Circumstances (English chapter 15)

The weather was now getting warmer and he miserably reminded himself that it was already three months since he became a monk. It was high time, he decided, for a break.

Taking a supply of money with him, he left the monastery and struck out on a path that led down the slopes of Shaoshi Mountain to the market town of Tantoupu. At an outfitter's in the town he bought himself a complete new set of clothing, including hat and shoes, which he carried off to a cave he had passed on his way across the mountain.

There he changed into his new purchases, made his monk's clothes into a bundle, and went off to admire his reflection in the still, deep part of a mountain stream. Satisfied with what he saw there, he made his way back to Tantoupu, carrying his bundle with him.

The first thing he did when he was back in the town was to find a good restaurant, where he treated himself to a substantial meal of chicken, duck, fish, and pork. Then, having satisfied his most pressing craving, he set out to look for somewhere where he could hear once more the shouts of gamblers and the merry rattle of dice. After walking the length of seven or eight little back streets, he heard a cry of 'Aces up!' from the depths of a house he was passing. The sound was sweet music to his ears. He knocked at the door. A man of forty or so with a rakish tilt to his hat came out to answer.

'What do you want?'

Trinket took out a silver ingot and juggled it in his palm.

'I've got itchy fingers,' he said. 'I want to lose some of these.'

'This isn't a gaming-house, sonny,' said the man, 'it's a whore-house. And if it's girls you're after, you'd better come back in two or three years' time.'

Trinket was not to be discouraged.

'That's all right,' he said, 'Find me a few of the free girls, enough to make up three tables, and we'll have a party.'

He pressed the ingot, weighing all of two taels, into the man's palm and gave him a wink.

'To buy yourself a drink, friend.'

At the feel of the money the man's manner underwent an instant transformation.

'Why, thank you, sir. Come inside, sir,' he said affably; and as Trinket entered, he turned and bawled in a great voice to those within:

'Visitor!'

The bawd came hurrying out, all smiles when she saw this fifteen-year-old in his expensive, flashy clothes.

'Here's a young lad who's stolen from his parents and gone on the town to spend the money,' she thought. 'We'll pluck you well, my pigeon, don't you worry!'

She took him by the hand.

'I expect you want to see the girls, my dear. We ask for a little present first, that's the rule. Like a deposit.'

The smile fled from Trinket's face.

'Who are you trying to fool? I'm no innocent babe, lady. I was *born* in the trade.' He slapped a wad of notes, three or four hundred taels' worth, on the table. 'One tea-round, five pennyweights a girl; flower-top, three taels; server of the big pot, five pennyweights; and five pennyweights for the auntie. And I'm feeling generous so make it all double.'

The bawd's jaw dropped. Only someone brought up in brothel could have so fluent a command of the language.

'How silly of me! I should have seen at once you were a professional. Now just say what you want, my dear, and we'll do our best for you.'

'I suppose in a small place like this you wouldn't have any Suzhou girls or any from Datong?' said Trinket.

The bawd looked embarrassed.

'Well, yes and no. We've got one who passes for a Suzhou girl, but she isn't really. She can fool our ordinary customers, but I wouldn't recommend her for *you*, dear.'

'Never mind,' said Trinket cheerfully. 'Call them *all* in. Tell them three taels each, with my compliments.'

Soon the room was full of twittering, excited young women. No beauties these: most of them were big-footed country girls, crudely made up, and far too gaudily dressed. But Trinket was happy. All his young life he had dreamed of playing the big shot, the seriously rich customer who treats all the girls, and for whom the brothel puts on its smiling best. He sat in their midst, a girl in either arm, on one of whom he planted a big kiss, savouring as he did so a very strong reek of garlic.

There was a movement in the doorway as two more young women came elbowing their way in.

'Two more!' he said. 'Welcome, welcome! Come over and let me give you both a smacker!'

Next moment he jumped up with a cry of dismay, upsetting the two girls at his sides. The two who had just come in were the Blue Girl and the Green Girl! The Blue Girl laughted mirthlessly at his confusion.

'We've been following you ever since you got to town,' she said, 'wondering what mischief you would get up to next.'

Trinket's back was clammy with cold sweat.

'You — no, not you, the other one — are you...I mean, is it...is your throat better now?' he asked faintly.

The Green Girl ignored him. The Blue Girl continued as if he had said nothing:

'We've been waiting outside the monastery day after day for you to come out. Now our patience has at last been rewarded and we are going to have our revenge. We are going to cut you up into little tiny pieces.'

'When I grabbed you that time,' Trinket said to the Green Girl pleadingly, 'it wasn't...I mean, I didn't...I think...'

The Green Girl reddened and her eyes flashed.

'And what about what you said just now when we came in?' said the Blue Girl angrily.

'Don't talk to him, Sister, he isn't worth it,' said the Green Girl. 'Let's kill him now and get it over with!'

She drew her sword from its scabbard. There were screams from the girls as the blade flashed out, catching the tip of Trinket's hat as he ducked to avoid it. The hat fell off, revealing his bald head.

'I advise you two to get out of here,' Trinket shouted, crouching behind one of the girls. 'This is a whore-house. Only prostitutes come in here. What about your reputations?'

The Blue Girl and the Green Girl were now both slashing with their swords. In the crowded room they narrowly missed decapitating one of the young whores.

'I told you, this is a whore-house,' Trinket shouted. 'Don't you understand why I came here? I'm going to undress now. I'll be taking my trousers off in a minute.'

He had already begun unbuttoning and tossed a garment out to show that he meant business. The Green Girl turned and fled. The Blue Girl stared angrily for a second, then turned and followed her. The bawd and one of the tapsters were knocked over as she and the Green Girl rushed out of the house.

Trinket knew that he had only gained a momentary respite. The girls would wait outside and cut him down as soon as he emerged. Inside the brothel, meanwhile, it was pandemonium.

'Calm down, everybody!' he shouted 'there's ten taels for every one of you. That's a promise. Only just calm down!'

At once there was silence. He took out twenty taels and gave it to one of the tapsters.

'Get me a horse from somewhere, and have it waiting for me at the end of the lane.'

The man ran off to do his bidding. Trinket took out another twenty taels and held it out to one of the young whores.

'Here's twenty taels if you'll change clothes with me.'

The young woman was only too willing to oblige.

'Those two who came in just now are my wives,' said Trinket. 'They shaved my hair off to stop me going out, so that I wouldn't be able to go to places like this. Now they've found out that I escaped, they're trying to kill me.'

The bawd and the young whores were fascinated. They were used to wives following their husbands to the brothel and quarrelling with them outside; but shaving a husband's hair off to keep him at home, and going out sword in hand to kill him — such things were quite outside their experience.

Meanwile Trinket was changing into the young woman's clothes. The others entered into the spirit of the thing, some of them fetching rouge and eye-black to make up his face for him while others offered advice. Male customers drifted in from other parts of the house to watch the fun. To hide his baldness, Trinket tied a floral kerchief over his head.

Presently the tapster returned to say that he had got a horse.

'You want to be careful, sir. Your older missus is outside the front door and your Number Two is round the back. They've both got their swords drawn waiting for you!'

'Spiteful bitches!' said the bawd. 'The like of them take the food out of our mouths. We should all be starving if they had their way. I'd divorce them, my dear, if I was you. Then you can come here and enjoy yourself whenever you like.'

'Good idea,' said Trinket. 'but right now, could you do me a favour? Could you go to the front door and give that bitch in the blue dress there a piece of your mind? Keep her occupied. Don't go outside though, or you might get yourself hurt.'

This was a task that the bawd was both willing and well-qualified to perform. Soon such a violent stream of abuse was issuing from the front of the house that even Trinket might have learned from it if he had been listening. But he was too busy handing out the promised money to the whores.

'When I give the word, I want you all to rush out of the back door with me,' he said. 'If we go out together, those filthy wives of mine won't be able to catch me.'

Emboldened by the sight of so much silver, the young whores, fairly hopping with excitement, enthusiastically agreed. Just at that moment there was a sudden break in the stream of invective from the front, followed by a cry of pain.

'Ow! Aiyo!'

Trinket concluded that the Blue Girl had finally lost patience with the bawd and stepped inside to strike her.

'Now!' he said, and the twenty-odd whores, with him in their midst, streamed through the back door in a promiscuous mass, while the Green Girl, sword in hand, stood helplessly by, not knowing what to make of this sudden exodus.

The Blue Girl, however, sensing that something was up, abandoned the bawd and rushed round to the back of the house. But Trinket was already astride the horse and galloping away. The whores laughed jeeringly and taunted the 'jealous wives'.

'Run after him! Hurry!' the Blue Girl shouted; but it was obviously too late.

Once out of the town, Trinket began taking off the whore's clothing garment by garment and tossing it away as he rode along. He had left his bundle of monk's clothes behind in the brothel, so when he dismounted on the lower rear slopes of the mountain, leaving the horse to make its way back alone, he had to climb up to the monastery in his underwear. He managed somehow to sneak inside unobserved and, hiding his face in his hands, to make his way back to his cell. Once inside his cell, he washed the make-up from his face and put on a fresh habit.

'Now,' he thought, 'if those two wives of mine come back here to make trouble, I'll deny the whole thing.'

III. Envoi

What if anything can we learn from this selection of a dozen episodes? I believe that they point to one inescapable conclusion; that there is in translating this kind of popular fiction a compelling need for a greater freedom on the part of the translator, a freedom in terms of abridgment and adaptation, a playful freedom in terms of sheer invention if necessary. This freedom calls out for a concomitant generosity on the part of the "host" culture (i.e. the author and reader/critic), and abandonment of the judgmental and possessive cultural attitudes that have characterised so much of the past. This is necessary (and long overdue) if Chinese literature is ever to flow into the global mainstream, just as for the past three thousand years in Europe and the greater Mediterranean area, Jewish, Christian, Greek, Roman, and Arab cultures have allowed each others' literatures and philosophies to interweave through translation; just as over fifteen hundred years ago the Chinese body cultural allowed itself to be permeated by the translations of the Buddhist canon, with far reaching and hugely enriching consequences; just as Chinese culture has itself been disseminated (often with major if subtle change) into the neighbouring cultures of Japan, Korea and Vietnam.

On a more practical, cautionary note, that freedom can only be effective if it is coupled with an unstinting expenditure of time on the part of the translators, invested in endless revision and devotion to detail. Martial Arts fiction is not composed slowly. The author tosses it off at a terrific rate, just as Dumas did. But it is impossible to imagine the same ever being true of the translator.

Translating Jin Yong:
A Review of Four English Translations

Sharon Lai (賴慈芸)
Department of Applied English
Ming Chuan University

Abstract

The paper reviews four existing English translations of Jin Yong's works, and discusses the translation strategies applied.

The four translations discussed are Robin Wu's *Flying Fox of Snow Mountain* (1972), translated from *Xue-shan fei-hu* 雪山飛狐; Olivia Mok's *Fox Volant of the Snowy Mountain* (1994), also translated from the same work; Graham Earnshaw's *The Book and the Sword* (1995), translated from *Shu-jian en-chou lu* 書劍恩仇錄; and John Minford's *The Deer and the Cauldron: Book I* (1997), translated from the first volume of *Lu-ding ji* 鹿鼎記.

The challenges Jin Yong's translators face include how to translate culture-bound text, how to translate a good novel, and how to create a new genre. Omission, expansion and editorial are some of the strategies appiled. This review concluder thar, 1) both Wu and Earnshaw have some difficulties in dealing with cultural heritage; 2) both Earnshaw and Minford produce good novels in translation; and 3)Minford contributes most in gener-creating through building up a rich lexicon of martial arts fiction.

I. Introduction

Jin Yong is one of the best writers of contemporary martial arts fiction, the adventure literature of Chinese culture. His works would qualify for inclusion in Martin Green's list of "respectable adventures", side by side with the Icelandic Sagas and *The Three Musketeers*. Although good adventures are often neglected by literary critics and scholars, they deserve translation, partly because reading them is an important way to understand the culture that gave birth to them, and partly because they are simply good stories.

Nevertheless, it is a daunting enterprise to translate Jin Yong into English. Some of the obstacles are obvious: the gap between the source culture and the target culture, the absence of martial arts tradition and martial arts literature, the lack of corresponding lexicon, etc. Other obstacles are implicit. For example, the novels of Jin Yong are deliberate celebrations of Chineseness, full of nostalgic touches. Who knows whether the endless displays of Chinese culture in the novels bore or attract the non-Chinese readers?

Kungfu films (*gong-fu pian* 工夫片) bring another problem. Thanks to the popularity of the movies of Bruce Lee and Jackie Chan, and TV programs like the Carradine Kung Fu series, Chinese martial arts are no longer a totally strange spectacle for the general reader in the West. However, the martial arts in these movies, TV series and games, and the kungfu practised by western enthusiasts, is different from what can be found in martial arts fiction. To a Chinese viewer, kungfu films and martial arts films (*wu-xia pian* 武俠片),[1] which are mostly based on martial arts fiction, are two different genres. The former should be found in the "Action" section of a video shop, the latter, in the "Fantasy"

---

1   In its 1981 programme, the Hong Kong International Film Festival used "martial arts films" to translate *gong-fu pian*, and "swordplay films" for *wu-xia pian* (Urban Council of Hong Kong, 1996).

section.[2]   The heroes in martial arts films and fiction usually use swords and many fantastic weapons, while the kungfu heroes mostly depend on their hands and feet. In a sense, the western reception of kungfu films can be misleading if transferred to martial arts fiction.[3]   Actually, a martial arts novel is more like a cloak-and-dagger romance, a historical romance, or a fantasy, rather than an action story.

Whatever the reasons, English translations of Jin Yong's works are far behind the translations of some Eastern Asian languages. Jin Yong's works had been translated into several Southeast Asian languages[4]   as early as the 1950s and 1960s, when the author was first serializing them, but English translations had not appeared until 1972. The first English translation, *Flying Fox of Snow Mountain*, was the only English rendition for more than two decades.

In recent years, however, there has been a new wave of international interest in Jin Yong. Fourteen out of the total of Jin Yong's fifteen works had been translated into Korean between 1986 and 1989 (Li, 80-82). Translators in both the Japanese and English-speaking worlds also began to join their counterparts working in other languages. Since 1996, the Japanese publisher Tokuma Shoten 德間書店 has started to issue twelve of Jin Yong's works in Japanese translation, almost his complete works. As for English translations, *Fox Volant of the Snowy Mountain*, translated by Olivia Mok, was published in Hong Kong in 1994. In the same year, the first two chapters of *The Deer and the Cauldron*, translated by John Minford, were published in Australia. In 1995, *The Book and the Sword* translated by Graham Earnshaw was posted on the World

---

2   Although in reality, the video shops in Chinese communities usually have a special section for martial arts films, rather than a "fantasy" section.

3   Translators sometimes compound the confusion. For example, Graham Earnshaw, calls his original work a "kung fu novel".

4   These languages included Vietnamese, Thai (Lin Yiliang, 19), and Indonesian. In Indonesia, some of Jin Yong's works have been translated more than once. There are also imitations by local writers (Buckingham, 6).

Wide Web. The next year, the first chapter of *Eagles and Heroes* translated by John Minford and myself was distributed at a conference in Hong Kong and later published in *Translation Quarterly*. In October 1997, the first volume of *The Deer and the Cauldron* translated by John Minford was published by Oxford University Press (Hong Kong). The publisher also plans to issue other translations of Jin Yong in the near future.

In this paper, I will review four of the English translations, with the emphasis on the challenges these translators faced, their strategies and effects. Possible approaches for future translations will also be discussed.

II. A Sketch of the Reviewed Translations

Robin Wu's *Flying Fox of Snow Mountain*, translated from Jin Yong's *Xue-shan fei-hu* 雪山飛狐, appeared in four instalments in *Bridge* bimonthly in 1972. This New York-based bimonthly was published by the Asian-American Resource Center, an organization founded by a group of Asian Americans in 1971. Robin Wu was probably a Chinese American[5] living in New York.

Xue-shan fei-hu is one of Jin Yong's early works. Compared to most other works by Jin Yong, it is quite short: only about one hundred and twenty thousand Chinese characters. This novel is not one of Jin Yong's major works, but it is quite a special one: the element of the detective story is even stronger than that of martial arts fiction. People with different aims gather together to make clear the truth of a murder that happened twenty-seven years previously, a murder related to a treasure handed down over a period of more than a hundred years. The protagonist, Hu Fei 胡斐 or the Flying Fox, is the orphaned son of the murdered martial arts master. When the story begins, the Flying Fox is ready to take revenge.

5　His romanization of some names differs from pinyin. All the "r" sounds are replaced by "y". For example, "Ruan" 阮 is spelt "Yuan"; "Ren" 人 is spelt "Yuan"; "Ruo" 若 is spelt "Yu".

Jin Yong first serialized this novel in 1959, when he was working for the film industry. The technique of this novel is clearly influenced greatly by western drama. All the events happen within one day and at one place; the main activity of the whole novel is the story-telling by different parties.[6]

Robin Wu's translation was based on the first edition of the novel, since Jin Yong first revised this novel in 1976. It is an abridged translation, especially of the second half of the novel. The first three instalments were devoted to the first five chapters of the original story, while the last instalment covered all the remaining five chapters. It seems that the translator changed his plan during the later phase of translation and rushed through the last instalment, leaving an uneven translation: the first half of the translation is merely abridged, but the second half is actually drastically retold. As a version it is reasonably readable, but over-simplified. The translator's insufficient knowledge of Chinese history and culture constitute another problem.[7]

Olivia Mok chose the same novel as Robin Wu. Although not one of Jin Yong's major works, *Xue-shan fei-hu* is the first one to have been fully translated into English. One may attribute the fact to the book's manageable length and comparatively fewer characters. This novel's compact structure is also probably one of the reasons. Robin Wu abridged, while Olivia Mok did a complete translation, with a map, illustrations of Chinese weapons and paralytic points, as well as an introduction to the story and the characters. Like Pearl Buck's *All Men Are Brothers*, this translation follows the original so closely that it sometimes sacrifices idiom.

---

6   Wen Rui'an has analysed this novel in great detail in his *Xi xue-shan fei-hu yu yuan-yang dao* 析雪 山飛狐與鴛鴦刀 (Taipei: Yuan-liu, 1985). It is also the first novel by Jin Yong to be studied in depth by a Western scholar. Kai Portmann's *Der Fliegende Fuchs vom Schneeberg: Die Gattung des chinesischen Ritterromans (wuxia xiaoshuo) und der Erfolgsautor Jin Yong* (Bochum: Brockmeyer, 1994) also focuses on an analysis of this novel.

7   The most serious example is his mistaking the Ming Dynasty for the Manchu regime. There are also many minor mistakes at the level of vocabulary. For example, the chief servant refers to his mistress as *zhu-mu* 主母, which is mistakenly translated as "the mother of the master".

Graham Earnshaw's *The Book and the Sword*, translated and abridged from Jin Yong's *Shu-jian en-chou lu* 書劍恩仇錄, has been posted on the World Wide Web since late 1995, but has not been published in book form yet.

Shu-jian en-chou lu is Jin Yong's first novel. Like *Xue-shan fei-hu*, the background of this novel is set in the early Qing Dynasty. But *Shu-jian* is more complicated than *Xue-shan*: it deals with ethnic conflict between the Han Chinese, the Manchus and the Muslims; a palace secret; a talented-scholar-and-beauty romance, and the brotherhood of a secret society.

Although still a shorter work by Jin Yong's standards, the length of *Shu-jian* is four times that of *Xue-shan*, still much longer than the average English novel. This makes an abridgement defensible. The original novel is composed of twenty chapters, while Earnshaw's version has only nine "parts". Except for Part Six which covers four original chapters, each of the remaining eight parts covers two original chapters. Most of the plot has been kept, but the "co-ordinate description" or *descriptio*,[8] the background of the characters, the details of their psychological make-up, fighting details, and allusions have been heavily cut. Only in Part Six (the original eleventh to thirteenth chapters) does the translator remove part of the main plot: the story about two supportive couples is completely removed. The translator has certain difficulties in translating passages in the literary language, especially poems and allusions.[9] But this translation is much more idiomatic than the earlier two.

8　The so-called *descriptio* is mentioned by Patrick Hanan (21). It is one of the most popular techniques of story-telling: the narrator or story-teller inserts seemingly irrelevant paragraphs into the story, maybe a piece of historical or geographical information, or a strange local custom.

9　For example, in the first chapter, Lu Feiqing leaves a note for his girl pupil Li Yuanzhi. The note is written in the literary language, and the translator does not understand it well. In the same chapter, Lu Feiqing chants a ci-poem by Xin Qiji 辛棄疾 of the Song Dynasty. Earnshaw's reads: "His body and name scarred by a hundred battles/The general approaches a bridge across a river/And turns to look back 10,000 miles/At the dead men left behind" (將軍百戰身名裂／向河梁，回首萬里，故人長絕). Although there is no specific name in the original poem, the poet alludes to the story of the General Li Ling 李陵 and his good friend Su Wu 蘇武 of the Han Dynasty.

John Minford's First Book of *The Deer and the Cauldron*, translated from Jin Yong's last novel *Lu-ding ji* 鹿鼎記, was published by Oxford University Press in late 1997. Before that, the first two chapters had been published in the Australian National University journal *East Asian History* in 1994, especially for Jin Yong's visit to the Sydney Festival Writers Week and the accompanying forum on martial arts fiction. In 1996, these two sample chapters were exposed to a variety of opinions from scholars at a conference entitled "The Question of Reception: Martial Arts Fiction in English Translation", held at Lingnan college in Hong Kong. This is the first translation of one of Jin Yong's major works, and the first translation to have been seriously discussed in this manner.

The five-volume *Lu-ding ji* is one of Jin Yong's longest novels. It is, again, a story set in the early Qing Dynasty. But it is much more admired by critics than *Xue-shan* and *Shu-jian*, and more popular with the general public. Wei Xiaobao 韋小寶, the hero of this novel, has become one of the best known fictional figures in the contemporary worldwide Chinese community. As Gereme Barmé says, Wei Xiaobao "has achieved the status of a common cultural property"(41).

The Deer and the Cauldron: First Book is a complete translation of the first volume of the original with slight editorial changes, including the renumbering of chapters.[10]

III. The Challenges

To discuss the challenges of translation, one has to examine the nature of Jin Yong's novels first. Jin Yong is the heir of traditional Chinese fiction in the vernacular. In Pearl Buck's term, martial arts fiction belongs to the tradition of

---

Since Li Ling surrendered to barbarian *xiongnu* 匈奴 tribe, Su Wu decided to break with him and bid him farewell. It is obvious that the translator has no knowledge of this story and has made several mistakes, including mistranslating gu-ren 故人 [friend] as "dead men".

10   The original first chapter is renamed "Prologue", and the original second chapter thus becomes the first chapter in this translation.

the "indigenous Chinese novel", a tradition that has all but died out in modern Chinese writing. Unlike most contemporary Chinese novels which are greatly influenced by western writing, martial arts fiction has its own tradition, its own conventions and language, part of which can be traced back a thousand years. The stories of Jin Yong all occur in an imagined pre-modern China, and his narrative mimics that of traditional Chinese fiction. In this respect, translating Jin Yong's works has much in common with translating classical Chinese fiction.

But Jin Yong is still a contemporary writer. His martial arts novels are contemporary works for contemporary readers, despite the archaistic language of both the narrative and the dialogue, and their historical setting. These novels are created to appeal to modern readers. The plots are complicated and exciting; the characters have modern views about such subjects as nationhood and love. The formulaic fighting scenes of military romances and the doggerel poems of *Water Margin* are replaced by cinematically vivid descriptions, which are more enjoyable for modern readers. In this respect, translators have to pay attention to the reading habit of the novel readers in the target language. The translations themselves should be enjoyable novels.

And Jin Yong's works belong to the genre known as martial arts fiction. As one of the popular genres, martial arts fiction has clearly recognizable core elements, its own format, rules and language. Jin Yong writes in the context of martial arts fiction: he repeatedly alludes to previous works of the same tradition, and uses the shared language and expressions of the genre. He does not need to explain the cosmology or ideas shared by martial arts writers and readers. In this respect, the challenge is how to constitute a genre which is absent in the target culture.

Therefore, a translator has to face the three challenges at the same time: how to translate culture-bound text, how to translate a good novel, and how to create a new genre.

IV. Strategies and Effects

With the three challenges in mind, I am going to discuss some translation strategies applied by different translators, as well as their effects. Among these strategies, omission and expansion is mainly for culture-bound parts, editorial changes and style is for the requirement of a good novel, and the lexicon is for the creation of a new genre.

1. Omission and Expansion

Jin Yong had his readers firmly in mind when he created his novels. His original readers are Chinese who have grown up, or are growing up, in a Chinese community. That is, they are familiar, to a greater or lesser extent, with Chinese history, culture, values and numerous customs. Moreover, it is very likely that the readers have read other martial arts novels, or come to know many stories in the martial arts tradition, before encountering Jin Yong's works. There is no need for Jin Yong to tell his readers what *Water Margin* is, or who General Yue Fei 岳飛 is.

The target readers of the English translation of Jin Yong — readers from a western background — are not on an equal footing with the original readers. They are not even on an equal footing with the readers of Asian language translations of Jin Yong, such as Korean or Japanese translations. To bridge the gap between the original readers and the target readers, one can either omit the foreign parts, or inform the reader what he or she may not know, through footnotes and other types of annotation.

If the translation is for academic purposes, the translator surely should provide the reader as with much information as possible. As William H. Nienhauser, Jr., the translator of *Shi-ji* 史記 declares, "...we modern translators (of *Shi-ji*) must provide our readers with all the material we know they should possess to reach an equal footing with the reader Ssu-ma Ch'ien in mind"(19). However, none of Jin Yong's existing translations are for academic purposes. To provide readers with an exhaustive knowledge of Chinese culture and the martial arts tradition in a single novel seems not practical. Therefore, the problem is: how much information should the translator omit or add? And how?

The description of Miss Miao Ruolan 苗若蘭 in *Xue-shan* is a typical example for Robin Wu's approach. In the original story, Miss Miao is pictured as an well-educated young lady of a rich family. She is served by a clever maid and two servant women who carry a cat, a pot containing an orchid which "would wither at the smell of a male",[11] and a white parrot which can chant poems. She asks her maid to burn different kinds of incense on different occasions and drinks Oolong tea with rose petals. She plays the classical instrument the *qin* 琴, and chants poems from *The Book of Songs* as an implicit way of conveying her feelings. These are typical, even stereotyped, descriptions for a young lady in classical Chinese fiction. The translator simply omits cat, orchid, parrot, incense, tea and the musical instrument all together, making Miss Miao an ordinary girl. Although this omission does not change the story, the flavour of classical Chinese fiction is lost.

Another problem of this translation is, Robin Wu sometimes uses Western allusions. Expressions such as "Adam's apple", "Achilles' heel", "meet Emperor Li in Hades", and "the marriage between beauty and beast" just destroy the aura of ancient China.

Earnshaw also omits cultural details systematically. For example, there are densely packed allusions in the original tenth chapter of *Shu-jian*, when the emperor is watching a beauty competition on Western Lake, and flirting with a famous singsong girl. The decoration of every boat alludes to famous love stories, like "Western Chamber" and "The Dream of Du Liniang". The judges in the competition are all famous men of letters of that time, such as Yuan Mei 袁枚 (1716-1797), Ji Xiaolan 紀曉嵐 (1724-1805) and Zheng Banqiao 鄭板橋 (1693-1765). Every song the singsong girl sings alludes to a well-known love story. And the gifts the emperor gives her are all paintings by famous painters of

---

11　「聞不得男人氣」(52).

the Ming Dynasty, such as Zhu Yunming 祝允明 (1460–1526) and Tang Yin 唐寅 (1470–1523).

It is indeed very difficult to deal with these allusions. It may take pages to explain these stories and people. Earnshaw keeps the event but removes all these specific names and the stories behind them. This is basically not a bad choice, since these allusions would not arouse much feeling in the English reader. But sometimes the omission changes the whole cultural image. For example, in the above episode, the singsong girl gives the emperor a perfumed letter, on which she writes a doggerel poem to suggest a rendezvous the next day:

> The Verdant Tower is immersed in the perfume;
> The songs tell the stories of the romantic Six Dynasties.
> The spring is still tender this evening,
> But if you return tomorrow, you will see the full blossom around the Tower.
> 暖翠樓前粉黛香
> 六朝風致説平康
> 踏青歸去春猶淺
> 明日重來花滿樓

In classical Chinese society, many famous singsong girls were able to write poems (though not necessarily good ones) as a means of flirting with men of letters. In Earnshaw's translation, the poem is replaced by a single word: "Tomorrow". A Western lady in a cloak-and-dagger romance (like Milady in *The Three Musketeers*) might have written such a note, but surely not a famous Chinese singsong girl by the shores of Western Lake. Although Earnshaw declared that he has changed nothing, but has only omitted certain things,[12] this example shows that omission can in fact entail change.

Olivia Mok seldom removes things, but expands a lot. She often inserts

---

12 "There are some differences between the original and my translation, but they are differences only of omission." (http://village.ios.com./~earnshaw/B&s.htm)

explanations within the text. For example, *hu-kou* 虎口 is translated as "the Tiger's Mouth, the web between the thumb and first finger"(34), and *nei-gong* 內功 is translated as "endomarts, the martial art of developing strength through breathing and other exercises of his internal organs"(46).

This is sometimes a handy strategy to inform readers about foreign expressions or objects, but it becomes inappropriate in dialogue. Take the following dialogue between two sworn brothers as an example. In the third chapter of *Xue-shan*, Paladin Hu (The great grand-father of the Flying Fox) is attacked from the back by his three sworn brothers. He cries before dying: "We four are sworn brothers, why... why are you attacking me from behind?" Paladin Miao answers him: "You ... dare to mention our sworn brotherhood?"(my translation)

（胡衛士）喝道：「咱四人義結金蘭，幹麼……幹麼施暗算於我？」
（苗衛士）叫道：「你……還有臉提到義氣兩字？」(67)

This impassioned dialogue at a tragic moment, is translated in a very long-winded way by Olivia Mok:

Then he cried out, "We four *have pledged ourselves in sworn Brotherhood to owe allegiance to each other, to realize the same common ambition and to commit ourselves to the same common cause.* Yet... yet... why have you attacked me like cowards?"
(Myrmidon Miao) shouted: "You...still assume airs, bragging about *integrity, principles, valiance, altruism, chivalry, loyalty, righteousness,* and all the rest!"(100)

It seems that the translator is trying to explain the expression *yi-jie jin-lan* 義結金蘭 and the term *yi-qi* 義氣 within the text. As a result, she uses twenty-seven words (my underlining) in the first sentence to translate the four characters of Hu's exclamation, totally betraying the original style. In the second sentence, she goes even further, lining up seven definitions to translate a two-character term. The translator has provided a lot of information for her readers, but she ends up failing to catch the style of the novel.

Minford also incorporates a number of hidden notes in the text, especially to explain the allusions. For example, in the original first chapter of *Lu ding ji*, the scholar Lü Liuliang 呂留良 makes an allusion to Peach Blossom Spring (*Tao-yuan* 桃源). The translator incorporates the following passage in the text:

> He thought of the poet Tao Yuanming's story about the fisherman who, by following a stream that flowed between flowering peach trees, had stumbled on an earthly paradise — a place where refugees from ancient tyranny had found a haven.(10)

This passage merges in with the text smoothly, without a trace of the translator's interference.

In some cases, however, Minford steps further in and sneaks his own interpretation into the text. For example, in the original Chapter Eight (the seventh chapter in the translation), the hero Wei Xiaobao is initiated into the Triad Society. The translator omits the text of the Induction oath, paraphrases some of the content, and expresses his own opinion through the mouth of Wei Xiaobao:

> Apart from what it said about the Great Ming being the rightful rulers and expelling the foreign foe, *there wasn't a great deal in it that Trinket could understand.* It seemed that they all belonged to a family called "Hong" in which Heaven was their father, Earth was their mother, the sun was their brother, and the moon was their sister. Apart from the surname "Hong", each of them, on entering the Society, acquired the secret name "Jinlan" — meaning Golden Orchid. (*"What's the good of a name," thought Trinket, "if everyone's got the same one?"*). . .They were all supposed to have been born on the same day. Old Cai even read out the date. (*Trinket knew this didn't make sense, but decided he'd better not to ask about it.*) They prayed 'in the words of the oath made in the Peach Garden' that they might all die on the same day. And there was more besides."(338-339)
> 天地萬有，回復大明，滅絶胡虜。吾人當同生同死，倣桃園故事，約爲兄弟，姓洪名金蘭，合爲一家。拜天爲父，拜地爲母，日爲兄，月爲姊妹，復拜五祖及始祖萬

雲龍爲洪家之全神靈。吾人以甲寅七月二十五日丑時爲生時……(309)

The three sentences I underline are all added by the translator. In the original, there is no indication that Wei Xiaobao didn't understand the oath. His questions about the name "Hong Jinlan" and the supposed date of birth are actually asked by the translator, for himself and for his fellow readers. The original oath, which is the same as the one found in historical documents about the Triad Society, is not difficult to understand in Chinese; the practice of using a fabricated name (including supposed parents and supposed date of birth) as a collective identity is not unusual in Chinese secret societies. Here the translator has interfered and substantially altered the original text.

To deal with the cultural gap between source and target cultures, the four translators apply omission and expansion quite often. Robin Wu omits too much to preserve the Chineseness, while Olivia Mok expands too much to keep the story going. Earnshaw's omission of some proper names and allusions are defensible as are certain paraphrasings of Minford's. Among the four translators, Minford is the most experienced to deal with classical Chinese fiction. Unlike Olivia Mok's wordy explination, his hidden annotations are so smooth that few readers will know they are added to the text. But his interpretation for some passages may arguable.[13]

2. Editorial efforts and style

In many ways, Jin Yong's novels are very different from contemporary English novels. To produce an enjoyable novel in English, some editorial changes are defensible. Abridgement is the most often used strategy for this purpose.

Although these novels are not particularly long by the standard of the genre of martial arts fiction, they are still immensely long for his translators and for the English-language readers. Each of his major works contains over a million

---

13 Such "disloyal" parts are very interesting to discuss. I think that these parts remind Chinese readers with the difference between cultures which we otherwise would not notice.

characters. If fully translated, each of the English versions would easily run to more than two thousand pages. Even for shorter works like *Shu-jian*, an unabridged English version would be almost one thousand pages long. A novel this size is obviously overlong for modern English readers, and abridgement should be considered as a realistic strategy.

Both Robin Wu's and Earnshaw's translations are abridged. Minford's first book of *The Deer and the Cauldron* is a full translation, but the rest of the version will be abridged. Our on-going project *Eagles and Heroes* will also be an abridged version. How to abridge is a real concern for Jin Yong's translators.

At first glance, Jin Yong's works do not seem difficult to abridge. There are many fighting details, and lots of passages of *descriptio* which seem not directly related to the story, such as the history of certain weapons, a historical anecdote concerning some place, or a piece of information about wine. Translators tend to remove these passages when there is a need of abridgement. However, this seemingly convenient strategy is actually quite risky. Fighting is the essential element of martial arts fiction, and *descriptio* is one of the most important characteristics which distinguish Jin Yong from most other martial arts novelists. It is through these "irrelevant" stories of weapons, historical anecdotes, or even details concerning certain types of wine, that Jin Yong creates the aura of Chineseness of his novels. A translation without these passages seriously betrays Jin Yong.

Robin Wu and Graham Earnshaw basically apply the same strategy: they follow the main plot, but remove many details. Robin Wu removes almost all fighting details from the novel. A page-long fight is often retold in a single sentence. For example, in the ninth chapter, there is a fight between Flying Fox and his nine enemies. But the complicated, three-page-long fight is encapsulated in the following three sentences:

> He (Flying Fox) leaps from the bed and saves Gold-Face Buddha in the nick of time. He challenges Martial Fan to a duel. The latter loses and is forced to free Gold-Face Buddha. (IV, 45)

A passage like this is deprived of the essential characteristic of martial arts fiction. Robin Wu's abridgement strategy seems inappropriate for a martial arts novel.

Earnshaw preserves more fighting scenes than Robin Wu does, only omitting certain details or names of moves. He also removes a lot of "irrelevant description", including passages concerning the background and psychological status of the characters. However, being the first of Jin Yong's martial arts novels, *Shu-jian* has one obvious shortcoming: given the length of the novel, there are too many important characters — the fifteen chieftains of the anti-Manchu Red Flower Society, the Manchu Emperor and his numerous followers, the two Muslim princesses and their kinsmen, the dart-escorts, and other characters in the River and Lake community. Unfortunately, Earnshaw's abridgement only serves to underline this shortcoming. The result is a crowd of characters jostling around in the story without distinct personalities.[14]

Neither translator successes. Trimming seemingly irrelevant descriptions will greatly alter Jin Yong's style. In this respect, the selective abridgement method used by H. S. in translating "The Adventure of a Chinese Giant" (*Shui-hu*), and by Arthur Waley in his *Monkey*, is worth consideration. H. S. chooses the story of Lu Da 魯達. When dealing with Lu Da, he seldom misses a single sentence; when dealing with other characters, he abridges drastically. For example, he devotes four chapters of the translation to the original Chapter Four in Shui-hu, which is all about Lu Da; but just uses one chapter of the translation to cover the story about Lin Chong 林沖 in the original Chapters Seven and Eight. Since H. S. translates every detail about Lu Da, the hero of his story, this character is very impressive. Lin Chong may also be a very impressive character, but that is another story. Arthur Waley applies the same approach: "I ... omit many episodes, but translate those that are retained almost in full, ..."(7). I think this

---

14　The translator himself sometimes makes further confusion. For example, the Thirteenth Brother of the Red Flower Society Jiang Sigen 蔣四根, has a nickname "Copper-head Crocodile". In the first half of the story, the translator calls him "Crocodile Jiang", but later "Copper-head Jiang".

approach suit Jin Yong's works better than "all over" trimming.

Since the second volume of *The Deer and the Cauldron* has not been published, there is no way for us to discuss the abridgement policy of the translator. But in the first volume, Minford has made some editorial efforts to appeal to the reading habit for his readers. The rearrangement of chapters is an example. The first chapter of *Lu-ding ji*, which describes the historical background of the novel, is written in a style very different from the following chapters. The translator then makes a reasonable rearrangement: treating the original first chapter as "prologue".

Chapter and section headings are another example. Minford replaces the original couplet titles with chapter headings in the style of the older-style British romance, such as Howard Pyle's *The Merry Adventures of Robin Hood*, and divides each chapter into several sections, each with a shorter heading. The content pages go like this:

> **Chapter 1** — *In which Trinket and Whiskers set out from Yangzhou for the Capital; of their Adventures on the Way; and of the Stories Trinket tells concerning the Golden Age, Heroes and Mongols, Turtles, Elephants, and Mice*
> Yangzhou, City of Pleasure — Trinket and Whiskers become acquainted on the Road to Victory Hill — Goatee Wu and Baldy Wang — The Troopers Arrive — Trinket on Horseback — The Satrap's Men — Whiskers the Would-be Master — Trinket the Storyteller

Compare this with a section from the content page of *Robin Hood*:

> **Part Second** — *In which shall be told how Robin Hood turned Butcher, and how he revenged himself upon the Sheriff. Also, of the famous adventures that befel Little John at the Nottingham Archery Match, and how he entered the Sheriff's service.*
> Chapter I. Robin Hood turns Butcher.
> Chapter II. Little John goes to the Fair at Nottingham Town.
> Chapter III. How Little John Lived at the Sheriff's House.

Although the translator does not actually change his "chapters" into "parts", nor call his sections "chapters", it is clearly in the same style as *Robin Hood*. Earnshaw also rearranges the chapters of *The Book and the Sword* in a similar way: he calls the original chapters "parts", and divides each "part" into several sections. Both translators are aware of the different reading habits of the source readers and target readers: Chinese readers enjoy very long undivided chapters, while English readers are used to shorter chapters. Earnshaw's "parts" and "sections" are just numbered without any title, while Minford's have somewhat archaic titles and convey more the flavour of the historical romance.

Among the four translators, Mok makes least editorial changes (She occasionally changes the sentence sequence for logical reasons). Unfortunately, her translation is also the least to satisfy the requirement of a good novel. The style of narration is the most obvious example.

Because of the huge linguistic difference between Chinese and English, it is impossible to require identify syntactic movement in the translation between the two languages. But Olivia Mok sometimes makes such a great shift of syntactic movement that the style of the original is totally changed. The following passage is a typical example of Mok's style of translation:

> 只見一個黃衣少女笑吟吟的站在門口，膚光勝雪，雙目猶如一泓清水，在每個人臉上轉了一轉。這少女容貌秀麗之極，當真如明珠生暈，美玉瑩光，眉目間隱然有一股書卷的清氣。廳上這些人都是浪跡江湖的武林豪客，斗然間與這樣一個文秀少女相遇，宛似走進了另一個世界，不自禁的爲她一副清雅高華的氣派所懾，各似自慚形穢，不敢褻瀆。(53)

The translator chops the first two flowing sentences into six simpler sentences (76):

1. A young damsel clad in gamboge was seen smiling from the portal (只見一個黃衣少女笑吟吟的站在門口).
2. She had a fair complexion (膚光勝雪).

3. Her eyes were like limpid pools and she cast a couple of glances at the people assembled (雙目猶如一泓清水，在每個人臉上轉了一轉).

4. Her looks and manners showed unusual refinement and inexpressible grace (這少女容貌秀麗之極).

5. Her brows gave her the air of a literateur (眉目間隱然有一股書卷的清氣).

6. She seemed like an orient pearl or an effulgent jadeite (當眞如明珠生暈，美玉瑩光).

And she chops the third sentence into four shorter sentences (76-77):

7. All those present in the hall were bold and brave members of the Martial Brotherhood, outlaws who had adventured across the kingdom (廳上這些人都是浪跡江湖的武林豪客).

8. They seemed to be mesmerized by suddenly chancing upon a damsel as fair and fine as she (斗然間與這樣一個文秀少女相遇，宛似走進了另一個世界).

9. They were all captivated by the ethereal grace of her poise, and were quelled by her beauty (不自禁的爲她一副清雅高華的氣派所懾).

10. They stood uncomfortably, spellbound and enraptured (各似自慚形穢，不敢褻瀆).

As a result, she uses a total of ten sentences to translate the original three. Moreover, nine out of these ten sentences begin with nouns (A young damsel/ She/ Her eyes/ Her looks/ Her brows/ She/ They/ They/ They), making the whole passage monotonous. The translator has altered the text on at least two counts: she has cut every sentence into shorter ones, and she has made the flowing description plain. She has tried to translate everything, but the style has been changed.

It seems Wu has no consistent policy in abridgement: sometimes he trims, and sometimes he retells. Earnshaw is aware of the problem of reading habit. He divides the chapter into sections and makes a more even abridgement than Wu does: every two original chapters become one "part" in the translation. Unfortunately, this strategy seems not very successful. Minford makes more editorial efforts for his readers. He rearranges the chapters and even makes-up romance-like headings, offering the target readers a highly enjoyable novel.

3. Lexicon: For the Creation of a New Genre

One of the most interesting things about translating Jin Yong is, martial arts fiction in English translation is in effect a brand-new literary genre. The translators are pioneers, and they have the license to try out many innovative strategies, in order to create what will be a new genre in English.

Like science fiction, fantasy or romance, martial arts fiction has its own language, which has been mutually created and recognized by all individual writers of the genre. Part of this lexicon is handed down from traditional martial arts works, and part of it has been created by modern writers. The weapons, martial arts styles, different schools or organizations in the community, conventions, customs, the martial arts ethic, cliches and stock expressions, and some half-imagined types of martial arts, such as *dian-xue* 點穴 or *qing-gong* 輕功 are all included here. This is the martial arts novelist's stock in trade. A writer of martial arts fiction may add some new terms, usually the names of strange weapons, schools, and martial arts styles. But all martial arts writers and readers respect the existing language — the rules of the game.

To build up such a lexicon, translations of classical fiction on martial arts themes can help little. This is partly because the number of Chinese special terms in modern martial arts fiction is far greater than that in traditional fiction, and partly because few English translators of traditional fiction have been aware of the importance of a martial arts lexicon.

The most radical (and "foreignizing") way to create such a lexicon is through romanization. This can effectively re-create an alien world. James Clavell's *Shogun* is a good example: this popular novel about seventeenth-century Japan contains a large number of romanized Japanese words (again, often provided with explanations), and the effect is to conjure up a world full of Japanese colour. Some romanized Japanese words, like samurai, have been already well accepted in English. But romanization has its risks. Many translators of Chinese fiction have complained about the confusing effect of romanized Chinese. With so many people's names and place names to be romanized, an excess of romanized terms can become a grave burden for readers.

Another, quite different, source for this lexicon may include the vocabulary of Medieval knighthood, the Order of the Knights Templars, Robin Hood tales and the like. Lexicon of this type can enhance the fantastic colour of the novel without burdening the reader with hard-to-remember romanized words. However, the risk of this domesticating approach lies in the sense of anachronism, and a mix of register.[15] Besides, words of this type may bring with them undesirable cultural connotations.

Some translators try to avoid this problem of lexicon. Both Robin Wu and Earnshaw omit a lot of martial arts terms when they abridge the story. For example, in the first chapter of *Xue-shan*, there is a fight in which six martial arts practitioners are involved. Each of the six has his or her own weapon, including a flying dagger (*fei-dao*飛刀), chained maces (*lian-zi-chui*鏈子錘), a monk's broadsword (*jie-dao*戒刀), a steel rod (*gang-bien*鋼鞭), twin hooks (*shuang-guai*雙拐), and a broadsword (*dan-dao*單刀). In Robin Wu's version, however, five out of the six are described as using plain swords as their weapons.[16]   In this way, the translator avoids the problem of how to translate the different weapons, and the names and details of special moves corresponding to each individual weapon. Even the most important fight in the story, the duel between the Flying Fox and the opponent of his late father, is simplified in the same way. Flying Fox's broadsword is replaced, again, by a sword. This saves the translator the trouble of translating the author's complicated theory as to the difference between broadsword and sword. But it also sacrifices some of the richness of the martial arts world. Earnshaw also omits some martial arts terms. For instance, in the first chapter of *Shu-jian*, the term *jiang-hu* 江湖 appears eight times and Earnshaw

---

15 Barry Asker has complained to this effect when reading Minford's *The Deer and The Cauldron* (159).

16 The only weapon he kept was *gang-bian* or "steel whip" in his translation. But this is a mistranslation. There are two kinds of *bian* among Chinese weapons. One is whip, and the other is something like a rod. The *gang-bian* is the second.

simply omits it each time. (In later chapters, he sometimes translates it as "underworld".)

As for Olivia Mok, she is hampered by her "one-word-for-many" policy. Being hesitant to coin a new lexicon for martial arts fiction, she applies a limited range of general words in many different places, thereby confusing her readers. Although she does not skip any word, she confuses many terms and fails to clarify the relation among them.

For example, "master" is used in the following seven terms:

1. "Grand Master" for *zhang-men* 掌門 (head of a martial arts school)
2. "Great Master" for *da-shi* 大師 (respectful term of address for a Buddhist monk)
3. "kind master" for *en-shi* 恩師 (teacher, so called by his or her disciples)
4. "master" for *zhuang-zhu* 莊主 (lord of an estate)
5. "master" for *zhai-zhu* 寨主 (lord of a robbers' den)
6. "master" for *jia-zhu* 家主 (lord, so called by his servants)
7. "master" for *gao-shou* 高手 (expert or adept)

They are all correct in their own context. However, the use of one word to represent seven different terms just confuses readers. Similarly, "outlawry" is involved in the following five expressions:

1. "the outlawry" for *jiang-hu* 江湖 (River and Lake)
2. "filthy outlaws" for *jian-zei* 奸賊 (brats)
3. "the outlawry" for *wu-lin* 武林 (martial arts community)
4. "the outlawry" for *lü-lin* 綠林 (Greenwood or robbers' community)
5. "the Outlawry" for *Gai-bang* 丐幫 (Guild of Beggars)

Jiang-hu, *wu-lin* and *lü-lin* are different concepts in martial arts fiction. *Jiang-hu* or River and Lake is the overall world in which all the stories of martial arts fiction take place. *Wu-lin* or the martial arts community, a narrower term than River and Lake, is the community made up of the various schools of martial arts, often good or well-known martial arts schools. *Lü-lin* or Greenwood is quite a negative term in contemporary martial arts fiction, representing the community of bandits. The Greenwood is one constituent member of River and Lake, but is often despised by the martial arts community. In terms of Science Fiction, River and Lake is the space; the martial arts community is the community of "good" spaceships and their crews; and the Greenwood is the community of despised space-bandits.

Olivia Mok uses "outlawry" to translate the three key words, simply removing their differences. It is a serious loss from the perspective of the genre. Moreover, she even uses the same word to translate *Gai-bang*, or the Guild of Beggars, compounding the confusion. Moreover, since all members of River and Lake are in a sense outlaws, it sounds odd for them to curse each other as "filthy outlaws".

John Minford is the first translator to consciously attempt to create a lexicon for martial arts fiction in translation. He romanizes some terms, like "Shifu" (*Shi-fu* 師父, the instructor of martial arts); coins some, like River and Lake (*jiang-hu* 江湖); and borrows some from other languages, like nom de guerre (*wai-hao* 外號, nicknames used by martial arts practitioners). He also applies some stock terms, like "Brave Man and True" (*Ying-xiong hao-han* 英雄好漢), to replace the simple "heroes" often used by other translators. Through this lexicon, the translator successfully establishes a series of conventions, a style that is different from that of the other translations of Jin Yong, and that can serve as a useful reference for later translations.

I would like to argue that, since martial arts fiction has a special lexicon in the original language, it also needs a special lexicon in translation. Take *jiang-hu* as an example. This word represents an imagined world in which all the martial arts stories happen. It has its own members, organizations, hierarchy, moral code, laws, objectives, etc. "Our circle", "the outlawry" (Mok), or "the underworld" (Earnshaw) all fail to communicate the uniqueness of the genre. By contrast, "River and Lake" used systematically by John Minford (and explained at considerable length in his General Glossary of Terms) preserves more of the colour of the genre. For the same reason, Earnshaw's "Martial Brother" and

Minford's "Brother-in-arms" for *Shi-xiong* 師兄 (the form of address used between disciples of the same kungfu master) are both better than Mok's plain "Brother". "*Nom de guerre*" (war name) used by Minford conveys something of the special aura of the world of River and Lake, while the plain "nickname" used by Earnshaw cannot.

But there is another difficulty here: how to enable translators to apply a "standard" English lexicon. No Chinese writer of martial arts fiction would alter the exact terms used in this system; *dian-xue* (literally "strike the vital points") cannot be arbitrarily changed into *an-xue* 按穴 (literally "press the vital points"), nor can *qing-gong* (literally "lightness" and "kungfu") be changed into *fei-gong* 飛功 (literally "flying" and "kungfu"). It would help establish the genre in translation if English readers could also enjoy a "standard" martial arts lexicon, rather than having to cope with a random and inconsistent system. For example, at present every translator coins his or her own rendition of *qing-gong*, including "levitational arts" (Mok), "Lightness Kung Fu" (Earnshaw) and "the art of flying" (Minford). All of these translations are still pioneer efforts, and it is hard to tell which one will be more welcomed by readers. Maybe this problem will solve itself as more translations of martial arts fiction come onto the market. As more translators apply the same system, it more likely to be accepted by readers.

Aside from the creation of lexicon, the code of life portrayed in martial arts fiction, things such as nom de guerre of important figures, kungfu moves, and the unspoken laws of martial arts society should be dealt with carefully. Excessive omission or simplification in this area may deprive martial arts fiction of its very special flavour and ethnic colour, which are in a sense its raison d'être.

Robin Wu's translation reads not like a martial arts fiction, mainly because of his extensive omission of fighting details and simplification of weapons. Some omissions of Earnshaw are reasonable, but some omissions of the martial arts element are not. For example, there is a clever and beautiful Muslim girl in *Shu-jian*. Earnshaw abandons her colourful *nom de guerre*, "Yellow robe and green feather" 翠羽黃衫, and instead uses her full pinyin name, Huo Qingtong 霍青桐. This may not be such a very desirable omission. First, a pinyin name is certainly less appealing than a translated nickname. Second, a *nom de guerre* preserves the flavour of martial arts fiction. Moreover, the iron lotus seeds she uses as weapons are all engraved with the mark of a feather, which is of course a reference to the "Green Feather". Without knowing her *nom de guerre*, readers can never decipher the meaning of that mark.

Apart from her name, all the kungfu moves of her "Mount Tian School" swordcraft, such as "Falling Glacier" (冰河倒瀉), "Floating Sands" (千里流沙), "Giant Lotus in the Snow" (雪中奇蓮), "Lonely Smoke in the Desert" (大漠孤煙) and "Mirage" (海市蜃樓), are omitted without exception. I would like to suggest at least two reasons for keeping them. First, the fact that every move in Chinese kungfu has a name is very special. None of the sword moves used by the Three Musketeers has a name. Secondly, each of these names contains an image which helps to enhance the Muslim colour of the girl.

From the perspective of genre, Robin Wu's contribution is the least. He simply removes too much martial arts stuff. Although Olivia Mok does not remove things like Robin Wu does, she hesitates to coin new expressions for the genre. Her "one-word-for-many" policy will not provide later translators much help with such lexicon. Earnshaw seems not aware of the characteristics of the genre sometimes, but he invents some interesting and usable entries in the lexicon, such as "Yuedao kungfu"[17] for Dian-xue and "Lightness kungfu" for qing-gong. Minford contributes most in the genre-creation. He is fully aware of the necessity of a martial arts lexicon, and tries various ways to build it up. *The Deer* can be a good reference for later translations of Jin Yong, and even of other martial arts writers.

---

17 "Yuedao" is *Xue-dao* 穴道 in Shanghai dialect. Since Earnshaw has lived in Shanghai for a long time, some of his romanizations are influenced by Shanghai dialect. Another example is General Zhao Hui 兆惠. Earnshaw's romanization is "Zhao Wei", also influenced by Shanghai dialect.

IV. Conclusion

One has to face many challenges to translate Jin Yong. The problems of language, and the problems of bringing to life a historical period and a sense of cultural heritage, are not radically different from the problems encountered in translating other traditional Chinese novels. But Jin Yong's works are contemporary popular novels. The readership of Jin Yong's work in translation should differ from, although it will inevitably overlap with, the readership of traditional Chinese novels in translation. That is, the reading habits of the general reader should be considered. However, the reading habits of the target reader and those of the original reader are so different that the translator has to apply many strategies, even experimental ones, to produce a translation that will be enjoyed by the target reader. Various decisions — omission, expansion, and abridgement — have been tried by different translators, and some have proved effective. Finally, martial arts fiction in translation is a new genre. Translators have to produce a new lexicon to render martial arts novels.

From the perspective of cultural heritage, Robin Wu and Earnshaw meet more difficulties. It is obvious that Robin Wu is not familiar with Chinese history, and Earnshaw has certain difficulties in dealing with literary language. Olivia Mok and Minford make far fewer mistakes.[18] The omission strategy used by Robin Wu and Earnshaw proves not very appropriate for the translation of Jin Yong.

From the perspective of readable novel, Earnshaw's and Minford's

---

18　But Olivia Mok sometimes makes mistakes in certain customs. For example, in the third chapter, the son of Paladin Hu appears at the anniversary of his father's death, in *cu-bu ma-yi* 粗布麻衣 (coarse hempen clothes, the mourning wear of the Chinese). She translates this as "coarsely garbed in the everyday vestment of a knave"(107). Wearing hempen-clothes to mourn for one's parents is still a very popular practice in Chinese communities today, but she seems not familiar with it.

translations are much better than the earlier two. Robin Wu's translation is fluent, but at the expense of almost all the characteristics of martial arts fiction. Olivia Mok tries to translate everything, but in the end betrays the style. Although Earnshaw's abridgement policy let him down, he catches some flavour of Jin Yong, especially when he does not trim too many details. Minford pays more attention than other translators to the reading habits of the target reader, and provides a highly readable version.

However, to create an enjoyable novel, I think there is still room for more approaches of translation, such as adaptation. Adaptation is a more drastic strategy than abridgement and chapter-heading make-up. There have been various adaptations of Jin Yong's works, for TV series, motion pictures, stage plays, comics and computer games. Many of them have been very popular. Although many of them may not be loyal to Jin Yong's story and style, some of the adaptation strategies used are still worth considering by translators. For example, many adaptations based on Jin Yong's major works just tell part of the original story. In this way, there are not so many characters, and the characters chosen are allowed to develop fully. A limited number of impressive characters can often achieve a better effect than a crowd of vague personalities. Early translators H. S. and Arthur Waley have proved this.

Finally, from the perspective of genre, Minford has made the biggest contributions. Through romanizing, coining, borrowing, and other approaches, he systematically builds up a rich lexicon, greatly helping to establish the characteristic of a new genre: Chinese martial arts fiction in English translation.

Reviewing the English translations of Jin Yong is rewarding. In the process of translation, the Chineseness within the lines, the difference of reading habits between the original reader and the target reader, and the particularity of martial arts fiction are manifested. In a sense, all translators are pioneers. Effective or not, their efforts should be appreciated by future translators.

Works Cited

Asker, Barry

1997   "The Reception of Kungfu Fiction: Problems of Register, Problems of Culture." Liu Ching-chih, eds. *The Question of Reception: Martial Arts Fiction in English Translation*. Hong Kong: Center for Literature and Translation at Lingnan College.

Barmé, Gereme

1997   "Trinket, a Common Property." *Translation Quarterly*, 5 & 6 (April): 43-67.

Buck, Pearl S

1939   *The Chinese Novel*. New York: John Day.

Buckingham, Edward

1996   "Jin Yong in Indonesia." Paper at the conference, "The Question of Reception: Martial Arts Fiction in English Translation," Hong Kong, March 22-23.

Clavell, James

1975   *Shogun*. London: Hodder and Stoughton.

Earnshaw, Graham, trans.

      The Book and the Sword (書劍恩仇錄). Http://village.Ios.com/~earnshaw/B&S.htm

Green, Martin B.

1991   *Seven Types of Adventure Tale: An Etiology of a Major Genre*. University Park: Penn State University Press.

Hanan, Patrick

1981   *The Chinese Vernacular Story*. Cambridge: Harvard University Press.

Jin Yong 金庸 (Zha Liangyong 查良鏞 or Louis Cha)

1995   *Shu-jian en-chou lu* 書劍恩仇錄 (Book and Sword). First serialized in *Xin-wan-bao* 新晚報 (Hong Kong).   Revised, Hong Kong: Ming-he 明河, 1976. Reprint.

1969-72   *Lu ding ji* 鹿鼎記 (*The Deer and the Cauldron*). First serialized in

Ming-bao 明報, Revised, Hong Kong: Ming-he 明河, 1981; reprint, 1995.

1959   *Xue-shan fei-hu* 雪山飛狐 (*The Flying Fox of the Snowy Mountains*). First serialized in *Xin-wan-bao* 新晚報. Revised, Hong Kong: Ming-he 明河, 1976; reprint, 1995.

Li Zhizhu 李致洙

1993   "Zhong-guo wu-xia xiao-shuo zai han-guo de fan-yi jie-shao yu ying-xiang" 中國武俠小說在韓國的翻譯介紹與影響. *Xia yu zhong-guo wen-hua* 俠與中國文化, eds. by Chinese Department of Tamkang University. Taipei: Xue-sheng 學生, 77-90.

Lin Yiliang 林以亮

1985   "Jin-yong fang-wen ji" 金庸訪問記. *Chun wen-xue* (Hong Kong) 5:4 (October 1969). Reprinted in Shen Deng'en 沈登恩 ed. *Zhu-zi bai-jia kan jin yong* vol.3 諸子百家看金庸(三). Taipei: Yuan-jing 遠景, 11-20.

Minford, John and Sharon Lai (賴慈芸), trans.

1997   "Eagles and Heroes (Chapter I)" [射鵰英雄傳]. *Translation Quarterly* (Hong Kong), 5 & 6 (April):161-94.

Minford, John, trans. and ed.

1997   *The Deer & the Cauldron* (鹿鼎記). Hong Kong: Oxford University Press.

Mok, Olivia (莫慧嫻), trans.

1994   *The Fox Volant of the Snowy Mountain* (雪山飛狐). Hong Kong: Chinese University Press.

Nienhauser, William H. Jr.

1995   "The Implied Reader and Translation." Eoyang, Eugene and Lin Yao-fu (林耀幅), eds. *Translating Chinese Literature*. Bloomington: Indiana University Press. 15-40.

Portmann, Kai

1994   *Der Fliegende Fuchs vom Schneeberg: die Gattung des chinesischen Ritterromans (wuxia xiaoshuo) und der erfolgsautor Jin Yong*. Bochum: Brockmeyer.

Pyle, Howard

1985   *The Merry Adventures of Robin Hood*. First published, 1883. Reprint, New York: Penguin.

S., H. trans.

   1872-73   "The Adventure of a Chinese Giant". *China Review*, vol. I (July
            1872-January 1873): 13-25, 71-86, 144-151, 220-228. Microfilm.

Urban Council of Hong Kong

   1981   *A Study of the Hong Kong Swordplay Film* (1945—1980). Hong Kong:
          The Urban Council of Hong Kong, Revised, 1996.

Van Gulik, Robert, trans.

   1976   *Celebrated Cases of Judge Dee* (狄公案). Tokyo: by the author, 1949.
          Reprint, New York: Dover.

Waley, Arthur, trans.

   1958   *Monkey* (西遊記). London: Allen and Unwin, 1943. Reprint, New York:
          Grove.

Wen Rui'an 溫瑞安

   1985   *Xi Xue-shan fei-hu yu yuan-yang dao* 析雪山飛狐與鴛鴦刀. Taipei:
          Yuan-jing 遠景.

Wu, Robin, trans.

   1972   "Flying Fox of Snow Mountain" (雪山飛狐). *Bridge*, vol. I: 4, 5, 6 & vol.
          II:1 (March, May, July, September):42-49, 36-44, 17-50, 40-45.

從《三劍樓隨筆》看金庸、梁羽生、百劍堂主在五十年代中期的旨趣

馬　幼　垣

香港嶺南大學中文系

摘　要

　　新派武俠小說五十年代初在香港登場。筆路藍縷的梁羽生、金庸、和百劍堂主（依首次發表作品的次序）先後在左派報紙的副刊開始其寫作武俠小說的生涯，故香港《大公報》於 1956 年 10 月底爲他們設一專欄，取名《三劍樓隨筆》，每日一題，不限範圍，由他們三人不定循環次序地各書己見。專欄維持了三個多月，得文八十餘篇，便無疾而終。

　　四十年歲月定乾坤，三人之所成判若日月。這事史有定論，不用多說。要說的是三人（特別是日後成就最著的金庸）在寫武俠小說之初，關心的是什麼問題。因爲梁羽生和金庸在封筆之前很少現身說法地談論其作品（百劍堂主封筆得早，不必多講），《三劍樓隨筆》應可助理解他們當時讀書和寫作的旨趣究在何處。

一、《三劍樓隨筆》的出版背景和研究狀況

　　五十年代初期，新派武俠小說崛起香港。作者的才華、作品的風格均大異於三、四十年代在中國大陸流行的武俠小說。[1]

1　雖然新派武俠小說是五十年代港臺文壇新興的寵兒，作品既均與舊派武俠小說有別，
　　且有共通特徵，但兩地早期的發展鮮有影響性的關連。發展過程當中，最廣爲人誤解

自這段始創時期至金庸和梁羽生（陳文統,1926-）於 1972 年及 1984 年
先後分別封刀,香港風起雲湧的武俠小說文壇長期由金、梁二人任盟主。他
們的作品緊接地連續出版,寫作期間現身說法的解釋則很有限。其中金庸對
自己和時人作品的解釋比梁羽生還是少得多。其實,要理解他們開始寫武俠
小說時的讀書和著作旨趣,倒是有一份相當現成的資料,那就是本文要析述
的《三劍樓隨筆》。

1956 年 10 月 22 日,香港《大公報》〈大公園〉版登了一段預告:

> 《三劍樓隨筆》:自梁羽生先生的《龍虎鬥京華》、《草莽龍蛇傳》、《七劍下天山》;
> 金庸先生的《書劍恩仇錄》、《碧血劍》;百劍堂主的《風虎雲龍傳》等武俠小說在
> 本港各報連載後,大受讀者歡迎,成為武俠小說中一個新的流派。現在我們約得
> 這三位作者給〈大公園〉用另一種筆法撰寫散文隨筆,日內刊出,敬請讀者們注
> 意。──編者

隔了一日,金庸就首先為這系列寫第一篇隨筆。隨後在間有跳期,和三人不
按次序登文（未嘗一人連寫兩日）的情形下,刊至 1957 年 1 月 30 日,便無
疾而終,得文 84 篇（每篇之後,均有作者手書簽名）。其中金庸、梁羽生、
百劍堂主各寫 28 篇（最後一篇是百劍堂主拉雜的結語,或不能算是正常的一
篇）。

以《三劍樓隨筆》為名的單行本很快便由香港的文宗出版社在 1957 年 5
月刊印出來。書籍和報刊性質不同,單行本和見於副刊者確有小別:篇目次
序有小異、百劍堂主刪去他認為已失去價值的一篇、若干讀者來函收為附錄、
標題偶有改動、各篇之末易手書簽名為（百）、（羽）、（庸）字樣。既然這些
改動都是作者在原文脫稿後迅即作出的決定,我們就不必拘泥刊於報章者的
純真了。

這八十多篇文章對理解金庸等三人在啟創香港武俠小說文壇時的旨趣十

的一點是新派武俠小說始自香港。其實按發展次序而言,是臺先港後,故不論推舉那
一位香港作家為新派武俠小說之祖（指工作發軔期,不是指影響力）,都是錯誤的說
法;見曹正文,《中國俠文化》（上海:上海文藝出版社,1994）,頁 129（此書另有繁
體字 1997 年臺灣重排本）。新派武俠小說在香港的出現雖較臺灣稍遲,但因為兩地基
本上是獨立發展,故當其發軔,仍可說崛起香港。

分重要。這點雖夠明顯，但一般研究者因難有檢閱五十年代香港《大公報》的機會，而出版已四十多年的單行本又同樣罕見。[2] 故此，迄今很可能僅得一篇專題討論《三劍樓隨筆》（且是直接根據副刊版本）的研究文字。[3] 這篇作者署名爲陳永康的文章寫得很不錯。但雖僅發表了一年，卻因刊登在香港的報紙副版，找來一看（即使在香港）並非易事。這些都是在討論《三劍樓隨筆》前，得先弄清楚的。

二、百劍堂主究爲何人？

正如《大公報》發表《三劍樓隨筆》前的預告所說的，在香港撰寫武俠小說的風氣始自梁羽生、金庸、百劍堂主三人。

《大公報》開始刊登《三劍樓隨筆》時，梁羽生已刊完《龍虎鬥京華》（《新晚報》〈天方夜譚〉版，1954 年 1 月 20 日-1954 年 8 月 1 日）、《塞外奇俠傳》（《週末報》，1954 年 5 月-？），[4] 和《草莽龍蛇傳》（《新晚報》〈天方

---

2 此書雖有 1988 年臺灣風雲時代出版公司影印本，但流通極有限。1997 年上海學林出版社亦曾以簡體字重新排版刊行，流通情形似已有改進。這些複本都不加出版說明，也不交代百劍堂主是誰。

3 陳永康，〈金庸、梁羽生、百劍堂主〉，《東方日報》〈G 版〉，1997 年 10 月 3 日-11 日。

4 《塞外奇俠傳》的詳細撰期，待找到《週末報》原物始能確實。此書複雜的撰期問題，現在還是可以解決若干的。梁羽生，〈與武俠小說的不解緣〉，收入劉紹銘、陳永明編，《武俠小說論卷》下冊（香港：明河社，1998），頁 676-702，內所含附錄〈梁羽生作品初次發表日期〉，頁 696，說此書初見《週末報》之日期爲「1954 年 5 月-？」。作者自記，紀錄應夠準確才對（這張作品初刊日期表聲明是按劉文良所提供的資料而編成的，且表中復有別的作品說不出原刊日期，可見連梁羽生本人都沒有保留足夠的原刊資料）。這本小說的撰期尚有一說。羅立群，《開創新派的宗師：梁羽生小說藝術談》（上海：學林出版社，1996），頁 192，說是「約 1957-1958 之交」刊於《週末報》的。羅書另有書名易導人誤以爲別爲一書之繁體字臺灣重排本：《梁羽生小說藝術世界》（臺北：知書房出版社，1997）。按此說，《塞外奇俠傳》撰寫時，《三劍樓隨筆》系列早已結束了。另外，《大公報》〈大公園〉版的編輯在推介《三劍樓隨筆》時也沒有提《塞外奇俠傳》。這和羅說合起來看，就似證明《塞外奇俠傳》是後出之作。事實卻不然。《塞外奇俠傳》和《七劍下天山》的故事是前後相連的。怎會先寫後集，然後才補撰前集？因此，梁羽生在寫《三劍樓隨筆》前所撰小說應包括《塞外奇俠傳》。這樣說來，難道羅立群根本沒有看過《塞外奇俠傳》？糊塗之例，還有一個。韓雲波，《俠林玄珠》（成都：四川人民出版社，1995），頁 167-168，說《草莽龍蛇傳》和《塞外奇俠傳》之

夜譚〉版，1954 年 8 月 11 日-1955 年 2 月 5 日），以及正在《大公報》〈小說林〉版發表《七劍下天山》（1956 年 2 月 15 日-1957 年 3 月 31 日）；金庸已刊完《書劍恩仇錄》（《新晚報》〈天方夜譚〉版，1955 年 2 月 8 日-1956 年 9 月 5 日），和正在《香港商報》〈說月〉版發表《碧血劍》（1956 年 1 月 1 日-1956 年 12 月 31 日）；百劍堂主的《風虎雲龍傳》則僅開始發表了幾天（《新晚報》〈天方夜譚〉版，1956 年 9 月 9 日-1957 年 7 月 29 日）。

這樣說來，百劍堂主動筆最晚，出版量也最少。按常理（且不說日後知名度之別），三人中居領導地位者應不是他。實情卻相反。

《三劍樓隨筆》初刊報章時，因分日不按次序地刊登，作者並無名次之別。刊印單行本時，則排名總應有先後之分。按現今的觀念，金、梁、百的排次當是眾無異論的。書的排名卻是百、梁、金。連刊登副刊時和出單行本時的《三劍樓隨筆》五字標題也出自百劍堂主之手（對照簽名即知）。最後的結語（內含報刊和單行本兩版本分別的解釋），和在單行本書首加的〈正傳之前的閒話〉介紹文字悉由百劍堂主一人執筆。從這些角度去看，說三人同意以百劍堂主為首，應不是臆度之言。

這情形有一可能的解釋，就是百劍堂主年長於金、梁二人（金長梁二歲，分別不算大）。解決之法，還是得先弄清楚百劍堂士是誰。

究竟百劍堂主是誰，不要說一般讀者不知道，連研究者亦多不曉得。[5]

潘亞暾、汪義生的《金庸梁羽生通俗小說欣賞》指百劍堂主為左派報人

間，還有一本《白髮魔女傳》。把梁羽生的第六本小說（《新晚報》〈天方夜譚〉版，1957 年 8 月 5 日-1958 年 9 月 8 日）算是他的第三本小說，還把《塞外奇俠傳》和《草莽龍蛇傳》的次序顛倒過來，掌握信息差勁的程度可以想見。

5　出版得重重複複的金庸傳記，不時提及金庸參加撰寫《三劍樓隨筆》之事。但檢及到的都說不出百劍堂主是誰。冷夏（鄭祖貴），《金庸傳》（香港：明報出版有限公司，1994），雖為與金庸有關係的機構之刊物，不無「官書」的意味，在頁 62-64 屢次講次百劍堂主，卻始終點不出他的本名，便是一例。至於此書之「官書」程度，見列孚，〈《金庸傳》引發爭議〉，《聯合報》〈讀書人〉，1998 年 11 月 2 日。另一例就是唯一撰寫《三劍樓隨筆》專題研究的陳文康。他承認不知道百劍堂主是誰，還斬釘截鐵地說沒有追查的必要；見其〈金庸、梁羽生、百劍堂主(一)〉，《東方日報》〈G 版〉，1997 年 10 月 3 日。

陳凡（1915-1997）。[6] 可靠與否，不易判斷。但陳凡有自傳，見劉以鬯主編的《香港文學作家傳略》，傳中列出年月日齊全的誕生日期。（按陳凡的知名度，祇有他本人才說得出來），[7] 內全不提百劍堂主這筆名和用此筆名寫的《風虎雲龍傳》。在這情形之下，要指百劍堂主為陳凡，確很難敎人信服。

　　證據還是有的。陳凡在前年（1997）9 月 29 日逝世後幾天，梁羽生在香港《大公報》〈大公園〉版刊一詩追悼，編者亦附加說明：

輓陳凡大兄

三劍樓見證平生　亦狂亦俠真名士
卅年事何堪回首　能哭能歌邁俗流

梁羽生

按：《三劍樓隨筆》係當年由陳凡、梁羽生、金庸三人輪流执筆撰寫的雜文專欄，膾炙人口，極受歡迎。

至此，百劍堂主之為陳凡始不復再有疑問。

　　百劍堂主的身份雖確定了，但他和他寫的《風虎雲龍傳》在武俠小說史上幾乎無紀錄可言。在近年為數不少，往往頗厚的武俠小說辭典當中，尚未

6　潘亞暾、汪義生，《金庸梁羽生通俗小說欣賞》（南寧：廣西敎育出版社，1993），頁 276、282。

7　參見劉以鬯主編的《香港文學作家傳略》（香港：市政局公共圖書館，1996），頁 601。

見有任何一種提及百劍堂主或其武俠小說。[8] 完全不理百劍堂主及其《風虎
雲龍傳》，當然是編撰這些辭典者之失。[9] 擺在眼前的事實還是很簡單。陳凡
寫完那本說不上有什麼影響力的《風虎雲龍傳》後，意興闌珊，再不沾手武
俠小說了。他以後的成績，除了替香港的左派報紙寫政論外，其他就沒有給
讀者留下明顯的印象。

　　《三劍樓隨筆》不是一本值得獨立研究的書。僅從幫助我們理解武俠小
說在香港創始時主要作家的興趣所在這角度去看，此本閒書才有探研的價
值。說明了這一點，以下的討論不多講百劍堂主就不用再解釋了。

三、棋話連篇

　　《三劍樓隨筆》話題很雜，分析起來，不能每樣都講。況且書中不少新
聞意味很重的篇章，過了四十多年，早成明日黃花，自可不論。雖則如此，
祇要僅以金、梁二人為談論中心，篇章按類歸納，這本書還是不難處理的。

　　按講的次數而言，書中最突出的話題是棋藝（圍棋和象棋）——梁羽生
七篇、金庸三篇（百劍堂主不談棋藝，下遇這種情形，不再註明）。

　　金庸寫的雖僅為介紹性文字，他已特別指出他在《碧血劍》中如何利用
奕棋佈置情節。[10] 其實《書劍恩仇錄》早有對棋的描寫了。金庸後續發揮以
棋局入稗的手法，在《倚天屠龍記》（1961 年）、《天龍八部》（1963-1965 年），
和《笑傲江湖》（1967 年）幾臻化境，雖是後話，串連起來看，該有助於明瞭

8　查檢過的辭典，包括胡文彬主編，《中國武俠小說辭典》（石家莊：花山文藝出版社，
　　1992）；寧宗一主編，《中國武俠小說鑒賞辭典》（北京：國際文化出版社，1992）；劉
　　新風、陳墨等，《中國現代武俠小說鑒賞辭典》（北京：中國民族學院出版社，1993）；
　　溫子健編，《武俠小說鑒賞大典》（桂林：漓江出版社，1994）。

9　《風虎雲龍傳》在《新晚報》刊完後，還有香港三育圖書公司的四冊單行本（1957-1960）。
　　辭典求全務準，不以褒貶定取捨。就算那些辭典編者以資訊不足為自辯之辭，但香港
　　左派文人刊書而不為大陸學界所留意，始終是具反諷意味之事。

10　金庸，〈圍棋雜說〉（1956 年 11 月 7 日），頁 33-35（前者為原見《大公報》的日期，
　　後者為單行本的頁數。為省篇幅，倘收入單行本時，題目有別，亦不註明。下同）。

金庸作為一個小說家的成長過程。[11]

　　梁羽生的情形則不同。他之於博奕，著迷入痴之程度尤過金庸。雖然他亦以棋局入小說，如《萍踪俠影錄》（1959 年），但他在《三劍樓隨筆》講的棋話卻不易和他寫的小說連起來看。理由很簡單。梁羽生在《三劍樓隨筆》寫的七題棋話，講的僅是當日棋壇（圍棋和象棋）高手如楊官璘、朱劍秋、吳清源（1914- ）、何頌安、王嘉良和他們當時的戰績。[12] 金庸棋話三題中，亦有一篇是講吳清源的。[13] 江山代有才人出，四十餘年過去了，這些名字所代表的自然大大不同。隨筆應一時興緻與價值觀念而寫，久存性難免受局限。佔了《三劍樓隨筆》幾乎八分之一篇目的棋藝話題，除了有助說明金、梁二人因何以奕入稗外，對分析有關小說書中涉及棋的情節，並不能說有很大的關聯。

　　與棋並稱的琴、書、畫又如何？這些在金、梁小說中層出不窮，而讀者也百看不厭的技藝，《三劍樓隨筆》全欠奉。有的僅是金庸談香港女水彩畫家李克玲的作品，不必與武俠小說強拉上關係的一篇。[14]

四、數理精微

　　金庸和梁羽生均以才高八斗，縱橫雜學見稱。他們雖然不在這系列談琴、書和畫，奇招還是有的。其中最教一般治文史者摸不著頭腦的是數學。[15]

11　無端，〈圍棋與金庸的武俠小說〉，收入餘子等，《諸子百家看金庸㈤》（臺北：遠景出版公司，1986），頁 33-44；溫瑞安，《天龍八部欣賞舉隅》（臺北：遠景出版公司，1986），頁 79-88；陳墨，《技藝金庸》（臺北：雲龍出版社，1997），頁 67-83。

12　梁羽生，〈閒話楊朱一局棋〉（1956 年 11 月 1 日），頁 20-22；〈談楊官璘的殘棋〉（1956 年 11 月 11 日），頁 48-50；〈圍棋聖手吳清源〉（1956 年 11 月 29 日），頁 82-85；〈棋壇歷史開新頁：寫在全國象棋大比賽之前〉（1956 年 12 月 13 日）〔增附錄〕），頁 111-113；〈縱談南北棋壇〉（1956 年 12 月 23 日），頁 132-134；〈永留佳話在棋壇：談何頌安「歷史性的一局棋」〉（1956 年 12 月 30 日），頁 145-147；〈談棋手的實力〉（1957 年 1 月 3 日，頁 149-152）。

13　金庸，〈歷史性的一局棋〉（1956 年 12 月 8 日），頁 101-104。

14　金庸，〈看李克玲的畫〉（1956 年 10 月 27 日），頁 10-12。

15　陳墨在《技藝金庸》書中，談論金庸小說中的醫、詩、琴、棋等十項技藝，方志遠，《彈指驚雷俠客行：港派新武俠小說面面觀》（南昌：江西人民出版社，1991），頁 311-355，綜論金庸、梁羽生小說中的琴、棋、書、酒、花五趣，均不提數學，可以為例。

　　《三劍樓隨筆》中，梁羽生和金庸各有一篇發表日期很接近的數學文章。[16] 梁羽生的一篇還算是一般性的介紹之作，金庸談圓周率則綜引古今，深入淺出，很見功力。早晚會有人在談金、梁小說的技藝時，擴展範圍及於數學的。這兩篇隨筆該有參考價值。

　　談完圓周率，金庸還在該篇提供一項寫作《書劍恩仇錄》過程的資料。他寫《書劍恩仇錄》時追查過海寧陳家的史事，眾所周知。但一般讀者並沒有他於參考史家孟森（1868-1938）那篇著名遺作〈海寧陳家〉之餘，[17] 還做過不少獨立探究的印象。在這篇講圓周率的隨筆末段，金庸說他追查到與陳家洛父陳世倌同輩的陳世仁（1676-1722）不僅為康熙翰林，更是一個所學有成的數學家，並指出所著《少廣補遺》「一直研究到奇數偶數平方立方的級數和等問題」。金學研究固早精細入微，知見所及似尚無人通過這項資料去證明金庸撰寫《書劍恩仇錄》的艱辛。

五、西方電影和小說的影響

　　金庸曾從事電影事業，且以電影手法入小說。這雖早是金學領域裡的老生常談，[18] 讀《三劍樓隨筆》者還是希望在書中能看到有關電影的討論。

　　金庸不教讀者失望。系列開宗明義的第一篇就是談美國小說家該隱（James M. Cain, 1892-1977）《相思曲》（*Serenade*, 1937），小說原書和電影改編版的異同。金庸毫不留情地抨擊荷里活電影界的庸俗市場傾向如何向一本文字優美、故事感人的小說作出各種粗暴的任意改動。[19]

　　這是金庸初撰武俠小說時不滿市場主導文學創作和作品改編的明確表

16　梁羽生，〈數學與邏輯〉（1957 年 1 月 17 日），頁 180-181；金庸，〈圓周率的推算〉
　　（1957 年 1 月 22 日），頁 191-194。

17　孟森此作雖實為一般長度的論文，但 1948 年以遺著形式首次發表時，北京大學出版
　　部是印為單行本刊售的，並列之為《國立北京大學五十週年紀念論文集》內文學院第
　　一種。其後此文收入好幾種合刊，如孟森，《清代史》（臺北：正中書局，1960），頁
　　511-532；孟森，《明清史論著集刊續編》（北京：中華書局，1986），頁 318-348。

18　最近一例為嚴家炎，〈金庸談讀書及小說、電影寫作〉，《明報月刊》，33：12（1998 年
　　12 月），頁 34-35。

19　金庸，〈《相思曲》與小說〉（1956 年 10 月 24 日），頁 2-5。

示。這裡帶出一個不在本文討論範圍而早晚該有人試圖回答的問題——金庸撰寫小說與市場需求的關係，特別是由原本改寫爲今本時（以及現在再進行別一次修改時）的關係。

討論小說《相思曲》時，金庸一併談及海明威（Ernest Hemmingway, 1899-1961）、費茲路（Francis Scott Fitzerald, 1896-1940）、福克納（William Faulkner, 1897-1962）幾個他傾心佩服的美國小說家。這樣一來，讀者不難會以爲金庸對盛名的美國小說家有偏好，因而敎人聯想到此等作家的小說對金庸究竟有何影響的問題。

《三劍樓隨筆》能幫得上忙的例子確有一個，就是點出《倚天屠龍記》的金毛獅謝遜出自梅爾維（Herman Melville, 1819-1891）筆下大白鯨無比敵（書名一樣，*Moby Dick*, 1851）。原來在《明報》開始發表《倚天屠龍記》（1961 年 7 月 6 日）前四年半，金庸的腦海中已印上謝遜的形象。

金庸在《三劍樓隨筆》一連用無比敵爲題寫過兩次。[20] 西方文評家對無比敵的詮釋五花八門，理論掛帥，亂套「主義」。金庸依從英國小說家毛姆（W. Somerset Maugham, 1874-1965）的看法，不相信那些解夢式的玩意兒。他相信的是書中表達出來的憤世嫉俗的強烈呼聲，和接近瘋狂的憎恨感與復仇慾，以及模稜兩可的善惡觀念。單說謝遜是無比敵的化身是不夠的，說他是大白鯨和亞海勃船長（Captain Ahab）的混合化身固然較切實情，還不如說金庸在移植的基因上做了一次中國化和眞實化的成功實驗。[21]

梁羽生的情形有幾分近似。梁羽生第一次爲《三劍樓隨筆》系列寫稿時，就坦然講出一件他樂於承認之事。他說有個中學生讀者看出《七劍下天山》的重要人物凌未風就是英國女作家伏尼契（Ethel Lilian Voynich, 1864-1960）處女作《牛虻》（*The Godfly*, 1897）中的十九世紀初義大利革命份子牛虻，並驕傲地承認不單事實確如此，還指出牛虻的化身是一析爲二的，由凌未風和易蘭珠（天山七劍客中二人）來分任。[22]

20　金庸，〈無比敵有什麼意義？〉（1956 年 12 月 1 日），頁 88-93；〈無比敵有什麼好處？〉（1956 年 12 月 5 日），頁 93-96。

21　這點吳靄儀，《金庸小說的男子》（香港：明窗出版社，1989），頁 82-88，有很漂亮的分析。

22　梁羽生，〈凌未風、易蘭珠、牛虻〉（1956 年 10 月 25 日），頁 5-8。此文近收入梁羽生，《筆花六照》（香港：天地圖書公司，1999），頁 50-52。

梁羽生點明《牛虻》和《七劍下天山》的關係也不止這一次。差不多十年後，他在那篇故弄玄虛，託名自褒，暗貶金庸，在武俠小説研究史上成爲異品的文章裡仍樂書不倦。[23]

國內研究武俠小説史者亦有附和的，把梁羽生的襲用牛虻説成是傳奇性的文壇盛事。[24]

這種美譽，不管是自誇的，還是人封的，確有説明究竟的必要。

《七劍下天山》和《牛虻》的關聯連一個買不起書，要在書店把書讀完的中學生（沒有低估其能耐之意）也看得出來，襲用者之消化不良本不必代辯。可是我們要管的並不是消化程度的問題，而是梁羽生怎會選中一本雖原以英文書寫，在西方文壇卻給人遺忘得幾乎一乾二淨的小説作爲模仿的對象？

首先我們應明白，伏尼契及其賴以存名的小説《牛虻》的聲譽絕不如一般中國讀者印象中崇高。其實她是一個《大英百科全書》（*Encyclopedia Britannica*）〈微知卷〉（Micropedia）部分不管，連專紀錄世界女作家的辭典如 Katharina M. Wilson, et al., *Women Writers of the Great Britain and Europe: An Encyclopedia* (New York: Garland Publishing Inc., 1997) 也不理的愛爾蘭女作家（她的姓不是愛爾蘭姓氏，因她從大之波蘭姓）。即使是僅以愛爾蘭作家爲記述範圍的辭典也有不少撇開她不提。[25] 她的書

23　佟碩之，〈新派武俠小説兩大名家：金庸梁羽生合論〉，《海光文藝》，1966 年 1 月號（創刊號），頁 4-6。此文在《海光文藝》連刊三期，其措辭顯欲令讀者以爲是最先約梁羽生、金庸、百劍堂主在《新晚報》發表武俠小説的羅孚所寫，實則文出梁羽生之手。此文雖屢經轉載，但遇到這種情形，爲了鎖定原作日期和保證文字無誤，還是應參據原版。

24　最明顯之例爲羅立群，《開創新派的宗師》，書中有一章標明以〈天山劍客有牛虻〉爲題，頁 96-108。但不知羅立群看過《三劍樓隨筆》沒有？梁羽生説牛虻化身爲凌未風和易蘭珠，他却説除凌未風外，書中還有劉郁芳和韓志邦二人是牛虻的化身。如果梁羽生和羅立群所説都對，牛虻在《七劍下天山》豈非一化爲四了！

25　提及她的愛爾蘭作家辭典當然有，不提她的還是不少，例如 Alexander G. Gonzalez, *Modern Irish Writers: A Bio-Critical Source Book* (Westport, Conn.: Greenwood Press, 1967); Anne M. Brady and Brian Cleeve, *A Biographical Dictionary of Irish Writers* (New York: St. Martin's Press, 1985)，都不覺得有爲她存紀錄的必要。至於西方文評家對她的研究，值得一提者恐怕僅得一篇四十多年前發表的短文：

不祇《牛虻》一本，但其它的僅能算是在出版史上查考得到紀錄之物而已。

這本遭西方文壇摒棄的小說爲何不單會變成梁羽生心愛之書，中國的研究者還可以抄錄若干段落來和《七劍下天山》作比較，[26] 甚至連靠在書店揩油的香港中學生也熟悉？無他，這本小說在西方雖不受歡迎，它之講革命和歌頌愛國情操卻使其成爲蘇聯和東歐共產國家的暢銷書。五十年代的中國唯蘇是從，還以爲《牛虻》是普及世界的作品，遂於 1953 年由李俍民譯成中文，印行一百多萬冊，使之頓成爲中國人眼中的西方名著。文革以後，此書各種新版本的相繼出現更使其在中國的流通歷久不衰。這雖是後來之事，也足以說明當日梁羽生受假象影響的程度。

就算沒有給假象誤導，梁羽生喜歡政治掛帥的作品也是事實。在《三劍樓隨筆》裡，他有一篇介紹蘇聯小說（讀的應是中譯本）的文章。原來連《鋼鐵是怎樣鍊成的》，那類歌頌共產主義支配的國家萬樣好的作品，他也讀得津津有味！[27]

講完這些，就不難看出五十年代中期的金庸和梁羽生雖同在赤報工作，後者的思想要比前者左得多。至於二人同受西方文學的影響，也有一很明顯的分別。金庸直接讀原書，選擇是自己決定的。梁羽生依靠譯本，選擇是別人圈定的。選擇性質之異是否會影響到接納、消化、運用等方面，續談下去，涉連很廣，就不必在此討論了。

六、《七劍下天山》中的納蘭性德和傅山

武俠小說講過去的故事，讓歷史人物穿插其間，不管他們是要角還是閒角，對增加小說的眞實感總有補益。如果金庸和梁羽生在《三劍樓隨筆》解釋一下他們選用的歷史人物，該多理想。

話雖如此，局限性仍難免。《三劍樓隨筆》出爐的時候，金庸和梁羽生已寫和正在發表的武俠小說合共僅六本，涉及的歷史人物不算多。幸而在這本

Arnold Kettle, "E. L. Voynich: A Forgotten English Novelist," *Essays in Criticism*, 7: 2 (April 1957), pp.163-174.

26　如羅立群，《開創新派的宗師》，頁 102-106，所抄錄者。

27　梁羽生，〈讀蘇聯的小說〉（1957 年 1 月 24 日），頁 196-199。

隨筆集內，還是能夠找到兩個配合說明的例子——《七劍下天山》中的納蘭性德（1655-1685）和傅山（1607-1684）。後者在書中的份量比前者重，但在《三劍樓隨筆》中梁羽生僅提供他對納蘭性德的看法。梁羽生爲這系列寫了三篇講納蘭性德的隨筆。[28] 首兩篇講納蘭性德的生平和推崇他的詞在詞史上的古今獨步，還沒有超越一般文學史事討論的範圍。第三篇就奇了。他解釋《七劍下天山》如何用暗示的手法點明納蘭性德懂武，且武藝不算差，但距離高手的程度甚遠，更無法和他在文學史上的成就相較。這豈非止是梁羽生的讀者夢寐以求的說明！

看見梁羽生談得高興，金庸也加入討論，並開闢一新話題，講納蘭性德好友吳兆騫（1631-1684）因科場事件而充軍新疆的冤獄，以及納蘭和另一摯友顧貞觀（號梁汾，1637-1714）經歷十年設法營救之事。[29] 香港和上海的讀者對這一連串的討論反應熱烈，甚至有爬疏鉤玄，參加探索者。[30] 這顯然是整本《三劍樓隨筆》談得最起勁，所講最歷久如新的話題。

梁羽生沒有談在《七劍下天山》書中較納蘭性德扮演更重要角色的傅山。倒是百劍堂主越俎代庖，寫了一篇簡介傅山的文字。[31] 該文僅說明傅山是明末清初志崇節高的隱士而已，完全沒有交代梁羽生如何配套此歷史人物入《七劍下天山》的情節內。[32]

要明瞭金、梁二人創作武俠小說之初怎樣利用和處理歷史人物，以求達到虛實相配和平衡，《三劍樓隨筆》幫得上點忙。它有梁羽生的例子，但沒有金庸的例子。

利用《三劍樓隨筆》的園地，說明當時已發表的作品，梁羽生比金庸積極。除了解說如何表達出納蘭性德懂武藝外，他還詮釋《七劍下天山》中一

28　梁羽生，〈才華絕代的納蘭詞〉（1956 年 10 月 28 日），頁 13-15；〈翩翩濁世佳公子、富貴功名總等閒：再談容若的詞〉（1956 年 11 月 4 日），頁 28-30；〈納蘭容若的武藝〉（1956 年 11 月 8 日），頁 35-37。

29　金庸，〈顧梁汾賦贖命詞〉（1956 年 11 月 10 日），頁 41-43。

30　《三劍樓隨筆》，頁 43-47，所收的兩篇讀者來函均很有份量。

31　百劍堂主，〈傅青主不武而俠〉（1957 年 1 月 23 日），頁 194-196。

32　陳永康評百劍堂主在《三劍樓隨筆》所寫諸文爲祇知搜集資料，左抄右湊，而無個人觀點，並非虛言；見其〈金庸、梁羽生、百劍堂主(二)〉，《東方日報》〈G 版〉，1997 年 10 月 4 日。

段冒浣蓮替桂仲明解夢（兩人均列名天山七劍客），因而助其恢復記憶的故事，是根據佛洛伊德（Sigmund Freud, 1856-1939）釋夢學說而寫成的。[33]這種消息雖屬一鱗半爪，對賞析他的作品還是有「夫子自道」的作用的。

認爲《三劍樓隨筆》有助理解梁羽生早期作品的話，還得留意梁羽生和金庸之間有一分別。梁羽生絕大多數作品成於寫作《三劍樓隨筆》之後（後期和前期作品數量的比例爲 31 對 4），比例較金庸大多了（金庸的後期前期數量比例爲 12 對 2，僅算長篇作品）。《三劍樓隨筆》以後，金庸沒有出版過隨筆集。[34] 梁羽生其後最少有四本個人隨筆集。[35] 若要整體討論梁羽生的小說，這些隨筆集自然不可或缺。這些題外話是有說明的必要的。

七、其他歷史人物的討論

除納蘭性德外，梁羽生還談到玄奘（602-664）。[36] 那是很難以要角形式寫入武俠小說的人物，可以不論。

金庸寫小說，對歷史忠誠交代的執著，和梁羽生一樣強烈。小說初在報紙或期刊發表時，受時空之限，史觀的詮釋和複雜史事的陳述都很難和諧地安插入文內。金庸在七十年代修改原本爲今本時，沒有了這些限制，歷史方面的補充話不少就用附錄的方式向讀者交代。[37] 這些附錄也給金庸提供了講明他對某些史事有特別觀感的機會。

金庸雖然這樣究心歷史眞相，卻沒有在《三劍樓隨筆》裡講及《書劍恩仇錄》和《碧血劍》兩書中的歷史人物。那麼他有沒有談到以後續寫各書中

33　梁羽生，〈夢的化裝〉（1956 年 11 月 22 日），頁 72-74。

34　金庸有一本社論集，《香港的前途》（香港：明報有限公司，1984），那是另一回事。

35　梁羽生的四本隨筆集爲《筆、劍、書》（香港：天地圖書公司，1985）；《筆不花雜記》（廣州：花城出版社，1986）；《筆不花》（香港：三聯書店，1989）；以及本文註 22 所列的新刊隨筆集《筆花六照》。

36　梁羽生，〈辯才無礙說玄奘〉（1956 年 12 月 6 日），頁 96-98。

37　〈康熙朝的機密奏摺〉，收入《鹿鼎記》；〈袁崇煥評傳〉，收入《碧血劍》；〈卅三劍俠圖〉，收入《俠客行》；〈成吉思汗家族〉、〈關於全眞教〉，收入《射鵰英雄傳》。其中也有早已發表，並非爲修訂本而寫的，如〈卅三劍俠圖〉原刊於 1970 年 1-2 月的《明報晚報》。

的歷史人物？這顯然是喜讀金庸小說者關心的問題。

　　按人物的先後年代，金庸在《三劍樓隨筆》談到兩組歷史人物：

　　㈠馬援（前14-後49）、漢光武帝劉秀，和在交趾起義而被馬援剿殺的二徵王（徵側、徵貳兩姊妹）。[38]

　　㈡郭子儀（697-781）、唐代宗李俶、沈后、昇平公主（打金枝故事的女主角）。[39]

兩者都可以構思為曲折離奇的故事。但金庸從未採用漢唐為武俠小說的時代背景，已封之刀也不會啓封，難道他對這兩題材的喜愛就真的沒有進一步發展的可能？

　　這事涉及一個金庸和梁羽生共同的情況。他們都想在再執筆創作時寫歷史小說。[40]

　　梁羽生的計劃似較易實現。梁羽生在未入嶺南大學念經濟前（1949年畢業）已師事太平天國史家簡又文（1896-1979）。[41] 他以太平天國為題寫歷史小說是理所當然之事。外界報導說他遷居澳洲後，已於1990年開始潛心寫太平天國歷史小說。[42] 消息如屬真，這本小說或者已快脫稿了。

　　金庸的情形沒有這樣明顯。金庸社交繁忙，且又開始再修改全部作品，刊為線裝本的繁重工作，[43] 能否分暇撰寫從未嘗試過的歷史小說，不能不說是疑問。假如確動筆寫歷史小說，會否自馬援和郭子儀兩題選一？讀過《三劍樓隨筆》的大多會提出此問題。這問題別人是不能代金庸回答的。

38　金庸，〈馬援見漢光武〉（1956年11月24日），頁75-77；〈馬援與二徵王〉（1956年11月28日），頁79-81。

39　金庸，〈郭子儀的故事〉（1956年11月17日），頁61-64；〈代宗、沈后、昇平公主〉（1956年11月21日），頁69-72。

40　金庸在封刀以後，經常講及倘再寫小說，當寫歷史小說。其中一例為林翠芬紀錄，〈金庸談武俠小說〉，《明報月刊》，30：1（1995.1），頁51-53。

41　費勇、鍾曉毅，《梁羽生傳奇》（廣州：廣東人民出版社，1996），頁6-8。

42　潘亞暾、汪義生，《金庸梁羽生通俗小說欣賞》，頁286。

43　金庸，〈小說創作的幾點思考〉，《明報月刊》，33：8（1998.8），頁48。

八、結　語

　　寫《三劍樓隨筆》的時候，金庸和梁羽生僅發表了以後全部武俠小說作品的一小部分。況且這些選題隨意，長度受制，還要照顧話題的多元性、可讀性和時事性的短文，基本上不是爲詮釋已刊的武俠小說而寫的。雖然書中確有爲提供這種詮釋而寫的文章，數目畢竟不多。那幾個刻意爲自己的武俠小說加註的例子也全是梁羽生的，金庸沒有這樣直接的說明。從這角度去看，《三劍樓隨筆》的史料價值是有限的，零碎的。

　　從另一角度去看，金庸、梁羽生二人寫作武俠小說的時期不算短，期間發表的現身說法之言卻量少質稀（最具實質的還是梁羽生那篇別有用心的託名之作）。《三劍樓隨筆》直接講武俠小說的地方雖不多，但對理解金、梁二人在五十年代中期讀書和寫作的旨趣，幫助不少。這本隨筆集的價值不該僅是羽片吉光而已。

金庸小說版本學

林　保　淳

淡江大學中文系

摘　要

　　金庸小說有新、舊版本的區別，所謂「新版」，指金庸自 1973 年始，十年修訂後的「修訂本」；「舊本」，則包括了早期刊載於報章的「刊本」、坊間刊印的「舊本」及臺灣盜印的「盜本」。由於金庸修訂幅度甚大，因此新、舊本有極大的差別。

　　金庸「修訂本」主要有三方面的易動，一是文辭（包含回目）的修飾，二是情節的刪易，三是歷史意識的增強。其刪削的標準，一是補苴罅漏，二是袪除神怪的情節，三是強調史識。

　　透過金庸新、舊版本的比較，我們可以推究出幾點重大的意義：(1)可以瞭解臺灣盜版的歷史背景及現象，為研究臺灣文化歷史重要的資料；(2)可以明白金庸創作的心路歷程，且窺探出金庸的思想、觀念的轉變；(3)可以為金庸作武俠小說史上確切的定位，並消解獨尊金庸的排擠效應；(4)可以透過金庸苦心孤詣的修訂過程，重新正視通俗小說的意義與價值。

一、前　言

　　版本研究向來是中國文學研究中相當重要的一環。版本研究的基本信念，在於肯定文本「歷時性」或「同時性」所呈顯的差異現象，足以作為文化分析的對象。從索緒爾（Ferdinand de Saussure）的語言學角度而言，文

本在「歷時性」的發展過程中，充分受到當代語言體系的制約與影響，這不僅包括了當代文化思潮、政經因素等對語言的干擾，也包含了作者個人（或繼起者）運用語言的不同階段特色。以《紅樓夢》爲例，「脂評本」與「高鶚續本」分別處在不同「歷時性」的階段，所代表的自然是不同時間中各異的觀念，「紅學」專家正可自其版本的易變中，或言索隱，或言自傳，或林林總總不同的議論。至於「同時性」的差異，則往往肇因於地域上的差別，張愛玲的《半生緣》，在舊版中題名爲《十八春》，結局迥異於在臺出版的今本，「張迷」亦自不妨從其差異中，分析探討文本「同時性」所牽涉到的整個不同思想領域中的變化。基本上，文本的版本探討有三個定點，一是作爲始點的文本（未必是最早的文本）；一是作爲比較的文本（未必是最晚的文本），一是比較者。這三個定點，都各自牽涉到當代不同的文化體系，而其中有傳承、有取捨、有變易，綜合起來，頗能略窺文化系統中某種程度的演變痕跡。

金庸武俠小說的研究，論者美其名爲「金學研究」，相較於《紅樓夢》的「紅學」、《金瓶梅》的「金學」，學術研究成果固然還是遠遜，但「金學研究」在當代卻因擁有天時（現代性，整個創作的文化背景非常具體）、地利（完整性，作者及創作脈絡非常明晰）及人和（普遍性，作品流傳廣遠、讀者眾多），事實上擁有最多的「研究人力」，茶餘飯後、街頭巷尾，無時無處不可見到一副儼若「金學專家」的讀者，有意無意間推動了金庸小說研究的風潮。儘管從學術研究的角度而言，這些「研究」充其量不過是主觀見解的抒發，而且蒙昧淺陋，零金碎玉，不成系統；但卻是文學研究中的一個特殊現象，意謂著文學不該僅止於學院，而應考量到更普遍廣大的讀者，作更進一步的調整與發展。本文之作，正企圖藉此爲調合溝通的手段，爲通俗小說的研究拋磚引玉。

二、金庸小說版本系統

金庸從 1955 年開始創作《書劍恩仇錄》，至 1972 年《鹿鼎記》完稿，一共創造了十五部武俠小說；1973 年金庸封筆，開始著手作修訂工作；1980 年，修訂版問世，這就是坊間常見的《金庸作品集》。

金庸作品的版本很多，基本上可以分成三大系統：一是報紙或雜誌上直

接刊載的版本，可以稱爲「刊本」，這是金庸作品問世的首度面貌，但並未正式發行印售。「刊本」在各報章、雜誌逐日（週）刊載，鮮少中斷，爲配合讀者的閱讀需求，除了各單元自有其章回外，每日均有一提淸眉目的小標題（以《天龍八部》爲例，第一回〈無量玉璧〉，前五日的小標有〈白衣少年段譽〉、〈滿手抓的是蛇〉、〈樑上少女，玩弄毒蛇〉、〈「禹穴四靈」的金靈子〉、〈神農幫採藥取麝〉等），或文或白，判斷應是編者所加；此外，有雲君所繪的插圖，相當精緻，與早年臺北眞善美出版社的插圖高手另人，可謂武俠插畫的「雙絕」。就在小說連載期間，由於金庸聲名的迅速播揚，坊間書店往往應時集結成小冊發售（應無授權），這是從報紙迻錄、隨寫隨刊的版本，可以稱爲「舊本」。此一版本最接近金庸的「原創意」，在修訂本未面世之前，無論是香港各書局（如三民、武史、娛樂等出版社）所出的版本，或臺灣盜印的諸作，甚至海外華人社會所流傳的各種版式，皆屬這一系統。「舊本」與「刊本」最大的區別，在於刪除了每日刊載的小標，其餘的略無更動，因此可以視爲同系。

一是臺灣的「盜版」系統，此一系統變化相當複雜，既有直接影印港版諸書而成的，也有張冠李戴、改頭換面的版本，更有據內容改編的魚目混珠之作，不過，基本而論，是依據「舊本」改換的。其間比較重要的易動爲：(1)作者及書名的改換（請參考下表）；(2)章回的重新擬定。在某些書中，章回的變換幅度極大（如《鹿鼎記》「刊本」前三章爲〈楔子：如此冰霜如此路，痛哭流涕有若是〉、〈紅巾方見劇賊走，白鬚又報官軍過〉、〈琢磨頗望成全璧，激烈何須到碎琴〉；臺灣盜版的《神武門》一回分成三章，〈楔子〉分爲〈逐鹿中原〉、〈君子遭禍〉、〈雪中奇丐〉），大抵是爲了配合臺灣出版 32 開本的慣例。

金庸武俠之飽受盜印摧殘，自然是受政治因素的影響，自〈戒嚴法〉頒布以來，金庸的小說一直在「禁書」目錄中（全面的查禁，則自 1959 年底實施「暴雨專案」始）。據《查禁圖書目錄》[1] 所載，金庸小說中的《書劍恩仇錄》、《碧血劍》及《射鵰英雄傳》三部最早的作品，曾在 1957 年「登臺」過（由

1　此書由臺灣省政府、臺北市政府、臺灣警備總司令部聯合編印，首度刊行於民國 66 年，其後逐年有所增訂。

時時出版社印行），但均遭禁毀（甚至直到 1980 年，遠景出版《金庸作品集》，
已刻意更名的《大漠英雄傳》仍赫然入列），故此後臺灣武俠出版社只能以各
種名目盜版印行，以下是筆者經見的目錄：

今書名	盜版印行書名
《射鵰英雄傳》	《萍蹤俠影錄》，綠文著，32 集，莫愁出版社，民 47.3～48. 5，17、18 至 27、28 兩集合訂爲一冊，共 26 冊。慧明書局於民 61 年亦重印。
	案：此書明顯爲據香港書翻印，且所據版本不同，故內文字體往往各集不一，且集數參差不齊。《射鵰》於 1957 至 1959 年連載於《香港商報》，顯見臺灣此書也是「舊本」，唯獨藉梁羽生的書名爲題，並捏造作者姓名而已。
	《英雄傳》，27 冊，新興書局，民 63 年印行。
《倚天屠龍記》	《至尊刀》，歐陽生著，33 集（未完或缺），四維出版社，民 53.7～54.3。
	案：此書幾乎完全依據金庸原著，連文字亦大體未改，然書中人名一律改換，如張無忌—葛百陽，張翠山—葛慎之，殷素素—尹薇薇，謝遜—穆謙，張三豐 葛聖倫（葛慎之之祖父）等，武當派也改爲終南派。[2]《倚天》於 1961 至 1963 年連載於《明報》，故此書當是金書完成後改編者。
	《天龍之龍》，12 冊，奔雷出版社，民 53 年印行。
	《天劍龍刀》，30 冊，新興書局，民 66 年印行。
	《懺情記》，4 冊，司馬翎著，南琪出版社，民 68 年 25 開本。
	案：南琪出版社是臺灣專業武俠小說出版社的「八大書系」之一，從民國 61 年起，即以司馬翎、古龍名目印行金庸諸作，先是 32 開本，68 年後改爲 25 開本，一律改換書名，自擬回目，偶爾變更主角名姓。

---

2 此書作者不知是誰，但國學根柢顯然不足，武當在湖北，終南在陝西，分明地域不同，
   但還是依舊本將終南派寫成在湖北，連改頭換面的功力都很糟，令人啼笑皆非。

《鹿鼎記》	《神武門》，司馬翎著，32 集，南琪出版社，民 61 底～62 初，民 66 再版。 《小白龍》，司馬翎著，31 集，南琪出版社，民 62.5～63.2，民 66 再版。 案：此二書割裂原書，且據原小説中的相關地點及人物外號命名。書中的韋小寶（小桂子）之名改成任大同（小柱子）。
《笑傲江湖》	《一劍光寒四十洲》，司馬翎著，25 集，南琪出版社，民 62 左右，民 66 再版。 《獨孤九劍》，司馬翎著，29 集，南琪出版社，民 63.10～63.12，民 66 再版。 案：亦割裂原書而成，前半部改換諸葛青雲之《一劍光寒十四洲》書名，後半部則從小説中之劍法而來。
《書劍恩仇錄》	《劍客書生》，司馬翎著，28 冊，南琪出版社，民 66 年；又，68 年重印 25 開本，3 冊。
《俠客行》	《玄鐵令》，古龍著，上下二冊，南琪出版社，民 68 年 25 開本。
《連城訣》	《飄泊英雄傳》，古龍著，上下二冊，南琪出版社，民 68 年 25 開本。
《神鵰俠侶》等	依原書名、作者名印行，新星書局，民 64 左右，32 開本。 案：這是臺灣正式以金庸之名印行的小説，但並未獲得授權。據筆者所見，有《飛狐外傳》、《倚天屠龍記》、《神鵰俠侶》、《射鵰英雄傳》（改名《大漠英雄傳》）、《碧血劍》、《天龍八部》等。

　　一是「修訂本」，1980 年金庸將十年修訂的成果授權臺北遠景出版社出版，共計 25 開 15 種 36 冊，其後則由遠流接手，這是流傳最廣、最普遍的版本。依其版式，有文庫本（48 開）、平裝本及典藏本、線裝本等。據聞金庸已經開始進行第三度的修訂，遠流亦策劃出版「評點本」。此外，大陸三聯書局、香港明河社（以新、馬地區為發行網）則有簡體字版本。這些版本，儘管外觀、版式或序跋有所差異，但文本內容皆是一致的。

　　除此之外，金庸的作品至今已有多種外文譯本。據廖建裕所述，東南亞

的印尼在五〇年代已有金庸小說譯本，[3] 據年代考察，譯本所據當是舊本；修訂本方面，1986 年起，韓國翻譯家金一江、朴永昌等，陸續翻譯了全套的金庸作品；[4] 日本則有 1997 年岡崎由美等人翻譯的《書劍恩仇錄》（德間書屋出版）；英文譯本，最早是有 Robin Wu 於 1972 年據舊本翻譯的《雪山飛狐》（*Flying Fox of Snow Mountain*）；其後 1994 年，Olivia Mok 也譯有此書（*Fox Volant of the Snowy Mountain*）；最近出版 John Minford 的《鹿鼎記》（*The Deer and the Cauldorn*），則屬修訂本系統。

金庸的舊版作品，目前零星流散於私人藏書家之手，匯集起來，定有完本；但是藏書家寶愛逾恆，輕易不肯外示，因此究竟世面上曾出現過多少種不同的舊版，至今仍無法斷定。在無法完整蒐羅金庸舊版小說的情況下，欲作所謂的「金庸版本學」研究，可能是個奢談；然而，版本研究的目的是可以多向度的，在此，我們將整個重心置於新、舊本情節、內容的差異上，藉新、舊本的比對，一則探討其文學性的優劣，一則深究金庸「歷時性」的創作心理，再綜合二者，討論相關的意義。

基本上，我以金庸早期在報章上的「刊本」為始點，但在資料不足下，部分則取香港出版的「舊本」，更不得不在「舊本」難尋的窘境下，藉助於臺灣的「盜本」。所幸，這幾個版本雖互有差異（如回目），但大體上均與原「刊本」相差無幾，已足夠具體分析、解決相關問題。至於「修訂版」方面，我用的是遠景於 1980 年出版的《金庸作品集》。

三、金庸小說的「新」與「舊」

金庸的作品雖僅十五部，但以字數來算，卻將近三千萬言；而且，金庸潛心案首，大到情節、人物，小至文字修辭，修定、更動之處極多，自不可能（也無必要）一一臚列標舉。在此，我將舉其犖犖大者，作具體的分析。

金庸「修訂版」小說，相對於舊版，變動的幅度極大，基本上，有以下

3　見〈金庸的武俠小說在印尼〉，收入《諸子百家看金庸（四）》（臺北：遠流出版公司，1987），頁 147-158。廖文提及最先出現的譯本為顏國梁所譯的《神鵰俠侶》。

4　見李致洙，〈中國武俠小說在韓國的翻譯介紹與影響〉，淡江大學編，《俠與中國文化》（臺北：學生書局，1993），頁 83。

幾種重要的易動：

一是文字、修辭上的更易，包含了內文的修飾與回目的重新設計；

二是情節的改換，包含了人物的性格、關係及情節的鋪排；

三是歷史性的增強，包含了相關史實的增入及附註說明。

㈠文字修辭方面

金庸修訂舊本小說，可謂達到了鉅細靡遺的地步，在文字修辭部分，幾乎每處皆有，是更動最多的地方。文辭的修訂，使金庸文字的風格更見典雅朗暢、流麗高華，可讀性也增強；尤其是金庸將若干仍饒具「說書」格套的「且說」、「話說」、「暫且不表」等盡行刪削，[5] 使小說內文更見純淨。論者謂金庸小說「達到了白話文的新高峰」，[6] 雖未免誇張，但就通俗小說而言，金庸的文字風格確實有其獨特的魅力，可作爲初入文章門徑者的津梁。當然，這瑣碎細微的修辭工夫，雖也展現了金庸自我嚴肅要求的意義，但相對於我們探討的主題，反而是較不重要的。

回目的重新設計，是金庸修訂版中下得工夫甚深的部分，從《雪山飛狐》之不著一字（僅用一、二、三區隔），到《笑傲江湖》二字擬目（如「滅門」、「聆秘」、「救難」），《射鵰英雄傳》、《神鵰俠侶》之四字擬目（前者如「風雪驚變」、「江南七怪」；後者如「風月無情」、「故人之子」），到《飛狐外傳》等三、五、六字不等的白話「章」（如「血印石」、「大雨商家堡」、「風雨深宵古廟」）；再從《書劍恩仇錄》的七字聯對（如「古道騰駒驚白髮，危巒快劍識青翎」）、《碧血劍》的五字聯對（如「危邦行蜀道，亂世壞長城」），到《倚天屠龍記》的「柏梁臺體」擬目（從「天涯思君不可忘，武當山頂松柏長」以下共 40 句，句句押韻）、《天龍八部》的自創新詞（分別以〈少年游〉、〈蘇慕遮〉等五個詞調分卷），到《鹿鼎記》集清人查慎行的詩句（如「縱橫鉤黨清

---

5 見葉洪生，〈「偷天換日」的是與非──比較金庸新、舊版《射鵰英雄傳》〉，收入《武俠小說談藝錄》（臺北：聯經出版公司，1994），頁 336。

6 在 1998 年 5 月，美國科羅拉多大學舉辦的「金庸小說與二十世紀中國文學國際學術討論會」（International Conference on Jin Yong and Twentieth-Century Chinese Literature）中，多數學者均自此角度評價金庸小說的文字，其中，李陀的〈金庸寫作中的「言」和「文」〉最具代表性。

流禍，峭蒨風期月旦評」、「絕世奇事傳聞裡，最好交情見面初」），變化繁複，風格各有差異。

回目的編次，是作者匠心及創意的設計，在中國古典說部中有淵遠流長的傳統，大體上，古典說部以「聯對」見長，我們所熟知的「四大奇書」與《紅樓夢》，正是以五、七、八字的聯對擬目的。武俠小說在回目的擬定上，是最具有傳統古典風味的，從平江不肖生的《江湖奇俠傳》（首回「裝乞丐童子尋師，起寶塔深山遇俠」），到還珠樓主的《蜀山劍俠傳》（一集首回「月夜棹孤舟巫峽啼猿登棧道，天涯逢知己移家結伴隱名山」），著名的武俠作品，幾乎都延續著此一傳統。就是如文藝腔十足的王度廬，儘管內容可以寫得宛若現代的言情小說，悱惻纏綿，但回目仍以聯對爲之（如《寶劍金釵》首回之「銀髯鐵臂老鏢頭隱居，美景芳春小俠女救父」）；而平生向以創作武俠爲屈辱的宮白羽，一鳴驚人之作《十二金錢鏢》，也得依循故轍（如首回之「小隱俠蹤閒居傳劍術，頻聞盜警登門借鏢旗」）。據張贛生所論，武俠小說中的還珠樓主，在這方面表現得最爲出色，「真正把這種回目的特色著意發揮，充分顯示其獨具的審美價值」，並舉《蜀山劍俠傳》之「生死故人情更堪早歲恩仇忍見鴛鴦同并命，蒼茫高世感爲了前因魔障甘聯鶼鰈不羨仙」爲例，許其「詩情奔放，意味雋永」。[7]

以聯對爲回目的「古典味」，在三〇年代，曾因其代表的「封建」意味，受到某些專家的批判，如沈雁冰即以「作品中每回書的字數必須大略相等，回目要用一個對子」等，「把章回體的弱點赤裸裸的暴露出來了」，[8] 極力加以抨擊。處在當時左翼文學勢力如日中天的壓力下，若干武俠作家也自有一套相應的更張；當然，武俠小說既以「通俗」形式存在，在面對通俗作品讀者逐漸匱乏古典文學素養的情況下，如何以更妥善的方式處理回目，以博取讀者的接納，也是一個思考的重點。在此，朱貞木是一個重要的範例。朱貞木的武俠小說，無論遣詞用字，都有十足的現代性，儘管寫的是古代背景的武俠小說，但是流行的新興名詞卻敢於大量運用。[9] 在回目上，朱貞木亦多所

7　見《民國通俗小說論稿》（重慶：重慶出版社，1991），頁 20。
8　見沈雁冰〈自然主義與中國現代小說〉，轉引自張贛生《民國通俗小說論稿》，頁 18。
9　張贛生曾引一例（前揭書，頁 310），轉引如下，以見一斑：
　　「沐天瀾載美而歸，理應歡天喜地；無奈背上的人頭，老在他心裡作怪，老是懷著一則

更張，以白話短詞、短句擬目，如《羅剎夫人》之「英雄黑裡俏」（第 1 章）、「美男計」（第 15 章）、「肚內的秘密」（第 23 章），《七殺碑》之「新娘子步步下蛋」（第 1 章）、「詭計」（第 11 章）、「大佛頭上請客」（第 17 章），「現代」的風味，一望即知。葉洪生曾謂「由於朱氏曾首創白話章回，而其小說筆法、內容又多爲五十年代港、臺武俠作家所仿效，因有『新派武俠小說之祖』的美譽」，[10] 可以說是一語中的，尤其是熟知古龍的讀者，看到「活寶」、「陳大娘的紙捻兒」、「賣荷包的家」等回目，定然會覺得非常眼熟吧？

　　回目的擬定，不但關涉到作者創作時全文情節的設計、主要內容的提示，更是藉以吸引讀者目光的噱頭。傳統聯對式的擬目，「精練、醒目，且具有形式美」，[11] 所長在其詩化語言的文字藝術功力及明顯而扼要的欏括內容，但由於讀者之疏離於古典詩文，故所短則在文字障，如前所舉還珠樓主的「生死故人情更堪早歲恩仇忍見鴛鴦同并命，蒼茫高世感爲了前因魔障甘聯鶼鰈不羨仙」，一般讀者恐怕連標點都會感到困難，同時，自不易明瞭此回主要內容。自朱貞木而下的現代擬目法，所長在文字簡易明瞭、重點顯豁，且具有懸疑性，以古龍的《蕭十一郎》爲例，從「情人的手・風四娘的手・花平的手」[12] 而下，主要都是藉「□□的□」標回目，文字儘管淺白，但重點十分清楚，且讓讀者不禁會饒有興致地欲窺知「究竟這些手有何特色？」而具先聲奪人的懸疑作用；但所短則在於作者任情標目，往往故弄玄虛，回目與內文根本無法繫聯，如溫瑞安《殺人寫好詩・深喉》之以「不管白狗黑狗，咬主人的就是衰狗」、「不論白馬黑馬，跑不動的就是劣馬」擬目，不過是書中人物的一句話，就不免走火入魔了。傳統與現代，互有短長，但看不同時期讀者的抉擇。

　　以喜一則以憂的觀念。女羅剎忐忑不寧的心情，他也一樣意識得到。不過此時他是主體，他明白自己家中的環境。進城門時，在馬上打好了應付環境的計劃草案；走到沐公府相近處所，馬頭一轉不進轅門，特地從僻道繞到自己府後花園圍牆外面。兩人一縱下馬，一聽府內正打二更，牆外悄無人影。兩人戚戚低語了一陣，便把沐天瀾的計劃草案通過了。」

　　文字的優劣與否不論，此段文字在用語上的大膽前進，是可以看出來的。

10　見《中國近代武俠小說名著大系・總編序》（臺北：聯經出版公司，1984）。

11　見張贛生前揭書，頁 20。

12　這是古龍於 1969 年 12 月，在《武俠春秋》創刊號標示的回目。

　　金庸修訂本小說的擬目，有若干配合小說內容的成分，如《雪山飛狐》以嶄新的西方模式「不結之結」創作，留下一個懸疑讓讀者揣摩，因此在回目上，也僅以一、二、三、四標出，倒也頗能相得益彰；不過，大體上以興到筆隨爲主，無一定成見，有時候僅僅取舊文重新編次，有時即興作詩、塡詞，更有時爲了推揚先人而集句。茲將其重要的編目簡說如下：

(1)重新編次者：《射鵰英雄傳》，舊本 80 回，修訂本 40 回，大致上取二
　　　　　　　　回併成一回，如舊本 1、2 回〈雪地鋤奸〉、〈午夜驚變〉
　　　　　　　　縮成〈風雪驚變〉；79、80 回〈異地重逢〉、〈華山論劍〉
　　　　　　　　縮成〈華山論劍〉。各回起訖不劃一，蓋因有所增刪之故。
　　　　　　　　《書劍恩仇錄》，舊本 40 回，修訂本 20 回，變化幅度較
　　　　　　　　多，主要是改單句爲聯對，其中既有直接取舊目而不改
　　　　　　　　易者，如舊本 23、24 回，併成 12 回〈盈盈彩燭三生約，
　　　　　　　　霍霍青霜萬里行〉；亦有取舊目櫽括者，如舊本 3、4 回
　　　　　　　　〈秋風野店書生笛〉、〈夕照荒莊俠士心〉，修訂本 2 回作
　　　　　　　　〈金風野店書生笛，鐵膽荒莊俠士心〉；更有重新擬定
　　　　　　　　者，如舊本 35、36 回〈竟託古禮完夙願〉、〈還從遺書悟
　　　　　　　　平生〉，修訂本 18 回作〈驅驢有術居奇貨，除惡無方從
　　　　　　　　佳人〉，回名不同，顯見重點有異。[13]
　　　　　　　　《神鵰俠侶》，刊本 30 回，修訂本 40 回，變化也很大，
　　　　　　　　不過原有的四字成詞結構並未改變，主要是重新編次
　　　　　　　　後，再據內容主體擬目，如舊本前 2 回爲〈深宵怪客〉、
　　　　　　　　〈桃花島上〉，修訂本的相應回目是〈風月無情〉；刊本末
　　　　　　　　3 回爲〈三世恩怨〉、〈襄陽鏖兵〉、〈尾聲〉，修訂本則爲
　　　　　　　　〈大戰襄陽〉、〈華山之巔〉。

(2)作詩塡詞者：《倚天屠龍記》，刊本分正續集，共 33 回，原爲四字回
　　　　　　　　目，如前 2 回爲〈花落花開〉、〈屠龍寶刀〉，末 2 回爲〈共

_____

13　此回改訂的優劣，可能人各有所見，但舊本強調的重點是李沅芷與余魚同的「針笛奇
　　緣」和紅花會前總舵主于萬亭的遺書，就與情節內容的配合而言，顯然要強過修訂本
　　之以驅驢（胡蘿蔔懸於驢前，可使驢拼命向前，書中用以影射張召重）及張召重最後
　　膏於狼吻的結局。

舉義旗〉、〈是耶非耶〉；修訂本 40 回，每回改爲七言一句，合爲 40 句的七言古詩：「天涯思君不可忘，武當山頂松柏長。寶刀百鍊生玄光，字作喪亂意徬徨。……」爲句句押韻的「柏梁臺體」古詩。

《天龍八部》，刊本分八部 64 回，四字回目，前 2 回爲〈無量玉璧〉、〈神馳目眩〉，末 2 回爲〈佳兵不祥〉、〈雁門關外〉；修訂本 50 回，每 10 回成一詞調，依序爲〈少年遊〉、〈破陣子〉、〈蘇幕遮〉、〈洞仙歌〉、〈水龍吟〉，由於詞調句數不定，故每回單、雙句不一。

(3)集句者：《鹿鼎記》，刊本 22 回，修訂本 50 回。除了楔子〈如此冰霜如此路，痛哭流涕有若是〉外，均爲七言聯對，刊本首回〈紅巾方見劇賊走，白鬚又報官軍過〉，修訂本首回則作〈縱橫鈎黨清流禍，峭蒨風期月旦評〉；刊本末回〈雲點旌旗秋出塞，風傳鼓角夜臨關〉，修訂本末回則爲〈鶚立雲端原矯矯，鴻飛天外又冥冥〉。這些聯對，均是自查慎行《敬業堂詩集》中輯出的，作者自言「所用的方法，不是像一般集句那樣從不同詩篇中選錄單句，甚至是從不同作者的詩中選集單句，而是選用一個人詩作的整個聯句」，[14] 之所以鍾情於查慎行，「康熙曾經看過」固是原因，但眞正的用意，恐怕還是在「替自己祖先的詩句宣揚一下」。[15]

總體而言，金庸修訂本的回目，「露才揚己（包含了祖先）」的意義，遠大於回目本身的適切性。經過修訂後的回目，典雅精緻，處處透顯文人色彩，因此高華流麗，與其內容上的文字同一風格；但是若要說到回目與內文的相關性，發揮相輔相成的效果，恐怕仍有一間之未達。其中尤以自作詩詞與集句者爲最，蓋詩詞創作較受格律牽拘，欲藉此鉤勒每回要旨，本就甚難（此所以聯對回目逐漸消失），尤其是用「集句」（又限於某人之詩）的方式，更是

14　見《鹿鼎記》第 1 冊（臺北：遠景出版社，1981），頁 44 自註。

15　同上註。

夐夐乎其難尤甚。因此，作者自己固然不得不承認其中「有些回目難免不很貼切」，[16] 學者更是很容易就發現此一類似「兒戲」的編目，「多少對小說有所損失」[17] 的弊病。平心而論，金庸修訂過後的回目，較諸舊本，實未見精采；而諸所撰詩詞聯對，恐怕也是平穩有餘，神氣不足。從通俗的角度而言，過度的「露才揚己」及文人化，勢將造成作品與讀者間的隔閡，楊興安謂「看回目便摸不著頭腦」，[18] 正指出了這個問題。事實上，金庸未必不明白這點，因此屢以加註的方式彌補，「回目中有生僻詞語或用典故的，在每回文末稍作注解」，[19] 問題是，金庸固然用心良苦，卻模糊、混淆了小說的特色，我們很難想像，如果金庸不是如今的「金大俠」，讀者接受的可能究竟有多大。

㈡情節的改換

就通俗小說而言，情節（plot）永遠是最吸引讀者的聚焦點，因此，不但金庸的「十年修訂」以此為重心，就是論者也多半集矢於此。金庸改換的情節相當多，倪匡最先提出《倚天屠龍記》中有關「玉面火猴」被刪掉一事，[20] 繼而潘國森、楊興安也提到《碧血劍》、《書劍恩仇錄》、《射鵰英雄傳》、《倚天屠龍記》、《笑傲江湖》等多處增刪之處，[21] 如果花些精力，將金庸新舊版本加以比對，相信一定遠比想像中為多。在此，僅取其具代表性的改換部分，略述如下：

(1)刪除的情節

金庸增刪的情節，向來頗為老讀者矚目，其中較重要的有《射鵰英雄傳》中「蛙蛤大戰」、《倚天屠龍記》中「玉面火猴」，及《神鵰俠侶》中楊過的生母秦南琴。茲簡述如下：

【玉面火猴】

在《倚天屠龍記》中，誕生於海外絕域冰火島的張無忌，原本有一玩伴

16　同註 14。

17　見陳墨，《金庸小說與中國文化》（南昌：百花洲文藝出版社，1995），頁 221。

18　見《金庸小說十談・談翻譯與增刪》（臺北：遠流出版公司，1998），頁 122。

19　同註 14。

20　見《我看金庸小說》（臺北：遠流出版公司，1997），頁 23。

21　潘國森，《話說金庸》（1987）；楊興安，《金庸小說十談》（1998），均由臺北遠流出版。

「玉面火猴」，修訂本則加以刪除。據舊本，「玉面火猴」爲張無忌在冰火島上的童年玩伴，之所以稱爲「火猴」，是因其「入火不焦」，堪稱神物。倪匡對金庸刪去此物，大致不滿。[22]

【秦南琴與蛙蛤大戰】

在修訂本中，已不見秦南琴的蹤影，但在舊本中，秦南琴是楊過的生母，其父秦老漢捕蛇爲生，由於縣太爺藉口需索毒蛇，強搶此女作抵；郭靖仗義相助，並收服了血鳥。其後，秦南琴爲鐵掌幫所擄，裘千仞命父女二人驅蛙、蛇、蛤蟆相鬥，欲從中習得破解歐陽鋒「蛤蟆功」的武學；接著，將她轉送給楊康，慘遭汚辱，以此懷了楊過。由於刪改的幅度甚大，因此舊本中許多重要的情節也隨之簡省，其中如秦南琴對郭靖的微妙情愫、秦南琴受辱後的激烈性情（與楊過頗類似）、秦南琴撕毀《武穆遺書》、毒蛇剋星「血鳥」、「蛙蛤大戰」[23] 等，皆完全不見蹤影；而爲了改穆念慈爲楊過生母，也只得將原來殉情楊康的穆念慈，重新還魂。粗略估計之下，相關情節被刪除不下於一萬五千字。

(2)改換的情節

【小說開場】

修訂本中，金庸於《碧血劍》、《射鵰英雄傳》等書的開場，均作過大幅度的修訂。《碧血劍》原由明末四公子之一的侯方域開場，引出袁承志；修訂本則改爲以一心嚮慕中原文化的張朝唐串場。《射鵰英雄傳》原來僅由「山外青山樓外樓，西湖歌舞幾時休，晚風薰得遊人醉，直把杭州作汴州」一詩，點出時代背景的輪廓；修訂本則篇幅擴增，以張十五說書，將詳細的歷史現象及人民觀感一一申說分明。

【韋小寶的武功】

22　同註20，頁 23-25。

23　楊興安對金庸刪除「蛙蛤大戰」及「血鳥」之處，頗致不滿，以爲這是一段「極精采、極匪夷所思」、令人「眼界大開」、「眉飛色舞」的文字（〈談翻譯與增刪〉，前揭書，頁 120）。平心而論，就文字上說，舊本此段果然精采，但是類似的描寫，自《鏡花緣》第 21 回〈逢惡獸唐生被難，施神槍魏女解圍〉以來，早期武俠小說家頗致力於類此「動物大戰」的情節刻畫，創意並不十足，同時亦頗具神怪色彩；且其事攸關秦南琴，既刪此人，自不得不忍痛割愛。

　　說韋小寶是個「武林低手」，相信閱讀過修訂本《鹿鼎記》的讀者，都會發出會心的微笑。在尚武的江湖世界中，韋小寶不能不會武功；因此，金庸也賦予了他某些「必要」的武功，如打鬥危急時出奇制勝用的「救命六招」（「美人三招」和「英雄三招」）、「三十六計走爲上計」的「腳底抹油功」（「神行百變」），但也不讓他專精，僅僅點到爲止。不過，很少有人注意到，金庸的舊本《鹿鼎記》中，韋小寶剛開始時是頗具一般武俠小說中的「俠客架勢」的。他不但「肯」虛心學習陳近南所傳授的武功，以致武功大有進展；同時天性聰慧精明，海老公所傳的「大擒拿手」、「大慈大悲千葉手」，可以「輕易」學會；甚至還安排了一部海老公與《四十二章經》一起收藏的「圖經」，韋小寶用陳近南的秘訣導引，「津津有味」地練成了四圖，金庸謂韋小寶「無意之間，已將兩門截不相同的武功揉合在一起」，「成爲武學中從所未有之奇」。[24] 順此發展，韋小寶之與其他俠客般，自創絕學，成爲「武林高手」，應是可以水到渠成的。可是，後來金庸構想改變，不但以前所學會的初級武功派不上用場，一味死纏爛打、狡獪脫困，連這一「自創武功」圖經，也消聲匿跡了。其實，據舊本看來，韋小寶未必不懂武功，而是作者金庸「廢」了韋小寶武功——不但在舊本中半途易轍地「廢」，更在修訂本中彌補了前後設計不一的缺陷，大力刪削，[25] 終究形成了武俠小說中唯一不懂武功卻能在江湖世界中大放異采的「千古人物」！

　　【鐵膽莊風雲】

　　《書劍恩仇錄》中，張召重大索鐵膽莊，搜出文泰來；陳家洛率群雄興問罪之師，大鬧鐵膽莊一段，寫得相當精采，其中尤以莊主周仲英徘徊於朋友義氣及親情之間的矛盾複雜、辛酸悲痛，更是入木三分，令人盪氣迴腸。修訂本中，文泰來的藏身之所，是張召重以言詞相激，周英傑小孩好勝，脫口而出，因而敗露；其後，周仲英氣怒責子，誤拋鐵膽，傷其性命。舊本則寫張召重以西洋千里鏡（望遠鏡）爲餌，步步爲誘，終於搜出文泰來；而周仲英在得知情實後，則先命周英傑交待未完的心願、向母親叩謝懷養之恩，

24　見臺版《神武門》第 10 集，頁 18。此節「刊本」連載 148 期中，以「兩種武功，混合爲一」當小標題，顯見是一設計重點。

25　有關金庸如何廢了韋小寶武功，筆者學生錢天善有〈金庸廢了韋小寶武功〉一文，羅列新舊本差異，頗有可取。

然後「在周英傑天靈蓋上一掌，『噗』的一聲，孩子雙目突出，頓時氣絕」。[26]

【降龍十八掌】

「降龍十八掌」是金庸武俠小說中最引人矚目的武學，究竟這十八掌名目爲何，討論的人多如過江之鯽。[27]「降龍十八掌」之所以吸引讀者，不但是因爲此武功正氣威猛，而且在《射鵰英雄傳》、《神鵰俠侶》、《天龍八部》中，皆與眾所喜愛的洪七公、郭靖、蕭峯緊緊繫聯；更由於其名目取之於《易經》，卻模糊籠統，讓讀者一時無法確定。[28] 以「降龍」爲名的武功設計，最直接的聯想便是與龍有關，金庸於此轉化一層，將《易經・乾卦》中的概念化入武功，而「乾卦」六爻中可用者原不過四爻（潛龍勿用、見龍在田、飛龍在天、亢龍有悔），故不得不借他卦經文補足（有無龍字就不予考量了），而成爲如今膾炙人口的武學——這是金庸修訂本中的構想。不過，舊本原先的設計，是純粹以「龍」爲主的，如「雙龍搶珠」（後改「履霜冰至」，且增加一段闡釋武學的說明）、[29]「雲龍三現」（後改「羝羊觸藩」）、「六龍迴旋」（已刪）均曾用過；而「神龍擺尾」，原爲舊招，卻「一氣化三清」，分別轉成「鴻漸於陸」、「震驚百里」、「神龍擺尾」（此招金庸曾特別說明，其原名爲出自《易經・履卦》的「履虎尾」，因嫌其「文謅謅」，故改名如此；[30] 但舊本則無，可見金庸重新設計的苦心）三招。換句話說，修訂本充實且深化了「降龍十八掌」，使得金庸的武學設計更上一層樓。[31]

金庸新舊本情節的優劣，論者各有不同的看法，尤其是針對其間單一的情節，更是人各一詞。不過，大多數人似乎偏好舊本，如倪匡、潘國森、楊

26　見香港光榮本《書劍恩仇錄》第 1 冊（無出版年月），頁 107。

27　在臺灣各大學 BBS 的武俠版上，這問題始終是熱門的討論話題。

28　據統計，降龍十八掌除了「亢龍有悔」(1)、「飛龍在天」(2)、「突如其來」(11)、「見龍在田」(15)、「履霜冰至」(16)等五招有明確序次外，其他十三掌均不詳其序次；而且，「龍戰於野」／「戰龍在野」、「或躍在淵」／「魚躍於淵」兩招，未作劃一；「笑言啞啞」亦難斷定是否屬十八掌之一。

29　見《射鵰英雄傳》第 3 冊，頁 1147。

30　見《射鵰英雄傳》第 2 冊，頁 616-617。

31　案：金庸的「打狗棒法」也經重新設計，原來的「當頭棒喝」、「大鬧天宮」等招數，均改爲與狗有關者，如「棒打狗頭」、「反戳狗臀」等，蓋既是「打狗棒法」，理應招招以狗爲對象。

興安等皆明白言之，[32] 後者甚至認為金庸改得最好的，只有「語嫣」兩字。[33]
不過，我個人傾向於認同修訂本。以「降龍十八掌」的重新設計而言，我們
不得不承認，金庸在「武學文藝化」的功力上，的確是精益求精、造詣非凡
的了。同時，在修訂本中，金庸重塑韋小寶，使此一機智伶俐、油腔滑調的
「不學無術」人物，跳脫了舊有武俠小說的格局，更彰顯了此一角色在武俠小
說上的獨創性。的確，韋小寶以一介市井混混，夤緣廟堂，於江湖、宮廷兩
個截然不同的世界中縱橫得意，無往而不利，真的是個「異數」。宮廷之間，
以傾軋鬥爭、爾虞我詐為能事，韋小寶的機智伶俐，於此場合中可以如魚得
水，這倒不見希奇；而江湖——這個「尚武」的世界，韋小寶的「三腳貓」
功夫，居然也能折服三山五嶽的武林高手，就真的讓人意外了。《鹿鼎記》在
本質上是武俠小說，但經金庸如此設計，卻整個「顛覆」了武俠小說的體質，
這真的是「前無古人」的創舉。

當然，優劣的論評往往仁智互見，甚難劃一，大體上，天機流行、情感
自然充沛，為舊本所長；而精密謹嚴、妥貼穩重，則修訂本為優勝，相信是
新、舊本公允的評價。

在此，我們姑且不論其優與劣，而試著探討一下金庸修訂所持的標準。

金庸是武壇中第一個嚴肅面對自己作品的作家，頗有以其作品鳴於世的
雄心，因此，在求好心切之下，不滿於當時受限於倉促、急迫、間歇時間壓
力下的連載作品，而欲出之以精密之思，一修再修乃至於三修，是很容易理
解的。平心而論，舊本中不乏前後無法貫串的矛盾（如韋小寶的武功），及牽
強違理的情節（如周仲英之為友殺子），修訂本一一予以更換，自是必要之舉，
因此，且補罅漏，當是金庸修訂的標準之一。

其次，誠如楊興安所指出，金庸「刪筆尺度，務求不致過於神異而求可

---

32 倪匡謂「喜歡舊版多於新版」（前揭書，頁 25），潘國森謂「確是舊不如新」（前揭書，
　頁 1），楊興安謂「不改勝於刪改，原版勝於新版」（前揭文，頁 114）。
33 《天龍八部》中，王語嫣舊本作「王玉燕」，楊興安認為「玉燕太平凡了，而『語嫣』
　則別具姿韻，很切合主人翁仙霧迷漫般的身分」（前揭文，頁 122）。平心而論，金庸
　小說中的角色姓名，一般都很平凡，較之古龍、溫瑞安取名之飄逸瀟灑（如楚留香、
　李尋歡，蕭秋水、方振眉），略嫌板實，但全部小說風格一致，兀然凸顯出一「語嫣」，
　究竟是優是劣，倒不易判斷。

信性」；[34] 倪匡亦指出，金庸刪除「玉面火猴」，是因爲「這種靈異的猴子曾在許多武俠小說中出現過，爲了不想落入『俗套』」。[35] 所謂的「神異」，當指「蛙蛤大戰」、「血鳥」之類的異物異事，熟悉武俠作品的讀者，當然不會忘記「舊派」名家還珠樓主《蜀山劍俠傳》（甚至臺灣早期的「舊派」如墨餘生《瓊海騰蛟》、衡山向夢葵《紫龍珮》等）中的許多神物靈怪，金庸創造這些作品之時，尚頗多沿襲前輩大家之處，[36] 居十數年之後，以刪削當開新，亦未嘗不是金庸精益求精之意，所謂「不落俗套」，正可此角度視之。金庸刻意避免「神異」之處，也可由「蝮蛇寶血」中窺出。郭靖之學「降龍十八掌」，以其駑鈍之資質，儘管具有「人家練一朝，我就練十天」[37] 的不懈精神，但「降龍十八掌」奧妙不在招式，而是內力，郭靖此時根本未習上乘內功，如何能學成，相信讀者不免滋疑。事實上，在舊本中，郭靖誤飮「蝮蛇寶血」，內力明顯增強，正是爲後來習「降龍十八掌」作伏線；但是，類似的情節，幾已成爲武俠俗套，且未免過於「神異」，因此金庸於修訂時大力刪削，卻忘了予以補救。至於「可信性」，則是金庸整個刪削事業中最明顯的標準，將於下文論之。

㈢歷史意識的強調

金庸的小說，向來以其濃厚的歷史氛圍，爲讀者所津津樂道。一方面，作者刻意在作品中凸顯出重大歷史事件或歷史背景，如《天龍八部》取北宋初年宋、遼爭持的場域爲背景，「射鵰三部曲」則從南宋之宋、金對峙，歷元蒙崛起到元末群雄幷起的初期，《碧血劍》寫明末流寇倡亂、清人入關，《鹿鼎記》敍康熙一朝盛事，《書劍恩仇錄》則述乾隆皇帝身世秘辛。其中雖然以「虛構」爲主，但是正史、野史、軼聞相互參雜，主脈朗顯，令人印象深刻。

34　同註18，頁123。

35　同註20，頁23。

36　葉洪生經常提出金庸受還珠樓主的影響，1998 年 5 月於美國科羅拉多大學「金庸小説與二十世紀中國文學國際學術討論會」中，更以〈論金庸小説美學及其武俠原型〉一文，洋洋乎言之。

　　金庸於閉幕致辭，一一答辯，頗不以爲然。然筆者認爲，蓄意模仿，當不至於，而所受影響，自當不少。

37　見《射鵰英雄傳》第 2 冊，頁 472。

一方面，作者在正文中隨處附加了註文、按語和楔子，如《天龍八部》正文前的一段〈釋名〉，就在解說完《天龍八部》書名之由來後，清楚地標示整個故事的確實年代在「北宋哲宗元祐、紹聖年間，公元 1094 年前後」。[38] 有時候，作者更不惜長篇大論，引述史料，加強其歷史眞實感，如《鹿鼎記》中有關吳六奇、查愼行之事，以按語方式，增錄了《聊齋誌異》和《孤賸》的記載，詳述構思過程，並引介查愼行《敬業堂詩集》之詩，篇幅長達三千餘字，有如學術論文。[39] 金庸小説「歷史感」之強烈，往往使讀者分辨不出究竟他是在寫「歷史小說」還是「武俠小說」，尤其是《鹿鼎記》，連金庸自己都說「毋寧說是歷史小說」；[40] 而且，金庸武俠小說中有關歷史部分的可靠與翔實，甚至也博得了專門史家的贊賞；[41] 誠如倪匡所說，「歷史在金庸筆下，要圓就圓，要方就方，隨心所欲，無不如意。可以一本正經敍述史實，也可以隨便開歷史玩笑。可以史實俱在，不容置辯，也可以子虛烏有，純屬遊戲」；[42] 套句王國維的話，歷史在武俠小說中的運用，到了金庸，才眞正的「眼界始大，感慨遂深」；[43] 金庸出神入化、虛實相生的筆法，委實是令人嘆爲觀止的。[44]

歷史意識的增強，是金庸修訂本中最明顯的企圖，事實上，許多情節的易動，也與欲以歷史故實增強其可信度、展現金庸的史識有關。眾所周知的《射鵰英雄傳》「張十五說書」一段，金庸雖以「傳統小說發源於說書，以說書作引子，以示不忘本源之意」[45] 爲解，然眞正用心，卻在藉張十五的說書內容，詳細交代當時的歷史背景，以及更重要的，金庸對這段歷史的評論——

---

38 見《天龍八部》第 1 冊，頁 7-8。

39 見《鹿鼎記》第 1 冊，頁 37 及 40-44。

40 見《鹿鼎記‧後記》。

41 如崑華山曾致函金庸，稱許其《倚天屠龍記》中對摩尼教的闡述和教規、習慣的描寫，「眞是難得的準確」，見《人民日報》1993 年 12 月 10 日第八版頭條，轉引自陳墨，《金庸小説與中國文化》（南昌：百花洲文藝出版社，1995），頁 16-17。

42 同註 20，頁 79。

43 見《人間詞話》（臺北：漢京文化事業公司，1980），頁 8。

44 請參見筆者〈通俗小説的類型整合——試論金庸的武俠與歷史〉一文，「金庸小説與二十世紀中國文學學術討論會」會議論文（即將刊印成書）。

45 見《射鵰英雄傳‧後記》。

畢竟，若眞的不忘本源，則「且說」、「話說」等語不必盡刪；而張十五以兩宋之人，居然會有類似「這兩個昏君自作自受，那也罷了，可害苦了我中國千千萬萬百姓」[46] 的「大逆不道」之語，也未免荒唐。類似的情形，在修訂本中俯拾可見，除了在可以尋找到任何歷史證據之處，隨時以各種夾注說明外，很明顯的一個趨勢就是將具體的年代標示出來或增入史料，如《天龍八部》的〈釋名〉中，舊版原無「據歷史記載，大理國的皇帝中，聖德帝、孝德帝、保定帝、宣仁帝、正廉帝、神宗等都避位爲僧」、「本書故事發生於北宋哲宗元祐、紹聖年間，公元 1094 年前後」[47] 等語；《碧血劍》中，金庸將原來的引首人物侯朝宗，改換爲渤泥國的張朝唐，因而大引史料入文，都是同樣情形下的產物。

就金庸的小說而言，「歷史感」是無論新、舊本皆「一以貫之」的。大體上，舊本的「歷史感」，著重於鉤勒背景；修訂本的「歷史感」，則在強調「史識」——金庸嫻熟書史，旣「藉歷史寫武俠」，[48] 自然也不會放過在傳述信史的過程中，展現他的「史識」。可以如是說，金庸在修訂本中表現得最顯豁的，就是他的「歷史癖」。

四、「金庸小說版本學」的意義

金庸小說的版本，連同刊本、舊本、修訂本及各地授權發行、外國譯本，林林總總加起來，至少有數十種之多，僅僅從金庸小說版本的數量，我們就可明白，金庸是近代以來最受歡迎的中國作家，論者謂「有華人的地方就有金庸小說」，絕非謬讚之語！

金庸小說版本的差異，有屬於「同時性」受地域影響的部分，如臺灣的「盜版」系統，肇因於政治因素，在 1979 年以前，金庸因《明報》（或曰因《射鵰英雄傳》書名暗用了毛澤東〈沁園春〉「彎弓射大鵰」之語）被歸爲「附匪文人」之列，以致遭到臺灣當局全面禁止。因此，臺灣早期出版金庸小說，

46　見《射鵰英雄傳》第 1 冊，頁 11。
47　見《天龍八部》第 1 冊，頁 7-8。
48　同註 43。

只能以暗度陳倉的方式盜版，或變易作者（其中司馬翎是被借用最多的），或改其書名（如《萍蹤俠影錄》等），或據原書改編（如歐陽生《至尊刀》），或更動主角姓名（如《神武門》及《小白龍》）。金庸小說的盜版現象，可以窺見臺灣在「白色恐怖」時期中，出版商（或文化工作者）如何突破防禁的苦心孤詣（當然，不能諱言，「商機」也是一大誘因），不失爲研究臺灣文化發展的重要史料。

　　不過，大多數的金庸小說版本，是屬於「歷時性」的差異的。金庸的修訂工作始於 1973 年，誠如葉洪生所言，「金庸是用一九七三年的見識眼光來修改十六年前的『舊作』」，「迥異於一般修飾、整理，殆可視爲脫胎換骨，重新改造」，[49] 因此，如果取金庸的新、舊本予以核對，自當可以深入瞭解金庸從開始創作以來的心路歷程，有助於讀者更進一層而瞭解金庸的作品。從最簡單的地方說起，歷來論者對金庸《天龍八部》書名的意涵，饒具興趣，卻往往無法直探其微，無論是將八部天龍一一附會於書中人物，或是取其寓意，視爲一種象徵，總覺主觀意識過濃，不愜人心。然而，「刊本」卻可提供一些切入的線索。在「刊本」中，此書原分「八部」，作者自云「這部小說將包括八個故事，每個故事爲一部。但八個故事互相有連繫，組成一個大故事」，[50]而第一部是「摩呼羅迦（梵文 Maharaga）之部」，這是「八部天龍」中的「樂神，其形蛇首人身」，「無足、腹行之神，因毀戒、邪諂、多瞋、少布施、貪嗜酒肉、怠慢持戒，遂墮爲鬼神；其體內多瞋蟲唂食其身，痛苦異常」。[51] 熟悉此書的讀者，當然知道這一故事以段譽爲主角，主要在敍述雲南大理國糾結複雜的恩怨情仇、冤孽果報。細窺金庸原意，各部之名，應在呈顯故事的「內容」，而非「人物」。不過，金庸寫到一半，似乎就改變了主意，故自第二部起，就不再標示「某部」，而「八個故事」的構想，也告中道而廢了。至於金庸於修訂本序言中所說的「只是借用這個佛經名詞，以象徵一些現世人物，就像《水滸》中有母夜叉孫二娘、摩雲金翅歐鵬」，[52] 顯然只能代表「修訂時」的構想了。

49　同註 5，頁 336。

50　見《明報》連載《天龍八部》第 1 期。

51　見《佛光大辭典》，頁 6086。

52　見《天龍八部》第 1 冊，頁 8。

　　此處之所以強調「修訂時」，主要是欲表明，金庸在修訂時，整個思想、觀念均與原創時期有極大的差異，而此一差異，透過新、舊版的比對，是相當清晰的。以「鐵膽莊事件」爲例，舊版的情節安排周仲英「親手」殺子，並相當戲劇性地演出「交代遺願」、「叩謝生養」的場面，震撼力十足；周仲英爲朋友義氣，不惜泯滅父子親情，很明顯是繼承舊有的俠客形象而來的，我們在《史記‧游俠列傳》郭解不爲外甥報仇、《太平廣記‧豪俠》賈人妻狠心戕殺親子及歷來流傳甚廣的「趙氏孤兒」故事，也依稀可見到類似的影子。俠客的生命重心在「廣交游」，透過義氣朋友的網絡，建構自我聲名，而支撐起這個架構的，就是所謂的「江湖道義」。周英傑「出賣」文泰來，是「見利忘義」，因此「周英傑受賄賣友之事，鐵膽莊的人全都認爲奇恥大辱」，[53] 如果不是因爲周英傑僅僅只是個「十歲小兒」，周仲英如此講究「江湖道義」手刃親子，恐怕眞的是「大仁大義」了。然而，朋友之道果眞遠較父子之情爲重要嗎？假如周英傑是成年人，周仲英應不應該「大義滅親」？此處，實際上牽涉到俠客「義氣」施用於社會現實面的難題及缺憾。而且，周英傑年方十歲，江湖對他而言，根本是虛幻的世界，周仲英強將「江湖道義」加諸小孩身上，不惜以犧牲其生命爲祭獻；而「紅花會」得理不饒人，大興問罪之師，實在令人懷疑，所謂的俠客果眞就是如此不近情理嗎？在眞相大白之後，章駝子這個直性人，居然僅僅用「一揖」，就掩蓋了此一人倫悲劇，暗示了此一不近情理的行爲之「理直氣壯」。很明顯地，金庸此時對俠客的觀念，還是相當傳統而模糊。修訂後，金庸將「受賄」改成「相激」，「親手」改爲「誤殺」，「一揖」改成「磕頭」，正是思考到此「爲義氣殺子」的不合理，而作的改絃更張，也代表了金庸自身俠義觀念的改變——不過，金庸事實上還是迴避了「義氣施用」的問題，這是相當可惜的。

　　此外，金庸在修訂本中所凸顯的「歷史癖」，也是值得探討的心路歷程之一。文學作品，如金庸一般以大量的史料、注腳、夾注、說明充斥其間的，金庸小說算是絕無僅有。讀者不妨激賞，不妨贊嘆，但是卻不能將此視爲其作品的一部分，從而誤認爲這是一種高超的表現方式。誠如陳墨批評《碧血劍》，「作者過多地關注歷史和歷史人物，固然使我們談『史』時眉飛色舞，

53　見《書劍恩仇錄》第 1 冊（香港光榮本），頁 22。

但小說本身卻不免要大受影響」，[54] 是相當一針見血的。不過，在濃厚的「歷史癖」中，金庸似乎並未察覺出自身的問題。金庸的「歷史癖」使他在小說中往往忽略了眞實與虛構的分際，以《鹿鼎記》中的建寧公主爲例，金庸以按語謂「建寧公主其實是清太宗之女，順治之妹。建寧長公主的封號也要到康熙十六年才封。順治的女兒和碩公主是康熙的姊姊，下嫁鼇拜之姪。但稗官小說不求事事與正史相合，學者通人不必深究」，[55] 金庸的「歷史癖」於此顯露無遺，但也往往自相矛盾，混淆了小說與歷史的界限。以建寧公主而言，事實上最適當的定位就是「純屬虛構」，蓋因書中的建寧公主，未婚前即不守婦道，且又分明有性虐待的癖好，自當與歷史上實有的建寧公主區別開來（小說中當然不妨有另一個虛構且名爲建寧公主的角色），但金庸爲了滿足其歷史癖，反而刻意強調其虛構的「建寧公主」的歷史性，牛頭驢嘴，不免自亂陣腳。如硬要與史上的「建寧公主」相符，則此一滿清公主之能否下嫁韋小寶，不僅令人滋疑，且與史實不符，何況更牽涉到「私德」問題，原無必要作此澄清，逕視之爲一虛構的建寧公主即可。

　　金庸寫武俠，同時也以武俠成名，但金庸實際上對其賴以成名的武俠小說（指類型而言）並沒有多大的好感（這是大多數武俠作家的共同觀點，據筆者所知，除了古龍和溫瑞安外，沒有一個作家認爲武俠小說可以當做一個文人的終身志業），甚至，武俠小說連歷史小說也比不上，如果說通俗小說是「次級文類」的話，則金庸心目中的武俠小說，極可能是「次次級文類」。因此，金庸頗沾沾自喜於《鹿鼎記》「毋寧說是歷史小說」之語；同時，在許多場合，寧可以「小說家」爲名，而諱言「武俠小說家」。[56] 說《鹿鼎記》是「歷

54　同註 17，頁 11。

55　見《鹿鼎記》第 3 冊，頁 847。

56　很遺憾地，至目前爲止，大多數研究金庸的學者，或多或少也仍持有此一看法，因此對其他武俠作品，每吝於論列；而討論金庸，也好像非得說他「超越了武俠小說的界限」，才能愜懷。在前述會議中，筆者即曾經提問：稱金庸爲「武俠小說家」或「小說家」，哪一個比較偉大？會提這問題的原因，是當時與會學者似乎頗忌諱「武俠小說」此一詞語。事實上，如果瞭解「武俠」二字只是一種方便的門類區劃，「武俠小說家」意味的是「精擅寫作武俠題材的作家」，實際上也還是「小說家」，金庸固不必耿耿於懷，學者更應擴展心胸。眞正優秀的作家，是無分門類的；而學術研究，更應無所不包，初不必劃地自限，更不當有如含羞忍恥，處處避忌。

史小說」，不僅混淆了歷史小說與武俠小說的界限，甚至，也代表了金庸對武俠小說愛恨交加、迷離糾結的觀念。

有關金庸小說的評價，自倪匡以「古今中外，空前絕後」[57] 盛加稱譽以來，論者幾乎眾口一詞，頗有「無所不用其極」的意味；然而，也因此而造成了影響極大的「排擠效應」，金庸武俠，在某種意義上就代表了全部的武俠小說，彷彿除了金庸，其他為數達三千種以上的作品，均無一可觀。這不僅僅使得許多優秀的作品、作家，深罹蒙塵、遺珠之憾，實際上也模糊了武俠小說發展史的客觀現象。由於金庸小說創始的年代，正值武俠小說重新出發的時期，金庸挾盛名之力，往往也被誤認為是所有「新派武俠」的鼻祖，自金庸以下，所有的武俠小說都是在金庸影響下創作的；而且，所有的作家，無論再如何能夠創新，也都在金庸的籠罩之下。換句話說，金庸一個人就可以抵敵所有的武俠，金庸成了武俠的「唯一」——唯一值得讀，也唯一值得研究的武俠。

關於武俠小說發展史的實際面相，筆者在〈民國以來「武俠研究」評議〉及〈解構金庸〉二文中，均有所論列，主要是強調：港、臺的武俠創作，基本上是同步進行、雙峰並峙的；同時，金庸的作品固然優秀，但無法奄有眾家之長，金庸無法涵蓋所有的武俠作品。從金庸小說新、舊本的比對中，我們可以發現：金庸小說的早期面貌，與修訂後有相當大的差距，修訂本已將舊本中許多明顯的罅漏彌補完成（如韋小寶的武功）——雖未必即無懈可擊（金庸打算三度修訂，正是為此）。因此，如果我們欲研究金庸在武俠小說上的獨特成就，修訂本當然是「蓋棺論定」所依；但是，如果欲將金庸置於武俠小說歷史的發展中窺其成就或影響，則「舊本」才是最確實可靠的，因為，金庸於此曾花了十年的精力，而其他作家，則一仍舊貌，沒有提供最佳面目的機會。

最後，從金庸小說版本的研究中，我們可以窺出金庸對通俗作品（儘管金庸意不在此，但對象卻正在此）的嚴肅要求，這是極具意義的。武俠小說此一文類，向來有「不登大雅」之譏，讀者固然以休閒消遣視之，以情趣為主，隨閱隨棄，就是作者，亦多半為稻粱而謀，隨寫隨忘，極罕得有人以嚴肅的態度面對。金庸肯以十年精力，潛心修訂，且不厭其瑣碎，博納雅言，

57　同註20，頁2。

一改再改，可以說是有史以來第一個嚴肅認眞的通俗作家，這是具有深刻意義的。我們雖不敢就此論斷武俠小說從此就步入文學殿堂，足以與典雅文學作品等量齊觀，但卻不能不承認，金庸以如此嚴謹的態度面對自己的作品，無疑將一新論者耳目，且有助於其他通俗作者對自我的肯定與要求。以此更進一步，相信通俗文學與典雅文學雙峰並峙的日子，將爲期不遠了。

Creating Classic Literature:
On the Revision of Jin Yong's *Sword of Loyalty*

John Christopher Hamm
University of Washington, Seattle

Abstract

Jin Yong's martial arts novels, now universally available in a standardized complete edition, are generally approached by both readers and critics alike as a stable and coherent body of work. Often overlooked are two different kinds of diachronic change within the corpus of Jin Yong's fiction: changes in the author's imagining of his fictional world over the nearly twenty years between the composition of his first novel and that of his last; and changes in the texts of the novels during the ten-year period of revision for the standard edition. Jin Yong's second novel, *Bixue jian* [Sword of Loyalty], presents an esample of both kinds of change. The novel was originally serialized in *Xianggang shangbao* in 1956. Jin Yong's final novel, *Liding ji* [The Deer and the Cauldron], serialized between 1969 and 1972, reincorporated some of the key characters and historical situations of the earlier work. The author visited this material yet again in 1975 with his *Yuan chonghuan pingzhuan* [A Critical Biography of yuan Chonghuan], a non-fictional treatment of the historical character who inspired *Sword of Loyalty*. And the same year saw the publication of that novel's revised edition — by the author's own account, the most drastically revised of the texts of any of his works. This constellation of variant texts and retreatments of similar material affords us an invaluable opportunity to explore the development of jin Yong's ideas and artistry. The present study undertakes a preliminary exploration of two aspects of this development: the representation of the political issues involved in a historic change of dynasties; and the figuration of china's literary and cultural traditions. It examines both the relationship between these two aspects within Jin Yong's fictional world, and the reflection of their relationship in the changing circumstances of the circulation and reception of Jin Yong's fiction. These investigations throw light on the question of how Jin Yong's works have attained the status of "classics" for twentieth-century Chinese readerships.

I. Introduction

In a recent paper, Li Yijian 李以建 reminds us that a significant part of Jin Yong's accomplishment rests on the effort the author has put into revising the texts originally serialized in Hong Kong's newspapers. Of Jin Yong's twenty-five year career as an author of fiction, fully ten years, two-fifths of the total, were spent in rewriting and revision, not in producing new works. It is the revised texts that are now in universal circulation, and it is on the strength of these revised texts that Jin Yong's fame has moved beyond the confines of genre fiction, to the point where he now receives consideration as one of the great novelists of twentieth-century China.[1]

One of the essential tasks awaiting scholars of Jin Yong's fiction and the modern martial arts novel is analysis of the process of revision. Such analysis must begin with systematic comparison of the serialized and revised texts of Jin Yong's novels. While many commentators on Jin Yong's work mention the fact of revision, most restrict their comments to remarks on a small number of

---

1   Li Yijian 李以建, "Yi jingdian wenxue 'gaixie' de Jin Yong xiaoshuo: jian tan zuowei baozhi lianzai ti de wuxia xiaoshuo (shang)" 以經典文學「改寫」的金庸小説：兼談作爲報紙連載體的武俠小説（上）[On the "rewriting" of Jin Yong's fiction as classic literature, with remarks on martial arts fiction in newspaper serialization (part one)]. Paper presented at the International Conference on Jin Yong and Twentieth-Century Chinese Literature, University of Colorado at Boulder, May 17-19, 1998.

examples either cited by Jin Yong himself in remarks appended to the revised editions, or mentioned by Ni Kuang 倪匡 in his path-breaking volumes of Jinology, *Wo kan Jin Yong xiaoshuo* 我看金庸小說 and its sequels.[2] The absence of new material is understandable, given the extreme difficulty of consulting either the original newspaper serializations or the earliest pre-revision book editions. Nonetheless, the continual recycling of a few treasured examples and anecdotes — such as the creation of the storyteller Zhang Shiwu 張十五 for the opening of *Shediao yingxiong zhuan* 射鵰英雄傳, or Ni Kuang's decision to blind the character A Zi 阿紫 while taking over the serialization of *Tianlong babu* 天龍八部 from the vacationing Jin Yong — raises these cases to an almost mythic status, while doing little to deepen our actual understanding of the nature and extent of Jin Yong's revisions.

This paper aims to make a modest contribution to the study of Jin Yong's revisions of his novels by comparing the original and revised texts of *Bixue Jian* 碧血劍 [Sword of Loyalty]. It also uses this particular case to broach some larger questions involved in the revision process and the changing status of Jin Yong's fiction. Li Yijian's valuable work addresses the importance of revision in terms of improvements made to the text. He argues that the revised texts are "better" in the sense of being more literary; they transcend the formulae and limitations of popular newspaper fiction and more closely approach the standards and values of "classic" literature.[3] My aim in this study is not to pass judgement on the

---

2   Ni Kuang 倪匡, *Wo kan Jin Yong xiaoshuo* 我看金庸小說 [A look at Jin Yong's fiction] (Taipei: Yuanjing 遠景, 1980).

3   It is interesting to compare Li Yijian's Judgement here with that of Ni Kuang, who laments the revised text's loss of the original's rough-hewn vitality (*Wo kan Jin Yong xiaoshuo*, 14-18); and with that of Ye Hongsheng 葉洪生, who views the "literarization" of Jin Yong's novels as unfair to the practice of other martial arts authors (see "'Toutian huanri' de shi yu fei: bijiao Jin Yong xin, jiuban *Shediao yingxiong zhuan*" 「偷天換日」的是與非：比較金庸新、舊版《射鵰英雄傳》 [The rights and wrongs of the "Switch of the Century:" A comparision of the old and new editions of Jin Yong's *The Eagle-Shooting Heroes*] in *Ye Hongsheng lun jian: wuxia xiaoshuo tan yi lu* 葉洪生論劍：武俠小說談藝錄 [Ye Hongsheng speaks of the sword: Talks on the art of martial

literary merits of Jin Yong's work. I am interested rather in the related but rather different process of how the texts themselves are engaged in the process of establishing literary and cultural value; how one aspect of the revision process is the delineation of standards of value, and the presentation of the revised texts as conforming to these same standards; how, to overstate the case a bit, the revised texts of the *Jin Yong zuopin ji* 金庸作品集 [Collected works of Jin Yong] undertake to canonize themselves.

II. Sword of Loyalty

Sword of Loyalty is far from the most well known or most highly regarded of Jin Yong's works. Ni Kuang 倪匡, for instance, imitating traditional aesthetic criticism by providing rankings of novels and characters, rates *Sword of Loyalty* only twelfth among Jin Yong's fourteen works.[4] Despite the relatively low esteem in which the novel is held by some readers, however, the extent of the changes wrought between the original and the revised text makes it a valuable source for the study of Jin Yong's practices of revision. First serialized in *Xianggang shangbao* 香港商報 in 1956, it was only the second martial arts novel that the author composed. In general, Jin Yong seems to have revised his early works more extensively than the later ones.[5] This circumstance presumably reflects a reconsideration of this early efforts in the light of standards and preferences developed over the course of his writing career. With regard to *Sword of Loyalty* in particular, Jin Yong has several times remarked on the extent of his revisions. A revised text was first serialized in *Mingbao wanbao* 明報晚報 beginning May 24, 1971. Here the novel is entitled *Bixue Jinshe jian* 碧血金蛇劍 [the Golden Serpent's Sword of Loytalty], and in his introductory remarks to the first day's installment, the author describes the process of revision as follows:

---

arts fiction] (Taipei: Lianjing 聯經, 1994), 333-363).

4   Ni Kuang, 22.

5   This point awaits verification through systematic comparison of the original and revised editions.

原作結尾太過草率，全部重新寫過。有一些次要角色如侯方城、祖太壽等，都另行改換。原作中前後不相呼應、文字粗疏的地方，均加潤飾修改。原書共二十五回，現改爲十二回，回目也有變動。

The conclusion to the original work was far too perfunctory and has been completely rewritten. A few secondary characters, such as Hou Fangcheng, Zu Dashou, Zu Zhongshou and others, have also been reworked. Internal discrepancies and careless language have been polished and revised. The original book's twenty-five chapters have been changed to twelve, and the chapter titles also altered.

In the "Afterword" to the Ming He edition of 1975, he explicitly states that this is the most throughly reworked of all his novels:

《碧血劍》曾作了兩次頗大修改，增加了五分之一左右的篇幅。修訂的心力，在這部書上付出最多。

Sword of Loyalty has undergone two fairly major revisions, which have added some twenty percent to its length. The effort I have put into revision has been greatest for this book. [Ming He, 864]

Beyond the extent of the revisions, *Sword of Loyalty* holds particular interest for a study of the development of Jin Yong's art and thought because of the fact that the author returned several times to the material of this early novel. From May 23 through June 28, 1975, *Mingbao* 明報 serialized Jin Yong's *Guangdong yingxiong Yuan Manzi: Yuan Chonghuan pingzhuan* 廣東英雄袁蠻子：袁崇煥評傳 [The Guangdong Hero "Yuan the Barbarian": A Critical Biography of Yuan Chonghuan], an account of the historical father of *Sword of Loyalty*'s fictional protagonist. This short work was inspired by the author's researches in connection with the second revision of the novel.[6]   In revised and expanded

---

6   See the author's comments at the head of the first installment, *Mingbao*, June 23, 1975; also the "Afterword" in the Ming He edition, 864, References to the revised edition, here referred to as Ming He, are keyed to: Jin Yong 金庸，*Bixue jian* 碧血劍 [*Sword of Loyalty*] (Hong Kong: Ming He 明河，1975.

form, with the title simplified to *Yuan Chonghuan pingzhuan* [A critical biography of Yuan Chonghuan] (hereafter *Critical Biography*), it is included as an appendix in the book edition of the revised novel.[7] In addition to the *Critical Biography*, Jin Yong revisited *Sword of Loyalty* in his final and most astonishing work of fiction, *Luding ji* 鹿鼎記 [The Deer and the Cauldron]. This novel, serialized in *Mingbao* from October 4, 1969 through September 23, 1972 (i.e. contemporaneously with *Mingbao wanbao*'s presentation of the first revision of *Sword of Loyalty*), not only incorporates several of the earlier work's characters, but also represents, as we shall see, a statement on certain questions which *Sword of Loyalty* had originally propounded.

III. Types of Changes to the Text

If we compare the text of the Ming He revised edition with that of the 1956 newspaper serialization, a first impression is that the alterations are ubiquitous and minute. Almost every sentence in the newspaper version can be matched with one in the book; but within nearly every sentence the author has recalculated his choice of one or two items of vocabulary, adjusted the syntax and sentence structure, shifted the punctuation. Commenting on the revision of his first novel, *Shujian enchou lu* 書劍恩仇錄 [Book and sword, gratitude and revenge], Jin Yong remarks that "nearly every sentence has been altered at some point;"[8] and the identical process is evident in the revision of *Sword of Loyalty*.

Such ubiquitous stylistic alterations are further joined by changes in the information narrated by the text. While these occasionally constitute modifications in the action or in various characters' roles, they most frequently take the form of clarifications of the characters' motivations and expanded exploration of their thought and emotions. Here, for instance, is the 1956 text's

---

7   Ming He, 737-863.

8   "Houji" 後記 [Afterword], *Shujian enchou lu* 書劍恩仇錄 [Book and Sword, Gratitude and Revenge] (Taipei: Yuanliu 遠流, 1990), 870:「幾乎每一句句子都曾改過」.

account of Wen Qingqing's 溫青青 realization that Ironhand He 何鐵手, mistress of the Five Venom Sect, has fallen in love with her:

> 青青一想何鐵手這幾日對自己的神情説話，果然是情有所鍾的樣子，原來她一見傾心，竟没再留神自己的女扮男裝，不覺好笑，問道：「怎麼辦呢？」承志道：「你娶了這位五毒夫人算啦！」【11月6日】
> Qingqing thought about Ironhand He's speech and bearing towards her these last few days; she really did appear as if she had set her heart on someone. She had been smitten at first sight, and hadn't realized how she herself was a woman in man's disguise. She couldn't help but feel amused. "What can I do?" she asked. "You'll just have to take Madam Five Venoms as your wife!" said Chengzhi. [November 6, 1956]

The revised text offers a fuller explanation of how her erstwhile captors had failed to perceive her true gender:

> 青青回想何鐵手這幾日對自己的神情説話，果然是含情脈脈的模樣。原來她一見傾心，神智胡塗了。那何紅藥則是滿腔怨毒，怒氣沖天。這兩個女子本來都見多識廣，但一個鍾情，一個懷恨，竟都似瞎了眼一般，再也没留神自己是女扮男裝，不覺好笑，問道：「怎麼辦呢？」袁承志笑道：「你娶了這位五毒夫人算啦！」【616頁】
> Qingqing thought back on Ironhand He's speech and bearing towards her these last few days; she really had seemed to be brimming with affection. She had been smitten at first sight, and her wits were all befuddled. He Hongyao for her part had been poisoned by resentment and ready to burst with rage. These two women were actually quite canny in the ways of the world, but one was smitten by love while the other nursed her hate; both of them in the end were as good as blind, and hadn't realized that she herself was a woman in man's disguise. She couldn't help but feel amused. "What can I do?" she asked. "You'll just have to take madam Five Venoms as your wife!" laughed Yuan Chengzhi. [Ming He, 616]

Another example occurs when Yuan Chengzhi 袁承志, who yearns to assassinate the Ming emperor in vengeance for his father's execution, ends up saving his life in order to foil a plot by traitors in league with the Manchus. The emperor is unaware of his savior's identity:

> 袁承志望著崇禎，想起父親捨命衛國，立下大功，卻被這皇帝凌遲而死，悲憤痛恨之極。崇禎那裡知道，溫言道：「你叫甚麼名字？在那個衙門當差？」【11 月 15 日】
> Yuan Chengzhi gazed at Chongzhen, and thought how his father had given his life to protect his country, rendering heroic service, only to have this very emperor send him to death by dismemberment. He felt grief, pain, rage and hatred. Chongzhen had no notion of this. He spoke in a kindly voice: "What is your name? In which department do you serve?" [November 15, 1956]

The revised text adds to Yuna Chengzhi's vengeful thoughts a sudden spasm of compassion:

> 袁承志望著崇禎，想起父親捨命衛國，立下大功，卻被這皇帝凌遲而死，心中悲憤痛恨之極，細看這殺父仇人時，只見他兩邊臉頰都凹陷進去，鬢邊已有不少白髮，眼中滿是紅絲，神色甚是憔悴。此時奪位的奸謀已然平定，首惡已除，但崇禎臉上只是顯得煩躁不安，殊無歡愉之色。袁承志心想：「他做皇帝只是受罪，心裡一點也不快活！」
> 崇禎卻那裡知道袁承志心中這許多念頭，溫言道：「你叫甚麼名字？在那裡當差？」【頁 633-634】
> Yung Chengzhi gazed at Chongzhen, and thought how his father had given his life to protect his country, rendering heroic service, only to have this very emperor send him to death by dismemberment. Grief, pain, range and hatred filled his heart. But when he looked closely at his foe, his father's murderer, he saw that his cheeks were deeply sunken, the hair on his temples white, and his eyes shot through with red — an utterly haggard appearance. By now the plot to dethrone him had been foiled and the chief villain eliminated, but Chongzhen's face showed nothing but care and unease, without the slightest trace of gladness. Yuan Chengzhi thought: "Being emperor is nothing but a torture to him; he isn't happy at all!"
> Chongzhen had no notion of the thoughts passing through Yuan Chengzhi's mind. He spoke in a kindly voice: "What is your name? Where do you serve?" [Ming He, 633-634]

Changes such as these tighten the narrative logic of the tale and add some depth to the character's psychological lives. They do not, however, alter the overall contours of the plot. For the most part it is possible to match the original and final texts scene by scene, paragraph by paragraph, and even (allowing for such expansions as just described) sentence by sentence. Extended and substantial alterations to the plot and narrative of the original text occur at only four points. The first is an expansion and modification of the novel's opening sequence. The second is the addition of the episode of Yuan Chengzhi's attempt to assassinate the Manchu emperor. The third is an elaboration of events in Beijing after the capital's fall to Li Zicheng 李自成. And the fourth, mentioned by the author himself in his earliest comments on the revision (see above), is a fuller development of the original text's rather abrupt conclusion.

IV. The Manchu Emperor

In both versions of the text, Yuan Chengzhi, journeying to Beijing in order to assassinate the Ming emperor, encounters a group of Portuguese soldiers, destroys their cannon (intended by the emperor for use against Li Zicheng's rebellion), and receives from them a map to an island in the southern seas. He then proceeds to the capital, where, in the 1956 text, he makes his first entry into the imperial palace. In the revised text, however, the sufferings of the war-plagued populace along the road arouse in him the determination to assassinate the Manchu ruler, Huang Taiji 皇太極. He therefore merely pauses in Beijing before journeying on to the northeast and the Qing capital at Shengjing 盛京. Infiltrating the palace, he is astounded to find the Manchu emperor speaking the Chinese tongue, quoting Chinese classics and histories in his deliberations with his Chinese-born advisors, sighing over the follies of the Ming court and vowing to ease the people's sufferings when he attains the throne. Yuan proceeds with his assassination attempt nonetheless, fired by his aversion to foreign rule and by knowledge of Huang Taiji's role in his father's ruin. He fails, is captured and entrusted to a lieutenant of his late father, now serving the foe;

when this worthy releases him, he enters the palace for a second attempt, only to witness Huang Taiji's murder at the hands of his brother, Dorgon 多爾袞. Yuan Chengzhi then returns to Beijing, and the revised text's plot merges once again with that of the newspaper text. The entire episode, inserted at the point of Yuan's arrival in the capital in the September 5 installment of the serialization, occupies some 29 pages in the Ming He edition (487-516, including a chapter break and illustration), comprising nearly 18,000 characters.

V. Li Zicheng and the Fall of Beijing

The next major amendment in the text occurs after Li Zicheng's seizure of the capital. Certain minor change appear during the course of Li Zicheng's assault. The revised text omits, for instance, the 1956 text's account of Yuan Chengzhi's bribing the Ming soldiery to relax their defense, presumably deeming this strategy rather unheroic (November 25, absent from Ming He 652); it adds Li Zicheng's address to his troops, forbidding them to loot or harm the capital's inhabitants (Ming He 660, absent from November 28). The primary revision, however, appears with Yuan Chengzhi's audience with Li Zicheng after the city's fall and the Ming emperor's suicide. In the November 30 installment of the serialization, Yuan refuses Li Zicheng's offer to marry him to the Ming princess and is gazed at with suspicion by Li's chief advisor. When a messenger reports looting by some of Li Zicheng's troops, and the advisors begin debating how to handle this matter, Yuan takes his leave. Returning to his residence, he finds a summons from his master, and (in the December 2 installment) leaves the capital for the novel's final sequence of adventures.

Before Yuan's departure from Beijing, the revised text adds over 7000 characters (Ming He 663-674), dramatizing the matter mentioned so briefly in the serializations's audience scene — the new regime's rapid plunge into pillaging and internal strife. Returning from his audience, Yuan Chengzhi is drawn into a brawl with rebel troops seeking to pillage his own residence. He returns to the palace, expecting Li Zicheng to enforce his earlier decree, but finds him at feast, surrounded by greedy generals and treacherous advisors, drunken with wine and besotted with lust for the ravishing Chen Yuanyuan 陳圓圓. Li Zicheng's desire for this beauty leads him to betray the general Wu Sangui 吳三桂, who holds the passes against the Manchu armies. Yuan departs, heavy-hearted, and witnesses ever greater excesses of looting and rapine. The next day Li Zicheng, closeted with his new paramour and swayed by his advisors' whispers of treachery, refuses him audience; Yuan wanders the terrorized capital and hears a blind street-singer's ominous lament; returning home, he receive his master's summons, and so prepares to depart.

VI. The Revised Ending

The revision of the novel's ending has clear aesthetic motivations, and also reinforces the themes brought out in the expanded treatment of Li Zicheng's victory. Jin Yong replaces the last several hundred characters of the final newspaper installment (December 31, 1956) with six pages of new text (Ming He 730-736), some 4000 characters in all. The new material narrates in some detail Yuan Chengzhi's journey to aid his beleaguered comrade Li Yan 李岩, their meeting, Li Yan's despair over the corruption of the rebellion, and the suicides of Li Yan and his wife. The additions ameliorate the abruptness of the original conclusion (brought about in part, perhaps, by the need to finish the story on the last day of the calendar year), and further develop a certain structural symmetry. The novel's opening sequence (discussed in detail below) features a young student attacked by rapacious Ming soldiery as he travels through China. In the original conclusion this student, now ageing and careworn, appears suddenly at Li Yan's tomb to recite a lament, then disappears once again. In the expanded conclusion Yuan Chengzhi encounters the student on the road — assaulted not by Ming troops this time, but by Li Zicheng's rampaging followers. The episode both mirrors the opening more closely, and re-emphasizes the degeneration of Li Zicheng's uprising. Indeed, these paired scenes of the ravages of the Ming and rebel troops can be further matched with the scenes of Manchu depredation at the beginning of the Shengjing episode, demonstrating the sufferings of the populace at the hands of all three contenders for the throne and justifying Yuan Chengzhi's final departure for an island far from the suffering empire.

VII. A Revised Political Perspective

The three major revisions discussed so far, in fact, all affect the novel's treatment of its historical background and the protagonist's response to China's political crisis — not his tangled romantic adventures or the debts and vendettas within the world of the martial arts that occupy so great a part of the narrative. A primary overall effect of the revisions Jin Yong has made to *Sword of Loyalty* is to adjust and amplify the novel's vision of China's political situation at this moment of historical crisis. The novel's fundamental assumption is that political legitimacy rests upon the ruler's concern for the best interests of the common people. By this yardstick, the Ming brings about its own downfall. "The Ming dynasty destroyed itself, it was not overthrown by the Manchus," states the *Critical Biography*.[9] This point is implicit in the first days of the serialization, showing Ming troops ravaging the coutryside, and is explicitly stated by Yuan Chengzhi as he views Chongzhen emperor's corpse:

> 「要是你早知道愛惜百性，不是逼得天下饑民無路可走，那裡會到今日這部田地。」
> 【11 月 29 日】
> "If you had understood to begin with what it meant to cherish the people, instead of driving the starving masses of the empire to desperation, you would never have come to the state you're in today." [November 29, 1956; cf. Ming He 661]

What the revised text adds to this assignation of blame for the Ming collapse is, as we have seen, a more developed representation of Li Zicheng's failure to

---

9　Ming He, 784：「明朝是自己覆滅的，並非給滿清打垮。」

achieve legitimacy by the same criteria. More surprisingly, perhaps, it also adds a more complex and even sympathetic view of the eventual victors in the imperial struggle, the Manchu Qing. The original text operates within the parameters of an anti-Manchu patriotism common to much martial arts fiction, and takes its protagonist's resistance to the Qing for granted. But in the revised text, Yuan Chengzhi, poised to assassinate Huang Taiji, is impressed not only by his formidable cunning (which he suspects is superior to that of the Ming emperor and even of Li Zicheng, and which reminds him of the devious wisdom of the text from which he himself has studied the martial arts), but by his knowledge of Chinese language and history, and by his concern for the sufferings of the common people. Yuan proceeds with his assassination attempt nonetheless; capitulation to Manchu rule is not an option for this character, the son of a renowned anti-Manchu general. Yet the depiction of the capable and compassionate Huang Taiji brings the vision of the novel as a whole much closer to the point of view expressed in Jin Yong's *Critical Biography* of that general: "It was necessary that the Ming dynasty perish. For the Chinese people, the Qing dynasty was far better than the Ming,"[10] This same viewpoint receives an even more compelling fictional expression in *The Deer and the Cauldron*. Here the narrative's adulatory representation of the Kangxi 康熙 emperor as an enlightened ruler is matched by the conversion of the novel's protagonist, Wei Xiaobao 韋小寶. Wei Xiaobao spends much of the novel bouncing between the Qing court and an anti-Manchu revolutionary society, first cynically playing both sides to his personal advantage, then torn between their rival claims to his loyalty. By the end of the tale, however, he admits that he "can't jump his way out of his imperial highness's Buddha palm,"[11] and happily accepts the wealth and honors that await him under Kangxi's benevolent rule.

If, as I have argued, these changes bring the 1975 revised text of *Sword of Loyalty* closer to the point of view of the 1975 *Critical Biography* and the 1969–

10   Ming He, 857：「明朝當然應該亡，對於中國人民，清朝比明朝好得多。」
11   1960：「總之是跳不出萬歲爺這如來佛的手掌心。」

1972 *The Deer and the Cauldron*; if they subtly reframe the tale of Yuan Chengzhi's despair over the fate of China in such a way as to allow the possibility of Wei Xiaobao's capitulation to the new order of things — what then? Do these revisions hold interest or significance beyond their evidence of this particular author's judgement on this specific moment in Chinese history? I believe they do; I also believe that the broader significance of the revisions lies not so much in the judgement they pass on history as in the criteria by which this judgement is rendered. And to begin to understand this broader significance, we shall turn to the last of the major changes in the text of *Sword of Loyalty*, the first to appear in the progression of the narrative — the rewriting of the novel's opening.

VIII. The Revised Opening and its Implications

As narrated in *Xianggang shangbao* beginning January 1, 1956, the story opens during the reign of the Ming Chongzhen 崇禎 emperor with the young student Hou Chaozong 侯朝宗, son of a retired official from Henan 河南, who, despite his parents' warnings about the perilous state of the country, sets out with his servant to see a bit of the world. He witnesses the misery of the peasantry and soon runs afoul of a troop of rapacious Ming soldiers. Only the fortuitous appearance of the caravan guard Yang Pengju 楊鵬舉 saves him from robbery and worse at the hands of the government troops. The warrior Yang and the scholar Hou receive aid from a group of mysterious recluses who are training a young boy in the arts of war. The eventually find themselves at a gathering of the followers of the patriotic general Yuan Chonghuan 袁崇煥, and learn that the child is the general's orphaned son, Yuan Chengzhi, who is being raised to take vengeance on the traitors who executed his sire. Thus it is by gradual stages that the narrative leads the reader to the tale's protagonist: presenting first a stranger to the "rivers and lakes," the callow and bookish Hou Chazong; then a classic type of the "goodfellow," the formidable and chivalrous Yang Pengju; and finally then the particular characters and situations that will structure the rest of the novel.

The revised text provides an even more circuitous entry to the main characters and events of the story. It tell how the King of Brunei travelled to the court of the Ming Chengzu 成祖 emperor in 1408. "Although [Brunei] was separated from the mainland by thousands of leagues of ocean, it had long held China in reverence."[12]   The narrative details the gifts presented by the King, and traces the history of Brunei's tributary missions since Song times. The present King of Brunei, entranced by the splendors of the Middle Kingdom, lingers there and passes away. The Ming emperor enfeoffs his son and indites an elegy which is subsequently inscribed on Brunei's sacred mountain. Brunei continues to send tribute to the Ming court, and Chinese travel to Brunei, often serving there as court officials. In later years one of these overseas Chinese, remembering his homeland, names his only son Zhang Chaotan 張朝唐 ("facing the Tang," i.e. the Chinese empire), secures for him a classical education from an itinerant scholar, and sends him back to his native land to complete his education and win success through the imperial examinations. The revised text's Zhang Chaotang is the reincarnation of the earlier version's Hou Chaozong. When he arrives on the mainland, only to find it ravaged by bandits and equally rapacious government soldiery, the two versions of the text begin to run parallel.

The revised opening does nothing to alter the tale of Yuan Chengzhi's adventures, whether private or public. Its function is to offer a larger frame for the significance of the Yuan's personal and political travails. It foregrounds the importance of China as the fountainhead of cultural meaning. Brunei's reverence for Chinese culture, the King's visit and presentation of tribute, and the importance of Chinese officials and merchants in Brunei's government and society, all affirm the preeminence and influence of the Chinese cultural tradition. One of the few alterations between the opening in the first revised version serialized in *Mingbao wanbao* and the final text presented in book form makes this point even more strongly. In the *Mingbao wanbao* version the King appears as something of an awestruck tourist:

---

12   Ming He, 7：雖和中土相隔海程萬里，但向來仰慕中華。

……國王來到中國之後，眼見花花世界，事事新鮮，明帝又相待甚厚，竟然留戀不去。

...When the King had arrived in China, he beheld this dazzling world, strange and novel in every way; the Ming emperor moreover received him with the greatest generosity, and in the end he simply could not bear to take his leave. [May 24, 1971]

The final version, however, explicitly attributes his response to an admiration of Chin's cultural achievements:

……國王眼見天朝上國民豐物阜，文治教化，衣冠器具，無不令他歡喜贊嘆，明帝又相待甚厚，竟然留戀不去。

...the King beheld the imperial court of this exalted nation, the people's prosperity and the abundance of goods, the cultured governance and the civilizing balm of the teachings, the elegant attire and cunning utensils — none of these but gladdened his heart and made him sigh with admiration. The Ming emperor moreover received him with the greatest generosity, and in the end he simply could not bear to take his leave. [Ming He 7]

The conjoining of "cultured governance and the civilizing balm of the teachings" with "elegant attire and cunning utensils" suggests that virtuous government is inseparable from the artifacts of the cultural tradition. This same linkage is evident in Yuan Chengzhi's perception of the Manchu emperor Huang Taiji, and associated there even more specifically with the linguistic and literary manifestations of the tradition: Yuan's understanding that this supposed tyrant actually feels concern for the people dawns in the wake of the realization that he speaks the Chinese language and is versed in China's histories and scriptures. The intimate association of the Word and the Way, of language and literature with moral bearing in both private and public life, is of course a persistent current in the stream of Chinese traditions. The adage *wen yi zai dao* 文以載道, "text serves as vehicle for the Way," enjoins literature to perform its proper function, and at the same time elevates it through a privileged association with the most central concern of human life, the transmission and realization of the Way.

If the King of Brunei's respect for China's culture parallels that of the Manchu emperor, it also matches that of the character with whom the monarch shares the revised text's opening — Zhang Chaotang. This youth's schooling in the classics and return to the mainland to seek advancement through the examinations reflects an acceptance of the centrality of China's cultural and literary traditions equivalent to that of the king. There is nothing particularly extraordinary in these characters' embrace of traditional attitudes. There *is* particular significance, I believe, in Jin Yong's foregrounding these characters' experiences by placing them at the opening of his revised version of the novel. The significance is twofold.

IX. Textual and Cultural Stewardship

The first point to note is that the revised text does not merely narrate the story of two individuals seeking instruction in the Chinese cultural tradition. It also enacts such a process of cultural initiation: it makes gestures towards providing the reader with instruction in the content and value of the Chinese literary and cultural heritage similar to that undergone by Zhang Chaotang and the King of Brunei. On the narrative level, the story of the King of Brunei has but a tenuous link to the events of the primary narrative. The main purpose of this episode, as already noted, is to establish an image of Chinese cultural supremacy. In the course of establishing this image, the text takes pains to offer explanations of geographic and linguistic material likely to be unfamiliar to the modern reader. It reproduces in full the text of the Ming emperor's verses for Brunei's sacred mountain; and in an endnote to the first chapter, it explicates these verses in modern vernacular Chinese.[13]

Huang Weiliang 黃維樑, in an article recommending Jin Yong's novels as primers in Chinese language and cultural knowledge, notes how much geographical and historical information is implicit in the opening lines of Jin

---

13   Ming He, 8 and 40.

Yong's first novel, *Shujian enchou lu*.[14]　The revised opening of *Sword of Loyalty* goes beyond such tacit transmission of knowledge to offer explicit glosses on its own statements. The explanations are sometimes enclosed in parentheses or set off by a variant typeface. This typographical practice highlights the authorial voice's departure from simple narrative and engagement in a more schoolmasterly practice of instruction. The adoption of an instructional stance extends far beyond the revised opening. Several of the later chapters of the novel are provided with endnotes explaining the background of the tale, elucidating historical and literary allusions, or quoting historical sources. At several points the author takes pains to make clear his story's divergence from the verifiable historical record. "Historians need not inquire too closely into a novelist's tales."[15]　By so carefully circumscribing the territory of fiction, of course, he demonstates a consciousness of responsibilities beyond those of a mere entertainer — responsibilities explored in the extended piece of historical writing appended to the revised novel, the *Critical Biography*.

　　Similar chapter endnotes appear in many volumes of Jin Yong's revised works, and explanatory appendices in several. But perhaps the most evident and comprehensive expression of the instructional impulse is the inclusion at the head of each of the thirty-six volumes of the *Jin Yong zuopin ji* of captioned colored plates reproducing works of art, cultural relics, historical documents, maps, portraits, and photographs of famous sites associated with the events of the novels. The 1975 "Afterword" to *Book and Sword* introduces the plates as follows:

　　「金庸作品集」全部預計出四十冊左右。每一冊中都附印彩色插圖，希望讓讀者們（尤

14　Huang Weiliang 黃維樑, "Tongmeng ke du ci er xue wen: Jin Young wuxia xiaoshuo yuyan de chouyang fenxi" 童蒙可讀此而學文：金庸武俠小說語言的抽樣分析 [A path to literacy for youth: A selective analysis of the language of Jin Yong's martial arts fiction], in *Wuxia xiaoshuo lun juan*, ed. Liu Shaoming and Chen Yongming (Hong Kong: Minghe, 1998), 651-653.

15　Ming He, 524：「小說家言，史家不必深究也。」

其是身在外國的讀者）多接觸一些中國的文物和藝術作品。〔遠流版，頁 870〕

We estimate that the *Colected Works of Jin Yong* will comprise about forty volumes in all. Full-color illustrations will be added to each volume; we hope that this will allow our readers (especially our readers abroad) to gain some further acquaintance with China's cultural artifacts and works of art. [Yuanliu, 870]

The educational ambition, expressed extra-textually through such features as the inclusion of these illustrations, is first evident within the text and on the diegetic level through the revised *Sword of Loyalty*'s expansion of the story of Zhang Chaotang and inclusion of the episode of the King of Brunei.

X. The Overseas Chinese

Beside explicitly stating the educational agenda of the *Collected Works of Jin Yong*, the remark just quoted also bring us to the second point that I wish to draw out in this discussion of *Sword of Loyalty*'s revised opening: the essential role played by individuals from outside the Chinese heartland in the validation and sustenance of China's cultural traditions. The King of Brunei, whose story frames the tale from a certain distance, is a foreigner, drawn to China by its glories and unable to depart. Zhang Chaotang, whose travels and travails lead directly into the primary narrative, is not the Henan native of the original text but an overseas Chinese, schooled in the traditional arts while growing up abroad, then sent by his father to fulfill his cultural destiny back in his ancestral land. On the structural level, Zhang Chaotang's arrival from abroad establishes a parallelism with his final departure in Yuan Chengzhi's company for a haven overseas. In terms of emotional impact, the idealism of his vision of the cultural heartland augments the poignancy of his encounter with the brutal reality of the empire's condition; his teacher, who has instructed him in the classics, is slaughtered by pirates as soon as they reach the mainland. At the same time, though, the tragic state of the Chinese mainland only highlights the importance of its admirers and grandsons overseas — both in affirming the central culture through their adulation, and in sustaining it through their extra-territorial transmission of its literature and values.

Just as the revised text's celebration of literature's importance as a steward of the cultural inheritance is replicated extra-textually in the presentation and marketing of Jin Yong's revised and collected works, so its vision of the role of expatriate Chinese in the preservation of that inheritance is played out in the history of the production and circulation of Jin Yong's novels. Jin Yong's earliest work was originally serialized in several newspapers in the British colony of Hong Kong. Largely on the basis of his fiction's success, the author founded his own paper. Then, through the continual mutual reinforcement of his novels' popularity and his publishing concerns' commercial achievements, he created an expanding network of newspapers and periodicals in Hong Kong, Southeast Asia, and among the Chinese communities abroad. Among the enterprises he established was a publishing company, Ming He 明河, exclusively devoted to producing the 36-volume *Collected Works of Jin Yong*. In Taiwan, with its own unique political and cultural relationship to the Chinese mainland, his novels circulated in contraband editions for years prior to the first authorized Yuanjing 遠景 publication in 1980. And finally, in the 1980s, Jin Yong's vision of China, born and fostered among the Chinese overseas, returned to the homeland of which it had dreamed so long. With China's economic reforms and opening to the outside world, millions of readers whose sense of being sundered from a tradition stemmed not from geographic displacement but from socio-political trauma, found in Jin Yong's work the double appeal of a voice from the wide world outside and the echo of their own remembered or imagined birthright.

XI. Conclusion

In an earlier paper I have suggested that one of the impulses shaping Jin Yong's early fiction was a sense of exile and displacement which can be associated with the experience of many of Hong Kong's Chinese residents in the years following the Pacific War and the establishment of the People's Republic of

China.[16]   From a certain perspective, the adventures of Yuan Chengzhi and other protagonists allegorize the refugee experience; and distress over the nation's plight and over separation from the homeland find partial expression in the martial arts novel's nostalgic recreation of a mythicized Chinese past. The present study of the revisions made to *Sword of Loyalty* reveals a related and yet significantly reoriented consciousness. By complication and qualifying its portrayal of the political issues involved in the historical Ming-Qing crisis, the revised text foregrounds the importance of a mass cultural identity that supersedes particular political allegiances. The revised narrative frame further suggests the crucial role played by Chinese outside the mainland in the definition and transmission of China's cultural heritage — a confident transmutation of the earlier sense of loss and nostalgia. And by emblematizing the role of textuality in cultural transmission, and consciously appropriating this educative role for itself, the text stakes a claim for its own importance as cultural gatekeeper.

The changes made to the text itself in the process of revision are mirrored and supported by the extra-textual circumstances of the circulation of Jin Yong's work: the publication of the 36-volume *Jin Yong zuopin ji* embellished with figures of the glories of China's history and art; the extension of Zha Liagnyong's publishing empire beyond Hong Kong into Southeast Asia and the worldwide Chinese diaspora. It may be worthwhile to clarity here what I intend, and what I do not intend, to suggest about the causality of the process here described. I am not arguing that the reimagined text magically generates the conditions of the novel's circulation and reception, but neither am I saying that the text's revision simply embodies a mechanical mirroring of the works' social context. I believe that the relationship is reciprocal: that the author's revisions reflect his changing perception of his work, its social function, and its influence; and that this reenvisioning of the martial arts novel's role, and the consequent revision of the

16   "The Marshes of Mount Liang Beyond the Sea: Jin Yong's Early Fiction and 1950s Hong Kong." Paper presented at the International Conference on Jin Yong and Twentieth-Century Chinese Literature

texts, supports in turn an increasing acceptance (whether conscious or unconscious) of the possibility that these novels might have an honorable role to play in the transmission of a cultural heritage to an expatriated or otherwise culturally uprooted readership. Readers and, increasingly, the scholarly and critical communities now welcome Jin Yong's works as masterpieces of 20th century Chinese literature. Jin Yong's revision of his works has been a crucial element in their attaining this status. We must understand the role of the revision process, however, not merely as the refining of the texts into some quintessence of artistic excellence, but as one part of an active engagement in the definition and appropriation of those very standards by which literary and cultural value is acknowledged. It is in this way that Jin Yong's novels erase the traditionally assumed gap between popular and elite literature, and in this way that they create themselves as modern classics.

第四輯　小說評論

《唐吉訶德》與《鹿鼎記》比較初論

陳 墨

北京中國電影藝術中心

摘 要

「金庸小說與世界文學」是「金學」研究中一個不可忽視的課題。金庸小說不僅「好在傳統文化」，同時也好在世界性及其現代性。

《鹿鼎記》與西方文學名著《唐吉訶德》的比較研究，可以給我們提供有益的啓示。

首先是二者的可比性有五：一、西方騎士小說與中國的武俠小說；二、《唐吉訶德》的「反騎士小說性質」與《鹿鼎記》的「反武俠小說性質」；三、《唐吉訶德》的諷刺性與《鹿鼎記》的幽默感；四、《唐吉訶德》的創新精神與《鹿鼎記》的突破文類局限；五、二者共有的雅俗共賞的審美特徵及文化寓言性質。

其次是進行小說中人物的比較：一是比較《鹿鼎記》的主人公韋小寶與《唐吉訶德》的第二主人公喬桑・潘薩，以二者的相似性作爲切入點，如二者均爲平民出身、具有豐富的俗語知識、注重功利、懶惰狡黠與自私怕死等習性、勝者爲王的觀念，其性格均深受環境的影響等等；二是比較韋小寶與唐吉訶德的獨特個性人格與普遍性人文精神；三是比較「唐吉訶德精神」與「韋小寶作風」。

最後是進行文本與泛文本的比較：一、《唐吉訶德》是通過一個可笑的騎士的故事表現對西班牙社會現實的認識和思索；《鹿鼎記》則是透過一個可樂的小人的故事表達一種對千百年中國歷史文化的審視與反思。二、《唐吉訶德》是感文藝復興之先聲而作；《鹿鼎記》爲思「文化大革命」之後果而創。

三、西方與中國，《唐吉訶德》與《鹿鼎記》之間三百年以上的歷史「時間差」。

四、東西文化的參考性文本。

一

「金庸小說與世界文學」是「金學」研究中一個不可忽視的課題。

本文篇幅有限，只能大題小做，專談金庸小說《鹿鼎記》與西班牙作家塞萬提斯的世界名著《唐吉訶德》的比較。[1]

首先看看二者之間的可比性。

其一，《唐吉訶德》是西班牙騎士小說的絕響，而《鹿鼎記》則是中國武俠小說的傑出代表作。西方的騎士、騎士文學及其騎士小說，與中國的俠士、俠文學及其武俠小說，均源遠流長，既見於歷史記載，又被文學藝術所再造，形成了各自獨立且連綿不斷的文化傳統，但二者之間卻有很大的可比性。美國史丹福大學劉若愚教授的著作《中國之俠》第五章「結論和比較」中就有〈中國游俠與西方騎士的比較〉一節。[2] 更能說明問題的是，《唐吉訶德》在中國，最早由林紓和陳家麟二人用文言文節譯出版，譯名即是《魔俠傳》（1922年），即可見二者的中心概念及其文學類型有其內在的互通性及可比性。

其二，《唐吉訶德》雖然在文類上是一部騎士小說，但在其精神實質上卻是一部「反騎士小說」。同樣，《鹿鼎記》也可稱之為一部「反武俠小說」。

《唐吉訶德》的創作目的，是對流行的騎士小說的反諷，並企圖借此清除騎士小說的一些「流行病」。這在該書的上卷前言中已經說得十分明確──作者借一位朋友之口指出──「這本書是諷刺騎士小說的。」「實際上，你的目的就是要推翻騎士小說胡編濫造的那套虛幻的東西。很多人厭惡騎士小說，但更多的人喜歡它。你要是能達到你的目的，收獲不小呢。」[3]

對騎士小說的反諷和批判，貫穿了《唐吉訶德》一書。除了上卷前言開

---

1 《唐吉訶德》有多種中文譯本，本文所據，是劉京勝的譯本（灕江出版社，1995年10月）。金庸的《鹿鼎記》則依據北京三聯書店1994年5月版。

2 本書有多種中文譯本，最好的是周清霖先生的譯本，上海三聯書店1991年9月第1版，係根據 Routledge & Kegan Paul Ltd 1967 年英文版翻譯。

3 同註1，頁2。

宗明義外，上卷的第六章寫了「神甫和理髮師在足智多謀的貴族書房裡進行了別有風趣的大檢查」，這是一場別開生面的對騎士小說的「審判」。例如對《希臘的阿馬迪斯》，神甫的判詞是「都扔到畜欄裡」，「什麼平蒂內斯特拉女王達里內爾牧人以及他的牧歌，還有作者的種種醜惡悖謬，統統燒掉。即使養育了我的父親打扮成游俠騎士的模樣，也要連同這些東西一起燒掉。」對於《勞拉的唐奧利萬》，神甫說：「這本書的作者就是寫《芳菲園》的那個人，我也不知道這兩本書裡究竟哪一本真話多，或者最好說，哪一本書說假話少。我只知道這本胡言亂語、目空一切的書也應該扔到畜欄去。」這位神甫顯然也代表了作者的觀點。有趣的是，他並非對所有的書都是如此，對有些騎士小說，也會網開一面（只要它有某些可取之處）。可見作者並非一味的蠻來，而是有分析和評判。這一章大可以作為了解西班牙及歐洲騎士小說的一種教科書。

在小說的最後，作者這樣寫道：「我的願望無非是讓人們對那些騎士小說裡的人物的荒誕行徑深惡痛絕。現在，我首先享受到了這種成果，已經心滿意足。由於我這本關於唐吉訶德的真實故事，騎士小說將日趨衰落，並且最終將徹底消亡。再見。」（下卷第七十四章）

值得一說的是，塞萬提斯的願望實現了。在《唐吉訶德》出版之後，歐洲的騎士小說便真的再也沒有多少市場，迅速衰落而且消亡了。

再看金庸的《鹿鼎記》。

金庸的創作道路與塞萬提斯大不相同，在《鹿鼎記》之前，金庸創作了一系列武俠小說，並且獲得了巨大的成功。看起來，金庸不太可能像塞萬提斯那樣對武俠小說提出那麼直接而又強烈的批評，甚至要將它們付之一炬。但這不表明金庸對武俠小說沒有絲毫意見。只不過，金庸將自己對武俠小說通常的各種各樣的弊病的認識，作為對自己的一種警戒，從而在創作中自覺地加以避免。這使得金庸的小說別有風貌，既不重複他人，亦不重複自己。金庸的小說力避荒誕，盡可能寫得有趣而又有意義，力求在其武俠小說中「抒寫世間的悲歡，抒發作者的人生感慨」（《天龍八部》後記）；力求做到「寫人性」（《神鵰俠侶》、《笑傲江湖》等書的後記）。這樣，金庸的小說便不斷開創新模式，創造新人物，拓展新境界。從而，金庸小說創作歷程經歷了「俠之正」、「俠之變」、「俠之疑」等不同階段之後，終於走向了「俠之反」，寫出了

《鹿鼎記》這部武俠小說史上從未有過的奇書。這部書可以稱之爲一部「反武俠小說」，雖然，金庸沒有而且也不可能像塞萬提斯那樣公然反對和抨擊武俠小說；正如他不可能像塞萬提斯那樣在自己的小說中不斷稱讚自己的作品是「偉大的」、「傑出的」的著作。因爲那不是金庸的性格，而且這樣做也不是中國人的習慣。

《鹿鼎記》反一般武俠小說之道而行之，具體表現爲：一、他的主人公不再是一位通常意義上的俠士，而是韋小寶這麼一個不文不武、不俠不士的小流氓。二、書中的俠義道，即常規武俠世界中的正派群體，不再是理想的正派世界，而是充滿了權力鬥爭及各式各樣的私心雜念的可悲的烏合之眾。如天地會青木堂內的堂主之爭、天地會及臺灣鄭家兩兄弟的權力之爭、天地會與沐王府的「擁唐」與「擁桂」之爭等，使這個俠士世界充滿了火藥味和陰謀詭計。書中的第一大英雄陳近南居然被其少主所殺，可謂死得極爲不值。其它人事更不堪多言。三、進而，具有反諷意味的是，書中正面英雄人物反清復明之「復」的目標固然是始終不明；而他們所反的對象，即滿清皇帝康熙恰恰又是一位英明的少年君主。四、小說的故事，即主人公韋小寶的一系列奇遇，也大反一般武俠小說的常規。韋小寶的遭遇，顯然是對武俠及其武俠世界的深刻的反諷。由此，我們不妨認爲，《鹿鼎記》是一部「反武俠小說」。

塞萬提斯對騎士小說一向反感，因而寫出一部「反騎士小說」，固屬不易；金庸由一位成功的武俠小說家，最後居然也寫出一部「反武俠小說」來，應該說更加難得。

其三，在寫作風格上，這兩部小說也有近似之處。《唐吉訶德》是一部傑出的諷刺藝術佳作；《鹿鼎記》則是一部優異的幽默藝術傑作。

塞萬提斯的小說中，不僅有對西班牙及歐洲騎士小說的直接了當的批評和挖苦，更有利用其小說的故事情節及人物形象對騎士小說進行絕妙的諷刺。如唐吉訶德出門征險及其後大戰風車等，無不是因爲他看了騎士小說而走火入魔。《唐吉訶德》的敍事及其語言亦莊亦諧，充滿了諷刺意味，矛頭所指，入木三分。而金庸在其小說《鹿鼎記》中，亦對筆下的主人公及其奇妙的經歷懷有一種獨特的情感態度，韋小寶的性格、言行舉止，和他所經歷的一切，無不讓人莞爾，乃至噴飯。書中的幽默趣味，相信給所有的讀者都留下了深刻的印象。

　　其四，《唐吉訶德》與《鹿鼎記》都充滿了創新精神，而且都突破了各自文類的局限。

　　《唐吉訶德》的作者不僅是要以此書諷刺騎士小說，並希望騎士小說從此走向衰朽，而且還有更高的審美目標及其藝術追求。諸如恢復理智良知、發揚人文精神、揭示生活真實，以及寓教於趣的活潑形式等即是。小說中的那位牧師有這樣一段話：「雖然列舉了騎士小說的許多壞處，可它還有一個好處，那就是可以在內容上讓有想像力的人充分表現自己。它提供了廣闊的創作天地，讓人無拘無束地任意編寫」；「只要筆意超逸，構思巧妙，而且盡可能地接近於現實，就一定會做到主題新穎，達到完美的境地，實現作品的最佳目的，就像我剛才說的，就是寓教於趣。這種不受約束的寫作可以使作者以詩與議論的各種美妙手法寫出史詩、抒情詩、悲劇、喜劇等。」（上卷第47章）由此可見，作者所反對的只是那種荒誕不經而又千篇一律的寫作方法，而對「不受拘束」的想像與寫作卻並不否定，反而大加讚揚。關鍵在於要「編得越接近真實越好，編得越減少讀者的懷疑，越具有可能性才越好。」我們無妨將這些話當做作者的創作宣言。而《唐吉訶德》也確實做到了。

　　金庸在《鹿鼎記》的〈後記〉中也這樣寫道：「《鹿鼎記》和我以前的武俠小說完全不同，那是故意的。一個作者不應當總是重複自己的風格形式，要盡可能的嘗試一些新的創造。」「在康熙時代的中國，有韋小寶那樣的人物並不是不可能的。」可見金庸的小說是在自覺地打破文類的局限，以其天馬行空的幻想來表現歷史的可能性。《鹿鼎記》與《唐吉訶德》一樣，不是一般的武俠小說或騎士小說，甚至也不是簡單的「反武俠」或「反騎士」，而是所謂「非法，非非法」。

　　其五，二者共有的雅俗共賞的審美特徵和文化寓言的性質。

　　《唐吉訶德》不僅具有明顯的可讀性，而且內涵深廣。它以一個看似純粹虛構的騎士傳奇故事為其外殼，包含了一幅幅當時西班牙社會的美妙的風俗畫。它寫到了社會各階層的人物，貴族、僧侶、地主、農民、兵士、市民、商人、演員、小店主、理髮師、學生、騾夫、牧羊人、強盜、罪犯等；寫到了鄉村和城鎮，寫到了路邊客店和貴族城堡，寫到了高山密林和無邊大海，寫到了政治、經濟、宗教、戰爭、愛情、習俗、詩歌、喜劇、騎士小說。進而，唐吉訶德和他的伙伴桑喬的性格及奇遇，形成了一部奇妙而又豐富的寓

言。《唐吉訶德》可以從各種層次和不同的角度去看。

　　《鹿鼎記》比《唐吉訶德》更加妙趣天然，鬼斧神工。韋小寶的經歷比唐吉訶德更離奇、豐富而又複雜。韋小寶當過小流氓、小太監、小和尚、小將軍、小伯爵乃至小公爵、小香主、小令主、小欽差、小囚徒、小島主、小英雄、小狗熊。他的足跡遍及妓院、賭館、書場、市井、宮廷、官場、寺院、軍隊、武林、江湖、民間、荒島、黑社會，乃至俄羅斯首都。這一切看似匪夷所思而又似乎合情合埋，實則作者在不動聲色地撕開了中國歷史及其傳統文化的幃幕，讓有心的讀者看到種種神秘的眞相。《鹿鼎記》以虛寫實，奇而至眞，一物兩面，渾然一體，將傳奇情節與歷史眞實結合得天衣無縫，在故事情節層面、人物形象層面、寓言眞義層面，每個讀者都有「路」可通，而且都會有所收獲。《唐吉訶德》的寓言深度已被廣泛地發掘，《鹿鼎記》則有待於進一步認識。

二

　　下面我們將對《鹿鼎記》的主人公韋小寶和《唐吉訶德》的二號人物桑喬‧潘薩進行比較。此二人有極大的相似之處，若能相見，定會結爲知交。照韋小寶的個性，弄不好還要結拜兄弟，而且還是眞心結拜。

　　此二人的相似點之一，都是出身平民，都來自民間世俗社會。這一點看似無關緊要，實則對二者的性格及其意義有著關鍵性的影響。

　　相似點之二，是二者都不識字，看似無知，桑喬的主人經常罵他是傻瓜、笨蛋，韋小寶亦被認爲不文不武不俠；實際上此二人雖不學但卻有術，極富民間的生存智慧。桑喬喜歡說話，且開口便是俗語，經常弄得唐吉訶德無可奈何，甚至被他影響，也說起俗語來。韋小寶自幼在書場、戲院學會「文腔」，又在妓院、賭館學會「俗罵」，論嘴上功夫，韋小寶少有匹敵。這還只是外在功夫，說到「內功」，即生存智慧，他們也端的不凡。在《唐吉訶德》下卷的四十五、四十七、四十九、五十一、五十三等章中，桑喬被公爵封爲巴拉托里亞總督，原本只是想出他的洋相，卻不料桑喬竟當得有聲有色，成就斐然。雖僅十日，亦可見桑喬內秀不凡。韋小寶的成就遠遠大於桑喬，用反推法，可以證明他比桑喬更加內秀。當然，二人所處的社會環境大不相同，也是二

人成就不同的原因。

相似點之三，二者都是典型的功利主義者。桑喬隨唐吉訶德出門征險，是爲了掙錢養家餬口，更何況主人還許以總督（後來果然當了）、伯爵（始終沒當上）之位。平生做事，有利便幹，無利便罷。桑喬的口號是「勝者爲王」（下卷第二十章），中文的意思是「有奶便是娘」。韋小寶更是如此。桑喬做總督還是兩袖清風，韋小寶第一天做臺灣代理行政長官便貪污了百萬兩銀子。韋小寶既是皇帝面前的紅人，又是反皇帝的天地會組織中的香主，還是神龍教的五龍令主。他的原則是生存第一，一切爲我，其它價值原則全都不在話下。

相似點之四，是二者都懶惰而且滑頭。桑喬做事，一向不很認眞，凡有機會總免不了要偷一偷懶。典型的例子是小說的下卷第十章，他騙主人說見過杜爾西內亞；兩人去托博索城時，他又建議讓他一人去尋，然後他獨自一人，編好一套謊話，休息半天，恰好碰見三位農婦，便去對主人說他找到了杜爾西內亞。韋小寶更是一個天生的懶骨頭。幾乎無論做任何正經事，都要偷懶耍滑，他拜過多位武功一流的師傅，但始終都不能入流，原因是他壓根兒就沒認眞練過，而且也不打算認眞練。其他的例子不必多舉。韋小寶的懶惰和滑頭，正如他的伶俐和好運一樣，給人留下了極深刻的印象。

相似點之五，是二人都有快樂的天性。他們都是爲自己而活，因而活得甚爲快樂；因爲快樂，且能自得其樂，他們便顯得非常之可愛。桑喬在這方面與他的主人形成了鮮明的對比。唐吉訶德心懷天下，苦多樂少，難得有片刻的歡娛；而桑喬卻不論在哪裡，總能找到快樂的理由，或者說總能找到逃避不快樂的方法。因爲不快樂，他寧願不當總督。韋小寶更是如此，看戲之樂、賭博之快、散漫之閒、熱鬧之歡，是他畢生的追求；當官、發財、出名、立德、立功、立言，倘無快樂和歡愉，他決計不想幹。即使是非幹不可，他也會尋歡作樂，一旦時機成熟，則立馬設法開溜。

相似點之六，是二人都自私自利、貪生怕死。不僅怕死，還怕苦怕痛。平心而論，桑喬不失爲一個忠僕，韋小寶也講點義氣；倘不過份，他們倒也想表現出一點大方英雄氣概。但若失利或痛苦，那就只好不客氣了。《唐吉訶德》下卷第三十五章，公爵和公爵夫人說可以破除杜爾西內亞的魔法，辦法是要桑喬在光天化日之下，裸露身體，自抽三千三百鞭，須疼痛難忍，方能

見效。桑喬一聽，頓時光火，毫不猶豫地大呼「急（拒）絕！」後來講妥多少錢一鞭，才可以商量。他的條件是讓他一人在樹林中打，結果是，他的每一鞭都抽在樹上。韋小寶自私怕苦而花招百出，例子更多，那也不必多言。對此當做認眞的分析，不宜做簡單的道德判斷。

韋小寶與桑喬相似之處甚多。其根本的原因在於，他們都是各自生活世界中的凡俗小人，或者說是世俗之中的常人。他們的個性及其生存智慧，都由世俗生活中來；他們的形象及其審美意義，必須歸於對生活及其世俗的深刻理解。韋小寶這一人物形象是否受到了桑喬形象的影響？這很難說。原因是，桑喬是西班牙的桑喬，而韋小寶則是中國的韋小寶。

韋小寶與桑喬也有不同之處。例如，桑喬生活在鄉村，而韋小寶則生長於都市；桑喬比較質樸，而韋小寶則更油滑；桑喬有宗教信仰，而韋小寶則什麼也不信；桑喬還有法律意識，而韋小寶則無法無天；桑喬只能是別人的僕從、書中的配角，而韋小寶則是書中絕對的主人公。桑喬與韋小寶是西班牙和中國兩種完全不同的歷史文化傳統及其社會環境的產物。

在美學意義層面上，桑喬形象很難與韋小寶相提並論。桑喬形象畢竟太過單純扁平了，而韋小寶形象則要豐富、複雜得多。因而，我們就有必要對韋小寶這一形象進行更深入的研究和分析。

三

以下將是韋小寶形象與唐吉訶德形象的比較。

隨著時間的推移，人們對唐吉訶德這一形象的認識也在不斷深入。人們越來越認識到這一人物的豐富性與複雜性。人們已經發現，此人不僅是一位發瘋的騎士，同時也是一位受難的英雄；進而，他也不僅是作者諷刺的對象，同時也是作者思想的傳聲筒；因此，此人不僅有著個性形象意義，同時還代表著一種普遍的人文精神。他並不總是發瘋發癲，有時卻又清醒明智；他有時讓人發笑，有時卻又讓人肅然起敬。對此，文學史早有公論，不必多言。

在《唐吉訶德》一書中，桑喬的形象與唐吉訶德的形象處處形成對比。一高瘦、一矮胖；一糊塗、一清醒；一貴族、一平民；一高貴、一卑俗；一理想、一現實；一忘我、一自私；一喜歡空想、一注重功利；一執著痛苦、

一馬虎快樂……。韋小寶既然與桑喬相似點多、相異點少，自然就處於與唐吉訶德相對的多、相近的少。

唐吉訶德是一位西方的騎士，韋小寶是一位中國的小人。騎士出身高貴，小人出身卑賤。兩種不同的出身，影響了他們的性格。中國古代一位哲人說：君子喻於義，小人喻於利；中國當代一位大人物則說：卑賤者最聰明，高貴者最愚蠢。智與愚、義與利，最好是具體問題具體分析。

唐吉訶德是一位發了瘋的騎士，韋小寶是一位清醒明白的小人。唐吉訶德之發瘋，是因爲他看多了騎士小說，尤其是對騎士小說信以爲眞，太過執著，以至成癡。韋小寶雖也愛聽書看戲，且能模仿一二，但卻不會太過當眞，更不會執著，所以永遠不會發瘋。

唐吉訶德是一個典型的理想主義者，韋小寶則是一位典型的現實主義者。唐吉訶德能爲、也願爲自己的理想而獻身；韋小寶則沒什麼理想，更不會爲之而獻身。韋小寶的大志不過是想將來開幾家像麗春院那樣的大妓院，能否做到，卻是無可無不可。他當然有各種各樣的欲望，並且有強烈的功利心，但這些都要在現實中求得滿足，且要服從現實原則。

唐吉訶德是一位行動主義者，既有理想，就要追求，就要主動進擊；既發現現實與理想不符，那就要向現實發出挑戰，就要改變現實。韋小寶是一位享樂主義者，隨波逐流，得過且過，最大的願望是有錢可賭、有戲可看、有熱鬧可乘，而獲得這些，最好又要得來全不費功夫，千萬不要踏破鐵鞋無覓處。

唐吉訶德是一位眞正的騎士，他把騎士的榮譽看得高於一切。韋小寶則是一位眞正的小人，自幼受輕受賤、挨打挨罵，習慣了沒有人格的存活；榮譽感淡到了幾乎沒有，至於尊嚴，則連聽也沒聽說過。正因如此，他可以隨時準備跪倒在任何威脅到他的強者面前，也可以隨時拜給予他好處的人爲師、爲父。只要能避難、得好處，做什麼樣的人，全不在乎。

唐吉訶德嚴於律己，時時處處以騎士的道德標準約束自己，言行舉止自戒自修，誠實勇敢，品行高貴。韋小寶懶於修身，談不上有何嚴格的道德標準、人生規範。性喜吹牛拍馬、撒謊騙人，怕苦怕疼、怯弱滑頭。善於隨機應變、見風駛舵、自私自利、無德無品。

唐吉訶德對自己想像中的愛情忠貞不逾，願爲他的杜爾西內亞不惜一

切，並把自己的一切德行與榮譽都敬獻給她，堪稱騎士之愛的典範，是情之聖者。韋小寶好色無厭，多欲寡情。《鹿鼎記》第三十三回書中，對此有精采的刻劃：韋小寶見百勝刀王胡逸之對著名美女陳圓圓鍾情極深，以爲可做同道，便想拜他爲師；胡逸之知他對陳圓圓之女欲得之而後快，便與他結拜兄弟。其實二人的愛欲觀念，判若雲泥。胡逸之之愛是忘我傾心、純粹的精神之慕──這與唐吉訶德之愛十分相似；而韋小寶之愛則不過是「一定要她做我的老婆」而已。

唐吉訶德是一位失敗的騎士，韋小寶是一位成功的小人。唐吉訶德的種種努力，常常只會被人嘲笑；他之不畏艱險、挑戰俗世，被認爲是自不量力和自討苦吃。韋小寶的樁樁胡鬧，則贏得一片掌聲；他之左右逢源、溜鬚拍馬，被看成是聰明機智和妙人妙事。

唐吉訶德死了，而韋小寶卻還活著。唐吉訶德最後清醒，壽終正寢；韋小寶始終明白，卻不知所終。

唐吉訶德死後，參孫‧卡拉斯科學士（也就是那位扮成白月騎士打敗唐吉訶德並逼他立誓一年內不出家門的人）在他的墓碑上寫下了這樣的墓誌銘：「高尙貴族，長眠此地，英勇絕倫，雖死猶生，功蓋天地。雄居世界，震撼寰宇，身經百難，生前瘋癲，死後穎異。」（下卷七十四章）韋小寶呢，這小子溜了。年方二十，便要「告老還鄉」；說是還鄉，卻又並不眞的還鄉，而是金蟬脫殼，躲起來了。有一點可以肯定，那就是他沒有死、也不會死。不死，當然就沒有墓誌銘，不能蓋棺論定了。若勉強要說，那只能借用二十世紀中國詩人北島的兩句詩：「高尙是高尙者的墓誌銘，卑鄙是卑鄙者的通行證。」──前一句屬於唐吉訶德，後一句才屬於韋小寶。

四

對唐吉訶德與韋小寶這兩個人物形象，還可以作進一步的比較。這兩個人物不僅具有個性形象的審美意義，而且還代表著兩種不同的文化精神。我們可以稱之爲「唐吉訶德精神」與「韋小寶作風」。

「唐吉訶德精神」的基礎層面自然是一種騎士精神，正如「韋小寶作風」的基礎層面是一種小人作風。不過，在這裡，對騎士精神和小人作風都不能

作簡單化的理解。唐吉訶德與韋小寶這兩個人物形象所包含的精神內涵，要比一般意義上的騎士精神與小人作風更加豐富，也更有深度。

唐吉訶德與韋小寶之間最本質的區別是，唐吉訶德總是力圖去改變自己所處的社會，而韋小寶則總是想要去適應自己所處的環境。

在上文中我們說到，唐吉訶德是一位發了瘋的騎士。他之出門征險，確似發瘋的行為。但我們應該追問一下，他的行為是發瘋，他的思想也是發瘋嗎？退一步說，他的思想看起來似發瘋，實質上也是發瘋嗎？再退一步，他的思想就算當時是發瘋，如今看起來還是發瘋嗎？深究下去，我們不能不說，他的出門征險，雖似發瘋，卻包含著一種合理的、令人肅然起敬的濟世精神。在唐吉訶德第一次出征之前，書中寫道：「事已就緒，他迫不及待地把自己的想法付諸實施。他要鏟除暴劣，撥亂反正，制止無理，改進陋習，清理債務，如果現在不做，為時晚矣。」（上卷第二章）在他第二次出征前則說：「他說世界上最需要的就是游俠騎士，而且他對游俠騎士的崛起責無旁貸。」（上卷第七章）在唐吉訶德第三次出征前，書中寫得更多：「你們費心勞神地想讓我不從事天意所指、命運所定、情理所求，尤其是我的意志希望我去做的事，那只能是枉費心機。因為我知道游俠騎士須付出的無數辛勞，也知道靠游俠騎士能得到的各種利益。我知道這條路非常狹窄，而惡習之路卻很寬廣，但是他們的結局卻不相同。惡習之路雖然寬廣，卻只能導致死亡，而道德之路儘管狹窄艱苦，導致的卻是生機，而且不是有生而止，是永生而無窮盡，就像我們偉大的西班牙詩人說的：『沿著這崎嶇的道路／／通向不朽的境界／／怯者無指望。』」（下卷第六章）——這表明唐吉訶德精神實質是要改革社會。雖感「惡習之路寬廣」，卻是責無旁貸，堅持走自己的崎嶇道德之路。這與只是追求愛情和個人榮譽的騎士不可同日而語。

韋小寶之出門遠行，則完全是另一種情形。他是見人欺侮他的媽媽，不得不反抗；後來幫茅十八殺了史松，不得不逃走。剛到北京，便當了太監海大富的俘虜，從此身不由己，只能走一步算一步，走到哪算哪。隨波逐流，見風駛舵，一切均屬迫不得已、不得不為。對韋小寶的性格，大儒查繼佐等人看得透徹：「韋小寶無甚知識，要曉以大義，他只講小義，不講大義；要喻以大勢，他也只明小勢，不明大勢。」（第五十回）——韋小寶作風的基礎是一種小人見識：道德、真理之大義，國家、民族之大勢，他是一概不懂，

也完全不想去搞懂。那不是他的事。事不關己，高高掛起，這是通例。他所注重的是小義、小勢，即個人所處的實際環境、具體利害關係及求生之法、求存之道。這需要眼觀四路、耳聽八方、照方抓藥、見風駛舵，以求得一席生存之地。

進而，唐吉訶德的騎士精神，本質上是一種理想主義精神；韋小寶的小人作風，本質上是一種功利主義作風。

奇妙的是，唐吉訶德看似一位發瘋的騎士，他的精神追求卻是一種合乎理性的社會理想。其實，很多的讀者都忽視了，唐吉訶德並非一直瘋癲。他是時而清醒時而糊塗，他的行為及其行為意識或許是糊塗而瘋癲的，但他對客觀存在的社會現實的批判卻是清醒而又深刻的。而且，在此基礎上提出的道德理想，也是富有理性的。小説的作者不止一次地提醒讀者，不要以為唐吉訶德是一位純粹的瘋子，他也有清醒的一面。例如，在桑喬被任命為總督時，唐吉訶德對桑喬有一番嘉言教訓。其後，作者如此寫道：「聽了唐吉訶德這番話，誰會不把他當成一個足智多謀、識見萬里的人呢？不過，就像這部巨著裡記述的那樣，他只是在談論騎士道時才胡言亂語，而談起其它事情時則頭腦清晰，所以他時時表現出言行不符的情況。」（下卷第四十三章）

進而，我們還必須考慮，唐吉訶德為什麼發瘋、以及發了瘋又怎樣？他固然是因為看多了騎士小説而發瘋發癡；更深刻的原因則是他的理想與現實的衝突。正如英國大文豪拜倫爵士所説：「《唐吉訶德》是一個令人感傷的故事，它越是使人發笑，則越使人感到難過。這位英雄是主持正義的，制服壞人是他的唯一宗旨，正是這些美德使他發了瘋。」[4]

韋小寶的情況與之相反。此人一向清醒明白，可是卻缺乏真正的理性，基本上是依靠自己的社會本能活著。個體的生存是他最重要的、乃至唯一的人生課題；滿足生存的欲望便成了他的生活目標。自我發展，不是他力所能及的；或者説白了，他根本就想不到這個。至於社會理想，那更不是他所能懂得的。對於他，社會理想是一個莫明其妙而又滑稽可笑的概念。韋小寶的精神層次之低，乃是有目共睹，不需多言。

---

4 轉引自《中國大百科全書·外國文學卷(二)》（北京：中國大百科全書出版社，1982），頁 890。

　　韋小寶的奇蹟，與唐吉訶德的遭遇恰成對比。面對強大的現實，理想主義歸於失敗，而功利主義則獲得勝利。韋小寶成功的訣竅，或者說韋小寶作風的實質，是無條件地服從現實的遊戲規則，無條件地與現實同流合污。看起來，他似乎也有一定的價值觀念，他甚至還自稱忠、義兩全。但他的價值觀念的本質是一切爲我。他根本就不會去考慮對康熙的忠和對天地會兄弟的義之間會有怎樣的深刻矛盾。他之忠、義的奧秘，是康熙對他很好，所以他對康熙也很好；陳近南及天地會兄弟對他不錯，所以他對他們也不錯。別人對他怎樣，他就怎樣回之；投桃報李，利益共享，有利才能有禮，有利就是有理，這是韋小寶的最大原則。

　　唐吉訶德精神與韋小寶作風的第三個本質區別是，唐吉訶德精神是一種西方近代人文精神；韋小寶作風則是一種中國傳統的人格形式。

　　許多《唐吉訶德》的研究者，尤其是中國的學者，常以爲塞萬提斯的這部小說是「在嘲笑騎士制度的同時，以理想化的騎士精神來反對沒落的封建階級。他揭露了西班牙的醜惡現實，然而他的理想卻是恢復到古代純樸的社會中去。」[5] 這樣的結論，恐怕大有商榷的餘地，至少是只知其一，不知其二。《唐吉訶德》既是反對沒落的封建制度，又從何見得其作者是要恢復古代社會純樸的理想？單看唐吉訶德作爲騎士，似乎能得出恢復古代社會理想的結論；若看到《唐吉訶德》是一部「反騎士小說」，則能見識其近代人文精神。唐吉訶德所扮演的是古代的騎士，但他所思所言則是近代的精神。他的關於法律、政治、愛情、人性、人生的種種議論，可以爲證。他將人的尊嚴、情感、個性和利益置於重要的地位加以考慮，更可以爲證。應該說，唐吉訶德既是西方社會的最後一位騎士，同時又是西班牙第一位近代人文精神的啓蒙者。

　　韋小寶之屬於中國傳統社會和傳統文化，自不待言。實際上，不僅在康熙時代有韋小寶這樣的人物是可能的；在整個中國古代歷史之中，韋小寶這樣的人物的存在，都是可能的。進而，我們還必須認識到，只要傳統的社會體制存在，只要傳統的文明形式存在，韋小寶的存在就不僅只是可能，而且還是必然。說到底，韋小寶及其作風，乃是特定的社會歷史及其文化價值的產物。韋小寶這一形象的思想價值及其審美價值也正在這裡。

5　同註4。

　　《唐吉訶德》不止是一個有關瘋騎士的可笑的故事，更是一個有關人類精神的寓言。隨著對這部書的讀解的加深，人們從這部寓言中獲得的信息也就越加豐富。唐吉訶德死後，參孫・卡拉斯科學士代表他的鄉親在他的墓碑上寫下了「雖死猶生，功蓋天地」和「生前瘋癲，死後穎異」的銘文。這一「蓋棺論定」不似中國式的死後的無稽的胡吹亂捧，而是作者最後埋下的一個伏筆，表現出作者對唐吉訶德精神的高度的贊揚和堅定的信念。果然，其後西方的學者和文人，將塞萬提斯筆下的唐吉訶德和沙士比亞筆下的哈姆雷特並列為近代以來最有影響的兩大文學典型：唐吉訶德敢於行動，哈姆雷特善於思索。英國作家笛福稱自己筆下的魯濱遜「具有一種唐吉訶德精神」；俄國大作家杜思妥也夫斯基則說要想讀懂他的《白癡》，必須首先閱讀《唐吉訶德》；美國作家福克納居然自稱每年都要讀一遍《唐吉訶德》，說「就像別人讀《聖經》似的」。[6] ……可見唐吉訶德精神有一種巨大的感召力。無論是在小說出版的當時還是以後，這種感召力都是人類精神的一種寶貴的財富。

　　韋小寶形象乃是中國文學史中極少見的傑出的藝術典型。這一典型的審美意義及其豐富的內涵還遠遠沒有被認識和發掘；對於「韋小寶作風」的文化內涵和思想意義更缺乏應有的重視和認真的研究。韋小寶是中國文化的一個精靈，又是一個怪胎；他是傳統文化及其社會關係的必然產物，既是一種膠合物，更是一種腐蝕劑。韋小寶形象隱含了中國文化的大秘密，而「韋小寶作風」則是中國歷史文化中最大的國情特色。

五

　　關於《唐吉訶德》和《鹿鼎記》這兩部書，要說的當然不止是桑喬、唐吉訶德、韋小寶這幾個人物形象，也不僅是可以抽象出來的「唐吉訶德精神」和「韋小寶作風」；還應該看到這兩部書對各自的社會、歷史、文化所作的深刻的闡釋和卓越的再現。

　　《唐吉訶德》所描繪的是西班牙的社會風情、各階層人們的生活。西班牙歷史風貌，如著名的萊潘托戰役；西班牙文化風俗，如主人公及其所見所

6　同註1，《唐吉訶德・譯本序言》，頁1-2。

聞的有關生死、宗教、婚姻、權力、財富、愛情、榮譽、尊嚴、自由、個性、法制、和平、戰爭等相互衝突的觀念和矛盾複雜的心理；以及當時人對於文學、藝術、文化的理解、思索和探討等等，歷來的文學史家和理論批評家已經有夠多夠好的研究和總結。其中最讓人深思的是杜思妥也夫斯基的這樣一段話：「到了地球的盡頭問人們：『你們可明白了你們在地球上的生活？你們該怎樣總結這一生活呢？』那時，人們便可以默默地把《唐吉訶德》遞上去，說：『這就是我給生活做的總結。你們難道能因為這個而責備我嗎？』」[7]——這就是說，《唐吉訶德》這部小說對整個人類生活的認識和總結，有某種普遍的意義。唐吉訶德這位可笑的騎士所代表的一種精神和他所面對的現實之間的矛盾關係，是人類生活的某種寓言。當然，杜思妥也夫斯基的這種評價，不無誇大的成分。小說《唐吉訶德》的寓言意義，嚴格地說，只有相對於西方基督教世界，才能得到充分的解釋和佐證。而對於東方古老的中國，這種解釋就多少有些文不對題了。

　　杜思妥也夫斯基的評價對於金庸小說《鹿鼎記》來說其實也非常合適。只是要加一個小小的注解，即對於中國的歷史文化及其社會生活，《鹿鼎記》具有極其深刻的寓言意義。這部小說對中國的歷史奧秘、文化精神、社會規則、生存環境以及中國人的文化心理、價值觀念、生活態度、思維方式等作了全面而又深刻的展示。這是一部關於中國人的最絕妙的精神生活大百科。韋小寶這位快樂的小人物的生動形象，是我們中國人最熟悉，也最容易產生好感，最能揭示我們的文化心理奧妙，卻又最不容易言說的。韋小寶的所見所聞、所遇所求，看似異想天開的奇蹟，實則是古老的中國社會中最平凡的故事。在它的傳奇故事的背後，有著最真實的生活經驗和人生智慧。當然這裡指的是中國的生活經驗和人生智慧。韋小寶與小說中的一系列人物的關係，如他與茅十八、海大富、陳近南、康熙、洪安通、晦聰和尚、九難師太、陶紅英、胡逸之、吳三桂、索額圖、明珠、康親王、胖頭陀、陸高軒和天地會眾兄弟，以及沐劍屏、方怡、雙兒、曾柔、蘇荃、建寧公主、阿珂和他的母親韋春芳等等，組成了一個巨大的網絡，包括了社會的方方面面。無論是敵是友、是帝王是賊寇、是高官是平民，或是男是女、是愛是恨、是出家是

7　同註6，頁3。

在家、是奇人是凡夫，韋小寶與他們的關係都是我中有你、你中有我。每一個人都是他的老師、他的朋友，又都是他的學生、他的敵人。更準確地說，每個人都是他的鏡子，都是他的形象的一個有機的組成部分。這也就是：人是他的社會關係的各方面的總和。韋小寶只有母親，沒有父親，這不僅意味著韋小寶的父親有可能是漢人、滿人、回人、蒙古人或藏族人，即韋小寶是一個「雜種」；而且還意味著，是全社會所有的這些人塑造了韋小寶，這些人都是韋小寶的精神和人格的生父生母。人是環境的產物。韋小寶不是孫悟空，不是從石頭裡面蹦出來的。這就是說，韋小寶和他的社會，是一而二，又是二而一的。此人左右逢源、四方通吃、八面玲瓏，並非他天生異稟、才智卓絕，而是他的那一套在社會上行得通。甚至說也只有他的那一套才行得通。他的不學之術是從社會生活中學到的，而且事實證明，他所學到的生存之術應用於社會，雖非高明，卻極實用。這就是韋小寶的傳奇故事的眞正意義，也是《鹿鼎記》一書的眞正價值。一個不認識韋小寶的人，很難說他能認識中國社會；不認識韋小寶，更難以認識中國的歷史與文化。——韋小寶自認爲既忠且義，進而，只怕還會認爲自己既仁且孝吧？這雖然似乎有些好笑，但你能說這是純粹的無稽之談嗎？如若有人認爲韋小寶忠孝節義、仁禮智信，當然是過分地抬舉他了；但若認爲他不忠不孝、不仁不義、不智不信、不禮不節，那恐怕又過分地苛求他了吧。對韋小寶這一人物進行道德的評判，不是我們的目的；而對這個人物的道德品質、價值觀念、行爲規範進行分析和研究，則無疑會有助於我們更好去認識中國歷史文化的奧妙。即可以使我們看到，忠孝節義、仁義禮智這樣一些堂皇的概念，在實際社會歷史之中是怎樣被操作運用，又是怎樣被談論和認識的。通過韋小寶，我們知道了，所有的這一切都大有「商量」的餘地，即所謂「假做眞時眞亦假，無爲有處有還無」。所有中國文化的概念，都「虛實相生」，都是「運用之妙，存乎一心」，都說是一套而做是另一套，都口頭上仁義道德肚子裡男盜女娼，都是說你行你就行不行也行，說不行就不行行也不行。所以，韋小寶雖然「不學」，卻仍然「有術」。這叫做，卑賤者最聰明，可以不學而有術；高貴者最愚蠢，蓋只會引經據典、空想清談。總之一句話，中國文化的無窮奧妙，盡在「韋小寶神功」之中。而《鹿鼎記》，則正是韋小寶神功的「葵花寶典」。其成就的奧秒，也還是那句話：「欲練神功，揮刀自宮。」即需要模糊性別、自毀人格，

方能無敵於天下。韋小寶能在俄羅斯建立功勳，揚威異域，正是此理。這使得韋小寶的後代，自傲無比，而且想欲非非。只不知，韋小寶碰到了唐吉訶德會怎樣？這二人無緣相見，實在遺憾千秋。好在有《唐吉訶德》和《鹿鼎記》在，隨時都可以讓他們比試一番。看一看東西方的文化武功，究竟孰高孰下？

　　欲讓這兩位主人公比試，尚須對《唐吉訶德》與《鹿鼎記》二書進行更進一步的比較。《唐吉訶德》是感西方近代文藝復興的先聲而作；而《鹿鼎記》則是思中國當代「文化大革命」的後果而寫。

　　對於《唐吉訶德》的思想傾向，學界有不同的認識。不少學者，尤其中國的學者，認為《唐吉訶德》及其作者塞萬提斯是「恢復到古代純樸的社會中去」。這話當然不無道理，卻又多少有些自相矛盾：既是「反對沒落的封建階級」，何以又「恢復到古代純樸的社會中去」？這等於說，這部書既「反古」而又「復古」，豈不矛盾？這部書確實有矛盾。唐吉訶德有時發瘋、有時清醒，該書是騎士小說、又是「反騎士小說」，這就是矛盾的根源。如何認識和評判，可真不是一件簡單的事。不過，我們似乎可以在西方的文藝復興運動本身得到啓發。文藝復興是要恢復古希臘傳統，它形似復古，意卻在立新。這也可以看做是《唐吉訶德》的精神傾向吧！塞萬提斯所處的時代正是文藝復興開始的時代，他受其影響，有史為證。他於 1566 至 1569 年在馬德里的人文主義者胡安·洛佩斯·德奧約斯甫的學校就讀，被神甫稱為詩人；於 1569 年開始軍旅生涯，並且作為胡里奧·阿夸比瓦樞機主教的侍從，出行文藝復興的重鎮羅馬；1572 年加入洛佩·德菲羅亞兵團開赴希臘的科孚島參加戰鬥；1574 至 1575 年又輾轉於義大利的薩丁、熱那亞、那不勒斯和西西里。[8] 這些經歷對塞萬提斯的影響不必多說。他感受了文藝復興的時代先聲，同時也獲得了新的價值標準，對自己祖國的社會現實和文化氛圍當然也就更加不滿。由此我們可以把握塞萬提斯創作《唐吉訶德》的真正動機。

　　《鹿鼎記》與中國「文化大革命」的關係，相對容易說明。我們可以從小說中的洪安通這一人物，及其所創的神龍教的種種活動儀式和整體氛圍中找到證據。這部書與作者前此寫作的《笑傲江湖》都是寫於「文化大革命」中，從而二者都有意無意、自覺或不自覺，都帶有這一時代的痕跡，有對這

8　同註 1，《唐吉訶德·附錄》。

一時代的直接或間接的反映。金庸學貫中西，是五四新文化運動哺育出來的自由主義知識分子，在香港這一自由世界中，對中國大陸興起的「文化大革命」的狂潮，有極爲痛苦的感受和思索，並以文字的形式表達出來。《明報》社論是一種，小說《笑傲江湖》、《鹿鼎記》又是一種。實際上，金庸在這兩部書的前言、後記或註釋中已經提到了這一點。《鹿鼎記》以寫與全書正文不太相干的文字獄開篇，即是對「文化大革命」的最直接的反應。「文化大革命」是一個「忠字舞」和「文字獄」並行的時代。然而，金庸對「文化大革命」的思考，並沒有停留在對它的一些表面現象的再現和嘲諷，而是深入地探索它的成因、它的可能而又極其可怕的後果。這才是韋小寶這一人物形象及《鹿鼎記》這部小說產生的眞正的原因。看起來，韋小寶及其康熙時代的傳奇故事與數百年後的「文化大革命」沒什麼相干；實質上，不僅康熙時代的文字獄和後來的文字獄沒有絲毫的區別，而且，沒有知識、沒有文化、沒有人格、沒有規範的「韋小寶作風」正是「文化大革命」能夠產生的社會基礎和文化根源。而「文化大革命」的結果則必然是沒有眞理、沒有科學、沒有操行、沒有知識、尤其沒有知識分子人格節操和科學理念的「韋小寶作風」更進一步的惡性膨脹、流毒深廣！——從韋小寶形象與「韋小寶作風」這樣一個特殊的角度去看「文化大革命」；以及從「文化大革命」的前因後果去看韋小寶形象及《鹿鼎記》一書，將無疑會有巨大的收獲。而這也正是我們應該積極認眞地去做的。

由此，我們不難看到，塞萬提斯感文藝復興的先聲而創作《唐吉訶德》，必然是對現實社會的批判，並且提出新的社會理想；以一位爲社會理想的實現而奮勇戰鬥、絕不妥協的瘋騎士的形象，樹立一種看似產自過去、實則面向未來的人格榜樣。因爲有這樣的榜樣，後來人就會不斷地批判現實、改造現實，追求理想社會、實現社會理想。而金庸思「文化大革命」的因果來寫作《鹿鼎記》，則必然是對歷史文化的思考，並總結出這一文化歷史的根蒂和眞相；從而創造出韋小寶這一歷史文化的精靈與怪胎，且讓我們認識到這一怪胎的幽靈至今仍在生存繁衍。「文化大革命」的興起，未嘗沒有發動者改變現實的夢想動機，「革命」一詞即可爲證；結果卻是全民族人民對殘酷現實的無條件的認同，其原因正是韋小寶的幽靈在作怪。「皇帝聖明」，韋小寶只能耍點小聰明，而不能跳出康熙的手心，這一歷史的積澱，也是原因之一。對

此，我們當然還須做更深入的研究。比較《唐吉訶德》和《鹿鼎記》二書的寫作動機和成因，當是一個重要的角度，和一個重要的課題。

　　《唐吉訶德》的上卷出版於 1605 年，而《鹿鼎記》則成書於 1972 年，其間有三百六十餘年的時間差距。二者的時間差距，看似偶然，實則由深層次的必然因素決定著。這一必然的因素，其實就是中西的現代文明興起和發展的時間差異。我們都知道《唐吉訶德》的誕生，標誌著西方騎士文學的終結；騎士的時代迅速地被由法律保護自由、公正的時代所取代。這是西方現代文明的開端。而《鹿鼎記》誕生的時代，中國的武俠文學仍在大量流行，廣大的讀者仍沉浸在刀光劍影的冷兵器世界，在無法無天的往日「江湖」夢中。中國人對武俠文化的喜好，固然不能簡單地附會於時代的落後；然而這種喜好，至少在心理上潛隱著古代農業文明的文化價值積澱。中國現代化之步履艱難，其實大可以在這種文化心理中找尋某些重要的根源。《鹿鼎記》一書之「反武俠」精神的價值，在未來的文學史家的筆下，一定會有《唐吉訶德》之「反騎士」同等的價值。只是它的覺悟已經晚了三百餘年。而且，不僅當下的讀者、評論家對此並沒有真正透徹的認識；有些研究專家，以及想「吃武俠飯」的人更是看不到《鹿鼎記》的反武俠精神；或者，看到了也莫明其妙乃至避而不談。甚至連它的作者本人，對於此也是含糊其辭、不願深究。由此更可見三百多年的現代文明歷史的時間差距，當真是非同小可。

　　唐吉訶德及其「唐吉訶德精神」與韋小寶及其「韋小寶作風」，可以看做是東西方文化差異及其比較的極具代表性的參照物。前者行為似乎可笑，但卻有一種不可忽視的精神；後者行為靈活，卻是對一切精神價值的腐蝕。前者追求理想，後者認同現實；前者面向未來，後者倚仗過去。二者都是各自作者在各自的時代中的卓越的藝術創作，而且也是對各自時代的最敏感、最深刻的把握。至於二者之間三百餘年的時間差距，那正是兩個不同民族和兩種不同文化之不同命運所決定的。金庸的《鹿鼎記》寫作在後，其實無損於它的創造性價值。對於中國、中國人、中國歷史和中國文化，《鹿鼎記》具有不可取代的認識價值。即使是偉大的《唐吉訶德》，也只能與之比較，而不能掩蓋《鹿鼎記》的耀眼光芒。更何況，《鹿鼎記》的藝術成就，比之三百多年前的《唐吉訶德》要大得多。遺憾的是，本文篇幅所限，對此不能進一步舉證分析了。本文只是比較初論，不過想提出問題，以期拋磚引玉而已。

《笑傲江湖》總論

馮 其 庸

中國藝術研究院

摘　要

《笑傲江湖》是通過江湖上武林爭霸來描寫人性的。

本書描寫了形形色色的各種人性。

劉正風、曲洋的故事是人性的光輝，它的內涵豐富，是以往「高山流水，知音難遇」故事的昇華。

令狐冲的性格是經過百折千難、重重冤屈、誤解而最後塑造完成的，他的人生之路是一條特殊的人生之路。任盈盈對令狐冲的愛，是純潔無我的愛，是至高無上的愛；儀琳對令狐冲的愛是聖潔的愛；寧中則對令狐冲的愛是師愛兼母愛。

本書所寫的岳不群，是一個完善的極端虛偽的典型，這個典型在文學史上有特殊的意義和貢獻。

至於任我行，是另一種性格典型，也具有很深的內涵和現實意義。

金庸的文章如行雲流水，是最高境界的敍事散文，他的文章遠得之於莊子，近得之於東坡。

本書中描寫音樂和評論酒具、酒品之處，都是絕妙好辭，令人百讀不厭。

一、前　言

金庸在《笑傲江湖》的〈後記〉裡說：

> 我寫武俠小說是想寫人性，就像大多數小說一樣……

這部小說並非有意的影射文革，而是通過書中一些人物，企圖刻劃中國三千多年來政治生活中的若干普遍現象。影射性的小說並無多大意義，政治情況很快就會改變，只有刻劃人性，才有較長期的價值。不顧一切的奪取權力，是古今中外政治生活的基本情況，過去幾千年是這樣，今後幾千年恐怕仍會是這樣。任我行、東方不敗、岳不羣、左冷禪這些人，在我設想時主要不是武林高手，而是政治人物。林平之、向問天、方證大師、冲虛道人、定閒師太、莫大先生、余滄海等人也是政治人物。這種形形色色的人物，每一個朝代中都有，大概在別的國家中也都有。

「千秋萬載，一統江湖」的口號，在六十年代時就寫在書中了。任我行因掌握大權而腐化，都是人性的普遍現象。這些都不是書成後的增添或改作。

以上這段話，是理解《笑傲江湖》乃至於金庸全部作品的鑰匙。金庸這裡所說的政治生活和政治人物，當然是從本質上講的，並非說《笑傲江湖》是一部政治鬥爭書，方證大師、東方不敗等都是政界的領袖。《笑傲江湖》所寫的當然還是武林爭霸的故事，只是這種不擇手段的權力的爭奪，本質上與政治權力的爭奪是一樣的。所以讀《笑傲江湖》所見的武林爭霸，亦可以概見歷史上的政治爭霸的情況。

金庸著重說明，他所描寫的是人性而不是影射，我讀《笑傲江湖》（包括金庸的其他作品）所深切感受到的，與金庸所說的是一致的。可以說在《笑傲江湖》裡，繼他以往已出的十多部小說，繼續充分展現了各色各樣的人性。

二、人性的光輝

在《笑傲江湖》裡，給人心靈上震撼的，首先是劉正風、曲洋的故事。劉正風、曲洋是音樂上的知音，兩人的音樂造詣已達到登峰造極的地步，而且相引為生死知己。但兩人卻分別屬於不同的門派：劉正風是衡山派的第二高手，而曲洋卻是魔教的長老。衡山派是江湖上的名門正派，而魔教卻是邪教，為正派所不容。而衡山派又隸屬於五嶽劍派，五嶽劍派的總掌門是左冷禪，此人心機深而野心大，企圖合泰山、衡山、恒山、華山、嵩山為一派，實則是以自己的嵩山派併吞消滅其他各派，由他為唯一的武林霸主，然後再

企圖消滅少林、武當各派以及魔敎，實現其武林一統、唯我獨尊的野心。因此他利用所謂正、邪不容的藉口，逼劉正風誅滅曲洋，屈服聽命於自己。

劉正風是一位大義凜然、正直高尙的俠士，又是音樂上第一流的高手，品簫的專家，他對音樂的愛好，已同他的生命融成一體，可以說音樂就是他的生命，因此他與曲洋結爲音樂上的生死知己。而曲洋則是第一流的琴手，品格高尙，翛然世外，唯願以音樂終其一生。而尤其視劉正風爲第二生命。而他們倆的琴簫合奏，是他們的生命的融合，精神和意志的融合，可以說是天地間自然合成的天籟。

劉正風預感到江湖門派之爭的不可避免，特別是五嶽岳劍派與魔敎之間的生死博鬥已逼在眉睫，而他與曲洋早已心在音樂的天國而看穿並厭棄了這種江湖門派之間的殺戮，甚至連一般的世俗名利都早已不屑一顧，惟願以音樂終其一生。他爲了躱避這不可避免的浩劫，故想出了一個逃避之計，買一個小官，作爲自己熱衷於俗而又俗的當官「美夢」，以避世人的眼目。實際上是想永遠脫離此江湖門派，以隱於市，以隱於官。如此庶幾得與曲洋盡其音樂之天年。豈知他的這種避世的想法也無法實現，因爲一入門派，便終身難逃。特別是左冷禪野心彌天，妒賢忌能，務必消滅異己，以遂其獨霸的野心，恰好劉正風結交的曲洋是屬於與五岳派對立的魔敎，所以以此爲藉口欲加誅滅。劉正風此時所面臨的形勢是要麼出賣朋友以自保，要麼甘願全家殺身以全友情。劉正風面對生死抉擇，却毫無猶豫毫無畏縮退避，昂然地說：

> 費師兄不妨就此動手，殺了劉某全家！
> 劉某結交朋友，貴在肝膽相照，豈能殺害朋友，以求自保……要動手便即動手，又等何時？

當岳不羣勸他說魔敎是妖人邪派，作惡多端，「不要因爲一時琴簫投緣，便將全副身家性命都交給了他」，受他的騙，劉正風却說：

> 岳師兄，你不喜音律，不明白小弟的意思。言語文字可以撒謊作僞，琴簫之音却是心聲，萬萬裝不得假。小弟和曲大哥相交，以琴簫唱和，心意互通。小弟願意以全副身家性命擔保，曲大哥是魔敎中人，却無一點一毫魔敎的邪惡之氣。

劉正風的弟子向大年也朗聲說：

我們受師門重恩，義不相負，劉門弟子，和恩師同生共死。

實際上這是一場正義與邪惡的鬥爭，不過正義恰恰屬於劉正風曲洋一邊，而一向以正派自居的五嶽劍派恰恰是屬於邪惡，結果在一場血腥的屠殺之下，劉正風全家被殺，劉正風則被曲洋所救，但在脫險之時，劉、曲二人均是身受重傷，命已垂危。他們在臨終前，還合奏一曲《笑傲江湖》，在奏完這一曲後，他們有一段對話：

> 只聽得一人緩緩說道：「劉賢弟，你我今日畢命於此，那也是大數使然，只是愚兄未能及早出手，累得你家眷弟子盡數殉難，愚兄心下實是不安。」另一個道：「你我肝膽相照，還說這些話幹麼……」
>
> ……
>
> 只聽劉正風續道：「人生莫不有死，得一知己，死亦無憾。」另一人道：「劉賢弟，聽你簫中之意，卻猶有遺恨，莫不是爲了令郎臨危之際，貪生怕死，差辱了你的令名？」劉正風長嘆一聲，道：「曲大哥猜得不錯，芹兒這孩子我平日太過溺愛，少了教誨，沒想到竟是個沒半點氣節的軟骨頭。」曲洋道：「有氣節也好，沒氣節也好，百年之後，均歸黃土，又有甚麼分別？愚兄早已伏在屋頂，本該及早出手，只是料想賢弟不願爲我之故，與五嶽劍派的故人傷了和氣，又想到愚兄曾爲賢弟立下重誓，決不傷害俠義道中人士，是以遲遲不發，又誰知嵩山派爲五嶽盟主，下手竟如此毒辣。」
>
> 劉正風半晌不語，長長嘆了口氣，說道：「此輩俗人，怎懂得你我以音律相交的高情雅致，他們以常情猜度，自是料定你我結交，將大不利於五嶽劍派與俠義道。唉，他們不懂，須也怪他們不得。曲大哥，你是大椎穴受傷，震動了心脈？」曲洋道：「正是，嵩山派內功果然厲害，沒料到我背上挺受了這一擊，內力所及，居然將你的心脈也震斷了。早知賢弟也是不免，那一叢黑血神針倒也不必再發了，多傷無辜，於事無補，幸好針上並沒餵毒。」
>
> ……
>
> 劉正風輕輕一笑，說道：「但你我卻也因此而得再合奏一曲，從今而後，世上再也無此琴簫之音了。」曲洋一聲長嘆，說道：「昔日嵇康臨刑，撫琴一曲，嘆息《廣陵散》從此絕響。嘿嘿，《廣陵散》縱然精妙，又怎及得上咱們這一曲《笑傲

江湖》？只是當年嵇康的心情，卻也和你我一般。」劉正風笑道：「曲大哥剛才還甚達觀，卻又爲何執著起來？你我今晚合奏，將這一曲《笑傲江湖》發揮得淋漓盡致。世上已有過了這一曲，夫復何恨？」

上面所引這一大段話，是這個故事裡最爲精彩的地方。按關於音樂知音的故事，最著名的莫過於兪伯牙、鍾子期的故事。此故事最早出於《列子・湯問》，說：

> 伯牙善鼓琴，鍾子期善聽。伯牙鼓琴，志在高山。鍾子期曰：「善哉！峨峨兮若泰山。」志在流水。鍾子期曰：「善哉！洋洋兮若江河！」

後來到了《警世通言》裡就成爲《兪伯牙摔琴謝知音》一個短篇小說，之後又被選入《今古奇觀》，但故事內容，仍不出《列子・湯問》，不過小說加上了兪伯牙與鍾子期結爲兄弟，第二年兪伯牙往訪鍾子期，子期已死，伯牙乃哭祭其墳，撫琴一曲，摔琴而歸的情節。從故事的意義來說，仍是知音難遇的意思，並未增加新的思想內容。但是這個故事到了金庸的《笑傲江湖》裡，不但是人物和故事情節都完全不同了，更重要的是它的內涵大大豐富了，除了原先的知音難遇之外，更增加了共同反抗強暴，共同不屈於壓力，寧可犧牲全家的性命，也不肯出賣朋友，眞正是肝膽相照，義薄雲天。而且在音樂上，亦只但求知音共賞，無復有世俗名利之思想。從品質上來說，兩位更是高人一等的高人。儘管敵人如此凶殘，滅了他們全家還殺了他自己，但劉正風卻只是淡淡地說：「此輩俗人，怎懂得你我以音律相交的高情雅致？」「他們不懂須也怪他們不得。」曲洋則說：「早知賢弟也是不免，那一叢黑血神針倒也不必再發了，多傷無辜，於事無補，幸好針上並沒餵毒。」而他們自己呢，卻說：「人生莫不有死，得一知己，死亦無憾。」「結交朋友，貴在肝膽相照。」「你我今晚合奏，將這一曲《笑傲江湖》發揮得淋漓盡致。世上已有過了這一曲，你我已奏過了這一曲，人生於世，夫復何恨？」這是他們兩人被敵人重傷後臨終前在荒山月夜的私下對話，並不是對眾演講。把這些話與前面那些劊子手殺人的凶殘行徑相對照，人性的善惡自然十分明了。

不僅如此，劉正風的弟子，以向大年、米爲義爲代表，「受師門重恩，義不相負」，「和恩師同生共死」。向、米兩人的言行，讀之催人淚下。要知道這

是一場正義與邪惡的生死鬥爭，並不是私人恩怨的仇殺。我覺得金庸把這個故事昇華了，把這個故事的思想內涵昇華了。寧可自己殺身，決不肯出賣朋友，師門重恩，義不相負，得一知己，可以無恨，這是何等高尚的品質！對照著有些人爲了自己的升官發財，不擇手段地陷害人，誣蔑人，更顯得這個故事的思想光輝和諷喻的意義太豐富太適時了！這個故事單獨的思想意義，我認爲甚至超過後來令狐冲與任盈盈的「曲諧」「歸隱」。

金庸通過這個故事，把人性的光輝，發揮到了極致，發揮到了淋漓盡致的程度！

三、人性的展示

在《笑傲江湖》裡，金庸確實展現了一大批各色各樣的人性。

其中岳不羣是描寫得最爲飽滿充分的一個。岳不羣現在成爲僞君子的代名詞，文學上的典型。在中國古典文學中，假仁假義、虛僞奸詐的典型，莫過於《三國演義》裡的曹操，但曹操的虛僞和假仁假義，時時不免露出馬腳，他的「寧可我負天下人，不可天下人負我」，就是他的不加掩飾的本質暴露。但是岳不羣卻不是這樣。他虛僞得徹底，虛僞得到家，虛僞得不露任何一點痕跡，虛僞得連他的夫人都看不透他。讀《笑傲江湖》如果不讀到底，是會以爲岳不羣是眞君子，是大好人，不是連少林寺的方證大師，武當山的冲虛道長等等都把他作爲正人君子看待的嗎？其實他是一個虛僞透頂的卑鄙小人：辟邪劍譜明明是他趁令狐冲昏迷之際從他身上搜去的，他卻硬賴令狐冲，並把他逐出門派，這樣讓人看來，令狐冲再也無從洗刷了。他明知勞德諾是嵩山派左冷禪派進來的臥底坐探，卻不揭露他，故意讓他把已經改過了的辟邪劍譜偷去，讓他們上當，在嵩山比劍之時，他故意讓女兒岳靈珊露幾手華山石洞中的武功秘密，以誘使左冷禪上當，誘使舉世武林高手進洞觀看，以實現其一網打盡的毒計。在少林寺與令狐冲比劍的時候，又用劍招迷惑他，示意他可以重歸華山派並以女兒相許，借此使令狐冲意亂情迷，當他足踢令狐冲的時候，故意用內勁將自己的腿骨震斷，借此可讓左冷禪等輕視他，使他們疏於防範。特別是在少林寺中殺死定靜、定逸師太，令狐冲、任盈盈等都以爲是左冷禪所殺，讀者當然也作如是想，殊不知卻是岳不羣所殺。岳不

羣竊取了辟邪劍譜，暗自偷學，與東方不敗一樣他的最厲害的武器是一枚繡花針，定靜、定逸就是死在繡花針上的，這當然無人能料到是他所爲了。他對令狐冲、也曾想拉攏利用，但更主要的是想消滅他，特別是到最後是必欲誅之而甘心。明明岳靈珊是林平之所殺，他却硬誣陷令狐冲逼姦不遂，才殺岳靈珊。岳不羣之所以必欲殺令狐冲，一則是自己明明偷了辟邪劍譜，却誣陷令狐冲，令狐冲自然要追查到底，這就總有一天被徹底揭露。二則是自己偷學辟邪劍法而自宮等等，已爲任盈盈揭穿，則如果不誅殺令狐冲和任盈盈，必然事情敗露，爲武林所不齒。所以爲了自己的虛僞面目不被揭穿，他必須殺令狐冲。終於他在追殺令狐冲的過程中，種種惡行徹底敗露，而且爲寧女俠所親見，於是這個僞君子的假面才徹底被撕掉，寧女俠在傷心之餘最後拔劍自殺。寧女俠的自殺，是對岳不羣的徹底拋棄，徹底揭露。

　　縱觀岳不羣的形象，我看在中國文學史上，還沒有第二個虛僞得如此徹底、如此嚴密的藝術形象。這無疑是金庸的一大貢獻，是金庸對人性認識和描寫的突出成就。

　　任我行是另一個具有特殊意義的形象，作爲性格來看，也是一個特殊的個性。讀者初見他時是在西湖地室牢底，加上向問天用計見他的一套特殊設計，令人對他旣感到神秘而又有幾分同情。任我行是被他的部下東方不敗篡權以後被囚湖底地牢的，他因爲精研武功，心無旁騖，才使東方不敗得以趁隙篡權。但任我行是一個有特殊心機的人，他獲得了武功秘笈《葵花寶典》之後，深知練《葵花寶典》必將陷入邪魔而不可自拔。他竟將這一秘笈賜給了東方不敗，從表面來看，是他對這個自己選定的後繼者的器重和絕對信任，而暗底裡是爲了將他引向迷路，陷入迷阱。後來發展雖然奪得了權位，但終於敗在學習《葵花寶典》上。使任我行最後奪回了權位。這樣的深沉比岳不羣又深了一層，令人感到其心可怕。

　　更令人可怕的是他在得勢以後的「一統江湖，千秋萬載」的野心和天下獨尊的威風和排場，眞正是氣焰燻天，不可一世，順我者昌，逆我者亡。特別具有諷刺意義的是當他在華山朝陽峯上接受五嶽派朝拜的時候，却已是各派的首領死滅殆盡，無人可來了。能來的只是一些名不見經傳的三四流角色。唯一一位頂天立地、武功蓋世的人物是恒山派掌門令狐冲，但偏偏是他和他的恒山派弟子，旣不朝拜更不屈服，以至令狐冲和他的恒山派弟子當場與任

我行決絕，痛飲絕交酒以備日後的一場生死決戰。

這是對任我行的最最辛辣的諷刺，實際上也是對世上一切迷信權力，作威作福，迷信個人的一種深刻、無情的諷刺。這個形象既具有認識意義也具有現實意義，每一個讀者看到這個形象和他後來的排場、口號，自然會有所領悟的，尤其是最後一段，可說是「春秋」之筆：

> 上官雲大聲說道：「聖教主智珠在握，天下大事，都早在他老人家的算計之中。他老人家說甚麼，大夥兒就幹甚麼，再也沒有錯的。」鮑大楚道：「聖教主只要小指頭抬一抬，咱們水裡水裡去，火裡火裡去，萬死不辭。」秦偉邦道：「為聖教主辦事，就算死十萬次，也比糊裡糊塗地活著快活得多。」又一人道：「眾兄弟都說，一生之中，最有意思的就是這幾天了，咱們每天都能見到聖教主。見聖教主一次，渾身有勁，心頭火熱，勝於苦練內功十年。」另一人道：「聖教主光照天下，猶似我日月神教澤被蒼生，又如大旱天降下了甘霖，人人見了歡喜，心中感恩不盡。」又有一人道：「古往今來的大英雄、大豪傑、大聖賢中，沒一個能及得上聖教主的。孔夫子的武功哪有聖教主高強？關王爺是匹夫之勇，哪有聖教主的智謀？諸葛亮計策雖高，叫他提一把劍來，跟咱們聖教主比比劍法看？」諸教眾齊聲喝采，叫道：「孔夫子、關王爺、諸葛亮，誰都比不上我們聖教主！」
>
> 鮑大楚道：「咱們神教一統江湖之後，把天下文廟中的孔夫子神像搬出來，又把天下武廟中關王爺的神像請出來，請他們兩位讓讓位，供上咱們聖教主的長生祿位！」
>
> 上官雲道：「聖教主活一千歲，一萬歲！咱們的子子孫孫，十八代的灰孫子，都在聖教主麾下聽由他老人家驅策。」
>
> 眾人齊聲高叫：「聖教主千秋萬載，一統江湖！千秋萬載，一統江湖！」
>
> 任我行聽著屬下教眾諛詞如潮，雖然有些言語未免荒誕不經，但聽在耳中，著實受用，心想：「這些話其實也沒錯。諸葛武功固然非我敵手，他六出祁山，未建尺寸之功，說到智謀，難道又及得上我了？關雲長過五關、斬六將，固是神勇，可是若和我單打獨鬥，又怎能勝得我的『吸星大法』？孔夫子弟子不過三千，我屬下教眾何止三萬？他率領三千弟子，悽悽惶惶地東奔西走，絕糧在陳，束手無策。我率數萬之眾，橫行天下，從心所欲，一無阻難。孔夫子的才智和我相比，卻又差得遠了。」

但聽得「千秋萬載，一統江湖！千秋萬載，一統江湖！」之聲震動天地，站在峰腰的江湖豪士跟著齊聲吶喊，四周群山均有回聲。任我行躊躇滿志，站起身來。教衆見他站起，一齊拜伏在地。霎時之間，朝陽峯上一片寂靜，更無半點聲息。陽光照射在任我行臉上、身上，這日月神教教主威風凜凜，宛若天神。

任我行哈哈大笑，說道：「但願千秋萬載，永如今……」說到那「今」字，突就聲音啞了。他一運氣，要將下面那個「日」字說了出來，只覺胸口抽搐，那「日」字無論如何說不出口。他右手按胸，要將一股湧上喉頭的熱血壓將下去，只覺頭腦暈眩，陽光耀眼。

　　上面這一大段文字，是金庸的神來之筆，也是對任我行的最後的最淋漓盡致的刻劃。從個性來說，任我行又是另一種獨特的個性，也是完全獨立的個性，與岳不羣一樣，古今中外，找不到重複的形象，這實在是獨創！當然，這個形象是有生活依據的，也正是因爲有生活依據，才能有此獨創，如果失去了生活依據，那這個形象必然站立不起來的，那也就無所獨創了！

　　在《笑傲江湖》裡，另一個值得一談的是左冷禪。左冷禪有岳不羣虛僞的一面，但却十分表面化，易被識破；有余滄海殘暴的一面，但却又時時想掩蓋其殘暴，不像余滄海那樣赤裸裸的殘暴。

　　左冷禪第一件令人怵目驚心的事就是他派人殺劉正風全家以及劉正風、曲洋兩人，一開始還假仁假義，說甚麼是爲劉正風好等等，緊接著就是一場預先布置好的大屠殺。雖然劉正風全家是被殺害了。但其結果是連正派的定逸師太都罵他們是「禽獸！」劉正風的女兒劉菁則「怒罵，奸賊，你嵩山派比魔教奸惡萬倍！」第二件事，就是派陸柏、魯連榮、封不平、成不憂等到華山奪權，結果以成不憂被裂屍而告終，接著就有藥王廟的夜襲，雖然岳不羣已被擒，寧中則重傷，危在頃刻，却又以令狐冲破封不平的「狂風快劍」，以破箭式刺瞎十五個蒙面客的眼睛而告終。第三件事，就是仙霞嶺喬裝魔教伏擊恒山派，廿八鋪鎮用迷藥俘獲恒山派，然後脅逼定靜同意將恒山派合併入五嶽派，在遭定靜嚴拒之下，又在鑄劍谷圍困恒山派及定靜師太，致定靜師太傷重而死。第四件事，就是派樂厚等人奉五嶽派的令旗不准令狐冲就任恒山派的掌門，並派上官雲、賈布等在恒山後面的翠屏山懸空寺天橋上設計害死令狐冲、少林寺方證大師、冲虛道長等，雖然事先布置得很周密，但最

終還是被任盈盈識破，殺掉賈布，上官雲投降，樂厚則鎩羽而去。第五件事，就是嵩山封禪臺上五派合併爲五嶽派，由他來當五嶽派的掌門以實現他的武林爭霸的最終目的。他事先的準備工作已經做得相當周密了，此時，恒山三定已然在他和岳不羣的陰謀下被殺害，泰山派與天門道長又在封禪臺比武時被激上當遭到慘死，令狐冲又在與岳靈珊比武中墮岳不羣的奸計中劍受傷，瀟湘夜雨莫大先生雖在與岳靈珊比武中擊敗了岳靈珊，却在他好意挽扶岳靈珊的時候爲岳靈珊偷襲受傷，岳不羣又當場表示他贊成五派合併，此時封禪臺上似乎只有左冷禪是當然的掌門了，你看：

> 左冷禪縱起身子，輕飄飄落在封禪臺上。他身穿杏黄色布袍，其時夕陽即將下山，日光斜照，映射其身，顯得金光燦爛，大增堂皇氣象。他抱拳轉身，向臺下衆人作了個四方揖，說道：「旣承衆位朋友推愛，在下倘若再不答允，出任艱巨，倒顯得過於保身自愛，不肯爲武林同道盡力了。」嵩山門下數百人歡聲雷動，大力鼓掌。

這一番姿態何等得意，顯然已是勝劵在握，大功告成，却不料想還有岳不羣出來比武。岳不羣不是明明已經贊成五派合併成五嶽創派了嗎？這一點不錯。但狡猾的岳不羣只是贊成五派合併，並未贊成左冷禪當五嶽派的掌門。至於掌門，當然還要以比武來定。至於左冷禪之勝岳靈珊，那當然不等於勝岳不羣，所以最後岳不羣出來與左冷禪比武，是順理成章的事。論武功，左冷禪原也不怕岳不羣，但岳不羣却早下伏筆，在少林寺比劍時故意在足踢令狐冲時自己以內力震斷腿骨，使左冷禪輕視於他；在封禪臺上比劍時又故意讓岳靈珊盡露嵩山派武功秘學十三招，使左冷禪更覺得已盡知對方的底細。到正式比劍時，在緊要關頭又使出辟邪劍法以誘使對方也用此法，其實左冷禪所使，已是經岳不羣篡改過的辟邪劍法，當然經不起岳不羣正宗的辟邪劍法，特別是到生死關頭，岳不羣故意將長劍讓左冷禪震飛，然後使出葵花寶典中之絕招，以繡花針刺瞎左冷禪雙目。於是左冷禪十年經營，半生陰謀併派，却成爲他人作嫁，只落得拱手讓岳不羣當五嶽派的掌門。

綜觀左冷禪一生，爲人陰險狠毒，時時刻刻在陰謀計算人，爲了實現他武林爭霸的野心，用各種陰謀手段，收買黨羽，暗派坐探，布置殺手，剪除敵手，有時表面上也裝一點虛僞的仁義，但這只是一層薄薄的面紗，很快就

自動揭去，露出兇惡的本相。封禪台比武失敗，是他完全意想不到的。但客觀上與他爭奪霸主的對手是比他更陰險、更毒辣的岳不羣。岳不羣之所以能戰勝他，從武功上說是他學得了真正的辟邪劍法而左冷禪只是學到的經過篡改的假辟邪劍法；從陰謀來說，他自以為布置得很巧妙，而實際上岳不羣的陰謀比他高出多多。如果說武功上他可以是岳不羣的對手甚至勝過岳不羣（不計後來岳不羣秘密學到的辟邪劍法）的話，在陰謀上他遠遠不是岳不羣的對手，大概也只是蔣幹與周瑜之比。但作為一個獨立的性格，左冷禪卻是完整無缺的一個性格，在華山山洞中的最後被殺，是他的性格完滿的最後一筆，這就是這個性格是到死也不知自己已輸了，到死也仍然要陰謀害人！

這樣的性格是深刻的，是足以警世的！

《笑傲江湖》中另一個值得一談的是衡山派的掌門瀟湘夜雨莫大先生。莫大先生第一次露臉是在衡山城中的茶館裡，有人胡說劉正風金盆洗手是因為他們師兄弟不和，言辭頗失分寸，所以有一位「身材瘦長的老者，臉色枯槁，披著一件青布長衫，手中拉著胡琴的人」說：「你胡說八道！」「忽然眼前青光一閃，一柄細細的長劍晃向桌上，叮叮叮地響了幾下」，桌上的七隻茶杯，「每一隻都被削去了半寸來高的一圈，七個瓷圈跌在茶杯之旁，茶杯卻一個也沒有傾倒。」這就是莫大先生。

莫大先生第二次出現時，是在衡山城外荒山之中，正當劉正風、曲洋絕命前奏完一曲《笑傲江湖》的時候，嵩山派的殺手大嵩陽手費彬到了，費彬殘忍地殺死曲非煙之後，企圖一手殺死劉正風、曲洋、令狐冲、儀琳四人，以滅活口，忽然間：

> 耳中傳入幾下幽幽的胡琴聲，琴聲淒涼，似是嘆息，又似哭泣，跟著琴聲顫抖，發出瑟瑟瑟斷續之音，如是一滴滴小雨落上樹葉。
>
> ……
>
> 費彬心頭一震：「瀟湘夜雨莫大先生到了。……」
>
> 費彬見他並無惡意，又素知他和劉正風不睦，便道：「多謝莫大先生，俺師哥好。貴派的劉正風和魔教妖人結交，意欲不利我五嶽劍派。莫大先生，你說說當如何處置？」
>
> 莫大先生向劉正風走近幾步，森然道：「該殺！」這「殺」字剛出口，寒氣陡閃，

手中已多了一柄又薄又窄的長劍，猛地反刺，直指費彬胸口。這一下出招快極，抑且如夢如幻，正是「百變千幻衡山雲霧十三式」中的絕招。費彬在劉府曾著了劉正風這門武功的道兒，此刻再度中計，大駭之下，急向後退，哧的一聲，胸口已給利劍割了一道長長的口子，衣衫盡裂，胸口肌肉也給割傷了，受傷雖然不重，卻已驚怒交集，銳氣大失。

費彬立即還劍相刺，但莫大先生一劍既佔先機，後著綿綿而至，一柄薄劍猶如靈蛇，顫動不絕，在費彬的劍氣中穿來插去，只逼得費彬連連倒退，半句喝罵也叫不出口。

曲洋、劉正風、令狐冲三人眼見莫大先生劍招變幻，猶如鬼魅，無不心驚神眩。劉正風和他同門學藝，做了數十年師兄弟，卻也萬萬料不到師兄的劍術竟一精至斯。

一點點鮮血從兩柄長劍間濺了出來，費彬騰挪閃躍，竭力招架，始終脫不出莫大先生的劍光籠罩，鮮血漸漸在二人身周濺成了一個紅圈。猛聽得費彬長聲慘呼，高躍而起。莫大先生退後兩步，將長劍插入胡琴，轉身便走，一曲「瀟湘夜雨」在松樹後響起，漸漸遠去。

費彬躍起後便即摔倒，胸口一道血箭如湧泉般向上噴出，適才激戰，他運起了嵩山派內力，胸口中劍後內力未消，將鮮血逼得從傷口中急噴而去，既詭異，又可怖。

第一次出場，莫大先生只說了一句話：「你胡說八道！」第二次出場，莫大先生說了兩句話，第一句是：「費師兄，左盟主好。」第二句是：「該殺！」這第二句話剛說出，費彬已身受劍傷，終於死在莫大先生的劍下，莫大先生的「該殺」兩字，無異是對這個劊子手的宣判。

莫大先生的第三次出現，是在夏口附近，漢水以北的小鎮雞鳴渡的小酒店裡。這回他與令狐冲促膝長談，他極口稱讚令狐冲「不但不是無行浪子，實是一位守禮君子」、「似你這般男子漢、大丈夫，當真是古今罕有，我莫大好生佩服」、「來來來，我莫大敬你一杯」、「你後來助我劉正風師弟，我心中對你生了好感，只想趕將上來，善言相勸，不料卻見到後一輩英俠之中，竟有你老弟這樣了不起的少年英雄，很好很好！來來來，咱們同乾三杯！」、「幾碗酒一下肚，一個寒酸落拓的莫大先生突然顯得逸興遄飛，連連呼酒，只是

他量和令狐冲差得甚遠，喝得幾碗後，已是滿臉通紅，說道：『令狐老弟，我知你最喜喝酒。莫大無以爲敬，只好陪你多喝幾碗。嘿嘿，武林之中，莫大肯陪他喝酒的，却也沒有幾人。那日嵩山大會，座上有個大嵩陽手費彬。此人飛揚跋扈，不可一世，莫大越瞧越不順眼，當時便一滴不飲。』」「魔敎雖毒，却也未必毒得過左冷禪。令狐兄弟，你現下已不在華山派門下，閑雲野鶴，無拘無束，也不必管他甚麼正敎魔敎。我勸你和尙倒也不必做，也不用爲此傷心，盡管去將那位任大小姐救了出來，娶他爲妻便是。別人不來喝你的喜酒，我莫大偏來喝你三杯。」「莫大先生嘆道：『這位任大小姐雖然出身魔敎，但待你的至誠至，情却令人好生相敬。少林派中，辛國樑、易國梓、黃國柏、覺月彈師四名大弟子命喪她手。她去到少林，自無生還之望，但爲了救你，她……她是全不顧自己了。』」這一席談話，莫大先生的是非正義之感十分鮮明，他心中沒有正敎魔敎的殭死界限，只有正義與非正義的標準。他認爲魔敎未必毒得過左冷禪，他勸令狐冲娶任大小姐爲妻，不能辜負任大小姐的至誠至情。凡此種種，可見莫大先生不但是非分明，見解開闊，而且確是性情中人。後來嵩山封禪台比武，他遭岳靈珊暗算受傷，也只是說了「將門虎女，果然不凡」一句，並未與岳靈珊計較，足見其性格之深沉寬容，確是高賢風範。到最後令狐冲與任盈盈新婚之夜，莫大先生還以琴聲祝賀，實現前諾，足見其行止，決不受世俗門派之所羈靡。所以莫大先生，實是武林中的隱逸，世外之高人。當然在音樂上他與劉正風似是兩途。劉正風應是雅樂，是嵇康之遺，而莫大先生是民樂俗樂。昔我鄉有二胡聖手瞎子阿炳華彥鈞，以琴聲街頭乞食，而琴語如訴，一曲《二泉映月》令人泣下。余青年時數數與之相接，其心胸境界之高，爲世人之所難識，後以貧病嘔血而死。莫大先生除武功神超外，其外觀其樂趣其行止亦阿炳之流乎？

　　《笑傲江湖》中如方證大師、冲虛道長、定逸、定靜、定聞師太，不戒大師、田伯光、向問天以及孤山梅莊四隱等這些人物，也都是個性凸出，令人讀後難忘的人物，惜乎篇幅有限，不能縱談。

　　《笑傲江湖》中的余滄海，木高峰之流，自是武林之梟雄惡霸，其等次又低於左冷禪多矣！

　　《笑傲江湖》中另一類人物，如鮑大楚、桑三娘，原先是奉東方不敗之命去查西湖梅莊地牢裡任我行的行蹤的，初到梅莊，氣焰燻天，但任我行一

出現，一舉手即被制住，立即俯首貼耳，忠心不二，此類人物，實爲見風使舵，唯權勢是從的武林棍徒。還有一種如遊迅、仇松年、嚴三星之流，都是翻雲覆雨、兩面三刀、爾虞我詐之徒，他們結夥爲惡，唯利是從，誰也信不過誰，到時候就可隨時出賣同伙，此類人實爲武林中蟊賊，社會上的下三流角色，書中也把他們寫得活靈活現，實際上此類人物，實爲歷史社會的現實寫照，每個時代都有，讀後令人百感叢生。

四、令狐冲的道路

令狐冲是《笑傲江湖》的主角，但直到第五回才正式出場，以前關於令狐冲的種種，一部分是他師弟陸大有、勞德諾、師妹岳靈珊等人講出來的，關於他捨命救儀琳，智鬥田伯光的事則是由儀琳口述的，到了第五回，令狐冲重傷後由曲洋所救，才正面出場。但在此之前由於種種介紹，令狐冲其人早已呼之欲出了。

令狐冲的道路，是一條充滿著艱難曲折的道路，是一條充滿著誤解、誹謗、陷害和蒙冤的道路，令狐冲就是在這樣的一條世途上走過來的，令狐冲的道路，具有特殊的社會內涵和認識價值。

令狐冲是一個連自己的父母都不知道的孤兒，他是由岳不羣、寧中則收養長大並收爲首徒的。所以他對師父和師娘具有特殊深厚的感情，可以說是父母加師父的感情。

他是一個至性仁厚，心胸開朗，放浪形骸，不拘小節的人物。他好酒如命，有時行爲任情所至，少加檢點，以至招來非議。但他卻心無半點邪念，是一個豪情高義，殺身成仁，捨身取義的俠士，又是一個厭惡權力，厭惡名利，崇尚自由閑散、不受拘束、向往於隱逸的逸士。這《笑傲江湖》一曲，無異是他個人的主題。

令狐冲一開始由於救恒山小尼姑儀琳而蒙受許多怨毒誹謗和誤解。實則若非他捨身拼命，儀琳就勢必遭田伯光之強暴。而他卻爲救儀琳而身負重傷，復受青城派羅人杰的重創至於垂死，幸得魔教長老曲洋相救，又得儀琳所敷恒山派治傷聖藥天香斷續膏才得以復活。然而，這件事給令狐冲帶來的卻是岳不羣責令他在華山思過崖山洞中面壁思過一年。原因是他在與田伯光搏鬥

時出言無狀，損害了恒山派。其實這完全是小題大做，他救下了儀琳這件大功偏偏不計，却計較他在救人時為逼儀琳先逃而說見尼姑不利，逢睹必輸等等的小節。

但是，思過崖山洞中的一年，却是令狐冲畢生道路上具有決定性意義的一年。

在這一年中，他失去了岳靈珊。初時他與岳靈珊熱戀，岳靈珊對他更是不能一日不見，但後來岳靈珊移情別戀林平之，抛棄了令狐冲，這對令狐冲的打擊是十分沉重而持久的。但客觀來看並不是壞事，對令狐冲的道路減去了一份羈絆。

在這一年中，他看到了思過崖山洞中的武功秘圖，並且通曉破解各派武功的秘法，這使他在武學道路上大開眼界，無異是進入了武學的新天地。從此深知華山派也好，別派也好，並不是武學的頂峰。更重要的是他得知華山派氣宗戰勝劍宗是靠的陰謀而不是武功，這對他心靈中的華山派形象是嚴重的一擊。

但是在這一年中最根本的收穫，是他得到了華山派前輩風清揚的眞傳，並學到了「獨孤九劍」。領會了獨孤劍法的精義：「無招勝有招」、「如行雲流水，任意所之」、「做到出手無招，那才眞是踏入了高手的境界」、「一切須當順其自然。行乎其不得不行，止乎其不得不止。」要把學到的劍招「全部將他忘了，忘得乾乾淨淨，一招也不可留在心中」、「獨孤大俠是絕頂聰明之人，學他的劍法，要旨是在一個『悟』字，決不在死記硬記。等到通曉了這九劍的劍意，則無所施而不可，便是將全部變化盡數忘記，也不相干，臨敵之際，更是忘記得越乾淨徹底，越不受原來劍法的拘束。」這許多言論，確是武學的精華，其實何止武學，施之於其他方面，又何嘗不是要言妙義。

令狐冲一年中的這三件事，都緊關著他畢生的前途，而且對他來說全是好事。失岳靈珊在他心靈創傷甚巨，但其實却是至關重要的一環，如岳靈珊不棄他而去，則令狐冲始終擺脫不了岳不羣的牢籠羈絆，則「獨孤九劍」的妙義便不可能眞正領會和學到，也就不可能有後來的令狐冲。

令狐冲蒙受的冤枉可謂多矣。第一是誣他藏匿岳不羣的「紫霞秘笈」和殺害師弟陸大有。第二是誣陷他偷了林震南家的「辟邪劍譜」，他後來的出神入化的劍術，就是偷學「辟邪劍譜」得來。這眞正是「千古奇冤」！由於這種

誣陷，致使令狐冲在藥王廟一劍刺瞎十五個蒙面客的眼睛，救了岳不羣、岳夫人及華山派全伙，却反被岳不羣認為其劍術就是從「辟邪劍譜」而來，就是偷「辟邪劍譜」的證據，以至到了洛陽王元霸家，會逕被王家駿質問：「我姑丈有一部辟邪劍譜，托你交給平之表弟，你怎地至今未交出？」隨即趁令狐冲內力全失之際，竟壓斷他的手肘，扭脫他左臂肩關節，使他無從反抗，然後對他進行搜身，結果竟錯把他懷中藏的《笑傲江湖》的曲譜當作了「辟邪劍譜」，以為拿到了贓證。這真正是令狐冲畢生的奇恥大辱。而且這樁冤案望不到頭，雖然經綠竹翁和「婆婆」演奏後，已知這確是琴簫譜而不是劍譜。但不久令狐冲到福州向陽巷林家老宅調查辟邪劍譜時，恰遇嵩山派白頭仙翁卜沉，禿鷹沙天江點倒了林平之、岳靈珊，獲取了寫著辟邪劍譜的袈裟。令狐冲跟蹤追擊，殺死兩人，奪回了袈裟劍譜，又因傷重暈死過去，為岳夫人所救，袈裟即被岳不羣取去。岳不羣却反誣袈裟是令狐冲隱匿不交，並當著眾弟子宣布，令狐冲結交魔教妖人，是華山派的「死敵」，致使令狐冲冤上加冤。令狐冲第一樁冤案的昭雪，是在第二十五回由於偷竊「紫霞秘笈」的勞德諾自己不小心將「紫霞秘笈」掉了出來而敗露了，隨之陸大有的被殺也就真相大白，立即清楚是勞德諾所殺，於是案情才得清楚。令狐冲隱匿「辟邪劍譜」的冤案，則一直死死地纏住了他。直到最後在嵩山封禪台上比武，岳不羣使出了辟邪劍法，用繡花針刺瞎了左冷禪雙目，才被令狐冲、任盈盈等人看出了他是偷學了辟邪劍法，因此真相得以大白，岳不羣確是做賊喊捉賊的偽君子。

但是更使真相得以大白的還有岳靈珊與林平之的一大段夫妻對話：

> 只聽得林平之說道：「我的劍譜早已盡數交給你爹爹了，自己沒私自留下一招半式，你又何必苦苦地跟著我？」岳靈珊道：「你老是疑心我爹爹圖你的劍譜，當真好沒來由……」林平之道：「我林家的辟邪劍法天下知名，余滄海、木高峰他們在我爹爹身上搜查不得，便來找我。我怎知你不是受了爹爹、媽媽的囑咐，故意來向我賣好？」
>
> ……
>
> 林平之恨恨地道：「他要殺我，不是為我待你不好，而是為我學了辟邪劍法。」岳靈珊道：「這件事我可真不明白了。你和爹爹這幾日來所使的劍法古怪之極，

可是威力卻又強大無比。爹爹打敗左冷禪，奪得五嶽派掌門，你殺了余滄海、木高峰，難道……難道這當眞便是辟邪劍法嗎？」

林平之道：「正是！這便是我福州林家的辟邪劍法！……

岳靈珊道：「可是，你一直沒跟我說已學會了這套劍法。」林平之道：「我怎麼敢說？令狐冲在福州搶到了那件袈裟，畢竟還是拿不去，只不過錄著劍譜的這件袈裟，卻落入了你爹爹手中……」岳靈珊尖聲叫道：「不，不會的！爹爹說，劍譜給大師哥拿了去，我曾求他還給你，他說甚麼也不肯。」林平之哼的一聲冷笑。

岳靈珊又道：「大師哥劍法厲害，連爹爹也敵他不過，難道他們使的不是辟邪劍法？不是從你家的辟邪劍譜學的？」

林平之又是一聲冷笑，説道：「令狐冲雖然奸滑，但比起你爹爹來，可又差得遠了。再説，他們劍法亂七八糟，怎能和我家的辟邪劍法相比？」

……

岳靈珊道：「原來大師哥所使的不是辟邪劍法，那爲甚麼爹爹一直怪他偷了你家的辟邪劍譜？那日爹爹將他逐出華山門牆，宣布他罪名之時，那也是一條大罪。這麼説來，我……我可錯怪他了。林平之冷笑道：「有甚麼錯怪，令狐冲又不是不想奪我的劍譜，實則他確已奪去了。只不過強盜遇著賊爺爺，他重傷之後，暈了過去，你爹爹從他身上搜了出來，乘機賴他偷了去，以便掩人耳目，這叫做賊喊捉賊……」岳靈珊怒道：「甚麼賊不賊的，説得這麼難聽！」林平之道：「你爹爹做這種事，就不難聽？他做得，我便説不得？」

岳靈珊嘆了口氣，説道：「那日在向陽巷中，這件袈裟是給嵩山派的壞人奪了去的。大師哥殺了這二人，將袈裟奪回，未必是想據爲己有。大師哥氣量大得很，從小就不貪圖旁人的物事。爹爹説他取了你的劍譜，我一直有些懷疑，只是爹爹既這麼説，又見大師哥劍法突然大進，連爹也及不上，這才不由得不信。」

……

只聽林平之續道：「你媽説道：『他和魔教中人結交，自是沒冤枉他。我説你冤枉他偷了平兒的辟邪劍譜。』你爹道：『難道劍譜不是他偷的？他劍術突飛猛進，比你比我還要高明，你又不是沒見過？』你媽道：『那定是他另有際遇，我斷定他決計沒拿辟邪劍譜。冲兒任性胡鬧，不聽你的教訓，那是有的。但他自小光明磊落，決不做偷偷摸摸的事。自從珊兒跟平兒要好，將他撇下之後，他這等傲性之人，便是平兒雙手將劍譜奉送給他，他也決計不收。』」……

林平之續道：「你爹哼了一聲，道：『你這麼說，咱們將令狐冲這小子逐出門牆，你倒似好生後悔。』你媽道：「他犯了門規，你執行祖訓，清理門戶，無人可以非議。但你說他結交左道，罪名已經夠了，爲何再冤枉他偷盜劍譜？其實你比我還明白很多。你明知他没拿平兒的辟邪劍譜。」你爹叫了起來：「我怎麼知道？我怎麼知道？』」……

隔了一會，才聽他續道：「你媽媽緩緩地道：『你自然知道，只因爲這部劍譜，是你取了去的。』你爹怒聲吼叫：「你……你說……是我」但只說了幾個字，突然住口。你媽聲音十分平靜，說道：「那日冲兒受傷昏迷，我替他止血治傷之時，見到他身上有件裂裟，寫滿了字，似乎是劍法之類。第二次替他換藥，那件裂裟已經不見了，其時冲兒仍然昏迷未醒。這段時候之中，除了你我二人，並無別人進房。這件裂裟可不是我拿的。』」

這一大段對話把事情的前前後後說得清清楚楚，令狐冲的冤案在讀者的心目中才得以徹底昭雪。

對令狐冲構成壓力的還有魔教。

壓力有三種：一是社會輿論的壓力，因爲魔教名聲不好，爲正派之所不齒，非但不齒而且都引以爲仇。而令狐冲却交了魔教的朋友，還承魔教長老曲洋救了自己的性命。盈盈則更是多次捨命相救自己的紅顏知己，曲非煙是曲洋的孫女兒，也是爲搭救自己出了大力的。另一個是向問天，是令狐冲的把兄弟，向問天的爲人也是令狐冲深爲欽佩的。更重要的是他還直接與魔教的教主任我行有來往，這樣從正派這方面構成的社會輿論就造成了對他的強大壓力。他被岳不羣逐出華山派，這就是他的主要罪狀。第二種是這種社會輿論的壓力轉過來形成了令狐冲內心的心理壓力，這個問題經常在他的心裡打鼓，形成交戰，使他陷於困惑。原因是魔教固然有壞人，甚至有極壞的人，但也有好人乃至極好的人，這兩種人他都親自見過。要將這兩種人一律看作是壞人，舉刀便殺，他思想上就想不通。第三種是魔教教主任我行堅持要令狐冲入魔教，並希望他將來繼承魔教的教主。這在令狐冲是絕對不幹的，但逼他就範的形勢明擺著，然就形成了對他的一種壓力。

面對著這樣的壓力，令狐冲不屈服，當任我行在朝陽峯上宣稱一個月內殺得恒山見性峯雞犬不留時，令狐冲却哈哈一笑，說：「令狐冲在見性峯上，

恭候諸位大駕！」

令狐沖就是在這樣的重重冤枉，種種誹謗、陷害、誤解中走過來的。

當然令狐沖也有愛。師母寧中則，是一個真正愛他的人，她代替了他的慈母的愛，所以到寧女俠臨將自殺前，還爲令狐沖裹傷。令狐沖所受的冤屈，寧女俠心裡是雪亮的，她始終愛撫和信賴這個像兒子一樣的徒弟。

魔教的「聖姑」，任我行的女兒任盈盈，是真正全身心地愛令狐沖的，她爲著令狐沖，寧可自己去少林寺送死，只要少林寺能治好令狐沖的傷。當岳不羣來殺令狐沖時，她冒著自身立即被殺的危險，出聲呼叫令狐沖，告訴他岳不羣要殺他。當著令狐沖拒絕加入日月神教，眼看著令狐沖終究在劫難逃的時候，她已悄悄作好與令狐沖同歸於盡的準備。她愛令狐沖勝於愛自己。所以只要是令狐沖想做的，她總是盡力去做，讓令狐沖得到安慰。應該說令狐沖從任盈盈那裡得到的愛是純金的，沒有絲毫雜質的，是純晶的，是通體透亮的，是純玉的，雖億萬年而不變的！

恒山派的小尼姑儀琳，外貌非常美麗，人也非常純潔善良，她是在危難中得到令狐沖的捨命相救的。她也是非常愛令狐沖的，她也曾冒著生命危險去救令狐沖，當人們在誣陷令狐沖時，她極力爲令狐沖辯解，稱令狐沖是大好人。當著令狐沖的生命受到威脅時，她默頌經文以求保佑令狐沖。當她的父母不戒大師和恒山「啞婆」得知她愛令狐沖因而要迫使令狐沖娶她時，她堅決反對，爲的是不讓令狐沖爲難。總之她的愛是聖潔的愛，是超塵俗的愛。岳靈珊對令狐沖也曾有過愛，也曾愛得熾熱過，但當令狐沖在思過崖受禁時，沒有經多久，她就從原來的熾熱漸漸冷卻了，冰凍了。甚而至於反目成仇了。只要讀一讀第二十四回岳靈珊逼著令狐沖交出辟邪劍譜的一大段對話時，就可以知道她已把令狐沖恨到何等程度了。讀這一大段文字，令人對岳靈珊其人寒心。我個人認爲岳靈珊離開令狐沖是好事，岳靈珊很快就愛上了林平之可能有岳不羣的作用在，這從後來林平之與岳靈珊的談話裡可以證實。岳靈珊後來向林平之解釋說她對令狐沖只是把他當「親哥哥」看，沒有男女之間的愛情，這是不符合事實的，只要看看令狐沖初上思過崖時岳靈珊送飯的情景就能明白了。總之，岳靈珊是一個嬌驕二氣都較重的一位小姐，由於她是岳不羣的女兒，所以她的地位特殊。她的愛情是要別人對她奉獻和供養的。她的自尊心比別人強得多，損傷了她的自尊心也就損傷了一切。她對林平之

的服從，也是她的自尊心的輻射。

令狐冲還有一批與他惺惺相惜的武林同道和前輩，也是令狐冲成長過程中不可忽視的一種重要社會因素。老一輩或兩輩的如風清揚、莫大先生、方證、方生、冲虛、恒山三定，都是對他能另眼相看的，有的則是在經過誤會後才得到正確的認識的，風清揚則更是他的實際上的恩師，無怪方生大師等會覺得他是風清揚的傳人。與他同輩的則有向問天，也不失是一位磊落英豪，其杯酒自酌，睥睨群兇的氣概，足以壓倒一切。就是那位行為不檢，污名周知的田伯光，當其能以打賭而不犯儀琳，復能擔酒上華山與令狐冲痛飲而後比劍，令狐冲比劍不贏而竟能讓令狐冲再學再比以至反而自己輸了，最後能棄惡從善、皈依佛門，得證善果的人物，在令狐冲的生活道路上，也是留下一定的影響的。

總之，令狐冲就是在這樣一條艱難曲折的道路上成長的，在他的身上凝聚著愛與恨，苦與甜，凝聚著社會的種種印記。

五、脈絡與結構

《笑傲江湖》是一部百餘萬字的大書，人物眾多，頭緒紛繁，而文筆又如行雲流水，一氣讀下，無復窒礙。及至讀完，掩卷細想，要掌握其脈絡姞構，却頗費思索。幸而金庸在書後有後記，雖未及脈絡結構，但其命意大致可知，我歸結為「武林爭霸」。以此為故事核心，一切都圍繞此點而來。

爭霸有二起，一起是以左冷禪為首的嵩山派，企圖兼併華山派、衡山派、恒山派、泰山派而成為五嶽劍派，而後再行消滅少林、武當各派。左冷禪派人制止劉正風金盆洗手，殺害劉正風全家，派人偽裝魔教，襲擊恒山派，致定靜師太戰死，派人阻止令狐冲任恒山掌門，企圖暗害令狐冲、方證大師、冲虛道長等都是為了這個目的。而為了同樣的目的，華山派岳不羣派人去福州窺視林家辟邪劍譜，青城派余滄海則直接屠殺林震南全家以圖搶到辟邪劍譜，因為獲得了辟邪劍譜就可以稱霸武林，達到爭霸的目的。

爭霸的另一起，是日月神教教主任我行，企圖一舉消滅武林各派，實現其「千秋萬代，一統江湖」的野心，所以以日月神教即魔教任我行為一方，以武林其他各派為另一方的一場爭霸和反爭霸的鬥爭亦在廣闊展開。其高潮

就是任我行在朝陽峯會見五嶽各派掌門的大會。但是那時原五嶽各派的掌門已死亡，就連任我行雖然當時還巍然獨存，但連這個會還未開完，也就病發倒下再也不起了。這個日月神教就由任盈盈接掌，任盈盈一反其父所行，實行和平方針，繼而又將教主之位傳給了向問天，向問天亦非野心分子，因這一場爭霸鬥爭才算自然終止，而令狐冲與任盈盈亦終遂隱隊居之樂。

以上是全書的大結構，總脈絡。

在此大結構、總脈絡之下，又有小結構、小脈絡。

例如華山派內部氣宗與劍宗之爭。華山思過崖山洞中所反映的一場大鬥爭，就是以往鬥爭的記錄。而魯連榮、封不平、成不憂等公然前來逼令岳不羣退位，讓出掌門，這就是現實的華山派劍宗與氣宗之爭。實際上封不平等已不屬華山派，不過是借原有的名義以實現其奪權的野心而已。而這次奪權行動的背景，仍是左冷禪的指揮。

再如泰山派天門道人在嵩山封禪台上與玉璣子、玉磬子、玉音子之爭，又是本派內部之爭。天門道人反對五派合成五嶽劍派，玉璣子等則主張併派，實則仍是權力之爭。背景是左冷禪買通玉璣子等，製造泰山派的內部分裂，以實現其奪權的野心。結果天門道人固然被他們的陰謀活活害死，連剛搶到權的玉璣子也成了獨腳廢人。

至於日月神教主這一面，也存在著內部奪權的鬥爭。任我行一時被東方不敗篡權，自己被囚於西湖地牢，終身監禁。但任我行在被奪權之前，已預感到東方不敗的權力野心，因而將《葵花寶典》賜給了他，表面上對他親密有加，實際上是讓他上當。果然東方不敗上當，為《葵花寶典》將大權交給了楊蓮亭，楊蓮亭又借此剪除異己，削弱東方不敗的力量。最後任我行被向問天、令狐冲救出，復奪了日月神教的教權，並殺了東方不敗和楊蓮亭。

總之，《笑傲江湖》情節結構的中心是武林爭霸奪權，為了達到目的，又奪得辟邪劍譜和葵花寶典，最後兩派都敗在辟邪劍譜和葵花寶典上。而主人公令狐冲則是一個志在放浪隱逸之人，經過千回萬折的鬥爭，終於實現了劉正風、曲洋未能實現的夙願——笑傲江湖。

六、行雲流水之文

「劍術之道，講究如行雲流水，任意所之。」

「一切當順其自然。行乎其不得不行，止乎其不得不止……」

以上是風清揚傳授令狐冲的劍術的要言妙義，其實這就是文章的最高境界。昔東坡論文，就指出文章如行雲流水，當行於所當行，止乎所不可不止。東坡的文論，源於莊子，莊子文章，浩無涯際，要渺無窮，我認為金庸的文章，近得之於東坡，遠得之於莊子。

金庸文章之妙，狀物寫景敘事，皆能得其神理，尤其是塑造人物，不僅外形刻劃得如目見親睹，更重要的是能栩栩如生。金庸的筆下，沒有刻板呆滯的人物，讀他的書，一些主要人物，皆可閉目即得，如多年老友。

《笑傲江湖》是金庸的後期作品，其敘事狀物，已到爐火純青，出神入化的境界，所謂文有餘思，筆無滯礙，信筆所至，皆成妙諦。

《笑傲江湖》裡所涉及的場景、人物以及各類武林人物交手搏鬥的場面不可勝數，但歷歷寫來，景隨情轉，變化無窮而皆能貼合生活，讓你如同身歷其境。例如第五回儀琳抱著重傷的令狐冲從群玉院逃出來到荒山裡，為令狐冲摘瓜，又為令狐冲講《百喻經》故事一段，簡直如讀第一流的回憶童年的散文，到第七回捉螢火蟲的一段，更是文如秋水，情如童夢：

> 這日傍晚，兩人背倚石壁，望著草叢間流螢飛來舞去，點點星火，煞是好看。
>
> 令狐冲道：「前年夏天，我曾捉了幾千隻螢火蟲兒，裝在十幾隻紗囊之中，掛在房裡，當真有趣。」儀琳心想，憑他的性子，決不會去縫製十幾隻紗囊，問道：「你小師妹叫你捉的，是不是？」令狐冲笑道：「你真聰明，猜得好準，怎麼知道是小師妹叫我捉的？」儀琳微笑道：「你性子這麼急，又不是小孩子了，怎會這般好耐心，去捉幾千隻螢火蟲來玩。」又問：「後來怎樣？」令狐冲笑道：「師妹拿來掛在她帳子裡，說道滿床晶光閃爍，她像是睡在天上雲端裡，一睜眼，前後左右都是星星。」儀琳道：「小師妹真會玩，偏你這個師哥也真肯湊趣，她就是要你去捉天上的星空，只怕你也肯。」
>
> 令狐冲笑道：「捉螢火蟲兒，原是為捉天上的星星而起。那天晚上我跟她一起乘

涼，看到天上星星燦爛，小師妹忽就嘆了一口氣，說道：「可惜過一會兒，便要去睡了，我真想睡在露天，半夜裡醒來，見到滿天星星都在向我眨眼，那多有趣。但媽媽一定不會答應。」我就說：「咱倆捉些螢火蟲來，放在蚊帳裡，不是像星星一樣嗎？」

　　這一段文章，就是放在最上等的散文集裡也不遜色。這一段文章下面還有很長的文字，限於篇幅，不能全錄。再看劉正風、曲洋在臨終前在荒山月夜彈琴的一段：

忽聽得遠處傳來錚錚幾聲，似乎有人彈琴。令狐冲和儀琳對望了一眼，都是大感奇怪：「怎地這荒山野嶺之中有人彈琴？」琴聲不斷傳來，甚是優雅，過得片刻，有幾下柔和的笛聲夾入琴韻之中。七弦琴的琴音和平中正，夾著清幽的洞簫，更是動人，琴韻簫聲似在一問一答，同時漸漸移近。令狐冲湊身過去，在儀琳耳邊低聲道：「這音樂來得古怪，只怕於我們不利，不論有甚麼事，你千萬別出聲。」儀琳點了點頭，只聽琴音漸漸高亢，簫聲卻慢慢低沉下去，但簫聲低而不斷，有如游絲隨風飄蕩，卻連綿不斷，更增回腸蕩氣之意。

只見山石後轉出三個人影，其時月亮被一片浮雲遮住了，夜色朦朧，依稀可見三人二高一矮，高的是兩個男子，矮的是個女子。兩個男子緩步走到一塊大岩石旁，坐了下來，一個拉琴，一個吹簫，那女子站在拉琴者的身側。令狐冲縮身石壁之後，不敢再看，生恐給那三個人發現。只聽琴簫悠揚，甚是和諧。令狐冲心道：「瀑布便在旁邊，但流水轟轟，竟然掩不住柔和的琴簫之音，看來拉琴吹簫的二人內功著實不淺。嗯，是了，他們所以到這裡吹奏，正是為了這裡有瀑布聲響，那麼跟我們是不相干的。」當下便放寬了心。

忽聽瑤琴中突然發出錚錚之音，似有殺伐之意，但簫聲仍是溫雅婉轉。過了一會，琴聲也柔和，兩音忽高忽低，驀地琴韻簫聲陡變，便如七八具瑤琴、七八支洞簫同時在奏樂一般。琴簫之聲雖然極盡繁複變幻，每個聲音卻又抑揚頓挫，悅耳動心。令狐冲只聽得血脈賁張，忍不住便要站起身來，又聽了一會，琴簫之聲又是一變，簫聲變了主調，那七弦琴只是叮叮璫璫的伴奏，但簫聲卻越來越高。令狐冲心中莫明其妙的感到一陣酸楚，側頭看儀琳時，只見她淚水正涔涔而下。突然間錚的一聲急響，琴音立止，簫聲也即住了。霎時間四下裡一片寂靜，唯見明月當空，樹影在地。

只聽一人緩緩説道：「劉賢弟，你我今日畢命於此，那也是大數使然，只是愚兄未能及早出手，累得你家眷弟子盡數殉，難愚兄心下實是不安。」另一個道：「你我肝膽相照，説這些話幹麼……」

再看後來洛陽綠竹巷中「婆婆」演奏的這曲《笑傲江湖》：

令狐冲又驚又喜，依稀記得便是那天晚上所聽到曲洋所奏的琴韻。

這一曲時而慷慨激昂，時而溫柔雅致，令狐冲雖不明樂理，但覺這位婆婆所奏，和曲洋所奏的曲調雖同，意趣卻大有差別。這婆婆所奏的曲調平和中正，令人聽著只覺音樂之美，卻無曲洋所奏熱血如沸的激奮。奏了良久，琴韻漸緩，似乎音樂在不住遠去，倒像奏琴之人走出了數十丈之遙，又走到數里之外，細微幾不可再聞。

琴音似止未止之際，卻有一二下極低極細的簫聲在琴音旁響了起來。回旋婉轉，簫聲漸響，恰似吹簫人一面吹，一面慢慢走近，簫聲清麗，忽高忽低，忽輕忽響，低到極處之際，幾個盤旋之後，又低沉下去，雖極低極細，每個音都仍清晰可聞。漸漸低音中偶有珠玉跳躍，清脆短促，此伏彼起，繁音漸增，先如鳴泉飛濺，繼而如群卉爭豔，花團錦簇，更夾著間關鳥語，彼鳴我和，漸漸成百鳥離去，春殘花落，但聞雨聲蕭蕭，　片淒涼蕭殺之象，細雨綿綿，若有若無，終於萬籟俱寂。簫聲停頓良久，眾人這才如夢初醒。王元霸、岳不羣等雖都不懂音律，卻也不禁心馳神醉。易師爺更是猶如喪魂落魄一般。

　　古往今來寫琴簫的文章多矣，但是能寫到如此深入細微而貼切的，恐不多見，特別是寫到同一曲子，不同的人演奏出來有不同的效果。劉正風、曲洋合奏此曲，自然是生命之曲的回蕩，其內涵和效果自然不同，到綠竹巷的「婆婆」演奏，自然又是一種純正的音樂之美，截然不同。這種情景並不難理解，記得我當年聽吾鄉瞎子阿炳拉《二泉映月》時，琴語如泣如訴，催人淚下，中間又有幾次頓挫，絃語如咽，令人淒然欲絕。後來此曲改編成管弦樂合奏，雖然還是那個旋律，但已是一支輕柔悅耳的輕音樂，無復當年阿炳的生命之曲的生死之感了。現在阿炳的原奏錄音和改編成管弦樂合奏的錄音俱在，有心的讀者不妨可以一比，以領略其中的妙諦。

　　當然，綠竹巷中「婆婆」所奏《笑傲江湖》應視作是此曲的正樂，故這

一大段描寫神妙至於極點，而劉正風、曲洋所奏，因爲變故在前，且臨命之際心情可知，我以爲他們二人所奏，雖極平生之懷，可以無恨，但却反而是帶有變徵之音，不可作爲此曲的正調。

所以綠竹巷「婆婆」所奏《笑傲江湖》之曲，至珍至貴，非後來改編瞎子阿炳《二泉映月》之可比也。

《笑傲江湖》裡這種絕世妙文，連篇都是，再看一段祖千秋論酒的妙文，本人也是酒友，故讀此頓增豪情：

> 祖千秋見令狐冲遞過酒碗，卻不便接，說道：「令狐兄雖有好酒，卻無好器皿，可惜啊可惜。」令狐冲道：「旅途之中，只有些粗碗粗盞，祖先生將就著些。」祖千秋搖頭道：「萬萬不可，萬萬不可。你對酒具如此馬虎，於飲酒之道，顯是未明其三昧。飲酒須得講究酒具，喝甚麼酒，使用甚麼酒杯。喝汾酒當用玉杯，唐人有詩云：『玉碗盛來琥珀光。』可見玉碗玉杯，能增酒色。」令狐冲道：「正是。」
>
> 祖千秋指著一壜酒，說道：「令狐冲這一壜關外白酒，酒味是極好的，只可惜少了一股芳冽之氣，最好是用犀角杯盛之而飲，那就醇美無比，須知玉杯增酒之色，犀角杯增酒之香，古人誠不我欺。」
>
> 令狐冲在洛陽聽綠竹翁談論講解，於天下美酒的來歷、氣味、釀酒之道、窖藏之法，已十知八九，但對酒具一道卻一竅不通，此刻聽得祖千秋侃侃而談，大有茅塞頓開之感。
>
> 只聽他又道：「至於飲葡萄酒嘛，當然要用夜光杯了。古人詩云：『葡萄美酒夜光杯，欲飲琵琶馬上催。』要知葡萄美酒作豔紅之色，我輩鬚眉男兒飲之，未免豪氣不足。葡萄美酒盛入夜光杯之後，酒色便與鮮血一般無異，飲酒有如飲血。岳武穆詞云：『壯志飢餐胡虜肉，笑談渴飲匈奴血』，豈不壯哉！」
>
> 令狐冲連連點頭，他讀書甚少，聽得祖千秋引證詩詞，於文義不甚了了，只是『笑談渴飲匈奴血』一句，確是豪氣干雲，令人胸懷大暢。
>
> 祖千秋指著一壜酒道：「至於這高粱美酒，乃是最古之酒。夏禹時儀狄作酒，禹飲而甘之，那便是高粱酒了。令狐兄，世人眼光短淺，只道大禹治水，造福後世，殊不知治水甚麼的，那也罷了，大禹真正的大功，你可知道麼？」
>
> 令狐冲和桃六仙齊聲道：「造酒！」祖千秋道：「正是！」八人一齊大笑。

祖千秋又道：「飲這高粱酒，須用青銅酒爵，始有古意。至於那米酒呢，上佳米酒，其味雖美，失之於甘，略稍淡薄，當用大斗飲之，方顯氣概。」

令狐冲道：「在下草莽之人，不明白這酒漿和酒具之間，竟有這許多講究。」

祖千秋拍著一只寫著『百草美酒』字樣的酒罈，說道：「這百草酒，乃採集百草，浸入美酒，故酒氣清香，如行春郊，令人未飲先醉。飲這百草酒須用古藤杯。百年古藤雕而成杯，以飲百草酒則大增芳香之氣。」令狐冲道：「百草古藤，倒是很難得的。」祖千秋正色道：「令狐兄言之差矣，百年美酒比之百年古藤，可更為難得。你想，百年古藤，盡可求之於深山野嶺，但百年美酒，人人想飲，一飲之後，就沒有了。一隻古藤杯，就算飲上千次萬次，還是好端端的一隻古藤杯。」

令狐冲道：「正是。在下無知，承先生指教。」

岳不羣一直在留神聽那祖千秋說話，聽他言辭誇張，卻又非無理，眼見桃枝仙、桃幹仙等捧起了那罈百草美酒，倒得滿桌淋漓，全沒當是十分珍貴的美酒。岳不羣雖不嗜飲，卻聞到酒香撲鼻，甚是醇美，情知那確是上佳好酒，桃谷六仙如此糟蹋，未免可惜。

祖千秋又道：「飲這紹興狀元紅須用古瓷杯，最好是北宋瓷杯，南宋瓷杯勉強可用，但已有衰敗氣象，至於元瓷，則不免粗俗了。飲這罈梨花酒呢？那該用翡翠杯。白樂天杭州春望詩云：『紅袖織綾誇柿蔕，青旗沽酒趁梨花。』你想，杭州酒家賣這梨花酒，掛的是滴翠也似的青旗，映得那梨花酒分外精神，飲這梨花酒，自然也當是翡翠杯了。飲這玉露酒，當用玻璃杯。玉露酒中有如珠細泡，盛在透明的杯中而飲，方可見其佳處。」

　　古人飲酒，講究酒具，故至今出土文物中還有唐代的犀角形瑪瑙杯，也有翡翠杯、白玉杯，至於金碗銀盞，那就不足為奇了。但在小說裡，這樣的講論酒杯與酒的關係，而且具有這麼高的文化色彩，實在是前所未有。

　　在本書裡，還有一段論酒的，也可以作為奇文，引出來供大家一賞：

令狐冲自幼嗜酒，只是師父、師娘沒給他多少錢零花，自來有酒便喝，也不容他辦選好惡。自從在洛陽聽綠竹翁細論酒道，又得他示以各樣美酒，一來天性相投，二來得了名師指點，此後便賞鑒甚精，一聞到這酒香，便道：「好啊，這兒有三鍋頭的陳年汾酒。唔，這百草酒只怕已有七十五年，那猴兒酒更是難得。」他聞到猴兒酒的酒香，登時想起六師弟陸大有來，忍不住心中一酸。

丹青生拊掌大笑，叫道：「妙極，妙極！風兄弟一進我酒室，便將我們三種最佳名釀報了出來，當眞是大名家，了不起！了不起！」

令狐冲見室中琳瑯滿目，到處都是酒罈、酒瓶、酒葫蘆、酒杯，說道：「前輩所藏，豈止三釀三種而已。這紹興女兒紅固是極品，這西域吐魯番的葡萄酒，四蒸四釀，在當世也是首屈一指的了。」丹青生又驚又喜，問道：「這吐魯番四蒸四釀葡萄酒密封於木桶之中，老弟怎地也嗅得出來？」令狐冲微笑道：「這等好酒，即使是於地下數丈的地窖之中，也掩不住他的酒香。」

丹青生叫道：「來來來，咱們便來喝這四蒸四釀葡萄酒。」將屋角落中一隻大木桶搬了出來。那木桶已然舊得發黑。上面彎彎曲曲的寫著許多西域文字，木塞上用火漆封住，火漆上蓋了印，顯得極爲鄭重。丹青生握住木塞，輕輕拔開，登時滿室酒香。

施令威向來滴酒不霑唇，聞到這股濃烈的酒氣，不禁便有醺醺之意。

丹青生揮手笑道：「你出去，你出去，可別醉倒了你。」將三隻酒杯並排放了，抱起酒桶往杯中斟去。那酒殷紅如血，酒高於杯緣，卻不溢出半點。令狐冲心中喝一聲采：「此人武功了得，抱住這百來斤的大木桶向小小酒杯中倒酒，居然齊口而止，實是難能。」

丹青生將木桶挾在肋下，左手舉杯，道：「請，請！」雙目凝視令狐冲的臉色，瞧他喝酒之後的神情。令狐冲舉杯喝了半杯，大聲辨味，只是他臉上塗了厚粉，瞧上去一片漠然，似乎不甚喜歡。丹青生神色惴惴，似乎生怕這位酒中行家覺得他這桶酒平平無奇。

令狐冲閉目半晌，睜開眼來，說道：「奇怪，奇怪！」丹青生問道：「甚麼奇怪？」

令狐冲道：「此事難以索解，晚輩可當眞不明白了。」丹青生眼中閃動著十分喜悅的光芒，道：「你問的是……」令狐冲道：「這酒晚輩生平只在洛陽城中喝過一次，雖然醇美之極，酒中卻有微微的酸味。據一位酒前輩言道，那是由於運來之時沿途顚動之故。這四蒸四釀的吐魯番葡萄酒，多搬一次，便減色一次。從吐魯番來到杭州，不知有幾萬里路，可是前輩此酒，竟然絕無酸味，這個……」

丹青生哈哈大笑，得意之極，說道：「這是我們不傳之秘。我是用三招劍法向西域劍豪英花爾徹換來的秘訣，你想不想知道？」

令狐冲搖頭道：「晚輩得賞此酒，已是心滿意足，前輩這秘訣卻不敢多問了。」

丹青生道：「喝酒，喝酒。」又倒了三杯，他見令狐冲不問這秘訣，不禁心癢難

搔，說道：「其實這秘訣說出來不值一文，可說毫不稀奇」。令狐冲知道自己越不想聽，他越是要說，忙謠手道：「前輩千萬別說，你這三招劍招，定然非同小可。以如此重大代價換來的秘訣，晚輩輕輕易易地便學了去，於心何安？常言道：無功不受祿……」丹青生道：「你陪我喝酒，說得出此酒的來歷，便是大大的功勞了。這秘訣你非聽不可。」

令狐冲：「晚輩蒙前輩接見，又賜以極品美酒，已是感激之至，怎可……」丹青生道：「我願意說，你就聽好了。」向問天勸道：「四莊主一番美意，風兄弟不用推辭了。」

丹青生道：「對，對」笑咪咪的道：「我再考你一考，你可知道這酒已有多少年份？」

令狐冲將杯中酒喝乾，辨味多時，說道：「這酒另有一個怪處，似乎已有一百二十年，又似只有十二三年。新中有陳，陳中有新，比之尋常百年以上的美酒，另有一股風味。」

向問天眉頭微蹙，心道：「這一下可獻醜了。一百二十年和十二三年相差百年以上，怎可相提並論。」他生怕丹青生聽了不愉，卻見這老兒哈哈大笑，一部大髯子吹得筆直，笑道：「好兄弟，果然厲害。我這秘訣便在於此。我跟你說，那西域劍豪莫花爾徹送了我十桶三蒸三釀的一百二十年吐魯番美酒，用五匹大宛良馬駄到杭州來，然後我依然再加一蒸一釀，十桶酒，釀成一桶。屈指算來，正是十二年半以前之事。這美酒歷關山萬里而不酸，酒味陳中有新，新中有陳，便在於此」

似上這段「酒話」，可說是酒國的絕世妙品。昔年我曾到過通化葡萄酒廠的酒窖，看過儲藏葡萄酒的大木桶，木桶甚大，決非丹青生所能搬動，也都是陳年老窖，可惜我沒有令狐冲的品酒本領，所以未能領略其殊美，我也曾喝過一瓶真正的乾隆陳紹，其味芳香醇厚而溫雅，所以讀這段文章，真是逸興遄飛。但我知道金庸並不能喝酒，至少他多次請我喝酒時他自己不飲。不管他自己喝不喝酒，這段「酒話」，無論如何是酒文化的極品。

金庸小說裡，特別是《笑傲江湖》裡，這樣的逸趣橫生的「絕妙好辭」實在太多了，可說是舉不勝舉。這也是金庸的文章百讀不厭的原因之一。

要品評金庸的文章，那可談的問題太多了。總而言之，我認為他的文章，

發源於莊周，也得力於東坡。他是我們時代的文章大師，是我們時代的光榮和驕傲。去年我曾有詩贈金庸，現在寫在下面，以作本文的收尾：

奇才天下說金庸。帕米東來第一峰。

九曲黃河波浪闊，千層雪嶺煙霞重。

幻情壯采文變豹，豪氣干雲筆屠龍。

昔日韓生歌石鼓，今朝寰宇唱金鏞。

一九九七年八月二十七日夜十一時

於京東且住草堂

離奇與鬆散
——從武俠衍出的中國小說敘事傳統

張　大　春

輔仁大學中文系

摘　要

　　如果說武俠小說是西風東漸後中文創作裡最後的敘事堡壘，那麼檢視武俠作品的類型質素便亦發具有勘掘中國小說敘事傳統的意味。二十世紀的傳媒效應將武俠小說作者金庸推上該文類的盟主地位，甚至形成了強大無比的「文類黑洞」現象，在這個形勢之下，金庸一方面完成了武俠小說現代化的工作，同時却也造成該文類的解體。

　　本文試圖引領武俠讀者回溯到平江不肖生一九二〇年代所寫的《江湖奇俠傳》，說明其人為武俠小說所做的一項重要發明，即：為俠建立一個系譜。有了這個系譜，金庸筆下的江湖才可能成立。早期的俠義小說中俠客的出現本身就是一個絕頂的離奇遭遇、一個無從解釋的巧合。可是到了不肖生那裡，便以一個合傳的架構處理數以百計的眾多角色之出現、遇合、交往等種種關係，進一步為俠客的身世、來歷「立傳」，從而俠客有了辨認座標，一個系譜。

楔　子

　　1966 年 4 月 22 日，美國加州大學柏克萊分校教授陳世驤先生在日本京都人文科學部研究所任教期間，由於買不到《天龍八部》的上市小本，特別致書作者金庸，請寄一套，而有所謂「求經求到佛家自己也」之語。這封信日後附錄於《天龍八部》書後，可以視之為「大學教授讀金庸武俠」之說的

一件最早的文獻。從這封（以及與之一併附錄、寫於 1970 年 11 月 20 日的第二封）信中的遣辭看來，陳氏和金庸並非時相過從的密友，陳之於金，倒像是一個浸潤既久、景慕亦深的讀者之於一個曠世無匹的作家；乃有將其在中研院集刊發表之文寄贈之舉、卻出之於以下之言：「本披砂析髮之學院文章，惟念　兄才如海，無書不讀，或亦將不細遺。此文雕鑽之作，宜以覆甕堆塵，聊以見　兄之一讀者，尚會讀書耳。」

　　無論出之於緬懷知音或借譽上庠，金庸披露的這些私人信函不意卻在一位比較文學學者的揄揚和讚賞之外，留下了一個值得推敲覆案的課題。在京都旅次的那封信裡，陳氏如此寫道：

> 書（按：指《天龍八部》）中的人物情節，可謂無人不冤、有情皆孽，要寫到盡致非把常人常情都寫成離奇不可；書中的世界是朗朗世界到處藏著魍魎和鬼蜮，隨時予以驚奇的揭發與諷刺，要供出這樣一個可憐芸芸眾生的世界，如何能不教結構鬆散？這樣的人物情節和世界，背後籠罩著佛法的無邊大超脫，時而透露出來。而在每逢動人處，我們會感到希臘悲劇理論中所謂恐怖與憐憫，再說句更陳腐的話，所謂「離奇與鬆散」，大概可叫做「形式與內容的統一」罷。

　　這段話之所以提到「離奇與鬆散」，實由於平素和陳氏往還聚談的「青年朋友諸生」之中，間或有認為《天龍八部》「稍鬆散」而「人物個性及情節太離奇」這樣的意見，陳氏信中所寫的一段正是對這些讀後感式的意見的答覆，也是對金庸作品的捍衛。是以在將近四年七個月之後的第二封信裡，陳氏復以王國維所謂「一言以蔽之曰，有意境而已」之語，稱道金庸：「至其終屬離奇而不失本真之感，則可與現代詩甚至造形美術之佳者互證」，甚至這樣睥睨慨嘆：「弟嘗以為其精英之出，可與元劇之異軍突起相比。既表天才，亦關世運。所不同者今世猶只見此一人而已。」

一個「文類黑洞」的形成

　　在陳氏言下，「今世猶只見此一人而已」顯然是極大的恭維，至少吾人無從考證陳氏是否像讀金庸之作那樣細讀過不肖生的《江湖奇俠傳》、《近代俠義英雄傳》、顧明道的《荒江女俠》、白羽的《十二金錢鏢》、鄭證因的《臥虎

藏龍》、《鐵騎銀瓶》和還珠樓主的《蜀山劍俠傳》等作。但是，這番恭維卻「不幸」而預言了二十世紀末金庸諸作在華文通俗小說閱讀世界裡所造成的強大擠壓效應。此際何祇陳氏（及其信中所提及的楊蓮生（聯陞）、陳省身、夏濟安等三數學者）而已？「金庸小說與二十世紀中國文學」國際研討會甫於今（1998）春在科羅拉多大學閉幕，半年後的臺北文壇復推出「金庸小說國際學術研討會」，推波助瀾，務期使金作、金學得一正典出身，與夫一再經由電影、電視、漫畫等其它媒介改編而擴大的原著市場比合而觀，金庸的作品非但可稱為武俠小說這一文類的集大成者，其書寫活動亦且被譽為「在審美內涵上突破了中國現代文學的單維現象（只有『國家、社會、歷史』之維），增添了超驗世界（神奇世界）和內自然世界（人性）的維度」（劉再復語），以及「在他手中形成了一種成熟的獨特的白話文，我們甚至不妨稱之為『金氏白話文』」（李陀語），金庸顯然成了他本人未必願意明白恭維的武林盟主；一個文化現象的核心。關於這一文化現象的種種討論——無論是文本內在的爬梳衍繹、抑或作品外緣的附會參詳，無一不是在增加金作、金學的擠壓效應，使成「捨金庸而無武、非金庸而何俠？」的「文類黑洞」之勢，席捲八荒、包羅萬象；從而也才會有「可以斷言：不會有超出金庸的武俠小說，因為金庸已成功地完成了武俠小說的現代化實驗，其結果是武俠小說的解體。」（見楊春時〈俠的現代闡釋與武俠小說的終結〉）這樣匆促而悲壯的結論。不過，在黑洞尚未形成之初，那個如慧芒星閃般乍現即逝的小小質疑尚懸而未解——陳世驤先生在私函中拈出、旋即又以「掉了兩句文學批評的書袋」之言解嘲放過的課題是否應再探究竟？「離奇與鬆散」難道果真是內容與形式的統一？這種統一是如何產生的？它的產生若非祇能在金庸名下始得彰顯，則是否自有淵源？質言云：倘若「離奇的內容」可以和「鬆散的形式」共生而形成一個美學典範，且非「鬆散的形式」不足以表現「離奇的內容」、非「離奇的內容」不足以寄託「鬆散的形式」；那麼，這個共生關係的根柢又從何而來？這個課題使我們可以離金庸此一黑洞稍遠，略見之前中國武俠小說所延展衍生的一種敘事傳統。蓋金庸亦嘗於答覆評者及其某些作品「結構不好」時曾經如此說道：「我寫小說，結構是一個弱點，好像 Thomas Hardy 的 *The Return of the Native*（《還鄉記》）、Charles Dickens 的 *A Tale of Two Cities*（《雙城記》）那樣精彩的結構，又如莫泊桑的一些小說結構的勻

稱渾成，是我絕對及不上的。現在我祇好老了臉皮地說：結構鬆懈，是中國
小說的傳統。」（見《明報月刊》1998 年 8 月號，金庸〈小說創作的幾點思考〉）
如果不以此言爲金庸個人老下臉皮自辯之辭而已，或者說「結構鬆散」的確
有可能是中國小說的一個特色或通病；那麼，它是否與陳氏所謂的離奇相呼
應、相表裡？設若俗見所認爲的鬆散的確又是一個小說結構上的毛病，則基
於什麼樣的觀點能指之爲病？

並無半個閑字

　　前揭陳氏的第一封信所謂「『離奇與鬆散』，大概可叫做『形式與內容的
統一』罷。」當然不是一句嚴格的評語；但是，其中頗有值得「披砂析髮」、
仔細尋繹的道理。

　　視「形式與內容的統一」爲一美學標準的這種意見，可以一直追溯到古
希臘時代亞里斯多德在他的《詩學》第八章中便提到：「戲劇情節的各個部
分必須用這樣一種方式連接在一起，以致任何一部分如果挪動或置換，就會
使整部作品鬆動脫節。要是某一部分可有可無，並不引起顯著的差異，就絕
不是整體中的有機部分。」

　　這個「有機論」的理性哲學背景促使抱持此論的批評家們相信：「統一」
（unity）這一概念和性質應用在藝術作品上的時候，得以檢驗、過濾或篩選出
多餘的、不適當的、不符合整體需要的部分。換言之：爲了吻合統一性，作
品的各個元素必須彼此鞏固、支持——如果以建築物作爲一部作品的類喻，
則不能彼此鞏固、支持的元素便失去統一性而使結構鬆散。

　　從這個建築物的類喻出發，中國古典說部章回體的作品恐怕絕少合格
者。毋怪乎胡適會在〈建設的文學革命論〉裡這樣指斥：「至於布局一方面，
除了幾首實在好的詩之外，幾乎沒有一篇東西當得『布局』兩個字！——所
以我說，從文學方法一方面看去，中國的文學實在不夠給我們作模範。」這
是 1918 年間胡適的意見。七年之後，他寫〈海上花列傳序〉，仍隱然秉持著
這一套看法，認爲《海上花列傳》的結構「實在遠勝於《儒林外史》」；從而，
胡適特別從一本名爲《海上奇書》的雜誌上抄錄下來《海上花列傳》作者韓
子雲自己的小說主張。韓氏身爲小說家，他自豪地表示：《海上花列傳》的

筆法雖然「從《儒林外史》脫化出來」，但是「惟穿插藏閃之法則爲從來說部所未有」。

　　無論「從來說部所未有」是不是韓子雲自矜夸誕之辭，重要的是他那穿插藏閃之法的例言中，有著看來似乎吻合統一性、有機論和建築物類喻的美學考慮：

> 一波未平，一波又起；或竟接連起十餘波，忽東忽西、忽南忽北，隨手敘來，並無一事完全，卻並無一絲挂漏，閱之覺其背面無文字處尚有許多文字，雖未明明敘出，而可以意會得之；此穿插之法也。劈空而來，使閱者茫然不解其如何緣故，急欲觀後文，而後文又舍而敘他事矣；及他事敘畢，再敘明其緣故，而其緣故仍未盡明；直至全體盡露，乃知前文所敘並無半個閑字：此藏閃之法也。

　　即使不勞借助於亞里斯多德的《詩學》第八章，韓子雲顯然亦申明了他「並無一事完全，卻並無一絲挂漏」以及「並無半個閑字」的要求，這一暗合於統一性、有機論乃至於建築物類喻的美學考慮正是彼一指稱結構鬆散爲病的基礎。韓子雲以迄於胡適卻不會看得起小說中那些多餘的、不適當的、不符合整體需要的元素，它們是「閑字」——也就是廢話的意思。

不許說廢話

　　韓子雲主張的「無挂漏、無閑字」乃至於胡適講究的「布局」所著眼者，恐怕也祇是後出而益趨緻密之結構論中的事件結構而已。強調事件結構的評者首先將一部小說分割成各種細小的情節單位，並以其間因果關係之必然與否來判斷某個情節單位是否能與其它的情節單位彼此鞏固、支持；若否則是爲結構上的不必要、也就是結構上的缺點。韓子雲的另一則例言是這樣說的：「合傳之體有三難。一曰無雷同……二曰無矛盾……三曰無挂漏：寫一人而無結局，挂漏也；敘一事而無收場，亦挂漏也。」這段話的「一曰」「二曰」指的是小說人物的塑造，惟「三曰」的部分所申言者，正是事件結構的琢磨。值得注意的是韓子雲用了「合傳」這個詞。

　　由於韓子雲用了這個詞，胡適便不得不沿用之、甚至附會之。他把「合傳」的來歷上溯到《史記》，並且爲司馬遷所寫的合傳定出優劣；認爲「有自

然連絡的合傳」是好的，相反則是不好的。什麼是「有自然連絡」呢？那就是「凡一個故事裡的人物可以合傳；幾個不同的故事裡的人物不可以合傳」。這個怪論非但涉嫌以小說的繩墨去規範歷史的寫作，甚且暗含著一個糾彈不完美的歷史的荒唐想法。不過，也正在這個怪論上，胡適暴露了晚清以迄民初之際，一個從韓子雲到胡適本人皆未曾想過要去質疑或抗拒的理念：小說是一種傳記。

基於「小說是一種傳記」的認識，便衍生出如下的許多主張：首先，小說以人物為主，而且這些人物在現實世界中是本有其依據、得以索隱而辨識的。其次，由於現實世界中的人的面目、性情、言語、行為有其不得度越的生理和物理限制，小說中的人物亦必須服膺同樣的法度。其三，中國的史傳自有其不容駢枝冗贅的精簡傳統，小說自然也沒有敷設筆墨描寫不相干事件的特權。其四，史的書寫一向不曾乖違過那個觀興亡、知得失的訓誡目的，小說也不應悖離其對家國社會等大我所應須負起的教化責任。

小說之為「一種傳記」不祇呼應了它隸籍稗官、歸途野史的宿命，同時也在上述這些寫實、求真、布局嚴密、教化端謹的種種需索之下失去了說廢話的自由。是以劉鶚《老殘遊記》寫申子平遇黃龍子和與璵姑一節，被胡適斥之為「荒誕可笑」；書末讓賈家一十三口冤死者還魂復活，胡適又斥之為「無謂之至」。這種「嚴禁離奇」的氛圍似乎試圖指出一條小說的必行必經之路：小說勢須擺脫說話人在書場上的「滿紙荒唐言」，而後撫捧起文人作者心目中那個大歷史、大敘述的「一把辛酸淚」。這樣的小說旨在映照一幕又一幕的現實；問題在於現實世界並非「無挂漏、無閒字」且嚴密「布局」出來的小說的鏡象對稱，現實世界本來就是一個結構鬆散的世界；更妙的是，這個鬆散性質也正是中國傳統書場的敘事特質。

書場裡的鬆散

源自清代說話人底本的《七俠五義》顯然是一部結構鬆散之作的範例。它的前二十回是依據明人作品《龍圖公案》演成的包公故事。其後則是一批批與官僚和律法或近或遠的俠客之間的勾鬥、以及俠客們如何輔助或正或邪的政治人物、並且在宮廷以至市井的各種小戰場上演習其勤王和謀逆的衝

突。由於本非出自一個完整的故事，是以沒有一個貫穿全局的主人翁；說話人在這部堪稱「群戲」的作品中對於人物所應負的責任更不是「立傳」，而是如何讓他們在原本不屬於自己的故事之中亮相，隨即消失，等到讀者（其實是聽眾）已經被另一個故事所吸引而幾乎忘記這個亮過相的人物之際，再另生一枝節，召之使來，令聽者忽生如見故人之感。就這個敘事技術的應用來看，它已經是日後韓子雲自稱自道「從來說部所未有」的穿插藏閃之法。

例言之：在《七俠五義》第三回中，包公攜包興赴京師會試，在一小店裡巧遇一人──「武生打扮，疊暴著英雄精神，面帶俠氣。」包公愛他氣宇軒昂，便邀來入座同飲；此人正是南俠展昭。展昭隨即於當晚將包公主僕從金龍寺惡僧手中救下性命。是後，小說屢述包公中試、任職、斷案、罷官、遇寇。忽忽說到第六回上，才又在土龍崗重逢展昭。此番一別又過了五回，包公復斷了幾個奇案。到第十一回末，說話人猛地一陣「忽東忽西」，另起爐灶；劈空硬切到展昭母喪之後往陳州漫遊，導出下一回「巧換藏春酒」，和戲弄龐昱手下勇士項福的一節。至此看來故事又是往展昭乃至陷空島五鼠的一條線上岔去，殊不知龐昱的這條線又是下一段包公故事的伏筆。

在說話人那裡，穿插加上藏閃之法是一個不得不爾的技術，非如此不能將來歷不同、底細無關的人物和他們各自的故事拼湊到一處去。這種拼湊之所以能夠奏效，顯然與說書這門藝術訴諸過耳即去的聽覺有著本質上的關連。和訴諸視覺的閱讀活動截然不同的──從事講述（兼帶表演、吟唱和口技）的說話人往往能夠利用現場的臨即性、突發、隨興的機智、群眾間的互動互染的常態而吸引其受眾進入當下的故事情境，這個在傳播效果上看來的確佔據優勢的書場敘事傳統一旦書面化、文本化之後，卻極可能暴露出一個失去臨場語境的問題。當彼一臨場語境不再，小說的讀者會更清楚地意識到穿插藏閃之際的時間問題──質言之：較諸書場受眾，小說讀者將更不耐於過分突兀或隱晦的穿插以及略嫌匆促或漫長的藏閃，小說的讀者也要比書場的受眾敏感於其實原本亦不應定於一尊的結構美學；說話人的廢話在書場上也許不顯，到了紙面上卻可能是令人觸目煩心的「閑字」了。可是，反過來說，無法體貼書場裡的小說與夫紙面上的小說之別，而逕以「無挂漏、無閑字」的主張和「布局」的講究一律衡之，究竟能否見識到：在尚未失去彼一臨場語境的那些說話人口中，鬆散可能正是小說的趣味之所在呢──那是一

種「不急欲觀後文」、不忙於尋求結果的趣味。

拒絕因果關係

前文已敍及：一部小說可分割成若干情節單位，各個情節單位之間又有一種可以彼此鞏固、支持的因果關係。然而，從另一方面看來，因果關係亦非必然。比方說：《七俠五義》第十五回述包公至天齊廟遇見貧婆自呼「哀家」、稱之「包卿」；包公不以爲忤，這乃是因爲在第六回中包公曾獲寇殊冤魂預囑，是以這兩個情節單位之間有一看似的因果關係。但是，先前也曾提及的包公途遇展昭的一節卻無前跡可尋，我們稱這種全無原由、來歷的情節單位爲巧合。巧合在小說裡非徒不需要符合因果律，它甚至是對簡便因果關係的一種拒絕。

巧合，一個離奇的遭遇；在小說裡面，他祇有兩種極端相反的、與因果關係之間的辯證。第一、巧合是完全沒有、也不需要解釋的；換言之，巧合的構成是排除因果律的。第二、必須經過錯綜複雜的因果關係，最後拐彎抹角獲致一個出奇但合理的解釋。金庸作品《天龍八部》裡的段譽便一身而兼俱這兩種巧合

在《天龍八部》第十四回〈劇飲千杯男兒事〉中，段譽離開曼陀山莊、失魂落魄地來到無錫城畔的松鶴樓，就像包公主僕那般沒來由地遇上展昭一樣、撞見了喬峯，二人縱酒劇飲，竟爾結爲異姓兄弟。此其一。到了第四十八回〈王孫落魄　怎生消得　楊枝玉露〉裡，歷盡波折眼見可成眷屬的段譽和王語嫣在王夫人突如其來的告白之下搖身一變、成爲亂倫的兄妹，然而情節急轉直下：段母刀白鳳隨即揭露原來她也有一段不爲人所知的私情；是以段譽和王語嫣的生父段正淳並無血緣關係。此其二。

作爲傳奇（romance）這個類型的關鍵性元素，巧合——離奇遭遇的高度象徵，可以稱之爲傳奇的敍述者的識別證。我們甚至可以將讀者對巧合的接受程度當作作品的試紙。設若一個讀者能夠認同其它屬於傳奇的文本元素——比方說：認同那些超自然能力與經驗和人類的日常生活相互融合、錯綜複雜的角色關係構成異乎常人所能承受的連續及巨大衝突、典型化甚至刻板化的個性或性格描述、相對立的信仰和價值之間過度誇張的不妥協性、一波

未平一波又起的重大磨難或成就、具有不可思議控制力的道德制約，以及許多無法通過經驗法則、邏輯推理和科學實驗來證明的神奇事蹟之描寫；但是，這個讀者卻不能相信或接受巧合的話，那麼傳奇之於此人便根本無法成立；此人之於傳奇也不會是一個有效的讀者。這裡牽涉到一個深刻的底蘊：傳奇必須透過巧合這一拒絕簡易因果關係的設計才得以展開其敍述。換言之：傳奇的內在原本預存著一個反事件結構的動能。

　　一個高明的作者會想盡辦法讓巧合看起來「事出有因」。如前述《七俠五義》第十五回包公至天齊廟巧遇李妃的一節。根據俞曲園（樾）為此書所寫的序言來看，俞氏依據說話人石玉崑《三俠五義》的本子，刪去原書第一回〈設陰謀臨產換太子／奮俠義替死救皇娘〉中很大一部分的細節描寫，祇是因為「狸貓換太子」的故事既不符合歷史的真實、也不吻合常識的原則。把 1889年經俞氏改訂且更名出版的《七俠五義》和 1925 年亞東圖書館請俞平伯標點、胡適作序的《三俠五義》本子對照看去，可知俞氏祇刪減了敷染故事的感覺、動作和對話細節，卻未更動或刪削事件本身。他甚至還保留了《三俠五義》第六回中寇珠冤魂托夢，和第十五到第十九回、也就是從遇李妃到戮郭槐的諸事始末；質言之，俞氏固然聲稱「援據史傳，訂正俗說」，卻沒有真正做到。他言刪而實未刪。提到這一節乃是因為俞氏從未試圖真地「訂正俗說」、將「狸貓換太子」這個在當時已經流傳了九百年的傳說故事從大歷史、大敍述的縫隙中湮滅，否則他大可以將第一、六和十五到十九回一切關於宋仁宗身世之訛謠一舉盡除之。倘使俞氏僅僅保留十五到十九回的部分，卻一定會招致一重大的質疑：包公剛剛鍘了太師龐吉的兒子龐昱，便立刻又揭發一段適足以觸怒天顏、冒犯龍威的宮廷秘辛，這種在政治現實裡想當然耳的危險無可避免會令讀者益加意識到天齊廟遇國母的巧合性。俞氏為了保留這整個故事，不得不順帶保留了第一和第六回中《三俠五義》原作者石玉崑為了掩飾日後的巧合而設計的伏筆。進一步說：在石玉崑那裡，伏筆──敍述時間及事件發生時間在前的情節單位，會使敍述時間和事件發生時間在後的情節單位看來像是具有「前」因「後」果的關係。石玉崑（乃至無數精熟此道的傳奇作者）深深瞭解：傳奇既然需要巧合這個反事件結構的動能，而當讀者一旦意識到「天下哪有這樣的巧事？」又偏能動搖作品的成立基礎時，作者祇好設法讓讀者不去注意那巧合之巧、之稀罕、之不可能。假「前」為

因、假「後」爲果的這個手段，也就是利用喚起讀者對伏筆的記憶的這個手段，因此實際上是巧合的掩護、是傳奇內在反事件結構動能的掩護。

暫時回到金庸

段譽和王語嫣居然差一點是同父異母的兄妹、又居然果眞不是同父異母的兄妹；「天下哪有這樣巧事？」可是且慢：這段奇上加奇、巧中生巧的情節有兩個伏筆——段譽在《天龍八部》第七回〈無計悔多情〉和第九回〈換巢鸞鳳〉曾分別發現：同他都有情愫的木婉清和鍾靈正是他同父異母的妹子。這兩次發現並不是第四十八回後文（也就是段譽與王語嫣生身之謎的赫然揭露）的「前」因；然而，一旦讀者在第四十八回上忽生「天下哪有這樣巧事？」之疑的同時，第七、九回前事的記憶立刻因其相似性而被喚起，一旦喚起便使沒有來歷的巧合看上去有了來歷。在這種掩護之下，讀者不會因爲段譽總是在亂倫邊緣而狐疑金庸利用段正淳的風流來註銷他越寫越不滿意的女主角人選與英雄終成眷屬的資格，他們甚至不會注意到段譽一再遇上失散多年的妹子的機率問題。於是，巧合之巧、之稀罕、之不可能等等顧慮就這樣揮發掉了。倒過來說，《天龍八部》第四十八回的奇上奇、巧中巧既未見疑，它本身反而也呼應了第七、九回的前事，成爲那兩次發現的收束和「後」果。前文與後文、伏筆與應筆之間明明是幾個相互全無因果關係的情節單位、欠缺形成緊密事件結構的條件，可是敍述卻創造了它們相互掩護的條件。這是利用敍述結構來彌縫、救濟事件結構的秘訣。

在這裡，讓我們重回本文稍早時設下的一個伏筆：金庸承認他寫小說（按：指『改也改不回來』的《天龍八部》等）「結構是一個弱點」，並謂「現在我祇好老了臉皮地說：結構鬆懈，是中國小說的傳統。」金庸的辯護顯然是將自己的作品托蔽於一個想像中的大傳統之下，藉由「共有而難免」彼一「結構鬆散」的「弱點」來承接那個傳統。有趣的是：如何辨識那個傳統和它的「弱點」呢？金庸的說法是一個帶有明顯價值判斷的對比；他說哈代、說狄更斯、說莫泊桑，還說這些西方作家作品「精彩的結構」「是我絕對及不上的」。我們無從也不必追究金庸所指的結構是小說的事件結構、敍述結構，甚或治絲愈棼的角色結構、符碼結構、主題結構……；我們祇能假設：金庸把

說話人書場裡那種在胡適眼中毫無「布局」可言的鬆散放置在自己作品的行列之前，以及西方十九世紀經典名作的對立面。的確，金庸的辯護讓我們想起胡適，聽見他「中國的文學實在不夠給我們作模範」的疾呼，嗅著他爲中國新文學運動所施放的、氣味並不純粹的歷史主義（historicism）薰香。

再次提到胡適

　　如果胡適是一個純粹一點的歷史主義者，他應該清楚：企圖將歷史簡化成一種演替模式其實已然違悖了認識歷史的基本倫理。但是，胡適對這樣的悖倫並不措意；他從赫爾德（Johann Gottfreio von Heroer, 1744-1803）這位歷史主義者先驅那裡繼承過來的恐怕祇是《人類歷史哲學大綱》（*Ideen Zur Philosophie der Geschichte der Menschheit*, 1784-91）裡那種對各別民族本土文化發展的關切和焦慮。赫爾德關心的是強勢民族對弱勢民族的宰制所可能造成的、對後者之民族精神的打擊，以及此一打擊反過頭來對全人類文化成長的傷害，這是赫爾德採集民謠、編製成書的底蘊。但是，胡適從事古典小說考證、寫作《白話文學史》（上卷）（1912-8）的工作卻萌芽於一個弱勢民族如何迅速改變其劣等地位或體質的憂忡。正因爲這份憂忡的巨大和沈重，遂讓整個呼擁圍繞著新文學運動的知識界觀察歷史、體驗歷史、以及重塑歷史的行動偏出了狄爾泰（Wilheim Dilthey, 1833-1911）式將材料置入歷史脈絡中加以檢驗的方法論，而走上了染有實用色彩、且明顯傾進於目的論的相反的路子──他們投注大量的心血精力編寫各種適合青年學子「快速浸潤」（一個異化了的詞）的「史」。固然，自晚清倡新式高等教育學堂伊始，一部部帶有講義性質的經學史、思想史、文學史……已森然出現，可是到了五四運動前後，史著所代表的意義和所具備的功能已非昔比。胡適於1917 年留美學成返北大任教，1918 年任《新青年》雜誌編輯；反文言、唱白話、主張文學革命。他同時還爲那個撰寫歷史的書寫活動添加了佐料。一方面，從他的老師杜威（John Dewey，1859-1952）那裡，胡適移植來一套論題：經驗是有機體和環境相互作用的結果，科學實驗則是在環境內經過精心設計的改造。從而，歷史書寫不必然是還原過去的眞相（雖然它不排斥這一點），卻更可以在透過精心設計的書寫之後，著史者已然重新解釋了、也改造

了歷史。《白話文學史》正是一部這樣的著作。另一方面，胡適未嘗放鬆他擴大史著意義和功能的文化包袱，於是才有「以合傳立體」喻小說這樣的筆墨。

爲俠立傳

1923 年 1 月間出版的《紅雜誌》第二十二期上隆重刊出一部由施濟群評贊、不肖生撰寫的「長篇武俠小說」《江湖奇俠傳》〈第一回〉。此作卷帙浩大計八十六回，洋洋近百萬言。連載雖未每期刊出，但是大體上和它的讀者圈維持了一個可以用「經年累月」稱之的親即關係。全書四十六回起轉至同一書局新創的《紅玫瑰》雜誌續刊，甚至有藉一連載而號召全刊讀者的聲勢。在開篇之初，隨文附評的施濟群有相當多的筆墨分析、介紹，甚至可以說吹捧此作。值得注意的是：他不時地提醒讀者，不肖生的小說是在爲一群俠立傳。「作者欲寫許多奇俠，正如一部廿四史。」「寫柳遲狀貌十分醜陋，而性質反極聰穎；其種種舉動，已是一篇奇人小傳。」（以上第一回後）「笑道人述金羅漢行狀，彷彿封神傳中人物。」「余初疑爲誕，叩之向君（按：不肖生本名向愷然），向君言此書取材，大率湘湖事實，非盡嚮壁虛構者也。然則茫茫天壤，何奇弗有？管蠡之見，安能謬測天下恢奇事哉？」（第三回後）施氏除了強調《江湖奇俠傳》隱然是一部可稽、可考、可索隱、有本事的、並不荒誕虛構的史傳之外，更有這樣的用語：「下半回在甘瘤子傳中，忽爾夾寫桂武小傳，乃作者行文變化處。」（第九回後）則是明明指出：書中所述者非一「角色眾多的傳奇」，而是諸多實有所本的俠的「合傳」。倘若作者所述甚爲離奇，讀之令人不忍信其爲實，評者更會這樣覆案：「此回敍向樂山辮功事，頗奇特；讀者或又疑爲誕，惟余則深信之，並引一事以爲證……（中略）由此觀之，則練功及辮，亦技擊家之常事，不可目爲誕妄矣。」（第十三回後）這裡面評者爲小說幫腔助陣之語即或未可深信，但是評者認爲小說讀者可能相信他的評語則是昭然若揭的；質言之，爲了讓《紅雜誌》讀者成爲《江湖奇俠傳》這部武俠小說（傳奇）的有效讀者，他的說服方式是用各種方式爲這部作品掙一個史傳的身分，甚至不惜在評中爲過分離奇的情節經營一段「事不孤立而可證」的互文。即令是六十年後的研究者在評及不肖生續作的《近代俠義英雄傳》時也不得不如此寫道：「書中所寫的人物如大刀王五、霍元

甲、趙玉堂、山西老董、農勁蓀、孫祿堂等，都是歷史上真有其人的，所記載的事蹟，十之八九也都是武術家們認可的。此書寫法與《江湖奇俠傳》相同，都是採取《儒林外史》式的結構，由一個故事引出另一個故事，集短篇而成長篇。」（梁守中《武俠小說話古今》，臺北遠流版）此話若是說在胡適口裡，他想必會把《儒林外史》式的結構形容成「鬆散的結構」。然而諷刺的是：他那個時代的武俠小說家卻也打著史傳的旗號向寫實的需索繳交離奇的故事，他們甚至和文學出版工業的其它環節共謀（由媒體邀聘知名的文士評者），誘導讀者相信武俠小說是「史」的一種形式。而這個文類所運用的敘述手段，卻又來自胡適不祇一次輕詆過的、「沒有布局」的《儒林外史》；一種胡適所反對的、將不屬於同一個故事裡的人物串連、拼湊在一部大「合傳」中的技術。既離奇、且鬆散，它正是本文前引陳世驤先生所說的：「書中的世界是朗朗世界到處藏著魍魎和鬼蜮，隨時予以驚奇的揭發與諷刺，要供出這樣一個可憐芸芸眾生的世界，如何能不教結構鬆散？」

武俠小說的結構

　　從說話人石玉崑的《三俠五義》到經學家俞曲園的《七俠五義》，旁及文康的《兒女英雄傳》、佚名作者的《七劍十三俠》，乃至眾多仿說話人底本所寫成的章回說部之公案、俠義糅合體諸作，都沒有觸及《江湖奇俠傳》所從事的一項發明；這項發明又非待「為俠立傳」的這個自覺出現而不能成立。那就是：不肖生為俠建立了一個系譜。

　　在《江湖奇俠傳》問世之前，身懷絕技的俠客之所以離奇非徒恃其絕技而已，還有的是他們都沒有一個可供察考探溯的身世、來歷；也就是辨識座標。俠客的出現本身就是一個絕頂的離奇遭遇、一個無從解釋的巧合。聽說書人演述故事的讀者不會追問：展昭的父祖師尊是誰？黃三泰、黃天霸父子的武藝又是出自哪個門派？早期恐怕祇有《兒女英雄傳》裡的「十三妹」何玉鳳有個師父鄧九公，因為何是女人——以一介女子而能身懷絕技是很難令那個時代的一般讀者接受的；是以非給她安插一位男性師父以絕疑杜口不可。此外，也祇在《七劍十三俠》中，我們發現了非常簡單的、尚未形成網絡的、甚至往往是分散的、一對一的師承關係。如：主人翁徐鳴皋有個師父

叫海鷗子，海鷗子又有六個道友，「皆是劍客俠士，平日各無定處，每年相聚一處，大家痛飲一回，再約後期。」

可是到了不肖生那裡，扛起了「此書取材，大率湘湖事實」的「立傳」的招牌，作者不得不爲數以百計的眾多角色之出現、遇合、交往等種種關係找到一個「合傳」的架構。他不能祇再大量依靠不相識的兩人巧遇酒樓，互慕對方「疊暴著英雄精神」、「器宇軒昂」，遂結成異姓兄弟的手段。再者，爲一個充斥著魑魅鬼蜮的芸芸眾生世界（一個結構原本鬆散的世界）添加一份寫實（大率事實）的要求，則非但巧合不足爲功，恐怕連那個假「前」爲因、假「後」爲果、令敍述結構彌補事件結構的書場慣技都未必足以應付，於是不肖生非另闢蹊徑不可。

這一條蹊徑是俠客的身世、來歷；俠客的辨認座標，一個系譜。俠不再是憑空從天而下的「機械降神」（*deus ex machina*）裝置（這個裝置要保留到重大磨難臨身之際讓俠客絕處逢生之用）；俠必須像常人一樣有他的血緣、親族、師承、交友或其它社會關係上的位置。此一系譜涵攝了幾個重要因素：其一，俠倫理構成，這個部分又包括俠對（通常是）父系自動承繼的種種能力、特質、恩情和仇恨的負債以及使命等等。其二，俠的教養構成，這個部分又包括俠從師門（或意外的教育和啓蒙者）被動承繼的特殊訓練、義務、身分和尊嚴的認定，以及社會關係和使命等等。以上兩個承繼關係讓身爲主人翁的俠比其它次要角色多了一個加速裝置，此一加速裝置使主人翁的行爲能力（武術、內功和知識）得以在其壯年時代（甚至青、少年時代）即已充盈飽滿、超越同儕乃至前輩。其三，俠的允諾構成，這個部分既容有來自父系和師門的道德教訓和正義規範，也包括了俠個人在其冒險經歷中所涉入與擔負的情感盟約、所發現和追求的理想抱負；而這個構成也往往和前兩個構成發生不可預期的衝突，突顯了個人與體制的決裂可能。這是由於允諾是有種種優先性考慮的──如：較早提出的允諾應比較晚提出的允諾具優先性、關乎大群體利害的允諾應比關乎私人利害的允諾具優先性、情感道義的允諾應比權益的允諾具優先性……等等；但是，質諸俠所面對的現實，這些優先性又常常彼此扞格繆輵。於是，俠的允諾構成，反而時時對他的倫理構成和教養構成提出挑戰、干擾和騷動。

這三個構成固然個別地、也點綴性地出現在中國古典小說敍事傳統之

中，起碼《小五義》和《續小五義》的主角們其實與《三俠五義》或《七俠五義》有著可以系聯的倫理構成；早在《西遊記》裡，吳承恩也敎孫悟空在靈台方寸山斜月三星洞須菩提祖師那裡迅速完成了他超凡入聖的法術敎養；甚至在《水滸傳》中，從「聚義廳」到「忠義堂」之轉變即已埋伏下一百單八將在誓義和效忠間的允諾衝突原型。但是，直要到一個奠基於「合傳」自覺與要求的不肖生手上，這三個構成才綿密地打造了眾多俠客的系譜；這系譜也果眞讓「傳主」看起來像活過的人——學經歷完整、情事理具足。

系譜的鬆散

　　厚達兩千頁的《江湖奇俠傳》所打造的百數十個俠的系譜原本祇是「崑崙」和「崆峒」兩派（練氣的劍派／練形的劍派）之間的勾鬥，根源於崑崙派的祖師金羅漢呂宣良在一次被迫之下的比武過程中以肩上的大鷹啄瞎崆峒派董祿堂的左眼取勝。日後兩派徒子徒孫又因種種巧合互涉恩仇。看似較屬「名門正派」的崑崙派自有行止不檢的後輩（如貫大元）；看似站在對立面的崆峒派亦有尚義任俠的傳人（如常德慶）。眾多人物亦如《儒林外史》般各於自己的「本傳」中獨當一面，管領風騷，並穿插藏閃於其他俠客的「本傳」以維繫整個合傳的系譜，形成彼此鞏固、支持的結構性力量。正是這個力量帶領讀者在閱讀過程中產生一目的性的疑問：崑崙派與崆峒派是否終將如全書第四回利用平江、瀏陽兩地鄉民爭趙家坪水陸碼頭的年度大決戰所隱喻的那樣——拚得一個你死我活的勝負？爭出一個魔消道長的是非？來一個圓滿的解決？

　　這個追求解決的目的性疑問，其實原來是不肖生打造的系譜必然會牽引出來的；因爲俠客各自的身世和來歷一經細節化的勾勒而納入系譜之後，他的結果就一如他的出身那樣不能不被納入系譜的辨識座標去解決。這也就是說：系譜中的俠的結局非在系譜中完成不可；甲俠和乙俠丙俠丁俠旣然分享一個糾結著複雜關係的出身和來歷，就不能祇有純屬甲俠個人的結局，他個人離開故事的解決至少要和乙丙丁諸俠有關。

　　可是不肖生不此之圖，非但未曾讓崑崙、崆峒兩派的大解決在趙家坪「畢其功於一役」，甚至原來幾乎是設計成爲一個了斷的紅蓮寺爭鋒也落了空。從

第七十一回起,他掉出筆鋒,幾乎盡棄兩派爭鬥,開始寫晚清四大奇案之一的「張汶祥刺馬(新貽)」故事,一寫十六回,幾至全書的五分之一,他的解釋(夾雜在七十一回正文之間)是:

> 因爲有刺殺馬心儀(按:不肖生在小說中改動了遇刺者兩江總督馬新貽的名字)那樁驚天動地的大案,前人筆記上很有不少的記載。並有編爲小說的,更有編爲戲劇的。不過那案在當時,因爲有許多忌諱,不但做筆記編小說戲劇的得不著實情,就得著了實情,也不敢照實做出來編出來。便是當時奉旨同審理張汶祥的人,除了刑部尚書鄭敦謹而外,所知道的供詞情節,也都是曾國藩一手遮天捏造出來的,與事實完全不對。在下因調查紅蓮寺的來由出處,找著鄭敦謹的女婿,爲當日在屏風後竊聽張汶祥供詞的人,才探得了一個究竟。這樣情節不照實記出來,一則湮沒了可惜,二則這一部奇俠傳,非有這一段情節加進去,荒唐詭怪的紅蓮寺未免太沒來由。因此儘管是婦孺皆知的張汶祥刺馬故事,也得不憚辭費,依據在下所探得的、從頭至尾寫出來,替屈死專制淫威下的英雄出一出氣。

不肖生這一大段作者現身自道的解釋主要就是在重申這部小說作爲社會或歷史實錄的「傳」的意義。他所間接聞之於鄭敦謹女婿的材料是否可靠?是否存眞?不肖生並不在意;他所要完成的是一個不同於官方、對立於專制、源出於民間的論述。這個論述是他一面寫奇俠合傳時才一面「調查探得」的,它不屬於原已具足的「布局」,前文自未預留「伏筆」;它更逸出了之前近一千六百頁正文所打造的系譜之外。相對於之前的故事,純屬那個說話人臨場橫生的「廢話」,而且,它絕對是全書的一大鬆散之處。這個大鬆散寫完之後,不肖生居然祇花了五頁多的篇幅草草交代了奇俠們火燒紅蓮寺的過節,然後說:

> 至於兩派的仇怨,直到現在還沒有完全消釋。不過在下寫到這裡,已不高興再延長寫下去了,暫且與看官們告別了。以中國之大,寫不盡的奇人奇事還不知有多少。等到一時興起,或者再寫幾部出來,給看官們消遣。

《江湖奇俠傳》就這麼結束了。不肖生剛發明了一個結構裝置,反手就終結了這個裝置——系譜,徒然提供後之評者一個離奇與鬆散的口實。在此,除了淺薄地指責不肖生無能之外,我們恐怕得回到前面提出的那個「解決」

上去看。

解決不了

「不高興寫下去」是不肖生留下來的一個謎。後人無從究竟得知：他是不高興些什麼？不過，張汶祥行刺馬新貽這個處處啓人疑竇的案子恐怕是不肖生整部《江湖奇俠傳》中最令作者難捺鬱忿不平之氣的一個部分；也是唯一現身再三，向「看官們」辯護他不得不「照實記出來」、「從頭至尾寫出來」的一個部分。不肖生甚至在八十六回中宣稱：他這部奇俠傳和施耐庵寫《水滸傳》以及曹雪芹寫《紅樓夢》不同，因爲這兩部書「都是從一條總線寫下來，所以不致有拋荒正傳、久寫旁文的弊病。」他也承認：自己這部奇俠傳（指的是第七十一至八十六回的大鬆散處）「所寫的人物，雖兼有不俠的，卻沒有不奇的。」如此一來，這十幾回內容竟然連俠字都擺脫了。

不肖生的「不高興」到此初露端倪：他在試著「調查探得」和「照實寫出」──也就是一個動機不在寫俠客奇遇，而是基於記錄、暴露、墾掘現實的書寫活動當中，發現他不能爲先前七十回辛苦建立的俠的系譜在小說裡面找到解決，因爲：

> 兩派的仇怨，直到現在還沒有完全消釋。

此處所說的「現在」，當然是指一九二〇年代不肖生寫作《江湖奇俠傳》已至終篇的那個現實的時間，上距同治九年（1870）的刺馬案已將半世紀。有趣的是：令不肖生阢隉不安的恐怕不是這近五十年間奇俠與奇俠之間的干戈擾攘未息，而是刺馬案這個從屬現實之中發生過的、不俠而奇的事件，如此逼真寫實地從他打造的俠的系譜之中延伸、迫近到不肖生這個作者的現實世界裡來。他原本那個「立傳」的基礎直到遇上刺馬案才眞正吻合「取材大率事實」的要求（因爲此案在上下數十年間一直是政壇、民間、媒體和藝文界不停挖探咀嚼的公認材料），可是它卻不能納入小說打造的系譜之中去解決；此案之懸而未解、解而未決、以至於決而不能平息物議，非但令不肖生試圖藉小說「出一出氣」；當它被納入小說之後又造成一龐大的累贅，因爲它與崑崙、崆峒兩派的系譜迥不相容──解決不了。

　　不肖生畢竟不是說話人，可以野草閑花、無罣無礙地「說廢話」，因為他不但沒有說話人那個臨場語境所容許的扯淡特權，還基於立傳需要而打造了一個畢現各個俠客出身和來歷的巨大系譜，以求其人「像一個個活過的人」。到頭來最像是「活過」的部分的確自行解決掉了；但是，四百多頁可說是「自生自滅」的內容卻「拋荒正傳」，摧毀了其他諸俠那個系譜。

系譜再現江湖

　　然而，系譜這個結構裝置畢竟為日後的武俠小說家接收起來，它甚至可以作為武俠小說這個類型之所以有別於中國古典公案、俠義小說的執照。一套系譜有時不祇出現在一部小說之中，它也可以同時出現在一個作家的好幾部作品之中。比方說：在寫了八十八部武俠小說的鄭證因筆下，《天南逸叟》、《子母離魂圈》、《五鳳朝陽》、《淮上風雲》等多部都和作者的成名鉅製共有同一套系譜。而一套系譜也不祇為一位作家所獨佔，比方說：金庸就曾經在多部武俠小說中讓他的俠客進駐崑崙、崆峒、丐幫等不肖生的系譜，驅逐了金羅漢、董祿堂、紅姑、甘瘤子，還為這個系譜平添上族祖的名諱。此外，金庸更擴大這系譜的規模，比方說：在《射鵰英雄傳》裡，他不祇接收了金羅漢兩肩上的一對大鷹，使之變種成白鵰，轉手讓郭靖、黃蓉飼養；還向《水滸傳》裡討來一位賽仁貴郭盛，向《岳傳》裡討來一位楊再興，權充郭靖、楊康的先人。至於《書劍恩仇錄》裡的乾隆、兆惠、《碧血劍》裡的袁崇煥、《射鵰英雄傳》裡的鐵木真父子和丘處機、《倚天屠龍記》裡的張三丰、《天龍八部》裡的鳩摩智……以迄於《鹿鼎記》中的康熙等等，無一不是擴大這系譜領域的棋子。

　　這些滾雪球一般越滾越大的系譜再也不像在不肖生那裡一樣、祇是讓傳主看起來彷彿一個個有身世的、來歷的、曾經活過的人；它們反而是在另行建構一個在大敍述、大歷史縫隙之間的世界，而想要讓大敍述、大歷史看起來像是這縫隙間的世界的一部分。這個輕微的差異其實顯示了一個重大的轉折：藉辭「立傳」、「取材大率事實」以寫離奇之人、離奇之事的企圖，轉變成讓傳奇收編史實的企圖。

　　至於陳世驤先生提出的那個問題：「要供出這樣一個可憐芸芸眾生的世

界，如何能不教結構鬆散？」我們祇能說：從武俠衍出的中國小說敘事傳統
從未因循「形式與內容的統一」而立法，無論是現實、史傳或傳奇，也都沒
有一個像建築物的類喻式結構。結構不是美學上的回答；它祇是說話人和小
說家爲了完成敘述而提出的種種假設。

《天龍八部》的傳奇結構

廖 朝 陽

國立臺灣大學外國語文學系

摘 要

　　《天龍八部》規模龐大，人物眾多，在佈局剪裁方面有許多地方似乎不甚嚴謹。其實如果捨棄寫實文類所服膺的亞理斯多德式密合結構觀，按照傳奇文類的特性來解釋，《天龍八部》的多線敘事較接近中世紀歐洲騎士傳奇與後來的傳奇史詩，自然不必遵守水平方向的敘事統一。歐洲傳奇的典型是「垂直透視」，也就是以意義的掩映重疊為中心，不重邏輯次序與水平連接。《天龍八部》在細節上不完全符合這個典型，而是透過人物意義的缺少發展，以及因此產生的，不合情理的突兀情節來架構另一個整體觀照的意義層次，產生「垂直透視」，同時也形成追求與拖延兩個層次同時存在，在等待、偏離中成就目標的傳奇結構。

　　佛經裡面的「天龍八部，人非人等」總是齊聚在佛前聽法，但是在有漏世界裡，他們仍舊各為不同的物類，成就佛法的途徑也各各不同。八種神道的獨立或孤立可以顯示，《天龍八部》的文化理想不在普遍化的道德自覺或同理心，而是在承受物類之身，面對物類本身不落常情常理的根本面，接受物類可以有絕對自主，非他人甚至也非自己所能臆測的選擇，並基於「異理心」，對其中不合常情常理的愚癡愛著寄予同情。佛經所說的無緣慈悲雖有願求卻無所攀緣，正是透過異理心的發揚來保存對象的特殊性，在超越特殊性的層次向平等溝通開放。《天龍八部》堅持人物癖性，對欲望驅力的自動反覆存而不化，使情節本身的現實性、合理性脫落於意義之外，形成兩截式的意義結構。本文以無崖子佈下的珍瓏棋局為例，說明其中產生許多敘事不合理之處，

其實是因爲書中其他部分的意義框架不斷滲入、干擾，沒有一個分離的「頂層」觀點就無法解釋得周全。這就是「依義不依語，依智不依識」。另外，段延慶發現段譽是自己的兒子，放棄對大理國帝位的主張，情節頗似英國史詩《仙后》裡無常女神向天帝朱彼德要求讓位的故事。兩個故事都呈現了正義與惡的密切關連，並且用「垂直透視」來解決惡的存在：自然含有無常的垂直對映，段譽則是段延慶的垂直對映。兩者都指向認知世界的大轉變，接近西谷啓治所說的大死，是無緣慈悲的拖延與顯現。

按哈瑪赫對班雅民的解釋，律法的施行是宣成性動作，純粹暴力或毀法暴力則是開成性動作，是成立各種宣成動作，同時也超乎其外，可以中斷或取消律法的力量。從無緣慈悲的觀點看，段譽的不入俗緣包孕、安置了虛竹與蕭峯的入世意義。從暴力與權力的觀點看，段譽處於毀法暴力的核心，是脫序可能性的顯露點，而虛竹對執法暴力的堅持與蕭峯對制法暴力的駕馭與克服各以不同的方式維持了敍事秩序，緩和了直接面對毀法暴力的壓迫感。所以段譽的福報不能單純的用「傻人有傻福」之類的說法來解釋，而是顯示出敍事過程在淺顯的層次從俗，在隱密的層次歸眞。只有這樣看，我們才能回歸傳奇結構的文類特性，掌握意義的多重疊覆，了解到《天龍八部》含有對權力的純粹形式的理解與批判，已經超出律法的斡旋而隱隱指向毀法暴力。

> 俗不定俗，俗名眞俗；眞不定眞，眞名俗眞。
>
> ——吉藏，《二諦義》112a
>
> 結構不會，也不該，走上街頭。結構並不屬於日常生活裡
> 構成現實的種種關係，而是屬於眞實的層次。
>
> —— Copjec 1994: 11

一

金庸的小說《天龍八部》規模龐大，人物眾多，在敍事上轉換焦點的幅度特別大是很自然的。段譽、蕭峯、虛竹在書中不同部分分別佔有主要角色的位置、當然可以說是針對多元化內容進行敍事管理必然產生的結果。但是

情節的交互迴環在這裡似乎不僅是一個佈局剪裁的問題、而是涉及人物癖性的獨立發展與不可溝通。雖然第四十一回後寫蕭峯率燕雲十八騎趕上少室山，展開蕭峯、段譽、虛竹聯手對抗群雄，丁春秋潰敗，慕容博、蕭遠山現身，無名老僧說法點化等情節，重要人物幾乎到齊，算是對全書各段落作了一大收束，但是在這場「八音繁會」的總結之後，蕭峯等三人仍將分別走向各自不同的最後結局，而慕容復、鳩摩智乃至大理段氏家族的恩怨以及遼漢之爭也還有待解決。這就像佛經裡面的「天龍八部，人非人等」總是齊聚在佛前聽法，但是一旦回到有漏世界，他們仍舊各為不同的物類，成就佛法的途徑也各各不同。即使接近「廢權顯實」立場的《大佛頂首楞嚴經》卷六也透過觀世音菩薩的自敍肯定物類的特殊性：

> 若有諸天，樂出天倫，我現天身而為說法，令其成就。若有諸龍，樂出龍倫，我現龍身而為說法，令其成就。……若諸非人，有形無形，有想無想，樂度其倫。我於彼前皆現其身，而為說法，令其成就。(129a)

這裡的意思顯然是說：說法已經是第二義的溝通，身像的跨越、移轉與對映才能根本消去物類之間的距離，撐起語言層次的意義傳遞。但是身像的幻化是菩薩的神通，就世俗意義來說等於是不可能實現的終極假設，也構成語言意義的黑洞。

要談《天龍八部》的結構，這個不同物類（在世俗意義上）終究不可溝通的原則是不可放過的重點。據說《天龍八部》代表金庸從比較狹隘的民族主義轉向「國際主義」及「和平主義」的超然觀點（陳墨 1997: 239）。其實八種神道的獨立或孤立正顯示，民族間的和平不但不是建立在追求融合、同化的「熔爐」觀念上，也不能簡化成中國儒家「淨除私累」，「化成世界」的道德自覺（羅龍治 1997b: 50）或普同化的「超然的同情」（溫瑞安 1997: 192），而是必須以接受個別性，承認民族身像不可跨越為前提。這就是為什麼小說描寫蕭峯跨越了民族界限，卻仍然處處顯露出不願抹煞民族特殊性的消息：「只有契丹人才有蕭峯這樣的英雄」（陳墨 1997: 242）。即使就善惡的界限來說，阿紫的故事的確帶有無限的同情：「凡是不解同情阿紫的人……亦不會自覺他自己生命黑暗的痛苦」（羅龍治 1997a: 43），但是如果只用「如果你是阿紫，你也會如何如何」這樣「設身處地」的同理心來為阿紫辯護，就不能

眞正切入阿紫的身像(總是有人會說：即使我是阿紫，我也不會或不該那樣；而另外有些人會說：如果你是被阿紫所害的人，你就會知道眞正値得同情的人是誰)，只有承受阿紫之身，以阿紫就是阿紫，再無其他條件的認知來面對她不落常情常理的根本面，才能接受她可以有絕對自主，非他人甚至也非自己所能臆測的選擇，而在這樣的選擇脫離道德常規，造成他人與自己的痛苦時，也才能基於「異理心」，對其中與常情常理根本「不同」的愚癡愛著寄予同情。

如果我們把這裡的阿紫換成近年來臺灣的首號罪犯陳進興，我們就可以了解到：在閱讀動作裡極易用常情常理說明的精緻文化價値(同理心、寬恕、同情等等)在面對現實世界時是多麼脆弱(任何針對犯罪行爲所作的解釋只要有一點點爲罪犯「設身處地」的嫌疑，立即會招來主流輿論「將犯罪行爲合理化」的無情抨擊)。這裡從相反的角度提出「異理心」的說法，並不是要否定同理心在一定的應用範圍內(通常就是在同類之間)有其文化價値，而是要指出一旦涉及絕對的惡(差異)，陷入意義的黑洞，同理心往往就會變成避免面對道德矛盾的托辭；在陳進興的例子裡，罪犯選任辯護人之權根本不受主流價値肯定(罪犯或罪犯家屬的辯護律師常被冠予污名，成爲「魔鬼」)，因爲這樣的罪犯已經「不是人」，也不得與人「同理」。另一方面，一旦陳進興成爲訪談分析的對象，使「設身處地」成爲可能公開傳佈的議題，罪犯「也有隱私權」卻立即被搬出來，封死黑洞(陳進興的世界)的進出口，因爲相較於黑洞的絕對乖離以及把黑洞誤認爲平地的危險，罪犯權利的評斷到底是較易用言語戲論來沖淡的問題。異理心的解釋直接承認異類之間不可溝通，至少不會落入閃避黑洞的盲點，也比較符合《天龍八部》與佛教思想的淵源。

佛經裡把慈悲分成三種：「緣於五陰願與其樂」，「如緣父母妻子親屬」，這是眾生緣慈悲；「緣諸眾生所須之物而施與之」，「不見父母妻子親屬見一切法，皆從緣生」，這是法緣慈悲；「緣於如來」，「不住法相及眾生相」，這是無緣慈悲(《大般涅槃經》452c)。眾生緣慈悲以人爲對象，法緣慈悲以事理爲對象，無緣慈悲則「無對象」(中村元 1956: 105)。眾生緣慈悲是以同理心爲基礎(我與對象認同)，法緣慈悲已經轉向異理心，分出施與者與受施與者(法)的層次，但還只是我與對象的分離相對；到了無緣慈悲，我與對象已經隔絕不相對，卻無損於慈悲的存在，「譬如日月不作往來照明之心。以諸

眾生福德力故。自行往反壞諸暗冥」（延壽 528a 引），所以無緣慈悲雖無對象卻反而能「心無分別，普救一切」（陳義孝 1996「三種慈悲」條）。這樣的慈悲觀念本身就形成斷裂的兩截式結構：如果慈是願使生樂，悲是願使離苦，那麼有願求卻無所攀緣，一方面是失去對象而無助於物類之間的溝通，可能成為無法落實的空談，另一方面卻也因為不攀緣而更能保存對象的特殊性，「雖觀無相，不捨大悲」（《大乘理趣六波羅蜜多經》909c），反而在更高的層次向平等溝通開放。在《天龍八部》裡，這兩個層次的斷裂是敘事結構的基礎，也使敘事本身因為不避私累（特殊性）反而超越了張牙舞爪的「化成世界」的層次。例如段譽的北冥神功與丁春秋的化功大法在形式上沒有什麼差別，小說把兩者定位為一正一邪，原本極為勉強，直到鳩摩智因錯學少林絕技，在即將走火入魔之際卻誤打誤撞，被段譽吸去功力而留下性命，才在一個更高的層次顯示出正邪觀念的本身就是一種簡化：化功大法在能化與所化兩方面都只有功力得失、消長的單一考量，而北冥神功卻因為段譽的不求甚解而時靈時不靈，也就是「化」不去特殊情境的偶然因素，反而能各因其類，演變出種種不同的結果。

這樣的兩截式層次分斷是歐洲文學裡寓言解釋成立多重意義的觀念基礎，卻不必然會表現為明確的寓言結構。另一方面，這裡的層次區分既然無所攀緣，自然也不會與單一層次的解釋形成衝突，而是以至柔的巧勁，容受各種對立的解釋，為種種特殊性的呈現求得安置，「為其成就」。例如陳世驤在一九六六年四月二十四日致金庸的信函中提到，《天龍八部》一書因為結構「稍鬆散」，「人物個性及情節太離奇」，在愛好者當中難免受到批評。而陳氏則常為之辯護：

> 書中的人物情節，可謂無人不冤，有情皆孽，要寫到盡致非把常人常情都寫成離奇不可；書中的世界是朗朗世界到處藏著魍魎的鬼蜮，隨時予以驚奇的揭發與諷刺，要供出這樣一個可憐芸芸眾生的世界，如何能不教結構鬆散？這樣的人物情節和世界，背後籠罩著佛法的無邊大超脫，時而透露出來。而在每逢動人處，我們會感到希臘悲劇理論中所謂恐怖與憐憫，再說句更陳腐的話，所謂「離奇與鬆散」，大概可叫做「形式與內容的統一」罷。（1966: 2486f）

這段評論引用亞里斯多德的文學觀念，當然說得過於簡單，未必真有意思要

建立一種解釋的原則。另一方面，這樣的比附卻也不見得只有「陳腐」，反而可能含有深刻的洞見，並且潛藏著一些文類區分的問題，隱約顯露出古老的西方批評觀念與《天龍八部》之間可以形成相當複雜的緊張關係。比如說，這裡的形式與內容似乎分別指的是鬆散的結構與離奇的人物情節，那麼統一指的似乎就該是鬆散與離奇的整合。但是這裡首先遇到的問題就是：如果鬆散與離奇具有同質性（離奇之事無所不在而無法求得條理，使敘事不得不鬆散），那麼兩者的整合應該是加倍鬆散，加倍離奇，而形式與內容之間應該也要形成鬆散，也就是離奇的關係，根本不應該是合理、統一。反過來說，如果鬆散與離奇是對立的（既然「常人常情都寫成離奇」，那麼離奇是不變的規律，是鬆散的反面），那麼形式與內容的統一指的只能是離奇壓倒鬆散，而這樣的統一本身也要克服鬆散，所以也必須以令人「驚奇」為先決條件，也就是說，要先成立不統一的鬆散關係，再用統一來壓倒不統一，但是這樣的結果片面揚升「離奇」、「驚奇」的面向，顯然只能重覆、加深小說內容所描寫的冤孽而沒有超脫可言。

　　這些矛盾的產生都是因為「統一」的原則不但必須用於內容與形式兩種對象，也必須「以己之道，還施己身」，用於內容與形式之間的關係，所以陳世驤的解釋如果還能成立，顯然就必須以「形式與內容的統一」這一層次兩離內容與形式，獨立於對象之外，不受對象拘束，從而封死「自作自受」的可能為前提。這樣一來，解釋也就回歸兩截式層次分斷的整體結構，雖然講的仍舊是整合、統一，卻已經不是原先那種一氣呵成的古典式單截密合體，而是把鬆散離奇看成魍魎鬼蜮的悲苦壓抑，把藝術的統一看成朗朗世界的得救狀態的雙重解釋了。按照現代批評理論對古典觀念的引申，形式與內容不可分離「與鮮血與鮮血當中的生命不可分離一樣」，兩者「既不分別存在，也不能想像成分別存在」，評論者可以從各種不同的角度來拆解、分析這個密合體，但是就終極價值來說，任何評論都只能以「重演」這個密合整所產生出來的，不可分割的整體經驗，使它「更豐富，更真實，更深刻」為理想（Bradley 1909: 705）。而如果上述鬆散與離奇如果要統一，就必然要以另立一個分離的觀點為前提的講法可以成立，那麼不但鬆散與離奇都是可以分別觀察的經驗，「統一」的要求顯然也不能「重演」鬆散或離奇以免變成自己的反面。所以陳世驤的評論雖然是以「陳腐」的古典密合體語言來陳述，其實卻是在最

富洞見的地方「重演」了小說本身的分斷結構。在後來的評論者當中，承接這個古典解釋路線（特別是「恐怖與憐憫」背後的希臘悲劇理論）的並不乏人（如溫瑞安 1997: 190ff），而小說的分斷結構似乎也頗能體現無緣慈悲的寬大，並不排斥這類來自特殊價值的文學觀，對冤孽與超脫的差別也沒有明確的堅持。一方面，各類「統派」解釋的確有許多發揮的餘地，並不會在細節的閱讀上遭遇結構性的困難；另一方面，細節解釋背後的層次分斷被排除於認知之外而成為無意識，也因為個人閱讀經驗過度密合，只能不斷「重演」自己而不能對外溝通，反而造成各種意義的歧出與不確定。

二

　　但是小說畢竟是俗緣的鉤連會聚，不求甚解到底不是敘事閱讀的常規。《天龍八部》含有無緣慈悲的觀照，雖然產生了超出俗緣之外的層次而在充滿悲憫的難捨中捨離了抹煞物類特殊性的我慢，在解釋方面產生的問題卻會妨礙到文化意義的形成。也就是說，無所攀緣不能成為解釋者不作為的藉口，而是必須保留一個跨越身像、開放溝通的層次，為各類解釋者的癖性留下轉變的可能。就佈局剪裁來說，陳世驤的解釋對意義重疊的重要性還有相當深入的認知，陳世驤之後的評論者卻往往走向純粹形式的考量：有人認為《天龍八部》的多線敘事不是問題，因為其中的無數人物各有所屬，「也不難理出一個頭緒來」（吳靄儀 1998: 309），甚至有人說小說的結構「嚴密已極，前後呼應十分緊密」，「在整部鉅構千絲萬縷的情節中，每項情節的接筍互應仍脈絡分明」（溫瑞安 1997: 103, 106）。其實這樣的辯護（甚至問題的提法）對密合式統一的觀念毫不置疑，可以說並不能抓住解釋工作的困難點。通俗小說雖然可以有系統化的意義托寓，在敘事形式的層次來說到底並不是八股文或哲學論文；它吸引人的地方並不在起承轉合的進退合度，對稱平衡，也不在整體間架的綱舉目張，條理分明。以西方的敘事文類來說，《天龍八部》的多線敘事較接近中世紀歐洲文學裡的騎士傳奇（chivalric romance）與後來的傳奇史詩，特別是敘事結構也曾引起長期爭議的文藝復興時期義大利史詩。但是在歐洲文學裡，即使是從現代讀者的角度來為傳奇辯護，重點也不在多重敘事線的穿插合度，而是透過敘事的穿插與分派產生出來的對照意義。也

就是說，因爲文字敍述在同一時間只能有一個對象，多線分敍其實是任何敍事文類都會碰到的問題，所以就傳奇來說，何處「接筍」、是否前後呼應等等敍事管理的細節其實只是較不重要的技術性考量；傳奇結構往往在分敍之上再產生一個交織（entrelacement）的層次，才是其特點所在：

> 一個人物的故事告一段落之後我們離開他，轉向其他人物，經過許多事件之後才接回第一段，而這時因爲插入許多事件，使得原先人物的心理狀態或成立意義的條件受到牽引，當他再度出現時早已不能接回原點。不僅如此，中斷原先的敍事而插入另一段，雖然看起來是偏離了主題，就最後結果而論如果不是這乍看似乎毫不相干的，「偏離主題」的第二條敍事線加入了某種東西，原先的敍事線根本就接不下去。（Tuve 1966: 363）

這個傳奇文學的著名解釋隱藏著不少問題（例如第二條敍事線是否純粹只是爲第一條敍事線服務），這裡無法詳細討論；《天龍八部》雖然也可能找出類似意義交織的例子（如蕭峯早出場卻令人懾服，慕容復晚出場卻虎頭蛇尾所形成的對照），其實卻不十分符合這裡局部意義交織的要求。這並不是說《天龍八部》完全不同於歐洲的傳奇；它的兩截式層次分斷主要來自佛家思想（參見吳靄儀 1998: 308, 314），卻符合歐洲傳奇「垂直透視」的敍事表現。所謂「垂直透視」不只是善惡、貴賤等等「道德或精神秩序的上下面向」（Macpherson 1990: 620b），而是由意義的掩映重疊所產生的表述結構：寫實文類重視邏輯次序與水平連接，關心的是如何「把我們帶進故事的結局」，而傳奇文類則喜歡「在一連串互不相關的事件中折騰挪移，似乎想要把我們帶到故事的頂層」（Frye 1976: 49f）。如果意義交織只是「垂直透視」的一種呈現方式，那麼我們就可以說《天龍八部》其實是以與意義交織幾乎完全相反的方式，透過人物意義的缺少發展，以及因此產生的，不合情理的突兀情節來架構另一個整體觀照的意義層次，產生「垂直透視」。

　　這是個極重要的原則，下面我們就以無崖子佈下的珍瓏棋局爲例，作較詳細的說明。大家都知道，這個棋局難倒諸大高手，是因爲它像一面鏡子：「這個珍瓏變幻百端，因人而施，愛財者因貪失誤，易怒者由憤壞事。段譽之敗，在於愛心太重，不肯棄子；慕容復之失，由於執著權勢，勇於棄子，卻說什麼也不肯失勢……」（金庸 1997: 7.1533）。虛竹所以能破解棋局，是因爲

他志在救人，對棋局本身心無繫絆，胡亂在白棋活氣處下了一子，自己擠死一大塊活棋，卻反而因易於迴旋而取得優勢，成為破解珍瓏的關鍵。這段描寫結合棋理、佛理、心理、事理等多重意義層次，也透過如實照映、無所攀緣的鏡子比喻串連了書中各有癖性的幾個主要角色，是全書敘事的高點之一，也是文學史上不可多得的精彩場面。但是仔細觀察，即使是這樣自成段落的描寫其實也不甚「統一」，而其主要原因則是書中其他部分的意義框架不斷滲入、干擾，產生了情節不能隨常理而變的現象，沒有一個分離的「頂層」觀點就無法解釋得周全。例如首先下場的段譽與蘇星河推演了十餘手棋，結果無法破解，雙方各將所下棋子撿起，「棋局上仍然留著原來的陣勢」（1521），這是一般解珍瓏的正當程序。中間慕容復試解，不由蘇星河應對而是鳩摩智代下黑棋，雖然違反遊戲規則，倒還可以說是兩人隨興，蘇星河也不拘泥；書中沒有提到慕容復下完收拾棋子，也可以說是敘事者百忙之中無暇顧及細節（虛竹看到段延慶下的一著棋與慕容復相同，怕他「重蹈覆轍」，說明了段延慶解棋之前棋盤應有恢復原狀，見 1531）。到了虛竹出手，自殺大塊白子，救了即將走火入魔的段延慶，蘇星河卻問他下一手如何下，要求他非下完不可（1537），擺明了是虛竹接著段延慶下，也就是可以合兩人之力破解棋局，或者說虛竹破解的已經是無崖子的珍瓏加上段延慶已下的著手。這樣的改變可以說完全打破了段譽解棋時的遊戲規則，顯得逍遙派選取新掌門的程序不夠嚴謹。

　　讀者在這裡當然也可以有種種合理化的解釋：例如我們可以說虛竹自己下的一手棋是能否破解珍瓏的關鍵，其他皆是次要，或者說觀棋者本來就可以重覆前人的部份著手，或者說時間緊迫，規則可以變通等等。但是接下來段延慶以傳音入密的功夫指點虛竹下到終局，讓在場的旁觀者都以為是虛竹在下棋，顯然表示虛竹是否獨力解完珍瓏仍是重要的考量。唯一比較行得通的解釋是認定虛竹擠死自己的下法已經使段延慶先前的著手（以及蘇星河的回手）大半成為虛著，與第一手就擠死自己沒有實質上的差別；也只有這樣才能解決後來虛竹向天山童姥覆局，「當下第一子填塞一眼，將自己的白棋脹死了一大片」的矛盾（1728）。另一方面，這樣的解釋其實已經走向極端，事理上極偏僻，敘述上也需要更明確的說明。更重要的是：種種針對「邏輯次序與水平連接」來強化情節密合度的解釋都只能保守或修補敘事的條理，不

能進一步彰顯情境的必然性，就像解珍瓏的人心中只看到著手如何連接，走向何種結局，反而不能像虛竹那樣，捨棄水平方向的考慮，直接用擠死自己來改寫整個棋局，「不著意於生死……反而勘破了生死」（1541）。那麼這裡解釋者是否能勘破水平面向的現實情理呢？正因為《天龍八部》遵循的是傳奇結構，這裡虛竹的遭遇含有另一個意義層次其實是顯而易見的。按虛竹所見，段延慶的著手前三輪應該與慕容復的解法相同，然後黑白雙方又下了二十餘子，這時玄難插話說：「段施主，你起初十著走的是正道，第十一著起，走入旁門，越走越偏，再也難以挽救了。」這個觀察既是由玄難說出，自然也可能含有私見，但是接下來段延慶由棋局聯想到改習旁門左道的「生平第一恨事」，心神動搖，顯然表示他的解法的確反映了他的心事，客觀來說的確是「旁門」（1533）；如此虛竹解棋不但接受了段延慶這個天下第一大惡人的指引，其實一開始走的（或延續的）就已經是「旁門」。這樣的描寫具有必然性，是因為虛竹後來遇到天山童姥，被迫連犯殺戒、淫戒、葷戒、酒戒，甚至成為靈鷲宮主人，按和尚的規矩來說的確是走入邪道。如果要繼續引申，我們甚至可以說虛竹的出身（少林寺玄慈方丈與葉二娘的「冤孽」）在這裡已經可以看出端倪。這就是意義不能輕易「化」去，不能隨常理而變的關節所在：這裡的安排可以用種種方式來改寫，使情節的發展更合理，但是就傳奇結構的要求來說，不論何種改寫都不能化去段延慶與虛竹的癖性，也就是不能化去虛竹延續段延慶的「旁門左道」，從而預先「演出」他的未來遭遇這樣的意義層次。不能化去，是因為這是傳奇文類的趣味（也算是癖性）所在，大部分讀者既然接受了珍瓏棋局的誇大虛構，其實已經樂在其中，並不會注意到棋局進行中還有種種不合理之處。如果把這一段改寫成正常合理的棋局，卻失去意義的覆蓋與掩映，反而才會令人覺得味同嚼蠟，這或許就是佛經所說的「依義不依語，依智不依識」了（見《大般涅槃經》401b）。

解珍瓏這一段還有一個類似的破綻值得一提，就是慕容復「執著權勢，勇於棄子，卻說什麼也不肯失勢」這樣的說法。其實就棋理來說，勢是未實現但可以透過棋形來實現的利，是落子對鄰接空目的取得能力或外圍敵子的攻擊能力，通常只有在佈局階段或中盤之初，盤面落子不多，尚有大塊空地的時候才會有是否取勢的考量。無崖子的珍瓏擺了二百餘子，「一盤棋已下得接近完局」（1522），所以不論如何棄子，都只能在死活上與敵方交換，不可

能取勢。即使這裡「不肯失勢」的「勢」可以解成別的意思（如純粹佔先），敘事者對慕容復的評語也不符合前面的敘述：慕容復所以陷入幻境，拔劍自刎，幾乎喪命，是因爲鳩摩智的詰問：「慕容公子，你連我在邊角上的糾纏也擺脫不了，還想逐鹿中原麼？」（1528）但是一方面既然盤面已經「接近完局」，珍瓏的重點是在全局各處棋塊的死活攻殺，佈局階段先佔邊角，再圖中原之分在這裡根本沒有意義；另一方面如果慕容復真的是「邊角上的糾纏也擺脫不了」，那麼他顯然沒有放棄邊角的死活（邊角易圍地而不利於發展，往邊角取勢是極難採信的構想），後面「勇於棄子」的說法也就不能成立了。這個破綻解釋起來比虛竹的第一手棋還要困難，但是讀者通常也不會覺得有何不妥，因爲這裡的重點仍然不在事件的合情合理或前後連貫，而是在慕容復的癖性既然如此，那麼珍瓏的鏡子照出來的他也就應該如此。我們甚至可以說，慕容復到最後既然倒行逆施，寧可一掌擊斃忠心的家臣包不同也要與他早就認定是「天下一害」的段延慶（1534）結盟，締結一個雙方都顯然不會遵守的約定，那麼在這段描寫裡他不論是既不敢棄子，又無能取勢，還是自認爲只是不敢，其實總是無能，或者是認定還在佈子，不知已過中盤，豈不也都是在透過敘事的不連貫，預演後來他的無理與倒錯？也就是說，就算是這樣的錯誤人物闖進了這樣的錯誤敘事，其實也算是得其所哉，也符合「形式與內容統一」的要求。這樣的分斷統一自然是古典密合體的觀念萬萬不能接受的，對傳奇來說這卻是敘事條理的自虛如竹，是特殊性的存而不化，也是閱讀與解釋的樂趣所在。

　　虛竹與慕容復的例子都涉及個人癖性的預演，在意義上卻不追求意義的交織，而是隔空發力，預先將人物納入固定的框架。因爲有層次的分隔，這並不會造成意義的單調化或平面化。按金庸的自述，這一點大約可以用個性統一「容易加深印象」來解釋（盧玉瑩 1985: 27），但是《天龍八部》裡人物的一致性其實是超越了統一閱讀印象的層次，而是透過不斷重覆人物癖性的要求，成爲一種含有「支配力」的形式，與多變的內容（服膺現實原則的敘事情境）形成對抗關係（參見 Frye 1976: 35），並且在頑固與變化的對峙與互動中產生解釋分歧，設立意義空間。這樣的運作與歐洲文學裡的傳奇形成有趣的對比，卻仍然暗合其基本精神。如果說歐洲傳奇的敘事過程常常突顯自我定位的不確定，只有在「『從前從前』之前與『兩人永遠快樂的生活在一起』

之後」才有固定的自我認知可言 (54)，那麼《天龍八部》透過超穩定的人物一致性來架構敍事過程，在一定程度上是顛倒了這個原則。但是從另一個角度看，這裡所謂自我定位的不確定指的是人物定位轉換過程中的意義變化，所以其中的複雜性並不是來自心理現實或複雜的「人性」，而是由「程式化人物」到「心理原型」的擴張，往往散發出與現實主義小說人物不同的，「主體凝聚力的光彩」(Frye 1957: 304)。我們甚至可以說，歐洲傳奇的角色不重行動、事件，而是意義編派的一部分，是善惡爭戰過程中各種變化場面的「記錄器」(Jameson 1981: 112)。比較起來，《天龍八部》人物的一致性建立在特殊癖性上，雖然符合寓言體人物專一偏執的正格 (Fletcher 1964)，就心理反應來說反而比較接近（甚至過度接近）現實世界裡的具體個人。例如蕭峯部份前半段也是一個自我定位不確定，不知道自己是誰的故事，但是蕭峯沒有變成程式化人物或「原型」，他的個人特質與文化意義（俠義英雄、勇猛的契丹人）也始終不變，甚至可以說他的身分問題仍然是一致性太強引起的；情況與蕭峯相近的慕容復完全沒有受到「非我族類，其心必異」的猜忌，下場也完全不同，可見蕭峯的命運與他的癖性仍有相當的關係。如此說來，我們似乎可以說《天龍八部》是透過人物的頑固癖性來製造敍事內容的變化，而典型的歐洲傳奇則是透過人物典型的凝聚與擴張來突顯、引發或強化主體內部的裂變，但是兩者都含有分歧與對抗，都偏向「垂直透視」的層次分離，與單截式的寫實小說不同。就歐洲傳奇來說，不論是多線交織還是典型化的主體凝聚都是敍事過程化不掉過剩的意義，使局部意義溢出原解、顛覆人物的一致性，也就是另立層次的結果。《天龍八部》的人物癖性則是敍事過程化不掉欲望驅力的自動反覆，使情節本身的現實性、合理性脫落於意義之外，形成兩截式的意義結構。

所以《天龍八部》的人物框架雖然頑固，它的敍事變化並不會受到影響，因爲它的變化並不以人物的發展，而是以意義本身的重疊（陳世驤所說的「離奇」）爲重心。如果不拘泥歐洲傳奇意義交織或人物典型化的具體表現方式，回歸多線敍事在分述之外附加意義，形成「垂直透視」的大方向，我們仍然可以說《天龍八部》比較符合傳奇文類的基本結構而不是亞里斯多德式的統一觀。如果是這樣，那麼小說在佈局剪裁方面引起的爭議或許還是應該回到意義層次的問題來求解。也就是說，這裡的敍事所以不符合部份現代讀者的

期望，必須看成是意義交疊（大體上就是人物形式與情境內容的對抗）產生的解釋分歧，而不是人物情節的編排穿插有何不妥。例如敘事的嚴謹並不能解釋段譽為什麼會在小說前段屢逢奇遇，到江南之後卻過度「嚴謹」，在很長的一段時間內淪為單戀王語嫣的跟屁蟲，在武功、性格、動作、言語方面毫無發展變化，或者慕容復為什麼聰明一世，在其父受無名僧點化之後卻倒行逆施，完全僵化為失去現實感的復國機器。反過來說，敘事的不嚴謹當然也不能解釋這種人物自動記憶、還原、回歸固定狀態的現象。這類困難其實都是對文類本身的癖性沒有認知，不能就文類本身的特殊性來看文類所導致的結果。只有承認傳奇敘事基於層次分斷的結構性偏向，雖與其他敘事類型相通卻不講求面面俱到，才能認清《天龍八部》敘事觀點超脫俗緣的所在。

三

那麼敘事觀點的超脫如何解決人物癖性不可溝通，人世冤孽「化」不去的問題呢？這就要回到前面提過的身像跨越了。佛經講本生緣都是「過去久遠」、「無量世時」的事、其中的時空轉換都是不能用現實感去衡量的。《楞嚴經》所謂「現天身」、「現龍身」等等當然也涉及緩慢的果報與漫長的等待，幾乎沒有當世變回原身的可能，不像阿朱的化妝術那樣，只在片刻之間就要達成目的。如果我們把傳奇敘事裡的層次分斷往前再推一步，把其中的敘事過程看成追求與拖延兩個層次同時存在，在等待、偏離中成就目標（Parker 1979: 4），那麼不論是人物典型的似立而非立還是癖性的欲化而不化，都可以說是為了終結時間而陷入時間，呼應了身像跨越未度他人先失己身的背反。但是傳奇文類所以是「充滿異質性，而且不受現實原則拘束的敘事空間」，所以能「感知不一樣的歷史節奏」，並且突破現狀，「接受奇才異能，實現改造世界的理想」（Jameson 1981: 104），正是因為跨越者的等待本來就是參與癖性，反抗常情常理的偏離，本來就含有改變認知習慣的強烈顛覆力。亞瑟王傳奇裡的騎士到處漫遊，並不否定尋找聖杯始終是唯一的終極追求，也就是偏離與成就兩個面向並行不悖。《天龍八部》裡的無名老僧也說「佛法在求渡世，武功在求殺生，兩者背道而馳，相互剋制」，但是「慈悲之念越盛，武功絕技才能練得越多」（10.2120），目標與過程在背反中也含有接合。

　　如果就小說來求解，那麼段延慶的惡無可逃避，最後卻在段譽母親刀白鳳告訴他段譽其實是他兒子之後產生了現實感的大轉換，使他的惡業在等待中脫落於現實之外，以存而不化告終，是似反非反，欲渡未渡最明顯的例子。段延慶的反叛其實很像史賓色《仙后》第七卷殘篇裡無常女神（Mutabilitie）大鬧天庭的故事。無常是巨神族（Titans）的後代，當初巨神之祖將統治權讓給弟弟農神（Saturn），條件是農神必須吃掉所有子嗣，還位於兄，結果朱彼德（Jove）出生後被母親用計藏起來，逃過劫難，後來就篡位當了天帝，並且平定巨神族的反亂。無常認為自己是巨神之祖的嫡嗣，農神父子以不正當的手段取得權力，應該讓位給她，於是一路發飆，從人間打到月宮，再闖入天庭，逼得朱彼德不得不下令讓使神寫下狀紙，要求自然大神出面仲裁（Spenser 1977: 7.vi.1-35）。最後她雖然向自然大神證明天地萬物無一能逃過無常變易，所以她有資格取回帝位，自然大神卻只簡短的回覆她；雖然萬物無常，但「本態常駐無變化；歷變自體成其大」；當時間終結，萬物必將回歸正格，永駐不變，所以原告主張不能成立（vii.58）。這個判決引用了（新）柏拉圖式的理念不變說，承接了布伊覺思（Boethius）對天命的解釋，同時也回歸目標（變易的終結、永恆的到來）無限拖延的傳奇結構。段延慶的情況與無常稍有不同：他是大理國太子，因國內變亂，皇帝被弒而出逃，亂平後因為太子失蹤，只好由領導平亂的堂兄繼位（金庸 1997: 2.376）。數年後他習武有成，帶傷回國，發現帝位已經傳給另一個堂兄，新皇帝「寬仁愛民，很得民心……誰也不會再來記得前朝這個皇太子。如果他貿然在大理現身，勢必有性命之憂」。這時他走投無路，幾乎失去求生意志，在絕望中遇到刀白鳳因不滿丈夫風流而捨身相就。他以為是觀音菩薩點化，遠走他方養傷，並苦練武功，成為「四大惡人」之首（10.2350-54）。後來他屢次想憑武功強行要回王位，都未成功，最後發現刀白鳳在他一次回國時懷了一個孩子，也就是即將成為太子的段譽，所以他不必復位也等於可以復位：「我雖不做皇帝，卻也如做皇帝一般」，終於解開心結，飄然而去（2384）。

　　無常女神與段延慶的故事相近之處倒不完全在情節的類似，而是在兩者都呈現了正義與惡的密切關連，並且用「垂直透視」來解決惡的存在。無常得到許多禮遇（朱彼德惑於她的美色當然也有關係），她的法統主張符合當時歐洲王朝處理繼承權的慣例，自然大神也承認萬物皆受無常節制，但是她的

造反卻危及整個宇宙秩序，幾乎可以視爲天下第一大惡神。《仙后》這裡的處理涉及英國都鐸王朝的統治法理，呼應了政治學裡國家與暴力的弔詭關係，使得無常盲目的毀滅力「散發出某種極端邪惡的意味」（見 McCabe 1989: 202, 209）。段延慶雖然表現了皇室氣質，做事比較有原則，跟丁春秋甚至慕容復比起來惡性其實並不重大，但小說以他爲四大惡人之首，外號「惡貫滿盈」，如果跳脫敍事是否嚴密的考量，正可以視爲小說對統治權力與暴力之間的關係表達了類似史賓色的立場。也就是說，段延慶的惡不在行事是否狠毒的層次，也不在道德是否有虧的層次，而是涉及現狀（可能是好勇鬥狠的朱彼德，也可能是大理國的好皇帝）一旦崩潰，暴力即將橫行的可能，所以是一種絕對惡，越是符合正義反而越可怕。這就是爲什麼大理皇室自知理虧，卻始終沒有採取任何補救行動，讀者也不會覺得不能認同；段延慶第一次回國時自認「如果他貿然在大理現身，勢必有性命之憂」，並非沒有道理。

　　另一方面，絕對惡的兩面性也打開了「垂直透視」的可能。無常女神勢力雄厚，一旦反亂，必然震動三界。但是《仙后》安排自然大神主持仲裁，其實已經含有身像的跨越，因爲無常召喚季節、月令、晝夜、時辰、生死等仙職出庭作證，以爲可以申明時間改變一切的原則，卻沒有看到這些變化其實都遵循一定的規律，都指向更高的旨意與規劃。史賓色用三個背反來描寫自然大神，說她「青春永駐風燭齡，常時流轉位不移，隱形藏跡見分明」（Spenser 1977: 7.vii.13），顯示自然本身已經包孕無常的身像，只是其中除了分明可見的無常表相之外還有一個「青春永駐」、「位不移」、「隱形藏跡」的層次。也就是說，自然過於玄妙而不可見，無常則是去除玄妙，能爲肉眼所見的，自然的鏡中像，是凡夫俗子認知自然的唯一路徑，所以無常與自然的關係不是對立，而是同一（MacCaffrey 1976: 429n），是「病中有藥」的連鎖（McCabe 1989: 206）。既然如此，自然的簡短裁決就不是絕對惡的消除（無常並沒有像反叛朱彼德的古巨神族那樣，被打入地牢，永遠不得翻身），而是向惡顯露一個異世界以及其中所含的，惡的自身像，從而成就惡的安置與異化。同樣的，段延慶的回頭也是起於自身映像的顯現：刀白鳳如何認出段延慶就是當日的乞丐，自然有可疑之處，但是她一句「天龍寺外，菩提樹下，化子邋遢，觀音長髮」，正是一種當頭棒喝式的啓示，使段延慶在絕不可能溝通的自憐、自棄情境中忽然見到一條垂直上升之路，讓他知道原來在惡的絕

對孤寂中還有另外一個人知道他（或與他共有）最私密的記憶。這個「直如晴天霹靂一般」的轉變顛覆了他原來的世界，使他開始認知到另一個平行世界的存在（金庸 1997: 10.2354f）。接下來的情節安排確定了段譽就是他兒子，他所反叛的對象其實已經包孕了他的身像，他與大理皇室的關係也不是對立，而是同一。

西谷啓治認爲慈悲或愛可以分成兩個層次。第一個層次是講究待人如己的世俗道德觀，由愛自己的心（「主體自覺」）出發，產生人亦如我的同理心以及克制私欲的能力。第二個層次則是近一步否定自我，講究有人無己（也就是從克制私欲出發，引申爲待人〈不可〉如己）的宗教觀點，透過捨棄自己，遷就對方（經過「大死」，變成活死人）而進入連通自他的底體（subjectum 或 hypokeimenon），使自我一方面不離人身，一方面則解除了人的存在方式（Nishitani 1982: 272-80）。這裡慈悲的第二個層次標舉異理心，似乎可以包括上文所說的法緣慈悲與無緣慈悲。法緣慈悲要求有彼無我，「諸眾生所須之物而施與之」，是割肉餵鷹的境界，已經不是世俗道德的同理心所能解釋，但是如果停留在自他相對的意思，這究竟還只是自我的超越提昇，不能進入底體的同一。無緣慈悲則進一步透過如來的絕對超越化使如來成爲虛位，在自他隔絕，不可溝通的珍瓏死局中形成二次顛倒，在大死之後產生大活，也使異理心的兩截分斷同時浮現，成爲在拖延中成就，包孕了眾生緣與法緣而同時能超乎其外的傳奇結構。只有在這個層次，自我的絕對否定與自我的絕對肯定才可以會通，有彼無我與「在萬物中見自我」也才不會相礙（277，281）。

《天龍八部》裡的虛竹、蕭峯、段譽都經過類似大死的經驗，陷入失去自我、飄搖不定的存在狀態：虛竹成爲孤兒、入逍遙派、破戒；蕭峯眾叛親離，身世成謎，又失去阿朱；段譽則是一開始就跌入無量山劍湖谷底，迷上「神仙姊姊」，成爲痴人。但是三俠的失去自我並不表示他們沒有主體的自覺與「慧識」（羅龍治 1997b: 51），反而因爲他們都表現了無心狀態而使他們的俠義行爲超越有我層次的同理心，指向「譬如日月不作往來照明之心」的無緣自在。虛竹解珍瓏、救天山童姥、成爲「夢郎」等等都出於無心，蕭峯陷入偵探小說式的解謎情節也非本意，段譽對六脈神劍的收發、與諸女是否爲兄妹等更不能隨心所欲。另一方面，他們三人各自又都以不同的方式回歸俗緣，成爲無緣慈悲的三重現身。虛竹爲三十六洞洞主、七十二島島主拔除生

死符，又用生死符收服丁春秋，是回到懲惡勸善，發揚公共價值（也就是俠義）的世俗道德。蕭峯終於捨命阻止大遼攻宋，是利人濟物的大菩薩。段譽則贏得神仙美眷，自做他的皇帝，似乎脫落在公共性之外，其實他的立足點卻已經包含了虛竹的世俗價值（個人情愛），蕭峯的入世實踐（大理國施政）以及絕對惡的超越與背反（段延慶身像的延續），指向無緣慈悲的分離與照映。所以虛竹與蕭峯的結局都是入無緣返有緣的傳奇式拖延，段譽更是拖延與實現同時浮顯，確立了整部小說善包孕惡，無我包孕有我，出世理想包孕世俗權力的分斷結構。沒有段譽，虛竹的馴順會顯得昏庸，蕭峯的高蹈也會有酷烈之嫌。有了段譽，兩人才能納入一個三緣互通的意義空間，成立底體的回互相入。

四

　　班雅民把暴力分為三種：執法暴力以維繫律法為目標，制法暴力則追求以力服人，遂行意志；這兩種暴力的作用都是在設立秩序，解決紛爭，分配利益，維持俗世的生產活動與生產條件；第三種暴力則是不講條件，沒有外在目標的展演，透過暴力的立即行使來推翻、中斷生產體制與律法秩序，是以本身為目標的純粹暴力。一般以改變生活或工作條件為目的的「政治性罷工」就是執法暴力與制法暴力的對抗，而「無產階級總罷工」則是純粹暴力的實現。前者是神話暴力的翻版，後者則體現了與神話暴力相對的，上帝的「毀法暴力」（Benjamin 1978）。純粹暴力因為沒有中介，沒有對象（不能用來謀取私利），其實已經可以視為非暴力或暴力當中的非暴力面向。按哈瑪赫的解釋，律法的施行是宣成性（performative）動作，純粹暴力則是開成性（afformative）動作，而且在律法宣成的過程中必然已經含有開成的一面（Hamacher 1994: 115）。這裡所謂宣成性，是說律法實質上並無外在規範可依而是在發為表述的過程中同時成立，而開成性則是成立各種宣成動作的可能性，同時卻超出宣成性之外，可以中斷或取消所有宣成項的力量；所以說開成性「是成立工具性、宣成性暴力的先決條件，同時也是阻止其完全成就的限制條件」（128n）。哈瑪赫所講的開成性與宣成性的關係其實就相當於上文已經提到的，追求與拖延兩個層次同時存在的傳奇結構：開成性是純粹形

式的顯現（129fn），是爲所有主體力量保存開顯可能的絕對倫理，就像是西谷的底體也可以視爲超出內容（人身）之外，與內容不相對卻爲所有內容保存溝通可能的形式（人的具體存在的反面）；而律法（主體）的內容雖然是在自我宣述當中形成，具有穩定性、延續性，同時卻也因爲要取得規範對象的認可而必須不斷追求與正義的絕對形式（也就是開成性）統一，從而因爲無法完全開放，無法眞正保存一切對體各自宣成的可能性而不斷拖延這個絕對形式的實現，不斷偏離普遍正義的目標。反過來說，也只有形式與內容不統一，純粹形式的開放才能不斷引進不同主體的宣述，不斷在宣成項陷入封閉狀態的時候引發改造現狀的契機，甚至保留推翻既成律法，產生革命（大死）的可能。

　　如果段譽的不入俗緣包孕、安置了虛竹與蕭峯的入世意義，那麼從暴力與權力的觀點看，虛竹對執法暴力的堅持（以領受少林寺杖責爲高點）與蕭峯對制法暴力的駕馭與克服（終結於爲反戰而自殺）就各自以不同的方式維持了小說的敍事秩序，沖淡了來自開成性的反秩序衝力，緩和了直接面對毀法暴力的壓迫感。而段譽正處於毀法暴力的核心，是脫序可能性的顯露點：他的故事不但以成爲「第一惡人」之子告終，也充滿了各種條理規範的中斷，是敍事層次開成性聚集的所在。小說一開始，他爲了不想學武而「罷工」出走，已經顯示他與開成性之間有密切的相關。然後他在劍湖宮失笑打斷別人比武，引出鍾靈、神農幫、靈鳩宮等暴力的更替。接下來是四大惡人使大理國陷入危機、倒收南海鱷神爲徒、搞亂段延慶棋局、一場戀愛忽然被新發現的兄妹關係所中斷、爲王語嫣失魂落魄、武功時靈時不靈等等，似乎暴力或欲望只要扯上段譽，就會宣而不成，開而難閉；大理皇室常常陷入權力轉換的危機，不是有人造反，就是皇帝要出家，正呼應了段譽處境的多變。這些細節在在顯示段譽雖然「愛心太重，不肯棄子」，但是他那種傾向抹煞自我的盲愛反而可能因爲內容應棄未棄，造成過剩，使純粹形式脫落於外，更容易造成宣成項的不穩定。另一方面，小說敍事的進行靠的是俗緣的水平連接、對垂直面向的異質揭顯不得不設立緩衝，以免失去讀者的閱讀興趣；虛竹、蕭峯的對照正是緩衝的一部分。另外，與段譽相關的情節充滿巧合（如「神仙姊姊」幾代的形貌都一樣，段正淳在外生的都是女兒等等），常常打破常情常理，也正是因爲敍事安排過度條理化、秩序化，可以補償毀法暴力帶來的

不穩定感。最後段譽忽然變成段延慶的兒子，說明段譽最後的福報不能單純的用「傻人有傻福」之類的說法來解釋，而是癖性所至，不得不放棄規矩秩序。也就是說，這部分敘事過程既要放棄常情常理，以無緣慈悲的超離觀點來面對暴力核心，又不能拋棄通俗敘事意義格局的限制，自然只能透過巧合、形式對照等設置來製造意義的分斷與垂直翻轉，在淺顯的層次從俗，在隱密的層次歸真。

　　只有這樣看，我們才不會以為用血緣的巧合來解決段延慶的毀法暴力是遷就權力的妥協，維護現狀的馴服，也才不會以為小說雖然反對民族仇恨，卻認為癖性不可溝通的立場是死抱「民族性格」的舊思想。開成性是純粹形式，本來就必須依附內容宣成的層次才能顯現，不可能離開內容，以廣告、文宣、口號、標語的陳述方式直接灌輸。同樣的，任何對權力體制的批判也不可能脫離制法暴力的對抗，甚至也難免有呈現為執法暴力的時刻。所以批判性的檢驗不在內容層次正確性的斤斤計較，而是在能不能維持毀法的可能性，形式上有沒有一個垂直上升的開放點。佛教思想常被視為空寂無為，消極保守，《天龍八部》也常令人產生內斂悲觀的感受。但是就像所有追求絕對與超越的思想，佛教思想自有其飽含革命可能的一面。如果我們能回歸傳奇結構的文類特性，切入更隱密，更超越的層次，我們也可以看到：《天龍八部》乃至金庸的其他小說要打破的，並不僅是師徒不能戀愛、正邪之分不可跨越、非我族類其心必異之類的文化教條，而是含有對教條背後的，權力的純粹形式的理解與批判。這樣的意義格局已經超出改良生產條件的層次而隱隱指向文化上的「無產階級總罷工」。

參考資料

Benjamin, Walter

　　1978　"Critique of Violence." In *Reflections: Essays, Aphorisms, Autobiographical Writings*. Ed. Peter Demetz. Trans. Edmund Jephcott. New York: Harcourt Brace Jovanovich. 277-300.

Bradley, A.C.

　　1992　"Poetry for Poetry's Sake" (1909).　Rpt. in Hazard Adams (ed.),

      Critical Theory since Plato. Rev. ed. Orlando: Harcourt Brace
      Jovanovich. 701-10.

陳　墨

    1997　《文化金庸》（中和：雲龍）。

陳世驤

    1966　致金庸函。四月廿二日。收入金庸 1997: 10.2486ff.

陳義孝編

    1996　《佛學常見詞彙》。下載程式。〈http://www.dharma.org.tw/canon/
      book/thes /ms.exe〉（1998.9.20 下載）。

Copjec, Joan

    1994　*Read My Desire: Lacan against the Historicists*. Cambridge: MIT
      Press.

《大乘理趣六波羅蜜多經》

      般若譯。大正新修大藏經，8.865a-917b。

《大般涅槃經》

      曇無讖譯。大正新修大藏經，12.365a-603c。

《大佛頂首楞嚴經》

      般刺蜜帝譯。大正新修大藏經，19.105b-155b。

Fletcher, Angus

    1967　*Allegory: The Theory of a Symbolic Mode*. Ithaca: Cornell Univ.
      Press.

Frye, Northrop

    1957　*Anatomy of Criticism: Four Essays*. Princeton: Princeton Univ.
      Press.

    1976　*The Secular Scripture: A Study of the Structure of Romance*.
      Cambridge: Harvard Univ. Press.

Hamacher, Werner

    1994　"Afformative, Strike: Benjamin's 'Critique of Violence.'" Trans.
      Dana Hollander. In Andrew Benjamin and Peter Osborne, eds.,
      Walter Benjamin's Philosophy: Destruction and Experience. Lon-
      don: Routledge. 110-38.

Jameson, Fredric

　1981　*The Political Unconscious: Narrative as a Socially Symbolic Act.* Ithaca: Cornell Univ. Press.

吉　藏

　　　　《二諦義》。大正新修大藏經，45.77b-115a。

金　庸

　1997　《天龍八部》10 冊（臺北：遠流，袖珍版）。

盧玉瑩

　1985　〈訪問金庸〉，翁靈文等，《諸子百家看金庸》第 3 輯（臺北：遠景），頁 21-32。

羅龍治

　1997a　〈我看《天龍八部》〉，羅龍治等，《諸子百家看金庸㈡》（臺北：遠流，第二版），頁 35-44。

　1997b　〈天龍九部：再論喬峯〉（1984），羅龍治等，《諸子百家看金庸㈡》（臺北：遠流，第二版），頁 45-52。

McCabe, Richard A.

　1989　*The Pillars of Eternity: Time and Providence in* The Faerie Queene. Dublin: Irish Academic Press.

MacCaffrey, Isabel G.

　1976　*Spenser's Allegory: The Anatomy of Imagination.* Princeton: Princeton Univ. Press.

Macpherson, Jay

　1990　"Romance since Spenser (English)." In A. C. Hamilton (ed.), *The Spenser Encyclopedia.* Toronto: Univ. of Toronto Press. 619b-21c.

中村元

　1956　《慈悲》（京都：平樂寺）。

Nishitani Keiji

　1982　*Religion and Nothingness.* Trans. Jan Van Bragt. Berkeley: Univ. of California Press.

Parker, Patricia A.

　1979　*Inescapable Romance: Studies in the Poetics of a Mode.* Princeton: Princeton Univ. Press.

Spenser, Edmund

 1977 *The Faerie Queene.* Ed. A. C. Hamilton. London: Longman.

Tuve, Rosemond

 1966 *Allegorical Imagery: Some Medieval Books and Their Posterity.* Princeton: Princeton Univ. Prss.

溫瑞安

 1997 《天龍八部欣賞舉隅》（臺北：遠流）。

吳靄儀

 1998 《金庸小說看人生》（臺北：遠流）。

延　壽

  《宗鏡錄》。大正新修大藏經，48.415a-957b。

第五輯

文學與社會

文學的雅俗對峙與金庸的歷史地位

嚴　家　炎

北京大學中文系

摘　要

　　五四以降的中文新小說在理論建構之初即有意識的以預先存在的「國語文學」——從《水滸傳》、《紅樓夢》、到《老殘遊記》等既有的成功的白話小說——爲典律，之前，這些「成功」的白話小說從不被認爲是學術研究的對象，在傳統學術視域下也幾無價值可言。從白話文學的系譜來看，基本上以原居於文字表達次要系統的民間的、世俗的語言系統置換長期居於主導地位的文言表達系統；爾後主流的五四文學在時間性上設定了以當下現實爲主要的場景，寫實主義的訴求內在的規定了物質符碼的時間性。時間性的設定同時相當程度地制約了白話文學產生的可能性，並且以那樣的時間性爲主導(如果不是唯一的話) 的意向。文學的啓蒙教化或揭露現實的功能也被內化，被上綱爲書寫的倫理。這種歷史長期發展中被合理化的傾向本身並不具有絕對的正當性，因爲它所依據的可能性邏輯並不是唯一的可能性。相對於這樣窄化的新文學格局，作爲「新派武俠小說」佼佼者的金庸武俠小說或許恰好可以提供一個突破口，回頭去質疑、重省白話文學的格局和書寫的可能。這是本文的第一個思考脈絡，把問題放回到五四文學的系譜，以古裝／時裝這一關鍵性的符碼問題爲焦點，把五四新文學中的一些重要的基本精神和特點(如感時憂國精神、抒情、浪漫、關於愛情、國族主義、民族情感) 等都拿出來和金庸小說做一番對比檢驗，藉此以重新思考新文學之中的現代性與中國性之調和或衝突，同時也可以反思不同時間符碼置換後的「文學性」——與傳統詩學的對話。

　　第二個思考脈絡是思想史脈絡。尤其是以 1949 年以後港臺新儒學運動爲基本的對比架構，以箇中所宣揚的文化價值、文化理想、文化精神、歷史精神、藝術精神等等爲焦點，初步探討這兩種對於價值的不同「敍述」方式。本文認爲，從文化史的角度來看，金庸武俠小說可以說是這一波文化價值再確認運動（「文化苦旅」）中非常重要的一環，從語言表達的角度來看，相對於前者不可思議的專門化、溝通對象的高度窄化、精英化，金庸武俠小說是一個重要的互補，建構了一個古代的場景來安頓、演出、證成既有的價值的同時，也恰好回應了白話文學原先的平民主張。

　　撇開雅／俗這樣的成見，本文企圖論證的是，金庸的武俠小說之所以會遠遠超過經典五四文學而獲得海內外不同階層的當代華人的廣泛接受，是因爲不論是在精神上還是文學上，它所完成的恐怕都比一般故步自封的文學研究者想像的多，甚至相當程度上回應了晚清時梁啓超等人對於小說的構想。

一

　　衡量金庸小說的歷史貢獻，必須放到二十世紀中國文學發展這個大背景，特別是小說雅俗對峙這個大格局中。

　　文學歷來是在高雅和通俗兩部分相互對峙中向前發展的。高雅和通俗兩部分既相互衝擊，又相互推動；既相互制約，又相互影響，構成了文學發展的內在動力。當然，所謂雅，所謂俗，都是歷史的概念，不同時代的人們會有不同的看法。在中國古代，詩文被認爲是文學的正宗，小說戲曲則是所謂「鄙俗」的「小道」，不能進入文學的大雅之堂，因此，雅俗對峙發生在詩文與小說戲曲中間。

　　到本世紀初，梁啓超等人受西方思潮影響，大聲吶喊著將小說提高到「文學之最上乘」。尤其到「五四」文學革命，師法西方小說的新體白話小說占據了文學的中心地位，進入了文學的殿堂，連歷史上那些有價值的小說也有幸沾光得到重新評價，脫去了「鄙俗」的帽子。但是，有一部分小說卻享受不到這種幸運，那就是二十世紀面對中國市民大眾的通俗小說。它們仍被新文學家、文學史家擯斥於現代文學之外。於是，雅俗對峙轉到了小說內部，形成新文學和通俗文學兩大陣營。「五四」文學革命拿「黑幕派」和「鴛鴦蝴蝶

派」來開刀，這些就都是通俗小說。其中「黑幕小說」污濁得很，沒有多少文學價值，「五四」當時對它的批判並不錯。但對鴛鴦蝴蝶派，否定得就太簡單了，把它說成是封建的小市民文藝，連同它所採取的傳統形式都不理睬。這種簡單化的批判效果不好，最多縮小了它在知識分子圈中的市場，而對廣大市民爭讀鴛鴦蝴蝶派作品的情況則幾乎毫無影響，反而使「五四」新文學本身不能較快克服語言形式歐化的缺點。這樣，雅俗對峙在二十世紀就成爲小說內部的事，成爲嚴肅小說、高雅小說和通俗小說、商品化小說之間的抗衡。

其實，從歷史上說，無論雅文學或者俗文學，都可能產生偉大的作品。中國的《水滸傳》、《紅樓夢》，當初也曾被封建士大夫看作鄙俗的書，只是到現代才上升爲文學史上的傑出經典。英國的狄更斯、司各特，法國的大仲馬，在十九世紀也都被認爲是通俗文學作家。直到本世紀八十年代中期，當中國作家協會副主席鄧友梅率領作家代表團訪問法國，談到巴爾扎克在中國作家中的崇高聲望和巨大影響時，負責接待的法國主人還說：「原來中國作家對巴爾扎克這樣的通俗作家感興趣。」在法國當代作家看來，巴爾扎克是暢銷書作家，地位低於雨果。了解了這種狀況，新文學家就沒有理由看不起通俗文學，而通俗小說家也大可不必在新文學面前自慚形穢。通俗絕不等同於庸俗。嚴肅文學中，其實也有大量思想和藝術上比較平庸的作品。起決定作用的，歸根結底還是作家自身素養的高低、體驗的深淺和文學表現才能的不同。

在文學史上長期以來的雅俗對峙中，高雅文學一般處於主導的地位。它逼得通俗文學吸取對方營養以提高自身的素質。但並不是說，高雅文學就不受到通俗文學的挑戰。這種挑戰，不但表現爲通俗文學往往比高雅文學擁有更多的讀者，而且表現爲通俗文學中有時也出現相當優秀的作品，其質量可能達到高雅作品的平均水平之上，甚至可與高雅文學中的優秀作品相抗衡。明清兩代的種種史料表明，當《三國演義》、《水滸傳》在長期說書和戲曲藝術的基礎上由羅貫中、施耐庵分別整理、加工、改定的時候，當《紅樓夢》最早的稿本開始流傳的時候，都曾出現人們爭相傳抄、洛陽爲之紙貴的盛況；這就是挑戰。金聖嘆在明末清初就把《水滸傳》拿來和《莊子》、《史記》相比，而且親手將這本書以及他自己在書上的批語交給十歲的兒子閱讀，此種見地和膽識，當時眞可謂驚世駭俗；這同樣也是挑戰。

二

　　進入二十世紀，一方面，占據主導地位的高雅小說對通俗小說保持著影響。這突出地表現在鴛鴦蝴蝶派文人密切注視新小說的發展並給予很高評價。有位署名「鳳兮」的鴛鴦蝴蝶派理論家，在 1921 年 2 月至 3 月間發表〈我國現在之創作小說〉，其中說：「魯迅先生《狂人日記》一篇，描寫中國禮敎好行其吃人之德，發千載之覆，洗生民之冤，殆眞爲志意之創作小說，置之世界諸大小說家中，當無異議，在我國則唯一無二矣。」又說：「文化運動之軒然大波，新體之小說群起。……若葉楚傖之《牛》，陳衡哲之《老夫妻》，某君（適忘其名）之《一個兵的家》，均令人滿意者。」[1] 他對胡適的《論短篇小說》也很推崇。鴛鴦蝴蝶派的秋山，還隨著新文學一起提倡寫社會小說。所以，張恨水這樣的小說家在二三十年代的出現以及抗戰爆發後終於靠攏新文學陣營，是一點也不奇怪的。這就是高雅文學的主導作用。

　　另一方面，通俗小說也常常以自己的某種優勢向高雅小說挑戰。二十年代後半期和三十年代前半期的張恨水，他的小說成就和影響就遠過於當時那些嚴肅作家所寫的大眾文學作品（即使僅僅按「大眾化」的標準來衡量也是如此），更不要說他擁有讀者的廣泛了。據荊有麟、許欽文回憶，魯迅的母親就很喜歡讀李涵秋、張恨水的小說，讀得津津有味，手不釋卷。有一次，老太太聽到許欽文和一兩個年輕人在魯迅家裡談論《故鄉》這篇小說寫得怎麼怎麼好時，老太太不服氣地說：「有這麼好的小說嗎？你們拿來給我看看！」當時老太太還不知道「魯迅」就是她自己兒子的筆名，她帶起老花眼鏡，把《故鄉》讀了一遍，然後用紹興話搖著頭對幾個年輕人說：「嘸啥稀奇！嘸啥好看！這種事情在我們鄉下多得很！」讓在座的這些年輕人聽了哈哈大笑，魯迅本人不插嘴只在一旁靜聽微笑。[2] 發生在魯迅家中的這場爭論很有意思，足以說明當時一些有成就的通俗小說掌握了多少讀者，並且培養了怎

1　1921 年 2 月 27 日至 3 月 6 日《申報・自由談》連載。

2　參閱荊有麟《魯迅回憶斷片》第一節〈母親的影響〉（上海：上海雜誌公司，1943 年 11 月）。

樣一種閱讀趣味（老太太用「稀奇」、「好看」做標準衡量小說，就是由通俗小說所培養的；至於老太太不以爲然地說到的「這種事情多得很」，恰恰是嚴肅文學所說的「眞實」或「概括性」）。

　　再舉張愛玲的例子，同樣可以說明通俗文學怎樣在向嚴肅文學挑戰。現在我們都知道，張愛玲是四十年代湧現的有獨特成就的新文學作家。其實，恰恰是張愛玲，具有與眾不同的通俗文學的背景。除了西方文化和英國作家毛姆等人的小說外，她努力從中國通俗小說中吸取著營養。她不但熟讀《紅樓夢》等古典小說，甚至喜歡公開談論上海商業文化（海派文化）和通俗文學對她的影響。她說她「從小就是小報的忠實讀者」，愛讀張恨水的小說，還對上海書攤上的通俗小說《海上花列傳》、《歇浦潮》推崇備至。在給胡適的信中，張愛玲說：「很久以前我讀你寫的《醒世姻緣》與《海上花》的考證，印象非常深，後來找了這兩部小說來看，這些年來，前後不知看了多少遍，自己以爲得到不少益處。」[3] 她十四歲時仿照鴛鴦蝴蝶派的筆法寫成《摩登紅樓夢》；最早發表的小說〈沉香屑·第一爐香〉也刊登在鴛鴦蝴蝶派刊物《紫羅蘭》上；無怪乎最初人們幾乎一致地把她看作是海派通俗作家。認眞閱讀她的作品，才眞正體味到這位晚清士大夫文化最後一個傳人的骨子裡的古典筆墨趣味，以及這位上海灘上才女在感受方式與藝術表達方面的深刻的現代性。張愛玲完全自由地出入於高雅與通俗之間、傳統與現代之間，達到了二者的溝通與交融；這正是她對中國現代文學的主要貢獻，同樣體現了通俗文學對高雅文學的挑戰。

　　如果說辛亥之後鴛鴦蝴蝶派的崛起只被新文學家當做對立面，那麼，張恨水的出現，張愛玲的成就，這些挑戰似乎並沒有使新文學界有所清醒，使他們的傲慢姿態有所收斂。他們只看到通俗文學和高雅文學相互對峙以爭奪讀者甚至給新文學構成威脅的方面，而看不到通俗文學對新文學還有相互推動、相互促進的另一方面。雖然抗戰爆發以後爲了動員群眾實現全民抗戰，新文學界也曾尋求通俗文學的支持，不少新文學家用通俗文藝的形式表現抗戰的內容，卻依然不曾改變居高臨下的態度。這時比較清醒的，似乎只有趙

3　轉引自胡適〈致張愛玲〉（1955 年 1 月 25 日），見張愛玲《張看》（香港：文化·生活出版社，1976），頁 161。

樹理。他眞正看到了新文學存在的某種歐化傾向以及不能被農民群眾接受的弱點，因而企圖汲取通俗文學經驗創制一種新的小說使它能在農民中扎根。這就是以《小二黑結婚》、《李有才板話》爲代表的一條新的道路。他的小說，眞正實現了農民化，是一種提高了的農民文學。人物是眞正農民中的人物，語言、形式也是充分農民化的，連感情內容、審美情趣也浸透著來自農民的質樸、平易、幽默和樂觀氣息，使人讀後耳目爲之一新。這對新文學界有所震動，使他們對通俗文學的態度有所反省。可惜，理論家們總喜歡搞模式化的東西，他們以爲從趙樹理那裡一下子發現了文學普遍規律，可以使高雅文學與通俗文學合二爲一，於是，趙樹理道路沒有被正確理解而走樣了，他文學營養、文學視野不夠寬廣的弱點反而被看成爲優點，他的道路被抬高誇大成爲「方向」，[4] 似乎所有作家都得普遍遵循，這就在實際上使文學單一化，使雅俗關係問題不能得到正確解決。

事實上，高雅文學和通俗文學，只能是一種長期共存的關係，永遠不可能誰吃掉誰而形成一統天下。陳平原教授把文學上雅俗對峙比做「一場永遠難解難分的拔河比賽」，可說頗爲貼切。確實，高雅小說和通俗小說，「雙方互有占便宜的時候，但誰也別想把對方完全扳倒。」而小說藝術則正是在這場沒完沒了的拉鋸戰中悄悄地「移步變形」。[5] 這原是一種正常現象。人爲地幻想用某類作品旣取代高雅文學又取代通俗文學，絕對行不通。即使像趙樹理這種很有新鮮氣息，很受農民歡迎的相當優秀的小說，也很難成爲以它作準的一桿標尺，讓矮的拔高、高的鋸矮。五十年代之所以出現大批旣不高雅也不通俗，只能說較爲平庸的作品，理論指導上的失誤，也是一個重要原因。我很贊成陳平原教授的這些見解。

三

金庸五六十年代在香港的出現，意味著本世紀以來長期困擾著人們的雅俗對峙問題，從實踐上和認識上得到了較好的解決。金庸小說的成就，是吸

4　陳荒煤，〈向趙樹理方向邁進〉，載 1947 年 8 月 10 日《人民日報》。

5　陳平原，《小說史：理論與實踐》（北京：北京大學出版社，1993），頁 274。

取了「雅」、「俗」雙方的文學經驗因而又是超越「雅」、「俗」之上的。金庸小說在以下四方面的經驗，對中國文學的發展，都具有根本性的意義。

第一，在創作觀念上，如果說嚴肅文學是「爲了人生」，通俗小說是「供人消遣」的話，金庸小說把這兩方面統一了起來，既供人娛樂，又有益於人生。朱自清在四十年代曾經說過：「鴛鴦蝴蝶派的小說意在供人們茶餘飯後消遣，倒是中國小說的正宗。」[6] 這話出自二十多年前反對將文學當消遣的文學研究會作家之口，很值得玩味。可見文學的娛樂性功能並沒有理由否定。金庸又不止於這方面。他的小說同樣還有「爲人生」的一面。金庸自己說：「武俠小說本身是娛樂性的東西，但是我希望它多少有一點人生哲理或個人的思想，通過小說可以表現一些自己對社會的看法。」[7] 金庸小說雖然寫的是虛幻的武林世界，卻寫出了眞切的現實人生，寫出了眞實豐富的人性，顯示了作者獨立的犀利的批判的眼光。當五六十年代大陸相當一部分作家受到左傾政治觀念與庸俗文藝觀念的影響而失去獨立見解時，金庸的創作與新文學的意識形態化形成了鮮明的對比。金庸保持了「爲人生」與「供消遣」相統一的自由創作心態，既以自娛，復以娛人，無拘無束，馳騁想像，寫出了一系列富有藝術魅力，又有著思想寄寓的作品，活潑輕鬆而有時又令人沉重，讓人休息卻又啓人深思。魯迅歷來主張眞正的文學要啓人之蒙，有益人生，又要令人愉悅，給人藝術享受，金庸的文藝觀可說與魯迅這樣的偉大作家根本上是相通的。

第二，本世紀中國文學（包括嚴肅文學和一部分通俗文學在內）的主潮是寫實主義，這種文學感時憂國，關心現實，反映民間疾苦，有很大的長處，但也存在一種有的學者稱之爲「單維」的現象——只有「國家、社會、歷史」之維，只有寫實主義之維，因而多少給人單調的感覺。有人曾開玩笑地說二十世紀中國文學的特徵是「涕淚飄零」（劉紹銘語）。這種文學最大弱點是缺少想像力，可以說和文學想像久違了。金庸小說在這方面有巨大的突破，他顯示了超凡的幾乎是天馬行空般的想像才能。金庸沒有到過大理，卻想像出

6　朱自清，〈論嚴肅〉，收入論文集《標準與尺度》（上海：文光書店，1948），此處引文引自《朱自清選集》第 1 卷（石家莊：河北教育出版社，1989 年 12 月），頁 437。

7　王力行，〈新聞文學一戶牖〉，收入《諸子百家看金庸》㈤（香港：明窗出版社，1997年 10 月），頁 71。

了無量玉壁那樣奇幻的景色；金庸沒有去過新疆，卻想像出了玉峰宮殿那樣神異的去處。武功的創造，更是無奇不有。《書劍恩仇錄》開頭，就是陸高止發金針釘蒼蠅的場面；以後各部小說更有什麼「九陰白骨爪」、「玉女素心劍」、「降龍十八掌」，什麼「吸星大法」、「六脈神劍」，乃至瑛姑的「泥鰍功」、楊過的「黯然銷魂掌」，等等，極盡想像之能事。《天龍八部》所寫的青年一代，幾乎每人都有一個獨特的身世之謎，這些謎相互錯綜，又交織成了整部小說極其複雜的人物關係網絡，它們完全超出了人們的想像，使讀者如書中人段譽那樣感受到「霹靂一個接著一個」般的巨大震撼，這在金庸以外的其他作品中，我們能夠讀到嗎？《鹿鼎記》第三十二回，寫到在昆明附近的三聖庵中，聚會了古往今來第一大反賊（李自成）、古往今來第一大漢奸（吳三桂）、古往今來第一大美人（陳圓圓）、古往今來第一武功大高手（九難，即長平公主）、古往今來第一小滑頭（韋小寶），這想像更是大膽之極！這種想像的神奇，滿足了多少讀者的好奇心，構成金庸小說異乎尋常的魅力！

　　第三，金庸小說堅持了傳統白話小說的形式和語言，而又有所改造和創新。劉再復先生最近在一篇文章中曾經指出：「如果平心靜氣看二十世紀初文學的變革，就會看到，由於社會變化和外來文學影響，中國文學已逐步分裂為兩種不同的文學流向：一種是占據舞台中心位置的五四文學革命催生的『新文學』；一種是保留中國文學傳統形式但富有新質的本土文學。新文學以啓蒙意識、外來文學的形式、歐化的白話文為其核心因素。它與此前文學的聯繫是次要的，充其量是某些作家採用了某些古代技法。它以前所未見的面貌出現於文學舞台，為那些贊同和傾向於『新思潮』的都市知識分子所認同，可以說新文學是表現這批活躍於都市的知識分子思想感情的。在新文學崛起的同時，另一種文學，即植根於古代文學悠長傳統的那部分文學也在發生緩慢的蛻變。它雖然不能像新文學那樣以耳目一新的形象示人，但文學史家戴著啓蒙意識的眼鏡，把它描繪成『封建文學』在清末民初的垂死沒落，是不合適的。我們姑且把這種文學命名為本土傳統的文學，它與新文學一起構成了二十世紀中國文學的兩大實在，或者說兩大流向。本土傳統的文學是在緩慢的積累中構造自己文學大廈的，在本世紀初有蘇曼殊、李伯元、劉鶚作為其代表，三、四十年代則有張恨水、張愛玲等作家，而金庸則是直接承繼本

土文學的傳統，並且在新的環境下集其大成，將它發揚光大。」[8] 雖然新文學
與此前文學的聯繫究竟如何，或許有待學術界深入討論，但從總體上說，我
比較贊成這種看法。金庸武俠小說在本土傳統形式方面所作的貢獻，可以說
完全適應了歷史的要求。早在四十年代，張恨水就多次提出過改造和弘揚章
回小說的願望。他在〈總答謝〉一文中說：「我覺得章回小說，不盡是可遺
棄的東西，不然，《紅樓》、《水滸》何以成爲世界名著呢？自然，章回小說有
其缺點存在，但這個缺點，不是無可挽救的（挽救的當然不是我）；而新派小
說，雖一切前進，而文法上的組織，非習慣讀中國書、說中國話的普通民眾
所能接受。正如雅頌之詩，高則高矣，美則美矣，而匹夫匹婦對之莫明其妙。
我們沒有理由遺棄這一班人，……大家若都鄙棄章回小說而不爲，讓這班人
永遠去看俠客口中吐白光，才子中狀元、佳人後花園私訂終身的故事，拿筆
桿的人，似乎要負一點責任。」[9] 在另一篇文章〈武俠小說在下層社會〉中，
張恨水又說：「中國下層社會，對於章回小說，能感到興趣的，第一是武俠
小說，第二是神怪小說，第三是歷史小說。……中國下層社會裡的人物，他
們的思想，始終有著模糊的英雄主義的色彩，那完全是武俠故事所教訓的。
這種教訓，有個極大的缺憾。第一，封建思想太濃，往往讓英雄變成奴才式
的。第二，完全幻想，不切實際。第三，告訴人鬥爭方法，也有許多錯誤。
自然，這裡也不是完全沒有意義的。武俠小說，會教讀者反抗暴力，反抗貪
汙，並且告訴被壓迫者聯合一致，犧牲小我。」在張恨水看來：「二三百年
的武俠小說執筆人若有今日先進文藝家的思想，我敢誇大一點，那會賽過許
多平民讀本的能力。可惜是恰站在反面。」[10] 張恨水呼籲有「先進思想」的新
文學家，不要拋棄中國的「普通民眾」，不要拋棄本土的章回體小說形式和傳
統的白話語言，這表明他很有卓見。歷史的發展與這類見解若合符節。就在
張恨水發出呼籲十年之後，金庸在香港出現了，而且他正是抓住了章回體中
影響最大的武俠小說這個類型，作了出色的實驗，證明張恨水之言絕非虛妄。
金庸對本土傳統小說形式的繼承和革新，既是用精英文化改造俗文學的成

8　劉再復，〈金庸小說在二十世紀中國文學史上的地位〉，載香港《明報月刊》，38:8（1998.
　　8），頁 43-46。

9　張恨水，〈總答謝——並自我檢討〉，載 1944 年 5 月 20 至 22 日重慶《新民報》。

10　張恨水，〈武俠小說在下層社會〉，載 1945 年 7 月 11 日《新華日報》。

功，又是以俗文學的經驗對新文學的偏見作了最切實的糾正。這確實具有「存亡繼絕」的重大意義。

在小說語言上，金庸吸取新文學的某些長處，卻又力避不少新文學作品語言的「惡性歐化」之弊。他扎根於本土傳統文學中，較多承繼了宋元以來傳統白話文乃至淺近文言的特點，形成了一個新鮮活潑、乾淨利索、富有表現力、相當優美而又親切自然的語言寶庫。金庸小說語言是「本土文學作家中交出的最好一份答卷」；[11] 或如李陀先生所說，金庸使傳統白話文得以「起死回生」。[12] 劉紹銘、黃維樑先生早在十年前就不約而同地提出金庸小說可用作海外華裔青年學中文的教本，[13] 足見學者們對金庸小說語言成就的高度重視。

第四，歷史上的高雅文學和通俗文學，原本各有自己的讀者，簡直涇渭分明，但金庸小說卻根本衝破了這種河水不犯井水的界限，他借用武俠這一通俗作品類型，出人意外地創造出一種文化學術品位很高的小說境界，實現了真正的雅俗共賞。金庸作品中包含的迷人的文化氣息、豐厚的歷史知識和深刻的民族精神，不但為廣大通俗作品所望塵莫及，而且也遠遠超過了許多嚴肅小說。金庸筆下的武技較量，固然能傳達出中華文化的內在精神；就連陳圓圓為一字不識的韋小寶彈唱吳梅村《圓圓曲》這個作者忽發奇想的情節，又包容了多少歷史興衰與個人際遇的滄桑之感。可以說，金庸是一位深得中華文化神髓的作家。他在法國被稱為「中國的大仲馬」。其實，如果按照作家本人對各自民族文化的理解程度以及小說創作所獲得的綜合成就而言，我個人以為，金庸恐怕已超越了大仲馬。他在文學史上的實際地位，應該介乎大仲馬與雨果之間的。

11　同註8。

12　李陀，〈金庸寫作中的「言」和「文」〉，載香港《明報月刊》1998年8月號。

13　參閱劉紹銘，〈金庸小說與僑教〉、黃維樑，〈童蒙可讀此而學文——金庸武俠小說語言的抽樣分析〉二文，收入《武俠小說論卷》上、下卷（香港：明河社，1998年5月）。

顯性與隱性

——金庸筆下的兩重社會

胡 小 偉

中國社會科學院文學研究所

摘 要

中國傳統社會一向具有兩重性質，一重是以君權爲中心，禮法爲構架，國家機器爲主幹形成的顯性社會，即正統社會；另一重或以信仰爲皈依，或以團體利益爲紐帶，信義爲構架，宗教或秘密社團的組織爲骨幹形成的隱性社會，即江湖秘密社會。這不但構成了最早的俠義長篇《水滸傳》的背景，也是金庸小說中的「俠義」人物、故事的生存基礎。

文章「解題」以後，從四個方面來分析金庸小說的兩重社會。

第一、小說選材與顯隱社會

《史記・游俠列傳序》引韓非語曰：「儒以文亂法，而俠以武犯禁。」但西漢以後儒法合一，儒生進入了主流，俠士依然沉淪下層。以司馬遷的慨嘆而論，「俠文化」應當與「儒文化」互補才能臻於理想。唐宋之際中國社會形態有了明顯變化，社會兩重性質出現新的分化，太史公所謂「匹夫」、「閭里」和「鄉曲」之俠也具有了完全不同的性質。金庸小說涉及的年代，絕大多數爲北宋以後，這正與歷史發展的大趨勢一致。明清之際尖銳的民族衝突，導致知識階層從秘密結社轉向到隱性社會，直到民初成爲熱點，也是「新派武俠小說」取之不盡的題材來源。

第二、時代變遷與顯隱互易

「大道廢，有仁義。智慧出，有大僞。」時代變遷使顯性社會構架發生危機，隱性社會的價值體系隨之凸現。金庸的創作多以不同時期民族政權引

起朝代變易作爲大背景,如宋元、元明之際的「射鵰三部曲」,北宋時期的《天龍八部》和明清之際的《書劍恩仇錄》、《碧血劍》、《飛狐外傳》和《雪山飛狐》等,突出人物的忠烈豪壯,任俠仗義,同時表現不同價值系統的激烈衝突。最後在《鹿鼎記》中金庸基於歷史觀念的變化,淡化了民族紛爭中「勢不兩立」的矛盾。

第三、三敎九流與隱性社會

「三敎九流」其實是古代對游民階層的統稱,諸如僧尼道姑,醫卜星相,倡優丐隸,等等,構成傳統中國社會豐富的人物譜系。其中宮廷內闈(包括神龍敎組織)作爲特殊的隱性社會,在《鹿鼎記》中得到充分的闡發。

第四、正邪人物與黑白兩道

隱性社會置身法律之外,其奇人逸士爲人行事常有出人意表者。金庸小說描繪的人物,從正邪分明(如袁承志)到亦正亦邪(如楊過)、再到無正無邪(如令狐冲)和無所謂正邪(如韋小寶),表明著作者極深的感喟,而江湖上所謂「黑白兩道」之界限也逐漸趨於模糊,與其說明作者表現江湖風波之詭異難測,不如感慨世道之沒落。

結語回到「社」和「會」的語義探討。即便在統一價值系統和法律環境的顯性社會中,仍應當給區域性(社)和行業性(會)團體以相當的自治空間,以發揮「俠文化」的道義功能補償作用。

一、解　題

金庸小說以獨立特行的人物,玄妙莫測的武功和曲折離奇的故事征服了無數讀者,同時還展示了一個個詭詭幻怪的世界。

金庸的熱心讀者都知道「黑白兩道」的說法。在金庸筆下,「黑白兩道」或者正邪分明,善惡對立,或者正邪不分,善惡互見,構成了一個個雲詭波譎,變幻莫測的世界,甚至在某種意義上構成了全篇的意象。這個世界不僅是他「成人童話」中形形色色人物活動的背景,而且或出於掌故舊典,或出於向壁虛構,本身就具有豐富的研究價值。

考慮到金庸先生的「顯性身份」是著名報人和時事評論家,他構築的種種小說世界自然不無隱喩,但「索隱」一道非本文旨趣所在,故不論。

其實「黑白兩道」不過是一種籠統之說，與現代社會中令司法當局頭痛的「黑社會」、「黑手黨」雖不能說了無關聯，但畢竟有本質區別。這是因為一，金庸小說虛構的「黑白兩道」，主要指江湖門派「正邪」之分，而非司法制度和與之衝突者之別。比如《笑傲江湖》中「白道」指「五岳派」，「黑道」則指「日月神教」。而《鹿鼎記》韋小寶統帶之驍騎營卻從未被視作「白道」或「正派」；二，金庸小說都是古代題材，或者說是可能發生在傳統社會架構中的故事，絕非討論現代司法制度及其「掃黑」問題。

傳統中國社會尤其是宋元以後，一向具有兩重性質，一重是以君權為中心，「禮」、「法」為構架，國家機器為主幹形成的顯性社會，即正統社會；另一重則或以信仰為皈依，或以團體利益為紐帶，「信」、「義」為構架，宗教或秘密社團組織為骨幹形成的隱性社會，即江湖秘密社會。這個社會的不同組織擁有自己的價值體系、語言體系（包括隱語、切口、手訣）、集會儀規、聯絡方式和管理系統，如天地會的切口「海底」，金庸就在《鹿鼎記》中有過詳盡描述。兩重社會雖然不時發生矛盾衝突，但常態則是互相包容，兩不相干。

本文論述就是基於這種認識展開的。

二、小說選材與顯隱社會

話說《史記‧游俠列傳序》開首，即引韓非語云：「儒以文亂法，而俠以武犯禁。」可知儒生和俠士在先秦社會中，都處於社會的反對派行列。金庸評論這句話時，以為「正統是只有統治者才重視的觀念，不一定與人民大眾的傳統觀念相符。韓非指責『儒以文亂法，俠以武犯禁』，是站在統治者的立場，指責儒家號召仁愛與人情，搞亂了嚴峻的統治，俠者以暴力為手段，侵犯了當局的鎮壓手段。」[1]　《淮南子‧泰族篇》曾載先秦時「墨子服役者百八十人，皆可使赴火蹈刃，死不還踵。」他們甚至建立了自己的法理，《呂氏春秋‧志秋篇》記述秦惠王欲赦殺人者，其父墨者鉅子腹䵍拒絕赦免，說「墨者之法曰：『殺人者死，傷人者刑。此所以禁殺傷人也。夫禁殺傷人者，天下之大義也。王雖為之賜而令吏弗誅，腹䵍不可不行墨者之法。』」以此觀之，

1　金庸〈韋小寶這小傢伙〉，見 http://www.xys.org。

「墨者」應該是最早的隱性俠義組織。但是自西漢選擇了「獨尊儒術」的文化政策後，儒法合一，儒生進入了主流，建立起正統社會，而俠士依然沉淪下層。

太史公曾感慨地說：「自秦以前，匹夫之俠湮滅不見，余甚恨之。」總結他之謂「俠」的特點有四：

一，修令譽。「修行砥名，聲施於天下，莫不稱賢」；

二，重然諾。「取予然諾，千里誦義，為死不顧世。」|其行雖不軌於正義，然其言必信，其行必果，已若必誠，不愛其軀，赴士之厄困」；

三，抗強暴，憫貧弱。「朋黨宗強，比周設財役貧，豪暴侵凌孤弱，恣欲自快，游俠亦醜之」；

四，行高潔。「雖時捍當世之文罔，私義廉潔退讓，有足稱者。名不虛立，士不虛附。」「既已寸亡死生矣，而不矜其能，羞伐其德。」這就特別強調了人格獨立和私德砥礪的重要意義。有人曾以「俠」為「文化離軌者」，[2] 竊以為未必確當。如說「俠」代表著中國的自由主義傳統，還較為切近。以司馬遷的慨歎而論，「俠文化」應當與「儒文化」互補，才能趨於理想境界。

概括言之，唐宋之際，中國社會形態有了明顯變化。「安史」亂後門閥制度解體，中晚唐藩鎮割據，則以多收「義子」攏絡部眾，如「十三太保」之屬，相沿成習，而《春秋》之「義」因而演化為「私誼」，而別析以「忠」。社會兩重性質出現新的分化，隱性社會得以建立。太史公所謂「匹夫」、「閭里」和「鄉曲」之俠，也具有了完全不同的性質。其中宋元人說話中的趙匡胤《飛龍傳》和梁山泊聚義《水滸傳》，尤能顯示當時豪俠於隱顯社會中之種種情態和轉化過程。明清之際秘密會黨及幫會大行於世，正如方以智《曼語草・任論》所曰：「上失其道，無以屬民，故游俠之徒以任得民」、「蓋任俠之教衰，而後游俠之勢行。」[3] 特別是知識階層由秘密結社轉向江湖隱性社

2　陳韻琳，〈俠世界與正邪論的顛覆・看金庸的武俠小說〉，見 http://www.cco.caltech.edu/awong/jin。本文所引凡未特別注明者，均出自 Internet 網金庸專題的這個網頁。

3　《墨經・經上》：「任，士損己而所為也。」〈經說上〉：「任，為身之所惡，以成人之所急。」

會，使其面貌爲之一變，傳說顧炎武曾參與創立、完善秘密組織，[4] 雖未得到確證，但足資想像。

曾有好事者羅列過金庸小說題材的歷史年代，[5] 其中《天龍八部》取材於北宋，「射鵰三部曲」爲南宋，《倚天屠龍記》爲元末，《俠客行》、《笑傲江湖》爲明代，《碧血劍》爲明末清初，《鹿鼎記》爲康熙朝，《書劍恩仇錄》、《雪山飛狐》、《飛狐外傳》爲乾隆朝，《鴛鴦刀》爲清代，《連城訣》爲清末。正與中國社會變遷的大趨勢一致，或者說是把握了中國歷史發展的趨勢。所述雖多「查無實據」，但畢竟「事出有因」。至於他對先秦至唐末「匹夫」、「閭里」和「鄉曲」之俠的愛重，除《越女劍》外，則以《三十三劍客圖》補足之。這些當然不是金庸小說的重心，故不論。

本世紀初，革命黨人藉海外爲基地開始反滿時，也開始了對秘密會黨的注意。孫中山先生不但身入洪門，並在《建國方略·有志竟成》中提出：「洪門者，創設於明朝遺老，起於康熙時代。蓋康熙以前，明朝之忠臣烈士，多欲力圖恢復，誓不臣清，捨生赴義，屢起屢蹶，與虜拼命，然卒不救明朝之亡。迨至康熙之世，清勢已盛，而明朝之忠烈亦死亡殆盡。二三遺老見大勢已去，無可挽回，乃欲以民族主義之根苗，流傳後代，故以反清復明之宗旨，結爲團體，以待後起者，可藉爲資助也。此殆洪門創設立本意也。」[6]

正是這個內憂外患的特定時期，引發了學者對明清之際中國社會變遷的特殊興趣，日人平山周著《中國秘密社會史》、《中國之秘密結社》（作者署「古研氏」）首開其端，而後有陶成章《教會源流考》、馮自由《革命逸史》、連橫

4　山西商幫票號雄視數百年，爲民間組織最嚴密而有成效者，徐珂《清稗類鈔·農商類·山西票號》亦曰：「相傳李自成擄巨資，敗走山西。及死，山西人得其資以設票號。其號中規則極嚴密，爲顧炎武所訂，遵行不廢，故稱雄於商界二百餘年。」（北京：中華書局 1987 年版，第 17 冊）。

5　見〈金庸小說的時代順序〉，其中未列入《白馬嘯西風》。儘管金庸在《笑傲江湖·後記》中曾鄭重聲明：「本書沒有歷史背景，這表示類似的情景可以發生在任何朝代。」但仍有好事者認定：「林震南的夫人是屬虎的，而在《笑》開始時她三十九歲，所以那一年是蛇年，即《笑》開始於紀元一四九七或紀元一五零九年。」見網文長江三俠〈笑傲江湖年代考〉。

6　《孫中山選集》（上）（北京：人民出版社，1961），頁 170-171。

《臺灣通史》、蕭一山先生《天地會起源考》等著作。[7] 尤其是二、三十年代學者的探討，其中包括一批極富情趣的題目，如孟心史《海寧陳家》、《袁督師後裔考序》、《董小宛考》、《香妃考實》、《太后下嫁考實》、《清世祖董鄂妃生死特殊典禮》、《世祖出家事考實》[8] 等等，深入清宮內闈秘聞的文章。而明史研究方面稍後亦出現吳晗〈明教與大明帝國〉[9] 上溯至元末的著述，拓展了研究隱性社會的範圍。這些討論涉及的問題，都或多或少地納入金庸小說的素材之中。

隱秘社會的話題，首先刺激了今稱「舊武俠小說派」的勃興，如平江不肖生、還珠樓主、王度廬、宮白羽、趙煥亭等。[10] 又葉洪生曾批校《近代中國武俠小說名著大系》，[11] 在〈論革命與武俠創作〉一文中還提及葉楚傖《古戍寒笳記》、蘇曼殊《焚劍記》等數十種作品。甚至新文學先行者魯迅亦寫過《非攻》、《鑄劍》、《奔月》諸篇。舊瓶新酒，正爲此也。「新派武俠」亦承襲了這個傳統，如梁羽生的三十五部武俠小說中，也刻意構築以時代社會變易爲背景的「江湖」隱秘社會。而香港以晚清黃飛鴻爲主角的武俠影視，變幻背景對象一拍再拍至百餘次，證明著觀眾興趣至今不衰。

金庸本人之經歷，實與近世國家民族內憂外患的命運休戚與共，時代特點造成的明清史學術旨趣直接導致了他的小說選材。金庸開手的第一部武俠小說《書劍恩仇錄》，就上承中山先生關於「洪門」創立之思想，描寫了「紅花會」這一隱性組織的抱負作爲。[12] 接著寫成的《碧血劍》又將時代上延，

7　平山周著作分別有商務印書館 1912 年 5 月和 1924 年中譯本，陶著載中華書局 1986 年版《陶成章集》，馮著中華書局 1986 年版，連著商務印書館 1983 年版，蕭著見《近代秘密社會史料》（上海：上海文藝出版社，1991 年影印本）。

8　孟森遺著輯爲《明清史論著集刊》正續編，由中華書局出版。上述文章即存於《續編》內。

9　輯入《吳晗史學論文集》（二）（北京：北京人民出版社，1986）。

10　如朱貞木《虎嘯龍吟》寫清初內家拳泰斗王征南與黃宗羲的友誼，文公直《碧血丹心大俠傳》三部曲寫謙匡扶社稷之事蹟，姚民哀《四海神龍記》寫晚清鎮江留日志士姜伯先的江湖俠義，平江不肖生《江湖奇俠傳》敍反清復明之崑崙派與江湖門派崆峒派的糾葛，最後爲「江南酒俠」曉以大義事，都有所寄寓。但大多數舊派武俠小說只述江湖恩怨，沒有明顯的時代背景。

11　由臺北聯經出版事業公司 1984 年出版。

12　按「天地會」典籍及傳說中本有「紅花亭」（有些記載寫作「洪花亭」），爲天地會盟誓之所。

創造出以袁崇煥舊部「山宗」爲代表的反清復明組織，然後逐漸延伸到宋、元，最後《鹿鼎記》又回到「天地會」這個隱秘社會的舊題目上來，只是旨趣與初始大有不同，下文再表。

　　此次會議中，金庸答疑時曾言，所以未以漢唐爲小說背景，是因爲生活細節睽隔太久，不易描述故也。愚以爲實則宋元以迄明清時代的生活細節，亦難復原，金庸小說這方面的描寫，揆之當時筆記所載，仍然可以挑剔出疵瑕。蓋緣漢唐時代的經濟及社會制度，尚不足以出現「隱性社會」，即使唐人小說鋪敍之事，仍然不出「匹夫」、「鄉曲」、「閭里」之俠的範圍，如金庸先生轉敍之《三十三劍俠傳》然，其中人物或可借鑒發揮，但其背景卻萬難敷衍成若許長篇。金庸小說選材所以限定於宋元以後，也是不自覺中的自然所爲。

三、朝代變遷與顯隱互易

　　武俠小說上承〈游俠列傳〉宗旨，向以「傳奇」（奇人奇事）爲皈依。要突出風雲際會，特立獨行，自必安排在「天崩地解」之社會大變革中，尤其是民族政權易手的當口，才能充分凸顯不同社會價值系統之激烈衝撞。老子曰：「大道廢，有仁義；智慧出，有大僞；六親不和，有孝慈；國家昏亂，有忠臣。」[13] 正謂此也。

　　朝代陵替和民族衝突引起的社會動蕩，百姓受盡苦難，在這種關頭，顯性社會的「禮」與「法」爲主的大架構已全然失去功用，反倒是深入民心的「忠」與「義」的觀念，成爲振刷舊朝積弊，振作民族精神的旗幟，民間結社團結抗戰成爲主流。據載金兵占領河東時，曾下令「今隨處既歸本朝，宜同風俗。亦仰削去頭髮，短巾，左衽。敢有違犯，即是猶懷舊國，當正典刑。不得錯失，付逐處。」宋欽宗《宋主與河北河東敕》諄諄勸降道：「民雖居大金，苟樂其生，猶吾民也，其勿懷顧戀之意。」與金人頗有唱和之妙。但是由齎送這道詔命的欽差聶昌《說諭河東士民》文告看，「昨者備坐聖旨，約知通以次出城面議。既不略至城外，審驗是非，諭問端的，輒下矢石，引兵

13　《老子》第十八章。

出戰，殆非體認朝廷危迫之意。昨晚又遣三輩齎敕書往，又復無報。不知公等意欲何爲？」[14] 顯然河東士民並不怕軟硬兼施的一套，相反卻反抗割讓，進行過堅決的抗金鬥爭，[15] 猶若金庸在《神鵰俠侶》中描述的郭靖、黃蓉夫婦由隱而顯，以丐幫幫主身份領袖群倫，組織襄陽守城，抗擊元軍達十數年之久然。而在《碧血劍》中，金庸敍袁崇煥餘部以明朝「官軍」之顯性身份，自結號爲「山宗」的隱秘組織，後來泰山人會上聯絡七省英豪，繼續抗清大業，則是由顯而隱的相反事例。

昔者莊子論劍，以江湖爭鬥、快意恩仇爲「庶人之劍」，「蓬頭突鬢，垂冠，曼胡之纓，短後之衣，瞋目而語難，相擊於前，上斬頸領，下決肝肺。此庶人之劍，無異於鬥雞，一旦命已絕矣，無所用於國事。」而安定天下的「天子之劍」則應「以燕谿石城爲鋒，齊岱爲鍔，晉衛爲脊，周宋爲鐔，韓魏爲夾，包以四夷，裹以四時，繞以渤海，帶以常山，制以五行，論以刑德，開以陰陽，持以春夏，行以秋冬。此劍直之無前，舉之無上，案之無下，運之無旁。上決浮雲，下絕地紀。此劍一用，匡諸侯，天下服矣。」安邦守土之「諸侯之劍，以知勇士爲鋒，以清廉士爲鍔，以賢良士爲脊，以忠聖士爲鐔，以豪桀士爲夾。此劍直之亦無前，舉之亦無上，案之亦無下，運之亦無旁。上法圓天，以順三光；下法方地，以順四時；中和民意，以安四鄉。此劍一用，如雷霆之震也，四封之內，無不賓服而聽從君命者矣。」[16] 三種境界決定了武俠小說的精神內涵、價值取向和設定品位。

金庸小說泰半取材於鼎革之際，把握這個關目，正欲以民族存亡、文化絕續的大題目、大關節，來提調讀者的關懷，並闡釋他的「俠義」觀念。其中《天龍八部》雖然寫北宋，但其時中原趙氏政權之外，尚有北部「分庭抗禮」之契丹政權、和偏安一隅的西夏李氏、大理段氏和吐蕃，彼此攻伐，動

---

14 上海書店影印神州國光社 1951 年版《中國內亂外禍歷史叢書》之《避戎夜話》卷3，上引同。

15 當時河東河北「紅巾軍」、「忠義社」以「懷土顧戀，以死堅守」爲號召，組織數十萬民兵堅持抗金，堅持數年以及終因長期失去支援而失敗的經過，鄧廣銘〈南宋初年對金鬥爭的幾個問題〉（《鄧廣銘治史叢稿》，北京：北京大學出版社，1997 年 6 月）曾有撮述，可以參看。

16 《莊子・雜篇・說劍第三十》。

亂不寧，可視爲同樣背景。

金庸嘗言：

> 我們中華民族遇到外族入侵時，常常能把外族打退，打不退的情況也很多，但卻
> 很難被征服。這是因爲一方面我們有一股韌力，一股很頑強的抵抗力量；一方面
> 我們又很開放，在文化上同它們融合在一起，經過一段時間，大家變成一個民族，
> 我們的民族從此又壯大起來。[17]
> 我初期所寫的小説，漢人皇朝的正統觀念很強。到了後期，中華民族各族一視同
> 仁的觀念成爲基調，那是我的歷史觀比較有了些進步之故。這在《天龍八部》、《白
> 馬嘯西風》、《鹿鼎記》中特別明顯。[18]

事實上，金庸小説在處理民族紛爭，政權易手的態度上凡有三變，謹略述之。

第一時期是承襲清末民初的「革命排滿」觀念和有關史料，描述明清之際遺民俠士和隱性社會在「反清復明」口號下的不屈抗爭，推崇以「漢民族主義」爲中心價值的正派隱性社會。代表作品爲《書劍恩仇錄》、《碧血劍》和《雪山飛狐》等。在《鴛鴦刀》的結束，還特地抖露「包袱」説：

> 「滿清皇帝聽説這雙刀之中，有一個能無敵於天下的大秘密，這果然不錯，可是他
> 便知道了這秘密，有能依著行麼？各位請看！」衆人湊近看時，只見鴛刀的刀刃
> 上刻著「仁者」，鴦刀上刻著「無敵」兩字。「仁者無敵」！這便是無敵於天下的大
> 秘密。[19]

17　〈金庸談中國文明〉，載《明報月刊》，1994 年 12 月號。

18　《金庸作品集·自序》，（北京：三聯書店，1994 年 5 月），頁 4。

19　《碧血劍》開首寫明末勃泥國華僑張朝唐回國趕考，遇見官兵搶掠，尤甚於匪的情狀，
　　也是有案可查的。明人馮夢龍在《甲申紀事自敍》中敍明末「兵害勝於寇害」曰：「有
　　兵而若無兵，且其害更甚於無兵，是以慮也。古者用兵，寧使餉浮於兵，不使兵浮於
　　餉。今未具餉而先聚兵，兵既具而餉不足，於是倡爲『打糧』之説，公然掃掠民間，
　　掠婦女則爲妻妾，掠丁壯則爲奴僕，一兵家屬多者至十餘人。朝廷養一兵，不能並養
　　其十餘人之家屬，其勢益不得不出於掃掠。而有兵之處閭裡皆空，未翦一二賊兵，先
　　添萬千兵賊，百姓嗷嗷，無所控訴，良可痛矣！不特此也，兵既有家屬，勢不能草居
　　露宿，於是民間之居，用民間之物，兵富而民貧，兵樂而民苦。才一徵調，則又有
　　安插家小之説，揀擇瘠肥，遷延月日，勢所必至，從設兵以來未有是也。……兵之戀

也是認定清室不能行「仁政」。

後來他超越了「漢民族主義」，從多民族視角主張融合共處，敍事亦爲之一變。如史書曾載遼、宋邊將常以「打草穀」爲名，相互劫掠人丁財物，金庸借以作爲《天龍八部》結撰蕭（喬）峯等一干人曲折恩怨的大關節。曾爲中原「丐幫幫主」的契丹人蕭峯之言述：

> 你可曾見過邊關之上，宋遼相互仇殺的慘狀？可曾見過宋人遼人妻離子散、家破人亡的情景？宋遼之間好容易罷兵數十年，倘若刀兵再起，契丹鐵騎侵入南朝，你可知將有多少宋人慘遭橫死？多少遼人死於非命？」「兵凶戰危，世間豈有必勝之事？大宋兵多財足，只須有一二名將，率兵奮戰，大遼、吐蕃聯手，未必便能取勝。咱們打一個血流成河，屍骨如山，欲讓你慕容氏來乘機興復燕國，我對大遼盡忠報國，是在保土安民，而不是爲了一己的榮華富貴，因而殺人取地、建功立業。

其義等同於墨者「禁殺傷人者，天下之大義也」。全書結末寫蕭峯不惜以死換取宋遼相安，成爲漢、契丹、鮮卑等各族人人嘆服的「大英雄」。他的觀念又得到全書的另外兩位中心人物，大理國主段譽和出身少林的西夏駙馬虛竹的極力推崇。而隨著蕭遠山、慕容博在少林掃地僧指點迷津後笑泯恩仇，吐蕃國師鳩摩智覺悟正果，「興復祖業狂」鮮卑慕容復瘋癲，金庸也完成了他賦予作品的主旨。

其後金庸參悟中國文化演進之謎，破除了漢滿政權交替，「夷夏大防」之「知見障」，觀念再爲之一變。

「中華」向來爲一文化概念。孔穎達疏有「中國有禮義之大，故稱之夏；有服章之美，故謂之華。」按照「諸候用夷禮則夷之，夷而進於中國則中國之」的觀念，滿族入關，改變了宋時女眞政權焚毀文物圖籍，劫掠人口財物北去的方針，加速了「全盤漢化」的進程，其中之變，乃是順治二年多爾袞

戀家室如此，即使驅之赴敵，亦內顧之意多，而進取之意少，求其死綏立功，尚安可得？此弊不革，恐餉終無時而足，兵終無時而可用也。見在之兵尚然，而更欲紛紛招募，將安用之？且昌平之亂由兵而不由民，淮陽之守由民而不由兵；京口一留兵，而即有西門焚殺之慘；金華一招兵，即有湯溪破城之變。兵之爲害，歷歷可見。」載鄭振鐸編輯，《玄覽堂叢書》（上海：玄覽堂，1941年線裝影印本）。

依山東人孫之獬的建議，下達「薙髮令」嚴令漢族變易明代衣冠之後，讓江南士人溫習了「披髮左袵」、文化變亂的故典，引起了「天崩地解」的憂慮，造成明遺民猛烈反抗，激起連韋小寶都念茲在茲的「揚州十日」、「嘉定三屠」等慘烈的大事件來。順治親政，尤其是康熙爲彌合民族矛盾做了很多値得肯定的工作，包括對明遺民的安置和尊重、輕徭薄賦、減輕戰亂地區負擔等，以致「清承明制」成爲史家定評。

《鹿鼎記》是金庸「金盆洗手」之作，第一主角其實是康熙，主幹事件則是除鰲拜，平三藩，收臺灣，尼布楚談判，也是史家以爲功績的系列事件。金庸一反前期作品的觀念，著力塑造了康熙的「仁君」形象，並借他之口，表達了「宮裡的一切使用，一兩銀子都是來自老百姓。百姓供養我錦衣玉食。我君臨萬民，就當盡心竭力，爲百姓辦事。你食君之祿，當忠君之事。我食民之祿，就當忠民之事。古書上說：『四海困窮，則天祿永終。』如果百姓窮困，那就是皇帝不好，上天震怒，我這皇帝也就做不成了。」在《鹿鼎記》後附的〈康熙朝的機密奏摺〉一文中，金庸並不掩飾他對康熙的好感，認爲「批示之中，可以見到康熙英明而謹愼，同時對待臣下和百姓都很寬仁」。他筆下的近世第一隱秘組織──「天地會」因而呈現出複雜的形態，不復「紅花會」之大義凜然。《鹿鼎記》與《碧血劍》人物故事時隱時現的接續，我猜亦有矯正前期偏頗之意。

當然，政權易幟、外族入主，會使顯性社會的中心價値觀念發生混亂或者崩解，引起紛亂，這恰爲作者創造隱性社會五花八門的幫派形象，開闢出巨人的空間。除刻意塑造的「名門正派」以外，金庸小說涉筆成趣的江湖門派甚多，雖似信手拈來，卻爲讀者會心一笑，或者津津樂道。其中因內廷陰謀導致領導權轉移，新的機制又造成整個組織變質的「日月神教」、領導人變質而使組織衰微的「華山派」（以上見《笑傲江湖》）、以拍馬屁唱頌歌爲標志的「星宿派」（《天龍八部》）、以下作手段控制組織，樹立領袖絕對權威的「神龍教」（《鹿鼎記》），等等。這在金庸後期創作中尤其突出，甚至具有某種「寓言」性質的警世意味，都給讀者留下難忘的印象。

四、三教九流與隱性社會

中國自周以來「以農立國」，「以農爲本」，長期還以「井田制」爲社會理想範式，並以此爲中心設計出一整套政治和管理制度來。「離土離鄉」意味著逸出傳統的範式制度之外，其流動隱秘，生計無常的特性，又使這些游民往往具有破壞力。常言道：「車船店腳牙，無罪也該殺」，從農本社會的觀念出發，這些離土離鄉、游蹤不定，或者以交通流通爲業的江湖角色，都是行事乖張，所爲可疑，坑蒙拐騙之輩。也是古代法制最難管理的一類。這類角色恰合莊子「不如相忘於江湖」（〈內篇・大宗師〉）中「江湖」二字的本意，構成傳統中國社會豐富的人物譜系。從宋元說話人開始，他們詭詭幻怪的生活和生存狀態，就是傳奇故事的基本題材。「三教九流」其實是古代對游民階層的統稱，諸如僧尼道姑，醫卜星相，倡優丐隸，商販盜賊，等等。

首先說「三教」問題。釋道儒「三教」從北朝開始「論衡」，到宋代的「圓融」，走過了由衝突、磨合到會通的漫長路程。筆者曾有〈三教論衡與唐代俗講〉[20] 一文論析，此不贅言。但以中國思想文化的主流，爲隱性社會的重要基礎，卻須略加辨析。

有讀者曾對金庸的宗教觀念有過論爭。[21] 我以爲出於對宗教的敬意，金庸小說中一向以少林、武當爲武林以及隱秘社會「名門正派」之首，這是不爭的事實。自禪門「叢林」制度化，並且影響到道觀和書院以後，釋道兩教儘管仍各有門派，但大體上形成了體系化、全國性的組織。少林地處中原，由於達摩曾經住錫，故向爲禪林名剎。近世武俠小說於禪叢中獨鍾少林，我以爲不一定起自「十八棍僧救秦王」的唐代傳說，恐怕與天地會「西魯傳說」中的少林事跡關連更密。[22] 金庸善以少林爲諸小說綰合情節，提調線索，領

20　拙文載《周紹良先生欣開九秩紀念文集》（北京：中華書局，1997 年 5 月），頁 405-422。

21　參見網文金剛〈歪批金庸〉及法雨〈金庸與佛〉。

22　參嘉慶十六年於廣西東蘭州武緣縣發現之天地會《會簿》（現存中國第一歷史檔案館）所載之「西魯傳說」，略謂康熙時西魯番作亂，康熙懸賞征帥。甘肅少林僧眾一百二十八人出征，凱旋後不受封賞。後爲奸臣迫害慘極，火燒少林，遂有十八僧走至「海石連天」，師尊萬提起法號雲龍，與門徒兄弟再集百零七人，指洪爲姓，與清兵血戰。

袖群倫之樞紐，即使驟臨群雄圍攻，也自有隱居高僧化解孽障，如《天龍八部》之掃地僧然。而少林眾僧也儼然自成系列，如于萬亭（俗家弟子，見《書劍恩仇錄》）、無色（《神鵰俠侶》）、覺遠、空聞、圓音（《倚天屠龍記》）、玄慈、虛竹（《天龍八部》）、妙諦（《俠客行》）、方證（《笑傲江湖》）、晦聰（《鹿鼎記》）等等。由於佛教有超越地域甚至國界的特點，所以金庸恆以吐蕃或西域之番僧胡僧，作爲神秘的外來門派，如靈智上人（《射鵰英雄傳》）、金輪法王（《神鵰俠侶》）、鳩摩智（《天龍八部》）等，以收出人意表，莫測變幻之功效。

　　武當之張三丰武學傳說本多，明時已被目爲神仙者流，[23] 作者以之與少林分庭抗禮，自是情理中事。而《倚天屠龍記》主角張無忌出身即爲武當。此外，金庸還在「射鵰」三部曲中著重介紹了全眞教（見《射鵰英雄傳》後附〈關於「全眞教」〉一文）的崛起，恐怕是金庸以《長春眞人西遊記》有關丘處機遠赴西域去見成吉思汗的事跡，與小說時代關合，引起的興趣所及。道教作爲中國本土宗敎，也影響到日本、朝鮮和越南，但不知爲何，金庸小說從未出現海外之道家高手助戰。[24]

　　倒是儒家向爲顯性社會之中堅，何以並列「三敎」，躋身隱性社會，尚需略論。

雲龍死後由五兄弟護至雲宵高溪廟安葬。這是有關天地會起始的主要傳說。又明末福王之堂叔痛禪上人遁跡少林，據說「今少林派開始第一手，以左手握拳，右手拊其背，即寓僅背國仇之義；地盆則以踏入中宮，以示不忘中國之旨。這就是痛禪上人傳下來的。」轉引自《中國武術史》（北京：人民體育出版社，1982 年 5 月），頁 46。

23 張氏生平關如，《明史》入〈方伎傳〉。明太祖、成祖都曾尋訪不遇，英宗敕封「通微顯化眞人」。關於張三丰的傳說最神奇的是說他「研磨太極陰陽之奧蘊，靜觀龜鶴之動態，探究其長壽之源，頓有所得。」（《大岳太和山志》），述武功最高妙的則是「夜夢玄帝授以拳法，厲明，以單丁殺賊百餘。」（黃宗義，《南雷文集·王征南墓志銘》）。武當道觀於明時獨顯，永樂初甚至發國帑工伕與紫禁城同時修建，主因還是其供奉之主神北方玄武（眞武）自宋初「降神」事件而地位漸尊，王欽若〈翊聖保德傳〉言：「翊聖眞君降盤崖民張守眞家，太祖、太宗皆崇信之……故道家都尊玄武。此所謂翊聖眞君，即玄武也。」（《四庫全書總目·子部·道家類存目》）「靖難」之役後又作爲朱棣之保護神，故特崇而祀之武當，其信仰沿襲至清。

24 歷史上之釋道「論衡」，時有可觀，如《廣弘明集》卷 4 高祖文宣皇帝〈廢李老道法詔〉所述北齊時道士陸修靜率徒與釋徒上統，雲顯鬥法，爲《西遊記》類似故事張本。但金庸小說未取此種描述。

蓋有宋文化普及以來，失意官僚和落第舉子居常時既具「處江湖之遠，則憂其君」之關懷，變亂中又有「天下興亡，匹夫有責」之憂憤，平民意識、遺民身份和結社風尚，使他們逐漸捲入隱秘社會的漩渦之中。《鹿鼎記》開首金庸回到明末清初重新以歷史為大構架，敍述起顧炎武、黃宗羲、呂留良、莊廷鑨「《明史》案」等掌故，[25] 後來又寫群雄大會推舉顧炎武為反清隱性社會之「總軍師」，就是出於這種認識。

儒者於武林的關涉，亦有可道者。大概是出於對王陽明學業事功，俱有大成，「內聖外王」的仰慕，據載：

> 明季中葉以後，科甲出身之人，頗有習武事者。《明史》所載，不一而足。如光州劉綸好擊劍，力挽六石弓，登嘉靖四年進士。宜黃譚綸，嘉靖廿三年進士，積首功二萬一千五百，嘗戰酣刃血漬腕，累沃乃脫。麻城梅之煥〔煥〕，萬曆三十二年進士，與材官角射，九發九中。嘉定孫元化，天啓舉人，善西洋炮法，綿竹劉宇亮，萬曆四十七年進士，善擊劍。萊陽沈迅，崇禎四年進士，短小精悍，馬上舞百斤鐵錐。而熊廷弼、盧象升二人尤以善射多力稱。蓋彼時科場陋習遂甚，究不致以小楷大卷桎梏其身。且從事學術之人亦究居少數，故得有餘閑鍛煉膂力也。清初尚存此風，如宋犖年十四以大臣子入宿衛，世祖渡桑乾，水闊數丈，犖躍馬以過，賜雕翎箭，見《碑傳集》。戴衢亨在阿濟格突圍場時，逸出一兔，即執之以獻。又于敏中於木蘭行帳中獲一鹿。均見乾隆《御制詩》。又康熙十八年學士孫在豐扈從南苑，授御用弓矢使射麋，獲之。見康熙《御制詩》。蓋自嘉、道以後，士大夫之高者講求精微之漢學，卑者汩沒於庸濫之場屋文字，風氣始日趨柔靡矣。此論世者所不可不知也。[26]

金庸小說雖也寫到了一批具有儒者風範，擅長琴棋書畫的人物，如「江

25　《鹿鼎記》中金庸寫及「莊氏史案」和顧炎武、黃宗羲、呂留良諸人，都以文士面目出現。史料有稱顧能手擒叛僕，數其罪而親沉之潭（《鮚埼亭集》，卷12〈亭林神道表〉）黃宗羲曾手錐父仇（《鮚埼亭集》卷11〈梨洲神道碑〉）；顏元嘗削竹為劍，擊敗「商水大俠李子青」（戴望，〈顏元傳〉，載《顏氏學記》卷1）。呂留良有「十年游俠千金盡，九世怨仇一劍知。為問門前車馬客，還能杯酒憶當時？」（《萬感集》卷5〈絕句〉）的詩，亦儼然自居大俠。

26　銖庵，《人物風俗制度談叢》（太原：山西古籍出版社，1997年7月），頁46-47。

南四友」(《笑傲江湖》)、以設計「珍瓏」教徒的「逍遙派」創始人無崖子(《天龍八部》)等,可惜風雅有餘,略嫌皮相,並未由此開掘。「三教」之武林風采,蓋有缺憾焉。

隱性社會與九流之關聯,比之三教要容易理解得多。其中乞丐是最典型的「游民」,金庸創造的「丐幫」在多部小說中出現過,其歷代幫主洪七公、黃蓉、喬峯、游坦之等也成為具有典型意義的人物系列。中國乞丐組織應該是始終存在,但是史料中卻從無「丐幫」之名。我猜金庸多少從雨果《巴黎聖母院》的描述的「乞丐王國」中得到過啟發。

九流人等,流品不一,諸色騙術歷來為其特色之一。金庸描述冒稱「鐵掌水上飄」之老兒裘千丈的吹牛功夫(《射鵰英雄傳》)頗有妙處。自《水滸傳》以來,綽號便是強調人物特點的不二法門,也與江湖豪傑「揚名立萬兒」的初衷不遠。《鴛鴦刀》刻劃小蟊賊如「太岳四俠」相當傳神:「咱大哥是煙霞神龍逍遙子,二哥是雙掌開碑常長風,三哥是流星趕月花劍影,區區在下是八步趕蟾、賽專諸、踏雪無痕、獨腳水上飛、雙刺蓋七省蓋一鳴!」而「二位夫人悄悄一張,見那人是個形容委瑣的瘦子,身旁還坐著三個古裡古怪的人物。」其作為卻也中規中矩,與「俠」的傳統定義不中不遠。結末網捕卓天雄,也算是全書「臨去秋波那一轉」的關鍵。他們是金庸筆下最富於喜劇色彩的人物組群之一。

宮廷內闈是一個特殊範疇。宮廷應該是「正統社會」的集中體現,但內闈卻完全是一個充滿陰謀、鬥爭和殘殺的世界。從這個意義上講,內闈無疑屬於「隱性社會」的範疇。金庸在《鹿鼎記》中,著意把江湖隱性社會的焦點,通過韋小寶這個「儱賴家伙」,集中在大內宮闈之內。這裡同時出現了「天地會」(韋小寶為其創始人陳近南之收關弟子和青木堂香主)、崇禎遺孤九難和李自成(《碧血劍》,韋小寶為九難「鐵劍門」之嫡傳弟子)、神龍教(仿佛《笑傲江湖》中的「日月神教」,韋小寶為其白龍使)等等隱秘組織,與宮廷密謀,內闈爭風絞結一起,五光十色。同事樓肇明兄言,金庸以為宮廷與妓院同為社會最虛偽的地方,不能不說是一個大膽的論點。此論極是。

牢獄從來是陽光不到之處。金庸描寫羈押囚禁之地甚多,但《笑傲江湖》囚任我行,與《俠客行》羈白自在略有雷同。《連城訣》中描寫丁典、狄雲之遭遇則較為獨特。而黃裳羈縻周伯通,老頑童卻於嫉妒孤獨之中,發明「雙

手互搏」之無上功夫，恐怕是由茨威格《象棋的故事》主人公自弈導致警世分裂的故事得到的啓發，只不過以喜劇方式處理罷了。

金庸糾結全篇樞紐，或組織情節高潮，調動隱密社會各派一時並現的基本手法有三：曰「武林大會」和尋訪「武林秘笈」或「藏寶圖籍」。「武林爭霸」（尋訪武林秘笈，亦爲爭霸而起）之大事，如「華山論劍」（《射鵰英雄傳》、《神鵰俠侶》），「倚天」、「屠龍」會（《倚天屠龍記》），「俠客島」邀請（《俠客行》）等等，幾乎每部都有。其事本無可能，後期金庸小說創造出一些準宗教組織，來豐富小說背景，設置怪異人物和魔幻武功，如被稱爲「魔教」、「邪教」之「日月神教」、「神龍教」、「星宿派」等，爲隱性社會中最隱密者。以其宗旨但奉現任教主，非關教化救渡，而殺人作孽，荼毒生靈以爲樂，隱然有王霸天下之志，因此每爲「爭霸」行釁爭端，挑起武林大亂。惟有「明教」是一例外。按明教爲歷史實有之宗教派別，其前身唐時由波斯傳入，但自北宋方臘即被視爲「食菜魔教」，以後一直受到壓制。[27] 金庸以其異域風情、神秘傳說、美麗人物，加諸小說鋪敍描寫之中，時有唐人韻味。小說寫明教抗元成就大業，卻以狡詐陰險之朱元璋位登九五，教主張無忌等「心灰意懶」，退隱山林爲結束。金庸認爲：「中國三千年的政治史，早就將結論明確地擺在那裡。中國成功的政治領袖，第一個條件是『忍』，包括克制自己之忍、容人之忍、以及對付政敵的殘忍。第二個條件是『決斷明快』。第三是極強的權力欲。張無忌半個條件也沒有。」（《倚天屠龍記》後記）

而尋寶故事向爲希臘神話所擅，本非中土故典。但金庸善以該事爲大關目，如「高昌迷宮寶藏」（《白馬嘯西風》）、「建文寶藏」（《碧血劍》）、「闖王寶藏」（《雪山飛狐》）和「滿州寶藏」（《鹿鼎記》）。其中「闖王寶藏」事並非空穴來風。《明史》卷三〇九〈李自成傳〉云：「自成至，悉熔所考索金及宮中帑藏、器皿、鑄爲餅，每餅千金，約數萬餅，騾車載歸西安。」未言終歸何處。後世傳言紛紜，如張一麔先生有歌曰：「莫打鼓來莫打鑼，聽我唱個因果歌。那李闖逼死崇禎帝，那文武百官一網羅。那闖將同聲敲夾烙，霎時

27　明教作爲宗教發展曲折，變化極大，已失本意。吳晗〈明教與大明帝國〉曰：「明教初始爲摩尼教，會昌禁斷後，已合於佛，已混於道，又與出自佛教之大乘教。三階教合。至北宋末又於出自佛教淨土宗之白蓮社合，與出自佛教淨土宗之彌勒教合。」頁401。明清以來參與政治鬥爭極多，已成專學。茲不贅。

間金銀堆積滿巖阿。沖冠一怒吳三桂，借清兵驅賊出京都。賊兵捨不得金銀走，馬上累累『沒奈何』（自註：金銀大塊名）。一路追兵潮湧至，把金銀向山西境上掩埋過。賊兵一去不復返，農夫掘地富翁多。三百年票莊稱雄久，不成文法孰嗟磨。相傳是亭林、青主兩公筆，這一椿公案確無訛。」[28] 寶藏引得秘密幫派鬥角鈎心，處心積慮，紛爭不已，從而凸現「名門正派」興復大業之苦心孤詣，同時迭宕情節，設置懸疑，平生無限曲折風波。惟韋小寶雖費盡周折，力挫群雄，從《四十二章經》中取得滿洲寶藏圖籍，結末「閑居無聊之際，想起雅克薩城鹿鼎山下尚有巨大寶藏未曾發掘，自覺富甲天下，心滿意足，只是念著康熙的交情，才不忍去斷他龍脈。」既與作者表達之主旨相合，又留下懸念供讀者玩味，是一意外安排。

五、正邪人物與黑白兩道

　　江湖社會所以分化產生了「黑白兩道」，區分在於其「道」之宗旨是否正大，手段是否光明，而核心在於領袖人物的人格指向。隱性社會置身法律之外，其奇人逸士為人行事，常有出人意表者。金庸小說描繪的主角，從強調「正邪分明」（如《碧血劍》之袁承志、《射鵰英雄傳》之主角郭靖），到「亦正亦邪」（如《神鵰俠侶》之楊過）、再到「無正無邪」（如《笑傲江湖》之令狐沖）和「無所謂正邪」（如《鹿鼎記》之韋小寶），表明著作者極深的感喟，而江湖上所謂「黑白兩道」之界限也逐漸趨於模糊。這種表述的變化，與其說是宣示江湖風波之詭異，不如說是表現了時代、社會價值觀念從一元到多元的流變。

　　莊子嘗言：「盜跖從卒九千人，橫行天下，侵暴諸侯。穴室樞戶，驅人牛馬，取人婦女。貪得忘親，不顧父母兄弟，不祭先祖。所過之邑，大國守城，小國入保，萬民苦之。」孔子往見，欲以「三德」說之。不意竟為盜跖所痛斥，以為「丘之所言，皆吾之所棄也。亟去走歸，無復言之！子之道狂狂汲汲，詐巧虛偽事也，非可以全真也，奚足論哉！」以致「出門上車，執轡三失，目芒然無見，色若死灰，據軾低頭，不能出氣。」其後子張詰難於

28　見〈五十年來國事叢譚〉，載《最近之五十年》（上海：申報館，1923），頁28。

滿苟得，竟爲其「無恥者富，多信者顯。夫名利之大者，幾在無恥而信」的言論和舉例所屈。（見〈雜篇・盜跖第二十九〉）莊子在這裡以寓言形式表述的，除了他一貫的「彼亦一是非，此亦一是非」（〈內篇・齊物論第二〉）觀念外，也道盡了社會變動時期價值觀念的轉移和多元化趨向的實情。

金庸當然不是「無是非」論者，而且中國武俠小說的靈魂和魅力，始終在於著力闡釋「俠義」二字的眞諦。金庸曾言：「我企圖在本書中寫一個急人之難、行俠仗義的俠士。武俠小說中眞正寫俠士的其實並不很多，大多數主角的所做所爲，主要是武而不是俠。孟子說：『富貴不能淫，貧賤不能移，威武不能屈，此之謂大丈夫。』武俠人物對富貴貧賤並不放在心上，更加不屈於威武，這大丈夫的三條標準，他們都不難做到。在本書之中，我想給胡斐增加一些要求，要他『不爲美色所動，不爲哀懇所動，不爲面子所動。』只是在我所寫的這許多男性人物中，胡斐、喬峯、楊過、郭靖、令狐冲這幾個是我比較特別喜歡的。」（《雪山飛狐》後記）即使被視爲「反英雄」代表形象之韋小寶，金庸也認爲「韋小寶重視義氣，那是好的品德。」（《鹿鼎記》後記）面臨康熙帝與天地會不可調和的衝突，韋小寶的解決方案倒也直截了當：「旣能讓皇上歡喜，又顧得了朋友義氣，而奴才自己這顆腦袋，仍是生得牢牢的。」「皇上要我滅了天地會，我不肯幹，那是講義氣。你們要我去刺殺皇帝，我也不幹，那也是講義氣。」（四十九回）

金庸小說的「正邪」人物已形成燦爛的譜系。如果說開初的主人公陳家洛、袁承志、郭靖都還是大義凜然、愛憎分明，頗有些「高大全」的話，一路寫下來變化紛呈，如《天龍八部》中多情如賈寶玉之段譽，豪爽類魯智深之蕭峯，篤厚似劉玄德之虛竹。金聖嘆批點《水滸傳》，以爲李逵是「一片天眞爛漫到底」，這其實是從戲劇臉譜發展出來的通俗小說傳統，金庸還把若干人物形象「符號化」，如阿朱的黠慧，阿紫的刁蠻，李莫愁的情怨，楊過的狂傲，小龍女的冷艷，等等等等，不一而足。江南玄素莊莊主石清、閔柔夫婦黑白分明，卻生了一對正邪分明的雙胞胎（《俠客行》），正所謂「龍生九種，種種不同」。尤其是華山論劍之「東邪西毒北丐南帝中神通」加上老頑童，更是刻意以人物正邪相間，性格差異造成的反差，來擴大小說容量。至於描述如戚長發之深機、岳不群之僞善，則需著意鋪排，逐次點染，在一個較長的過程中顯現出來，是要費些手段周章的。這類形象錯綜於金庸人物譜系之中，

無疑展現出作者對人生的感悟理解，也豐富了作品的內涵。

　　金庸的主人公們最終都歸於隱逸。莊子曰：「至人無己，神人無功，聖人無名。」（〈內篇‧逍遙遊第一〉）「俠」之謂「俠」，命運如是，理想亦當如是。〈游俠列傳〉謂：「太史公曰：昔者虞舜窘於井廩，伊尹負於鼎俎，傅說匿於傅險，呂尚困於棘津，夷吾桎梏，百里飯牛，仲尼畏匡，菜色陳蔡，此皆學士所謂有道仁人也，猶然遭此災，況以中材而涉亂世之末流乎？其遇害何可勝道哉！」金庸的讀者大抵是「以中材而涉亂世之末流」。他們從金庸的人物系列中各取所需，悠然心會，「黑白」「正邪」與否，或許倒是次要的了。

　　大率而言，金庸生活和寫作的時代，是一個意識形態至上的時代，而且相當長的一個時期，不同意識形態發生尖銳衝突，以致具體化到每個人的每件事都需要表明「立場態度」的地步。另一方面，「神聖化」的意識形態體系又在不斷地變化之中，從「排滿革命」到「五族共和」，從「大割資本主義尾巴」到「顧客是上帝」[29] 和「市場經濟」，價值體系的動盪搖擺，宛如一個無比巨大的萬花筒。金庸身處是非地外，自能更容易地覺察到其中蘊含著荒誕的幽默。

六、餘　論

　　《左傳‧昭公二十九年》：「共工氏有子曰句龍，為后土……后土為社。」《禮記》：「句龍為后土，能平九州，故祀以為社。」

　　「會」本義為聚合匯集，《易‧乾》：「亨者，嘉之會也。」《論語‧顏淵》：「君子以文會友。」鄭玄注《中庸》「仁」曰「與人相偶」，「偶者，會也。」引申為際會，《文選‧漢陳孔璋（琳）為袁紹檄豫州文》：「此乃忠臣肝腦涂地之秋，烈士立功之會。」

29　「顧客是上帝」是目前商界的流行口號。但上帝顯然不是消費者，確是整個西方價值系統的源泉。儘管「任何比喻都是有缺陷的」，但這個比喻實屬不倫。英人有「國王永遠是對的」的成語，後來營銷學強調市場需求，仿此造出「顧客永遠是對的」。此番議論自然與金庸小說無關，不過說明意識形態論者搖擺幅度之大，有令人瞠目結舌的感覺而已。

　　以此觀之，傳統中「社」與「會」，都是自治組織，且是中國社會不可分割之部分。分別而又咬文嚼字地說，「社」更接近於地域結合，「會」更合於同道聯絡。至於後世「社」「會」用於團體組織時，時有互訓之義。近世日人翻譯 society，首以「社會」一詞爲其對應。以西人眼光看，仍有「法理社會」和「禮俗社會」之別。[30] 我以爲，即便在統一價值系統和法律環境的顯性社會中，仍應當給區域性（社）和行業性（會）團體以相當的自治空間，以發揮「俠文化」的道義功能補償作用。

　　倘若中國仍須發揮「俠」的文化功能和社會功能，那麼「武俠小說」的產生發展自有它的必然，也自有繼續存在和提升的必要。我們希望，金庸先生如此精彩的著作，不至於成爲《廣陵散》似的絕響。

　　這當然是逸出金庸小說以外的話題了。王夫之《薑齋詩話》云：「作者用一致之思，而讀者各以其情遇。」這道破了「詮釋學」的眞諦要訣，讀者自有不問初衷，只論感受的特權。這番不管三七二十一的言論，絕無強作解人之意。如果有強加於金庸先生之處，應該是理論的偏頗，而非筆者之本意。

30　參考（美）托馬斯.F.奧戴與珍妮特.奧戴.阿維特著，《宗教社會學》（北京：中國社會科學出版社，1990），頁 66。

Grass-Roots Militarism and its Portrayal in the Novels of Jin Yong

Robert L. Chard

Institute for Chinese Studies, University of Oxford

Abstract

One of the more widely acknowledged characteristics of Jin Yong's work is the remarkable backdrop of historical detail in his novels. However, studies of the influences on his work, and on the *wuxia* 武俠 genre in general, tend to focus on literary antecedents, as reflected in early anecdotal literature such as the *Yan Danzi* 燕丹子, poetry, Tang fiction, later vernacular fiction, and a wealth of popular tales, folklore, and performance genres (as in James Liu's famous study, *The Chinese Knight-Errant*). Much less studied has been the historical basis for the world portrayed in martial arts novels, to what extent the fiction is based on actual fact.

This study will attempt to examine aspects of militarism and martial arts in traditional China from the standpoint of local society: the phenomenon of local militias and private armies (*yibing* 義兵), bandits and outlaws, the spread of fighting arts among the populace at large, and the existence of women fighters. The topic is a difficult one to study, and it is often impossible to disentangle reality from myth, but it will be argued that significant aspects of the counterculture world of the 'Rivers and Lakes' (*jianghu* 江湖) did exist, preserved in far greater detail in traditional fiction than in historical documents. To this day this counterculture world and its ethos are familiar throughout the Chinese world, deeply ingrained in Chinese culture and values. The detail and convincing realism with which Jin Yong has brought this world to life goes a long way toward explaining the enduring appeal of his novels to Chinese readers.

The imperial Chinese state claimed authority over all military activity, and often took explicit measures to prohibit the ownership of weapons, private armies, and martial arts training among the populace at large. It is clear that this met with limited success: a wide range of martial training and organized fighting groups thrived outside official control throughout Chinese history, and particularly during the late imperial period. The world of colorful martial adepts portrayed in such detail in the novels of Jin Yong (Louis Cha) was to some extent real. The modern *wuxia* 武俠 novel, and the long pre-modern traditions on which it is based, deserve study not just by scholars of literature, but also by military historians.

This paper will offer preliminary observations on *wuxia* fiction from a historian's perspective, and argue that this modern genre, and its pre-modern antecedents, are useful for understanding the martial side of Chinese life, especially at grass-roots level. This is not to claim that such material necessarily records actual events, or to deny that much of it is overtly fictional. However, it does offer a detailed picture of traditional Chinese martial culture, both in its reality and in the popular imagination, some of which can be found also in accounts from conventional historical sources. Significant aspects of traditional martial culture still survive in modern China, not just within the underworld and among young males, but also as a general familiarity with the *wuxia* ethos and values across society at large. This is one reason why Jin Yong's work strikes such a deep chord in the Chinese psyche, a part of what has been described as an essential "Chineseness," leading some to doubt whether his extraordinary success in China and elsewhere in Asia can ever be duplicated in the West.

In early times, the martial side of Chinese culture was much more prominent than it later became. Up until the Spring and Autumn Period, China was ruled by a warrior aristocracy which placed a premium on martial valor and success on the battlefield, and adhered to values which in some respects were not unlike those of the later *xia* 俠 tradition. Considerable changes took place during the Warring States period, when states sought to regiment their populations and establish centralized control over armies and warfare on a much larger scale, reflected in the arts of command as set out in the *Sunzi* 孫子 and other *bingfa* 兵法 literature. It was at this time that the basic pattern of military administration of the imperial period was established.[1]   And yet, although the documentary record of the early and medieval periods reveals little of life at the grass-roots level, there are occasionally signs of local martial activity outside official control.

Early sources such as the *Shiji* 史記 describe individuals from the Warring States period onward — some explicitly described as *xia* 俠, others not — possessing remarkable fighting skills, often shunning public life, and adhering to an ethos of rigorous honor, bravery, loyalty to friends, chivalry, and revenge; in short, very like the fighters in the novels of Jin Yong today.[2]   In contrast to the theories propounded in the *bingfa* 兵法 texts, one finds that feats of individual valor and single combat were still to be found on the battlefield; the *Shiji* "Annals of Xiang Yu" 項羽本記 contain striking examples of this.[3]

Mention of surreptitious military activity at the local level can also be found. For example, the *Shiji* "Annals of Xiang Yu" record Xiang Liang's 項梁 preparations for rebellion in the Wu 吳 region under Qin rule, saying that he exploited occasions such as funeral processions and corvée musterings to drill large numbers of people in military maneuvers.[4]   Fragments of the lost *Chu Han chunqiu* 楚漢春秋 record that Xiang Liang's men were also melting down coins to make weapons.[5]

---

1   Described in detail in Mark Lewis, *Sanctioned Violence in Early China* (Albany: SUNY Press, 1990).

2   The early *xia* have been extensively studied; in English see James Liu's famous study, *The Chinese Knight-Errant* (London: Routledge & Kegan Paul, 1967).

3   *Shiji* (Beijing: Zhonghua Shuju, 1972), 7.328 and 334–335 (Xiang Yu's challenge of single combat to Liu Bang; his encounter with the Loufan 樓煩 archer; and beheading Han commanders just prior to his final defeat).

4   *Shiji*, 7.296.

5   Preserved in *Taiping yulan* 太平御覽 (rpt. Beijing: Zhonghua Shuju, 1985), 835.3b.

More generally, the periodic occurrence of armed religious rebellions from Eastern Han times onward, and rapid militarization at local and regional level during times of disorder, might suggest widespread martial training and some form of military organization at grass-roots level, a substrate from which larger armies might quickly coalesce. For example, the Yellow Turbans of the late Han were able to muster enormous forces in relative secrecy over a wide area within a relatively short time. Of course grass-roots martial training and organization was to a considerable extent initiated officially, through conscription and garrisons under the control of the local administration, but we do know that from Eastern Han times onward powerful families used armed dependants to defend their estates, and it is possible that local communities would have formed militias in the same way as they did in the Song dynasty and later. Certainly at the county level and above regional armies and warlords inevitably appeared during times of disorder, but only those powerful enough to participate on the national stage were ever mentioned in the official histories. For example, the *Sanguo zhi* 三國志 records that in AD 194 Lü Bu 呂布 was defeated at Chengzhi 乘氏 by one Li Jin 李進, identified only as "a man of the county" (*xianren* 縣人), and not found anywhere else.[6] He appears only because he fought off Lü Bu, a major player; there must have been many others like him at the county level and below.

It is in sources of the Song period and later, particularly in unofficial histories and sources such as *biji* 筆記 collections that the full extent of local militarism becomes apparent. For much of this I rely on the sources presented in Chen Shan 陳山, *Zhongguo wuxia shi* 中國武俠史. In this study, Chen argues for a widespread popularization of the *wuxia* tradition and the practice of martial arts from the Song dynasty onward, though I would suggest that this might in part be a function of the much more detailed records available in late imperial times, more an evolution of the grass-roots militarism which had existed throughout Chinese history than something entirely new.[7] However, there is no question

---

6   *Sanguo zhi* 三國志 (Beijing: Zhonghua Shuju, 1973), 1.12.

7   Chen Shan, *Zhongguo wuxia shi* 中國武俠史 (Shanghai: Sanlian Shudian, 1992), pp. 162–165.

but that the Song and later sources reveal glimpses of a world strikingly similar to that depicted in traditional and modern *wuxia* fiction.

A principal feature of late imperial martiality is the awareness of and interest in martial arts at the popular level. Sophisticated training in fighting techniques is of course evident much earlier, from pre-Qin times, originally focused primarily on the sword (*jian* 劍). From Six Dynasties times onward a greater profusion of weapons and empty-handed techniques developed, spurred on in part by contacts with non-Chinese peoples.[8] Documentary evidence from the Song shows that martial arts were widely known, at least within urban society. Sources such as the *Meng liang lu* 夢粱錄 and *Wulin jiushi* 武林舊事 record street performances of armed and empty-hand fighting techniques by both men and women, and there were organizations (*she* 社) dedicated to martial arts training.[9] Other sources mention popular sayings which refer to the martial arts, and the names of particular fighters (often with colorful nicknames like those found in *wuxia* novels today) who had achieved reputations for consummate skill.[10] Oral anecdotes detailing deeds of chivalry and fighting skill were recorded in collections such as the *Yijian zhi* 夷堅志.[11] By Ming times various of the prominent martial arts schools had appeared, such as the Shaolin 少林 and Wudang 武當.[12]

The spread of martial arts among the general population was a cause of concern for the authorities. In 1263 the Yuan court issued the following decree:

All ritual weapons in temples must be replaced with objects made only of wood, earth, paper, or silk; the use of real weapons is prohibited... All Han people are prohibited from

---

8   Chen, pp. 177-183.

9   *Meng liang lu* 夢粱錄, in *Dongjing meng hua lu wai sizhong* 東京夢華錄外四種 (Beijing: Zhonghua Shuju, 1962), 20.312; *Xihu laoren fansheng lu* 西湖老人繁勝錄, in *ibid.*, 123; *Wulin jiu shi* 武林舊事, in *ibid.*, 3.377 and 6.462-463.

10   Chen, pp. 165-167.

11   Chen, pp. 210 and 163-164; one such anecdote from the *Yijian zhi* is translated below.

12   Chen, p. 182.

carrying weapons; only Han people in the army are not prohibited from carrying weapons... Those in private possession of complete suits of armor shall be put to death; in cases where the armor is not complete, they shall receive fifty-seven lashes and one year's imprisonment; in cases where there are only scattered pieces of armor which cannot be worn or used in defence against an enemy, they shall receive thirty-seven lashes. Those in private possession of ten spears, swords, or crossbows shall be put to death; those with five weapons or more shall receive ninety-seven strikes of the cane and three years' imprisonment; those with four weapons or fewer shall receive seventy-seven strokes and two years' imprisonment; in cases where the weapons are unusable they shall receive fifty-seven lashes. Those in private possession of ten sets of bows and arrows shall be put to death...

When there are those who abandon their proper occupations and train in or employ the sport of wrestling (or "unarmed combat," *juedi* 角牴) or study the arts of attack (*gong ci* 攻刺), both teacher and student shall receive seventy-seven strokes of the cane.[13]

Similar measures were adopted during the Ming and Qing.[14] There is no indication that these laws were effectively enforced.

Even more relevant to the phenomenon of local militarization during the Song period is the appearance of various "societies" (*she* 社 or *shehui* 社會) of a martial nature. One striking example is the "Bow and Arrow Societies" (*gongjian she* 弓箭社), local associations formed for defense on the northern frontier areas, as described by Su Shi 蘇軾:

At present, there is a frontier army stationed in western Heshuo 河朔, and since the peace agreement of Chanyuan 澶淵, the common people have themselves banded together to form Bow and Arrow Societies. Each household, no matter how high or low in status, contributes one person. From among themselves they choose men from families whose martial arts (*wuyi* 武藝) is generally regarded as the best to act as society leaders, assistant leaders, and secretaries; these are called "chiefs" (*toumu* 頭目). They carry bows when they till the soil, swords when they cut firewood; their eating habits

---

13 *Yuan shi* 元史 (Shanghai: Dianshizhai 點石齋 ed. of 1903), 105.4a-5a (*Zhi* 志, *Xingfa* 刑法 4).

14 Chen, p. 191.

and skills are the same as those of the enemy. They have established their own system or rewards and punishments, stricter than the official ones. They patrol in shifts, and keep watch between one house and the next. If a northern [enemy] rebel or local bandit slips through without being caught, then all those in the current shift are severely punished. When there is an emergency, a drum is beaten; more than a thousand men can be summoned in a short time. Their weapons, armor, and saddles are constantly in preparation, as if enemies had already arrived. It is clear that when people are fighting for the land where their families live and are buried, the enemy is always afraid of them. [15]

There were also urban societies dedicated to particular forms of martial arts, including archery, the staff, and various forms of unarmed fighting techniques. [16] Much larger in scope were the secret societies, such as the White Lotus (*Bailian jiao* 白蓮敎) and Heaven and Earth (*Tiandi hui* 天地會), which became so prominent in the Ming and Qing periods. These were fundamentally martial as well as religious in nature, and were a significant component of unofficial militarism during this time.[17]

Also significant was the vast underworld of criminals, assassins, fugitives, robbers, and bandits: many of these were highly skilled fighters, and they often banded together to form locally-based armed organizations. The definition of a "bandit" is of course subjective: it might refer to genuine criminals, people classified as rebels, or chivalrous heroes at odds with the law. There are records of "righteous robbers," Robin Hood-like figures who took from the rich to give to the poor.[18] In Qing times the threat of brigands and highwaymen sparked off an industry of armed bodyguards and escorts (*biaoshi* 鏢師 or *biaoke* 鏢客) who defended wealthy travellers and merchant convoys.[19]

---

15   *Song shi* 宋史 (Beijing: Zhonghua Shuju, 1985), 190.4726-4727.

16   *Wulin jiu shi*, 3.337; Chen, p. 167.

17   Chen, pp. 212-226.

18   Chen, p. 199.

19   Chen, pp. 194-196.

Viewed from a social perspective, the world of fighters, secret societies, and outlaws constituted a distinct if somewhat varied realm within society as a whole, a counterculture bound together by shared customs and values. Different subgroups within this counterculture world are denoted by various terms in the novels of Jin Yong and other twentieth-century *wuxia* writers: the *wulin* 武林, referring to the realm of fighters and martial arts; the *jianghu* 江湖, the realm of itinerants, including performers, healers, beggars, fortune-tellers, etc. as well as fighters; and the *lulin* 綠林, the world of outlaws, fugitives, and rebel bands. Common to all were the development of adept fighting skills; building up a reputation for remarkable deeds, usually linked to a descriptive nickname; a code of honor and chivalry harking back to the *xia* 俠 tradition of antiquity; extravagant acts of revenge and gratitude; unvarying adherence to one's word; and strong ties to friends and associates, often reinforced by oaths of brotherhood. This last feature is particularly significant as a mechanism for networking and bonding in a mode of existence outside the bounds of conventional family and social structures. The closest ties, those between martial arts master and student, and between fellow students of the same school, were explicitly likened to those between parent and child, and between siblings. Ties of friendship and association (often referred to as *jiaoqing* 交情 in various degrees) were also taken very seriously, an important asset in the counterculture world.[20]

The non-fiction record offers ample evidence that the world of fighters, criminals, escort agencies (*biaoju* 鏢局), and secret societies portrayed in the *wuxia* novels was to a considerable extent based on reality. The novels portray this world in vastly greater detail than the historical sources, but they are after all fictional, written as entertainment; many of them, particularly the pre-modern ones, contain elements of magic and obvious fantasy – immortals, marvellous periapts, monsters, and people capable of flying through the air. Even the anecdotal accounts in the *biji* literature are colorful and sometimes fantastic. Can we really justify the use of *wuxia* fiction as a historical source for the study of

---

20　Chen, pp. 200-203.

martial China?

My comments here will be general ones; I have neither the space nor the expertise to explore this question with detailed examples. However, it is important to remember that pre-modern *wuxia* fiction was produced within the conceptual universe of late imperial China, and even its most fanciful elements reveal beliefs deeply embedded within the Chinese martial tradition.

A prominent characteristic of *wuxia* fiction, one which more pragmatic readers might find difficult to appreciate, is descriptions of astonishing feats of skill and strength, which in many works (though not those of Jin Yong) include blatantly superhuman powers. Even arts which are represented as being physically possible strain the credulity of readers not steeped in *wuxia* fiction, such as the amazing powers achieved through "inner arts" (*neigong* 內功) or "inner power" (*neili* 內力 or *neijing* 內勁), the leaping and climbing abilities associated with the "arts of lightness" (*qinggong* 輕功), or the astonishing feats performed with throwing weapons (*anqi* 暗器). However, these derive not from the imagination of the modern *wuxia* author, but from the actual belief systems of those involved in the martial arts.

Martial arts training was linked to the overall Chinese tradition of self-cultivation, overlapping with meditation, breathing techniques, physical exercises, alchemy, the observation of moral precepts, and the like, through which it was believed that the more rarefied constituents of the human body and mind (such as *qi* 氣 and *jing* 精) could be strengthened and transformed, in some contexts ultimately leading to the greatly extended lifespan and superhuman powers of the "transcendent" (*xian* 仙). The overlap between martial arts and spiritual cultivation is clear in exercises designed to strengthen the practitioner's *qi*, part of the practice of the "inner arts", described in martial arts manuals at least since the Qing period.[21]   My view is that this overlap is much older: even in Tang dynasty stories esoteric cultivation and fighting arts are clearly linked. One example of this is the well-known story of Nie Yinniang 聶隱娘, a ten-year

---

21   Some of these are discussed in the study by Meir Shahar in this collection.

old girl spirited away from her family by a mysterious Buddhist nun for training as an assassin. She later describes her training to her parents:

> When I was first carried off by the nun, we travelled some distance, I don't know how many *li*. At dawn we reached a cave in a cliff several dozen paces above the ground. The area was completely uninhabited, with a great many gibbons and monkeys, and a dense growth of pines and creepers. There were already two girls there, both also ten years old, both clever and pretty. Neither ate ordinary food, and they could run at flying speed across cliffs and climb trees like monkeys, without the slightest misstep.
>
> The nun gave me a pill, and a precious sword, which she ordered me to carry with me at all times, with a blade two feet long, so sharp it would sever a hair blown against it. I climbed about with the other two girls, and over time felt my body growing light as the wind. After a year I could kill monkeys with the sword, not missing one in a hundred; later I killed tigers and leopards, cutting off their heads and bringing them back; after three years I had achieved the power to fly through the air, and was sent to kill eagles and hawks, which I never missed. The blade of the sword gradually shrank to five inches. Birds in flight encountering it could not tell it was coming.[22]

The nun then takes the girl to a large city, and sends her to assassinate evil men. Though the account does not spell out the details of the actual training (the effects of which seem to be due primarily to a miraculous pill), the link between spiritual training (under the guidance of a Buddhist nun) and fighting arts is clear.

A Song dynasty account from the *Yijian zhi* suggests a link between Daoists and fighting arts in the popular imagination:

> On the evening of the Lantern Festival, Guo Lun 郭倫, a man of the capital city, took his family out to view the lanterns. Returning home late, while traversing a winding alleyway, ten evil youths approached from the opposite direction, arms linked, singing,

---

22　*Taiping guangji* 太平廣記 (Beijing: Zhonghua Shuju, 1986), 194.1457, see also the translation in C.C. Wang, *Traditional Chinese Tales* (New York: Greenwood Press, 1944), 98-103.

shouting, and laughing. They peered and glared at [Guo and family], intending to bully them. Guo Lun could see that he was far too weak to stand against them, and grew anxious.

Suddenly a Daoist appeared, dressed in green garb and recluse's turban. He berated the crowd [of youths]:

"A man returns home by night with his family; how dare you insult them?"

The youths were furious. "We were having a little sport," they said. "What business is it of yours, crazy Daoist?"

With a great outcry the youths attacked. [Guo Lun's] wife and children managed to slip away in the confusion; Guo Lun remained behind.

The Daoist grew suddenly angry. "You really intend violence, do you? I'll fix you!"

Arms waving, he launched into them, as though beating small children. In a moment the youths were knocked to the ground, crying out abjectly. They fled, helping each other along.

The Daoist continued casually on his way. Guo Lun hurried after him, and bowed low in thanks.

"You and I are total strangers, honored master!" he said. "And yet you graciously assisted us, allowing my wife and children to escape from danger. Are you a man of unusual powers (yiren 異人)? I must express my gratitude! I wish to repay you in some way. May I ask if there is anything you would like?"

"I did not come here with the intention of assisting you," the Daoist said. "I happened to witness a wrong, and justice demanded I do something about it. I desire nothing worldly; certainly I had no thought of reward!"[23]

It was widely believed that ordinary human beings could develop superhuman fighting powers through prolonged and arduous training in esoteric techniques transmitted by masters. And of course the actual martial arts reached a level of skill and sophistication, with adepts performing feats which would have seemed nearly superhuman to the uninitiated.

As a sidenote, it is also worth mentioning that esoteric arts are associated not just with individual adepts but also whole armies. This is particularly evident in

---

23   *Yijian zhi* 夷堅志 (Beijing: Zhonghua Shuju, 1981), 14.1676.

religious uprisings (such as that of the Boxers *Yihe tuan* 義和團), but even official armies used divinatory techniques to read the strength and disposition of the enemy, and resorted to magical techniques to cause harm, examples of the latter being found in traditional novels.[24]

In addition, those belonging to the martial arts world shared in a folklore of tales and anecdotes about remarkable personalities, deeds, and events. Even in the present day, martial arts students exchange stories of this sort, many of which might strain the credulity of those not belonging to the group. Colorful, exaggerated accounts were a part of the martial arts and *wuxia* counterculture, and no doubt often circulated through general society as well. The anecdotes about fighters found in collections such as the *Yijian zhi* could well have derived from within the martial world itself.

Traditional accounts relating to grass-roots martiality, though not a true record of actual events, is an important source on the belief system surrounding the Chinese martial tradition, and perhaps also a part or the legend and folklore which helped shape it. This is not to claim that all readers would necessarily have believed everything in the stories. Rather, even the most fantastic elements in them operated according to patterns and conventions well known at the popular level in late imperial China. With careful evaluation, historians should be able to learn much about the patterns and extent of martiality in daily life at the grass-roots level, and the legends and folklore which went with it.

But what of the works of Jin Yong? Though obviously not a primary source for research into traditional China, they are a continuation and renewal of pre-modern literary traditions, one which interacts with the contemporary survivals of the real *wuxia* counterculture and the greater public's perception of that world, even though they are set in the past, not the present. The themes, conventions, and ethos of the *wuxia* world have always been deeply interlocked with the values of Chinese traditional culture, integral to the "Chineseness"

24　Magical techniques in a military context have been researched by Robin Yates; I understand the results are to appear in a forthcoming volume of *Science and Civilisation in China*.

which Louis Cha himself and others have cited as a reason for the enormous appeal of his work.

To make a perhaps obvious point, the novels of Jin Yong and other writers of the twentieth century *wuxia* genre stand in sharp contrast to the fiction of the May Fourth tradition: the latter sought to break away from traditional China in both style and content, and took a largely negative view of the old society; the former preserves the traditional style and content (though not without modification), and takes a much more positive view of pre-modern society. Jin Yong's novels are of course critical of the dark side of the old society and the suffering of the common people, but at the same time offer a solution from within the traditional Chinese culture in the heroism and chivalry of the *wuxia* fighters.

The essential "Chineseness" of Jin Yong's novels has been mentioned as a barrier to their acceptance in the West. Time will tell if this is indeed the case, but my feeling is that it is not. Once the formidable barriers to translation are overcome (John Minford's translation of *Lu Dingji* 鹿鼎記 is the best and most ambitious effort to date), there is no reason why his literary skills should not be communicable in Western languages.[25]   The "Chineseness," properly presented, might turn out to be an asset rather than a barrier. There is a great thirst for knowledge about China among the Western reading public; Jin Yong offers a rich and vivid introduction to the world of the Chinese past, comparing well to the best writers of historical fiction in the West. The added *wuxia* element should only add to its appeal.

---

25   For a detailed examination of problems in translating Jin Yong's work, see Olivia Mok, "Martial Arts Fiction: Translational Migrations East and West," PhD thesis, University of Warwick, 1998.

否想[1]金庸

——文化代現的雅俗、時間與地理

黃　錦　樹
國立暨南國際大學中文系

摘　要

　　五四以降的中文新小說在理論建構之初即有意識的以預先存在的「國語的文學」——從《水滸傳》、《紅樓夢》、到《老殘遊記》等既有的成功的白話小說——爲典律，之前，這些「成功」的白話小說從不被認爲是學術研究的對象，在傳統學術視域下也幾無價值可言。從白話文學的系譜來看，基本上以原居於文字表達次要系統的民間的、世俗的語言系統置換長期居於主導地位的文言表達系統；爾後主流的五四文學在時間性上設定了以當下現實爲主要的場景，寫實主義的訴求內在的規定了物質符碼的時間性。時間性的設定同時相當程度地制約了白話文學生產的可能性，並且以那樣的時間性爲主導（如果不是唯一的話）的意向。文學的啓蒙教化或揭露現實的功能也被內化，被上綱爲書寫的倫理。這種歷史長期發展中被合理化的傾向本身並不具有絕對的正當性，因爲它所依據的可能性邏輯並不是唯一的，相對於這樣逐漸窄化的新文學格局，作爲「新派武俠小說」佼佼者的金庸武俠小說或許恰好可以提供一個突破口，回頭去質疑、重省白話文學的格局和書寫的可能。這是本文的第一個思考脈絡，把問題放回到五四文學的系譜，以古裝／時裝這一關鍵性的符碼問題爲焦點，把五四新文學中的一些重要的基本精神和特點(如感時憂國精神、抒情、浪漫、關於愛情、國族主義、民族情感) 等都拿出

---

1 作爲所謂「海外華人」的接受者的閱讀的一些斷想及聯想。

來和金庸小說做一番對比檢驗，藉此以重新思考新文學之中的現代性與中國性之調和或衝突，同時也可以反思不同時間符碼置換後的「文學性」——與傳統詩學的對話。

第二個思考脈絡是思想史脈絡。尤其是以 1949 以後港台新儒學運動爲基本的對比架構，以箇中所宣揚的文化價值、文化理想、文化精神、歷史精神、藝術精神等等爲焦點，初步探討這兩種對於價值的不同「敍述」方式。本文認爲，從文化史的角度來看，金庸武俠小說可以說是這一波文化價值再確認運動（「文化苦旅」）中非常重要的一環，從語言表達的角度來看，相對於前者不可思議的專門化、溝通對象的高度窄化、菁英化，金庸武俠小說是一個重要的互補，建構了一個古代的場景來安頓、演出、證成既有的價值的同時，也恰好回應了白話文學原先的平民主張。

撇開雅／俗這樣的成見，本文企圖論證的是，金庸的武俠小說之所以會遠遠超過經典五四文學而獲得海內外不同階層的當代華人的廣泛接受，是因爲不論是在精神上還是文學上，它所完成的恐怕都比一般固步自封的文學研究者想像的多：甚至想當程度上回應了晚清時梁啓超等人對於小說的構想。

一、前　言

我醒來的時候，恐龍依然在那裡。
　　　　　　　　—— Augusto Monterroso[2]

金庸武俠小說在當代華語世界、華文閱讀市場獲得的跨地域、跨階層的普遍接受，甚至深獲學院知識分子的肯定（連番國際性研討會的召開，更是一項公開的「正典化」詔告——至少確認它的存在具有非比尋常的——至少不亞於所謂的「純文學」——的意義），使得它的存在業已超脫一般通俗文學的流行的正當性，而昇揚爲當代華人文化界一個不可忽略的文化現象。這樣的現象所揭櫫的金庸武俠小說的文化位置，大略在雅俗之間。從一個更廣泛的文化史脈絡來看，這其實是一個並不尋常的位置。

金庸和他的同時代人（所謂的「新派武俠小說」——但尤其是金庸）的

2　轉引自卡爾維諾著、楊德友譯，《未來千年備忘錄》（社會思想，1994），頁 54。

作品獲得雅俗共賞的成功；它的生產、改寫、改編與被接受擺在 1949 以後、歷史文化充滿了焦慮感的兩岸三地及海外華人閱讀圈，它詭譎複雜的上下文作為閱讀與詮釋的支援系統對於它存在的意義或許早已有了豐富的回饋。這一現象本身在某種程度上將迫使我們回頭重新評估晚清文化變遷、新文化運動以來對於文學（尤其是小說）的諸多構想和假設。和其他許多被知識分子早早的在正統新文學殿堂確立了正典位置的作品類似，金庸武俠小說同樣的也無法被排除在白話文運動的影響之外；如果我們摒棄了雅／俗之間的成見及學院未經充分檢驗的學術身段，重新檢視平等對待不同的文學類型——尤其是「較不成問題」[3] 的、在正典化過程中的金庸武俠小說，檢視它的相關機制（如「真實效果」、時間性等等），也許可以獲得一番不尋常的解碼。以下的討論大體依循兩個理解的框架，一是五四以來白話文學；二是 1949 中共掌權，晚清、五四新文化運動以來傳統被超自然化而造成的文化危機在華裔知識分子進一步離散之後越趨嚴重而導致相對的中國文化再造的脈絡。

　　首先把對象置入晚清文人對於小說的回顧及胡適之等人對於白話小說的原始構想，做一番概要的討論；接著進入金庸武俠小說的「世界」，從文本裝置的角度對比互襯金庸武俠小說和五四主流的寫實小說、五四個人主義、浪漫主義、感傷主義、抒情傾向與感時憂國之間的親密關係，以分解它們之間可能共享的，或可以對照的美學意識型態與文化假設。在這樣的基礎上，進入作為一種「通俗類型」（？）的武俠小說的成規，它特殊的文本裝置和母題，檢視作為浪漫文學之一端的武俠小說和歷史敘事、散文化的敘事和抒情詩之間的關係。接下的部分是分析金庸武俠小說中經由小說的文本裝置所設定的倫理價值，以對照唐君毅的「花果飄零」論述，並且進一步分析金庸武俠小說中刻意營造的文化詩境的文化旨趣，及這種文化旨趣和武俠小說特殊的時間性中包含的中國特性（對於海外華人）所能提供的文化想像共同體的建構，而和海外華人民族主義有所牽扯。

3　較沒有爭議的。諧擬。通俗類型作為一個有活力的系統。有才能的作家可以讓它的藝術質地上昇，同理，庸才也常把所謂的嚴肅文學的類型——即使是道德上十分正當的（如革命現實主義）寫得俗不可耐。

二、近現代白話小說：嚴肅的通俗，或嚴肅而不通俗

　　回到晚清知識分子對相關問題的討論，回到那近現代白話小說生產的初始時刻，原因在於——嚴格說來，當代以中文書寫的任何文化產品其實都無法脫離那個起源時刻所贈予的生產條件，彼時象徵既有秩序的物質和精神都瀕臨解體／在解體中，象徵雅文化的嚴密、固定的語言表達系統的正當性正逢嚴厲的考驗。對既有高度精煉的語言表達系統的質疑，其實也正是對那長期而合理存在的強大抒情傳統本身的挑戰，抒情的優先性被敘事的優先性所取代。[4] 抒情傳統被迫向一個新的、建構中的敘事傳統過渡。更準確的說，是文學表達上抒情的絕對優先性讓位於敘事，從邏輯上來看，抒情降爲輔助的系統，而並非全然被排除。[5] 歌頌、提倡小說和文言表達系統／白話表達系統位置上的顚倒[6] 雖然並不是同步發生，卻有內在的必然性——文的（默的）表達系統被一個相對的話的（喧囂的）表達系統所替代——以安頓時代的喧嘩，而非詩意的寧靜。

　　處於價值重估的時代，時代的聲音在走在前端的知識分子那兒體現爲一種意志，它要求一種可以讓它安頓的形式。而敘事，無非是在時間之中的敘事，因而蘊含了一種時間意識的確認。在這樣的脈絡下，小說被召喚。如同任何的創始時刻，故事（的形式）之被召喚，實則是在召喚一則共同的神話——當這樣的神話體現於維新論述、革命論述或啓蒙論述及時代傳奇人物的生平事跡，而虛構敘事——內容在生產中的文學的虛構敘事形式本身反而被賦予了神話般的本體位置：首先體現爲對小說功能的確認。

　　1897 年刊於《國聞報》上署名幾道、別士所撰的〈本館附印說部緣起〉

4　胡適的文學革命爲甚麼非得從詩這個最爲困難的領域開始不可——因爲在那裡遭到最嚴峻的抗拒——正說明了這樣的問題。胡適在《四十自述》（臺北：遠流，〔1986〕1997）的附錄〈逼上梁山〉中有一番清楚的敘述（頁 97-131）。而在古典文學研究的領域，從王國維的《宋元戲曲考》到胡適的小說考證，也說明了這種趨向。這是一個大問題，五四以來的白話文學，基本上離不開這樣的問題情境。

5　是以必然會有被壓抑的複返。詳後。

6　胡適〈文學改良芻議〉中對於「不用典」處理上的困難，可以清楚的看出：要把文言系統徹底的廢絕是不可能的，有效的策略是讓它從整體的優勢降爲局部性的存在。

（嚴復、夏曾佑）中明白的道出這樣的旨趣：「夫說部之興，其入人之深，行世之遠，幾幾乎出經史上，而天下之人心風格，遂不免爲說部所持。」[7] 以英雄、男女爲神話、歷史與虛構敍事共享的基本母題（頁 18-25），而且源於人的「公性情」——這同時是它們被創造和被接受的基礎。幾年後梁啓超在〈論小說與群治之關係〉（1902）對小說的感染力有更進一步的發揮，提出「小說支配人道」的四種力：熏、浸、刺、提；[8] 充分的認識到作爲虛構敍事的小說在功能上恰能製造出讓讀者沉浸的幻境，而在那樣的幻境裡與敍事中的角色認同，深深左右了讀者人格的養成——如同被敍述的角色那般自我養成，而爲「吾中國群治腐敗之總根源（頁 53）。同樣的感染力，可以導人墮落或者奮進。作爲大眾啓蒙教育之一環，梁啓超強調的是後者。這樣的論述總體上並沒有超出「夫說部之興，其入人之深，行世之遠，幾幾乎出經史上，而天下之人心風俗，遂不免爲說部所持」的基本論斷，可是從角色與讀者的人格養成的角度立論，卻幾乎已導向、深化至這樣的議題：小說攸關群眾文化想像、歷史意識的塑造。[9]

　　企圖借用小說的感染力來進行大眾人格型塑的梁啓超及其同時代人，充分意識到小說不僅僅是一種賞玩之物，而是一種活生生的事物，它會在社會大眾的意識裡生根。體認到經史的大傳統對於社會大眾的無能爲力，因而它是做爲文化敎養的輔助系統而被提倡的，在這樣的前提下，所提倡的必然是那種「意識正確」[10]——且具有感染力——的小說。[11] 這一構想中的小說，

7　收入陳平原、夏曉虹編，《二十世紀中國小說資料（第一卷）1897-1916》（北京：北京大學出版社，1997），頁 27。

8　同上註，頁 51。

9　如宋恕於同年（1902）的〈遵旨婉切勸諭解放婦女腳纏白話〉第二十一條中相當深刻的指出婦女纏足雖然明顯殘虐生理，卻依舊能行之久遠，「其病源深處在於『無才便是德』一句話上頭，淺處是在造小說、做戲、唱詞三種男人的筆頭、腳頭、舌頭呢。」指出演出型態的世俗文化敎育把某些世俗價值內化了，以理想自我的角色參與了肉體、人格的型塑。這已經相當接近把小說看成是特定時代集體心態的投影的看法（見胡珠生編，《宋恕集》上（北京：中華書局，1993），頁 341-342。）；民國以後，顧頡剛深受小說和民間故事啓發的新史學視域中，就包含了這一認知（見其《古史辨》第一冊的〈自序〉）。

10　換句話說，可以看出知識分子淑世的「寄託」——不一定就是說敎。

要求的是通俗而嚴肅，而非通俗而不嚴肅，或嚴肅而不通俗。而感染力，和抒情脫離不了干係。[12] 梁啓超也認識到，要達到那樣的功效，語言的選擇是非常重要的：「在文字中，則文言不如其俗語，莊論不如其寓言。」（頁 52）教條、經典訴諸理性及權威的說教不如以俗語說故事的感染力，而預設了較具可接受性、接近民間的俗語的選擇。梁啓超對小說的看法，大體上是同時代大多數人的共同看法，也就是那個時代對相關問題的共同視域。[13]

　　1902 年以後知識界對小說的豐富討論，明顯把小說和啓迪民智劃上等號，也充分意識到既有的經典教育只是少數人的教育，而注意到相對大多數有能力閱讀小說的人口，他們的人格養成與國民性之塑造，其實都和他們所可能接觸及接受的通俗讀物息息相關，箇中他們所能接受的語言——俗語——是一大關鍵。胡適對於小說的認知與召喚，大體是建立在這樣的知識準備之上。

　　以最困難的環節（古典詩）作突破口展開（白話）文學革命的胡適，在他建構他的國語論述——文學的國語，國語的文學——時，他那在〈文學改良芻議〉時期白開水似的白話文主張有了重要的轉折。認識到「國語」並不能只是一種在文化上貧乏的語言，而必須是「文學的國語」——以文學的語言作爲國語成立的條件。[14] 而他所認定的「文學語言」，卻是既存的成熟的白話小說的語言——它既是未來的「國語的文學」，也是「文學的國語」成立的條件。胡適的論證有其自相矛盾之處（既以前者爲後者成立的條件，又以後者爲前者成立的條件），可是卻蘊含著以下值得注意的提示：廣被接受的

---

11 有可讀性——在書寫上並不先行預設了對一般讀者閱讀期待的抗拒。或者我們也可以說，是「人的文學」。後文將據此來檢視金庸的武俠小說。

12 所有這些對於小說功能的談論，都離不開感染力：而訴諸情感、感動，其實也沒有脫離〈毛詩序〉對於抒情詩的政治功能及美學本體論基礎的基本論點：風。

13 《二十世紀中國小說資料（第一卷）1897-1916》所收錄的大量資料，有的文章從題目就可以看出旨趣，如：〈論小說與社會之關係〉、〈論寫情小說於新社會之關係〉、〈小說之功用比報紙之影響爲更普及〉、〈小說種類之區別實足移易社會之靈魂〉等。也有人唱反調，主張小說要當小說來讀，見摩西《〈小說林〉發刊詞》，同書，頁 253-255。

14 胡適，〈建設的文學革命論——國語的文學，文學的國語〉（1918），姜義華編，《胡適學術文集：新文學運動》（北京：中華書局，1993），頁 44-46。

小說，它的語言將可能是未來平民百姓的「國語」的模範，來自世俗的小說語言「俗語」)，在建構「文學的國語」的前提下，它不能太俗──它必須有一定程度的文雅──必須承載一定程度的文化的雅致。然而這樣的「一定程度的文化雅致」，它的上限卻在於文言表達式，下限在於俚俗──在某種程度的雅俗之間。

而古舊的文雅觀念在文學革命之後，甚至就在五四一代成熟的作家作品（魯迅以降）中，卻看到它們以一種現代的形式回歸：一種新青年精神所主導的寫作，一種基本上以城市小知識分子為讀者預設的寫作，問題小說的進路，夏志清先生所描繪的「感時憂國」的文學格局。[15] 它基本上是寫實的──其細節是同時代人熟悉的，來自於眼前，或並不遙遠的過去──小知識分子淑世的心態和相應的情緒（絕望、憤怒、沮喪），對當下問題的立即反應，從西方借來的有限的現代文學技術、作品和現實世界有著頗為緊密的對應關係，從而內在的規定了作品的時間性：向當下現實投注。這樣的文學在美學的實驗或形式的探討之前，就已先行的預設了一種有關書寫的道德，預設了一種嚴肅的功能（啓蒙、敎化，讓讀者覺醒等等），一種禁慾的目的──文學的閱讀不能是一種享樂。這種情況下「純文學」的文雅一方面是西方的格式，一方面是轉型期士大夫在書寫上設立的功能限定。這樣的大趨勢，一方面回應了晚清對於小說的期待和召喚（借小說以覺民，白話文）──嚴肅，一方面卻也偏離了箇中的相關要件──通俗。五四的感時憂國精神下的文學寫作，大體是嚴肅而不通俗的。[16]

就總體歷程來看，從晚清到五四，在中國近現代文學成立的過程中（同時也是現代中文成立的過程），在美學上是雅的被拆散，「文」被置入括弧，還原爲「質」，[17] 重新開始出發，以建立新的雅的基礎。[18] 以中國傳統文學

15　夏志清著、劉紹銘譯，《中國現代小説史》（臺北：傳記文學，1979）。

16　當然不可忽略的是王德威先生對於以魯迅爲主要象徵的感時憂國傳統之外另一傳統──老舍所象徵的喜劇傳統──的文學史建構，詳〈魯迅，還是老舍？──中國現代寫實小説的兩個方面〉，參見王德威，《從劉鶚到王禎和──中國現代寫實小説散論》，（臺北：時報，1986），頁103-126。可是在細節的時間性卻仍在「寫實」的總體趨向下。這一點對於非當代人，或者海外華人而言，在接受上都會造成相當的隔閡。

17　胡適，〈逼上梁山〉，頁105。

18　這個問題將另做專文討論。

批評的觀念和術語來表達，正是從文到史的過渡。只是這樣的史（敍事性）的位置在晚淸的思想脈絡下，淸楚的被定位爲俗──向俗取資──從文到質，即是從雅到俗的平行過渡。[19] 而箇中不斷經由辯證揚棄而回歸、復返的，是文、雅、抒情詩的意味。[20] 五四的嚴肅寫實取向，又讓這樣的「史」不僅僅是一種比喩而已。

武俠小說的「通俗」自不待言，是否可能「嚴肅」還可爭議。在這樣的敍事背景之下，我們可以嚴肅的估量一下金庸的武俠小說在文化代現（cultural representation）上的意義。

三、文化代現：時間、符碼，與世界

整體上，武俠小說在現當代學術研究裡的位階仍舊是「通俗小說」，[21] 陳平原教授對此一「學界的共識」雖頗表遺憾（頁 137），而企圖從小說類型學的角度來進行考察，然而在他那本頗具啓發性的論著裡，卻時時流露出這樣的訊息：武俠小說和純文學是有著顯著不同的（如頁 198），[22] 陳平原先生的立場很淸楚：武俠小說是一種通俗文學類型，認爲「不能像純文學研究那樣斷然否定程式化傾向，沒有程式化傾向也就沒有通俗文學；……」（同頁）可是在談到武俠小說的未來時，卻強調武俠小說如果要「有根本性的變革」卻必須「跳出已有的固定程式」──其敍述方式不能是「武俠小說」的（頁

19　至少在表達的語言上是如此。梁啓超〈小說叢話〉：「文學之進化有一大關鍵，即由古語之文學，變爲俗語之文學是也。」原刊於《新小說》第 7 號（1903）；後收入陳平原、夏曉虹編，《二十世紀中國小說資料（第一卷）1897-1916》，頁 82。

20　陳平原的《中國小說敍事模式的演變》（臺北：久大，1988）一書，對抒情詩的回歸這一問題做了頗爲詳致的討論。關於中國近代小說雅／俗之間的不同取向及其消長的概要敍述，詳陳平原，《二十世紀中國小說史（第一卷）1897-1916》（北京：北京大學出版社，1989）第四章〈由俗入雅與回雅向俗〉，頁 114-147。

21　陳平原，《千古文人俠客夢──武俠小說類型研究》（北京：人民文學出版社，1992），頁 186 的歸納。這本書仍然是目前討論中國武俠小說最好的論著，後文不少論述建立在陳教授分析的基礎上。

22　這一訊息伴隨著另一訊息：金庸往往是這些通俗作家中的例外（如他的急流勇退、勤於修改等）。這訊息至少說明了金庸相對而言比較有意識的去修正發表時受制於通俗文學市場機制的一些可能的缺失，而修正的方向無疑的是「文學」的。

220）──換言之，只有「不再是武俠小說」（在類型之外、逸出既有類型）方能在「純文學」中覓得一席之地。這幾乎預設了做為一種通俗類型的武俠小說本身本質上就不可能成為「純文學」。本文並不預設這樣的「純文學」立場。[23] 類型學的角度有它的方便卻也有它的局限。就以「純文學」的小說來說，幾乎每一種題材在長遠的書寫傳統中都已自成類型（每一種母題都可以說是一種廣義的類型──甚至魯迅的〈故鄉〉在中國現代小說上也可以說是該「類型」〔離鄉─返鄉〕的鼻祖──它也必然有更多的外國祖先），也都有各自的「程式」（同一種題材的開展，必然包含諸多類似的敘事要素，這些要素內在於題材的屬性）。故而「程式」的存在並非通俗小說的原罪；問題只在於依賴的程度。以下的論述嘗試在一定程度上擱置通俗、類型的框架，而檢視相關的文本機制，和寫實小說的基本「格式」做一番對照，以嘗試建立在武俠小說格局內的文學合理性基礎。

　　總體來看，和寫實小說相比較，它們之間最明顯的差別在於二者間經由技術規則操演出來的「世界」是大不相同的。清楚而可以辨識的，是符碼的選取：武俠小說的世界如同寫實小說，是借由特定的符碼構成的，且各自遵循著不同的符碼選取法則，以構成各自的肌理。可以借其中一個轉喻來說明──衣飾──有著古裝與時裝的根本差異，這象徵了二者間的總體差異。首先是時間性。寫實小說的時間性總是投注於當下的時間性，就算指涉過去也總是「並不很久以前」的、可以辨識的過去；敘事時間和寫作者所處的生活時間有著鄰近性，是可以參照、可以考核、確認的。五四感時憂國的寫實傳統尤其扣緊作者所處時空的當下現實，它的當下指涉不止是普遍符碼的時間性，更是所關切、思考的問題的時間性，甚至地域、語言也牢牢相扣──而構成「此時此地」的道德視景。這樣的書寫在許多的技術成規上，基本上已非常接近「客觀」歷史（當代史）寫作；書寫者所立足的時間基本上是「現在式」的──即使他以懷舊的方式想像的建構一段過去。它的可理解性訴諸於讀者對於這些具體現實性細節及問題的熟悉度，總是用「已經在那兒」（*having-been-there*）的事物來確證它的真實效果（*reality effect*），羅蘭巴特（Roland Barthes）把這種現象之稱為指涉的幻覺（*referential illusion*）它

23　「純文學」的概念在這裡或許該先行擱置。

的重要機制是「具體細節」（"*concrete detail*"），而具體細節「被建構於指涉物與能指的直接共謀；所指被從符號中驅逐出去，」而

> 這種幻覺的真理是：在實際言語行動中被當成外延所指而去除的「真實」（the "real"），作爲內涵所指而復返；當這些細節被拿來直接的指稱現實，它們所做的，也不過是意指（signify）它而已。……換句話說，就是那個所指的缺席，唯獨對於指涉物有利的，成爲寫實主義特殊的能指：真實效果被造就了，這一未言明的逼真性（vcrsimilitude）的準則，構成了所有標準現代作品的美學。[24]

這樣的真實效果，訴諸於歷史客觀性的幻覺法則，排除了經由語言操作可能達致的其他幻覺——真實效果。[25] 把敘事的符碼牢牢鎖在敘事者所在的鄰近歷史時間，這是真實文學的基本格式，[26] 所設定的認識論基礎離不開現實的擬真，和十九世紀以降的客觀史學共享了同一種代現法則（law of representation）。從言語行爲的角度來看，這並非唯一的代現法則，不過是諸多法則中的一種。以這樣的認識爲前提，或許可以發現許多不同的大的文學類型（如奇幻、神怪）都有它們各自遵守的代現法則，有各自的製造真實——幻覺效果的文本機制，也都有各自存在的合理性。

美學的逼真性造就了作品「世界」的肌理。武俠小說在時間上明顯的屬於過去，和書寫者、讀者所處的時間有著一個不可跨越的時差。時間猶如地理，在這樣的時間距離之下，書寫者有極大的彈性空間以採取不同的代現策略，甚至在某些共同的程式（不可減約的要素，如武和俠）之下可能存在著不同的類型；從帶有奇幻色彩的劍俠、劍仙神佛妖魔充斥、充滿他界事物的舊派武俠小說（接近於奇幻文學的類型），到神魔鬼怪這些他界的超越者缺席的新派武俠小說，奇幻因素的減弱，其實標誌著武俠小說本身的「寫實化」

24　Rolad Barthes, "The Reality Effect," in *The Rustle of Language*, Richard Howard trans, London: Basil Blackwell, pp.147-148.

25　依上述羅蘭巴特的語意，所謂的真實效果其時同時也即是一種幻覺效果。

26　此一問題的詳細討論見瓦特（Ian Watt）著，高原、董紅鈞譯，《小說的興起》（北京：三聯書店，1992）第一章對「形式寫實主義」的分析。同理，歷史小說也分享了同一種代現法制。

趨勢。[27] 這種寫實化以它的時間性爲限度，被設定於一段假擬的過去，近似於歷史的逼眞性；然而却又和歷史小說有一段距離（不像歷史小說儘管虛構，在很大的程度上受限於大量的歷史上下文），只是把某段設定的歷史時空作爲舞台，以最低限度的要素（不少於普遍的認知）構成它在該時間性中的美學逼眞性。從這個角度來看——就某方面而言——與寫實小說作比較，這種武俠小說所依循的代現原則在扣除了時間因素和二者間不同的基本類型程式之外，竟可能是近似的：或者說在金庸的作品裡，可以視爲是後者對前者有意識的擬仿。在這方面，它造成的閱讀上的眞實效果是：那些細節似乎可能曾經發生過。相對而言，有限的奇幻事物（如武術、兵器、奇遇等不可或缺的）之存在，該類型本身即提供了存在的合理性[28]（從讀者的立場來看，如果不那樣，哪還算得上是武俠小說？），裡頭蘊含的是另一種眞實效果、另一種逼眞性、另一種代現法則——接近於神話、民間傳說、夢、超自然，訴諸於集體心態與集體心理需求，超乎個體具體存在有限性的幻覺的眞實——是爲修辭的另一種幻覺效果。換言之，像金庸那樣減低奇幻色彩、具有「歷史—寫實」傾向的武俠小說，箇中其實包含了兩種不同的代現法則，兩者互相制約[29] 而達致一種美學的平衡：並沒有逾越彼此的「最低限度」。擬「歷史—寫實」在效果上取其不離常識太遠，在文本內在有著把該世界自然化的作用，取其常；反之，被類型本身合理化的奇幻色彩則在那樣的基礎上產生作用。而該最低限度的要素構成它的有限歷史逼眞性，被世俗文化意識混淆的歷史意義會在那裡被辨識出來。在那樣的世界的構成原則上，如果寫作者有

27　減弱的限度是：不能減至被認爲「不是武俠小說」。這和金庸武俠小說本身的著重點有關，談錫永在〈武俠小說的境界〉中拿金庸和其他兩位前輩武俠小說家比較，認爲「平江不肖生以江湖知識取勝」，「還珠樓主以地理知識取勝」，而「金庸以歷史知識取勝」；同時也指出相對於平氏之以「異聞」，還珠氏之以「神話」爲主，金庸則「以人世的悲歡爲小說的支柱」（見三毛等，《諸子百家看金庸》肆，臺北：遠流，1997，頁5-6）。

28　這也即是卡勒（Jonathan Culler）在《結構主義詩學》（北京：中國社會科學院，1991）所列五種逼眞性之中的第三種「體裁模式」（models of genre）：「一種範例爲所謂某個作家的想像世界：我們允許作品構成一個半自足的世界，其內在規律與我們周圍世界的規律不盡相同，然而它的內在規律卻使該範疇以內的行爲和事件有可理解性和逼眞性。」（頁216）

29　就武俠小說而言，後者相對而言具有一定的主導性——它不能不是武俠小說。

心，某種世界觀將依循文本的構成法則而寄寓著，合理的被建構——而並非僅只是「純文學」的特權。後文將揭示，在那樣的時間性設定內，某些建構將較其他文學類型更為方便（如中國文化——文化中國、中國性——文化在武藝俠客中回歸）；而另一些建構也不見得比其他類型不便——如人情、愛情、感時憂國等。

四、敍述：故事、母題和神奇事物

敍事者的時間和被敍述的時間之間的落差並非作品類型的原罪，反而在這樣的時差中拓開了一個書寫（意義）的空間。本節主要討論兩個問題。一、討論武俠類型之所以為類型的諸要素，它的奇幻要素的敍事學意義；二、在把時間性的因素釐清的前提下，作為一種「類型」的武俠小說被過度高估的類型限制在論述中可以獲得一部分的解除，以這樣的角度來討論諸如金庸這樣的武俠小說除了是武俠小說之外，還可能是甚麼。[30]

所謂的「類型程式」，基本上是一個「舞台及佈景」的概念。[31] 在設計上，泰半訴諸和讀者約定的要素，「程式」即讀者閱讀某一類類型時期待故事會給予的（如俠客必然有著離奇的遭遇，困頓時遇見神秘的或廢黜的智慧老人），在作者和讀者視域的融合處建立需求，在那樣的目光交會中構築起浪遊的俠客真正的家——一個抽象的超越位所。它的合理性就建立在這種心照不宣的約定上。[32] 在這基礎上，建立起它自身的敍事語法，各式各樣武俠小說專有的神奇事物構成的「神奇百寶箱」[33] 奇幻物象體系（諸如武術、武功秘訣、神劍、毒藥、山洞……等），武俠小說世界裡的自然：它擁有的不止是

30　類型的判定是後設的，而非先驗的。就書寫活動而言，類型的跨越就蘊含於書寫的可能性之中。

31　從符號配置的角度來看，中國現代小說中一樣也存在著「舞台」的問題，詳黃子平對於魯迅《故事新編》精采的討論，見〈《故事新編》：時間與敍述〉，《中國文化》（臺北：風雲時代出版社），第 2 期（1990.6），頁 124-132。

32　相對而言，五四現代小說即使是對讀者也有一種道德的強制性——一種小知識分子的倫理投射——凝視它所設定的現實。即使「頹廢」如郁達夫也不例外。

33　借戴俊《千古世人俠客夢——武俠小說縱橫談》中的修辭（臺北：臺灣商務，1994），例子見該書的詳舉，頁 68-89。

體裁（類型）的逼眞性，還有文化的逼眞性。[34] 經由這些敘事要素、敘事語法，故事所達到的，所經歷的，無非是一些人類基本的敘事母題（motif）——探險、尋覓、成長、復仇、愛、恨、生、死。

　　從金庸的武俠小說被普遍認爲是「情書」及無可否認的以情愛爲他武俠世界的中心來看，如果不以武俠的角度而以情愛爲關注的焦點，[35] 其實也可以把那樣的小說視爲是變形的才子佳人小說——只不過在那樣的世界裡的才子和佳人，都尚武而非從文——是俠客和俠女的舞台。在武俠的世界裡談情說愛仍不會令人覺得突兀，[36] 說明了它有著相對的合理性，原因在於，情感要素是大多數敘事作品可以被接受的共同基礎，植根於普遍的人的日常生活，不管那是一個怎樣的「世界」。當這一部分的效果被相對的強化，甚至其餘的部分都可以降爲配景。在金庸的武俠小說中，更可以看出作者刻意的經營：把戀愛場景作爲一種美學意境來經營。[37] 不只是郭靖和黃蓉、楊過和小龍女、張無忌和阿蛛／小趙／趙敏／周芷若、陳家洛和香香公主、令狐冲和任盈盈、胡斐和程靈素……這些作爲敘事主線的愛情，即如《射鵰英雄傳》中的周伯通和瑛姑、《神鵰俠侶》中的李莫愁……所營造出來的遺憾和悵惘，對於不同人物角色的愛戀（不論是歷經長程試練和磨難而「有情人終成眷屬」還是「此恨綿綿」）的著力經營，往往和古典詩詞的相關抒情意境可以會通，而渲染出強烈的抒情效果，成功的讓以情爲中心的美感經驗凌駕帶著陽剛色彩的江湖恩仇，這幾乎可以說是對武俠小說本身類型上的突破。這一特色幾乎貫穿了金庸所有的武俠小說，也構成他個人武俠世界的一大特色。這樣的

34　卡勒《結構主義詩學》對「文化逼眞性」（cultural vraisemblance）是指「一系列的文化範式或公試的常識」（頁 212）只比眞正的「自然」稍微不自然。

35　這裡借卡爾維諾（Italo Calvino）的談法：「……一個物體出現在一段敘述中的時刻，它就負載有某種特殊的力量，變得像是一個磁場的極，一種不可見的關係的核心……我們甚至可以說，在一篇敘事文中，每一件物體都是奇幻的。」（楊德友譯，社會思想出版社，1994，頁 34。）卡爾維諾這裡針對的是「一切敘事」。故而像魯迅〈藥〉中的血饅頭、〈長明燈〉中的燈火、〈祝福〉中的門檻等，也都可以說是「奇幻事物」，只是訴諸的逼眞性（眞實—幻覺效果）的參照系不同。

36　同樣的道理，愛情小說也可以加上武俠的要素。

37　談錫永，〈武俠小說的境界〉也指出金庸這種對愛情場景的經營，往往達致一種「『散文詩』似的境界」，而「增加了小說的文藝氣息」（頁 5）。

取向，甚至可以說，他潛在的更換了以江湖恩仇爲主要敍事動機（motiva-
tion）的傳統程式，而潛在的以男女情感來作爲敍事動機。這也幾乎決定了作
品的抒情性。對中國抒情傳統有深切瞭解的陳世驤先生在致金庸的函[38] 中即
已相當淸楚的指出金庸對於武俠小說類型上的突破，「以爲精英之出，可與元
劇之異軍突起相比」也借王國維對元劇的評估：「有意境」──「寫情則沁
人心脾，寫景則在人耳目，述事如出其口」──來鑑定金庸武俠小說。認爲
這在「情、景、述事必以離奇爲本」的武俠小說「爲尤難」（頁 58-59）換言
之，金庸在小說的技術和文學的意境上成功突破了「類型」所加諸的限制。
馮其庸在〈讀金庸的小說〉中也強調金庸小說的「文學性」塑造出的「詩的
境界」，「特別美好的境界」[39] 而以武俠小說而言，最關鍵的也許是把武鬥場
面（武俠小說的「戲肉」、死角）也盡其可能的藝術化，把最可能展現出暴虐、
血腥的場景也從可能的「暴力美學」向藝境轉化。在金庸的小說裡，有很多
例子可以讓人看出他這方面的用心──把武術的最高境界設定在《莊子》（以
〈養生主〉中的「庖丁解牛」爲基本格式）中所呈顯的美感境界；也把每一場
武鬥盡可能的展現爲武之道的展示，武者遊於武之藝，而讓讀者透過語言文
字的描繪「體道」──感受一種「中國藝術精神」。[40]

　　而且也相當明顯的，金庸的武俠小說幾乎也都可以算是「成長小說」：「江
湖」做爲必要的洗禮，和民間故事的程式類似，成長的歷程包含了作爲一個
（中國）人的各種價値的考驗，愛情是其中一端──在金庸，是尤其被強化的
一端──而其他的所有人倫範疇內的基本情感關係──武俠的程式──師、
友之義──也都成了小說主人公人格考驗的核心。在金庸的武俠世界裡，同
時也可以看到作者本身的道德感（或對小說人物道德上的潔癖）的投射（尤
其在小說主人公的身上）：小說主人公在道德上基本上是相當值得稱道的。放
浪如令狐冲、楊過，也都不嫖妓、不好色（對性有潔癖）、不三妻四妾[41]　（即
使有許多「始亂終棄」的露水姻緣的機會，也都「潔身自愛」、「從一而

38　1970.11.20，收入《諸子百家看金庸》貳（臺北：遠流，1997）。
39　《諸子百家看金庸》肆，頁 47。
40　借自徐復觀先生《中國藝術精神》（臺北：學生書局，1966 初版，1979 六版）
41　或許唯一的例外是韋小寶。

終」[42]）、不頹廢（縱使愛喝兩杯）的守禮英雄，「發乎情、止乎禮」，對於婚前性行為的禁絕、對於傳統婚姻的肯定。遵守基本的人倫秩序，雖然他們被設定在一個仕儒的體制之外。[43] 這樣的設計，使得金庸筆下的主人公們雖然有著江湖世界裡不盡的傳奇和浪漫，在那被設定的、本質上帶著過去時間性的時空地理，浪漫抒情的內部卻蘊含著一種頗為強烈的道德理想。就金庸對愛情的處理而言，主人公們頗為接近敢於尋求自由戀愛的五四新青年，如郭靖就比胡適還堅決，可是卻沒有擺向徐志摩、郁達夫那一端：江湖的浪漫情愛，有限的個人主義被限定在大致是傳統的（但經過一定程度修正的）格局內。在這方面，它自然不是甚麼「否定的藝術」，反而是相當明確的肯定了一些既有的價值。這或許也是它在中國人價值渙散時代中被廣泛接受的其中一個原因。

再和五四現代小說從類型上做比較，和五四浪漫個人主義[44] 有所共享也有其根本的分歧；作為一個想像的、有價值的過去的世界的武俠世界，它本質上即是浪漫的。然而就表達的方式（語用的型態）上來看，五四新文學中被上昇到至高位置的敘事者「我」在武俠世界裡卻往往被「他」所取代；[45]更遑論日記、書信等自我暴露的文學形式。就這一點來說，武俠小說本質上較接近於傳統的敘事體——傳奇說部。它之所以是那樣封閉的敘事體，時間性設定的緣故。

42　試看看令狐冲和狄雲之「移情別戀」是多麼的困難；楊過的專一又留下了多少「遺恨」；而張無忌雖然有一些「搖擺」，卻儘可能的不佔任何一方的便宜；袁承志則近乎迂儒。

43　包含愛情在內的「江湖道義」的強化而上昇為金庸武俠世界裡至高的道德守則，使得在那樣一個原本可以以武力為導向的世界裡，武的成份被道（德）所約：即使在武藝上可以「從心所欲」，也不能逾道德之矩。就師徒之義，《笑傲江湖》中令狐冲和岳不羣的戲碼，正清楚的展示了這一點；就同門之誼，《書劍恩仇錄》中陸菲青和張召重的衝突也是一個典型。

44　詳細的討論參普賽克的重要論文〈中國現代文學中的主觀主義和個人主義〉，收入氏著《普賽克中國現代文學論文集》（長沙：湖南文藝出版社，1987），頁 1-30；李歐梵，〈現代中國文學文學中的浪漫個人主義〉，收入氏著《現代性的追求——李歐梵文化評論精選集》（臺北：麥田，1996），頁 91-116。

45　一般而言，假定了過去時間性的武俠小說，第一人稱的設計在一般讀者的接受上會對它的「真實效果」打折扣。

　　在那樣封閉的敍事體的舞台／世界裡，角色都是一些浪游者。浪跡天涯是他們在敍事時間中存在的宿命。然而那樣的宿命在一則又一則對於「在朝」的價值否定和不信任中，「退隱」作爲結局或武林高人眞正的歸趣、以無爲有的存在之居所來看，卻隱然透顯了一股對衰世、亂世──武俠世界總是亂世──的傷悼。俠客高人終歸是「天下」之中的流離者。和歷史小說類似，一如唐傳奇〈虬髯客傳〉，即使依賴於特定的、眾所熟知的歷史背景，作爲「界碑」的已成事實的過去之歷史座標對於想像的限定，[46] 使得俠客們在本質上對於「大局」並不能改變甚麼：《碧血劍》中的袁承志之於明室傾覆、《鹿鼎記》中天地會之「反淸復明」、《書劍恩仇錄》紅花會眾之於乾隆帝……。[47]已成事實的結局反過來成爲這樣的武俠敍事中角色的歷史宿命；因而俠客們的飄泊沒有定點，除非在結局，或死亡，而隱沒於江湖。從這個角度來看，江湖中的浪遊者們在他們的「世界」背後，飄浮著典型現代人的幽靈；略爲誇張的說，那正是近代中國文化與歷史解體過程中釋放、游離出來的精神浪游的現代個人的意識。[48] 在那樣的世界裡，往返於家朝之間與及家─朝一體的傳統士大夫士宦格局，易爲家庭被解散的普遍狀態，江湖是沒有屋宇籠罩的江湖，一個更爲廣大卻也更爲抽象的世界：「所謂『人在江湖』，那『江湖』的意符直指『外面』的世界，與你我稱之爲『家』的地方是難免對立的；而『人在江湖』這句諺語，在一定的程度上，勾畫出個人置身於無限之中，是怎樣的漂泊與無主。」[49] 小說的主人公，浪遊者們，作者與及讀者，在神州土

46　相對而言，雖不能改變已成事實的「結果」，但可以修改、移易「前因」。

47　同樣的，香港特殊的地理位置（位處於「兩岸三地」之中的尷尬位置），金庸武俠小說生產的特殊歷史狀況（兩岸政治對抗、而香港又屬殖民地），兼之金庸某些小說要麼把時空背景設定在異族統治的淸初（存在著南明流亡政府），要麼對政治現實若有所隱射（如《天龍八部》、《笑傲江湖》中被權力腐化的武林高人），在在都容許讀者對它進行家國寓言的解讀。參韓倚松撰、何鯉譯，〈淺談金庸早期小說與五十年代的香港〉，《明報月刊》，33: 8（1988.8，總 392 期），頁 36-39。

48　對中國現代文學的一個有趣的討論參李歐梵，〈孤獨的旅行者──中國現代文學中自我的形象〉，收入氏著《現代性的追求》，頁 117-138。近代武俠小說誠然是中國近代化、大眾讀物、讀者閱讀市場成熟過程中的文化產物，它的原始性格離不開文化商品的市場機制，然而作爲文人的書寫品，書寫者同處於現代時間，卻也讓它和五四現代文學共享了同一個思想史大背景：傳統的「道的基礎」的解體，彷徨的現代個人。

49　王宏志、李小良、陳淸僑，《否想香港：歷史、文化、未來》（臺北：麥田，1997），頁 284。

地上地理的無限性中經由故事—經歷召喚意義。

五、花果飄零：中國性與想像的共同體

　　在那樣一個經由讀者、作品、作者間的類型契約而儘可能被自然化的世界裡，它的時間僅屬於過去，而且更僅屬於中國，甚至不無誇張的說：它的時間性具有純粹的中國性。武俠小說所設定的時間都是在中國的古典世界內，最多延伸到新舊交替的民國初年——但那已快要被排除出武俠的類型。金庸的下限更只到清朝初年，一個王朝仍然自足，中心依然穩固，中國自身的存在沒有被現代化所質疑的時代——那也是一個假定中國式的傳統武術可以自足而不受西方鎗炮威脅的時代。近代化讓中國的歷史時間重新依現代時間歸零起跳，在古／今之間劃出一道深重的分界線；也宣告了中國的過去屬於「古典世界」，它被現代所終結，而強迫完成。以古典世界的終結爲它的生產條件（現代的印刷、出版、讀者群、白話文、文人的邊緣化、城市庶民）的新派武俠小說，不管是有意還是無意的，都銘刻了一代世俗大眾的懷舊，和進行近代「國學」生產的袞袞諸公們其實共享著一種情懷，也共同參與了一場曠古的召喚——對於文化的，或歷史的精神。因從時間從屬於「過去」這一點更進一步界定，其實武俠小說之作爲一種類型，在本質上內含了時間的中國性——文化中國時間，內含了中國的古典世界——而且假設了相對於西方現代化的古中國的純粹性，如此也設定了它內在的地理景觀，仍然是天下一神州。

　　時間的設定讓武俠小說的世界成爲假擬的古典世界。在五四作家以「一種自覺改革的新精英主義：要除掉細節描述，以至所有傳統的繁文縟節」，且把「所有『中國』的東西都以死亡和疾病這等鬼魂式的形象」[50] 的那個時代，武俠小說卻以假擬的、奇幻化的中國事物、布景化非刻意講究但仍可以辨識出它似乎具有普遍性、尚未被現代變遷所摧毀的中國細節[51] 來構築它的世

50　周蕾，〈現代性和敘事——女性的細節描述〉，《婦女與中國現代性——東西方之間閱讀記》）（臺北：麥田，1995），頁 81。

51　這裡所謂的「中國細節」是被「奇幻事物」所中介的。也即是許多論者都會提及的金庸武俠小說所借用的傳統歷史文化材料，如陳世驤所說的「細至博奕醫術，上而惻隱

界；新文學中被鬼影、病體化的過去也相反的以俠客精神和肉體上精神的無
比剛健和超脫凡俗；一場規模龐大的世俗增補。在休閒消費之外，大眾對於
這種類型的異常心理需求倒也多少說明它的基本功能：一個體質超乎常人的
中國人的世界。平行對比，在近代中國思想史上，那也是一個轉型期士大夫
在召喚俠——剛健精神的時代。因而從思想史的角度來看，俠的召喚意味著
士大夫群體對柔弱的儒的精神上的修正，以佛的菩薩入世和墨者的兼愛勇
健。晚清以降的近代思想史把自漢以來所獨尊的儒術等移於諸子，在被壓抑
的諸子學裡企圖為一個衰弱的中國在固有的資源裡找到思想和精神上的出
路，佛、道與墨。墨的進取、民間色彩、尚武、群體行動、社會實踐；道家
的淡泊名利及藝術化的生命境界；佛家的捨身、菩薩之道。從康有為、章太
炎、譚嗣同、梁啟超、熊十力……到錢賓四，被五四一代視為保守反動、反
現代的國粹主義者們，紛紛以百科全書般漫無邊際的經典記憶、抽象幽深的
理論辯證、等身的著作，對古典時代作總體的招魂，以憂患和悲切，帶著深
濃古樸的過去時間，卻礙難下降至在現代時間裡忙於衣食的庶民，在語言文
字和意識的高樓。而產生於現代中國世俗而被金庸高度文人化——向上修
正[52]——的武俠小說，於若輩或竟是現代都市市街上一窪污黑積水中的他們
意識的照影。表面的差別是前者儒、文、雅而後者武、俠、世俗，然而跨越
俗雅之界而被深於中國傳統的博學者如陳世驤、楊聯陞先生所稱許（且在學
術上可以論證、辨識）達致一種高雅的藝術「境界」，使得照影和原像之間的
雅／俗、上／下、高／下、大／小……等價值的鴻溝似乎也變得十分可疑——
至少對於象牙塔外的接受者而言。但實際上對於廣大被唐君毅先生稱為「中
華民族飄散在世界各地的花果，在各地逐漸生根長葉……。但只在各地生根
長葉，而忘其本原，不更回念其本原，而對其本原有所盡責，則是一精神上
的大危機」的「海外中華兒女」[53] 而言，金庸小說中所呈現的歷史文化掌故及

佛理」（前揭文，頁 59）；馮其庸所說的諸子百家、三教九流、傳統詩詞（前揭文，頁
45），數量種類相當龐大且廣泛的遍及大小傳統的文化材料，「俱納入性格描寫與故事
結構」（陳世驤，同前）。

52　即以傳統文化資源為「創造性轉化」的材料。也意指金庸對於小說的有意修改。

53　引自唐君毅〈海外中華兒女之發心〉（1971），收於《唐君毅全集卷七‧中華人文與當
今世界（上）》（臺北：學生書局，1988），這是書中同一系列的第三篇，另兩篇是〈中

醫卜星相，琴棋書畫，武術毒藥等等，不管是確有所據，還是「想當然耳」的偽知識（pseudo-knowledge），由於他們大多數並無法擁有充分的學術參照，[54] 因而那被有機的溶入該世界裡的「中國細節」也即以（偽）百科全書的方式存在、被接受。一如學院知識分子之看待「國學大師」。從這個角度來看，金庸武俠小說恰好在雅俗之間的中間位置──如香港這個近代華人文化工業大國、向「海外」輸出俗或不俗的通俗文化的大本營的地理位置所象徵的──倒也近乎嘲諷、錯體的「實踐」了唐君毅先生文化想像共同體的召喚及杜維明教授對於「儒學第三期發展」[55] 及「文化中國」[56] 的構想：一個沒有

　　華民族之花果飄零〉、〈花果飄零及靈根自植〉。在〈海外中華兒女之發心〉文末，在反共的前提下，唐君毅呼籲這些飄零的花果們「發心」「建立一海外的中國文化長城」，最終目的則是「使中國在二十一世紀，成為人的文化之中國。」（頁 74）而企圖召喚一個想像的文化共同體。這種態度在 1973 年的未完手稿〈海外中華子孫安身之道〉（《唐君毅全集卷七·中華人文與當今世界補編（下）》，臺北：學生書局，1988）中有一番修正，修正為「只要求（這些花果們）在文化意識上為中華子孫」而不要求他們在國籍上也屬中國（頁 454），受到星加坡現況的啟發，認為「中華子孫在海外安身的問題和中國問題」可以分別處理。

54　即使有，如果沒有「考據癖」，大概也不會對小說當真。

55　杜維明教授在〈儒學第三期發展的前景問題〉（1985）中大體承繼唐君毅對飄零花果的文化召喚，以儒家傳統為「東亞文明的體現」，而言「如果把海外華人社團的價值取向也列入考慮，那麼，廣義地說，儒學傳統也是新加坡、東南亞、澳洲、歐美的。」（頁 301）這裡頭的關鍵修辭大概是「廣義地說」；廣義地說，那是一種並非新型態的文化民族主義。或許廣義地說，金庸也該算是新儒家罷。收入氏著《儒學第三期發展的前景問題──大陸講學，問難，和討論》（臺北：聯經，1989）。

56　1995 年，杜維明教授對「儒學第三期發展」做了些微的（修辭上）的修正，標舉外延所指較廣的「文化中國」，可是把儒學世界化、「全球化」的企圖並沒有改變，（見陳引馳編、杜維明作品精粹《一陽來復》（上海：上海文藝出版社，1997），「文化中國」條，頁 10-11）而以三個「象徵世界」（symbolic world）來展開論述，在他的劃分中，中國、臺灣、香港、澳門和新加坡「這些社會居民的絕大多數在文化和種族上都屬於華人（中國人）」所以是當然的「第一世界」、「當然的中心，絲毫不理會這些不同地區的「花果」們在歷史發展上已成事實的文化、與及文化認同上的差異（尤其離譜的是把新加坡列入），與及說是以文化為判準，不如說是以前現代的血緣做判準（華人文化認同的複雜程度，王賡武、陳志明等人的大量論著已有一番詳細的研究）。這從他把「力求從思想上理解中國」的「與日俱增的國際人仕」──外國／族人──雖然他們「的塑造作用毫無疑問勝過兩個世界的總和」列為「第三（象徵）世界」可以看得十分清楚。同樣有趣的是，馬來西亞華人和其他各地的華人被列入「第二象徵世界」（同前書，「象徵世界」條，頁 26-27），這「中間」的位子十分值得玩味──

精神負擔的桃花源，時間性投向過去的烏托邦，一個純粹的精神的王國，一個神州、天下、中原——爲他們想像中的「祖國」劃出一個帶著多少[57] 文化氣味的基本輪廓，讓他們殘存或永續、抽象且感傷[58] 的（文化）民族主義、[59] 內在中國有一個可以顯影的參照系，也界定了作爲文化想像共同體的物質顯影的那個世界的基本時空座標：過去、天下。一個不是被文言文，而是被白話文所表述的僞古典世界。借由閱讀而把自我意識投入那個被書寫的動人世界，在「沁人心脾」之情、「在人耳目」之景中，書本逐漸失去了物質性，「它們成爲意象、觀念、語詞，成爲純粹的精神實體」而「我」卻被一個「如出其口」的主體的意識所擄獲，而「我在這樣一種不再有權把它視爲我自己的方式中，被限定了。我被借給了另一個人，這個人在我之中思考、感覺、受難和行動。」[60] 經歷了那個世界的精神漫遊，被那文化借代的實體（假想裡頭有個「文化母體」？）裡頭的抒情、歷史、文化所哺育、贈予、包裹、含納，代價是主體的被借出：「由於我被另一個人的思想奇特地侵入，我就成了思考他人思想的經驗的一個自我，我成了我思想之外的思想主體。」（頁 5）在與現實無涉的世界，自我因而被一個具有強烈文化屬性的他人所寄寓，暫時

其實有一大部份的馬來西亞華人遠比新加坡華人「更中國」，而大馬華人總數還遠超過新加坡人口的總和，更別說是新加坡華人。如果是以對金庸武俠小說的接受做「文化判準」，「文化中國」的構想說不定會「落實」。王賡武教授對「文化中國」的概念也曾從文化中國的時間、地域限制等面向提出委婉的批評，見〈關於文化中國的四個疑問〉，陳其南、周英雄編，《文化中國：理念與世界》（臺北：允晨，1994），頁 6-10。

57 再少也比他們在非第一象徵世界的現代一般日常生活爲多。

58 「感傷」是因爲在政治現實中被邊緣化的緣故。

59 在〈南洋華人民族主義的限制 1912-1937 年〉，王賡武著、姚楠編，《東南亞與華人——王賡武教授論文選集》（北京：中國友誼出版社，1987）一文中王賡武教授早已指出，本世紀初南洋華人的民族主義基本上「並不是由一種熱情的自我發現所決定的，而大都是來自中國受過教育的華人巧妙游説所決定的」（頁 136-137），以一個抽象的想像承諾：「一個強大的中國將會保護他們。」（頁 137）這裡指的是維新、國民革命一直到國共內戰；而之後（新中國成立、南洋新興國家獨立），與中國的隔離使得新一代南洋華人民族主義更加抽象、更加純理論，是一種王教授稱之爲「束之高閣的民族主義」（頁 153）也即是文化的意味遠大過政治，情緒、情感的意味大過於理智；換言之，不是寫實的，而是「金庸武俠小說讀後感」式的。「文化中國」的實質或許也是如此。

60 普萊（George Poulet）著、龔見明譯，〈閱讀的現象學〉，王逢振、盛寧、李自修編，《最新西方文論選》（廣州：廣西新華書店，1991），頁 7。

的，或存續的。

　　同時，相對於五四感時憂國小說被苦難中國當下現實的時間性所牢牢吸附而黏貼在那「去古未遠」的近代中國的地表，太過中國而並不古典——是以反而「不夠中國」[61]——反而失去了作爲海外華人文化想像的條件（因爲他們有自己應接不暇的苦難），金庸武俠小說（當然或許不止金庸），恰好歪斜的實踐了相對於五四的另一種小說觀——嚴復、梁啓超等人在大中華帝國日欲落未落時對於白話小說改變人心的期待，以英雄男女爲基本母題，借敍事對讀者熏、浸（但不一定「刺、提」或一般不「刺、提」）而影響「群治」[62]——灌輸現代的理性價值、改良主義的思想。而今形式猶存，在這第一或第二象徵世界，內容卻被替換爲一種有限度的中華文化熏陶；也應證了「夫說部之興，其入人之深，行世之遠，幾幾乎出經史上」這樣的預言——尤其是對「海外」華人而言——經史早已浮昇爲大字木刻的「有字天書」。

　　只是不知道，「今之儒者」在構想「文化中國」[63] 時，腦中是否想及金庸？

61　被現代時間「污染」而相對的不夠「純粹」。

62　侯健〈武俠小說論〉：「武俠小說的問題癥結，不在一時一地的不良效果，而是長遠的腐蝕人心，破壞原則，妨害正常的適應，終至反社會，反文明。」見《中國小說比較研究》（臺北：東大，1983，頁 194），或許可以作爲正統晚清小說觀的現代版。

63　當代比杜維明先生更早提倡「文化中國」的，在臺灣，或許是以溫瑞安爲首領的神州詩社同人。在他們於戒嚴大中國時代編輯出版的《青年中國雜誌》（由他們自組的青年中國雜誌社出版，1979.11）的第 3 號即是「文化中國」專題（共出 3 期，第 1 期是「青年中國」專題；第 2 期是「歷史中國」專題）。而溫瑞安何許人也？讀金庸、古龍等人的武俠小說長大的「第二象徵世界」的大馬青年，早年的生活即已浸熏在武俠小說的世界裡，把那個世界當眞，成長過程中「相逢先問有仇無」，所寫的作品充斥著俠骨柔情刀光劍影；1974 年來到「第一象徵世界」臺灣，創立充滿江湖氣味、拼貼著武俠符碼的神州詩社。早年金庸是他的超級偶象，而今他所寫的武俠小說，在數量上，金庸已是「望塵莫及」。在〈古遠的回聲——談武俠小說〉一文中，指出武俠小說有「四種特殊的意義」：一、「它是民間」；二、「有讀者，有民間的力量」；三、「最能代表中國傳統文化精神」，「它的背景往往是一部厚重的歷史，發生在古遠的山河裡，無論是感情和思想，對君臣父子師長的觀念，都能代表中國文化的一種精神。」四、「時空比一切創作都要大，聯想的作用可以發揮得淋漓盡致」（見氏著《回首暮雲遠》（臺北：四季出版公司，1977，頁 221-223）第三點尤爲重要（雖然「君臣」二字是胡說八道），可借以管窺「第二象徵世界」中人對金庸是如何接受的。而文中舉證除了少許古龍的作品外，都是金庸的名著。對金庸武俠小說中的藝術成就和「文化意境」倒眞有深切的感受——他的文化中國裡頭是留有一個特大的位子給金庸坐的。

圓桌座談

——俠之變，俠之反

主持人：吳靜吉
貴　賓：金　庸
引言人：范秀珠、陳墨、瘂弦、司徒達賢、李仁芳、陳慶浩
紀　錄：張瀛太

吳靜吉（學術交流基金會）

　　今天座談會的立意在從各種不同角度看金庸小說；一方面，有從現代的企業管理直攻小說的俠義世界，有從文學的研究翻譯創作講到多媒體方面的整合，另一方面，也有從過去的追溯談到未來的計畫。最後的重頭戲，當然是請金庸先生來作總結和回應。以下先請遠從越南來的范秀珠女士，爲我們報告金庸小說的越文版翻譯情形。

金庸小說在越南

范秀珠（越南文學院）

　　金庸小說在越南的翻譯出版狀況可分爲三個階段。第一階段是 1975 年以前。當時很多冒牌貨紛紛出籠，魚目混珠。

　　第二階段是 1975 到 1995 年。金庸小說已被各階層讀者所接受，不過因爲翻譯品質不好，越南知識分子對金庸小說有所誤會，他們把金庸小說叫做「金庸掌書」，不是文學，只是武打。

　　第三階段是 1998 年 2 月迄今。我們覺得應該還原金庸小說的原貌，於是和越南作家協會出了金庸小說的專刊，翻譯《雪山飛狐》，謹守原著的精神、

詩詞、歷史，甫刊行就受到矚目。雖然長期以來對金庸小說的誤會還存在，但這已經是好的開始。

俠之變，俠之反

陳墨（北京中國電影藝術研究中心）

我之所以願意投入七年最美好的時間來做研究，最主要原因在於，金庸小說確實達到了傑作的標準：既不重複他人，又不重複自己。具體地說，它經歷過四個階段：「俠之立、俠之變、俠之疑、俠之反」。金庸是立中有變，集小變為大變；變中有疑，集小疑為大疑；疑中有反，集小反為大反。在早期幾部書中，他按照正宗的中國俠義觀念——儒家之俠這個觀念來書寫，這到郭靖是最高峰；但是到了楊過就開始變，而到張無忌則變異越大；在不斷變化中，對武俠世界的傳統價值慢慢產生懷疑，而懷疑的典型代表是《連城訣》，那真有點拔劍四顧心茫然的感覺，而《俠客行》中幾乎所有的人物都是被自己的慾念支配著，正宗「俠」的理念在這世界很難找到，《天龍八部》也是對武俠價值有著高度的懷疑。這是金庸不同於別的作家之處，而更與眾不同之處就是走向「俠之反」，對武俠價值、對武俠傳統寫作方式有種自覺或不自覺的顛覆或反諷。

金庸先生是左派？

瘂弦（作家）

多年來，金庸在臺灣既是個傳說，也是個謠言。我想藉這個機會請教一下金庸先生。

三、四十年代左翼文學以及 1949 年以後的大陸文學界，特別是官方欽定的文藝思想都視武俠小說為異端。雖然當年臺灣說中共用武俠小說來宣揚統戰思想，但到目前為止，我們還沒見過完全照毛澤東文藝思想所寫成的武俠小說。1966 年《幼獅文藝》開了座談會討論「中國武俠小說向何處去」，當時還有人說如何利用武俠小說來表現反共觀念，現在看起來都很有趣。

既然改革開放前，中共對武俠小說是採取貶抑態度，怎可能歡迎金庸作

品在大陸流傳？臺灣以前傳說金庸先生是左派，說《射鵰英雄傳》的射鵰二字是影射毛澤東〈沁園春〉裡的「彎弓射大鵰」等等，這對金庸是不公平的。

而在金庸作品還沒有在臺灣出現前，臺灣也有蓬勃的武俠小說創作活動，像臥龍生、諸葛青雲、司馬翎、古龍、慕容美、上官鼎、柳殘陽、獨孤紅、玉翎燕、雲中岳等等。能否請金庸先生說說他對這些小說家的評價。

大俠老婆管理學院

司徒達賢（政治大學企業管理研究所）

從管理觀點看金庸武俠小說，似乎「俠」的基本價值和文化與今天的組織現象、組織文化會有所牴觸、矛盾。管理，它的基層是組織，在今天的社會裡，人和人、組織和組織之間基本邏輯就是交易，相互間會有妥協和讓步、利益分配和行政規範。可是金庸小說的俠，都有非常奔放獨立的生命，他可以犧牲很多東西，就爲了追求單一目標。不需要和人家妥協，不用和人成群結隊，沒什麼利益交換，也不受組織規範，所以不容易從組織管理的角度來觀照他們。

雖然武俠小說裡也有組織，但試看長期存在於組織的人，或組織裡有效的領導者，似多平庸之輩。全眞教的道士們、少林寺的和尙們，武功高有什麼用？很俗氣！彼此之間的想法、溝通很複雜，不是個痛快的人生。

大俠還有一個特色，就是行政管理都不行。像郭靖、令狐冲、張無忌，雖然個人魅力很強，但他們帶領那麼多人，都是黃蓉、任盈盈、趙敏在管，就像有個老婆管理學院。最近很多女性主義者認爲金庸小說的女性不重要，我倒認爲金庸武俠小說反映了一個現實，就是男人在外面打拼，女人在後面遙控，眞正有能力、有影響力的是女人。

人性與俠性的解脫

甚至還有個現象就是，同一個人在組織內外表現特異。如向問天，流落江湖被人追打時多麼英雄豪傑，後來任我行平反後，讓他做了行政主管就俠義不起來了。金毛獅王謝遜在江湖闖蕩時多好，但以前在明教裡也很不快樂；

這跟《水滸傳》一樣，所有人入夥前都是英雄好漢、立體的人物，跑到梁山泊以後就變成平面的，只是一個名字而已。這種矛盾，其實解釋了全世界風起雲湧的金庸現象：因為在資本主義市場經濟之下，我們把自己的生活生命都投入了大大小小的各種組織結構，羈絆在裡面，使我們的人性、俠性受到太大的扼殺！現在閱讀武俠小說，不但可以解脫一下，也幫我們在現實生活中所埋沒的人性，取得一點新鮮空氣。

反權威的文字傳統

李仁芳（政治大學科技管理研究所）

　　金庸先生曾提到二十世紀的中國文學可以分主流、非主流。主流是受到歐美影響，不論是文字結構和感性都很西化。而非主流，就像張恨水，文字內容思想情感都比較傳統中國。金庸先生承認他是後者，他寫小說時，文字就特別避免西化。我之所以談這件事，是因為我覺得文字代表文化的認同和思想，文字意義和情感承載影響了我們的想像空間。可是現在的年輕人，在各種文字圖像影音的見聞裡，很缺乏華人的主體性，這會影響一整代的美學和生活品味。

陳慶浩（法國科研中心）

　　金庸講過，中國古典小說基本上是反教條、反權威，而武俠小說承繼了中國古典小說傳統，所以將武俠小說、中國古典小說、金庸小說連起來，其間的繼承關係就很明顯。

　　在當代，將小說作為一種教化工具並不適當，但它確是中國古典小說的基本傳統。從唐人說經到宋人說書，都將小說作為教化工具。而聽眾也不單是為了娛樂，他們也想在裡面吸收一些知識。例如歷史知識、日常生活方面的知識：包括醫藥保健、旅行須知、官司狀語、如何走後門等等，都非常實在。這種傳統甚至演變到有些小說就為了專門表現作者的知識而寫，像《野叟曝言》、《鏡花緣》、《三言》、《二拍》，都充滿知識性。

　　金庸的武俠小說也充滿了知識教育，歷史感特別強；另外，琴棋書畫、飲食、醫藥、歷史等也多所討論，不知道作者是否有意藉此傳達知識？若從

金庸小說目前受歡迎的程度，對照中國古小說帶有教育功能的想法，可見這種傳統還是有它的價值。

金庸答客問

金庸

臺灣武俠小說很蓬勃，事實上在我開始寫之前，臺灣的武俠小說已經寫得很成功了。上次在美國科羅拉多開會時，葉洪生先生說，臺灣在全盛時代，前前後後有五百作家在寫武俠小說，作品大概有四千部之多。而我個人最喜歡的作家，第一就是古龍，第二是上官鼎（劉兆玄），然後是司馬翎、臥龍生、慕容美。

司徒大俠提到的管理方式我很同意。明教管理有問題，丐幫的洪七公也管得不好，黃蓉就好了許多。所以有些女性質問我好像很男性中心，不重視女權。我當然答不出來。有位女讀者為我辯護，說查先生寫女性寫得很可愛，她問我什麼道理，我說我寫女性寫得可愛，因為我崇拜女性啊！

其實，在我的小說裡，女性地位比男性重要，男性在外衝鋒陷陣，後面作 CEO 的人其實是女性，看任盈盈、黃蓉、趙敏這些例子，就是如此。

再講到組織。紅花會好像組織得不錯。一個企業團體的管理，最重要的是戰略，基本戰略錯了，組織再嚴密也沒有用。領袖的決策錯誤，企業也就垮台了。我的小說裡，企業管理得最好的幫會，我看是《俠客行》裡頭的長樂幫。這是個很無聊、微不足道的幫會，只會為非作歹、做壞事，但它組織很嚴密，上面一指揮，大家就一體去執行。雖然這個幫會武功不好、做事也不正當，但他們相當團結，從企業眼光來看，可能是相當不錯的幫會。

但真正組織得最好的，我想是滿清。滿清跟明朝對抗的時候，滿清只有幾千兵，明朝有幾十萬大軍。但明朝打得過滿清嗎？主要原因是八旗兵的軍隊紀律好，組織嚴密，大家聽上面的命令，奮勇衝鋒，不敢後退。所以一個企業或組織成不成功，主要是策略對不對，紀律好不好，大家是否遵守。

李教授講到文字和語意方面的問題，我趁機補充一下。現在的中國文學有兩路：一路是歐化，一路是中國傳統文字的寫法。像大陸有些作家使用傳統方式來寫文章，受到讀者很大的歡迎，最初鄧友梅寫得很成功，後來汪曾

祺小說也寫得很好。這兩人我都喜歡。後來陳忠實、賈平凹也很受歡迎,都是用較傳統的方式來書寫。

藝術不一定要爲社會服務

　　陳慶浩教授提到小說作用的問題。我有個感想:當年毛澤東在延安講,文藝作品一定要爲革命服務,不然就是反革命,就要取消、打垮。所以有很長一段時間,在共產黨統治的地區,跟革命無關的創作根本就沒有人敢寫,寫一些風花雪月的東西就變成反革命了。任何藝術創作一定要爲革命目標服務、一定要有社會作用,這種思想不只在大陸,很多地方也有,一提到文學作品,人家就馬上問這個作品對社會有什麼好處害處,如果這小說流行的話,是不是會貽害青少年?我很不贊成把文學和社會功能相提並論,文學跟音樂、圖畫、雕刻都一樣,可以有、但不一定非要有社會功能不可,它本身就是純粹的藝術創作。

　　瘂弦先生問,《射鵰》是否在宣傳毛澤東思想?其實它完全不是。當年我拿這本書到遠景出版的時候,這裡的警備總部覺得有「射鵰」兩個字不好,所以就改成《大漠英雄傳》。其實我的解釋是,射鵰這兩個字最早在《史記》就有了,講李廣射死大鵰的故事;另外,王維有一首詩說道:「回看射鵰處,千里暮雲平」,寫大漠風光寫得很有氣派,這樣好的詩,毛澤東寫不出,何況他還沒出世呢。

　　感謝各位提供很多寶貴的意見。至於有人提到「金學」這兩個字,我愧不敢當。我覺得金庸小說不能成爲學問,李白、杜甫多偉大,也沒有李學、杜學啊!倒是對於中國傳統文字西化這個問題,希望大家能夠提倡改善,恢復我們中國傳統的優美白話,這是很有價值的工作。

後　記

王秋桂

　　1996 年底王榮文先生跟我說，他想和東吳大學中文系主任王國良教授合作，舉辦「金庸小說國際學術研討會」，希望我也能參與籌備事宜。由於他們兩人和我都是多年好友，我就一口答應。1997 年初，剛好陳慶浩先生在臺北，我就找了他到遠流出版公司。國良也帶了張曼娟副教授來。我們四人就和榮文在他的辦公室開了第一次籌備會議。我們的共識是金庸小說不能只當成文學作品來研究。他的作品已形成一種文化現象，應當從更寬廣的角度從事跨學科的探討。會中我們推舉張曼娟副教授來撰寫會議宗旨，但後來榮文還是要我執筆定稿。接著我建議邀請漢學研究中心為合辦單位，大家也都贊成。由於該中心自 1987 年來和我有七次合辦國際會議的經驗，當我打電話給聯絡組林如組長時，她很乾脆的就答應了。後來開的第二次籌備會議，她也出席並提醒我們要早日決定邀請與會學者的名單。

　　1997 年 2 月間我去美國，在普林斯頓大學和余英時教授提起要舉辦金庸小說研討會事，並商請他就「俠／士，儒／商」為題撰寫主題演講稿。他說可以考慮。但到了三月間榮文告訴我，和東吳大學合辦研討會事有了問題。他希望找其他的合辦單位。我問了清華大學中文系，但他們意願不高，這事就擱了下來。七月初慶浩再度來臺，我們二人和榮文再度會商。榮文強調研討會一定要辦，請我繼續和國外學者連絡。七月下旬，我接受蔣經國國際學術交流基金會委託，前往澳洲訪問十二所曾接受或有意申請補助的大學。到雪梨的 Macquarie University 時，我在訪問劉南強教授後乘便向他約稿；在坎培拉的澳洲國立大學，我跟柳存仁教授約稿。劉教授是研究明教的權威學者，雖是初識，我們談得很投機。他說對金庸先生聞名已久，但手頭沒有他的作品，我回旅館後即電請榮文寄一套《倚天屠龍記》給他。柳先生是非常照顧後輩的長者，我有幸認識他多年，1995 年 4 月時還曾邀他來臺參加漢

學研究中心和施合鄭民俗文化基金會合辦的「中國神話與傳說學術研討會」。他和金庸先生交情非凡，當下一口答應撰稿。

　　1997 年 10 月我到墨爾本大學擔任爲期一年的訪問研究員。11 月初適巧金庸先生和夫人來墨爾本小住，榮文要我去見他們。這是我初次見到金庸先生。我跟他提起會議的構想並徵求他的意見。他很客氣，說一切由我安排，並告訴我劉再復先生和 Howard Goldblatt 教授擬於 1998 年 5 月在美國科羅拉多大學召開「金庸小說與二十世紀中國文學國際學術研討會」，又提及牛津大學的 Robert Chard 對他的作品有研究興趣。於是我回墨爾本大學的研究室後就去函邀請他們三位與會。劉先生我慕名已久，無緣識荊；Goldblatt 教授是舊識。Robert Chard 是研究灶神的專家，我於 1994 年曾邀他來臺參加漢學研究中心主辦的「民間信仰與中國文化國際研討會」，1996 年又在牛津見過面。他這次很快回函同意參加。

　　十一月中我赴香港參加第五屆「中國飲食文化國際研討會」。在港期間我約了中文大學中國文化研究所陳方正所長，嶺南大學劉紹銘教授和馬幼垣教授，香港理工大學 John Minford 教授及香港科技大學呂宗力博士。他們基本上都同意與會。宗力還推薦他的同事危令敦博士；John 也推薦他的學生賴慈芸博士。方正兄雖是學物理出身，精通文史。中國文化研究所在他領導之下，業務蒸蒸日上。這是我每到香港必拜的碼頭。紹銘兄和幼垣兄，一是翻譯專家，一是考證名家。他們二人和方正兄都研究過金庸的作品。John 剛出版他英譯《鹿鼎記》的第一冊。香港翻譯學會出版的《翻譯季刊》（*Translation Quarterly*）在 1997 年 4 月出版的第 5/6 期合刊是「英譯武俠小說專號」，其中有紹銘兄的序言和 John，慈芸，宗力，令敦等人論金庸作品英譯的文章。宗力給了我一冊，正好做爲參考。

　　十一月下旬我順道回臺。榮文說已和中國時報人間副刊談定合辦研討會的事，並約我和楊澤先生及焦桐先生會面商討細節。在會中我們商定由遠流出版公司，漢學研究中心及中國時報人間副刊合辦研討會。後二者分別向有關單位申請補助，不足之數由遠流承擔。會議的時間，地點和形式也做了決定。另外邀請與會學者事宜也做了分工：我負責邀請海外學者，楊澤負責邀請國內學者，慶浩負責邀請大陸學者，榮文負責邀請圓桌會議的學者。這樣，整個研討會才算定案。十二月中旬我去哈佛大學參加慶祝韓南（Patrick

Hanan）教授榮退的研討會。在會中邀了王德威教授和 Meir Shahar 博士。
德威說很有興趣參加，但沒有把握是否抽得出時間。Meir 是韓南教授的高
足，學生時期曾在漢學研究中心做過訪問學員。1994 年我曾邀他來臺參加「民
間信仰與中國文化國際研討會」。我原只知道他是研究濟公的專家。在會上他
提的就是從中國武術史看金庸小說的論文。他當下答應增訂該篇論文。韓南
教授又推薦他過去的學生余珍珠博士（香港科技大學文學院副院長）。哈佛的
研討會結束後我又去普林斯頓大學看余英時先生。他說 1998 年 10 月他得回
去中研院史語所開會，11 月不可能再到臺北，不過論文還是可以考慮寫。

　　回墨爾本大學後，我就把前所邀的學者的傳眞號碼和地址傳給時報的張
定綺女士（楊澤先生和焦桐先生都是大忙人，找定綺來負責連絡的事），請她
安排發正式邀請函給他們。後來楊澤先生來傳眞抱怨我邀了太多海外學者，
影響國內學者的名額。因此雖然 David Johnson 教授和張洪年教授分別來函
推薦 Chris Hamm，我遲遲不敢接受。Chris 是第一個以金庸小說爲題撰寫博
士論文的學者，不邀他參加實在可惜。因此我再次分別打電話或傳眞給以前
邀的所有學者，希望能確定人數。結果劉再復先生，Goldblatt 教授，余珍珠
博士和陳方正所長回覆說無法參加，這我才放心的去傳眞邀 Chris Hamm 與
會。

　　1998 年 2 月我去河北邯鄲參加一研討會，再順道去山西考察。回程經北
京時和胡小偉先生見面，提及籌劃金庸小說研討會事。他說他很想參加。小
偉是多年舊識，我原也只知他近年來專心研究關公。他既有興趣，我就請他
直接與慶浩連絡。我又推薦中正大學中文系的陳益源副教授給楊澤先生。

　　1998 年 4 月我回臺參加蔣經國國際學術交流基金會的歐洲咨議委員會
議。在臺期間，跟榮文談了幾次，又去漢學研究中心和林如組長及承辦研討
會的李素娟小姐商討細節。她們二人和我有多次合作的經驗，因此我要她們
接手籌備後期的連絡工作。楊澤先生和慶浩邀約的學者大致也已確定。素娟
是老手，我可放心的把事務性的事交給她。

　　1998 年 5 月我赴香港中文大學參加 "Ethnography in China Today:
A Critical Assessment of Methods and Results" 研討會。期間就近再度
邀請方正兄，他還是找不出時間寫論文。跟 John Minford 和幼垣兄打了電
話，確定他們屆時與會；跟紹銘兄和宗力見了面，他們也沒問題。

　　七月間我再去普林斯頓大學見余英時先生，想跟他催稿。結果他說近來興趣轉到巫在中國思想史中的地位，沒有時間為研討會撰寫主題演講稿。這本來是我策劃研討會的王牌之一，行不通了只能失望而歸。另一王牌是請劉兆玄先生擔任圓桌會議的主席。他還任國科會主委時，我傳真邀請。後來他高升行政院副院長我就不便再提。這是另一件可惜的事。另外德威跟我說因系務繁忙他跑不開，無法與會。這又是件令人失望的事。

　　八月間素娟傳來所有論文的題目，我便初步排了議程。九月回國我去國家圖書館見新上任的館長莊芳榮先生。芳榮是多年老友，對研討會事表示支持，我也就放心。林如組長已離職隨夫婿祝基瀅先生赴瑞典，她的職務由館長秘書耿立群女士接任。立群以前一直在漢學研究中心，辦事認真。我跟她也有多年合作的經驗。當下和她及素娟把議程定案並請素娟即刻連絡邀請擔任主席的人選。本來我不安排評論員，但楊澤先生堅持要，而且每一論文找一評論員。我當時認為這是不可能的事，不過楊澤先生說他有辦法。我將信將疑就任由他安排。想不到他果然神通廣大，居然找齊二十六位評論員，使研討會大為生色。本來我性子急，而楊澤先生慢，在籌備過程中有幾度我生他的氣。但他安排評論員一事不得不令我佩服。

　　會議結束後，榮文要我負責編輯論文集。實際的編務由素娟執行，我只是出主意而已。今年八月素娟寄校稿給我，說應當有篇序文，我想起以前和彭鏡禧教授合編 *Death in a Cornfield and Other Stories from Contemporary Taiwan* （Hong Kong: Oxford University Press, 1994）時請德威寫序，收到畫龍點睛之效。而且德威原本答應提論文，正好趁此機會請他寫序以代替論文。當下我即打電話給德威，而他也一口答應。素娟把校稿寄給他後一個月內，他便把序文傳來。而我們也依據他的建議把論文的次序做了調整。另外，在此集中，我們尊重個別作者所使用的拼音系統和標點方式（英式或美式）以及西文大小寫的用法，而不予以統一。

　　經過幾番波折，「金庸小說國際學術研討會」總算成功的召開，圓滿的結束。榮文請我代他致謝。我們首先要感謝金庸先生，他提供作品讓我們從事研究，並全程參與研討會，且在圓桌會議上回答問題。連戰先生撥空前來致開幕詞；沈君山先生特別從美國趕回發表主題演講；中國時報黃肇松社長和漢學研究中心曾濟群先生和莊芳榮先生前後二位主任全力支持；行政院文化

建設委員會及大陸委員會給予經費補助；西華飯店董事長劉文治先生提供「射鵰英雄宴」的場所和設備。在此謹向上述諸位先生及機構致謝。特別要感謝的是所有與會學人和聽眾。沒有他們，這場戲就演不成。

順帶可以一提的是，在論文集出版前夕，榮文決定把本集全部文字和研討會全程錄音以及金庸先生訪臺的照片與答客問的影片製成光碟，留供紀念。這些數位資料將送上「金庸茶館網站」讓網友分享。

附
錄

「金庸小說國際學術研討會」
會議簡介

● **緣起**：

　　武俠小說是本世紀華人世界中最具魅力的「大眾文學」，這是值得注意的一種文化現象。但是困於傳統的觀念，學院長久以來將其排除在殿堂之外。在眾多的武俠小說作家中，金庸是最受矚目的一位。他從 1955 年《書劍恩仇錄》到 1972 年完成《鹿鼎記》，共出版十五部武俠作品。金庸作品的讀者群可以說是遠超過任何其他文學作品，而「金迷」更橫跨了社會的各個階層。已故哈佛大學講座教授楊聯陞先生在論劉若愚（James J. Y. Liu）教授所著的 *The Chinese Knight-errant*（Chicago: The University of Chicago Press, 1967）的書評中，以該書未能討論金庸的作品爲憾。近年來更有英、日文等譯本相繼出版，使金庸成爲一國際性的文學家。此次研討會擬集海內外金庸小說的研究者及相關學者專家，分別就文學、歷史、宗教、社會、政治、心理等不同領域，提出學術論文，擴大、加深「金學」的研究範圍，進一步闡釋金庸作品的藝術價值及時代與社會意識。

● **研討主題**：1. 金庸小說的作品分析與人物研究
　　　　　　　 2. 金庸小說的社會、政治結構研究
　　　　　　　 3. 金庸小說的宗教信仰、民俗及文化研究
　　　　　　　 4. 從其他學科（如心理學、數學等）探討金庸小說

● **會議時間**：民國 87 年 11 月 4 日（星期三）至 6 日（星期五）

● **會議地點**：國家圖書館國際會議廳（臺北市中山南路二十號）

● **與會人員**：國內外學人約 220 位（含觀察員）

● **主辦單位**：漢學研究中心、中國時報人間副刊、遠流出版公司

● **贊助單位**：行政院文化建設委員會、行政院大陸委員會

● **展覽主題**：《俠者風貌——金庸小說版本展》

● **展覽地點**：國家圖書館國際會議廳會客室

「金庸小說國際學術研討會」
會議議程

●11月4日（星期三）

報到　8:30～9:00

開幕式　9:00～10:10
貴賓致詞　連戰
專題演講　沈君山

茶敍　10:10～10:30

第一場會議　10:30～12:10
主持人　劉紹銘
1.柳存仁　《脫卜赤顏》・全眞教和《射鵰英雄傳》
　　講評人　李豐楙
2.Samuel N. C. Lieu (劉南強)　Fact or Fiction: Ming-chiao (Mani-chaeism) in Jin Yong's《倚天屠龍記》
　　講評人　王見川
3.洪萬生　全眞教與金元數學
　　講評人　龔鵬程

午餐　12:10～13:30

第二場會議　13:30～15:10
主持人　楊澤
1.張小虹　問金庸情是何物——禮物、信物、證物

　　講評人　易鵬

2. 黃宗慧　他不看她時她在嗎？——以《天龍八部》中段正淳身邊的女性爲
　　　　　　例談自戀、戀物、攻擊慾

　　講評人　蔡淑玲

3. 林保淳　金庸版本學

　　講評人　沈謙

茶敍　15:10～15:30

第三場會議　15:30～17:10

主持人　柳存仁

1. 馮其庸　《笑傲江湖》總論

　　講評人　呂正惠

2. 馬幼垣　從《三劍樓隨筆》看金庸、梁羽生、百劍堂主在五十年代中期的
　　　　　　旨趣

　　講評人　柯慶明

3. J. Christopher Hamm　Creating Classic Literature: On the Revision
　　　　　　of Jin Yong's *Sword of Loyalty*

　　講評人　林文淇

◉11月5日（星期四）

第四場會議　8:50～10:30

主持人　齊邦媛

1. 劉紹銘　《鹿鼎記》英譯漫談

　　講評人　林耀福

2. John Minford　Jin Yong through the Translator's Eyes

　　講評人　廖朝陽

3. 賴慈芸　Translating Jin Yong: A Review of Four English Transla-
　　　　　　tions

　　講評人　呂健忠

茶敘　10:30～10:40

第五場會議　10:40～12:20
主持人　羅宗濤
1.呂宗力　《鹿鼎記》中的粗口與韋小寶的形象塑造
　　講評人　王邦雄
2.陳芳英　絕世聰明絕世癡──《笑傲江湖》中的藝術與人物
　　講評人　許俊雅
3.陳益源　金庸小說人物的不倫之戀
　　講評人　李瑞騰

午餐　12:20～13:30

第六場會議　13:30～15:10
主持人　李亦園
1.嚴家炎　文學的雅俗對峙與金庸的歷史地位
　　講評人　張健
2.張大春　離奇與鬆散──從武俠衍出的中國小說敘事傳統
　　講評人　李孝悌
3.黃錦樹　否想金庸──文化代現的雅俗、時間與地理
　　講評人　廖咸浩

茶敘　15:10～15:30

第七場會議　15:30～17:10
主持人　陳慶浩
1.危令敦　楊過的遭遇：試論《神鵰俠侶》的構思和意識
　　講評人　胡錦媛
2.廖朝陽　《天龍八部》的傳奇結構

　　講評人　陳鵬翔

3.陳　墨　《唐吉訶德》與《鹿鼎記》比較初論

　　講評人　周英雄

◉**11月6日（星期五）**

第八場會議　8:50〜10:30

主持人　瞿海源

1.曾志朗、莊瓊如　認知能量，情緒指標與一心兩用——金學中的認知心理
　　　　　　　　面面觀

　　講評人　楊茂秀

2.胡小偉　顯性與隱性——金庸筆下的兩重社會

　　講評人　南方朔

茶敍　10:30〜10:40

第九場會議　10:40〜12:20

主持人　王秋桂

1.Robert L. Chard　Grass-Roots Militarism and Its Portrayal in the
　　　　　　　Novels of Jin Yong

　　講評人　廖炳惠

2.Meir Shahar　Martial-Arts Fiction and Martial-Arts Practice: The
　　　　　　Concept of *Qi* in Jin Yong's Novels

　　講評人　李振亞

3.林富士　武俠世界中的醫者

　　講評人　李永熾

午餐　12:20〜13:30

圓桌座談　13:30〜15:30

主持人　吳靜吉

貴　賓　金庸

引言人　司徒達賢　李仁芳　范秀珠　陳慶浩　陳墨　瘂弦

閉幕式　15:30～16:00

「金庸小說國際學術研討會」
與會人員名單

中國大陸
胡小偉　中國社會科學院文學研究所研究員
胡文彬　中國藝術研究院紅樓夢研究所研究員
陳　墨　北京中國電影藝術研究中心副研究員
馮其庸　中國藝術研究院副院長
嚴家炎　北京大學中文系教授

日本
松金公正　日本筑波大學歷史・人類學研究所博士研究生；漢學研究中心訪
　　　　　問學人

以色列
Meir Shahar（夏維明）　　Senior lecturer, Tel Aviv University

法國
陳慶浩　法國科研中心研究員

香港
John M. Minford（閔福德）　　Professor, Hong Kong Polytechnic Univer-
　　　　　sity
危令敦　香港科技大學人文學部助理教授
呂宗力　香港科技大學人文學部助理教授
馬幼垣　香港嶺南大學中文系教授
劉紹銘　香港嶺南大學翻譯系教授

美國

J. Christopher Hamm　Assistant professor, University of Washington

Thomas Moran（穆潤陶）　Assistant professor of Chinese, Middlebury
　　　　　College；漢學研究中心訪問學人

張克濟　美國密西根大學歷史系博士候選人

英國

Robert Chard（晁時傑）　University lecturer, University of Oxford

荷蘭

吳榮子　萊頓大學漢學研究院圖書館館長

越南

范秀珠　越南文學院研究員

陳紅雲　越南文學院研究員

陶俊影　越南文學院研究員

瑞士

Roland Altenburger（安如巒）　Associate scholar, Dept. of East Asian
　　　　　Languages and Civilizations, Harvard University；漢學研究中
　　　　　心訪問學人

澳洲

劉南強（Samuel N. C. Lieu）　Professor, Macquarie University

柳存仁（Liu Ts'un-yan）　Professor emeritus, Australian National Uni-
　　　　　versity

吳秀玲（Wu Hsiu-ling）　Doctoral candidtate, University of Melbourne

臺灣

丁圭惠　施合鄭民俗文化基金會編輯

王至誠　臺灣師範大學英語系副教授

王見川　圓光佛學研究所專任講師

王邦雄　中央大學中文系教授

王杏慶（南方朔）　文化評論家

王明月　中正大學外文所副教授

王芳雪　國家圖書館編審

王秋桂　清華大學人類學所教授

王釗芬　光武工專講師

王國良　東吳大學中文系教授

王雅萍　政治大學民族系講師

王榮文　遠流出版公司負責人

王慶麟（瘂弦）　作家

王錫璋　國家圖書館參考組編審兼代主任

王錦慧　銘傳大學應用中文系副教授

皮述民　文化大學中文所教授

司徒達賢　政治大學企業管理研究所教授

朱兆禹　光武工專講師

吳思華　政治大學科技管理研究所所長

吳敏嘉　輔仁大學翻譯所教授

吳靜吉　學術交流基金會執行長

宋　晞　文化大學史學所教授

汪雁秋　中國圖書館學會祕書長

李壬癸　中央研究院語言所研究員兼主任

李仁芳　政治大學科技管理研究所教授

李永熾　臺灣大學歷史系教授

李世珍　臺中僑光商專講師

李亦園　中央研究院院士

李孝悌　中央研究院史語所研究員

李振亞　中央大學英文系教授
李瑞騰　中央大學中文系教授
李壽菊　德明商專副教授
李豐楙　中央研究院中國文哲所研究員
杜麗琴　元定科技企劃主編
沈君山　清華大學教授
沈　謙　空中大學人文學系教授
呂正惠　清華大學中文系教授
呂健忠　東吳大學英文系教授
林文淇　中央大學英文系教授
林安梧　清華大學通識教育中心教授兼主任
林芷瑩　樹德工商專校講師
林保淳　淡江大學中文系教授
林淑雲　臺灣師範大學國文系講師
林富士　中央研究院史語所副研究員
林雅玲　崑山技術學院講師
林蕙麗　元定科技專題主編
林耀福　臺灣大學文學院院長
周英雄　中正大學副校長
易　鵬　交通大學外文系教授
邱彥彬　臺灣大學外文系講師
邱漢平　臺灣師範大學翻譯所副教授
胡錦媛　政治大學西語系副教授
柯慶明　臺灣大學中文系教授
侯坤宏　國史館協修
施懿琳　中正大學中文系副教授
洪淑苓　臺灣大學中文系副教授
洪萬生　臺灣師範大學數學系教授
洪銘水　東海大學中文系副教授
唐翼明　政治大學中文系教授

耿立群　漢學研究中心聯絡組組長

郝譽翔　東華大學中文系助理教授

馬漢寶　臺灣大學法律系教授

崔承宗　淡江大學中文系副教授

張大春　作家

張小虹　臺灣大學外文系教授

張玉欣　中國飲食文化基金會圖書館主任

張思賢　施合鄭民俗文化基金會編輯

張　健　臺灣大學中文系教授

張瑞芬　逢甲大學中文系副教授

張穗芳　醒吾商專講師

莊芳榮　國家圖書館館長；兼任漢學研究中心主任

莊淑芝　施合鄭民俗文化基金會編輯

莊瓊如　陽明大學通識教育中心行政助理

許俊雅　臺灣師範大學國文系教授

許健崑　東海大學中文系副教授

郭乃禎　臺灣師範大學國文系講師

郭　箏　作家

陳兆南　逢甲大學中文系副教授

陳君卿　科學工業園區管理局專員

陳芳明　靜宜大學中文系教授

陳芳英　國立藝術學院戲劇系副教授

陳金木　彰化師範大學國文系教授

陳建忠　清華大學中文系講師

陳益源　中正大學中文系副教授

陳　斌　金石堂圖書股份有限公司副總經理

陳義成　逢甲大學中文系副教授

陳鵬翔　世新大學英語系教授

焦　桐　中國時報人間副刊副主任

彭　慰　國家圖書館資訊組主任

曾志朗　陽明大學副校長

曾永義　臺灣大學中文系教授

游玉琪　元定科技網路記者

游秀雲　銘傳大學應用中文系副教授

湯熙勇　中央研究院社科所副研究員

黃天佑　大成報編譯

黃孝光　中原大學人文社會教育中心教授

黃季平　政治大學民族系講師

黃宗慧　臺灣大學外文系助理教授

黃純怡　中興大學歷史系助教

黃錦珠　中正大學中文系副教授

黃錦樹　國立暨南大學中文系講師

黃蘭亭　中國飲食文化基金會圖書館館員

楊永智　東海大學中文系助教

楊茂秀　臺東師範學院兒童文學研究所副教授

楊振良　花蓮師範學院教授兼所長

楊晉龍　中央研究院中國文哲所研究助理

楊淑娟　華僑高中教師

楊　澤　中國時報人間副刊主任

廖炳惠　清華大學外文系教授

廖咸浩　臺灣大學外文系教授

廖朝陽　臺灣大學外文系副教授

廖湘美　臺北科技大學講師

齊邦媛　臺灣大學外文系教授

劉石吉　中央研究院社科所研究員

劉顯叔　漢學研究中心資料組組長

蔡淑玲　淡江大學法文系教授

蔣秋華　中央研究院中國文哲所副研究員

鄭志明　南華管理學院宗教文化所教授

鄭恆雄　國家圖書館編目組主任；兼任漢學研究中心副主任

盧福志　光武工專講師
盧錦堂　國家圖書館特藏組主任
賴慈芸　銘傳大學應用英文系助理教授
錢佩文　中原大學人文社會教育中心講師
謝佩芬　銘傳大學應用中文系副教授
謝明勳　東華大學中文系副教授
簡瑛瑛　輔仁大學翻譯研究所教授
瞿海源　中央研究院社會所研究員
羅宗濤　政治大學中文系教授
羅美文　淡江大學英文系講師
羅賢淑　文化大學中文系講師
嚴鼎忠　國家圖書館編輯
嚴靈峰　輔仁大學教授
蘇墱基　中國時報副總編輯
龔鵬程　佛光大學籌備處校長

「金庸小說國際學術研討會」
籌備委員暨工作人員名單

籌備委員（依姓氏筆劃順序排列）

王秋桂　國立清華大學人類學研究所教授
王榮文　遠流出版公司負責人
莊芳榮　國家圖書館館長兼漢學研究中心主任
陳慶浩　法國科研中心研究員
焦　桐　中國時報人間副刊副主任
楊　澤　中國時報人間副刊主任

工作人員

秘書組	耿立群	李素娟	梁文芳		
議事組	秦東岱	孫秀玲	張定綺	鄭美里	
新聞組	崔燕慧	林映源	許毓眞		
接待組	李傳理	李佳穎	舒意雯	蘇安籐	
事務組	易明克	周瑞聰	林弘裕	莊有富	趙亞平　盧政志
財務組	王麗雪	蔡慶郎			
展覽組	吳興文	許翠華	鄭祥琳		
攝影組	陳輝明	徐志初	蔡沂均		
設　計	霍榮齡	周尙文	唐壽南		

金庸生平與著作年表

西元	年齡	大事記
1924	出生	本名查良鏞，生於浙江省海寧縣袁花鎮。
1929	5	入讀家鄉海寧縣袁花鎮小學。
1932	8	讀第一本武俠小說《荒江女俠》，作者顧明道，之後更閱讀平江不肖生的《江湖奇俠傳》與《近代俠義英雄傳》等。
1939	15	讀初三，與同學合著並出版第一本書《獻給投考初中者》，大獲成功。
1941	17	因在壁報刊文〈阿麗絲漫遊記〉譏諷訓導主任，被浙江省立聯合高中勒令退學。
1942	18	自浙江省衢州中學畢業。
1944	20	考入中央政治大學外文系，因與國民黨職業學生衝突，向校方投訴而被勒令退學。在中央圖書館閱覽室掛一職銜。
1945	21	在杭州任《東南日報》外勤記者及英語電訊收譯員。
1946	22	轉赴上海東吳法學院插班修習國際法課程。被錄取爲上海《大公報》國際電訊翻譯。
1948	24	被調派香港，續任國際電訊翻譯。
1949	25	發表國際法論文〈從國際法論中國人民在海外的產權〉等文。
1950	26	應邀北上赴京到外交部任職，不滿而歸。不久，其父查樞卿作爲「反動地主」在家鄉受到清算鎮壓。
1952	28	《新晚報》復刊，調任該報副刊編輯，並以姚馥蘭、林歡爲筆名撰寫影評。此外，又寫出《絕代佳人》、《蘭花花》等電影劇本。
1955	31	以「金庸」爲筆名，創作第一部武俠小說《書劍恩仇錄》，在《新晚報》連載一年，奠定武俠文學基業。
1956	32	《碧血劍》開始在《香港商報》連載。並與梁羽生、百劍堂主在《大公報》開闢「三劍樓隨筆」專欄。

1957	33	進入長城電影公司。寫《射鵰英雄傳》連載於《香港商報》。
1958	34	與程步高合導電影《有女懷春》。
1959	35	與胡小峰合導電影《王老虎搶親》。創辦《明報》,《神鵰俠侶》開始在《明報》創刊號連載。《雪山飛狐》連載於《新晚報》。
1960	36	爲《武俠與歷史》雜誌撰寫《飛狐外傳》。
1961	37	《倚天屠龍記》、《鴛鴦刀》、《白馬嘯西風》開始在《明報》連載。
1962	38	《明報》因報導「逃亡潮」而聲名大噪,發行量遽增。
1963	39	爲《東南亞周刊》撰寫《連城訣》。《天龍八部》開始在《明報》連載。
1964	40	發表〈寧要褲子,不要核彈〉社評。與《大公報》展開一系列筆戰。
1965	41	創辦《明報月刊》。創作《俠客行》。
1966	42	對「文革」做一系列分析。
1967	43	香港爆發「六七暴動」,《明報》成爲左派分子重點襲擊目標。在馬來西亞及新加坡創辦《新明日報》。在香港創辦《明報周刊》。創作《笑傲江湖》。
1969	45	創作、發表巓峰之作《鹿鼎記》。
1970	46	寫《越女劍》。開始修訂全部武俠小說作品。
1972	48	《鹿鼎記》連載完畢,宣布就此封筆不寫武俠小說。
1973	49	以《明報》記者身分赴臺訪問十天,會見嚴家淦、蔣經國等。之後於《明報》連載〈在臺所見・所聞・所思〉。
1979	55	參加臺北舉行之「建國會」,與丁中江共同爲小組討論會之主席。正式授權臺灣遠景出版社出版《金庸作品集》。
1980	56	廣州《武林》雜誌連載《射鵰英雄傳》,金庸武俠小說正式進入大陸。十五部三十六冊《金庸作品集》全部修訂完畢,前後花了十年時間。
1981	57	與妻子兒女回大陸訪問,會見鄧小平,並遊歷十三個城市。獲頒英國政府 O.B.E.勳銜。
1984	60	出版《香港的前途——明報社評之一》一書。再次赴北京訪問,會見中共中央總書記胡耀邦。

1985	61	任中華人民共和國香港特別行政區基本法起草委員會委員。

1986　62　被任命爲基本法起草委員會「政治禮制」小組港方負責人。正式授權臺灣遠流出版公司出版《金庸作品集》。獲頒香港大學名譽博士學位。

1988　64　「主流方案」事件在港引起軒然大波，發表〈平心靜氣談政制〉文章。獲香港大學名譽敎授榮銜。

1989　65　宣布辭去基本法草委、諮委職務。在《明報》創報三十週年慶祝茶會上，宣布卸下社長職務，只擔任明報集團有限公司董事長。

1991　67　明報企業掛牌上市。與于品海聯合宣布：智才管理顧問公司技術性收購明報企業。

1992　68　赴英國牛津大學做訪問學者，並於牛津近代中國研究中心主持講座，作〈香港和中國：一九九七年及其後五年〉的演講。回鄉尋師訪友，並爲嘉興市捐建「金庸圖書館」。獲加拿大 UBC 大學 D. Litt. 榮銜。

1993　69　發表〈功能選舉的突變〉長文。赴北京訪問，會見江澤民。宣布辭去明報企業有限公司董事局主席職務，改任名譽主席。在《明報》發表〈第三個和第四個理想〉一文，確定「退休」一事。

1994　70　香港中文大學出版金庸武俠小說第一部英譯本 *Fox Volant of the Snowy Mountain*（雪山飛狐）。正式授權北京三聯書店出版《金庸作品集》大陸簡體字版。《二十世紀中國文學大師文庫》出版，將金庸列爲本世紀中國小說家第四位。被授予北京大學名譽敎授。獲選英國牛津大學兩所學院之榮譽院士。

1995　71　明河社星馬分公司出版《金庸作品集》東南亞簡體字版。

1996　72　獲選英國劍橋大學兩所學院之榮譽院士。日本德間出版社取得版權，正式開始翻譯刊行《金庸武俠小說集》。

1997　73　香港回歸中國大陸，在《明報》發表〈河水井水　互不相犯——寫在回歸第一日〉一文。香港牛津大學出版社出版英譯本 *The Deer and the Cauldron*（鹿鼎記）。

1998　74　5月中旬，美國科羅拉多大學東亞語言文學系和中國現代文化研究所召開「金庸小說與二十世紀中國文學」國際學術討論會，各國四十餘位學者赴會或提出論文。獲香港政府市政局頒授「文學創作終身成就獎」；香港（及海外）文學藝術協會以最高之「當代文豪金龍獎」授予巴金、冰心、金庸三人。日本「潮」出版社、香港明河社、北京大學出版社、臺北遠流出版公司分別出版金庸與日本創價學會會長池田大作對話錄《探求一個燦爛的世紀》一書。11月上旬，由漢學研究中心、中國時報人間副刊、遠流出版公司在臺北舉辦「金庸小說國際學術研討會」，共有來自中、港、台及美、英、澳、以等國二十六位學者發表論文。

國家圖書館出版品預行編目資料

金庸小說國際學術研討會論文集=Proceedings
of the International Conference on Jin Yong's
Novels ／ 王秋桂主編.　--初版.
　--臺北市：遠流，　1999〔民88〕
　　　　面；　　公分.
　　ISBN　957-32-3813-6 (精裝).

1.金庸-作品研究　2.武俠小說-評論-論文,講詞等

857.907　　　　　　　　　　　88013140